THE
QUEEN'S NECKLACE

THE QUEEN'S NECKLACE

TERESA EDGERTON

An Imprint of HarperCollins*Publishers*

This is a work of fiction. Names, characters, places, and incidents are products of the author's imagination or are used fictitiously and are not to be construed as real. Any resemblance to actual events, locales, organizations, or persons, living or dead, is entirely coincidental.

EOS
An Imprint of HarperCollins *Publishers*
10 East 53rd Street
New York, New York 10022-5299

Copyright © 2001 by Teresa Edgerton
Interior design by Kellan Peck
Map by Ann Meyer Maglinte
ISBN: 0-380-78911-6
www.eosbooks.com
http://ecuador.junglevision.com/carolyn/teresa/te-home.htm

Library of Congress Cataloging-in-Publication Data

Edgerton, Teresa.
    The queen's necklace / Teresa Edgerton.
        p. cm.
    ISBN 0-380-78911-6
        I. Title.

PS3555.D473 Q44 2001
813'.54—dc21   00-047617

First Eos trade paperback printing: July 2001

Eos Trademark Reg. U.S. Pat. Off. and in Other Countries,
Marca Registrada, Hecho en U.S.A.
HarperCollins® is a trademark of HarperCollins Publishers Inc.

Printed in the U.S.A.

10 9 8 7 6 5 4 3 2 1

The following people offered aid, comfort, encouragement,
and advice during the writing of this book:

Tina Benz, Jennifer Carson, Carolyn Hill,
and Tom and Paula King.

Had eluki bes shahar not believed in it,
this book might never have seen print.

Therefore, to all these dear friends

The Queen's Necklace

is affectionately and respectfully dedicated.

Dramatis Personae

In Mountfalcon

CAPTAIN WILROWAN KROGAN-BLACKHEART—(otherwise "Will") A raffish young nobleman. Captain of Her Majesty's Guard.

BLAISE CROWSMEARE-TREFALLON—His closest friend. An ornament of the court.

SIR RUFUS MACQUAY—A fop.

FINN, PYECROFT, BARNABY—Drinking companions of Will and Blaise.

CORPORAL NATHANIEL DAGGET—of the City Guard. A very young officer.

LILLIANA BRAKEBURN-BLACKHEART—(otherwise "Lili") Wilrowan's wife. A young woman of character.

LORD BRAKEBURN—Lilliana's father. An insignificant gentleman, of large means but very small cunning.

MISS ALLORA BRAKEBURN—Lord Brakeburn's maiden aunt. Lilliana's mentor.

SIR BASTIAN JOSSLYN-MATHER—A gentleman magician.

LIEUTENANT KESTREL BRAKEBURN—(otherwise "Nick") Lili's young cousin. An officer in His Majesty's Guard.

WILOBIE CULPEPPER—(otherwise "Willie") A phantom. That is, a false identity invented by Will.

EULALIE—A wig-maker's daughter. On terms of considerable intimacy with Wilobie Culpepper.

CORPORAL SWALLOW—A junior member of Her Majesty's Guard, acting as Will's body-servant.

KING RODARIC OF MOUNTFALCON—A sober man, very much in love with his flighty young wife.

QUEEN DIONEE—The afore-mentioned wife. Wilrowan's foster-sister, related to him on both sides of the family.

LORD THADDEUS VAULT—A foreign nobleman. The ambassador from Nordfjall.

LORD-LIEUTENANT JACK MARZDEN—of the City Guard. Formerly Will's nemesis, now his friend.

A WRYNECK—A Goblin masquerading as a Man.

DOCTOR OCTAVIO PRENDERBY-FOX—An academic magician. A professor at Malachim College.

SIR FREDERIC TREGARON-MARLOWE—Also a Professor of Magic.

LADY LETITIA STEERPIKE—A woman of the court. A scheming hussy.

CRWCRWYL—A raven.

ALSO:

A Prostitute. A Gaoler. An Innkeeper. The Governor of Whitcomb Gaol. A Surgeon. Various courtiers, servants, guardsmen, tradesmen, pedestrians, magicians, felons, &c.

In Winterscar

KING JARRED OF WINTERSCAR—A grieving widower. An honorable young man.

LUCIUS SACKVILLE-GUILIAN—(otherwise "Luke") A witty young gentleman. Jarred's second-cousin and foster-brother. An amateur historian.

DOCTOR FRANCIS PURCELL—A natural philosopher. Formerly tutor to Jarred and Luke.

LORD HUGO SACKVILLE—Jarred's uncle. An aging rake.

PRINCESS SOPHRONISPA—(otherwise "Ys") The Princess Imperial.

LADY SOPHRONISPA—(otherwise "Sophie") Ys's aunt. An Imperial Princess.

VALENTINE SOLANGE—(otherwise "Madame Debrûle") Governess to Ys. A martyr to her duty.

MADAM ZAPHIR—An Ouph fortuneteller.

LORD VIF——(otherwise "Monsieur Debrûle") A person of little intelligence but considerable breeding, masquerading as Valentine's husband and Ys's uncle.

LORD WITTLESBECK——Jarred's Master of Ceremonies. A fussy old man.

ALONZO PERYS——Jarred's coachman.

LORD RUPERT WALBURG——Jarred's Heir-Apparent. A sporting gentleman, not much interested in affairs of government.

ZMAJ, JMEL, IZEK——Three handsome youths of Imperial descent.

A GRANT——A Goblin apothecary, ancient and venerable.

DOCTOR MATTHEW WILDEBADEN——A physician. Cousin to Francis Purcell.

ALSO:

A Padfoot Seamstress. A Major Domo. Two Footmen. The King's Secretary. An Invalid. Various courtiers, cabinet ministers, guardsmen, & servants residing at Lindenhoff.

On Shipboard

CAPTAIN PYKE——Master of the Pagan Queen. A man with a past.

SIMON PERYS——Lucius Guilian's valet. A loyal retainer.

RAITH——An Anti-demonist. Tutor and bodyguard to the children of the Crown Princess of Rijxland. A man of mystery.

ALSO:

A Linen-draper. A Goldsmith. A Grant. Three Ouphs. Sailors & passengers.

In Rijxland

KING IZAIAH OF RIJXLAND The Mad King. Formerly a man of rare genius.

PRINCESS MARJOTE——Izaiah's daughter, the Crown Princess. A woman of high principles but limited understanding.

LORD FLINX——Izaiah's nephew. An unscrupulous politician.

TREMEUR BROUILLARD—An orphan, his ward. A young female with a scandalous reputation.

LORD POLYPHANT—The ambassador from Winterscar. A man of fashion.

LORD CATTS—The Minister of Trade. A dandy.

VARIAN DOU—An earnest young parlimentarian, being groomed for a government post by the Princess Marjote.

ALSO:

A Hackney-coachman. The Princess's children. Various visitors, inmates, attendants, & physicians at the mad-house in Luden (including some giddy young women).

In Montagne-du-Soliel

LADY KROGAN—(formerly Odilia Rowan) Wilrowan's grandmother. A dowager of sinister reputation.

ALSO:

A Coachman and a Porter.

In Nordfjall, Chêneboix, Bridemoor, Catwitsen, & Herndyke

A RAG-AND-BOTTLE DEALER—An ancient Wryneck with some claim to gentility.

LIEUTENANT ODGERS, CORPORAL GILPIN—Guardsmen assigned to assist Wilrowan.

GENERAL PENGENNIS—Assigned to protect His Royal Highness, the Prince of Catwitsen's, frontiers.

ALSO:

A Grant. A Hired Coachman. Several innkeepers. Some border guards. Three constables. Sailors, fishermen, villagers, &c.

N
W
E
S
POLARWASTE
Tarnburgh
CIRCUMPOLAR MTS.
POLAR WASTE
R. Arcis
NORDFJALL
R. Szar
WINTERSCAR
KJELLMARK
LICHTENWALD
TÖLMARCH
zutlingen
mare
Frigorium
mare
Demonium
PHLEGRA
MONTES
R. Windle
R. Ounce
R. Eel
R. Catkin
penmorva
Fencaster
BRIDEMOOR
WÖLFEN-
BRÜCKE
R. Heron
HERNDYKE
chalkford
R. Ousel
germouline
CHÊNEBOIX
R. Weasel
FINGHYLL
The Troit
Cudan
MOUNTFALCON
Hawkesbridge
Eaudaimanté
MONTAGNE
du SOLIEL
mare
Sirenium
CHÂTEAU
ROUGE
MONTCIEUX
R. Zule
THOLIA
CALORIS MONTES
(ALPS)
R. Ounce
Voirdemare

Prologue

On a chilly autumn morning in the year 6509, a nondescript hackney coach jolted through the muddy streets of a great northern city and came to a halt in a dismal little square. The door flew open and two women—as discreetly colorless as to their gowns, hats, cloaks, and gloves as they had been in choosing a coach—stepped down to the slippery cobblestone pavement. The taller of the two dropped a few bright coins into the hand of the driver up on the box.

"Wait for us just here." Her voice was low and intense, with the accent of one accustomed to command. A filmy black scarf thrown over her wide-brimmed hat concealed her face and shoulders, but her figure was straight, her movements graceful. There was a rustle of silken petticoats under the sober skirts of her gown.

When the driver protested against keeping the horses standing, she silenced him with an upraised hand. "Our business is urgent—so may be our hasty departure."

Turning sharply on her heel, she started down the nearest narrow street, shouldering her way through a knot of rough-looking men unloading beechwood casks from a wagon. Her companion followed in her footsteps, darting nervous glances to either side.

A thick, oily fog had descended during the night, making it difficult to read the hand-lettered cards in the shop windows. But as she passed a tilted sign post, the smaller woman cried out. "Val—it is the wrong street. I knew there had to be some mistake."

"Hush, Sophie. It is a quarter of a mile distant. If there is trouble later, the driver should know as little as possible."

Sophie lengthened her steps, trying to keep pace. "But *such* a neighborhood. Could Chimena, even Chimena, abandon her child in a place like this?"

"If she was desperate enough. If they were pressing her very hard, and it was the only way to keep the child safe."

The street grew narrower and narrower still, finally dwindling to a dirty footpath. Val disappeared in the oily dimness up ahead; somewhere behind, Sophie thought she heard footsteps: the slow but firm tread of a very large man taking long, easy strides. She felt a sudden twinge of panic.

Then, a freshening breeze blew cold and sweet full in her face; the fog lifted. The ground seemed to fall away, and the path opened on a vast blue-grey expanse of mud and sky and water, and what appeared, at first glance, to be an infinite network of piers and catwalks and floating bridges, connecting a likewise infinite number of ramshackle little buildings built up on stilts, a shanty town made up of mud and ooze and sticks and every sort of flotsam and jetsam. They had reached the great mudflats west of the river Scar.

The two women descended a flight of rotting wooden steps and set out briskly across the piers and catwalks.

The houses, though flimsy, were two and three stories high, with unsavory little shops down below. There were ale-houses and opium dens and gin shops advertising their wares in crooked letters: *DRuNK FoR a PEnnY, DEaD DRuNK FoR TWo.* There were greasy little cookshops redolent of squid and pickled seaweed. There were decaying hulks of ships and smacks and fishing hoys, stranded in the mud ages past, now converted into more of the wretched little dwellings. Smoke rose lazily from a few chimneys, but most of the interiors looked cold and dark.

Gazing around her in wonder and disgust, Sophie came to a startling conclusion. "This is Goblin Town," she said.

"Yes," Val replied in a low voice, as they crossed a narrow plank bridge between two of the piers. "This is Goblin Town. A miserable existence to be sure—yet on dry land, these vile hovels would be so many fire-traps. Out here in the damps, where even seasoned firewood is slow to burn, the creatures feel safe."

Sophie looked down at the murky chemical stew that bubbled and seeped below the bridge. "But living right over the water! How can they—?"

"We are ninety miles from the sea. The river here is a perfect hell-broth of plagues and poisons," said Val, "but no more noxious to Goblins than it is to Men."

She came to a sudden stop before an untidy erection of driftwood and shingle. A dirty bow-front window jutted out from the worm eaten woodwork, and a number of faded signs had been stuck up at random. *Bottle, Bone, & Rag Shop,* said one. *Old Clothes. Fine Costumes for Gentlemen, Ladies, Goblins, & Goblines. To Be Had Cheap,* said another. And a third, equally faded but originally done in a bolder hand: *Old Iron Bought, Books Bought, Curios & Antiquities Bought & Sold. Inquire Within.*

"Unless I am mistaken, this is the place."

It was two steps down to the entry. The door creaked loudly when Val pushed it open, and a bell tinkled dully at the back of the shop.

Inside, the stale air caught at the back of Sophie's throat and made her cough. On every side there was dust and clutter: tottering piles of books and papers; heaps of old clothing, dark with mildew; a jumble of broken furniture; pyramids of chipped crockery, tarnished silver, ancient tea kettles.

And bottles everywhere—medicine bottles, ink bottles, scent bottles, dusty wine bottles with the dregs still in them, bottles of blue glass and green, bottles of every conceivable description— glinting in the light of a battered horn lantern hanging from a rusty iron bracket.

Sophie shivered at the sight of the bottles with the crusted sediments. Once she had held a similar vessel between her trembling hands, a slender glass phial containing a handful of silvery ashes, and a strip of parchment scrawled with the terrible message: *Your Maglore Princess is dead. Abandon the Dangerous course you follow, before you Destroy us all.*

"Chimena is gone. Betrayed and murdered by our own kind." Val's voice, directly in her ear, brought Sophie back to the present. "We can only hope she was somehow able to preserve the child."

Something rattled the papers in another part of the room; there was the sound of a hasty scurrying departure down an unseen aisle. A row of skeletons at the back of the shop, dressed up in ragged finery and suspended from a beam, began to sway like so many bodies on a gibbet. Then a second door creaked loudly open, and a grotesque figure came into the light. Sophie drew in her breath.

He was an old, old Goblin of a type not often seen: a Wryneck, all gangling limbs and long body, with a hump at the back of his neck that caused his head to thrust forward. He was the very picture of shabby Goblin respectability in a loose, snuff-colored coat, drab waistcoat and breeches, and grey woolen stockings, yet there were silver buckles on his shoes and his frizzled white hair had been tied back with a large black satin bow—marks of superiority far beyond the aspirations of his humbler Goblin neighbors, the Ouphs and the Padfoots.

When he caught sight of his two visitors, he started visibly. "Ladies—" he began. Then his sharp old eyes seemed to detect something and he bowed very low. "You have come for the child?"

Val lifted up her veil, drew forth a long, gleaming, pearl-tipped hat-pin, and fastened the veil back over her hat so that the silken folds fell down behind. "That remains to be seen. There are many questions which must be answered. The first one is: how such a child ever came under your protection."

The Wryneck bowed again. "She was left in my care, madam, soon after she was born. The mother gave birth in a room above this shop, lived here for a time, then left in haste the following summer. Alas, I can no longer say that the child remains under my protection. I did what I could for her as an infant, but as she grew—she became unmanageable."

Val stepped forward into the light. There had been reason for the concealing veil; if her face was not beautiful, yet it was memorable, with bold dark eyes, a high-bridged nose, and a vivid red mouth.

"Such children are often difficult; they are powerfully inclined to be stubborn and willful. Unless, that is, they are left in the care of those who know how to discipline them." Val made an impatient gesture. "So the child proved unmanageable. What then?"

"She turned feral. She lives for the most part out of doors, though she comes inside when the weather is bad. She is here now." Again there came a rustling among the moldering piles; a musky, bestial odor seemed to penetrate the dead air.

Sophie glanced nervously around her. But Val moved swiftly. Heedless of all—the rising dust, the scattered papers, the sudden clattering of the disturbed skeletons—she swooped down, caught hold of a retreating scrap of dirty cloth, and pulled a ragged child into the light.

The child shrieked and began to struggle. But a few sharp words, a smart blow to the head, and it cowered submissively at Val's feet.

"As I said—unless they are left in the care of those who know how to discipline them."

Sophie looked down at the child. So dirty, so wild, so abject. Stunted as it was, with a pinched face and tiny claw-like hands, it was

the size of a Human child just learning to take its first steps—but
there was something about the bright, wary eyes that betrayed a
considerably greater age and experience.

Sophie cleared her throat. "When was it—she—born?"

"Eleven years ago, madam, almost to the day."

The women exchanged a significant glance. "For all that, we
must make very certain." Val turned her brilliant dark eyes on Sophie. "Did you bring those things I told you?"

Sophie searched in her little jet-beaded purse and finally came up
with a white handkerchief and a silver phial. Meanwhile, Val produced a second wicked-looking hat-pin. "I'll hold her while you
prick her."

Another struggle ensued, when the child guessed their intentions, but one dirty finger was eventually pierced; three drops of
blood were squeezed out on the white handkerchief. Sophie unstop-
pered the silver phial and poured the contents over the red stain.

"Ahhh—" breathed the Wryneck, as the linen began to steam
where seawater touched blood.

"Maglore in any case." Val panted softly as she knelt on the floor
with the child crushed against her chest. "She's no Ouph or Padfoot
with that straight back and tiny feet. And perhaps, cleaned up, she
may resemble Chimena. Who else knows of her existence?"

"The Humans who frequent Goblin Town have seen her, certainly, but they pay small attention to feral children, of which there
are so many in the neighborhood. Aside from that—I imagine every
Goblin within five miles of this place knows what she is, but they
will say nothing."

"And do you tell me that no one else ever asked uncomfortable
questions?"

The Wryneck shook his head. "There were Men who came—I
will call them Men; they never told me otherwise. They asked many
questions about the mother. I told them what I knew of her, which

was essentially nothing, and as they did not seem to know there was a child, I saw no reason to enlighten them."

Val rose to her feet, still keeping a hard grip on the little girl's arm. "We will take the child with us, as you suggested in your letter. No doubt you will be glad to be rid of so tiresome, so *dangerous* a charge."

"Let us say," said the Wryneck, bowing, "that I shall be glad to place her in the care of those able to protect her."

Val moved toward the door, leading the child by the hand, while Sophie trailed behind with the phial and the handkerchief. But the old Goblin stopped them, asking to speak a private word to Val. She considered for a moment, then sent the others on to the coach without her.

The rag-and-bottle shop was suddenly very quiet as Val faced the old Goblin across a pile of broken furniture. "I suppose you expect to be rewarded," she said, her lips curling into a scornful smile.

In the pale yellow light of the horn lantern, the Wryneck looked immeasurably ancient. Val wondered how old he might be; his kind were fabulously long-lived, even among Goblins. It was impossible that his life and memory stretched all the way back fifteen hundred years to the glorious days of the Maglore Empire, but it was just possible that, as a very young Goblin, he had spoken with those of his own kind who *had* lived then and did remember.

"A reward? Madam, you wrong me. Rather, I wish to be unburdened of another responsibility that has been mine—most reluctantly mine—these ten years and more."

He disappeared into a room at the back, and reappeared several minutes later holding a small brass coffer. Placing the box carefully on a pile of books, he opened the lid and drew out a necklace: a double string of milky white stones. They looked like pearls, but they were not pearls, and Val knew they were something far colder and infinitely more perilous. At the point farthest from the clasp, linking the two strands together, there was a heart-shaped pendant of clouded crystal.

"Perhaps you have seen this before?" said the Wryneck.

Val reached out and took the cold stones into her hands. Even through her black gloves the chill penetrated. Yes, she had seen the necklace before. It was not one of the Great Jewels, which the Maglore of old had invested with such awesome power, but these artificial stones had been created at the same time and of the same elements as those in the greater Jewels. Though potent enough in its own way, it was doubtful the necklace had ever been intended as anything more than an amorous plaything for a Goblin princess, who had far greater forces at her command. It had never been more than a toy to Chimena, who had used its peculiar properties to attract and entrap, and sometimes to torment, her numerous lovers.

Holding the necklace, Val felt a queasy sense of wrongness. For a moment, it was as though she could actually see *inside* the old Goblin: *the long, thick, fibrous spinal cord, glowing with the scintillating colors of the astral light—that complex structure of tiny vessels which was the* rete mirabile, *at the base of the brain, busily transforming the red blood into a pure, subtle spirit—most of all those delicate branching nerves, which she might set vibrating either in ecstasy or in pain with the barest intention—*

A shiver passed over Val's skin, and she looked away. "How did you come by this?"

"It was sent to me by the mother, a few months after she left. I understood it was to be passed on to the child."

Val gazed down at the necklace, with a deep sense of revulsion. It seemed a peculiar gift from a mother to her innocent newborn child. "You might have sold this any time these last ten years."

The Wryneck looked at her reproachfully. "The necklace was not mine to sell. Madam, I'm only an humble shopkeeper, but I come of a distinguished family, an honorable race. My father and grandfather were philosophers, scientists—"

"Well, they must have been," Val interrupted him. "They could hardly have been otherwise."

"As you say," he agreed, blushing faintly. Wrynecks were as shy about discussing the details of their dry scientific conception as other creatures, more conventionally conceived, were reluctant to discuss theirs. "I, on the other hand, am as you see me—yet I am an honest Goblin. I had an idea this Jewel had never been profaned by Human hands, and I wished it to remain so."

Val slipped the necklace into the front of her gown. "If you are wise, you will forget that you ever saw these stones, the child, or her mother."

Back inside the coach, she pulled out the necklace and showed it to Sophie. Sophie shuddered distastefully, screwing up her face. "Oh Val, you had the thing there right next to your skin! I remember how Chimena—"

"Yes, yes. It is a wanton's plaything, but I doubt I'll be infected with a taste for perversion just by touching it." Nevertheless, Val wrapped the necklace up in a handkerchief before she slipped it back inside her gown.

"Will we sell it?" asked Sophie. "But how can we? Dangerous to sell, but much more dangerous to keep!"

The hackney lurched into motion. "I haven't decided. It is the only thing the girl will ever have of her mother's. And who knows— it may prove useful." Val looked down at the child, who had curled up under the other seat and apparently fallen asleep. "What a vile little thing she is. It will take months to undo the neglect of so many years. The first step will be to break her will."

Sophie smiled wistfully at her friend across the coach. Though they appeared much the same age, that appearance was deceptive. Val was considerably older and had played an important rôle in Sophie's upbringing. "I daresay it will go hard with her if she doesn't learn quickly."

"It will go hard with her regardless. She will be controlled; she *will* be disciplined. I'll not see her grow up to repeat her mother's mistakes."

Sophie raised her voice in order to be heard over the creaking of the wheels. "What of the Wryneck? Poor old fellow. Must we have him silenced?"

Val considered for a long time before she spoke. "I think—not immediately. It might cause others to draw dangerous conclusions. And perhaps not at all."

Sophie was amazed. "Compassion—from you, Val? I hardly expected it."

Her friend passed this off with a wave of one thin white hand. "He is honest and loyal; I believe we may rely on his discretion. Besides, like the necklace, he may prove useful."

Book I

She was an ancient city, grown gaunt and weather-beaten. Her origins were shrouded; she had been old when the Maglore Empire was still new; even then, no one had ventured to guess at her age. And when Men rose against the race of Goblin sorcerers who had ruled them so harshly for five thousand years, when they cast off their chains, shattered an empire, and reconfigured the map, they made Hawkesbridge the capital of one of their small new kingdoms.

For a time, she enjoyed a glorious renaissance: old buildings were razed; imposing public works—libraries, gardens, universities, observatories, palaces—rose in their place. The arts and the sciences flourished. Metaphysicians and philosophers flocked to her. For culture, sociability, novelty, there was no place to match her in all the world. But time was not kind to Hawkesbridge, the aging process was relentless, and all that she had once possessed in the way of beauty and charm had since withered away to little more than a frail skin of humanity on an angular skeleton of brick and stone.

Many of her buildings stood half empty. These Men of the new age were increasingly conservative, less and still less inclined to tamper with the work of their ancestors—those stalwart men and women who had brought down the Goblin civilization and created a new Society, nearly perfect, in its place—nor to remove anything created by previous generations. Nowhere was this so strikingly evident as in Hawkesbridge. When the lower floors of a house became dank and musty and uninhabitable, the owner simply erected new stories on top. When the whole pile collapsed, often with a great loss of lives and goods, instead of hauling the ruin away, he scavenged the better parts of marble and masonry and built a new house over the wreckage, as much like the house that had been there before as it was possible to make it. By now, Hawkesbridge was a city of crooked tall buildings with bow-front windows, cracked marble columns, and winding exterior staircases crawling up from the deep overshadowed streets and alleys below.

Yet sometimes of a cold winter's night, when the black north wind came roaring down those subterranean lanes—when the gas flares were lit and windows glowed with yellow firelight—when fine ladies and gentlemen came out in butterfly satins and jewel-toned velvets, and rode through the icy streets, uphill and downhill in gilded carriages and painted sedan-chairs, on the way to some brilliant dinner or theatrical event—when the very snow that piled on the roofs and drifted against the houses, and made the going in some of the steep places exceedingly difficult, nevertheless seemed to soften the broken outlines and the harsh corners of the ancient city—then a feverish gaiety set in, a hectic flush of youth was momentarily restored, and it was possible to envision Hawkesbridge as she had once been.

It could not last long. In the first grey light of dawn she lost her artificial bloom. When the fires died and the gas-lights were extinguished, when the chairmen trudged wearily through the streets and the gay gilded carriages went rumbling back home, to be supplanted by the rattling black wagons of the city tradesmen, then Hawkesbridge shriveled back into hideous old age.

1

J t was a raw morning, with a chill on the air that bit like steel
and went all the way through to the bone. But a large crowd
gathering in the long shadow of the Theomorphic church
seethed with excitement. Word of a duel about to be fought had
brought them together on a level stretch of ground between the
church and the frozen River Zule, and every man of them anticipated bloodshed.

Yet one of the seconds appeared to be reconsidering. He stood
arguing with his principal in low, urgent tones.

"Will, Will, I beg you to stop and think before this goes any further. That fool Macquay, so eager, so *insistent* about pressing a quarrel, when all the world knows you are the better swordsman. He
can't be so ready to die as it seems, and I thought more than once
during the night he was not so drunk as he pretended. There is mischief afoot. If you have any sense you'll refuse to meet him. As the
injured—"

"As the injured party, I intend to do nothing of the sort," Will
Blackheart replied, grinding his teeth. He was a small man in a
rough soot-colored coat many sizes too large for him and a wide-
brimmed hat of black beaver, pinned up at one side with some drag-

gled turkey feathers and a large brooch in the shape of a scarab bee-
tle. His long auburn hair had been loosely tied back with a piece of
frayed ribbon, and in the cold light of morning he looked pale and
dissipated.

Despite his slovenly appearance, despite that of his companions,
there was a certain something about them—inbred and entirely unconscious—which marked them all for exactly what they were:
rackety young aristocrats who had spent the night just past cele-
brating the New Year in taverns and gambling houses. The watching
tradesmen, the shipwrights, caulkers, and carpenters from the
docks and shipyards, even the handful of Ouphs and Padfoots hovering on the edge of the crowd, moved a few steps closer to hear what
was being said.

"By the Shades of the Damned, Blaise, what Macquay said was
unendurable!" Will gestured in the direction of his opponent, who
was holding a heated conference with one of his own seconds—
while Finn and Pyecroft, the other two men involved, met in the
center of the field to inspect the weapons and make the final
arrangements. Will lowered his voice to a hiss. "The fellow spoke
disparagingly of Lili. Am I to allow a man to insult my wife without
demanding satisfaction?"

Blaise released a heartfelt sigh. His appearance, in a patched blue
coat and a big tricorn hat, a dirty yellow handkerchief knotted
round his throat, and a pair of thin steel hoops piercing his left ear,
was almost as villainous as Will's, though he was actually the steadi-
est of all young Blackheart's friends.

"God love you, Wilrowan, it seems to me your entire existence
is an insult to your wife. Your wild behavior, your numerous love affairs, the way you go from scandal to scandal —Lilliana can scarcely
be ignorant, even if she does live in the country thirteen months out
of the year. And having endured so much, can you really suppose she
cares what a drunken fool like Macquay says at a private gathering?"

"No." Will clenched a small fist under the deep cuff of his sleeve. "But if she knew I was present to hear and I took no action, she would care about that."

"That makes no sense. I wish you would explain to me—"

"I can't explain to you." Will turned even paler than before; his hazel eyes went uncommonly bleak. "Not without touching on things that are neither decent nor right for me to discuss."

His friend looked away in patent disgust. Such scruples were not remarkable—but they did seem curiously out of place in Wilrowan, who otherwise treated Lili with so little consideration.

In any case, it was too late to draw back now. Pyecroft and Finn had already reached an agreement and Finn came back with Will's rapier.

"I tried to hold out for first blood, but Macquay refused. He means to make this a killing affair. Or at least to do you some serious injury."

"He can't." Will spoke curtly as he shrugged out of his coat, doffed his hat, unknotted his fringed neckcloth, and began to unbutton his ratskin waistcoat. He took the hilt of his rapier, made a few experimental passes with the blade.

The observers were quick to notice that his figure—now that he had stripped down to a loose-fitting white shirt, tight satin trousers, and thigh-high boots—possessed the wiry, muscular grace appropriate to a swordsman.

"I've no mind to accept first blood either," he said, showing his teeth. "I mean to teach Macquay a sharp, unforgettable lesson."

A flock of glossy black ravens had settled on the roof of the old limestone church, up among the stone sphinxes and the lion-headed women, as though they, too, took an interest in the proceedings. As the duelists met and saluted in the center of the field, the earthbound onlookers, Human and Goblin, moved in closer. After a few preliminary feints, there was a clash of steel as the two men engaged, then a rapid series of attacks and counter-attacks.

Wilrowan was swift and relentless, his swordplay dazzling, while the tall, loose-limbed Macquay fenced with a dogged determination, a lack of daring and imagination, which made him look slow and awkward, if only by comparison with young Blackheart's reckless brilliance. Despite the advantage of his extra inches, he remained purely on the defensive, which fact Will noted with grim satisfaction as he forced him back and back.

Seeing a chance when Macquay clumsily shifted his weight, Will lunged forward, beat the other blade aside, and continued on to strike just below the heart. But the rapier met unexpected resistance. Low and extended as he now was, Will was vulnerable when Macquay took a half step backward and slashed down at his head.

The thin blade hissed through empty air as Wilrowan ducked under the blow and sprang back, well out of reach.

"I believe I touched you," said Will, with a brief, mocking salute. "Do you wish to call a halt, while your seconds determine the damage?"

Macquay shook his head. "You are mistaken, Blackheart. I wasn't even scratched. Have at you!"

Certain that he was lying, fueled by a surge of indignation, Will obliged with a furious offensive, a series of feints and thrusts his opponent barely countered. Rotating his wrist to disengage from another of Macquay's awkward parries, Will lunged again. This time, the tip of his blade grazed the other man's shoulder.

Again, he experienced a curious impression of resistance, and Macquay continued on with his riposte, apparently unaffected. There was a slashing of cloth, a grating of steel against bone, and

Will felt a sharp pain in his right arm just above the wrist as Mac-quay's blade flicked past.

Startled, yet swiftly recovering, Will backed out of range, hold-ing his sword hand high, to keep the bright gush of blood from run-ning down his arm and making his grip on the hilt slippery.

"Undoubtedly, the first touch was mine." There was a sheen of perspiration on Macquay's bony forehead, his long fair hair was dripping wet, and his sword arm shook ever so slightly, yet he managed a broad grin. "Do *you* want a moment's pause, so your seconds may bind up that wrist?"

Before Wilrowan had a chance to accept or refuse, his friends had already rushed to his side. While Finn rolled up his sleeve, Blaise pulled out a clean handkerchief and contrived a quick band-age.

"You were right." Will spoke under his breath as Blaise finished knotting the linen in place. "There is mischief afoot. I touched him twice and yet—nothing. He's found some Padfoot magician to sew a spell of protection into his shirt, the beastly coward."

"You have the right to demand we examine him," said Finn. "It's not always possible to be certain, but—"

"No." Will shook his head stubbornly. "And look like a fool and a craven if nothing turns up? Besides, these spells are generally good for three hits only. I have but to touch him lightly one more time and then I'm free to skewer him like a damned pig."

Blaise stared at him in disbelief. "And never discover what this is about? Show a little sense! Cut him to pieces if you must, but at least leave him alive long enough to answer some questions."

But Will's mind was awhirl with thoughts of blood and revenge, he was only dimly aware of the pain in his wrist, and he hardly heard what his friend said.

This time, he led the attack with a beat and a straightening of his arm. Only at the last possible instant did Macquay turn his blade aside.

There followed a rapid series of attacks, parries, and disengages. When Macquay stumbled slightly, Will moved forward in an irresistible lunge, the point of his rapier driving full at his opponent's narrow chest for the third touch. As before, the force of his blade was mysteriously deflected. Yet now he attacked with even greater vigor, forcing Macquay to retreat.

A thunder of dark wings as every raven on the roof of the church rose into the air at once ought to have warned him, but Will was too intent on the duel. So intent, he failed to register the scuffling and shouting which began at the edge of the crowd, followed by an unnatural hush among the spectators. Nor did he heed Pyecroft's shouted warning or the sudden defection of all four seconds. The City Guard had already closed in before Wilrowan realized what was happening.

Two men seized him roughly from behind, while a third twisted the rapier out of his grasp. Between them, the three guardsmen forced Will to the icy ground and held him there, despite his struggles.

"Be damned to you! Don't you know who I am?"

"No, sir. And you have been caught dueling, which you ought to know is strictly forbidden except under warrant from the Lord Lieutenant. If you'll just come along peaceably to Whitcomb Gaol—"

"How the blazes," raged Will, glancing from one face to another and finding none of them familiar, "do you know that a warrant is lacking? You came in and broke up the fight without even asking. Raw recruits by the look of you, and how Jack Marzden came to let you out on your—"

"Lord Marzden has been out of the city these five days." The young officer spoke with quiet authority. Though he could hardly be more than eighteen or nineteen, he looked solid and capable in his scarlet coat. "No warrants have been issued during his absence. And if your duel were legal, I would imagine your friends had remained to say so."

There was a soft, deadly click in the vicinity of Will's ear; out of the corner of one eye he caught a glimpse of a large horse pistol with brass fittings, clenched in a white-knuckled hand. Abruptly, he ceased to struggle.

"There was no warrant and it might be said that my friends' involvement was—irregular—but the law does not apply to me. I am Wilrowan Krogan-Blackheart, formerly of the City Guard, now Captain of Her Majesty's Guard; as an officer in an elite company I don't require a warrant."

"Then it's unfortunate, sir, that you are out of uniform, as we have no way of knowing if you are who you say you are. Now if you please——" While the young corporal spoke, Will was raised to his feet and hustled in the direction of Whitcomb Gaol. "——if you'll just come along willingly, you can plead your case to the Lord Lieutenant when he returns."

Deciding he had no choice, Will permitted them to lead him through the snowy streets, though not without glancing around to see if his friends and his erstwhile opponent were in similar circumstances.

"Consign the lot of you to Eternal Darkness! Where is the man I was fighting? I suspect him of entering the duel with magical protections, which is a far more serious offense than the absence of your damned warrant."

"That is as may be," said the youth with the pistol. He handled his weapon in such a nervous, inexperienced way that, just watching him, Will broke into a cold sweat. "Sir Rufus Macquay was able to establish his identity, and because we know him to be an intimate of the king, we allowed him to depart on his own assurance he would appear before the magistrate in three days time. If you have any complaint, you may accuse him then, sir."

"If he actually appears, which begins to look doubtful," said Will under his breath. But resigning himself to the inevitable delay, he spent the rest of the journey to Whitcomb in dark contemplation of the revenge he would eventually take, if and when he finally caught up with Macquay.

2

*L*illiana felt as though she had been travelling for weeks. Her eyes felt dry and gritty, and a dull ache at the small of her back grew steadily worse in spite of the support of her whalebone stays. Leaning back against the black leather seat of the coach, Lili wondered if, by the time she and Aunt Allora finally reached their destination, she would be able to summon sufficient strength of mind and body to bring this arcane treasure hunt to its proper conclusion.

There was a jolt and a thump, followed by smoother going. Much of the light disappeared as the berlin left the dirt road, crossed an ancient iron bridge, and rolled down a cobblestone lane between rows of tall buildings. The horses began to labor up a steep incline.

"Hawkesbridge, I suppose," Lili said out loud.

And at last, she added to herself, taking a peek out the window.

"You are weary, Lilliana," her great-aunt said from the seat facing her.

A little old woman with a very flat bosom and very sharp eyes, Allora still looked surprisingly fresh, exquisitely neat as to her gown, her ribbons, and her laces, her tiny gloved hands folded demurely in her lap. But Lili's aunt was a lady of the old school, and eighteen hours spent rattling around in the coffinlike coach were not enough to ruffle her composure, or dim her indomitable spirit. Her expression softened ever so slightly as she viewed her great-niece across the carriage.

"Perhaps, my child, it is time to stop and rest and eat a hot meal."

"No." Lili leaned back again. Her stomach felt empty and her knees weak; she had not eaten anything since the night before, when Allora produced a wicker hamper from under the seat and they supped on cake, cold beef, and raspberry cordial. Yet she was more troubled now by an odd sense of urgency.

"I would much rather not. I admit that concentrating so hard makes my head ache—but we don't want to risk losing our quarry, just when we seem to be catching up to him." Her fingers closed around the metal divining rod she held in her lap. It was a curious device: a hollow brass tube enclosing a long needle of magnetized iron, bound by five alternating rings of copper and zinc, with a pyramid-shaped prism fastened at one end. "Only *think* how wearisome if we had to keep going for another day and night."

As she spoke, the wand moved in her hand and she felt a sudden mental wrench, so sharp and sickening the world turned dark for a moment. Even when her vision cleared, she could hardly focus her eyes, and the pain in her head was so fierce she could scarcely breathe. The crystal prism at the end of the divining rod now indicated an easterly direction.

"Make the coachman stop. We have passed the place and are moving away."

Aunt Allora used the ivory knob at the end of her walking stick to rap on the roof of the coach. The berlin lurched to a halt. "What shall I tell him?" she said, opening the door.

"Go back to the street or alley we just passed and turn to the right. And tell him—tell him to keep the horses to a slow walk." Lili rubbed the back of her neck as she spoke.

Allora relayed the instructions and slammed the door shut; the coach lunged forward, heading for some wider place where the coachman could turn the horses. Several minutes later, there was a creaking and a swaying as the berlin turned down the alley.

"Another hundred feet." Lili closed her eyes, the better to concentrate. The wand was a useful device, so long as nothing obstructed or deflected the magnetic lines of force to which it responded, but it was not so precise as her own native talent, honed by the magicians of the Specularii into a trained sixth sense. "I think—it must be a tavern or something of the sort."

Aunt Allora gave another sharp tattoo on the roof, and the coach stopped again. "Do you feel strong enough to proceed?"

Lili nodded, then wished she had not; the movement only increased her pain, made her vision blur again. She heard rather than saw the coachman open the door and let down the steps. Slipping the wand between the cushions for safekeeping, she followed Allora out the door, clutching gratefully at the hand of the driver as she stumbled from the narrow step to a patch of frosty ground.

When her vision cleared again, Lili found herself in a filthy alley at the foot of a crooked staircase leading up the side of a tall building. Craning her neck and gazing upward, Lilliana could just make out a ramshackle landing thirty or forty feet above, and a faded sign bearing the indistinct outline of some deep-sea monster and the even less distinct legend: *The Leviathan.*

"Can this possibly be the right place?"

Allora shook out the satin skirts of her biscuit-colored gown, anchored more firmly her flat straw hat. "It is for you to tell me. I was purposely kept ignorant of the scroll's whereabouts, for fear I might influence you."

Lili sighed. Though the place seemed unlikely, the pull of the ancient hierophantic papyrus was unmistakable. And she knew that if she passed this test, if she proved worthy of the arcane education which Aunt Allora and her mysterious friends had already invested in her, she might someday be asked to go into places equally daunting all on her own.

"I am certain the scroll is somewhere inside." Raising the hem of her brown velvet cloak, she began the long climb up the crooked staircase.

She knew that the sudden appearance of two unescorted gentlewomen would cause a commotion inside the tavern; the only way to carry it off was to proceed with as much dignity and authority as she could possibly muster. Arriving breathless, and more than a little apprehensive, at the top of the stairs, she hesitated on the threshold until her pulses stopped hammering and her eyes adjusted to the gloomy interior.

A pair of smokey green lanterns hung from the beamed ceiling; there was an inglenook and a blue gas-fire at the far end of the room. As she had expected, the taproom was crowded and noisy; the air was thick with the odors of pipeweed, raw spirits, and unwashed bodies. Even so, she found it easy to single out one solitary old gentleman—very much in the style of her grandfather's day, with his waist-length white hair, soft black hat, and long full-skirted grey coat—sitting quietly by the fire.

He is the one, thought Lili. Heedless of the catcalls and obscenities that greeted her entrance, she stepped boldly into the room. Every man in the place turned to watch her progress across the floor, though Lilliana knew there was not much about her to catch and hold the masculine eye. Only a slender figure, more angular than willowy, a head of chestnut curls, and a pale face with a broad forehead, a straight nose, and a pair of quizzical grey eyes.

"I believe, sir, that you have something for me."

The old gentleman gave her a severe glance. "That hardly seems likely. Indeed, it appears you are in the wrong place entirely. If I were you, madam, I would leave at once and find some more *suitable* location for—whatever assignation brings you here."

Lili felt herself blushing hotly. "Yet I am convinced I am not mistaken. If you will produce the—object—my friends have entrusted to you, I'll not trouble you further."

At this, the old gentleman sat up a little straighter on the bench. "Well, perhaps we do have some business. But I can hardly give you the—object—in question here before so many people. It is, as you may well apprehend, of some little value. Will you come up to my room?"

Lili shot Allora a questioning glance, but her great-aunt gave no response. "Naturally, sir, my companion and I will do whatever you think best. Though I think—"

"You mistake my meaning. You must accompany me upstairs, leaving your companion behind. What I have with me is for you and you alone."

Lili experienced a sharp twinge of apprehension. If she had somehow mistaken her man, if she allowed herself to be led into compromising circumstances—

Yet if he meant to test her courage and resolution, she must not fail. "I will do as you say." And with visions of rape and worse things besides dancing in her head, she followed him across the room, through a narrow doorway, and up another rickety flight of steps. The only light filtered in through a cracked and dingy window near the top of the stairwell.

She kept her head down as she climbed, in case they met anyone on the stairs. Perhaps that was why she scarcely noticed how her escort labored—until he stumbled on the top step and caught at the newel post to keep himself from falling. Then she glanced up and saw how he clutched one hand to his side under the slate-colored coat.

"Are you injured? I have been trained as a healer, sir, and if you have hurt yourself—"

"There is no injury." The man unbent with an obvious effort. "The pains have been with me since early morning, though not so severe. I begin to fear, Mrs. Blackheart, that someone has poisoned me."

Lili felt her heart skip a beat. "Let me help you to your room. Please don't hesitate to lean on me; I am stronger than you might think."

As he took her arm, she felt the heat of his skin through the sleeve of her gown. "Not poison, I think. You are burning with fever. With your permission, I'd like to examine you."

The old gentleman nodded weakly. He stopped outside a battered door and produced a large brass key, which Lili slipped into the lock. Still half-supporting him, she guided him into the dim bedchamber on the other side, helped him to lower himself to the sagging bed. Then she ran back down to the taproom to speak with Allora.

"He is fearfully ill, Aunt. We'll need a basin of water—of *clean* water, if you can get it. Also, candles, cloths, paper, pen and ink, and the little basket of simples I left in the coach." Before Allora had time to answer, Lili was climbing the stairs.

She found her patient sitting on the side of his rusty iron bed, glassy-eyed and panting, as though the pain had increased. She helped him to remove his hat, his coat, his blunt-toed shoes, then urged him to lie back. The bed was damp and smelled musty, but there was no help for that; she doubted there was a warming pan or a pair of clean sheets in the house.

When Allora arrived with the things she had asked for, Lili lit a candle and placed it on a stand by the bed. She reached down into her basket and pulled out a six-inch globe of clear glass, filled with a pale, viscous fluid. This she placed on a silver tripod in front of the candle to reflect and diffuse the light. Only then did she turn toward her patient.

Lili began her examination by carefully studying the old gentleman's hands. The nails were a dull leaden color, which she knew for a very bad sign. When she took his wrist between her fingers and thumb, his pulse was slight and irregular.

"Sir, have you been—I'm afraid I don't know your name."

"He is Sir Bastian Josslyn-Mather, my old friend," Allora offered, over Lili's shoulder.

"Sir Bastian, then. Have you been out of the country?" She unfastened the nickel-plated buttons of his waistcoat, ran a practiced hand over his upper abdomen.

"I was in Château-Rouge three weeks ago."

"In Château-Rouge, and so recently! I've heard the Black Bile Fever runs epidemic in the seaside towns there." As she had feared, the area just below his ribs was hard and swollen. "However, I know very well how the Fever is treated. I promise you, sir, I will do all I can."

"I am aware the disease is often fatal—and highly contagious," he whispered hoarsely. "You must not take this risk on my account. I implore you to send for a doctor, and leave before you contract the Fever yourselves. This is no place for gentlewomen under the best of circumstances."

Lili and her aunt exchanged a glance. They both knew that to stay at his side for even an hour was to court a lingering death.

But Lili stiffened her spine. "The Specularii have not secretly educated me these many years only so that I might turn coward and run away at the first sign of danger!"

"Nor were you taught to sacrifice yourself without good cause. You are far more valuable than I—or you will be, when your education is complete. Miss Brakeburn—I beg you to reason with your niece. This is no time for sentiment."

Allora smiled faintly. "My niece can be exceedingly stubborn. And she knows her duty as a healer-physician."

"Her duty to all Mankind is even greater." Sir Bastian continued to protest, though the breath rattled in his throat and it became more and more difficult for him to speak. "Eternal vigilance against the return of the Maglore—"

"My duty to Mankind begins here, or wherever I am needed." Lili searched through the basket Allora had brought in with her, extracted a smooth black stone from an indigo leather bag. "The Maglore may not reappear during our time. I certainly don't intend to spend the rest of my life sitting uselessly by, waiting for them to do so."

She lifted his shirt and placed the glassy stone on his swollen abdomen. "The principal cause of your disease is an excess of the melancholic humor, which has gathered here in the cavity just below your ribs. This stone is obsidian, and as like attracts like it will draw off some of the black bile. Is there someone trustworthy in this house? Someone we can send to an apothecary for medicine? I fear our borrowed coachman is as unfamiliar with these streets as we are."

"The woman in the room next door appears—amiable," Sir Bastian answered with a low moan. "And it is not likely she will be—engaged at her business at this early hour."

While Allora left the room to knock on the door of the adjacent chamber, Lili made use of pen, ink, and paper. *Rx. Senna, 2 oz.;* she wrote. *Polypody of oak, 6 oz.; Bay Berries (hulled), 4 oz.; Ash Keys, Rhubarb, Ginger, SassafrasWeed, and Clove, 1 oz. each. Bruise all but Senna, which must be kept whole, and steep in 1 pint Ale.* As she had no sand to set the ink, she blew softly on the paper in order to dry it.

By this time, Allora had returned with the woman from the next room: a flaunting, tawdry, ruined-looking creature in a shabby silk gown. Her ribbons and laces hung limp and dirty, the silver beads on her shoes were tarnished almost black, and she smelled strongly of gin. It was easy to guess what Sir Bastian had meant by "engaged at her business."

Lili handed over the paper, asking the woman to deliver her instructions, then wait while the apothecary prepared the medicine.

"Because it is vitally important that we physick him as soon as possible."

The prostitute nodded dully. Under a thick coating of rouge and white lead powder, her skin sagged, and her eyes were heavy and unutterably weary. But when the old gentleman addressed Lili and her aunt from the bed, she gave a sudden start and a spark of recognition came into her clouded eyes.

"Mrs. Blackheart—Miss Brakeburn," gasped Sir Bastian. "There is a purse in an inner pocket of my coat. You are not to go to any expense on my behalf."

The purse was found and two silver florins passed on to the harlot, who left the room with a sweep of her ragged petticoats.

"It's beyond endurance," Allora hissed in Lili's ear. "You saw how that low creature recognized your name. Even in a place such as this, you're continually reminded of his infidelities!"

"She is probably just someone Will knew when he was a student at the university, and even wilder than he is now." Lili spoke under her breath; she was painfully aware of Sir Bastian's presence. "His more recent—friendships—seem always to be with ladies of the court. And really, Aunt, it's hard on poor Will to hold him to account for his youthful follies, especially when he can hardly be blamed for this extraordinary meeting."

Aunt Allora sniffed loudly. "You always defend him."

Lili gathered up the rags the tavern-keeper had provided and began to soak them in the basin of water. Whatever pain Will had caused her over the years, she preferred to keep it to herself. "Will and I have a comfortable understanding. Though we can't love each other, we try to treat each other with—with unfailing kindness and toleration."

"It seems to me," snapped Allora, "the comfort is entirely on Wilrowan's side, the toleration all on yours. How any decent woman can condone such vicious habits—!"

Lili stopped with a wet cloth in her hand. "I don't condone anything. But what I can't forget, even if you do, is that Will was tricked into marrying me when he was barely seventeen—though to be sure, I was younger still, and as much a victim of Papa's machinations as he was. We agreed, then, to always be friends and never impose on each other more than necessary. If six years later the consequences of that promise seem burdensome to me, they probably seem much the same to Will.

"Besides," she added, wringing water out of the rag with a deft twist of her wrists, "I doubt you'd be better pleased if Will were more attentive, if he insisted I dangle after him in town! It has always suited you to keep us apart as much as possible."

"Because I knew his wayward nature. Because I saw how dangerous it would be to share your secrets with him."

"I suppose the queen trusts him with *her* secrets, or she would never have appointed him captain of her guards." Lili moved toward the bed with the wet cloths in her hand.

Aunt Allora gave another loud sniff. "Queen Dionee is a spoiled, mischievous child. Which is hardly surprising, since she and Wilrowan were raised in the same household and are more like brother and sister than cousins."

"Cousins *and* half-cousins—which practically is brother and sister," Lili remarked absently. Sir Bastian had lapsed into a restless doze and did not wake when she arranged the soaking strips of cloth over his forehead, hands, and feet. "And, if anything, Will seems to exert a steadying influence, as unlikely as that sounds."

"A spoiled, mischievous child," the old woman repeated as she moved around the bed. "And that was another unfortunate marriage. What a sensible man like King Rodaric was thinking when he chose Dionee, I don't know."

"He fell in love, I suppose," Lili responded sharply. Her headache was worse, and she did wish her great-aunt would find something to talk about besides Will and Dionee's all-too-numerous transgressions. It always put her on the defensive, somehow forced her to argue Will's side—a cause for which, in truth, she had small sympathy and no enthusiasm. "And so we see that love matches can be disappointing, too, and that civility and friendship may be the best way after all."

Aunt Allora shook her head, pounded her stick against the floor. "Do you honestly believe that?"

"What use is there believing anything else? What purpose could it possibly serve if I enacted great tragedies over his infidelities?

"If you will lift Sir Bastian's head," Lili added briskly, "I will arrange the pillows to make his breathing easier."

Still shaking her head, Allora moved to the other side of the bed and did as her great-niece instructed. In his new position, their patient seemed more comfortable. But as Lili bent to study his face, his skin took on a grey tinge and his lips turned almost black.

"What is it?" Allora asked, seeing her frown.

"I don't know." Lili took his pulse again, put an ear to his chest. "That is, I'm not certain but I fear the worst. You know, of course, there are vapors and essences within the body—what philosophers have named the vital and the animal spirits. In Sir Bastian, these appear to be failing so rapidly, he may die before the medicine even arrives."

Then, with a sudden grim determination: "There is only one way to keep him alive: to rapidly expel all the morbid humors out of his body."

Allora raised her eyebrows. "Without the aid of physick? But to do that—"

"To do that," said Lili, rummaging through her basket again, producing a small flask of purest olive oil scented with myrrh, cinnamon, and galingale, and proceeding to anoint the old gentleman at his temples and wrists, "I will have to risk a laying-on-of-hands."

The old woman frowned. "I don't mean to tell you your own business, but considering how tired you are, do you dare to attempt so delicate a procedure? If your mind should wander, if your concentration fails for even an instant—"

"Then he will die. But he is dying now, and there is no other way I know to save him." Lili placed both palms flat on Sir Bastian's narrow chest. "And as the result of any distractions may well prove fatal, the more reason for you to keep silent, Aunt Allora, and to make certain that nobody else disturbs me for the next half hour."

She fastened her eyes on the glass globe. In that dim room, it shone like a planet hanging in the void. She must focus her mind on that and on her task—on those things alone—for once she opened herself to the cosmic forces, there was always the danger that the fierce Centrifugal Winds of manifold time and space would sweep her away.

Taking a deep, long breath, Lili entered the healing trance. *Subtle vapors rose in her brain. Drawing magnetism up out of the earth, she sent it pulsing through her body.* A pure ray of astral light hit the shining globe and was deflected, piercing Sir Bastian's chest and penetrating to the very core of his being. He and Lili cried out in the same instant—then there was only darkness.

3

From without, it was as ugly, grim, and formidable as any great prison, in any great city, anywhere in the world. But within the mighty walls of Whitcomb Gaol there was a huddle of sordid little buildings, all connected by locks, gates, bars, grates, and dark passages, opening every now and again on some dismal yard where the prisoners took the air.

On the day following Wilrowan's duel and its unfortunate conclusion, an elegant gentleman appeared at the lodge by the outer gate and presented his credentials to the burly individual who answered his knock. The gaoler subjected him to a careful scrutiny, taking in the coat of flea's-blood satin lined with sable, the white silk stockings and immaculate small-clothes, the silver-hilted sword and point-lace ruffles, the fair hair perfumed and pomaded, the red-heeled shoes and the little jeweled eyeglass worn on a black velvet ribbon. Deciding that this was no man to be trifled with, the turnkey unlocked the gate and ushered him inside.

The visitor was relieved of his sword and escorted to a stifling small room, where he was presented, along with the documents he carried in one perfectly manicured hand, to the Governor of Whitcomb Gaol: a dried little husk of a man in a fox-colored wig, who sat hunched behind his desk like a Goblin.

"Blaise Crowsmeare-Trefallon." The visitor made a prodigiously elegant bow. "I have a warrant and a letter from the king, authorizing the release of one Wilrowan Krogan-Blackheart."

The governor hitched his chair an inch or two closer to the desk. He held out a clawlike hand to receive the papers, which he read through silently before replying. "These seem to be in order. But you must understand, there are certain procedures that must be followed—which may take as much as a day or two."

Trefallon bowed again. "As you must understand that the king and queen are impatient to see Captain Blackheart return to his duties at the Volary."

The governor scrutinized the letter. "It does not *say* immediate release. Nor anything about duties at the palace. His Majesty knows how these things are done, so in the absence of any clear instructions to the contrary—" Yet there was something in the visitor's cool, unwavering stare that made him add: "I see no reason to deny access to the prisoner in the meantime, if that is what you wish."

"I do," said Blaise, and followed the turnkey out of the room and through a series of chilly stone corridors, rotting gates, tunnels, yards, and more gates, until they came to a double iron grating facing on one of the wards.

A dozen or so prisoners stood or lounged in different parts of an icy yard, some of them hobbled with iron fetters, all of them rough, sullen, and dangerous looking. In that company it was easy to spot Wilrowan: a boyish figure in a long red coat embellished with a quantity of tarnished gold galloon. The familiar hat with the battered turkey feathers was drawn low over his eyes, and he was crouched on one knee close to the ground, apparently absorbed in a pair of black ravens scratching through a pile of frozen garbage at the edge of the yard.

When Blaise called his name, Will rose slowly to his feet, pushed back his hat, thrust his hands into the pockets of his gaudy coat, and sauntered over to the grating, the thin ice crunching beneath his feet as he walked. Amused by this consummate piece of play-acting, Blaise shook his head.

"I'm sorry not to have come to your rescue sooner. I was out last night when your message arrived." Lifting his eyeglass to examine Wilrowan at close quarters, he gave a delicate shudder. "If you don't mind my asking, where did you come by that hideous coat? Really, my dear, you should never wear scarlet with that ginger hair of yours."

Will responded with an appreciative grin. Blaise Trefallon in full dress was a creature of infinite refinement and exquisite taste, far removed from his companion of the taverns and gaming hells. "You can buy anything here. Wine, firewood—even whores, though I've not tried it. The only thing you can't buy is your way out, because the governor, they say, is incorruptible."

Blaise smiled faintly. "He is a petty tyrant who delights in his power. And in no hurry to release you, I regret to say. If there is anything you need in the meantime—" Blaise reached for the coin purse he carried in his pocket.

"I thank you, no. Put that away, Blaise; your money would only burden me. As it is, I only barely escaped being throttled once and bludgeoned another time, all for the sake of this worthless brooch— and the ring I wear on my hand." Will rested his right hand on the inner grating, so that Trefallon could see the silver intaglio ring.

"If I hadn't friends here to guard my back, you might have arrived here only in time to claim my body."

And it was typical of Will, thought Blaise, that he should find some of his former cronies residing in Whitcomb Gaol. But declining to discuss what had always been a sore point between them, he focused his attention on the ring instead. It was of antique design, heavy and intricate, the stone a great smoke-colored crystal deeply incised with ancient writing. It reminded Blaise of some of the minor Goblin artifacts—harmless curiosities all, though immensely valuable—he had seen in private collections.

The gaoler was stationed with his back to a wall about fifteen feet away from the grate, where he could watch Wilrowan's movements but not overhear the conversation. Nevertheless, Blaise lowered his voice.

"You had that from your grandmother, didn't you? I remember you once said it was the most precious thing you owned. Shall I take it away for safekeeping?"

Will hesitated. "I think not. She wore it, you know, through so many dangerous times, and yet she survived. I have an idea it brings me luck."

All the time they were speaking, not once had Will bothered to glance behind him, though twice there had been a shuffling and a muttering among the other prisoners, and once Blaise caught a cold glimmer of sunlight on metal, the impression that something long and exceedingly sharp had passed swiftly from hand to hand. Thinking of those attempts on Will's life, Trefallon shuddered inwardly, hoping the friends who had come to Wilrowan's aid before could really be trusted.

"Are you absolutely certain they only wanted to rob you? Don't you think there might be something else—something *more* at stake?"

"I have considered that, yes. And I've thought about the duel, as well. Macquay's damnable spell of protection. The way those guardsmen arrived just when he was finally in trouble. All arranged in advance—but why? Macquay has no particular grudge against me, not any I know about, anyway."

Will shifted his position from one foot to the other. "And there is another thing: we both know that Rufus Macquay lives well beyond his means. He hasn't paid his debts in six months. But it takes gold to buy spells, to bribe guardsmen. You can't put them off with empty promises, as you can some honest tradesman."

Blaise shook his head thoughtfully. "You can't put off tradesmen forever. Suppose that someone bribed Macquay himself—to provoke the quarrel? Gold in his pocket, his debts paid, men have been murdered for less." Trefallon frowned. "The worst of it is, he has disappeared. And we can't even question the striplings who arrested you, not until Marzden returns. In the meantime, is there anyone else who might be involved? Somebody with 'a particular grudge'?"

Will shrugged, putting his hands back into his pockets. "Beyond all the fathers, husbands, and brothers?"

Blaise raised his eyeglass again, favored his friend with a sardonic glance. "For simplicity's sake we'll confine ourselves to the male relations of your most recent conquests. No need to bring the half of—but stay a moment. What of your own father-in-law?"

A noisy argument had started up in the yard, between a pimple-faced boy and an immense brute in iron leg-shackles. Will did not seem to notice; he rocked slowly back on his heels, giving his full attention to Blaise's question.

"Lord Brakeburn? I don't doubt he wishes me dead and buried; I've hardly lived up to his expectations as a son-in-law. And he surely believes that Lili deserves a hundred times better. I think so myself. But to actually arrange my death?" Will gave a short, negative jerk of his head. "Besides, he would hardly ask Macquay to insult his own daughter."

"A master stroke to divert suspicion?"

Will smiled contemptuously. "I doubt he is capable of any such 'master stroke.' He tricked Lili and me into marrying with the stupidest, most transparent lie—if we hadn't been such children at the time, we'd have seen right through it. Nor would he expect me to take up the sword as Lili's champion. He can't begin to comprehend the nature of my feelings where she is concerned."

Blaise felt a brief twinge of sympathy for the unfortunate Lord Brakeburn; the nature of Wilrowan's feelings for his wife was a continuing mystery even to Will's best friend.

Meanwhile, the quarrel in the middle of the yard had grown ugly. The pimpled youth had taken an ill-advised swing at the gigantic felon; now the big man reached out with one huge hand, took him by the throat, and dashed the boy violently to the ground. The turnkey in the passage did nothing.

"Curse that pig of a governor!" Blaise whispered through the grating. "What does he mean by delaying your release? You're in danger every minute you remain here."

"My dear Trefallon, the only place more dangerous than Whitcomb Gaol is on the streets of Hawkesbridge." Will laughed softly. "You may not be so intimately acquainted with the denizens of the streets as I am, but you should know *that*. The governor may be doing me a favor by keeping me locked up."

Blaise ground his teeth audibly. The gaol ambiance—the great weight of stone and iron on every side, the brutality of the inmates—was beginning to wear on his composure. He simply did not know how Wilrowan could take it all so lightly.

But his present unease put Blaise in mind of something that had troubled him the day before. "There was one odd thing: I saw Goblins among the spectators during your duel. An Ouph or two, at least three Padfoots, and a tall young fellow with a crooked neck."

Will was immediately interested. "A Wryneck, do you think? I've never met a Wryneck or a Grant—they're said to be highly reclusive."

"I don't know. Except for the angle of his head he looked Human enough, but I've never met one either. What started me thinking was the fact that Goblins *invariably* stay clear of trouble. Of anything, in fact, that's likely to attract the attention of the authorities. Yet there they were, watching what may have been for all they knew an illegal duel. Do you have any enemies in the Goblin Quarter?"

"I know a handful by name and they know me, but that's the extent of it. But supposing there *was* a Goblin with a grudge—where would the creature come by enough gold to bribe a man like Macquay? If there really is a scheme to kill me or put me out of the way, I doubt that it's motivated by personal malice. I suspect it's only a matter of policy."

"Policy?" said Trefallon, only half attending. Behind Will's back, the big man had stooped to raise his smaller opponent, probably with an eye to inflicting further punishment. Again there was a flash of metal, and this time both men fell heavily to the ground. The gaoler remained stolid and apparently uninterested.

With an effort, Blaise refocused his attention on Will's last statement. "Do you mean that someone might envy your influence over the queen and seek to supplant you?"

"That, or someone might think there are still too many Rowans left in the world, *especially* in a position to influence Dionee."

Blaise groaned softly. "The Rowans. I was forgetting those notorious relations of yours. What were your parents thinking when they named you after them? But tell me this: Is there no *end* to the number of people who might be thirsting for your blood?"

A shadow passed over Wilrowan's face, and Blaise suddenly realized that his annoying air of careless insouciance was largely affected. "I really don't know," he replied with a wistful smile. "But I should imagine the list is a damnably long one."

The room was oppressive, so small and dark it might have been a cell, with its one high square window barred in iron, its stone-flagged floor, and scarred hickory furniture. But it was not a cell; it was the room where prisoners, their papers already processed, awaited release from Whitcomb Gaol.

At the present time, there was a single occupant, pacing the floor through a long, cold night, while a trencher of oysters and a tankard of ale sat untouched upon the table. Though the hour of Will's release remained uncertain, Trefallon's gold had bought him this one indulgence, removing him from the common wards and the prison yard to this place of comparative safety, procuring him this meal which he had not tasted.

As the first pale light of dawn crept through the window, there came a fluttering of wings in the air outside. Wilrowan glanced up, just in time to see a large black bird land on the window ledge between the iron bars.

<*Crwcrwyl*>. Will extended an arm and the raven hopped from the ledge to his wrist. <*What news do you bring from the Volary?*> The silver intaglio ring on Wilrowan's hand had come to life, glowing in that dreary little chamber with an uncanny blue light. To Will's heightened vision, a spark of similar light appeared deep within the raven's brain.

The raven folded its wings. <*A quarrel in the queen's apartments. Throughout the palace there has been much coming and going. Much whispering and intrigue. But nothing out of the ordinary.*>

The ring was ancient, as Blaise had suspected, though not so harmless an article as he supposed. It allowed Will to communicate with the great black birds that came and went almost unnoticed throughout the city. How it had first come into the possession of his relations, the mysterious Rowan family, Will did not know, but it had passed to him from his grandmother, Lady Krogan, on the day he was appointed Captain of the Queen's Guard. "*It may prove useful,*" the former Odilia Rowan had said as she bestowed the gift, and useful it had certainly proved to be. The Hawkesbridge ravens made an effective and utterly unsuspected network of spies.

<*What of Macquay? Has he returned to the palace?*> Will asked.

The bird stepped daintily up his arm. <*No. He has not been seen.*>

Will ground his teeth. <*Then you will have to search the entire city. Inform me immediately, should you or one of your lieutenants spot him.*>

<*If you are not alone, what token shall I bring you?*>

Wilrowan considered. A twig or a blade of grass was the usual signal when the ravens had any information to give him, but this was important and the sign should be a clear one. He reached into one pocket and drew out a small brass coin. <*Take this with you.*>

The raven lowered its glossy head, took the coin in its beak.

<*In the meantime, you should assign a watch on Pyecroft and Barnaby. On Finn, too. He's no great friend of mine, though he did act for me in the duel.*> Will created a vivid mental picture of each man's face, so there could be no mistake.

<*Pyecroft. Barnaby. Finn.*> Crwcrwyl gave the images back as confirmation. <*Not Trefallon?*>

Will hesitated. Not that he doubted Blaise for a moment, but perhaps he should ask the ravens to watch as a measure of protection?

Before he had time to decide, a clatter of footsteps in the corridor outside his door, the grate of an iron key in the lock, shattered his delicate communion with the bird. Startled, the raven fluttered up from his wrist, then flew out the window.

Once upon a time, in the bad old times, when Men were weak and timorous and an evil race of Goblins ruled the earth, a certain small village grew into a great city of brick and marble, slate, and cobblestone.

Men lived there, of course, as they lived elsewhere: ragged and humble, dirty and ignorant, which was just as the Maglore wished to keep them, and therefore fit only for the most grinding, laborious tasks, like working and maintaining the pumps and other underground machinery——for Tarnburgh was located in a volcanic region far to the north, and the machines brought heated air and boiling subterranean waters up through a series of pipes and radiators to heat the metropolis during the long arctic winter.

She was just such a city as the Goblins loved: vast and intricate, startling, beautiful, and perilous. In the great maze of her winding streets and small hidden courts were many neat little shops where the tireless Goblin craftsmen (Ouphs and Padfoots, mostly) worked long hours making singing roses, clockwork dragonflies, glass slippers, and other novelties for their Maglore masters. In Tarnburgh's great libraries and universities, the scholarly Grants and Wrynecks, bowed and ink-stained after centuries of study, drew elaborate star charts and leafed through ponderous old books on history, genealogy, and etiquette——for it was a characteristic of the long-lived races in those days that they delighted to look upward and inward, sideways and backward, but rarely more than a week or two forward in time.

But the beautiful Maglore in their mansions and palaces had little to do but amuse themselves, for tens of centuries had passed since they first created the intricate jeweled devices on which their power and their Empire rested. So they dreamed up endless tiny variations on spells they already knew by heart, became fanatic patrons of all the arts, and devoted themselves to those most elegant civilized pastimes: court intrigue, lovemaking, and delicate cruelty.

But when Mankind became restless, when they began to see the possibility of something more than poor rations, hard labor, and ignorance——when Men throughout the Empire first sought that knowledge of lives and fates, time and the universe, which the Maglore had denied them——when at last they took arms against the Goblin races, overthrew the universities and slaughtered the ancient scholars, herded the inoffensive Padfoots and Ouphs into the poorest parts of the cities and forced them to live ever afterward in damp cellars, drafty attics, and dingy small tenements—when, armed with fire and salt, Mankind carried the battle against the Maglore into every city, village, and town, and vowed not to be satisfied with anything less than total extermination—when Men remade the world according to a new and better pattern, when some cities faded and others appeared out of nowhere—Tarnburgh, like Hawkesbridge, endured.

Naturally, she underwent changes. For all their outward similarities, Men differ greatly from Maglore: numbers and measurements fascinate them, and they love what is useful as well as beautiful. So the city of portrait-painters, dancing masters, courtiers, astrologers, and toymakers became instead a city of clerks and notaries, lens-grinders, cartographers, inn-keepers, tailors, and bookbinders.

The Maglore, meanwhile, gone but not precisely forgotten, had entered into legend, the heroes and (more often) the villains of a thousand fantastic tales: as false black knights and scheming queens, wicked stepmothers, magical godmothers, and the like. And some indefinable hint of their presence still lingered in Tarnburgh, lending that city of fine old buildings and curious small shops an indefinable air, suggesting the kind of place where any sort of marvelous unexpected thing might happen.

4

The palace was ablaze with light. From the latticed window of an attic room two miles distant, Ys could not actually see Lindenhoff, but she had passed the palace five days earlier on her way into Tarnburgh, and given the golden glow she could see on the north side of town, over the dark irregular roofline of the intervening shops and houses, it was easy to picture how enchanting King Jarred's elegant white-and-gold jewelbox of a castle must look with the torches all lit.

The girl shivered and folded her arms across her chest. A square-necked grey taffeta gown, cut low across the bosom, with full skirts held stiffly out from her body by a set of baleen hoops, offered scant protection against the damps and drafts of this garret in the Goblin Quarter. But it was anticipation quite as much as the bitter cold of winter that nearly froze her already chilly blood.

She thought of the months just past, the long weeks of planning and scheming; she thought of the difficult years before that, the times when she had even lost faith in Madame Solange, her threats as well as her promises. But at last the great day had finally arrived, the hour was almost at hand, to go to the ball and enchant a king.

A large white rat skittered across the uneven floorboards; Ys drew in her breath sharply, felt her fingers curl instinctively. For just a moment, a memory struggled to surface. *The memory of something small and savage, a swift, sly, wary little creature that cringed in dark corners, that fought for every mouthful of food it ever ate, for the very pile of rags on which it huddled at night—* Then the memory faded, and Ys could breathe again.

The old nightmare, that was all it was. The old terror that came when she was lying in bed half-sleeping, half-waking, and made her feel as if she was being stifled to death with dust.

With an effort, Ys forced her thoughts into more pleasant channels. They said that King Jarred was young, elegant, and darkly handsome; educated, witty, and charming. With all this, she could only hope that he would not prove to be overly clever, or he might wear her to death with questions she dared not answer.

Her hands wandered to the glowing necklace at her throat, to the strange stones which always appeared at first glance to be pearls, but were something brighter, colder, and harder, to the crystal pendant burning like a lump of ice against her bare skin. She remembered, then, that Jarred was going to find her absolutely irresistible, and that would make everything so much easier.

The door behind her creaked open; there was a rustle of stiff petticoats. Ys whirled around just in time to see the slim, active figure of her governess sweep into the room. As always, Madame Solange appeared to be animated by a dark, malicious energy. "How much longer do you mean to keep us waiting? Do you imagine we have nothing better to do than to linger here at your pleasure?"

Ys flinched, though she knew the harsh words were not intended for her. They were meant for the tiny crooked Gobline who huddled on a low stool in one corner of the attic, sewing up a seam with quick, even stitches.

"I am just finished now." The little Padfoot seamstress made a final knot and snipped off the thread with her teeth. She was a queer little person, all skin, bone, and gristle, except for a rat's nest of unruly hair and a pair of large fleshy feet. "I have mended the spell as best I could, given so little time."

Madame Solange snatched up her handiwork, examining it minutely. It was a long sealskin cloak, very old, very tattered and fragile looking. Once, it had been a lady's garment and exceedingly fine. Around the edges, where the short dark hairs had been stripped away, there was an intricate border of crystal beadwork, and the fragile leather had been so deeply permeated with a rich, musky perfume that the scent still lingered. But it was not with an eye to its antiquated grandeur that Madame regarded it. When she reversed the cloak and spread it out across her skirts, the gossamer-light inner lining shimmered—and then *disappeared*, enabling Ys and the little seamstress to see right through Madame Solange to the dusty plank floor behind her.

"The young lady must wear the skin-side out until she reaches the palace," the Padfoot cautioned. "I can't vouch for such shoddy work on such short notice, but the spell should hold while she moves from the kitchen to the ballroom."

"If it does *not* hold, we will all regret it," Madame replied in a voice of suppressed passion. "You most of all."

She might have said more, but just then a dainty figure, vaguely masculine, appeared in the doorway, instantly claiming the attention of all three females.

Lord Vif was a sight to behold. Exquisitely attired in a coat of palest lilac satin with silver embroidery, he was rouged, patched, laced, powdered, tricked out to a remarkable degree. After a pause, which allowed the others to admire him sufficiently, he minced into the room, extended a slender silk-clad leg, and made a deep flourishing bow, toward a point strategically located somewhere between Ys and her daunting governess. "It is time. Your carriage and escort await you."

THE QUEEN'S NECKLACE ·☾ 49

Her "carriage," as Ys well knew, was nothing more than a rickety peddler's cart, her escort a rag-tag company of wandering entertainers led by a disreputable old Ouph woman who posed as a fortuneteller. It was ludicrous and degrading that she, who should have been empress of the entire world, was forced to arrive on the king's doorstep in a cart, but it could not be helped.

So Ys held her tongue and allowed Lord Vif to help her put on the cloak, draping the ancient sealskin to conceal her gown of taffeta and lace, then pulling up the deep hood to cover her profusion of powdered curls.

She was moving toward the door, when a small gnarled hand reached out and timidly touched a corner of her cloak. "My Lady, your shoes. They catch the light."

Ys stopped and looked down. So far as she could see, the tattered hem of her mantle reached all the way to the floor. Still, she imagined the creature had detected something, some flash of reflected light as she moved across the room. With a shrug, Ys bent down, raised her hoops and ruffled petticoats with one hand, removed her diamond-heeled brocade shoes with the other. Her stockings of finest pearl-grey silk would suffer, but that was a small price to pay, considering what she hoped to gain this night.

"The necklace," said Madame Solange. "It might be well to keep it hidden until the moment arrives."

Wordlessly, Ys unfastened the clasp and dropped the double string of cold stones down the front of her gown.

"Don't speak to me of the Maglore, I beg you." Lucius Sackville-Guilian gave a bitter laugh as he spoke. "Spin me no tales of those beautiful, terrifying Goblin sorcerers, for I am half-convinced they never existed. Or if they did, if they were anything more than an elaborate hoax on the part of our ancestors, then *we* are their lineal descendants."

Far from taking offense as Lucius might have intended, King

Jarred only responded by laughing, too. "Is this another page from the Great Revisionist History? Just how many *revisions* does that make?"

His cousin shrugged. "I believe at last count there were eighty-three." It was a conservative estimate; Lucius had been rewriting history since the age of eight, and the book's history—if not the history in the book—was a long and colorful one.

"You realize," said Jarred, "that you are being perfectly outrageous. And yet, your powers of persuasion are always so great, I wouldn't be surprised if Francis and I end up 'half-convinced' before you are through with us."

The third man present, Doctor Francis Purcell, said nothing, though the old man's eyes were troubled. At Purcell's invitation, the king and Lucius had met in the philosopher's workshop-laboratory for a light supper before the ball. That conversation around the mahogany dining table would eventually turn argumentative the older man might have foreseen, for he had been tutor in his time to both the young ones. That the discussion, over the final course of pigeons, chestnut soup, and game pie, would take on such a disturbing tone, he had clearly not anticipated.

"We are told," said Lucius, sitting back in his chair, crossing one muscular white-stockinged leg over the other, "that ever since Men brought down the Empire and harried the Maglore into extinction the world has existed in a state of near perfection. And why? Because Our Revered Ancestors, when they created their new civilization, made certain laws, handed down certain maxims, and incorporated certain habits and fears into the very fabric of Society, intended to maintain that state of near perfection practically forever. But have we really inherited the best of all possible worlds?"

The room was quiet for several moments, while the king and the scholar thought that over. Quiet, except for the movement of heavy machinery in the room above. For reasons that were obscure to Jarred—but perhaps only because Purcell found the sound of moving gears and wheels, the constant whirring and ticking, somehow soothing—the philosopher had chosen to locate his workshop in the Lindenhoff clock tower.

"You think we have not?" said Purcell, adjusting his gold-rimmed spectacles.

"I think we could hardly have inherited anything worse. We are a hundred tiny nations ruled by a hundred ruling houses, as vain, idle, weak, and sapless a collection of painted figureheads—excepting present company, of course—as one could hope to meet. Why are they inbred to the point of weakness? Because our ancestors placed a ban on marriage between the various royal houses. Why are they idle, vain, and frivolous? Because that is what people expect, that is what they *will* have. Because when the rare exception comes along, a visionary thinker, a great humanitarian, the world grows uneasy— just as our ancestors planned that it should —and everyone starts muttering about Imperial Ambitions."

Jarred put down his empty wine glass. With that movement, the candles on the table flickered and then grew bright again. "You're thinking of the King of Rijxland."

"The King of Rijxland as he once was, yes. But as he is now, he illustrates my point even better. The poor old fellow goes absolutely mad—I suppose that he *is* mad, and it's not just a convenient excuse for locking him up?"

"Oh, yes. I sent two of my own doctors to confirm the diagnosis, and so did the King of Kjellmark and the Prince of Catwitsen."

"Well then, Izaiah of Rijxland is undoubtedly insane. But do they depose him?" said Lucius. "Do they set up his daughter as regent to rule in his place? No. There is no precedent for either of those things in Rijxland, so they keep the lunatic on as their head of state and actually allow the business of government to be conducted from a *madhouse*. And what is even worse, nobody anywhere else seems to think the situation at all unnatural."

Jarred moved uneasily in his chair. Izaiah of Rijxland's original complaint had been a deep melancholia directly following the death of his queen, a melancholy which had lingered long and eventually declined into madness. As a heart-broken widower himself, Jarred sometimes felt he identified a little too closely with the old man's plight.

He gave another light, insincere laugh. "But to return to your interesting thesis: now that you have dismissed me and my kind, Cousin Luke, what can you tell me about the aristocracy? Surely you and yours have an important part to play in the 'perfect' Society our ancestors created."

"The aristocracy," Lucius said with a sneer, "are no better or worse than our sovereign princes. I wish I could say we were. We have trivialized everything, made fashion our religion—and religion no more than a passing fad. Yet what choice have we but to devote our lives to such weighty matters as the delicate contemplation of the perfect waistcoat, or the exquisite fall of lace at the edge of a brocade sleeve?"

Francis Purcell looked up from a brief inspection of his own discreet ruffles. Surely no one here deserved to be condemned on account of vanity. Purcell was dressed with neatness and propriety in sober broadcloth and thread lace, the king with somber elegance as became a man still in half-mourning, and as for Luke—his clothes were excellent and he had the kind of slim, broad-shouldered figure which ought to compliment them, but except on the most formal occasions he wore them so carelessly he was the despair of his valet.

"Let us become too energetic," Lucius was saying, "let us become too industrious, too inquisitive, and we'll go the same way the Rowans did, fifty years ago."

The king picked up an antique bronze flagon liberally embellished with tritons and fish-headed monsters, and poured himself another cup of the dry red wine. Doctor Purcell made a hard little sound at the back of his throat. "In the case of the Rowan family, there were those two dangerous marriages. One brother to the niece of the Duke of Nordfjall, another to a cousin of the Prince of Lichtenwald. Perfectly legal, all according to the letter of the law, but not in keeping with its spirit."

"Those marriages——" Lucius dismissed them with a wave of his hand. His handsome face was so pale and earnest, there was such a glow in his fine dark eyes, it was plain he was speaking from the heart now and not just choosing a cause at random, as was often his habit. "They certainly served to attract attention to the family. And once people started looking too closely, what did they find? That the Rowans, unlike other noble families who live by the sweated toil of their tenant farmers, had invested some of their money in trade. Also, they read too much, travelled too much, had too much influence in too many places, and two or three of them took rather too much interest in vegetable poisons——though merely, as it later developed, with an eye to exploiting their medicinal properties.

"All this stirs the public imagination to the point where wild stories start circulating: about murders, poisonings, and intrigues of every description. What follows next? Trials, imprisonments, executions, and the family is in a fair way to be wiped out."

He paused to take a sip of wine. Across the table, Jarred made an impatient gesture. "Go on, Luke. Don't leave us in suspense. I've always wondered why *any* Rowans survived."

"They survived because the winds of conservatism suddenly started blowing in their favor. It seems there have been Rowans——if not forever, at least since the fifty-first century when the world was perfected——so it naturally follows that the family must play some essential role in the Grand Scheme of Our Revered Ancestors. No Rowans at all would be almost as bad as too many and too powerful. So the surviving few are retried, and amazingly, the chief witnesses begin to recant. All too late, of course, for the men and women who had already been executed, or who died in prison under suspicion."

"You take a warm interest in the fate of a family not personally known to you," the scholar commented dryly.

"I hardly remember a time when I was not fascinated by the Rowans. When other boys were playing at rebels and Maglore, I always fancied myself as one of the Wicked Rowans going to the scaffold in high style, putting on a brave face while the mob screamed for my blood." Lucius turned to the king. "Surely you remember those games we played?"

"As I also remember you were invariably pardoned at the last possible moment, when one of the other boys came racing in with the necessary reprieve," Jarred replied, with a sardonic lift of his dark eyebrows. "Even in play, Luke, you never had to face the consequences of your odd ideas. I wonder if you believe you will always be immune?"

That should have been a home thrust, but Lucius affected to shrug it off. "Shall I continue my argument, or do I bore you?"

Jarred pulled out his crystal pocket watch, flicked it open, and glanced at the dial. "You don't bore me, but we have been talking here for two hours, and I have still to dress before my guests arrive. Perhaps you can present the rest a little more succinctly?"

His cousin sat gathering his thoughts for almost a minute, sitting with his brow furrowed, staring moodily into the soup.

"I've little to say about the middle class." Lucius bowed to Purcell across the table. "All the virtues that Man allows are embodied in the able, energetic middle class. A clever craftsman—say, a glassblower or a coach-maker—is always free to introduce some new trick or fancy, just as an inventive genius like Francis is perfectly free to play with his clocks and dancing automatons. But let either one of them, the craftsman or the philosopher, discover or invent a thing which improves the lot of his fellow Men in anything more than the smallest particular, or advances the total of Human knowledge by anything more than the tiniest fraction—and Society will brand him a renegade."

The scholar was quiet, evidently taking these words to heart. He had gained some fame as the creator of dancing dolls—clockwork figures ranging from the miniscule to the more than life-sized, from the comical to the sublimely beautiful—ormolu music boxes, miniature planetariums set with tiny gemstones, and other delicate mechanical toys of his own invention. He had gained a secondary fame as a collector of nautical clocks, astrolabes, and other instruments of scientific measurement. He had assembled a remarkable collection over the years, and he was always taking them apart and putting them back together again with small improvements.

But of rather more significance: in one corner of his laboratory there stood a curious device, made up of bronze wheels, lead weights, and rotating compound magnets. On this particular creation Purcell had bestowed the name of "Celestial Clock," hinting to his pupils that it would ultimately fulfill some hitherto undreamed of function—yet he had been working on his invention for eighteen years without ever daring to bring the design to its full perfection, or even explaining its purpose.

To cover the sudden awkward silence, Jarred spoke to Lucius. "And can you dispose of the lower classes so neatly and briefly?"

"Even more so. The lower classes live very little better than the Padfoots and the Ouphs, and the Ouphs and the Padfoots live like dogs."

"All very well," said the king. "But now you've dissected our entire society and found it wanting, what has that to do with what you said before? Why do you doubt—or pretend to doubt—that the Maglore ever existed?"

"Because the world is so sick and stagnant. Because—because without the dreadful example of the Maglore in all their wickedness to scare us into submission, how could Society hope to stifle our natural curiosity, our natural ambition, and our creative imagination?"

"And so——?" said Jarred, not quite following him.

Lucius laughed that bitter laugh again. "I doubt their existence for one reason only: because they are just too *damned* convenient."

5

Ys followed Lord Vif down three steep flights and out through a low door, to the moonlit alley where the Ouph fortuneteller and her troupe waited in the cart. Madame Solange whispered a few words in her ear, then someone offered Ys a large calloused hand. A moment later, she was sitting on a wide bench next to the driver: a great dirty brute of a Man, with bloodshot eyes and bristling jowls, who stank of sweat and cheap spirits.

Lord Vif stepped back, the driver spoke to the horses, and the cart began to move. They turned left at the end of the alley, jogged down a narrow street for a quarter of a mile, and then came out on a broad boulevard. It was nine o'clock, but it might have been any time between noon and midnight. All hours were the same, this far north, and would remain the same until the sun finally inched above the horizon two weeks hence.

But an immense blue-white moon with a silver halo hung just over the pointed roof tops, and the aurora borealis played in pastel streamers across a black velvet sky already studded with a thousand diamond pinpoints of light. The city shimmered, resembling nothing so much as a great spun-sugar confection, under its dusting of ice crystals and snow.

Progress through the town was noisy, between the rattling of the flimsy two-wheeled vehicle over the icy cobblestones, the twittering of Madam Zaphir's Prophetic Canaries, in two tin cages down in the straw under the seat, and the whispering and muffled laughter of the ragged entertainers. They took turns riding and walking, alternately tumbling in and out of the cart like acrobats.

Well, they were excited, Ys realized that. Though none but Madame Zaphir, with her ugly little eyes and her cringing, obsequious manner, had any idea what it was all about. They only knew they had been paid in gold to perform a mission of utmost importance to the grand lady who employed them. And since it was impossible for that gaudy company *not* to attract attention as they entered the center of Tarnburgh, where the moonlit streets were still crowded even at this hour, best to make their approach loudly and openly, so that no one could suspect any sinister purpose.

For all that, Ys felt a burning blush color her cheeks at the thought of being seen in such company. She sat stiff, silent, and embarrassed inside her sealskin cloak—until something about the route they followed forced out a protest.

"This is not the way to the palace gate! Where are you taking me?" Fear of treachery stabbed at her heart. If the fortuneteller had guessed who she really was, if the others knew they were harboring one whose very *existence* was a capital crime anywhere in the world—

From her place at the back of the cart, Madam Zaphir spoke. "We must enter Lindenhoff on the other side: the servants' entrance. What did Your Ladyship suppose? It's not as though we've been hired to entertain the king's guests. We are only there to amuse the cooks and potwashers after their labors."

With an effort at regaining her composure, Ys subsided. Bitter as it was to accept, the Gobline was right. How else to enter the king's house unannounced—which was the only way that Ys *could* get in—but through the servants' entrance?

For life as Ys knew it had rarely included elegant ballgowns or jeweled slippers. More often it meant wearisome travel, by mail coach, diligence, and packet, and an endless procession of cheap lodgings and second-rate inns. It meant changing names and playing new roles in every new city where she and Madame Solange happened to find themselves—here as a music teacher and her devoted daughter, there as a widow and her paid companion—and more often than not it meant dresses, once beautiful, that had to be mended, let out, and turned inside out, in order to maintain the illusion of genteel poverty.

"We dare not attract their attention," said Madame Solange, when Ys was still very small. *"That is something that every Goblin and Gobline knows."* As she grew older, Ys had come to realize that quite as much as it was for the Padfoots and Ouphs, the Grants and Wrynecks, this was the key to her own survival.

But all that began to change on the day Madame first gave Ys the necklace and the phial containing her mother's ashes. Remembering that day, Ys pressed her hand to the front of her dress, felt the strange stones and the heart-shaped pendant lying so cold and malignant between her corset and her skin.

"Those who murdered your mother are dead. The Maglore are no longer divided. Though our numbers are few, we are now united in one great purpose," Madame had announced. *"And while it is not possible that we could regain for you the entire world overnight, it has been decided that you should at least reclaim a small part of it. We are going to arrange—an advantageous marriage."*

After that memorable day, there was a flurry of activity, a frenzy of plotting, a calling-in of hidden resources, all leading up to this night. Ys could only hope that Madame Solange had not given in to a last frugal impulse and neglected to pay the fortuneteller so handsomely the thought of treachery never even entered her mind.

As the ugly cart continued its awkward, lurching progress, Ys glanced back at her disreputable companions. They had little enough, it was true. Yet, unlike Ys, they seemed to value what they had, to get the most enjoyment possible out of their rude, uncertain existence. She did not know whether to pity or to despise them.

Then she remembered something else Madame had said, the last words her governess whispered as Ys climbed into the cart. *"After all, any humiliation you suffer tonight can be easily erased. Just as soon as the first part of our plan is successfully completed, once Jarred falls in love with you and makes you his queen, we'll make certain nobody remembers."*

Ys knew what that meant: that tools once used may then be discarded, that those who knew the degrading details—Madam Zaphir, the seamstress, these other nameless wretches, even Lord Vif—could be ruthlessly and permanently eliminated.

But O Madame Solange, Ys thought with a shudder, *be careful what kind of monster you are raising me to be. Be careful lest someday I grow so heartless, I decide I can just as easily dispose of you!*

There was an uneasy silence in the clock tower workshop, as the king and Purcell, temporarily forgetting the ball and the guests so soon to arrive, sat and considered what Lucius had just said.

"Your arguments are tortuous," said Jarred at last. "And I wonder if you mean half you say. Or rather, I'm certain you mean every word of it now, but what will you mean tomorrow?"

The philosopher gave another dry little cough. "You said something; I am not quite certain if I heard or understood you correctly. You said, 'We are the Maglore.'"

Lucius tossed off the contents of his glass. "And when I said 'we,' I was naturally referring to all Mankind. I ask you to consider what we know about Goblins. Take any Ouph or Padfoot: bones brittle, sinews ropey, hair like straw, skin dry and cold, the whole combination highly combustible. They burn like paper at the touch of a flame, they can't eat more than minute quantities of salt or they die in agonies, and there's something in the blood that boils if it comes into contact with seawater. But what do the stories say of the Maglore? Why, that they were outwardly indistinguishable from Men. It seems likely that the Maglore were no more Goblins than you and I, and it is only the passage of time that has embellished their legend."

Jarred toyed with the remains of game-pie on his plate. "Stories do tend to alter with every telling."

"Consider this too: they say the Maglore had lost the ability to look more than a few days or weeks forward in time, and it was Man's own ability to imagine a future full of changes that finally gave him the advantage. But how far and fearlessly do we look ahead? How many months? How many years? It seems our vision grows shorter with every passing generation. If the Maglore were *not* Men to begin with, I very much fear that Men are becoming Maglore."

"But," said Francis Purcell, again with a troubled frown, "there are the Goblin Jewels. The Crystal Egg, with its delicate interior machinery, which His Majesty uses to regulate the volcanic fires under this city. The Orb of Mountfalcon. The great Silver Nef belonging to the King of Rijxland, which prevents the sea from breaking through the dikes and flooding a hundred miles of farmland, sweeping away a dozen villages and at least one great city. And all the others, equally miraculous. Could Human sorcerers have invented such wonders?"

"Why not?" Lucius leaned back in his chair. "We have no way of knowing the capabilities of our distant ancestors. We can only know what they *chose* for us to know about them. And think about this: a hundred pieces of jeweled clockwork, a hundred tiny kingdoms, principalities, and arch-duchies. Is this a coincidence or was it planned? Which came first—the Kingdom or the Crystal Egg?"

"That I can answer easily. There were many times a hundred Goblin treasures, both great and small, but only the Great Jewels survived the revolution. The others were destroyed, or else were lost or hidden away, and no one has discovered their whereabouts in all these years."

"But that is precisely my point. Fifteen hundred years, my dear Francis, and five thousand years before that. It was all so long ago, how can we hope to know the truth?"

In the room above, there was a grinding and a sliding, followed by a loud, vibrating peal, as the bronze giant in the clock tower moved down his track, raised his mighty hammer, and struck one of the twelve great bells. As the crashing note faded away, the laboratory and its contents continued to reverberate gently.

Jarred gave himself a sharp mental shake. "I am going to be late for my own ball. Shame on you, Luke, for keeping us here with your wild speculations." He pushed back his chair and the others did the same.

"Botheration!" said Lucius. "I've kept Perys and the barber waiting in my room this half hour. They say that it takes the better part of an evening to render me presentable—and I've hardly left them time to do the trick tonight."

Making a deep bow to Jarred and a polite inclination of his head toward the philosopher, Lucius moved toward the door. The king was about to follow him out of the room when Purcell put out a hand and lightly touched his black velvet sleeve.

With an inquisitive quirk of one dark eyebrow, Jarred turned to face his host. "Yes, Francis?"

"These are dangerous ideas. Very dangerous indeed. I wonder how Mr. Guilian comes by them?"

Jarred shrugged. "I suppose he gets them from you, at least indirectly. You are the one who taught us both to question everything. Perhaps you taught Luke even better than you knew."

"But what of this journey he is planning to make, this tour of the continent? And he actually talks now of publishing his book: *A Great History of the World, Refuting Everything*. The very title so exceedingly provocative! I cannot think any good will come of it."

The king put a friendly hand on the old man's shoulder. "You have a good heart, Francis. But only consider this: I have never seen Luke hold fast to a declared purpose in my entire life. I have a strong notion that whatever he intends to say in his book at the beginning, he'll end up *refuting* no one so much as himself."

"But while he is travelling from place to place, living among strangers, asking so many ill-advised questions—I cannot help thinking he will prove a danger to himself, once he leaves Winterscar and your protection."

"My dear old friend," said the king, "that is precisely the reason I have encouraged him to go."

The philosopher gave a violent start. "To put him into danger? Surely Your Majesty cannot possibly mean—"

"No, no," Jarred replied soothingly. "Nothing of the sort. But to teach Luke what it really takes for a man to make his way in the world. It was a great mistake, if you stop to think about it, when my father decided we should be reared together and Luke brought up like a young prince—but with none of the responsibilities. Secure in my favor and friendship, he can do as he likes, say what he pleases, create no end of a stir with his wild theories, and never have to consider the consequences. I hardly think he knows there *could* be consequences."

The philosopher gave a mournful shake of his head. "I cannot argue with anything you say. But I fail to see—"

The king began to wander around the room, picking up bits of clockwork and giving them a cursory examination, then putting them down again with an impatient gesture. "Luke has always fancied himself the Champion of the Common Man, though he has no more idea than I do how the common man really thinks and feels. He has pursued no career, not even those a gentleman might, as diplomat, military man, or academic. As a result, he simply does not know what it means to be forced to compromise or to regulate his impulses. He never *does* regulate his impulses——except, occasionally, according to the promptings of his own generous nature."

"All this is true. But how, Your Majesty, can any of this be mended at this late date?"

"Perhaps it can't be," said the king with a sigh. He touched a hidden spring on an amber and ivory casket; a tiny door opened in one side and a little golden clockwork serpent slid out and glided across the table, flickering a tiny red tongue. "Yet I still hope, with some broadening of his experience, that Luke may yet come close to becoming the man he might——nay, the man he *ought* to be. A man with so many inherent gifts and graces, so much could be made of him. So I encourage him to make this journey, to travel to places where no one knows him, to learn first-hand what it is like to be, if not a common laboring man, at least an ordinary private gentleman."

Jarred turned back to the philosopher with a wry smile. "In the end, I suppose, I hope he will gain——wisdom, which is the one great thing that he lacks."

"Indeed, I hope that he *may* gain wisdom," said Purcell, though he appeared to doubt the thing was even possible.

In happier days, the first dance had always belonged to Jarred and Zelene. Now that she was gone, it was up to him to choose another partner. But at this first ball since her death, he simply did not have the heart to lead out anyone else, and the idea of so many expectant faces turning his way as every female in the room waited to be chosen, their visible disappointment when they learned he was not dancing, was more than Jarred could bear. For that reason he had given the order, two days before, that his guests should begin the ball without him.

When the king finally arrived in the ballroom, the musicians were playing and the dance floor was already crowded with elegant men and women engaged in a stately minuet. Candlelight shimmered on pale rose silks, embroidered white satins, and tissue of silver and gold. And yet, Jarred thought as he paused on the threshold, they were dancing their measure, these dainty modern ladies and gentleman, on the very same white marble floor where (if history was truthful and Lucius mistaken) the last Goblin empress and the ladies of her court, ponderous in their wide farthingales and immense cartwheel ruffs, had danced their wild galliards and voltas.

Thinking of Luke, the king's eyes passed quickly over the ballroom, seeking him out. There he was, fresh from the hands of his barber and valet, unusually resplendent in claret-colored satin and antique bone lace, his dark hair tied back with a crimson bow. He was dancing with—

Jarred felt his mouth go suddenly dry, his heart begin to thump in his chest. He shook his head to clear it, wondering what could have possibly come over him. Surely *not* a glimpse of the unknown girl in pearl-grey satin who was dancing with Luke. And yet—no, he was sure they had never met. Though she was not precisely beautiful, there was something deeply appealing about her heart-shaped face, which he should have remembered, and as for those dark, dark eyes—

Without moving from the arched doorway, he signaled to his major-domo, who immediately wove a silent and unobtrusive path across the dance floor. "Who is the lady, the pale girl in the ash-colored gown, dancing with Mr. Guilian?"

"No one seems to know, Your Majesty. Indeed, it is what everyone seems to be talking about. We have just been waiting for you to arrive and tell us what ought to be done; not wishing to commit any discourtesy, should she prove to be the wife or daughter of some foreign dignitary. But if you wish her escorted out—"

"No. Let her stay for a time at least. A touch of mystery might—enliven this evening."

No lady's maid or seamstress dressed up in her mistress's finery could possibly feign that dainty air of hauteur. Or could she? Jarred moved toward the dais and took a seat in one of the two rose brocade chairs between the silver lions.

As always, he was uncomfortably aware of the empty seat on his right. If he closed his eyes, he could almost hear the whisper of Zelene's pale silken skirts, smell the faint, elusive scent of her perfume. But if he closed his eyes, when he opened them again the disappointment would be too sharp, too painful.

Shaking off these melancholy reflections, Jarred allowed his gaze to wander across the ballroom, and again his attention was caught by the girl in the grey gown and cobweb lace.

She was standing alone at the far end of the long room, because the music had stopped and Luke had deserted her. If she had come in with a proper chaperone, surely this was the moment for some solicitous female to appear and lend the girl countenance, yet nobody even moved in her direction.

But how extraordinary, Jarred thought, *for such a very young lady to come in without an escort. Particularly wearing a fortune in diamonds.* They sparkled in her powdered hair, on the bracelet she wore on one slender white arm, even on the high heels of her brocade slippers.

Without any conscious volition, he left his chair on the dais and crossed the ballroom. The girl tilted her head up at his approach, rewarded him with a dazzling smile.

"With your leave, this next dance is mine," he heard himself murmur.

She lowered her eyes and, without a word, allowed Jarred to lead her out to the center of the dance floor.

*   *   *

"So now Jarred is dancing with the fair unknown," drawled a lazy voice.

A portly figure in cherry-colored velvet swam on the fringes of Luke's vision. He turned to find that Jarred's uncle, Lord Hugo Sackville, had joined him at the edge of the ballroom, under a stained-glass window painted with the Walburg swans and lilies. "*Quite* a little beauty and so lavishly dressed. Now, I wonder who is keeping her? And who, among this brilliant company, is hiding his chagrin at the sight of the little baggage putting herself on display?"

"Do you think she is—a beauty, I mean?" Lucius ignored the nastier part of Lord Hugo's speech; the man was inclined to be vulgar, and Luke never liked to encourage him. "I suppose she is, if you admire the type. If you're not put off by that sharp little chin and the generally vixenish look to the face."

"If you are, then why did you ask her to dance?"

Lucius was not quite certain, as he indicated with a characteristic shrug. "Curiosity, most likely. My fatal flaw. Like everyone else, I wanted to know who she is."

"And did you find out?" Lord Hugo reached into a waistcoat pocket, brought out a gold snuffbox set with rubies and a large cameo, and flicked it open.

"No, I did not." With a slight shake of his head, Luke declined the offer of perfumed tobacco. "It was an odd conversation, now that I think of it. For all she was so evasive about who she was and where she had come from, she was impertinent enough to ask about *me*. And when I told her that Jarred and I were second cousins, she gave me such a look out of those black eyes of hers—"

"Yes," prompted the royal uncle, taking a pinch of snuff for himself before snapping the box shut.

"It was only a passing fancy. I thought to myself: This must be how a corpse feels, being measured for his shroud."

Lord Hugo gave an uneasy shout of laughter. "You'll be the death of me yet, young Guilian, you and your extraordinary notions. But tell me, dear boy, did you chance to mention that you were going abroad, that you'd be on your way to Kjellmark when the light returns in a few more weeks?"

"Yes, I did," answered Luke with a puzzled frown. "Though I can't tell you why I was so absolutely eager to tell her what she wanted to know!"

Going through the figures of the dance, breathing in the heavy scent of the musk and orris root his partner had mixed with the rice flour that powdered her hair, King Jarred felt increasingly baffled by his own reactions to the mysterious young woman. When he first took her cold hand in his, he had felt a deep shudder of revulsion, but now he was gripped by a powerful attraction, an urgent need as unexpected as it was embarrassing. No woman had attracted him at all since Zelene's death, and yet here he was: not merely aroused by this girl, but beginning to feel possessive, hungry, obsessed. It felt like betrayal.

To make matters worse, every time that he tore his eyes away from her, he became aware of a discomforting distortion in his vision: the marble pillars holding up the painted ceiling began to tilt alarmingly; the long windows and the silver gilt mirrors lining the room went out of square and seemed to hang crookedly; even the faces of the dancers to either side blurred and elongated. Only when he brought himself to look directly into her face did everything else settle back into its proper size and proportion. Somewhere at the back of his mind, the image of poor old King Izaiah in the madhouse pricked at him incessantly.

Am I going mad? The question occurred to him again and again, yet he was desperately determined not to believe it. He was only reacting to the heat of the crowded ballroom, the intoxicating scent of the girl's perfume. To cover his confusion, he tried to make conversation.

"Do I know you—mademoiselle?"

Though it had not yet been established that she came in with some foreign dignitary, how else to explain that uncanny something about her, the occasional odd inflection when she spoke, the merest hint of a lisp that he found so fascinating? He had heard that accent before, or one very like it, when travelling in the south many years before.

"Did we meet here in Tarnburgh—or somewhere abroad? But no, that's impossible. You must have been still in the nursery when Francis and I were touring the continent." Whenever their fingers touched in the course of the dance, a delicious shiver passed over his skin.

"Surely that would be for Your Majesty to say. I wouldn't presume to claim an acquaintance." She lowered her eyes demurely, but a smile played about the corners of her mouth. "Perhaps I merely *remind* you of someone. I have been told I am very like your late—" She broke off with a faint blush, as though suddenly conscious of an error in taste.

Jarred tried to see it. He tried very hard to trace a resemblance to his beautiful Zelene in that sharp little face, since that would explain the attraction. But there was no similarity beyond her size and her coloring, and the coincidental choice of the color of her gown.

"You are certainly very lovely. But that doesn't seem to be it."

The music stopped and she curtsied very low, going down almost to the floor in a welter of grey taffeta and rustling petticoats. "If we might be alone for a moment. I will show you something which may explain everything,"

Why he should be so quick to oblige, he did not know. Keeping his grip on her hand, he led her into a curtained alcove between two long mirrors. With his free hand, he drew the heavy curtains of gold brocade together behind them.

"I don't even know your name," he said with an embarrassed laugh.

He could hear the sudden buzz of comment out in the ballroom, the flurry of startled speculation. *But let them wonder and speculate,* said a new voice in his mind. *I may be a widower, but* I'm *not the one who is dead and buried.* And again he was shocked at his own disloyalty.

Somehow, her hand slid out of his grip. "My name is Ys, Your Majesty. You will not find it familiar, but perhaps you recognize this." She drew a string of—pearls?—out of her bosom and held the necklace invitingly before him. Something that looked like a heart cut out of ice glowed in her palm.

"Perhaps I do," said Jarred, reaching out. Viewed so close, he could see the necklace was made up of polished white stones, as lustrous as pearls, but lit with a cold internal fire. And he had handled something like them before, certainly, but the harder he tried to remember, the harder it became for him to think at all. *The fire of the milky stones was burning him in places he had not been touched in a long time, creating in him a craving, a deep body hunger that—*

"Look into the crystal heart," said Ys. And mindlessly, Jarred did as she told him.

Once he did so, he could not turn his gaze elsewhere. He felt a curious sensation at the base of his spine; every nerve in his body was thrumming like a lute. There was a voice speaking inside his head, the same voice which had prompted him a while before, so softly he had mistaken it, then, for a mere echo of his own thoughts, his own desires. But now it was speaking with a penetrating clarity which was like *her* voice, though with a strange quality infinitely sweeter. It was offering him the most alluring blandishments, promising him the most impossible pleasures, if he did what it said, if he did everything it wanted him to do. There was an edge to that sweetness which made him distrust it, which made him try to resist it, but with every struggle of his, the sweetness of that voice shivered along his nerves in a way that was half pleasurable, half painful. In the end, he knew that he had no choice but to obey.

As soon as he acknowledged this, the voice grew quieter, its tone became nearly matter-of-fact. No longer alluring, no longer hurting him, it simply told him what he must do.

So Jarred listened. As the voice continued to speak, a series of vivid pictures appeared in his mind and began to spin through his brain, faster and faster.

"Do you understand? Will you do as I told you?" The words, when at last she spoke out loud, sounded harsh in his ears.

"Yes." Once the promise was made, he discovered that he could shift his gaze. Yet he was shaken and confused; there was a deep sense of dissatisfaction, a baffled craving, as though something long desired had been denied him. What that something was, he did not know. Everything that had happened in the last few minutes was rapidly receding from his conscious memory.

Ys reached out, and wordlessly took back the necklace, and slipped it back inside the front of her gown.

"Then you may kiss me," she said, turning up her face, which glowed faintly pearlescent in the candlelit alcove.

Tentatively, reluctantly, Jarred bent forward and touched his lips to hers. And that kiss was longer, sweeter, colder, and more terrifying in its way, than anything he had ever experienced before.

6

The hour was well past midnight, but the tavern known as the Leviathan was alive with clandestine activity. In the taproom, two highwaymen divided their booty; in a private parlor, someone plotted an assassination; in one of the chambers above, a young man of good family but diminished fortune sat down to drink himself to death with gin and wormwood.

In Sir Bastian's room Lilliana woke with a start. She had been dozing in a ladderback chair beside her patient's bed, when someone rapped sharply on the door. Jumping to her feet, she hurried across the room.

"Who is there?"

"If you please, ma'am, you be needed mortal bad on t'floor up above." It was the voice of one of the Leviathan barmaids, and she sounded agitated. Lili opened the door a cautious few inches, saw that the thin, shabby female figure was the only one standing in the dark corridor, and opened the door a tiny bit wider. "We been told you and your aunt be doctors."

Lili's heart sank. It seemed that her fumigations and her other precautions had not been sufficient; the Black Bile Fever had claimed another victim. Her hand went instinctively to the tiny mousefoot soaked in camphor that she wore in a satin bag between her corset and her gown. "Someone is ill?"

"No, ma'am, not ill. There be a man bleeding to death near t'steps up above."

Lili hesitated. What was really needed here was a surgeon, not a physician, someone skilled in the treatment of wounds and broken bones. But there would be no time to send for anyone now. "I will come at once."

Stepping out into the corridor, Lili closed the door softly behind her. She followed the barmaid down the dark passage to the stairwell and there she went ahead.

In a pool of light at the top of the steps, the tavern-keeper was bending over what Lili first mistook for a pile of old clothes. But when the landlord straightened and moved aside to make room for her, holding high a cruet of burning fish oil which served him for a lamp, it came to her with an ugly start that what was lying at his feet was actually the battered body of a man, curled up on the floor in a tight ball of agony.

Lili went down on her knees in a rustle of petticoats. There was blood everywhere, the plank floor was already sticky with it; when she gently turned the body over, more came pumping out from a dozen different wounds. For a moment the world went grey around the edges; her vision blurred; Lili closed her eyes, struggling with a sudden nausea.

Coward! This is no time to grow faint or foolish. With an effort, she made herself look, and gradually her patient came back into focus. Yet she scarcely knew where to begin, his case was so hopeless.

Someone handed her a dirty sheet; realizing that she would be offered nothing better, Lili began to tear the old, fragile muslin into strips. She worked frantically, she never knew for how long, applying tourniquets, bandages, doing anything she could to stop the bleeding. Even when his heart gave a last feeble beat and then was quiet, even when the bleeding slowed to a dull trickle and then stopped altogether, she kept on—until she felt a hand on her shoulder and heard a familiar voice speaking directly in her ear.

"Enough, Lilliana. You have done your best, but the man is dead."

Lili looked up at her great-aunt, wondering how long Allora had been there beside her. She blinked twice, feeling strangely disoriented. She had never lost a patient before; the idea was almost inconceivable.

Over her head, Allora was questioning the landlord. To Lili their voices had a hollow sound, as though she were hearing them from a long way off. "Was he murdered right here on this spot?"

"In his own room, most like." The tavern-keeper made a vague gesture with the fish-oil lamp. "There be a trail of blood."

Lili stood up, and in doing so experienced an intense vertigo. She took several deep breaths until the corridor stopped spinning and the walls settled back into place. The voices of the others came closer.

"It's impossible such wounds were self-inflicted," Allora was saying sharply. "Did no one hear anything? Have you no idea at all who is responsible?"

The landlord shrugged. "Can't even tell you this feller's name; he didn't give none when he took a room. But he did have a meeting in t'taproom wi' another young gentleman, all very quiet-like in a corner by theyselves—'til it come to harsh words. Don't remember when they come upstairs."

There was blood on Lili's hands, which she wiped on her skirt. The dress was ruined anyway, so streaked with dirt and soaked with blood that it would never be clean again.

"And the other young gentleman—can you describe him?" It was dangerous, Lili realized, to even ask. Common prudence in a place like this, to say nothing of her own reasons for being there, argued that she should leave any investigation to the proper authorities. And yet, considering the dead man's fine linen and his velvet coat, considering something vaguely familiar about his face, she could not banish a suspicion that the murder of such a man in this particular place might be somehow related to her own business here.

"A stranger, same as this one." The landlord's expression was sullen. "His hat were pulled down to cover his face, and he wore a long cloak."

In fact, Lili realized, the whole story of the quarrel might be a lie, meant to avert suspicion from the tavern-keeper and the people he employed.

" 'Tweren't no Man at all."

Everyone turned to stare at the barmaid. She flushed and went on. "He did *look* like a man in his fine clothes, but I see he do have a kind of hump t'back of his neck. He were one of they Goblins t'other side of town."

The landlord drew in his breath sharply. "A Goblin—in my house?" He favored the girl with a sour look.

Lili was intrigued and also a little frightened. The presence of a Goblin in this terrible business—and no ordinary Ouph or Padfoot, either, but one of the rare, reclusive Wrynecks—was ominous to say the least.

"It would be best, I think, if my aunt and I were to look over the place where he was actually murdered. If you will give me the lamp—" Lili held out her hand with such an air of quiet determination, the landlord yielded the light without question and even stepped out of the way to let her go past.

With the dish of burning oil held high to show the way, Lilliana and Allora followed the trail of blood down the narrow corridor and into a cramped bedchamber at the far end.

Inside the small bedchamber, blood spattered the floor, the threadbare rug, the peeling walls, and the furniture. "Good Heavens!" said Allora, pausing shocked in the doorway. Then she shook herself and added briskly, "He put up a struggle, that much is certain."

"Yes," said Lili. "And nobody in any of the rooms on this floor or the one below heard a thing. Or else—which is worse!—they ignored what they did hear."

Putting the lamp down on a table by the door, she made a swift survey of the room, taking note of anything that might bear examination. The bed was unmade, the chamber was cluttered with clothes and toilet articles: two large wigs on a wicker stand by the door; patch boxes, curling tongs, razor and shaving brush; a collection of milk-glass and crystal perfume bottles on the flimsy dresser.

A man of fashion, thought Lili, wrinkling her nose. Two of the bottles were broken and the perfumes mixed unpleasantly with the lingering odors of blood and sweat. Yet again there came that faint nudge of familiarity at the back of her mind.

She began to explore the room. The fireplace had been raked out and a handful of sticks and some pine logs thrown carelessly on the grate. Behind them, in the sooty maw of the fireplace, she discovered a small pile of ashes on the bricks, a scrap of scorched paper, and some candle drippings, as though someone had burned a letter after the old fire was raked out and before the new one was laid. She gathered up the ashes in a clean white handkerchief.

Rising to her feet, she glanced over at her great-aunt. "Will you look through his clothes? I am going to try and discover the contents of this letter."

Allora nodded and went straight to work, picking up a coat of straw-colored satin lined with muskrat and turning out the pockets. She did not ask how Lili meant to reconstruct a letter that had been so thoroughly burned. The gift which had allowed Lilliana to trace the movements of the papyrus scroll across so many miles had other applications as well.

Taking the lamp with her, Lili spread out the handkerchief in a clear space on the dresser. Closing her eyes to aid concentration, she began delicately sifting the ashes through her fingers. She was rewarded with a swift series of letters and words that appeared in her mind like writing on a page, but all so jumbled and incoherent that it was impossible to make sense of them. Yet she persisted, sifting through the pile a second and a third time, hoping something would appear to provide a key to the message.

"It's no use," she said at last. "Whoever burned this took every precaution. He tore the letter up into small pieces before he set fire to it, and he mixed the ashes afterwards. I wish I were more experienced at this."

Just then, there was a thumping in the corridor outside the door. The landlord and two other men came in with the corpse and deposited him unceremoniously on the bed.

When the men went out again, Lili wandered over for a closer look. "I know him. At least—I don't remember his name or where I met him, but there is something about that long bony face—"

On the other side of the room, Allora made a faint exclamation of distress. "Lilliana, I want you to come over and look at this." She held up a white cambric shirt.

Lili moved closer and put out a hand to feel the material. The cambric was very soft and fine, but something considerably more important had attracted Allora's attention. Around the collar and wristbands there was a delicate embroidery worked in horsehair and silk: a spell sewn into the fabric of the shirt.

"Oh, Aunt—if only he had been wearing this!"

"Yes," said Allora. "The first blows, perhaps unexpected, would have left him unscathed, and he might have been able to defend himself afterward." She folded the shirt carefully and placed it back on the spindle-back chair where she had found it. "If he had been wearing this, he might be alive right now, and the Goblin dead in his place."

*　　*　　*

Evening shadows gathered in the snowy streets of Hawkesbridge. As the bells in all the myriad city churches chimed the quarter hour, the outer gate of Whitcomb Gaol creaked open, and Wilrowan stepped out, a free man.

A shiny black livery carriage with wheels picked out in scarlet waited for him in the street. Without a backward glance, he sprang inside, slammed the door shut, and threw himself down on one of the red velvet seats, with his hat pulled forward and his arms folded across his chest—the very picture of sulky dissatisfaction.

Lounging elegantly on the broad seat opposite him, Blaise Trefallon cleared his throat. "The atmosphere of Whitcomb, my dear, is—rather distinctive. Fortunately, it does wash off." He waved a handkerchief liberally scented with civet and neroli in his friend's direction.

Outside, the driver spoke gruffly to his horses; the carriage lurched into motion.

"Do you think so?" Will sat hunched in a corner, and all that Blaise could see of his face under the black beaver was a glitter of eyes and a three days' growth of rust-colored beard. "Yet I wonder, Trefallon, if this time my misdeeds will leave an indelible mark."

Blaise tucked the handkerchief up his sleeve, raised a shapely eyebrow. "If word of your imprisonment gets out, people will certainly talk, but the ladies, no doubt, will think it romantic. Do you really care? I've always supposed not."

"I care," said Will morosely. "Not for the tittle-tattle of tongues at court, but for the opinion of those I respect, yes."

Blaise continued to regard him with well-bred skepticism. "You amaze me, Blackheart. May I know the names of the favored few?"

The carriage turned a corner. Will braced himself with both booted feet on the floor. Trefallon put a hand on the seat.

"Spare me your sarcasm, please," said Will. "If I've ever shown

any restraint in my life, it was because I cared for your good opinion, and for Lili's."

"And you think Lilliana will hear about this and imagine—what?"

"That I fought Macquay over some wretched woman we were
both pursuing. What else is *anyone* to think, when I can hardly repeat
his vile insinuations?" Will moved restlessly on the seat. "I keep
thinking about what you said: that my whole way of life was an insult to Lili. And yet, Blaise, even when I mean well, as I swear I did
this time, it comes out ill." He sighed deeply. "Sometimes, I don't
care very much for my own company."

"Then why," said Blaise brutally, "do you continue to be so
damnably reckless?"

Wilrowan hesitated. "Because I grow bored, I suppose." There
was a glint of white teeth in the shadows. "So quickly, so fatally
bored, my dear," he said, in perfect imitation of his friend's most
worldly manner.

Blaise gave him a weary glance. "I wish to heaven you took life
more seriously. You might spare yourself and everyone else a great
deal of heartache."

"Really?" said Will. "You intrigue me, Trefallon. I'd no idea that
serious men were immune to heartache. I would have thought they
were the very ones most likely to succumb."

7

In the heart of Hawkesbridge stood a crumbling ancient wall: moated, gated, and triple-towered, part of the city's original fortifications. It had come to be regarded as a remote outer bastion of the Volary palace, though a full city mile lay between, and the iron-studded gates, facing each of the four cardinal points, were always guarded by the elite companies of the King's and the Queen's Guards, who took the duty in turn a week at a time. It was impossible, therefore, to approach the palace on horseback, by coach, or by chair, without first being identified and perhaps interrogated.

To one of these gates, in the early evening, came the shiny black carriage bringing Blaise and Will from Whitcomb Gaol. The job carriage rumbled across a wooden bridge and creaked to a halt. A few words passed between the driver and the men on duty, the door opened, and a trim military figure in the maroon-and-gold uniform of the King's Guard appeared in the gap.

"Mr. Trefallon." The young lieutenant nodded respectfully. His gaze moved on to the figure slouched in the corner, and he gave a start as he recognized the second passenger.

"Will, you bastard, where in blazes—that is, Captain Blackheart!" He clicked his heels and saluted. "There is a message from the queen. You are to attend her at the Volary, sir. I was instructed to emphasize *immediately*, before you speak with the king or see anyone else."

Will frowned, not liking the sound of this. He might have asked for further information, but the officer had already stepped back and was motioning to his subordinates to open the heavy oak-and-iron gate.

As the door slammed shut and the carriage rolled on, Blaise gave Wilrowan a quizzical glance. " 'Will, you bastard'—is that how your men address you? My dear Blackheart, how on earth do you manage to maintain discipline?"

Will pushed back his hat. "Not one of mine, as you should have known by the uniform. Oh, very well, I see what you mean. But it's Lili's cousin, Nick Brakeburn—Lieutenant Kestrel Brakeburn, I *should* say—and I've known the boy since—" He gave an embarrassed laugh. "Curse you, Blaise, I *do* maintain discipline; there isn't a better company anywhere. You can ask anyone."

The carriage crept slowly down a narrow lamplit avenue crowded with wagons, coaches, men on horseback, and a noisy mob of jostling mud-spattered pedestrians. Twice, the driver was forced to stop completely: once when a sedan-chair overturned in front of him, and again when the wheels of a dray and a pony cart locked together. There was a loud altercation, a shrill, whinnying protest from one of the panicked cart-horses, then the way was clear again.

The job carriage rounded a corner and the wheels began to creak as it moved uphill. Inside, Blaise yawned and closed his eyes; Will continued to brood in his corner. A vagrant breeze spiraled down the street, bringing with it a penetrating wild animal scent that quickly invaded the interior of the carriage. They were still some distance from the Volary, famous for its gardens, observatories, and menagerie, but the wind was in the east and the lion-scent became stronger as they moved along.

Without any warning, Will leaned forward and tapped Blaise on the knee. "Tell the driver to let me off by the dancing school."

Trefallon's eyes flew open. "Fiend seize you, Blackheart, what are you up to now?" But he obligingly knocked on the roof, and when a panel slid open, relayed the order.

"Nothing you need worry about. I'm going to visit—a friend."

"And the queen? Young Brakeburn said she wanted to see you at once."

"You can tell Dionee I'll appear presently, duly chastened and prepared if necessary to throw myself at her feet in an agony of abasement. No?" Will grinned at Trefallon's expression of well-bred dismay. "Then just tell her to expect me within the hour."

As soon as the carriage came to a halt, Will was out the door and elbowing his way through the crowd. Narrowly avoiding a collision with a sturdy chair-bearer, he ducked down a dark alley. Overhanging stories above blocked out the light from the stars. After two blocks, the alley ended at a rusty iron gate, illuminated by a blue gaslight. Pushing open the gate, he arrived at the foot of a steep staircase.

He climbed for several flights up the side of the building, until he came to the sixth floor and an anonymous door with a tarnished brass knocker.

Drawing a large iron key out of one pocket, Will opened the door and stepped boldly across the threshold. Then he felt in the darkness until he found a stub of greasy tallow candle and a dented tin box on a table by the door. The box contained flint, steel, and dry bits of tinder. He struck a spark, lit the candle, and glanced around him.

He stood in a small, shuttered room. There were books scattered everywhere, including much of the floor. Several maps had been pinned to the walls and a crude star chart sketched in charcoal on the planked ceiling. On a scarred table in one corner was a jumble of flasks and braziers, bottles of elixir, essences, and mineral salts, along with a telescope, a compass, and assorted prisms and lenses. A cursory glance told him that nothing had been disturbed during his absence, though oddly enough the room smelled strongly of smoke.

Will set the candle on a dish already filled with melted tallow. Shrugging out of and discarding the gaudy scarlet coat, impatiently tossing his hat on a chair already piled dangerously high with books, he crossed the room and unlatched one pair of shutters. Throwing them wide, he listened for an answering flutter of wings outside.

There was only silence. He waited for several minutes, then closed the shutter. He was just refastening the latch when someone rapped sharply on the door.

With a frown, Wilrowan started to answer it, then paused to think. That he had taken these rooms was a carefully guarded secret; he was known to his neighbors by an assumed name; he came and went mostly at night. On the other hand, he had never been arrested before or so nearly assassinated. The present circumstances seemed to call for unusual precautions. He opened a cabinet, took out a pistol with a walnut stock and a chased silver barrel, made sure it was loaded and primed. Then he opened the door a bare few inches, holding the pistol concealed but ready.

A slender young woman stood outside. "Wilobie Culpepper, is that you?"

Will gave a sigh of relief, recognizing his landlord's daughter. "Eulalie. Is there anyone with you?"

"No. I'm quite alone. But——" She broke off speaking as he opened the door wider and drew her inside, then slammed the door behind her. She put a hand to her hair, gave the skirt of her flowered muslin gown a twitch. "No need to pull me about like that. My Heavens! You've grown very eager for my company, haven't you?"

She was, as Will had noticed long before this, a remarkably pretty girl. She was particularly appealing now, flushed and still breathless from her climb upstairs.

And Will had never been one to resist feminine beauty. "Willie—" she began, and was again interrupted, when he tossed the pistol down on the table, took her impetuously into his arms, and covered her mouth forcefully with his own.

Eulalie returned his kiss with enthusiasm, molding her slim body against his. But then she seemed to remember why she had come; she gasped and pulled away. "It isn't safe. There was a fire down below that weakened some of the beams, and the house could collapse at any moment."

Will let her go at once. "A fire—here?" That explained the lingering scent of smoke. Then he reached out again, with both hands, and took her roughly by the shoulders. "Was it an accident, or did somebody try to burn down the house?"

She twisted out of his grip and moved toward the door. "Not now, Willie. I told you, it isn't safe." As if in confirmation, the entire building shuddered convulsively.

Convinced that at least some of her story was true, he picked up his coat and hat, retrieved the pistol, then followed her out the door and down the steps to the alley.

"Now," he said, when they stood on solid ground. "Tell me exactly how it happened."

She gave a slight shrug. "A coal from the stove rolled onto the floor; the next thing we knew, the room was ablaze." Eulalie made a grimace of distaste. "Would you mind putting that thing away? I don't quite care for the look of it. And why on earth should you suspect that somebody tried to burn down the house?"

He slipped the pistol into a pocket of his coat. "Because I have a low mind—as you of all people should know." He was at least suspicious enough to wonder if she was telling the truth even now.

Though he ought to be able to trust her. They had been sharing a bed together, on and off, for about a year: a pleasant arrangement that seemed as much to her liking as it was to his. Pleasant and prof-

itable, Will reminded himself, remembering some of the expensive
gifts he had given her.

"Eulalie—do you love me?" Even as he spoke the words, he
wished them back.

She raised an eyebrow. "Is that what you want? Would that make
things better?" In the dim glow of the flaring blue gaslight it was difficult for him to decide if her expression was angry, calculating, or
just surprised.

"No. Of course it wouldn't make things any better." Because if
Eulalie loved him, he would be a villain: seducing the girl with his
gifts and his flattery, deceiving her about his name, his rank, his
background.

If he *had* deceived her. Will sometimes wondered if he had been
less clever than he intended. Besides owning the house, Eulalie's father made wigs for the nobility. Every now and again, Will casually
recommended the wig-maker to his friends. Perhaps by doing so, he
had indirectly revealed his identity; or perhaps Eulalie had known all
along and had encouraged his advances merely for the sake of a connection at court.

She moved toward him now, sliding her arms under his coat,
pressing the palms of her hands against his back. He could feel the
heat of her skin through his thin cambric shirt. That he was filthy,
reeking, seemed to bother her not at all. He bent to kiss her, but
without much enthusiasm.

Because suddenly, painfully, standing there with another woman
held tightly in his arms, Will wanted Lili. It was senseless, confusing—Blaise, he supposed, would call it perverse—but there it was.

Except that Lili was a hundred miles from Hawkesbridge and had
never loved him, anyway. With that thought, his hold on Eulalie
tightened, the kiss deepened. And Eulalie was a clever girl, she knew
exactly how to arouse him. As his hands moved over her, she made
tiny, encouraging sounds.

Pushing the one woman up against the side of the building, Will pushed the other one just as deliberately out of his mind, and abandoned himself to the pleasure of the moment.

Three-quarters of an hour later, Wilrowan was again on his way to the Volary. He was avoiding the crowded streets, and had taken to the winding alleys, hidden stairs, and other back ways that led just as surely in their roundabout fashion uphill to the palace.

At last he emerged on one of the public boulevards. A vast and complex jumble of buildings, of towers and domes and odd projecting balconies, loomed up before him. The early rulers of Mountfalcon, products of an age noted for its appetite for knowledge, had been virtuosi: scientists, explorers, inventors, collectors. In adapting the ruinous shell of the old brick-and-timber Maglore palace to their own uses, they had added a glassed-in observatory, a planetarium, a dozen greenhouses, two museums, a menagerie, a great aviary full of wild birds, as well as numerous dizzying wall-walks and high observation platforms intended for star-gazing. Many of these structures were slowly collapsing into disrepair—the greenhouses and the garden mazes overgrown, the hundreds of glass panes in the observatory cracked and dimmed with age and weather—but the menagerie and the aviary were still well stocked. As evening and the feeding hour approached, the impatient roaring of lions, the screeching of hungry hawks and owls, could be plainly heard for a quarter of a mile.

Will entered through a gate on the south, moved down the Fountain Court, where marble men and monsters sent jets of water hundreds of feet into the air, and eventually penetrated the gloomy central pile of the palace itself.

Part palace, part museum, part zoo, that was the Volary—or, at least, so the newly betrothed Dionee had declared on her first visit, three years ago, as she wrinkled her pretty nose at the philosophical kickshaws in which the Volary abounded, as she took in, with ill-disguised dismay, the faded grandeur of the chilly state chambers, with their vaulted ceilings and queer scientific murals. A month after her wedding she asked if she might redecorate her apartments, and the king (whose own rooms were located in another wing, where his cherished peace would not be disrupted by the renovations) gave his consent, with the one restriction that she not alter the historic fabric of the palace in any way.

So, away went the moth-eaten velvet draperies shrouding the windows; silken hangings came in to conceal the peeling frescoes; richly figured carpets went down to cover the cold marble floors. Ruthlessly, Dionee plundered the other apartments of their prettiest and quaintest furnishings: lacquer tea-chests, ormolu tables, chairs of gilt and ivory. She brought in statues, and flowering plants in marble urns, and tiny songbirds in dainty cages of silver wire. When it was all done, the sober Rodaric had shaken his head at his young wife's reckless extravagance, but he had said nothing.

Arriving, at last, outside this unusual set of rooms, Wilrowan nodded to the green-coated guards stationed to either side of Dionee's bedchamber door, scratched on the painted panels to announce his presence, and walked boldly in without waiting for an invitation. He found her dressing for supper, surrounded by her pretty young attendants, as well as a dozen or so of the dandies and officers who made up her admiring court.

As Will crossed the room, a battery of quizzing glasses rose up to follow his progress. But a gesture from the queen, a whispered instruction to one of her maids-of-honor, and the ladies dropped curtsies, the men made elaborate bows, then they all filed discreetly out of the room—though not before several of the more ardent gentlemen cast darkling glances in Will's direction. The last one to leave rather pointedly left the door slightly ajar.

Undaunted by this reception, Wilrowan swept off his disreputable hat, went gracefully down on one knee, and raised one of

Dionee's little white hands to his lips. It was all very prettily done, but his cousin stepped back with a shudder of distaste.

"Will, you wretch, you look positively g-ghastly! And I can't even begin to say what you smell like."

Will grinned up at her, far from penitent. "I smell like a prison— or perhaps like a brothel." Eulalie's perfume lingered on his skin, along with the effluvium of Whitcomb Gaol. "I beg your pardon. I would have cleaned up before inflicting you with my presence, but I understood you wished to see me immediately."

She began to pace the room, picking up a trinket here and there, examining it briefly, then setting it down in a new place. Wondering what it was she found so difficult to say to him, Will sat back on his heels and waited for her to speak.

After several minutes, Dionee settled at a goat-legged dressing table. "I suppose I should warn you. You're in utter disgrace, and I don't even like to think what might happen if Rodaric sees you. He is absolutely furious over this latest escapade!"

"Escapade?" Will's eyebrows rose sharply. "Dionee, I haven't done anything wrong. It was just a stupid mistake by a company of inexperienced guardsmen."

"That's not how Barnaby and Pyecroft tell the tale. They told Rodaric it was all your doing, insisting that Sir Rufus fight you. They say they told you it was quite unfair, as *you* were permitted to enter a duel without a warrant, but none of *them* were so fortunately situated."

Will tried to remember. "I suppose someone may have said something like that. It wouldn't have stopped me. The only thing on my mind at the time was how much I wanted to murder Macquay." He scowled at the memory. "And did Pyecroft and Barnaby also tell Rodaric that Macquay spent the entire evening trying to provoke a quarrel—until he finally hit on the one insult I *couldn't* ignore?"

"Yes," said Dionee. "I don't believe they meant to make trouble for you. They even said you had hardly been drinking. Though I suppose, in the end, that went against you." Wilrowan nodded morosely. It never seemed to count in his favor that he invariably committed his follies stone-cold sober. "And, of course, they were much too discreet to tell the woman's name."

Will groaned and struck his forehead with the palm of his hand. "But *not* so discreet they failed to mention a woman was involved?"

Dionee gave a sarcastic little laugh. "Do you really think anyone would have supposed otherwise—no matter what story they might invent?"

He glanced up angrily. The elation he had felt on leaving Eulalie was rapidly fading. He was sliding toward depression, an all too familiar reaction. At Dionee's words, he began to wonder: had he truly become a byword for loose behavior? Or —worse—a joke? Between the man of many easy conquests and the hardened rake there was an ugly distinction. Had he, without knowing it, crossed the line? He was opening his mouth to ask the question, but Dionee forestalled him.

"Look at this, Wilrowan." She picked up a tiny blue glass bottle, pulled out its silver stopper, and sniffed the contents before she passed it on. "Do you think it pretty? It was a gift from your grandmama. And only imagine how clever—it's not really perfume, though it smells so divinely. Try to guess what it is."

Will declined to guess, with a shake of his head and a sinking sensation. Lady Krogan was the only grandparent they did not share in common; true to her Rowan heritage, she was always sending him potions and powders; that she sent similar gifts to his cousin he had never imagined.

"Well then, I'll tell you, since you are too stupid to guess. It's invisible ink. Isn't that cunning?"

"Very," said Will, with an inward sigh of relief. His grandmother's gifts to himself were seldom so innocent.

He rose to his feet, began to pace the floor. "But Dionee—how far do you think I should go to avoid meeting Rodaric? And for how long? Just how angry *is* he?"

"In a vile temper. He's done nothing but lecture me the last two days, on your follies and my own. He almost refused to sign that letter authorizing your release, and he said that he wished he might not see your face again for at least a fortnight."

"For at least a fortnight?" Only once in his life had Will seen the king so angry it took more than a day for him to cool down. "What have you done to put him in such a temper, during my absence? You've been flirting again, I suppose, and that's put down to my bad influence. Though Rodaric should know—"

"—that you lecture me even more than he does," Dionee finished for him. "I expect he will remember that, given enough time. Right now, he seems more concerned that you nearly got Finn and Pyecroft arrested."

Will thought about that. He had never perfectly understood Rodaric, who seemed to waver between regarding him as an ally, because of his influence over the queen, and resenting him for that same reason. But then he remembered that Pyecroft and Finn were the sons of two of the king's cabinet ministers. He could easily imagine the shock and dismay of those two highly respectable gentlemen, if their sons had been obliged to join him in Whitcomb Gaol.

"But this is dreadfully inconvenient for *me*, my dear. Letting you go off, precisely when I need you."

Will stopped pacing and cocked his head, instantly suspicious. "How inconvenient? You need me how?"

"Did you forget that you promised to go with me to the birthday fête at the embassy?" She picked up a fan of painted chicken-skin, unfurled it, and began to flirt it with practiced ease. "There's to be a picnic on the embassy roof, and fireworks at sunset—I thought we would have such a lovely time!"

Yes, he had forgotten, in the recent press of events, but now that he remembered, he was reminded, too, of a persistent worry. "You spend too much time with Lord Vault and those people from Nordfjall. You pay far too much attention to *all* the ambassadors. If you're not careful, everyone will start suspecting you of foreign intrigues."

She dismissed his warning with a light laugh. "What is the purpose of foreign ambassadors if no one is allowed to know or visit them, for fear of starting that sort of talk?"

"All very well, but there *is* a difference between knowing such people and visiting them occasionally, and living in the ambassador's pocket. Fire and Thunder, Dionee! I wish that I *might* escort you, if only to keep you out of mischief. But Coffin and Polmaric will have to serve in my place."

Then, as Dionee made a wry face over the fan, he asked sharply: "They're my lieutenants. Who else would you have me send?"

"Coffin's so old. And as for Polmaric—such a plain young man I've never seen, and he has no conversation at all." She dropped the fan, left it lying on the table with her ribbons and other trinkets. "I'll be bored to death in their company."

Will realized that he was growing weary of hearing his men criticized. First for laxity by Blaise, now for dull respectability by Dionee. He began to consider the prospect of leaving the city with real enthusiasm. "Do you mean to tell me that I should choose my officers for wit and for beauty rather than ability?"

"Well, why not?" Dionee picked up a delicate crystal hand-mirror set with glass roses; examining her reflection, she made a slight adjustment to one silvery curl. "They tell me the Queen's Guard in Tholia is entirely made up of handsome, strapping young men, all of them remarkably fair-spoken and accomplished, for she chooses them herself."

"Then the King of Tholia is remarkably forbearing. You had better not share this information with Rodaric; not if he's already in a jealous rage."

Dionee said nothing, just went on rearranging her curls, spoiling her hairdresser's careful work. Several minutes passed, during which she seemed to forget his presence entirely.

Will waited as long as his patience could bear, then cleared his throat loudly. "Am I dismissed then? May I go?"

"Well, of course," said Dionee, with a wave of her hand, though she immediately cancelled the effect of this airy dismissal by asking a question. "But where will you go?"

"I suppose I'll go home," said Will, without thinking.

His cousin raised her eyebrows in mock surprise. "Home to your papa? You'll distract him from his books, as likely as not, and you know how cross that always makes him."

"I meant that I'll go to visit Lili at Brakeburn," said Will, with icy dignity. Dionee was beginning to bore him. Worse, he was beginning to despise her, and that always meant that he despised himself, for they were much alike.

But Dionee failed to recognize, or perhaps just ignored, the dangerous note in his voice. "Wilrowan, you are just too amazingly funny. Now why should you say 'home' when you mean Brakeburn Hall? You're practically never there and you *hate* your in-laws." She gave a trill of laughter.

He shook his head, not certain what impulse had prompted him. Except that he somehow *needed* to see Lili, and that he would not feel comfortable again until he had done so.

"At least you should give her fair warning. Send a messenger ahead, so she can prepare for your visit. Why—she might not even be there."

Will was astonished. "Where else would Lili be, if not at Brakeburn? If she wanted to go anywhere else, she could visit me here."

Dionee gave him a roguish glance over one shoulder. "You're

mighty possessive for so careless, so wayward a husband. I wonder how Lili endures you, how she accepts your infrequent visits with such complaisance—if she really *is* complaisant."

He returned her smile with a bewildered frown. In her words, he had detected a faint echo of Macquay's insinuations, three days earlier. "Lili is always happy to see me. What have you heard to make you think otherwise?"

"I've heard nothing," said the queen with a shrug. "I've heard nothing, but just like anyone else, I can speculate."

She turned back to her mirror. "And really, Wilrowan, it would serve you right, you wicked boy, if you dropped in at Brakeburn some day and found Lili not waiting, but off having romantic adventures of her own!"

8

awn was just breaking as the *Pagan Queen* sailed out of Zutlingen harbor. A cold, sleety rain had fallen during the night, freezing on the shrouds and the bulwarks, casing the ancient vessel in ice, but a dim red glow that began at the horizon and spread across the sky like wildfire promised a day that would be cold but clear.

The captain stood on the forecastle: a rugged, white-haired old salt, no less weatherbeaten than his ship, with a scarred face and one false hand, which had been marvelously carved and articulated out of sea ivory, then strung on silver wires—a relic of more adventurous but also more prosperous days.

It would be difficult to imagine a wilder, more damaged-looking craft than the *Pagan Queen*. She had never been a beauty, and a life of hard knocks and rough seas had not improved her. Under her patchy armor of ice she was as battered and worn to splinters as a bit of old bone. An unlikely choice, it would seem, for a voyage on wintery seas, she was, quite simply, the only merchant ship willing to leave this northern port so late in autumn; those who had managed to secure a passage counted themselves lucky.

She was not long underweigh before the wind rose, shrill and

biting, and another icy rain began to fall. The gale increasing hour by
hour, the ship forged onward through an ugly head sea, with her
timbers creaking and her decks awash.

Alone in his tiny cabin, Lucius Sackville-Guilian tried to shut out
the noise of the storm. It was a forlorn effort. Throwing down his
goose-quill pen, putting aside the paper on which he had been dili-
gently scribbling for the past half hour, he pushed back his chair and
sprang to his feet.

The damp little cabin, already oppressive, had been made even
closer by a mountain of luggage that took up most of the floor space
not already occupied by the scanty furnishings. Luke knew that
somewhere in that baggage, perhaps buried in one of the horsehide
trunks—along with the books, coins, and other curiosities he had
picked up during his travels; his clothes; and, of course, the two
thousand six hundred and eight blotted, crossed-out, and amended
manuscript pages of Luke's *History of the World, Refuting Everything,*
which was still very much in progress, and which Perys, his valet,
had been obliged to find room for by cramming into every available
corner of the two trunks and miscellaneous baggage—somewhere
at the bottom of all this, there was a dog-eared pack of playing cards,
and also a flask of brandy. But having no mind for a game of Patience,
feeling too queasy to hunt out the brandy, Luke resigned himself to
a long morning and a weary afternoon.

But Rijxland and a thousand amazing discoveries beckoned to
him. During almost a year of adventure and travel—a year spent
thrusting himself into places and situations a wiser man might have
avoided—Luke had escaped the worst consequences of his own impulsive behavior again and again. Taking all things into account, he
would consider himself fortunate if a day, a week, even a fortnight
of tedium was the worst that he had to suffer—if Rijxland lived up
to his expectations.

Finding it impossible to continue writing, having no idea when Perys would return, Luke cast himself down on his narrow bunk and fell into a restless doze, lulled by the sound of the pumps in the hold below.

That day crept by slowly, and so did the next. The fourth and fifth days proved so interminable, he stopped taking note of the time altogether. The storm raged on. Every so often, Perys would come in with a plate of greasy unappetizing food that Luke was obliged to eat, or with a cracked basin full of soapy water. When this occurred, Lucius eyed the valet warily. The man's face had acquired a greenish tinge and his hands shook so that the shaving water danced in the bowl. Luke decided against trusting Perys with the gleaming two-edged razor and proceeded to shave himself.

While Luke scraped away at his face, Perys relayed all that he had learned about the other passengers. There were three other gentlemen on board.

"Not *real* gentlemen like yourself, Master Luke, but quite decent looking tradesmen, all going south on important business." Perys folded his hands primly across his drab waistcoat. "And a small party of Goblins, *if* you'll believe me. Two or three of those nasty little Ouphs, and another one, very like a man they say, but with his limbs all anyhow."

Luke turned away from the shaving mirror, his eyes alight with sudden interest. The higher sorts of Goblins, the Grants and the Wrynecks, were said to be highly intelligent—not to mention the fact that they sometimes lived practically forever. To speak with a creature who had already existed for six or seven centuries had long been Luke's ambition. "Is it a Grant, do you think?"

The valet sniffed audibly and managed to look haughty in spite of his interesting color. "I wouldn't know, Master Luke. I haven't seen the creature myself; nor do I want to. And they do say the whole lot of them have hidden themselves away in a compartment even smaller than this one, and haven't been seen since they came on board."

Luke felt his hopes plummet. It was unlikely, then, that the Grant would emerge. On the rare occasions when Goblins did embark on a voyage they were known to spend the entire time holed up in the most waterproof cabin available.

"A pity," he said with a sigh, as he rinsed the razor in the bowl of soapy water. "An opportunity to exchange views with a Grant might have served very well to while away some part of this interminable voyage."

One day, Luke woke uncertain of the time, and all was strangely quiet around him. The ship had ceased to buck and pitch; she was rolling gently; the pumps had ceased to labor. There was no sound louder than a muffled creaking, a gentle slap of waves on the other side of the wall, and the slow drip, drip, drip of water from the beams overhead to the deck below.

With a yawn and a stretch, he sat up. Reaching into a pocket of his ribbed-satin waistcoat, he consulted his watch. Noon or midnight? He tried to remember when he had first stretched out on the bunk. Noon, he decided, with another gaping yawn. Either way, he was weary to death of the damp little cabin, eager for a chance to go up on deck.

Unassisted, he struggled into his coat, straightened his lace-edged neckcloth, and retied the ribbon in his hair. Examining the result in the shaving mirror, he was far from satisfied. The neckcloth was looking a little wilted, and a deep crease marred one velvet sleeve. No doubt Perys would be scandalized. But the valet had no business wandering off when he was needed, and Luke was determined to catch a glimpse of the sky, a breath of fresh air.

As soon as he ventured out into the dim passageway he was up to his ankles in seawater. More came pouring down from a hatchway above the ladder leading to the upper decks. Hailing a passing sailor, he asked about the weather.

"Wind and sea do grow quieter, sir, but it still be raining fit to bust t'skies open. All t'gentleman been invited into t'captain's cabin for a bit of refreshment. Mayhap you'd care to join 'em?"

"Perhaps I would," said Luke. The sailor directed him to a door at the far end of the passageway, then continued on about his business, somewhere in the bowels of the ship.

Halfway down the passage, Lucius saw the cabin door open, yielding a brief glimpse of light and color. A dark figure in a long cloak and a black hat with a high crown and a wide stiff brim stepped through, heading in Luke's direction. As the passage was narrow, Luke stepped aside to make room, and the stranger nodded his appreciation as he slipped on past.

He was a tall man with a lean, impassive countenance and something grim about the unrelieved black of his clothes. Luke watched curiously as the man mounted the dripping ladder, his large sinewy hands gripping the sides as he ascended swiftly and fearlessly toward the stormy regions above.

Once the stranger had disappeared from sight, Luke headed on to the cabin. There he found three other men, answering the valet's description of "decent tradesmen," gathered around a small round table, drinking the captain's wine. At the others' invitation, Luke filled a glass from the dusty green bottle. Taking a cautious sip, he pronounced the wine tolerable.

Yet, though he entered into easy conversation with the other passengers, his thoughts still ran on the dark stranger. Not one of the sailors, not one of the officers, nor manservant to any of these men in the cabin. For all his somber attire, the cut of his coat and the cloth it was made of were much too good for that. Perys had failed to mention that any such person existed. And why had he chosen to brave the storm when there was warmth and company here below?

Finally, Luke's curiosity could no longer be denied; he asked if anyone knew the man who had just been leaving the cabin when he arrived.

"The Leveller, do you mean?" said a stout goldsmith in a sap-green coat and a scarlet waistcoat. "He came on at Ottarsburg. I know nothing else about him. They are a dour set of fellows, the Anti-demonists, and not so courteous as they might be, though this one seems well enough."

A religious fanatic, thought Luke. Which explained the cropped hair, the black garments devoid of lace or other trimming, the stern set of the stranger's features. Yet despite his distaste, Lucius was intrigued. He had never been acquainted with any member of the Anti-demonist sect—commonly known as Levellers—but he had listened to a number of open-air sermons and those had piqued his curiosity.

"His manners are certainly better than most," offered another passenger, who had previously identified himself as a linen-draper with a thriving business in Luden. "Yet I have also heard this particular Leveller can be dangerous to know."

Luke turned to stare at him. "Dangerous—how? Unless by that you mean his politics, which may agree with my own rather better than you think!"

The cloth-merchant hesitated, playing nervously with his nickel-plated watch fob. "When you reach Rijxland, you expect to make a long stay in Luden, I believe you said, and you mean to present letters of introduction at the embassy?"

Luke bowed the affirmative.

"Then you might find the Leveller a useful acquaintance. There is very little that happens in Luden that he doesn't know of it, and you could spend your time most profitably listening to what he might tell you. But as for anything you might say to *him*—I would advise you to weigh your words carefully, for they might be repeated in places where you never meant them to be heard at all."

Far from being daunted by this, Luke gave a shout of laughter. "My dear sir, I have no secrets. If the truth were told, I am generally considered a little too ready to share my opinions, and I tend to be crushed if the things that I say fail to be memorized and passed on to others."

At this, the linen-draper bowed, and he and Luke parted company. But those words of warning continued to echo at the back of Luke's mind. Eventually, he grew so curious, he took the other man aside for a few private words.

"I beg your pardon. I should not have made light of what was undoubtedly sincere and well-meant advice. I wish you would tell me exactly what you meant."

But now the merchant seemed reluctant to explain himself. He gave an uneasy glance in the direction of the cabin door. "It is I who must beg your pardon, for passing on what is probably only an idle rumor. I am only slightly acquainted with the man myself." Then he gave an embarrassed laugh. "And it occurs to me, Mr. Guilian, that I don't know *you*. It is possible that I've said too much already."

Naturally, having been strongly cautioned against doing so, Luke's first impulse must be to scrape up an acquaintance with the mysterious stranger and learn all his secrets.

What—he asked himself as he prowled the lower decks in search of the Leveller—had brought the fanatic on board to begin with? He could not have urgent business as the three tradesmen did, to justify a voyage on rough autumn seas. When Levellers engaged in trade, it was only in a modest way; they had no interest in accumulating worldly goods. And what had the cloth-merchant meant by his mysterious hints? Luke, who had a passion for plots and a penchant for detecting them whether they actually existed or not, found his mind pleasantly awhirl with Leveller conspiracies and other pleasing fancies. Members of the Anti-demonist sect did have a history of radical politics and were inclined to preach such revolutionary doctrines as Universal Equality.

For a day and a half he allowed his imagination to run wild, before he realized that the draper had actually hinted at something very different. *"Repeated in places where you never meant them to be heard at all."* A confidential agent for the Crown of Rijxland? Well, why not? Who better than a religious fanatic, ripe for martyrdom, if you wanted someone hardy under torture and willing to guard your secrets with his very life?

Intrigued, excited, wishing to know more, Luke was nevertheless doomed to frustration for the next several days. The Anti-demonist proved as reclusive in his own way as the Goblins were in theirs. The rain continued to fall, a stiff breeze blew steadily across the bows, keeping the other passengers to the lower decks, and it seemed that the Leveller preferred his own company and the wind, sea, and rain, to that of the men who continued to meet in the captain's cabin. He was known to take long walks on the rainy deck, to eat all his meals alone in his cabin. Though whether this was done in accordance with the precepts of his strange religion, or motivated by a desire for solitude, not even Captain Pyke could say.

The weather did not clear until shortly before the *Pagan Queen* landed in Herndyke. She sailed into the harbor at night, and Luke did not venture on deck until the next morning.

It was a fine, fresh, sunny day, and the leaden skies and the soaking wetness of the last fortnight seemed a million miles away. Luke took up a position by the rail and watched, with idle curiosity, the party of Goblins as they tottered gratefully down the gangplank.

In the natural way of things, Ouphs were inclined to a sallow rather than a ruddy complexion, but these appeared uncommonly yellow with seasickness and wobbly besides. Yet their taller companion moved with such dignity and self-possession that he might have been mistaken for some decent working-class patriarch, were it not for the odd articulations of his long arms and legs.

"Do Goblins have souls?" Luke wondered out loud. What had prompted the question, he was not quite certain, unless it was because that other mysterious passenger, the Leveller, was still very much on his mind.

"They do have souls, but of a vastly inferior nature, midway between the souls of animals and of Men," said a deep voice behind him and, turning, he saw a long figure emerge through the hatchway. It was the Leveller himself, moving in Luke's direction with his dark cloak billowing around him.

With an effort, Lucius controlled his surging elation, forced himself to keep his voice light and casual. "In what way 'vastly inferior'? If souls are, as all philosophers assure us, wholly immaterial, sublimely impalpable, how is it possible to measure or to quantify them?"

The stranger joined him beside the rail. "Perhaps I should have said undeveloped, rather than inferior. The souls of Goblins are darker in nature, less apt toward enlightenment."

Luke gave the Leveller a sideways puzzled glance. That statement opened up some intriguing possibilities, but it was also an entirely new line of thought. "Less apt, you say, but that would imply—not entirely incapable? Nor incapable, I suppose, of achieving salvation according to the precepts of your religion?"

Again the Leveller surprised Lucius with his response. "Surely anyone with a compassionate heart must hope so. It would be insupportable to think that so many of God's creatures were doomed from the very beginning."

Detecting some change in Luke's expression, he added quietly: "You think otherwise? Or perhaps—believing those of my faith cruel and inflexible—you are merely astonished to hear *me* say so?"

As this was *exactly* what Luke had been thinking, he had the grace to blush. For a moment, he could not imagine how he ought to answer.

"I beg your pardon," he said, recovering. He forced himself to meet the fanatic's steady gaze. "I really know very little about your religion. The truth is, I am very pleased to meet you." He put out one of his hands, determined to make the most of this opportunity. "If you will allow me—I am Lucius Sackville-Guilian, and I am planning to spend the winter at Luden."

The stranger barely touched the tips of Luke's fingers with the ends of his own. "How do you do, Mr. Guilian. They call me Raith."

Luke waited to hear more. But when no more came, he suddenly remembered that Levellers were not in the habit of giving their full names to anyone—something to do with hexes, though he could not perfectly recall the details. And he was not certain whether he ought to feel snubbed or encouraged. This Raith's manner was reserved, but it could hardly be called repulsive.

So Luke tried again. "I understand—that is, something that one of the other passengers said led me to believe that you are employed by the Rijxlander government—as a courier, or in some other confidential capacity."

The Leveller inclined his head, under the shadow of his stiff black hat. Almost it seemed that Lucius had amused him.

"As a secret agent do you mean, Mr. Guilian? But there, I believe, my appearance is against me. Have you ever met anyone whose face, whose dress, whose manner, whose entire aspect more clearly proclaimed the word 'spy'?"

With the question put to him in that way, Luke had to admit that he never had. "Which I suppose would make it impossible for you to be one. But if you don't mind my asking, what *do* you do?"

"I am employed by the Crown Princess of Rijxland, but in a purely private capacity. Indeed, I believe my position is unique: I am the governor of her five small children and also act as their body-guard."

Yet again, Luke was at a temporary loss for words. "Tutor *and* bodyguard," he managed at last. "That *is* an unusual position. I don't think that I have ever—"

"But a position for which I am peculiarly qualified. You frown, Mr. Guilian. Perhaps you have heard that those of my faith do not carry weapons. That is true, but it happens that I am remarkably quick and strong. If it were to come to a fight between us—and providing you did not take me *entirely* by surprise—it is likely that I could kill you in a matter of seconds, whether you were armed or not."

Luke continued to frown suspiciously, not quite certain whether his new acquaintance was making sport of him or not. But Levellers, as anyone might tell you, were singularly devoid of a sense of humor. Not that this Raith seemed to be a typical Leveller, or a typical any-thing else. Luke remembered, too, that the linen-draper had de-scribed the Rijxlander as dangerous to know, though he had seemed to mean something quite different at the time.

But then Lucius laughed, a laugh of pure delight. This Raith rep-resented a riddle, and there was nothing he liked more. "My dear sir," he said with a deep bow, "I believe I desire your further ac-quaintance."

Raith responded with a half bow of his own, and Luke returned to the original subject of their conversation.

"I wonder," he said, indicating with a motion of his head the Gob-lins, who were still gathering together their baggage on the pier below, searching among the casks and the bales the crew had already unloaded, "I wonder that the captain was willing to carry such un-usual—cargo. I have always heard that sea-going men are uncom-monly superstitious and regard the presence of Goblins on board as the very worst sort of ill luck. And certainly, we've had rough weather while they were with us."

Raith did not answer at once. He appeared to stare through and beyond the smaller Goblins as though he were hardly aware the Ouphs existed, though once or twice some movement on the part of the Grant attracted his attention. "Perhaps if we had ever been in real danger, the crew might have grown actively hostile. As for the captain: he tells me this is not the first party of Goblins he has taken on board. During the last year, he has fallen quite into the way of transporting Grants and Wrynecks in particular from one port to another."

"But how very—curious." Luke struggled to fit this extraordinary snippet of information in with his present theories on Goblins—theories that had mutated a number of times since he left Winterscar, theories that his cousin Jarred and his tutor Francis Purcell would have scarcely recognized by now—but the significance eluded him. "And did the captain tell you to what he attributes this unusual activity?"

The tide was rising, bringing with it swell after swell. The ship strained against her moorings, her ropes pulled taut.

"They appear to be disturbed about something," the Rijxlander answered gravely. "Also, they are invariably travelling from north to south. From which Captain Pyke concludes that there is something taking place in the far north that is making them all profoundly uneasy."

Luke felt a pang across his heart. "In the far north? My home is in Winterscar; my family is there. But I've been travelling for many months." He turned away from the docks, leaned back against the rail. "I've received very few letters during that time, and I expect that several have gone astray. If you will excuse my asking, I was told you had recently been in Nordfjall. In Ottarsburg, in fact, which is not very far from the Winterscar border. Would you have any idea what that disturbing 'something' might be?"

"I have not. I went to Nordfjall on personal business, searching for information on certain relatives of my own, from whom I have been long estranged. I am afraid I thought of very little else while I was there."

"And was your search successful?" Luke asked politely.

For the first time, Raith displayed a strong emotion. His eyes flashed in the shadows under his hat; his mouth compressed into a thin, hard line. "Unfortunately not," he said, in a voice of suppressed passion. "The people I was looking for died many years ago, and those who knew them best have all disappeared."

Then the Leveller collected himself, became so cold and calm and stern again, Luke almost believed he had imagined that moment of intense emotion. "I might have stayed longer, have asked further questions, but I had neglected my duties in Rijxland for some months already, and I was naturally eager to return home again."

9

The *Pagan Queen* weighed anchor the next morning. From the time she entered the Troit, the wide channel between Herndyke and the isle of Finghyll, the wind continued to blow cold and steadily. In the mornings, her sheets and her blocks were misted with ice; in the warmer afternoons, an unpleasant odor rose from the hold. She had taken on a cargo of uncured sealskins in Kjellmark, and because she was driven off course by the storm, and therefore already two weeks late delivering them, they had begun to rot.

Yet the days which followed were great days for Luke, as he strove to advance his acquaintance with the mysterious Rijxlander. They spent hours together walking the deck, while Lucius asked question after question, attempting to draw Raith out. He was particularly fascinated by the man's religion.

The people that Luke knew best changed their religion as they changed their fashions: They were today Proto-deists, next month Neoprotonists, and no one could say what fancy would strike them in six months' time. These conversions were easy, painless, unattended by spiritual or moral upheaval. Luke suspected that it was all a part of the Grand Scheme of "our damned interfering Ancestors"—though in this case he rather approved. Religion crossed national boundaries. It was therefore a little dangerous—it would be *very* dangerous, if taken too seriously. Fortunately, few people did take it seriously.

But Levellers were different. They were born, lived, and died in the same stern religion; from cradle to grave they devoted their lives to the precepts of a single demanding creed. What could possibly be the attraction?

"The Anti-demonists took me in," said Raith. "I was a dirty little orphan boy begging for my bread, and they had every reason to despise me, yet they were generous and offered me a home."

"Despise you—how?" said Luke. "Dirty and wretched you may have been, but still you were an innocent child."

Raith shrugged a broad shoulder under his voluminous cloak. "I was hardly innocent. My parents were—essentially—criminals, and I was born with the sins of my fathers lying heavy on my soul. Yet for all that, those good people were moved to accept me among them, and they struggled—how they struggled, against every inclination of my own wayward nature, against every obstacle I could throw in their way!—to make something decent of me."

Luke frowned. The picture in his mind was not an engaging one: a circle of grim fanatics attempting to beat and bully one small boy into submission. "I have been told," he said tentatively, "that Levellers use their children harshly. That they are swift to punish and slow to forgive, even ordinary childish transgressions."

Raith considered a moment, standing still and silent, a dark silhouette against the moving background of blue sky and wispy white clouds. Up on the forecastle, the first mate shouted to his men, ordering them to trim the yards as the wind was getting a bit ahead. There was a sudden bustle of activity on every side.

"Perhaps the discipline we practice *is* somewhat harsh. My own temperament being what it was, I needed that discipline, I craved that discipline. I would have been abandoned to sin without it. Being unacquainted with children my own age when I was a child myself, I cannot say if their other fosterlings feel such gratitude. For me, it was a great thing, a miraculous thing, that they were willing to take such pains to save me."

"And what of the young prince and princesses you have in your charge?" Luke brushed aside a lock of dark hair, which the wind had loosened from his satin hair ribbon and blown into his eyes. "Do you practice on *them* the same methods that were applied to you?"

"I could hardly do so," said Raith, with the hint of a smile. "Their mother would be horrified if I attempted it. And I must admit I have never found it necessary. My young charges are exceedingly conformable. A word or a look is usually enough to bring them into line—though I have been told they are less easily managed when I am not present."

He glanced across at Luke. Not for the first time, Lucius was struck by the depth and darkness of his eyes. The iris was as dark as the pupil; no ring of lighter color relieved the inky blackness. Yet there was a brilliance to those eyes, and something else, which Luke was inclined to identify as a restless intelligence.

"You, no doubt, were also raised on milder principles, and perhaps that suited you. Tell me, Mr. Guilian, are you entirely satisfied with the results?"

This, though perhaps not intended to be, was something of a poser. Luke gave a short false laugh. "I've never really thought about it. That is, I suppose I *am* tolerably pleased with the result, though others seem less so."

"You ask too many questions. I beg your pardon; I do not mean to say that I, personally, am offended. Only that other men, less given to examining their own actions, might find your habit of asking so many questions disturbing."

More often, as Luke knew very well, they were put off by his habit of answering his own questions. Yet somehow, in this new friendship, positions had been reversed; it was the Leveller who explained things, and Luke had slipped easily into the rôle of avid listener.

He laughed again, this time more naturally. "Then my questions aren't an intolerable annoyance? I am glad to hear it. I don't mean to be rude—or unbearably inquisitive."

Raith looked out across the Troit. The wind was ruffling the sea, and waves were hitting the ship with increasing force, sending up a wild white spray. "It is good to ask questions. The day may come, sooner than any of us think, when we are all required to explain ourselves to a Higher Power, to minutely and mercilessly examine our own hearts."

There was another long silence between them.

"The Apocalypse," Luke finally said, with a lift of his eyebrows. "So fondly described by all your preachers."

"Yes, the Apocalypse," replied Raith, apparently undisturbed by his sarcasm. "The earth will heave and the mountains slide; the sea will burn like wax. Kings and princes will topple from their thrones. An angry God will level all before him. It is coming soon, I think."

Luke cleared his throat, unaccountably embarrassed. "It all sounds terribly unpleasant. And now that I think of it, my old tutor, Doctor Francis Purcell, would dismiss the idea as errant Vulcanist nonsense. But perhaps you're not familiar with that scientific theory, which states that the present world was built out of the ashes of an older world, destroyed eons past by erupting volcanoes?"

"I am," Raith responded coolly, "and with the opposing theory, as well. Your Doctor Purcell, I take it, believes that all modern rock formations and sediments were laid down by ancient seas. I have studied the arguments on either side, but I fear I cannot call myself either a Vulcanist *or* a Sedimentarian, believing as I do that both the Fire and the Deluge are yet to come."

At this, Luke was again thrown into some slight confusion. As much as he respected his companion's mental powers, he had not supposed him a highly educated man—perhaps because he was employed to instruct such very young children, perhaps because of his devotion to his religion. To Luke's way of thinking, the basis of all religious doctrine and practice was a profound ignorance of the natural world.

So now he could not help feeling ashamed of himself. The question had not been asked in any generous spirit. There was something perhaps a bit petty, perhaps a bit mean, in trying to trip up this man who had answered all of his questions so patiently, so courteously.

"I beg your pardon," he said contritely. "I had no idea you were a scholar—and a natural philosopher at that."

"I have been many things in my time," said Raith, with his quiet smile. Though he did not expand, then or later, on that interesting statement.

In the evening, Luke invited Raith down to his cabin and presented him with a handful of dog-eared and blotted pages from his revisionist history. Having gained so high an opinion of the Leveller's perspicacity, he was naturally eager to share his theories. The Rijxlander read straight through the first fifty pages without so much as lifting an eyebrow. Luke watched him with growing impatience; he had expected some strong reaction, positive or negative, and was sharply disappointed at not having gained one.

"Your arguments are—original," Raith said at last. "I am particularly struck by this idea of yours that much of the history of the last fifteen hundred years is a flimsy tissue of lies. May I ask how it was you arrived at this startling conclusion?"

Luke, who had seated himself on the lower bunk, so that his long-legged visitor might enjoy the benefit of the one rickety chair, searched through his mind for the proper words. "In Kjell-

mark there is a great pile of stone: the remains of a fortress battered by cannon in a conflict that has—somehow—been overlooked in all of the history books. In Tölmarch, Lichtenwald, and
Wölfenbrücke I have seen whole cemeteries filled with unmarked
graves, whether of revolutionaries or plague victims no one could
tell me. On Finghyll, I learned that it is a crime to carry the portrait of a certain early patriot, Carolus Vosdijk by name.

"I used to think," Luke continued, "that other historians were
merely mistaken. That all of the things that I knew to be true, yet
were somehow omitted from official histories, were only the result
of careless copying. But I have seen so much, I have learned so much
since then, I believe I have uncovered evidence of something far
more sinister."

He reached into a pocket and drew out a curious old eight-
sided coin. "Look here." He held up the gold coin, the better to
display its peculiarities. "I found this in Catwitsen when I was
there, six—no, seven months ago. As you can see, it pretends to
offer a portrait of Grand Duke Willem, one of their early rulers.
But what an improbable picture it is. The face appears to have
two left eyes, the mouth is crooked, and the head seems utterly
detached from the neck and floats above the lace collar as though
it had no relation to the body at all. At the very least, I believe
we can safely say that no living man ever sat for this portrait!"

"But what then?" Raith accepted the coin into his hand, examined
it minutely. "Surely this would not be the first time an official portrait failed to do its subject justice."

"I believe that whoever designed this coin was trying to leave an
encoded message for future generations, attempting to tell us the
truth: no such person as Grand Duke Willem ever existed and every
story associated with his name is a deliberate fabrication."

"But what is the purpose of this great deception?"

"That," Luke said darkly, as he took back the gold coin and

slipped it back into his pocket, "is exactly what I mean to find out in Luden.

"But I appear to amuse you," he added, a shade resentfully. "Surely you, as a rational man, must admit that much of what we have heard about the earliest centuries of Man's Dominion sounds highly improbable."

"As so might the events of our own era, a thousand years in the future. You understand that I don't dispute your conclusions," Raith added carefully, "I merely wish to point out that the truth of our own times is considerably stranger than any fiction."

"Well, yes," Luke admitted, putting his chin in his hand. "We do live in bizarre times." He glanced slyly across at his companion. "The tales one hears out of Rijxland, for instance. I have heard of debtors taking their wives and children into prison with them, in order to keep the family together, but that a devoted daughter should follow her father into a *madhouse*, and the entire court of Rijxland follow her example? It hardly seems possible!"

"It is not possible—or at any rate, it is not true," the Leveller responded. "The Crown Princess and her children do occupy a house on the grounds of the hospital, but they do not mingle with the other inmates. Nor does the king precisely hold court at the asylum—although, visiting the hospital on certain days, one might easily suppose he did. The true situation is rather more complex than that.

"You must understand," Raith went on, in what Lucius assumed was his best pedagogical style, "that while the king has been reduced to a figurehead and the real power in Rijxland now lies in the hands of the Parliament, King Izaiah still nominally rules. His foreign doctors entertain a very real and a very lively fear that someone will accuse them of undue influence. At the same time, they are regrettably eager to display their medical prowess to the world at large. For this reason, they have made an ongoing experiment of the king."

Luke thought he detected some shade of emotion in the Leveller's last statement. "You have some.quarrel with their methods?"

Raith cleared his throat, moved the flimsy chair a little closer to the table. "Some of their treatments appear—grotesque—and calculated to do more harm than good. Nor do I like the way they make a public entertainment of the king and the other inmates, by throwing open the doors of the madhouse and allowing great crowds to flock inside."

Luke creased his brow. He had to admit the idea was faintly obscene. "I would think that so much attention would be rather trying, even distressing, to a sick old man."

"So I think also. Unfortunately, those in a position to act on his behalf do not seem to agree."

"And the Crown Princess?"

"The Princess Marjote is of much the same mind, but her influence at the moment is negligible. She is engaged in an ugly and extended power struggle with her cousin, Lord Flinx, and she appears to be losing." Raith's large hands gripped the table for a moment, then relaxed. "As for Lord Flinx, he is a gifted orator, though a very bad man, and his party grows stronger with every passing day."

Luke nodded thoughtfully, his dark eyebrows twitching together. Of the king's nephew, he had heard wildly conflicting accounts. "The stories they tell of Lord Flinx are gross and distasteful, yet one hears, too, that his behavior in Luden is generally impeccable."

"He commits his worse excesses on visits to his country estate, or to the house he keeps over the border in Montcieux for that very purpose," said Raith. "There he indulges his depraved appetites without any shame or disguise. Of course, all this is dismissed as malicious rumor by his supporters."

"And the young woman—his protegée? His niece, or his natural daughter, or—"

"Tremeur Brouillard." The name seemed to hang in the air, conjuring up any number of scandalous associations. Lucius seldom listened to bedroom gossip, but even he had heard stories about the enterprising and unscrupulous Mademoiselle Brouillard.

"Yes, Tremeur Brouillard. The adventuress Lord Flinx has reportedly insinuated, possibly incestuously, into the Mad King's bed. What is her influence?"

"I think you would find her somewhat different than you imagine her," said the Leveller, his dark glance grown suddenly keen. "The king is certainly attached to her, and she seems to be a young woman of considerable wit as well as beauty. But she is still very much under the control of Lord Flinx, who is her legal guardian.

"Her entire situation is highly ambiguous. And, in my opinion at least, extremely uncomfortable."

They were sailing along the coast of Rijxland when the wind rose and the waves grew choppy. Unable to sleep because of the rolling and pitching, Luke rose from his bunk early, shook Perys awake and demanded to be dressed, then stumbled up to the deck.

He found Raith already there before him, apparently glorying in the clash of the elements. He was standing by the rail with his long cloak floating around him and a look of ecstasy on his usually stern face.

"Is this your promised End of the World?" Lucius asked mockingly. A heavy sea was beating against the bows; the sails boomed overhead with a noise like thunder; on all sides, unintelligible orders were being shouted and carried out. Even as Luke spoke, a wave washed over the side of the ship, soaking them both to the knees.

"I have not said that the world will end. Only that it will be broken and remade. When the Day of Wrath arrives, it will be nothing like this. Though I admit that on days such as this——"

He might have said more, but just then the ship heeled over, and seemed to stand on its side in the water. Raith held on to the rail and was nearly washed away, but Luke was thrown backward. As the ship righted herself, there was a shout from the rigging, something flashed through the air over their heads, and then there was a splash, and a cry of, "Man overboard!"

Scrambling to his feet, Luke rushed back to the railing. He caught a brief glimpse of a dark head bobbing in the waves, a pair of wildly thrashing arms receding in the distance. Knowing that very few sailors knew how to swim, being a strong swimmer himself, Luke acted almost without thinking. He kicked off his shoes, tore off his coat, climbed up on the rail. "Is this wise, Mr. Guilian?" he heard Raith say, just before he launched himself into the air.

Luke landed in the water with a mighty splash. The force of that impact and the icy coldness of the channel momentarily stunned him. For several seconds after he rose to the surface, he could neither see nor breathe. Then the air rushed back into his lungs, his head cleared, and he was making powerful strokes in what he hoped was the direction of the drowning sailor.

Before long, he caught sight of a thrashing figure on his left, appearing and disappearing under the waves. He adjusted his course and arrived just in time to catch the sailor by the hair as he was going under, perhaps for the last time.

Luke felt for another hold, and was able to pull the man up by the neck of his shirt so that his head appeared above the water. The sailor gasped for air, then nearly knocked the wind out of Lucius with the violence of his struggles to remain afloat.

"Be still, can't you? I am trying to save you, but if you keep on like this, you'll drown us both."

Unfortunately, Luke's words fell on deaf ears. He was forced to gain the man's cooperation by the ruthless expedient of holding his head underwater until his struggles ceased. When Lucius brought him back up again, the sailor sputtered and coughed, but he remained quiet.

But now Luke had another problem. He could not see the ship, had no idea if the officers had launched a boat to rescue him. And while he had only a dim conception of the time already elapsed, he did not think he and the sailor could last very long in the deadly cold of the sea.

A great wave washed over his head. With immense and exhausting difficulty, Luke struggled with his burden back up to the surface. As his head broke through the water, he wondered how many more times he would be able to do it. Already, he felt as though iron weights had been attached to his arms and legs.

At last he heard a familiar voice. A moment later, a sleek dark head appeared in the sea beside him; a strong arm reached out to help him support the semiconscious sailor. With a vast sense of relief, Luke accepted this assistance.

"Raith, is this wise?" he could not resist saying.

"You must tell me. I am only following your heroic example. The ship has dropped anchor and they are lowering a longboat. It should be along soon to take us up."

There was a muffled shouting carried on the wind, and Luke realized that he had somehow gotten turned around, and the ship was behind him.

With Raith to assist him, Luke was able to tow the sailor in the direction of the approaching longboat. After what seemed an eternity, he heard the rise and fall of oars. At length, the boat pulled alongside and all three men were dragged on board.

The Leveller immediately collapsed in the bottom of the boat, the victim of a violent bout of vomiting. Limp and exhausted, Luke allowed himself to be wrapped in a piece of canvas while raw spirits were poured down his throat. That accomplished, he could only watch helplessly as Raith continued to heave and contort his long body.

At last the painful retching subsided; Raith recovered enough to pull himself up into a sitting position.

"Seawater sits ill on the stomach," said Luke with a sympathetic shudder. "But how did you manage to swallow enough to make yourself so amazingly sick?" Though very little had actually come up, by the violence of Raith's reaction he might have swallowed most of the Troit.

The boat hit a heavy swell and descended into the trough with a loud smack, washing oarsmen and passengers in foaming water. As the sea receded, Raith leaned back against one of the benches. "I am more accustomed to water that is still—not to the kind that swells up and slaps one in the face. I have never been in the sea before." He made a deprecating gesture. "And though I am strong, I am hardly what you would call an excellent swimmer."

Luke gazed at him with undisguised admiration. "Then what you did was remarkably brave. *I* had an arrogant confidence in my own ability to battle the waves, misplaced though it might be, but you— you're a hero! Allow me to shake your hand."

Raith smiled faintly as their fingers touched. "You flatter me. I have to inform you that I was solely motivated by self-interest." He closed his eyes, lay back against the bench. "It came to me, as I stood by the rail and watched you swim off, that death by water—particularly in an attempt to save a life—would serve to wash away a multitude of sins."

10

$\mathcal{J}$t was a sharp day, with severe frosts and the wind blowing shrewdly. Snow had fallen during the night; in all the low places where the wind had gathered it, the road was buried two feet deep. It made slow going for the horses. Inside the black berlin, Lili wondered if she would ever reach home.

She glanced across at the opposite seat. Allora's eyes were closed and she snored softly, yet she remained very straight as to her posture, very precise as to the placement of her tiny feet—even dozing, she looked an entirely formidable old lady.

As if in answer to Lili's question, Allora's eyes fluttered open. "Patience, Lilliana."

Lili sighed and shifted her position for the tenth time in as many minutes. "Did I disturb you? I beg your pardon. I don't even know why I feel so restless."

The horses plodded on. The sun set in a blaze of crimson behind a wooded hill. Lili tried not to fidget; she closed her eyes, but sleep eluded her; her feet were all pins and needles.

At last the coach passed through the gates of Brakeburn, creaked down the long avenue of oaks to the house, and jolted to a stop at the foot of the granite block staircase. When the coachman opened the door, Lili was out and halfway up the steps before she realized that her father was waiting for her at the top.

She dropped a dutiful curtsy. "Did you miss me, Papa?"

He did not answer her question, though he presented a grey-stubbled cheek for her to kiss. "You have company, Lili."

Too tired to quiz him, she entered the house through the stone-flagged entry and moved on toward the parlor. She had lowered her hood and was in the process of stripping off her gloves when she came to a sudden stop on the threshold of the sitting-room, with one glove on and the other off.

There was a fire roaring in the great stone fireplace; spermaceti candles burned in the iron chandelier. All this Lili might have expected with visitors in the house. What she was *not* prepared to see was a stern little man, meticulously dressed in mouse-grey velvet and old lace, pacing the hardwood floor with a restless tread. His face was grim, his manner impatient; it was a moment before she recognized, in the immaculate stranger, her usually careless husband.

As he caught sight of Lili, Will bridled up. He crossed the room, made a stiff bow, imprinted the back of her ungloved hand with an icy kiss. "You might have written to tell me you were planning a journey."

Lilliana was stunned, and then she was speechless. Will in the unfamiliar rôle of the injured husband was rather more than she was prepared to handle. And what was Wilrowan *doing* here, anyway, looking like a thundercloud?

"I suppose I might have, if I had any idea you cared to hear about it," she finally admitted. "But—but how agreeable it is to see you, Will. Have you been here long?"

He bowed again, even more stiffly. His hair was tied back with a black velvet bow and he smelled of bay rum; he wore a tiny black satin patch high on one cheek. He was dressed like a man who had come courting, but he never *had* dressed that way when he was reluctantly courting her.

"It is a pleasure for me also, madam. Though a pleasure long deferred. I have been here three days. Your father and I have not passed the time—amicably."

Feeling weak in the knees, Lili sat down on an old oak settle next to the fireplace. She felt a bubble of laughter rise in her throat at the thought of Will and Lord Brakeburn forced to endure each other's company for three long days. "Will, I am most d-dreadfully sorry. It must have been simply un-unbearable for both of you."

Slightly mollified, he unbent just a little. With punctilious courtesy, he moved a painted screen between Lili and the fire, sat down beside her on the hard oak seat. "Did you enjoy your visit?" he inquired politely. "Where did you go and who did you see? Your father neglected to tell me—or perhaps it was I who neglected to ask."

Lili unfastened her cloak strings, wondering what had gotten into him. She had often heard of his volatile temperament, but had never seen him in a mood like this. "It's not worth telling about, really. Most of the time I spent nursing a sick man back to health."

Inexplicably, Will went stiff again. "But how pleasant for the gentleman in question. I daresay he was in no particular hurry to recover, with so charming an attendant to see to his needs."

So that's it, thought Lili. *How can he possibly be so ridiculous?* "It is always worrisome when a man of seventy takes ill," she answered primly, "but this was particularly serious."

"Aaaah," said Will, on a long breath. "It was an elderly gentleman?" Then he relaxed and was the Wilrowan she knew. "My poor Lili," he said with a wry look, "do you never do anything more amusing than visit invalid old men?"

Lili thought about that before she answered. "Well—no. Not more *amusing* and not always particularly agreeable, but I do well enough." And she wished she might tell him how very exciting her journey had actually been—though mindful of Allora's warnings, she kept it all to herself. Really, he was so unpredictable, it was wise to be cautious.

"But you—I suppose you have been tolerably well amused in Hawkesbridge?"

"Tolerably well," he admitted, with a sheepish grin. "I wonder you need to ask. No doubt your aunt has already acquainted you with all of my follies, all my transgressions."

Lili sighed. Though living retired in the country, Allora maintained a wide correspondence; whatever gossip she heard about Will, she passed on to her great-niece. Lili studied Wilrowan's face, wondering if he had come all this way to tell her something—and how she would bear it if that something turned out to involve another woman.

"But we've both been away, you know. She'll be days sorting through all of her letters, she gets so many of them," said Lili, trying to make light of it. "Perhaps you had better confess—whatever it is you've been doing—and save Allora the trouble."

For a moment, it seemed he *would* tell her. He started to speak, then his eyes darkened, he shook his head, looked down at his feet. "What a vastly improper suggestion," he said under his breath. "Tell you the whole of it—even the half of it? I'd cut a pretty figure, laying my sins in your lap."

To her surprise, Lili experienced a pang of disappointment. But that was ridiculous. Could Will's confidences lessen the humiliation of his infidelities even a little? She sincerely doubted it.

Dinner that evening in the candle-lit dining hall was more than usually dreary, conducted as it was in a self-conscious hush, only occasionally broken by a little stilted conversation. For long minutes, the only sounds were the faint *tink-tink-tink* of silverware and the soft-footed steps of the servants as they circled the table. Lili was abstracted; Lord Brakeburn and Allora were formal and distant. As for Wilrowan, he scarcely touched anything but the soup, the mutton, and the red wine.

He was wondering what he was even doing there. He had come to Brakeburn with some vague idea of unburdening himself, of explaining about the duel, Macquay, Eulalie—

He scowled at Lili, seated on the other side of the table, divided from him by a wide expanse of damask table-cloth, flint glass, and rose-pattern china. She had stopped eating, was listening to something Allora was saying in a low voice, excluding the men. Lili smiled, shook her head. She had changed into a gown of russet silk and a shawl of black spider lace; despite her long day of travel, she looked cool, unruffled, serene. What a villain he would have to be, what a dog, to shatter that serenity with his sordid confessions.

When the ladies withdrew, Will did not linger over the port. He made his excuses to Lord Brakeburn, escaped from the dining room, and went for a walk in the frosty gardens. There he walked for about an hour, in the company of the leafless trees and the winter stars, until the thought of Lili waiting for him in the bedroom above warmed his blood and drew him back into the house.

Let it not be another night of sweet condescension, of ladylike submission, he thought as he climbed the stairs.

But she was sitting up reading in bed when he arrived in her bed-chamber, and Will felt a familiar chill as he entered the room.

Lili's four-poster bed was a veritable icon of respectability, with its immaculate linens, snowy counterpane, and the numerous horsehair bolsters and feather pillows that surrounded and supported her. Lili herself looked as chaste as ice, in a voluminous white nightgown discreetly trimmed with ribbons and lace.

The big four-poster could never be mistaken for anything but what it was: the Marriage Bed, hallowed by custom, sanctified with the cleanly scents of lavender and orange-flower water, where Lili

enacted her wifely duties and Will was obliged to bridle his unbri-
dled passions. It could never be the scene of wild, unrestrained
lovemaking—or could it?

Shrugging out of his coat and tossing it on a chair by the door,
Will cleared his throat. Lili glanced up from her book. "I hope," he
said, "you are not too tired for company this evening?"

"Of course not." Her smile was warm and friendly as he sat down
beside her, but by no means inviting.

He felt a vein begin to pulse in his throat. "What are you reading?"

"It is only Mandeville. I daresay you had enough of him at the
university." Lili closed the book and put it aside, and Will—more to
fill the suddenly awkward silence than because he was really curious—picked it up.

He examined the cover. It was bound in shark-skin and fastened
with a clasp of polished fishbone. Finding no title, he unfastened the
clasp and opened the book to a place at random. With a start of
recognition, he found himself staring at a familiar paragraph. "But
this isn't *Mandeville's Encyclopaedia of the Whole World*, it's his *Philosophy
of Magic*—much more rare and exceedingly difficult." He glanced up
at Lili, genuinely surprised. "I would never have guessed you would
be interested."

Lili twitched an eyebrow. "Have you read it, then? Now I am the
one who must admit to being surprised."

He closed the cover, put the book firmly aside. "I have read it,
yes. Studied it most carefully, I should say. Dash it, Lili, I didn't
spend the *whole* of my time at Malachim College on misbehavior."

Her chestnut curls were slightly damp after her bath, and she
smelled faintly of soap. A delicate color came and went in her
cheeks. She had never seemed more desirable.

"You look amazing. I can't think what has kept me in Hawkesbridge all of these months."

Lili smiled at him quizzically. "That was very prettily said. Really, Wilrowan, you've become so gallant, I can't help wondering if there is something you want from me."

Under the white nightgown, her breasts rose and fell; he knew by touch every one of the curves that lay hidden beneath those chaste folds of linen. *I want to rip off that damnable nightrail,* he thought. *I want to nail you to the bed, make love until we both grow weak, make you scream with passion.*

But he could not, of course, suggest any of those things. She was as much a victim of Lord Brakeburn's machinations as he was. Even more so, because her father's schemes had tied her for life to a man whose caresses left her singularly unmoved.

"I want you to visit me at the palace for a month or two this spring. Or if you can't bear the accommodations at the Volary, we could let a house. I want—I want to try and start a family."

Lilliana opened her eyes very wide. "But haven't we *been* trying? That is—we've been doing the sort of thing that generally does lead to babies, though I had no idea you were serious about setting up a nursery. If so, I must say you've been marvelously patient. It has been six years."

Will frowned, wondering if she meant to be sarcastic. "Blast it, Lili, I don't blame you. How on earth could I? I should visit you here more often than I do."

"I wouldn't say that it was anyone's fault. You have made it clear that I'm welcome to visit you whenever I please. It has been my decision to remain here most of the year. Though I must admit, you have hardly been pressing in your invitations."

"I don't mean to press you now. But I wish you would consider it." He captured her hand and raised it to his lips. "You are my best friend, Lili, and I don't mean to neglect you, but it is—difficult— living apart."

She began to look flustered. "That's very sweet of you, Will. I'm not reluctant to visit you in Hawkesbridge, but have you considered that a month or two of my company might eventually strike you as—tiresome? You do grow so easily bored."

Will shook his head, regarded her with a puzzled frown. "Bored with you? You are practically the only person who never *does* bore me."

It seemed, somehow, like the right moment to act, so he leaned over, drew her into his arms, and kissed her full on the mouth. Something fluttered inside her chest, he could feel it, something responded. For one giddy sweet moment, he allowed himself to hope that it would be different this time.

But as he drew away, a shiver passed over her and she averted her face. "Wilrowan," she said breathlessly, "you *will* blow out the candles before you come to bed?"

"Of course," he said, with a disappointed sigh. It was almost—but not quite—enough to cool his ardor. "The gods forbid that I should ever offend your modesty, my dear."

11

id-morning found Will and Lili at the breakfast table, carefully polite. They had been spared the company of Lord Brakeburn and Allora, both early risers, and the tea, cutlets, toast, and chocolate were consumed with a liberal seasoning of silence.

Will brooded amidst the willow-ware teacups. A man was at a distinct disadvantage wooing his own wife. He had an uneasy feeling he had made a fool of himself the night before. *"Thank you, Wilrowan, that was really very nice,"* Lili had declared, just before falling asleep. It had stung then and it stung now, in the cool light of morning.

Watching her narrowly across the breakfast table, he wondered (not for the first time) if his Lili concealed, under that gentle exterior, rather more of spite than she ever let on. Certainly, the girl he had married had been spirited enough—in fact, she had been most damnably outspoken. He cringed inwardly, remembering their first—no, their second meeting.

"What on earth are you doing in my bedchamber, Mr. Blackheart?" Lili had said. A thin girl in a white nightdress, she seemed to Will remarkably

self-possessed for a sixteen-year-old virgin faced with an intruder in the sanctity of her bedchamber.

The widowed Lord Brakeburn had rented a house in Hawkesbridge for the summer. Unfortunately, it was a house located too near the university; the street on which it stood was frequently the scene of spirited encounters between the more reckless students, the Watch, and occasionally the City Guard. This was the first time, however, that a disturbance below had extended to the upper floors of the house.

"I beg—I beg your pardon," Will managed to stammer. "It seems I have mistaken the house. I can only imagine what you must be thinking, but indeed, Miss—I regret to say that I don't recall your name, though you seem to know mine. Have we been properly introduced?"

"Yes, we have been introduced, though I'm hardly surprised you've forgotten the occasion," she responded tartly. "And of course you've mistaken the house. I never imagined for one moment you intended to climb through my bedroom window!"

Will was ready to sink through the floorboards. "Shades of Darkness!" he exclaimed. "Miss Brakeburn, isn't it? I didn't recognize you in your nightdr— that is, under the present circumstances."

Whether it was the white nightrail or the fact that he faced her on her own ground, she was certainly very different than he remembered her. More attractive, too, than she had appeared at a ball two months previously: overcorseted, hardly able to breathe, awkward in the wrong color, the wrong gown.

"I would be happy to leave by the same way I came," said Will. "But as you can see, it's a long drop. I'm always very well going up, but when I have to descend—" Just then, there came a loud pounding on Lili's door and the voice of her father demanding to be let in. Apparently, one of the servants had seen Wilrowan climbing the wall and alerted his master.

Will darted toward an open wardrobe, but Lili put out a hand to stop him. "If it is all the same to you, I'd rather not be discovered with a man cowering inside my closet!" She proceeded to unlock and throw open the bedroom door, admitting her father and the two servants with him.

THE QUEEN'S NECKLACE · 129

"Mr. Blackheart was just leaving, Papa. It was all a mistake," she said calmly. "He had somebody else in mind when he climbed through my window."

Will did not think it worthwhile to mention that he had actually been escaping from the City Guard, after an evening devoted to mischief and mayhem with some of his less savory friends. He simply bowed and took his leave, before the astonished Lord Brakeburn collected himself sufficiently to utter a single word.

But Lord Brakeburn clearly had the advantage of him six weeks later, when he summoned Wilrowan to his house in the country.

"I had imagined you—not precisely a gentleman, after our previous encounter, but at least above disgracing my daughter by speaking so freely of an incident that could hardly add to your own credit," Brakeburn said sternly.

"I beg your pardon," said Will, taken most profoundly and completely by surprise. "I've not said anything to anyone. As you say, it's not a story in which I appear, sir, in any flattering light."

Brakeburn appeared to unbend. "Perhaps I have misjudged you. Perhaps one of the neighbors chanced to witness your entry through Lili's window. In any case, the incident has created a scandal. My daughter is in hysterics, her reputation in shreds, and she is likely to die of the disgrace, unless you agree to do the honorable thing."

There had been a great deal more, all along the same lines, until Will, horrified by what he imagined must be Miss Brakeburn's situation, horrified, too, that he had brought the whole thing about by his irresponsible behavior, finally broke down and agreed to marry her. Little did he know that Lord Brakeburn's daughter—far from submitting to a bout of hysterics or threatening to perish from the disgrace—was being subjected to similar pressure, told she was endangering a young man's "brilliant academic career," warned that Will stood in danger of being disinherited by his grand relations, unless she allowed him to redeem himself. Allora was not there to advise her, and Lili was vulnerable. Will had been vulnerable, too, far too ashamed to consult his distant, uncaring father, or his formidable grandmother—and by no means as sophisticated and worldly-wise as he liked to pretend.

So they had married at the tender ages of sixteen and seventeen. And nei-
ther one of them learned, until it was much too late, that Lord Brakeburn had
deceived them both: the incident in Lili's bedchamber was known only to
themselves, Lord Brakeburn, and the two servants. For the Brakeburns had
money, an ancient name, an almost equally ancient estate—but nothing to
compare with the wealth and influence of the Rowans, the Krogans, and the
Blackhearts. Lord Brakeburn had simply been unable to resist the prospect of
such a brilliant match for his bookish daughter.

It was unfortunate that Brakeburn had failed to look beyond the daz-
zling name and inquire more closely into the character and habits of his
prospective son-in-law.

Will continued to study his wife across the table, remembering
that other Lili: so exasperating in her fearless honesty, yet so fresh,
so natural, she had won the heart right out of him before he knew
it. She had accomplished that, in fact, while he was chasing other
women. But when had *that* Lili gone away, to be replaced by this
handsome, composed young woman, friendly yet somehow distant?

Mechanically, Will lifted his cup to his lips, swallowed a mouthful of tea without tasting it. No wonder life was so flat and stale. The
women he knew in Hawkesbridge disgusted him: a collection of
shallow, mercenary schemers, empty-headed dolls, and jaded volup-
tuaries. His pursuit of them had taken on an air of desperation. And
the only woman he really wanted was the one he could bed whenever he chose—but who continually frustrated his attempts at true
intimacy.

One of the servants slipped into the breakfast room and discreetly deposited a letter on the table at Will's elbow. Sipping his tea,
continuing to mull over his dreary prospects, Will did not notice at
first. But then something about the letter—the pale blot of sealing
wax, the musky erotic scent wafting his way—intruded into his
thoughts.

He stared down at the folded slip of paper, with deep loathing in his soul. The direction was written in a flowery feminine hand—could it be that Eulalie or one of the others had been brazen enough to write to him here at Brakeburn Hall?

"You have a letter. Who is it from?" Lili's voice was casual and un-suspicious.

With the greatest reluctance, Will gingerly picked up the letter and was relieved to recognize Dionee's cypher impressed on the wax. "It comes from the queen." He took up a butter knife and pried loose the seal, unfolded the paper and sustained another shock. The sheet was absolutely blank.

"Is it bad news?"

"It's no news at all." But then he recognized the scent of Lady Krogan's perfume. Remembering Dionee's penchant for melodramatics, he reached out and moved one of the silver candlesticks closer.

Exposed to the flame, the invisible ink slowly appeared. Will blew on the paper in order to cool it. The message was brief, but un-doubtedly in Dionee's style. *Return at Once,* she had scrawled. *O Will, Will, Something so Dreadful has Happened, I cannot Describe it to You. I need You here NOW!*

"It *is* bad news," said Lili, reading his face as he read the letter.

"It is probably nothing more than some nonsense of Dionee's." Yet even for Dionee, the tone was rather frantic. Will felt his spirits sink even further. "For all that, I hardly see how I can safely ignore it. I'll have to return to Hawkesbridge immediately."

He spent the rest of the day on horseback, snatched a few hours of sleep at an Inn, wrapped up in his riding cloak by the fire in the coffee room. He woke after midnight, called for soup and a tankard of spiced ale, swallowed them hastily, and rode on toward Hawkes-bridge.

Wilrowan entered the ancient city just after daybreak, when the gas lamps were winking out, one by one, when the water-carts made their first appearance, and gardeners came out to gather up dung from the streets. Fog from the Zule had seeped into the narrow lanes and alleys, mixing with smoke from the coal fires being kindled in kitchens throughout the town, making the way dim. Will's grey mare shied at something moving in the shadows. Keeping his hands on the reins, he slid down from the saddle and, picking his way carefully, led the weary mare uphill toward the palace.

Harsh voices of ravens sounded overhead. A flock appeared out of the mist, circling just above the housetops, all calling out at once. It was hard to make sense of the clamor in his head, the confusion of sounds as the birds continued to wheel in the clammy air.

Then one of the ravens came swooping down and landed on the empty saddle. <*Coffin and Polmaric are dead, and another man injured. They say he may die of his wounds.*>

<*My lieutenants dead?*> Will stopped, his mind reeling. He stood in the narrow street with the condensed fog dripping off of his hat, and tried to imagine what it all meant. <*How did this happen?*> He extended an arm, and the raven made a short hop and landed on his wrist.

<*We are not certain. There are too many stories; we cannot make sense of them.*> The bird walked sideways up his arm until it reached his shoulder; the indigo spark at the base of its brain wavered and then grew bright again. <*The queen stays in her room, refusing to speak to anyone, except to ask for you.*>

"Gods!" said Wilrowan out loud. So it was more than Dionee's usual mischief after all. <*I want to hear more of this—listen at every keyhole and window in the city if you must. I'll speak to the queen and learn what I can there.*>

The raven flew off his shoulder and disappeared in the fog overhead.

*   *   *

At half past seven the Volary was already stirring. Coachmen, grooms, chair-men, and link-boys swarmed in the courtyards nearest the stables. A line of wagons was rumbling through the back gate: greengrocers, butchers, bakers, and confectioners. Smaller tradesmen pushing wheel-barrows full of crayfish, oysters, cabbages, eels, and round yellow cheeses jockeyed for position by the kitchen door. Inside the palace proper, the halls resounded with the quick patter of running feet, as valets, hair-dressers, barbers, and maid-servants bearing pots of chocolate and plates of buttered eggs scurried from one bedchamber to another, trying to meet a hundred different demands at once.

The queen's maids-of-honor had gathered in a nervous group outside her bedchamber door. Ignoring their questions, since they were unable to answer his, Will impatiently pushed open the door and entered the candlelit room beyond.

Inside, the songbirds were ominously silent in their silver cages. Dionee was pacing, half frantic, still in her satin corset and ruffled petticoats, only partly concealed by a flowered silk shawl thrown carelessly over her shoulders. Apparently, she had been up all night without completely undressing or brushing the powder out of her hair.

At the sight of Wilrowan, she burst into tears, cast herself into his arms, and wept all over the shoulder of his riding cloak. He did his best to calm her: smoothing her tousled white curls, kissing her on both wet cheeks, whispering he knew not what words of comfort in one tiny ear.

"O Will, my Will, I have been so wicked—so wicked. And Rodaric will never forgive me when he learns the truth."

"What have you done, Dionee? Tell me what it is, and I'll make it right if I possibly can."

She heaved a tremulous sigh and tried to speak, but choked on

the words. Realizing that it would be impossible to get anything useful out of her until she calmed down, he gave her a little shake by the
shoulders, then put her aside.

There was a silver flagon on a lacquer tea-table, and a pair of
crystal goblets. Pouring poppy-water into one of the glasses, he sat
Dionee down on a bamboo chair by one of the potted shrubs and instructed her to drink. When she seemed able to speak, he sank down
to his knees on the floor at her feet. "I shouldn't even be here. Blast
it, Dionee, you're only half-dressed. Tell me quickly what you have
to say to me, before we cause a scandal between us."

She leaned wearily back in her chair. "Non-nonsense. Everyone
knows you are as near to being my brother as it's possible for anyone but a brother to be."

"Yet for all that, I am *not* your brother." The Mad King of Rijxland, so rumor had it, was cohabiting with his own great-niece, a
scandal that had titillated the continent for almost a year. Will had
no idea whether the story was true or not, but if even that fine old
gentleman was vulnerable to gossip, what might the Hawkesbridge
tittle-tattles make of this?

"But let us be calm, let us be sensible. Tell me why you sent for
me and why two of my men are dead."

The queen began to sob, so loudly he was obliged to shake her
again. "It is too late to be calm or sensible. Or—no, perhaps it isn't.
Providing you can get the Chaos Machine back again, before Rodaric
learns it is missing."

Will sat back on his heels. He sent a silent plea for patience up
to the flaking painted sky twenty feet above. "You are not making
any kind of sense. Recollect that I have no idea what you have done,
and tell me your story from the very beginning."

Dionee tried to compose herself. "You know, at least, what the
Chaos Machine *is*?"

Wilrowan nodded. It was one of the curiosities in which the

Volary abounded: a miniature device much like a clockwork orrery, consisting of five tiny jeweled spheres and four figures of the elements which rotated around each other inside a rock crystal case in a complex and apparently random pattern.

"Well, I—I suppose it seems like a silly prank to you, but I smuggled the thing out of the palace the day that I went to the ambassador's fête. You may wonder why I chose to take such a childish toy with me, why I—"

"I wonder," said Will, "why you dared to take anything half so rare, half so valuable. That 'toy,' as you call it, is the only one of its kind in the world. Nobody knows when or how it was made, the metal is an unknown alloy, and as for the value of the diamonds, rubies, and emeralds— Darkness, Dionee! What were you thinking?"

"Lord Vault is a connoisseur—he collects these toys. And it was his birthday; I thought he would be amused."

"And was he amused?" asked Will, in ominous tones.

"N-no. He was as shocked as you are. Though really, it's not as though the thing were actually *useful*, or that Rodaric hadn't a thousand such knick-knacks and curios besides. Why *this* one should be locked up year after year, in a secret cabinet, so that nobody ever sees or plays with it—"

Will experienced a sinking sensation. "That is hardly for you or I to say, since the object in question isn't ours. Or Rodaric's either. Like everything else of value in the palace, the Chaos Machine belongs to the people of Mountfalcon."

Dionee heaved another tremulous sigh. "It doesn't belong to them now."

Will passed a hand over his face. "Are you trying to tell me that you mislaid the jewel?"

Dionee stiffened. "Do you think I would be so stupidly careless?" Will forbore to answer that question. "I kept it safe inside my muff the whole time—" He groaned inwardly. Ladies were always hiding their money and jewelry inside their muffs, a trick known only too well to thieves. "—and I never let it out of my hands. But on the way back from the fête, my carriage was stopped by disgusting f-foot-pads, who took the muff, the little orrery, and my diamonds as well."

Will frowned. Though he supposed some such disaster had been practically inevitable the moment Dionee decided to borrow the lit-tle jeweled engine without permission, he did not understand how anything like this could happen with a crowd of his men surround-ing the queen. "But your guards? I hope you don't mean to say they did nothing to defend you?"

"They tried to defend me, but there were only the four of them. And the coachman—he was very brave, but the thieves took his musket and beat him over the head until the blood ran down into his eyes." She wrung her hands and began to weep again.

This time, however, Will was unmoved by her distress.

"I begin to understand," he said coldly. "You went out wearing a fortune in jewels, carrying with you one of the palace heirlooms, and you went with only a minimal escort. As a result, two of my men are dead, your coachman is likely to die of a cracked skull, and the heirloom is missing. I congratulate you, Dionee. You have surpassed all your previous follies and have finally achieved something it will be difficult ever to match."

"But Wilrowan," she whispered, "I never left the city the whole time—and who would have thought that footpads would—would do anything so bold?"

Wilrowan blinked at her, much struck by that idea. "Now that I think of it, I've never heard of footpads holding up a coach—nor of highwaymen waylaying anyone *inside* the town. Yes, and four armed men should have been enough to discourage ordinary thieves. The whole thing is incredible."

He rose to his feet, began to pace the floor. "But you said that Rod-aric doesn't know what happened. How could he *not* know that you were robbed—particularly with half your escort murdered right there in the street?"

"Well, of course he knows I was robbed, but he doesn't know about the little orrery. I made certain that no one told him."

Will stopped walking. "If you tell me you bribed the two surviving men—*my* men—to keep silent, I don't know, Dionee, what I am likely to do to you."

"No, no, it was nothing like that. I begged them to keep my secret for a few days. They said it was a troublesome question of—of conflicting loyalties, and agreed to keep silent until they spoke to you. With your two lieutenants dead, that was the proper thing, wasn't it? It—it never occurred to me they might be bribed."

"You astonish me," he said, beginning to pace again. "I should have thought that suborning guardsmen—" He decided not to pursue it. "What of your maids-of-honor? There must have been one or two in the coach with you."

"Luisa was with me. She shrieked and fell into a dead faint before the robbers even entered the coach." Dionee gazed up at Will hopefully. "I thought you could go to some of your low friends, your pickpockets and highwaymen, and find out who is responsible." She wiped the tears off her cheeks with the back of one hand. "If you did that—if we found a way to buy it back again, Rodaric might never need to know that his precious heirloom was missing."

Will stopped in his tracks. "Eternal darkness, Dionee! I won't be a party to any such thing."

She began to cry again. "You won't help me to recover the little engine?"

"That, most certainly, if I am able. But I will not allow you to go on deceiving Rodaric. He will have to be told at once. No, I mean it, Dionee, you can go on weeping as much as you like, but on this point I will not be moved."

Then, relenting just a little, he went and stood over her, lifted one of her hands and dropped a kiss on it.

"Compose yourself, my dear. I can't condone any such dangerous deception, but if you feel you need me there at your side when you tell the king, I remind you that I am yours to command."

12

As Dionee needed time to dress and compose herself, Will made haste to his own rooms, in order to clean up after his journey and render himself presentable for a meeting with the king.

The barracks were located in an old brick pile at the back of the palace, where the clatter of men coming and going at all hours, the carousing that sometimes went on far into the night, would not disturb the king and the queen at their rest. The chambers were small, drafty, and dark, and the building was largely ruinous—doves nested in the rafters, winds whistled in the lower corridors, rain came hissing down the chimneys and put the fires out—but the men were content. With no wives, sisters, or mothers on hand to air out the rooms or tidy their things away, they were able to lead a rakish, rollicking bachelor existence and maintain an atmosphere made up in equal parts of tobacco, old boots, brandy, and gunpowder.

In his tiny bedchamber under the roof tiles, Will pulled on a worn velvet bell-cord, summoning the very junior guardsman who served as his valet. That worthy youth presenting himself several minutes later, Will demanded to be dressed in as little time as possible.

Young Swallow rose to the occasion. In half an hour, Will was washed and shaved, his hair immaculately dressed and powdered. In forty-five minutes he was in uniform—green coat, white waistcoat and breeches, black leather boots reaching past the knee—arranging the deep rows of Chêneboix lace at his wrists and throat. In two minutes more, he had strapped on a sword with a silver hilt, tucked a black three-cornered hat with a feather panache under one arm.

It was thus a supremely elegant Captain Blackheart, the very picture of a gallant young officer, who escorted the queen into King Rodaric's walnut-panelled study and set a chair for her beside the king's desk.

If Rodaric was somewhat taken aback by the sight of Wilrowan after hearing that Will had forsaken Hawkesbridge for at least a fortnight, Will and Dionee were totally unprepared for the explosion that followed her stammering confession. Sweeping aside the papers, pens, and silver inkstand on his desk with an uncharacteristic oath, Rodaric rose from his big oak armchair and began to pace the floor in an agitated manner.

A careful man of five-and-thirty, King Rodaric always had an eye toward appearances, and though his ire was easily aroused his rages were generally cold, controlled, and distinguished by sarcasm rather than by cursing or physical violence. He looked capable of violence now, however. Seeing this, Dionee grew agitated, too, and dropped her lace handkerchief. Will picked it up, handed it back without a word, and stationed himself behind her chair.

"But after all, I know that the Chaos Machine is very, very old and very, very valuable, but if it can't be recovered, it *can* be replaced," she protested. "If I sell everything I own: all of my jewels, both of my carriages—"

Rodaric continued to pace. In the clear light of a crystal oil lamp burning on his desk, his face was grim. "Not if you sold the Volary and everything in it. Dionee, you have lost the one thing in the palace, in Hawkesbridge, in all Mountfalcon —which—cannot—possibly—be—replaced." He bit off the words one by one for emphasis. "You have lost one of the Goblin Jewels."

Dionee clasped her hands in front of her face, shook her head in denial. "But, sir, how could I—how *could* I? It is the Orb of Mountfalcon, not some absurd toy—"

"It is the Orb of Mountfalcon that is a sham, a bauble, a toy. It has one purpose only: to serve as a decoy for traitors and thieves, and so keep the Chaos Machine safe."

Dionee continued to shake her head. "But I have seen—*everyone* has seen you open the little golden globe and display the intricate machinery inside."

"Ordinary clockwork, the merest counterfeit. How clumsy a counterfeit you would know if you had ever compared it with the infinitely more delicate machinery, the exquisite tiny gemstones inside the Chaos Machine."

Dionee sat with her head bowed. "But how can this be? And why—*why* was I never told?"

Rodaric ignored her question. "It is the same with all the other so-called Maglore treasures—the Silver Nef, the Blue Glass Swan—all of them. They were all created for the same purpose: to protect the real Jewels from ordinary thieves and to discourage any royal house with Ambitions from stealing the Jewels of the other houses and consolidating all of that power in one place."

He sat down on the edge of his desk beside the oil lamp, thrust his hands into the pockets of his full-skirted brown coat. "I do not, of course, know which are the genuine treasures elsewhere, though I entertain some strong suspicions. And this being so, I must conclude that neighboring rulers must entertain similar suspicions about the Chaos Machine."

Will cleared his throat. "If you will pardon my saying so, Your Majesty, it seems to be a—transparent deception."

Rodaric stiffened and turned his cold grey eyes in Will's direction, as if he had just received an unwelcome surprise. As perhaps he had; it was unlikely he would have said nearly so much had he remembered Will was present.

"Pointless, too, because at least a hundred people at any one time would know the truth. It hardly seems like a secret at all. Did whoever concocted this scheme *really* believe they could keep the Jewels safe with such an obvious ruse?"

"A naïve deception, perhaps," Rodaric allowed, "but one that has succeeded for fifteen hundred years. Perhaps because it *was* so simple. And even though so many people know a part of the truth, no one could identify *all* of the Jewels except the Maglore who created them—and the Maglore, of course, are all extinct."

"I expect," said Dionee, twisting her handkerchief, "that if the thieves—whoever they are—were to find out what it is they have, the ransom would be truly staggering."

Rodaric drew his hands out of his pockets. "If they were willing to negotiate, we would be fortunate indeed, whatever they might ask. Dionee, do you have any idea how much our people depend on the Mountfalcon Jewel? We are a land-locked nation, do you know what that means?"

"That we have to pay tolls and tariffs to our immediate neighbors to bring in trade goods, to get everything we need."

"And how do we pay these tolls and tariffs?"

"Sir, I do *know* these things. I'm not entirely frivolous. It's with iron and tin and—and coal, which they don't have."

"And iron, tin, and coal have to be dug up out of the ground, an arduous and even dangerous process. There are ancient mines in the mountains to the northeast and southwest of Hawkesbridge, mines which have been active for thousands of years. The veins run remarkably deep, and the mines are vast beyond your comprehension. Many of the pumps that keep them from flooding are so old and

primitive, the timbers that shore up the tunnels so ancient and fragile, you would think the miners would be terrified to enter them,
yet enter they do and bring up the ores we so desperately need. Do
you know why?"

"Because," Will answered for Dionee, "it's not just pumps that
keep the mines dry, not just timbers that shore up the tunnels. It's
the tiny engine inside the Mountfalcon Jewel, working at a distance."

"Precisely. But not at too great a distance. And those very small
gears and wheels need frequent adjustment, just as any ordinary
watch or clockwork does. In the wrong hands, it would eventually
run down. If the Chaos Machine is not restored to me within half a
year, the mines will become so dangerous, I could not in good conscience allow anyone to enter them."

"You say that you have half a year," said Will. "In those six and a
half months, you could send engineers down into the mines; they
could repair the ordinary machinery, make the tunnels safe."

"I doubt they could accomplish all that needs to be done in six
months or sixty months. You have little idea of the depth and im-
mensity of those mines. The first time I went down into one of
them, I was staggered by what seemed to me an infinity of branching tunnels. And if we attempted to do any such thing," Rodaric
added, "everyone would know that the Jewel was missing—and that
could be fatal."

He stood up. Beckoning Dionee to follow him, he picked up the
lamp from his desk. Crossing the floor in two long strides, Rodaric
swept aside the moth-eaten crimson draperies at one end of the
room, and led the way into the vast shadowy chamber beyond.
Though he had not been invited to do so, Wilrowan could not resist
following silently, several paces behind.

King Rodaric's library was one of the wonders of the Volary, rising shelf upon shelf, balcony above balcony, six stories high to a
domed ceiling. The air inside was heavy with the musty odor of ten

thousand books. On every balcony perched lindenwood statues, intricately carved and richly gilded, creatures symbolizing the four elements—harpies for air, mermaids for water, salamanders for fire, gorgons for earth—which gazed down from the heights with their blank wooden eyes: silent, inscrutable, old as the palace itself.

In the center of the floor there was painted a great map of the world: twenty-five feet across from corner to corner. Though the pigments had faded and grown dingy over the years, though the names of the cities and nations, originally done in spidery-thin letters of gold paint, had been worn by the passage of many feet until only a few dull metallic flecks remained, it was still possible to make out the dim outlines of five continents, and to gain a vague impression of mountains, rivers, and seas.

Taking Dionee by the hand, Rodaric drew her toward that part of the map occupied by Mountfalcon and her nearest neighbors. "The mountains I spoke of, I should perhaps remind you, border on Herndyke, Chêneboix, and Montagne-du-Soliel. If the thieves who took the Chaos Machine were not ordinary footpads but agents of some other ruler, if it became known that the Mountfalcon Jewel was in his hands, the people who live in our mining towns might conceivably decide they owe their allegiance to that man instead of to me. Someone may be trying to expand his borders, someone may be attempting to build—an empire."

Will felt a shiver pass over his skin; looking past Rodaric to Dionee, he saw that her eyes were wide with shock.

For nearly fifteen hundred years, the world had existed in a precious but perilous balance. No kingdom, arch-duchy, or principality was allowed to gain ascendency over the others. Alliances were forbidden; the ruling houses could not intermarry. Yet nightmarish memories of the Maglore Empire, its monstrous excesses, its long history of oppression and cruelty, still lingered on. Equally terrifying were tales of the early years of the Reign of Mankind. For three turbulent decades, wars had been waged across the globe as men of great ambition—rulers of the strongest of the newly formed nations—strove to impose their will on their weaker neighbors. The slaughter had been past reckoning.

Gradually, order had been restored. A new civilization had been painstakingly created: a perfect Society, magnificently static. It had been designed to endure for a thousand thousand years. It *must* endure. It was a Society not only of laws, but of minds and hearts. It taught Men how to think.

And yet—the fear of a New Empire rising continued to haunt them all, the one subject that decent people seldom discussed, but could never quite banish from their minds.

Wilrowan remembered when he was a student at Malachim, he had attended a number of midnight gatherings at a neighboring college, at which some of the bolder students actually dared to discuss some of the ways a ruthless leader might go about building an empire of his own. Will emerged from these meetings feeling profoundly shaken, but also immensely stimulated—as though he had been allowed to witness some gross indecent act, which both repelled and fascinated him. An anonymous paper on the subject was even circulated through the various colleges at the university. To no one's surprise, the paper was suppressed as soon as it came to the attention of the authorities, and everyone involved was instantly expelled. Unfortunately for Will, some of his friends had been deeply implicated, and though innocent himself for once in his life, those associations had counted against him later.

"The danger may not come from any direction we might expect," he said, staring down at the map. "It could even originate as far away as—Nordfjall." He turned suddenly toward Dionee. "You told me it was your own idea to surprise the ambassador—but was there nothing Lord Vault did or said that suggested the scheme to begin with?"

She wrinkled her brow, trying to remember. "He *mentioned* the

Chaos Machine in a general way, wondering how old it was and where it was made, but it was Rufus Macquay who said that it might be amusing——" She stopped and shook her head emphatically. "No, Will, no. There *can't* be a connection between your duel and what happened afterward."

"You think not?" he said grimly. "I was supposed to be dead or languishing in Whitcomb Gaol, and you were to go to the embassy with a less diligent escort." He gave a short, humorless laugh. "And even when nothing fell out as planned, I was still obliged to leave Hawkesbridge rather than face His Majesty's wrath."

Rodaric and Dionee exchanged a significant glance: surprised on his part, chagrined on hers. "I lied to you, Will," she said in a very small voice. "But it seemed such a harmless deception, how was I to know it would end so badly?"

Wilrowan blinked. "You lied to me—how? You told me the king was in a rage, you said he had all but banished me—was none of that true?"

"Rodaric *had* scolded me, but not about you. When Barnaby told him you challenged Sir Rufus only because he insulted Lili, he said what you had done was—was entirely understandable."

At this point, the king interrupted her. "I don't recall that I said precisely that. But I did indicate that Wilrowan's misdeeds might possibly be overlooked this one time. Why did you tell him otherwise?"

"Because *I* wanted him out of the way. He would have spoiled everything if he knew what I was planning."

Will ground his teeth. "So I would have done. My compliments, Dionee. You have apparently succeeded in doing Macquay's work for him, and in doing so, have undoubtedly brought disaster on us all." He flexed his hands. "I have half a mind to take you by the throat and strangle you."

But then, catching sight of the king, he added under his breath: "With His Majesty's permission, of course."

"Thank you, Wilrowan, that won't be necessary," Rodaric answered coldly. "I know she has lied to you and treated you abominably, but I'll thank you not to forget when you address her that she *is* the queen." He turned away from the map, led the way back into his study. "I suppose," he said, with a sigh, to Dionee, "that I might have stopped you from committing this folly as well as Wilrowan."

"But, sir, you didn't know. How could you know?"

"I would have known everything, had I decided to accompany you to the embassy that day. Of course, it is my custom to avoid these lengthy and crowded affairs—hardly the wisest course for a man with a young and flighty wife, as we see now. It is certainly a selfish policy, I have always known that. As for continuing to conceal from you the true nature of the Chaos Machine: indeed, Dionee, I think I should have trusted you. Flighty you are, but I can't believe you would be wicked enough to betray a confidence, or careless enough to do what you have done had you known the truth."

As the king returned to his seat behind the desk, Dionee knelt down beside his chair in a rustle of satin. "Then you are not really angry with me?"

Setting the oil lamp in its original location, Rodaric glared down at her. "Just at the moment, I could *murder* you, Dionee. But considering I'm hardly blameless myself, I rather suspect I'll eventually forgive you." He turned to Will. "You are not, perhaps, the first person I would have chosen to trust with this secret. But now that you are involved, I believe I am glad. I suppose I can rely on you to make inquiries among your—less savory connections?"

Reaching down, Will gave Dionee his hand and raised her to her feet. "If the Chaos Machine was taken by Hawkesbridge footpads, I will find a way to get it back. But if it's been spirited away by agents of some other king, prince, or duke—the thing has been missing for three days already and could conceivably be in Rijxland, Chêneboix,

Montagne-du-Soliel or Montcieux, and well on its way to Herndyke, Bridemoor, or Château-Rouge."

"No," said Rodaric. "I think not. In maintaining the mechanism, I have become attuned to it. There is a kind of vibration within the tiny gemstones that make up part of the machinery—in short, I don't believe the Chaos Machine could go very far or cross our borders without my knowing it."

Will frowned thoughtfully. "If there *is* a species of magical sympathy at work, that may prove useful in recovering the Jewel." He remembered sitting on Lili's big white bed, asking what she was reading. "I had Mandeville in my hands just two days ago—I wish I had the book now!"

But thinking of Mandeville suggested an idea. "The University of Hawkesbridge owes its very existence to the king's warrant. All the professors have taken an oath to serve the Crown. And the faculty at Malachim College is made up entirely of magicians and natural philosophers—who might be able to suggest a course of action."

Rodaric considered, then came to a swift decision. "I will write to the chancellor and ask him to arrange a meeting with his two best men.

"In the meantime," he added, "say nothing of this and trust no one. As you say, there is no telling how far this plot may extend—or who may be involved in it."

13

"It is the wrong house," said King Jarred. "I have never been here before, and I certainly never intended to come here now." As he spoke, an inexplicable creeping sensation, a clammy revulsion, moved across his skin.

His coachman and two footmen exchanged a puzzled glance. "Your Majesty—" the coachman began, but his voice died and he could only shake his head in total bewilderment as Jarred opened the door of his tiny, ornate coach, pulled down the steps for himself, and climbed back inside.

"You have simply made a mistake. You have not followed my directions precisely, and there is nothing more to be said."

But there *was* something more, as the coachman and the footmen all seemed to imply by their uneasy silence, by their continued stillness.

"Well?" said Jarred, with a deep sigh. "You do not mean to tell me this is the home of my friend, Marius Bouvreuil? We have been there a dozen times before!"

The coachman was a strapping young man: tall, fair, and muscular. Six feet eight from the top of his powdered wig to the soles of his well-polished boots, he made a broad, imposing figure in his fur-lined cloak and his long, full-skirted coat, as he stood with a whip in one hand, a big tricorn hat in the other; yet he shuffled his feet and looked abashed when Jarred questioned him.

"Well?" the king repeated.

For answer, the driver stuck his whip under one arm, reached into a pocket of his capacious velvet coat, and produced a folded triangle of thick paper. "You said nothing to me, sir, about Mr. Bouvreuil, when we set out at noon. And here is the direction, exactly as you wrote it yourself."

Jarred took the paper, opened it, examined the contents minutely. The writing was certainly his own, but he had no memory of penning the wor—

He felt a sudden mental wrench, and suddenly the memory was there. He gave an embarrassed laugh. "Yes, I remember now. I do beg your pardon. Mr. Bouvreuil has changed his lodgings. I can't think how I came to forget. Though I will admit, I never imagined he would live in a place like this."

The house in question was about a mile from the city, a decaying mansion set well back from the road against a dark backdrop of hemlocks and firs, surrounded by its own park. It was a terrifying old house—or, at least, so thought Jarred, as he descended from the coach a second time and peered through the wrought-iron gates.

If his own Lindenhoff palace was like something out of an old story, the white-and-gold castle of some extraordinarily blessed fairy-tale prince, these two wings with a single large turret sprouting like a mushroom between them made the perfect setting for one of the darker passages in the same kind of story. The tower was as round as a drum, though it ended in a wickedly elongated sharp-pointed roof. The white paint and plaster covering the original stone had grown patchy in places. Above all, there were too many strangulating vines climbing up the walls, twining around the balconies, too many windows peeking through the ivy and bramble, with too many tiny panes of glass glinting red in the dying sunlight, like the faceted eyes of some great insect. Jarred felt that he knew this place, though he had never been here before: it was the witch's house where the princess lay sleeping in a crystal coffin, under a pall of cobwebs, in a room full of dust.

At this, the king gave himself a sharp mental shake. There were many of these ancient mansions on the outskirts of Tarnburgh. The only question was: How had he come to be standing outside the gates of this one?

He had set out this frosty afternoon in his little gilt-and-mahogany coach to visit his invalid friend, Marius Bouvreuil. Something had impelled him to direct the coachman to this particular house—though up until today, he had always believed that Marius lived in another part of town.

He sat down on the steps of the coach, struggling to remember. He recalled that Marius had written asking him to visit. What he did *not* remember was any mention of this particular house, or a change of lodgings. Yet someone had told him—

He could hear the coachman and the footmen consulting together; though they spoke in whispers, he could guess the drift of their conversation. The coach-horses were steaming and stamping in the cold. Even without looking, Jarred knew that his guards and their high-spirited mounts must be growing equally restive.

There was a jingle of spurs, as one of the guards dismounted and came striding in Jarred's direction. Sweeping off his plumed hat, he went down on one knee before the king. "Your Majesty, are we to wait here longer, or go back to the palace?"

Suddenly, Jarred realized how bizarre his own behavior must appear. It was not like him to be thoughtless of his men and horses. He glanced up at the sky. The sun had disappeared behind the trees in back of the house, and the sky was streaked with the brilliant colors of an arctic sunset. He must have been sitting here, undecided, for at least an hour.

He signaled to one of the footmen. "Go up to the door and knock. I will follow in another minute."

The footman withdrew. Jarred picked up his hat and his sable cloak, rose slowly to his feet. Instructing his guards to stay where they were, he followed the lackey past the iron gates, down a meandering flagstone path, past a frozen fountain, then up a short flight of steps to a pair of heavy doors.

He arrived just as one of those doors was swinging wide open, and the porter inside bowing very low and respectfully invited him to enter.

As he crossed the threshold, Jarred shivered; the room was as chilly as the air outside. It had a great empty floor of black-and-white tiles, a vaulted ceiling, some tapestries worked in faded silks along one wall. There was also a fine oak staircase, leading up to a shadowy gallery. What it really needed was a roaring fire, and five or six branches of candles. But there was no fireplace, just a long dark shaft in the center of the floor, covered by a wrought-iron grating; the only light came from two brass lanterns, hanging by chains from the ceiling.

Jarred cleared his throat. "Mr. Bouvreuil—is at home this afternoon?"

The porter did not answer his question directly. He bowed, declared that he would inform his master that His Majesty had arrived; relieved Jarred of his hat, cloak, and gloves; and disappeared through a low doorway, leaving the king with a hundred questions spinning through his head, and nothing to occupy him while he waited.

Jarred glanced curiously around him. There was an odd sort of circular mirror on the wall near the stairs, the antique bronze frame in the form of a serpent—and a suit of Goblin armor up on the landing. Wandering over to look at the glass, he saw his vision blur, his image distort. The walls of the room tilted, and the entire perspective of the room shifted.

Dazed and confused, Jarred thought for a moment that he was going to faint; he reached out with one hand to steady himself by gripping a chair. But as soon as he shifted his gaze from the mirror to the old wainscot chair, he realized that it was the *glass* that was wrong, not anything the matter with him. Its misshapen reflection of the room and his own figure had created a visual disorientation, which alone was the source of his momentary confusion.

"Your Majesty, what an unexpected honor," said a high, sweet voice, apparently out of the air above him.

Jarred looked back over his shoulder. A fair-haired girl in a black silk gown was smiling down at him from the landing. Turning to get a better look at her, he drew in his breath sharply; there was something uncannily familiar about her face.

As he tried to remember where he had seen her before, the girl came tripping down the steps, one hand sliding along the polished oak banister, the other extended in welcome. It was not until she had reached the bottom of the stairs and dropped a curtsy, not until he was gallantly lifting her cold little hands, one after the other, and brushing kisses across her fingertips, that he finally recognized her.

"You are the girl who disappeared without a trace."

He experienced a brief twinge of pleasure, flavored by bewilderment. There was something—something unexpected about her. Of course—she had worn her hair powdered the night of the ball, and he would never have imagined, with those black, black eyes, these glittering masses of golden curls. But it was certainly her: dark eyes, white skin, pointed chin, high cheekbones, and all.

"Mademoiselle, I wonder if anyone told you: I've had men searching every corner of the city, trying to discover your whereabouts for the last twelve weeks. And then to find you here in the home of my old friend—"

His voice trailed off. He had just caught a glimpse of the neck-lace of milky white stones encircling her throat, the crystal pendant glowing against the black gauze scarf discreetly filling in her low neckline. Again, he was assailed by a dizzying disorientation, a sick-ening sense of total confusion. "This is—this *is* the home of Marius Bouvreuil?"

She shook her head until the blonde curls danced. "Oh no, Your Majesty. I'm afraid I don't know who your Mr. Bouvreuil is."

It was then that she apparently became aware of his incapacity. As his grip on her hand loosened, hers on his tightened. "Sir, you are ill. May I show you into the parlor?" Her pale face blurred, then came sharply back into focus.

Jarred nodded his head, unable to speak. But her cold little hand was pulling him inexorably on. Too giddy to think or to act on his own, he allowed her to lead him. He stumbled into a room that seemed to have too many mirrors, too many tiny dancing lights. In response to a gentle push, he sat down awkwardly on the narrow seat of a high-backed chair.

"I—I thank you," he managed, as the room continued to spin around him in a dazzle of mirrors and light. "I can't think what came over me. I can only apologize—"

"There is no need for you to apologize." As she spoke, she went down gracefully on her knees beside his chair. "And nothing for you to worry about either."

By concentrating on her and her alone, Jarred discovered that he could see much better. Her sharp little face was nearly on a level with his own; her silken gown, far from being an unrelieved black as he had first supposed, was covered with a design worked in fine sil-ver threads, like a network of cobwebs over the silk.

"You are the princess."

She gave a violent start. "The—princess, Your Majesty?"

"The princess in the story. The one who slept for hundreds and hundreds of years, waiting to reclaim her kingdom, while the great grey spiders covered her coffin with their webs." He gave an embarrassed laugh. "I beg your pardon, I seem to be babbling the most childish nonsense. But it is only because of the pattern on your gown."

Puzzled, she looked down at the dark silk. Then she gave a throaty laugh of her own. "You are quite right, Your Majesty. I *have* been asleep for—hundreds and hundreds of years, but I am awake now."

Jarred moved uneasily in his chair. Her pose, kneeling on the floor at his feet, was both submissive and mildly erotic. There had been, too, something deeply and oddly suggestive in her laugh, particularly coming from one so young. All this awoke in him a strange hunger, an intense craving he was uncertain how to define. It seemed to involve pleasures utterly unconnected with the ordinary lusts of the body, yet there was a perversity about it that made him feel suddenly ashamed.

Whether or not she guessed what he was feeling, he could not tell. A burning blush passed over him. Beyond all doubt it would be better for them both if she did not know. But her expression was entirely unreadable as, without a word, she reached up behind her neck and unclasped the double string of white stones.

A moment later, he felt the weight of the necklace in his hands. *A cold thrill passed over his skin and shivered along his nerves, an excess of pleasure as deeply disturbing as it was exquisite.* And suddenly—he was not certain why—Jarred was very, very frightened.

14

The hour was almost midnight and the moon had set, but the sky blazed with stars. Jarred stood at an open casement window in the Lindenhoff clock-tower, looking down at his city. In other places, spring was hastening on apace; here it would still be winter for many long weeks. The equinox had come and gone, but still there was snow in the streets of Tarnburgh and the dew froze on the roof tiles every night.

Jarred allowed his gaze to wander further: over the glittering rooftops—over the city walls—past the crumbling Maglore palaces on the outskirts of town—past the barren ice-fields and the tiny, isolated villages—all the way to the jagged white peaks of a mountain range on the distant horizon. One of the peaks was smoking; a pale glow of fire stained the snow the color of roses. Soon, he knew, the mountain would stir and grumble, there would be a fall of ash. But while the wind remained in the east, Tarnburgh and the surrounding villages would not be affected.

As for their own volcano, it slumbered peacefully and would continue to do so, so long as the king continued to maintain the tiny intricate mechanism inside the Winterscar Jewel.

Over his head, the bronze giant swung his hammer and the

twelve o'clock bell gave a resounding peal. Jarred closed the leaded-glass window and latched it, then turned back toward the homely light and warmth of the philosopher's laboratory.

"My dear Francis," he said, taking a seat by the brick fireplace, "I hardly know whether you will credit any of this, but I had the most amazing adventure today."

Doctor Purcell was at his workbench, making some small adjustments to one of his mechanical toys: a little silver canary with ruby eyes, which had a habit of falling over on its side if wound up too tightly. When the king spoke, the old man immediately put this task aside, and his eyes became suddenly keen behind the gold-rimmed spectacles.

"I did wonder, sir, when you first came in, why you looked so ill. But your color has returned in the last half hour. Perhaps you feel strong enough to explain this—adventure—whatever it was?"

"Yes, I think that I do. I think that I must." The king flexed his long white fingers. "For I admit to being at a total loss how to explain my own actions, and I hope you will help me to make some sense of them."

The philosopher left his workbench, took a seat on a stool opposite his former pupil, and assumed such an interested and sympathetic attitude that Jarred was encouraged to go on.

"You remember the girl that I met at the ball? The one I was so eager to find afterward? Well, I chanced to meet her today, under surprising circumstances. Though that is—comparatively speaking—nothing. It is what happened later that particularly concerns me."

The old man nodded and continued to look interested. But the king was caught up in his own disturbing reflections, and it was several minutes before he spoke.

"I suppose I should begin," said Jarred, very slowly, "by telling you a little about her. She lives with her uncle and his somewhat ter-

rifying wife—the name is Debrûle and they claim to be distantly related to the Montbarrons." The Montbarrons, as Jarred and Purcell
both knew, were a very ancient and noble family with estates in
Montcieux and Château-Rouge. "They are staying, just at this time,
in one of those old Goblin mansions south of the town. You know the
sort of place: as cold as ice because there are no open fires and no
place to put them; what little heat there is comes up in shafts from
the fires down below. All through the house, there are mirrors in
old-fashioned frames, and immense sideboards full of pewter and of
silver plate, so that the light of a single candle is reflected back a
hundred times."

Doctor Purcell cleared his throat. "I have been in such houses.
They are often let out to wealthy tradesmen and the shabby genteel.
But the girl, Your Majesty, was she able to explain what she was
doing at the ball—most improperly I have to say—without an escort?"

"Yes, she did. The family is in mourning, so naturally the aunt and
the uncle didn't think it proper to be seen in public. The young lady,
however, was simply chafing under these restrictions—and being
only sixteen or seventeen, she thought it might be an adventure to
slip secretly out of the house and go to the ball on her own.

"I am under the impression," Jarred added, his straight dark eyebrows drawing together as he pondered the point, "that she was escorted in by one of the young officers at the gate. She swept him
away with her beauty, no doubt, dazzled him with her diamonds. She
was a little evasive about exactly who and exactly how." He smiled
and shrugged. "As there was no harm done, I saw no reason to pursue the question further. Her presence at the ball being explained, I
made a long visit. I was introduced to a number of her relations.
Three young cousins came in—three young men—all of them remarkably handsome and proud. I gained an impression that one at
least had formed a passionate attachment to Mademoiselle. The

other two seemed to be baiting him somehow. It was really quite amusing, the way they all strutted about, striking poses and making fine speeches——"

But then Jarred's smile faded and his brow creased. This was where his memories of the day became so fragmented, so confused. *He was walking down long echoing corridors, passing through high vaulted chambers. His mind was bewildered, his steps erratic. At last he arrived in a room where there was a long table set with monogrammed silver and faceted crystal. Spread out on the table was a selection of cold dishes——jellies, creams, chantillies, aspics——inexplicably reminding him of a funeral banquet. When somebody pulled out a chair, Jarred sat down. He lifted a silver fork to his lips, felt something cool slide over his tongue——but it came to him, as he swallowed reflexively, that something was wrong, something was strangely lacking.*

With an effort, he collected himself. "We had——some sort of meal in the dining room. It all seemed so flat, so oddly tasteless. There may have been a chilled wine, but I'm not certain. It could have been water for all I know."

"Perhaps you were already beginning to feel ill?"

"Not in the least. Except for a headache that came much later, I was practically euphoric the whole time. And that might explain my remarkable behavior. After the meal, the men had some engagement elsewhere, and the aunt was called away too, leaving me and the girl alone in the sitting room."

Jarred's color fluctuated as the memory brought the blood racing to his cheeks. "It couldn't have lasted for more than a quarter of an hour, and our conversation was perfectly innocent, I swear to you, I *swear* to you. Yet when the aunt returned, I had the most extraordinary impression that I had just been caught doing something wrong——something shameful. I cannot explain how it was, but the moment that terrible woman walked into the parlor, I actually felt as though she had surprised me in the midst of some perfectly indecent act."

He rose from his chair. Signaling the scholar to remain seated, he began to pace the floor. "I found myself babbling —I don't remember what. The gist of it was that my intentions were honorable, that Mademoiselle Debrûle would take no harm from me, that I meant to do the right thing, that—" He turned back toward the older man. "Francis," he said bleakly, "I am very much afraid I have somehow gotten myself—betrothed."

There was a long, brittle silence.

Then the old man said: "Might there not have been some misunderstanding? You are the King of Winterscar, sir, but who is the girl? It hardly makes sense that you would ask her to marry you. It seems to me that you offered the young lady your protection only."

Jarred gave a short, mirthless laugh. "There was no misunderstanding. Francis, do you really think I would sink so low as to make indecent proposals to a sixteen-year-old girl? Particularly with her aunt right there in the room?"

The philosopher shook his head. Through Jarred had been reared at a court that put manners over morals, he had somehow acquired a delicacy of principle which ought to preclude the seduction of anyone quite so young—yet Purcell had hoped that Madame Debrûle and her niece might believe otherwise.

"But then, Your Majesty, am I to suppose there is no drawing back, that Mademoiselle accepted your proposal right on the spot?"

"My dear old friend, of course she accepted me! I will admit she was so flustered by my offer, it seemed for a moment she might actually refuse, but the aunt made very certain that she *did* accept me. Ys gave me her hand very prettily, said she would strive to be the most conformable wife imaginable—for a moment, I was actually giddy with joy—until I suddenly remembered how little I knew her, and that I didn't want to marry her at all."

There was another long silence, during which the only sounds in the laboratory were the ticking of the clocks, the gentle whirr of machinery in the room up above. Jarred circled the floor once, twice, a third time.

"I wonder, Your Majesty," the old man ventured at last, "if there might not have been some sort of trickery involved. You did say, did you not, there was something wrong with the food?"

Jarred laughed incredulously. "My dear Francis, I should have *tasted* poison, and since when did poison ever cause a man to make a complete fool of himself?"

"I was thinking, sir, of drugs or love potions. You are right, of course, when you say that you ought to have detected something. Nevertheless—"

"Nevertheless," the king interrupted him, "there was something very bizarre about my own behavior, long before we sat down to eat." And he described to the philosopher the puzzling series of events which had led him to the decaying mansion in the first place.

Purcell briefly considered the notion that the servants might have been bribed. But the coachman was Alonzo Perys, the brother of Luke's valet. His people had been serving Jarred's people for generations, and the two footmen also came of families that had been serving the Walburgs, the Sackvilles, and the Guilians practically forever.

"Perhaps, after all, we are making much out of little, out of events that only *seemed* to gain meaning by what followed after." The doctor clicked his teeth together in a way that he had when he was displeased with himself. "But supposing, then, that the entire situation came about by chance—might it not be possible to buy the girl off?"

The king gave the philosopher a reproachful look. "Unworthy, Francis. That is a suggestion I might have expected from my Uncle Hugo Sackville."

Purcell blushed. The suggestion might be distressingly crude, yet there *were* times when a practical man— But the king was an honorable man, not a pragmatic one; if he was repulsed by the suggestion, there was no more to be said about it.

So he tried again. "You say there is a cousin, young and good-looking. One assumes that he and the girl are often in each other's company. Might it not be possible——"

"——that some previous understanding exists between them? No, I doubt it. And even if there were, it would make no difference."

There was a jumble of images inside Jarred's brain. He struggled to make sense of them. Then came a moment of clarity, and he was briefly back at the crumbling mansion south of the town: *The girl was speaking. "This is Zmaj, Your Majesty." A hot-eyed youth in a black velvet coat and an immense white neckcloth was standing with his arms folded, a scornful smile curling his lips.*

As the memory faded, the king spread his hands in a hopeless gesture. "After I made such a fool of myself, the whole family miraculously reappeared, their engagement elsewhere apparently forgotten. The boy—Zmaj—was clearly attentive to her every look, her smallest gesture, but if I read his manner correctly, he would sooner cut out my liver and fry it, than stand by tamely and watch me break her heart."

"Dear me," said Purcell, with a half smile and a shake of his head. "He sounds quite formidable. Fully as bad as the terrible aunt."

"That would be impossible." Jarred continued to move around the room in the same restless manner. "You will understand what I mean when you finally meet her—as I suppose you must, if I marry her niece."

The philosopher straightened his glasses, racked his brain for another solution. "Well then, I wonder if it might be possible to convince the young lady she would be far happier, far better off in all ways, if she changed her mind and refused your flattering offer?"

Jarred stopped by the fireplace, picked up the heavy brass poker, stirred up the dying coals until the sparks flew. "How happier? How better off? I hope I'm a modest man—but I *am* the King of Winter-scar."

"Precisely," said Purcell, folding his hands together, tapping them thoughtfully against his chin. "And your wife will be the Queen of Winterscar, and expected to preside over one of the most elegant and traditional courts in the entire world. A somewhat daunting proposition, if I may say so, for a young and impulsive girl."

A gleam of humor came into his pale green eyes. "Invite her to visit you here at the palace. Not officially as your prospective bride—you must tell her that nothing of the sort is possible while you are still in half-mourning. Invite her here, and put her into the hands of your Master of Ceremonies. Tell him of your secret engagement, but tell him, also, that you think of reviving some of the more fantastic old rit-uals of your father and grandfather's day, that he is to instruct and make her letter perfect before the wedding. If I am not mistaken, he will drill her mercilessly: the rhymed words of welcome she must use in greeting a foreign ambassador—the depth of the reverence due an aging grand-duchess. There are a dozen old volumes in gilded leather gathering dust in the Archives, simply crammed with that sort of de-tail, and I am convinced that Lord Wittlesbeck knows them all by heart."

The king listened to all this with a faint, dubious smile. "But if I do as you suggest, people will talk. Everyone will believe I intend to marry her."

"Let them talk," said the philosopher. "Talk of that sort will do the young lady no harm. Meanwhile, she should have ample opportunity to form an attachment to the handsome, fire-eating cousin."

Jarred put down the poker and abandoned the fireplace. "Well, it is a clever plan and it might actually work. Providing I can get Mademoiselle alone afterward, away from the influence of the over-whelming aunt. But if it doesn't work?"

"Then we will simply think of something else."

Jarred continued to pace for another five minutes. There was something else on his mind, something that brought a sick, hollow feeling to the pit of his stomach, but he did not know exactly how to broach the subject. At last he came back to the chair and sat down again, facing the old man.

"All this aside, I feel a certain concern about my own behavior. This strange obsession with the girl, after a single meeting. And now I have actually seen her again, I admit to being attracted, but I'm not in love with her. I can't help wondering if my actions today were entirely—rational."

He gave the philosopher a pleading glance, brought out the fear that had haunted him for so many months. "Do you think, Francis, that I might be losing my mind?"

To Jarred's vast relief, a faint smile twitched at the corners of the old man's mouth. "Did you really believe that you would never again have these feelings for a woman? Considering how long it has been—how long I assume it has been since you last had a woman in your bed—believe me, Your Majesty, when it comes to the stirrings of the flesh, sometimes a brief spell of madness is entirely healthy."

Jarred leaned back in his chair. He gave a short laugh, half embarrassment, half self-disgust. "You think that is all it was? I can't begin to tell you how much I still feel Zelene's loss, yet for all that I do sometimes experience—stirrings, as you say. But I never expected to marry again so soon, or even to consider taking a mistress."

He gave his dark head a quick, involuntary shake. "A woman in my bed occasionally, I don't think Zelene, if she knew, would deny me that much, though up until now I have denied myself—but anything more than that? I could not. I don't believe that I should. Not when I loved her so well."

"Sir, you have explained far better than I could your own behavior," said Purcell soothingly. "Your relative inexperience in these matters—

having been married so young, having been joined in a union of such superior felicity—a sense that you were somehow betraying your late queen, the girl's youth and apparent innocence—all these things contributed to the impression that you were behaving badly. You reacted accordingly, as a man of honor would."

"Then you don't think I *am*—losing my mind?"

The philosopher shook his head emphatically. "What I think, Your Majesty, is that you are being unduly severe with yourself. I have watched you grow from boy to man, and I believe I know you better than anyone living, with the possible exception of your cousin, Mr. Guilian. This being so, I think my opinion must be worth something."

"It is," Jarred assured him. "And that's why I ask you to speak, not as my subject, not even as my old schoolmaster, but as what you truly are and always have been: a second father to me."

Much moved by this appeal, the old man leaned forward and covered the king's firm white hand with his own frail one. "Why then, speaking as your second father—but not without a father's pride and affection—I would have to say that you are the sanest man I know."

The city of Luden in Rijxland—Luden of the charming brick houses and the broad, pleasant canals—was entirely the invention of Men. She had not even existed during the days of the Maglore Empire, had been created out of whole cloth by the enterprising men and women of the fifty-third century, and had come to embody all the solid, comfortable public virtues and secret vices of a rising mercantile middle class. Though some Goblin taint eventually crept into the poorer part of the town, no Maglore princess had ever been carried in a litter down her pleasant cobblestone streets; no Grant or Wryneck scholar ever paced, with slow, measured tread, through the sacred precincts of her tiny university; nor did she owe a single one of her picturesque buildings to the labor or ingenuity of Goblin craftsmen. These were facts of which the citizens of Luden were inordinately proud. More than a thousand years later, they were still congratulating themselves.

Of Luden as she was—rather than as she might have been but thankfully was not—there they had reason enough for congratulation, because Luden had practically everything that makes a town pleasant to live in.

She had a quaint harbor, where the great, white-sailed ships lay anchored in neat rows, and she had warehouses filled with tea, porcelain, figured muslins, chocolate, sugar-cane and opium—which you might purchase openly as a headache remedy from any physician in the town. Beyond the warehouses were hundreds of remarkable little shops, where you could buy anything and everything: ostrich eggs and elephant tusks; rare old books; rings, cameos, and miniature portraits; tobacco, hemp, chinchona bark, and spices; scent bottles, etuis, and lace fans; quills, ink, and churchwarden pipes; combs made of ivory, tortoiseshell, and mother-of-pearl; patch boxes, jewel boxes, music boxes; silver tea canisters— If you could buy it anywhere, you could buy it in Luden.

She had baroque statues set in tiny jewel-like parks and gardens; she had delicate white bridges, spanning her brackish canals. She had churches known for the sweet music of their bells as well as the brevity of their sermons; and two fine old red brick Houses of Parliament where the bluff, independent members from the country districts—honest fellows with no use for pomp or *pretense*—regularly attended sessions in their mud-splashed top boots, and ate oranges and cracked nuts during debates.

She had all these things and she had more besides, because Luden prided herself on being a city of philanthropists. In the last hundred years alone there had been built a model workhouse, a model foundling hospital (where the grateful orphans were on view two times a week in their brown stuff gowns), and a model madhouse, so efficiently run and on such compassionate principles that even the King of Rijxland himself deigned to pay an extended visit.

So life in Luden rolled pleasantly along, with picnics, regattas, lotteries, and assemblies for the upper classes, honest labor for the lower, and a universal conviction among them all that even a crust in Luden was sweeter and more wholesome fare than a feast served elsewhere.

As for the frail, bewildered old gentleman who was her nominal ruler: he, too, was one of the sights of Luden. Those who had been privileged to see him at his daily routine, who had the pleasure of watching him eat, drink, dress, or otherwise disport himself, always brought encouraging reports back to their friends. His physicians were devoted and attentive; he was provided with every comfort; there could not possibly be a happier or more enviable madman in any other city, anywhere in the world.

15

"There is something a little giddy about walking on solid ground after so many weeks," said Lucius Guilian to his faithful valet, as they stood on the docks at Luden with their baggage piled around them. "I find I am so accustomed to walking at a tilt, if I don't find my land legs soon, I am very much afraid I will shortly fall flat on my face."

Though the hour was very early on a frosty morning, there was a stir of activity on every side: sailors shouting to their mates in the rigging, carpenters hammering, dockworkers stamping, passengers embarking and disembarking, wagons rumbling, and from somewhere came the scent of burning pitch.

"I will miss your pleasant ways, Mr. Guilian," said a voice behind him, and Luke turned to see the Leveller striding in his direction. An ice-tinged breeze was blowing in from the harbor; it lifted the edge of Raith's cloak as he crossed the wooden walkway. "However, I feel tolerably certain you will regain your ordinary sense of balance before any such ignominious fate befalls you."

Luke laughed, coloring slightly. He had spoken for his valet's benefit only.

"I have been able to hire a hackney coach," said the Leveller. "And

I wondered if you would give me the pleasure of your company as far as the embassy?"

Luke accepted the offer with gratitude, then looked around for someone to help Perys with his boxes and trunks. But Raith settled the matter decisively—and quite unexpectedly—by grasping the handle of the largest horsehide trunk, heaving the bulky thing over one shoulder, and striding off, leaving a flushed and indignant Luke to assist his valet with the remaining baggage.

"No, Master Luke, you mustn't!" Perys protested, as Luke caught the handle of the smaller trunk and tried to emulate the Leveller's feat of strength. "What will people say?"

Lucius had no idea what people would say, never having been in Rijxland before. He suspected the reaction would be much the same as it would be in Winterscar—if anyone recognized him, which was highly unlikely. Nevertheless, he thought grimly, as he managed to get the trunk on his back and set off in the Leveller's footsteps, he would be *damned* if he stood by and allowed a man like Raith to wait on him like a servant.

He smiled fiercely at Perys, who had loaded himself down with the remaining luggage and was struggling manfully to keep up. "I think of converting, Perys. Of spending the rest of my days in a strict Anti-demonic suppression of my infernal vanity. Only think how much easier that will make things for you: no ruffles, no laces, no velvets, no satins—just plain honest wool and linen."

"Master Luke, you wouldn't," said the horrified valet, as they shouldered their way through the press of humanity. "Master Luke, you never would!" He had seen Luke adopt a bewildering array of ideas and poses over the years, but this one seemed much the worst.

Lucius took pity on him. "More than likely I wouldn't. Or if I did, I could hardly be expected to stick with it long."

He was rewarded with a wan smile. "It was just your little joke, sir."

By now, they had left the docks and the red-brick warehouses behind and had come out on a broad avenue, where they found the hired coach waiting. They discovered that Raith and the driver between them had already fastened the large trunk on top with the Leveller's own baggage.

"This was hardly necessary," said Raith as he swung down from the roof, took the bags out of the valet's hands, and tossed them up to the coachman. "Mr. Perys and I would have managed very well."

Luke allowed his burden to slip to the ground with a thud. "No doubt you would have, but you're not my blasted servant," he answered between his teeth, as he flung open the door and climbed inside. He took the seat facing back, because that would be the least comfortable once the coach started to move, and crossed his arms over his chest.

Raith left Perys and the driver to arrange the rest of the baggage on the roof, and took the seat facing Luke. "I do not aspire to be your valet. But I feel no shame doing a service for a friend, believing as I do that we will all be equal on the Day of Wrath. For you, however—"

Luke continued to speak between clenched teeth. "Thank you, but I will be the judge of what is appropriate behavior for the King of Winterscar's cousin."

Then his sense of humor got the better of him, and he laughed, unfolded his arms, and relaxed against the cushions. "Raith, Raith, you are the very best of good fellows, but I wish you would consider my position. Back in Tarnburgh I am the gadfly, the iconoclast. I have even, occasionally, posed as the Champion of the Common Man. Then you come along with your honest principles, your sincere convictions, and you show me up for the hollow thing that I am."

The coach lurched into motion. Raith raised a dark eyebrow ever so slightly. "You were not a hollow man when you leaped into the sea to rescue that sailor."

Luke adjusted his broad embroidered cuffs, shook out his lace ruffles; the unaccustomed exertion with the baggage had somewhat disarranged him. "I believe I told you at the time that what I was, was an arrogant young fool. You were the real hero on that occasion. And to be brutally honest, you probably saved my life."

Raith smiled his quiet, conservative smile. "We will not argue about it. Perhaps there was heroism—and foolhardiness—on both sides. Instead, I wonder if I might ask you a question?"

"As I have certainly asked you a great many myself, I should think it only fair to allow you to do the same."

The Leveller studied Luke for several moments. "What is it that brings you to Rijxland just at this time? There is your book, of course, but why you should risk a voyage so late in the year, I cannot begin to guess."

Luke removed an invisible piece of lint from his sleeve. "The city, of course, is of some little interest. In Luden, I won't have to dig through five thousand years of Goblin history to get at the truth."

But then, under his companion's steady, courteous gaze, he found himself blurting out: "Is the King of Rijxland—truly mad? I should tell you I was once what you might call a disciple. I studied all of his early writings, and it's hard for me to imagine that such a superior mind could so easily become deranged. And while I was in Lichtenwald the idea that he might *not* be mad rather took hold of me, until I felt I could never rest until I satisfied my curiosity."

The Leveller did not answer his question directly. "You told me, I think, that your cousin sent his own physicians to examine King Izaiah. Was he not entirely satisfied by their report?"

"Yes, yes, he told me he was satisfied. But the information came to him at second hand. Whereas *you* were in Luden when the king was first confined."

Still, Raith did not answer his question. "You are wondering, I take it, whether the king was declared mad simply to discredit some of his more unpopular ideas, to keep him from putting any more of his radical policies into effect?"

Lucius leaned forward eagerly. "That is exactly what I am wondering. And so——?"

"And so, Mr. Guilian, I *was* in Luden at the time the king was first confined, and I have occasionally had the privilege of seeing him since. He is not a raving lunatic, but he is frequently delusional. And though his delusions are essentially harmless, and often quite whimsical, I am sure you will agree it is hardly desirable to leave the reins of government in the hands of a man who cannot always remember his own name—or worse, is able to convince himself that he is another person entirely."

Luke fell back in his seat, feeling oddly deflated. "I suppose you are right. Well, it's not an idea I had my mind absolutely set on. Though it is naturally humiliating to realize how far wrong I was."

"As to that," said the Leveller, in his slow, thoughtful way, "I do not say that your doubts on the subject are not perfectly understandable."

Seeing how Luke's face lit with interest, Raith continued on. "Like you, I believe that even if the king's condition were less serious than it is, he would still be exactly where he is now. I think, too, that if he ever begins to recover—which appears unlikely—there will be some effort made in the Parliament to suppress the information and prevent the king from regaining his freedom. There are those, after all—and Lord Flinx is a name which comes immediately to mind—whose power in Rijxland would be significantly reduced if that ever happened."

All the time that Raith had been speaking, Luke had been listening breathlessly. Now, in one long sigh, he released all the air he had been holding in. "But this is appalling. Has the king no friends, no well-wishers, to step in at need and secure his freedom?"

"The king's friends have been silent for a long time," Raith answered carefully. "Yet they are all of them still here in Luden, and I hardly imagine they are not perfectly aware of the things I have told you."

Luke's vivid imagination was working at full speed now, pouring forth a variety of pleasing scenarios. He cast Raith a glowing look across the coach. "You think there is already some conspiracy in place, already poised to effect a rescue should Izaiah show signs of recovering?"

The corners of Raith's mouth began to twitch. "I perceive that you are a romantic, Mr. Guilian. First you imagine a plot against the king, and now you ask me if there might be a second plot, this time in his favor. And naturally I recall the original theories you were so obliging as to explain to me during our voyage. If you will pardon my asking, I cannot help wondering: do you see conspiracies *everywhere?*"

"Why, to tell you the truth, I believe I do," answered Luke with a slight frown. "That is, I am not the sort of person who sees Imperialists lurking around every corner—"

"I had not thought so," Raith murmured, "for a fear of Imperialist plots is a little too commonplace to strike your fancy."

"—but I do believe there is a widespread, though largely unspoken, agreement among those in power to keep certain uncomfortable truths hidden from the lower orders—one that goes far beyond the falsification of historical records we discussed before."

The coach went over a bump and began to rattle and jolt so violently, Lucius took a peek out the window to see what was happening. They were passing over one of the arched white bridges, and that appeared to be the cause of their rough ride.

When he settled back against the leather cushions, he found that Raith was still regarding him. Did he detect a flicker of concern in the Leveller's dark eyes?

"Mr. Guilian, I believe you have made it your personal crusade to bring to light those uncomfortable truths that you mentioned just now."

Luke bowed the affirmative.

"Why then, I hope you will satisfy yourself with that. If there should be, as I very much doubt, anything in the nature of a conspiracy to rescue the king at need, I beg you will not ready your cloak and dagger and seek to join in. I must remind you that King Izaiah's friends have had a considerable period of time in which to lay their plans—if plans have been laid at all.

"I daresay they would find your precipitous entry into their affairs disconcerting to say the least, and your engaging enthusiasm even more so."

Luke's reception at the tall old house of brick and stucco which housed the Winterscar embassy was not exactly what he had come to expect. He was left kicking his heels for some little time in the chilly white marble entry hall, and even when he was admitted to the inner precincts, his welcome was not a warm one.

"I do not perfectly understand His Majesty's intentions," said Lord Polyphant, with a puzzled and slightly petulant air. He was a fussy little gentleman of uncertain age, who, after a hasty introduction, had spent a good fifteen minutes examining Luke's credentials. "Have you come here, Mr. Guilian, to oversee my endeavors—or to eventually replace me?"

Luke had been standing at a broad bay window, gazing down on the busy street below, while the ambassador paced the floor in his ridiculously high-heeled shoes and perused Jarred's letter and the accompanying passport. The scene taking place under that window was appealing in its way: there was very little hurry, very little noise, just neatly dressed people going about their business in what seemed to be a quiet, methodical manner. Every so often, by way of contrast, a brightly painted coach or sedan-chair would pass by, giving a momentary glimpse of a patched and painted face, or some incredible erection of hair and powder inside. Again for contrast, a lean figure would occasionally stalk by, a man in a stiff-brimmed black hat and long cloak, or a stern-faced woman in a black bonnet—there seemed to be quite a number of Levellers on the streets of Luden.

At the ambassador's extraordinary suggestion, Luke spun around. "Oversee or replace you? My dear Lord Polyphant, I can assure you: no such idea ever entered His Majesty's mind. He is very well pleased—that is, he's not actually confided in me, but I see no reason to suppose otherwise—he is very well pleased with the work you are doing here."

The ambassador continued to gaze at him doubtfully.

"If you will look at the date," Luke added helpfully, "you will see that the king wrote his letter almost a year ago. I've made a great many stops since leaving Winterscar, and my business here, I do assure you, is *entirely* my own."

Somewhat mollified, Lord Polyphant took a seat facing Luke and motioned him to be seated on a lyre-back chair. He regarded his visitor with a more benevolent eye. "Then what may I do for you, Mr. Guilian, while you are here? If there is anything I can possibly do, you will find me your most obliged and obedient servant." To emphasize the point, he took out an elegant little gold repoussé snuffbox with the mask of a lion embossed on the lid, and offered it to Luke.

Lucius helped himself to a generous pinch, inhaled, then drew out his clean pocket handkerchief and sneezed into it. "You can provide me with a roof over my head, at least for two or three days. I certainly don't intend to trespass on your hospitality any longer than that. What I would like—really, the only request I have to make—is for you or someone on your staff to assist me in finding some suitable lodgings."

"Well, well," said Lord Polyphant easily, now that friendly relations had been established. "We will arrange something." He smiled expansively. "And, of course, you are welcome to stay *here* just as long as you like."

This was a handsome offer, but not one that Luke was inclined to accept, having no desire to subject himself to a tedious round of embassy teas, embassy balls, and embassy dinners. "In fact," he said, determined to make his point and stick to it, "if you can't recommend any rooms yourself, I suppose I might ask Raith to advise me. He is bound to have some sort of suggestion to make; the man appears to know practically everything."

This casual mention of Raith's name produced the most extraordinary response. The ambassador stiffened and his already prominent eyes bulged. "Raith—did you say Raith? Excuse me, Mr. Guilian, but are you by any chance referring to *the* Raith, Raith the Anti-demonist?"

"Unless there is more than one gentleman by that name professing to the same religion," said Luke, affecting innocence, "I suppose I must be." He had not expected such a vehement reaction, though he was not, for that reason, above thoroughly enjoying it. "Why do you ask?"

Lord Polyphant was beginning to huff and puff. "But this is extraordinary. You have only been in Luden a matter of hours, a matter of minutes almost. How did you manage to make so vastly unsuitable an acquaintance?"

At this, Luke frowned. While it had been amusing enough to shock the ambassador, he did not enjoy hearing his friend criticized. "I had the pleasure of meeting Raith during the voyage over. As to being an unsuitable acquaintance: he is school-master to the children of the Crown Princess, surely a most respectable occupation."

"A respectable occupation—were that all!" Lord Polyphant said darkly. "But that is not the only work he is said to do for the Princess Marjote, and if you're to be staying with us here at the embassy—!"

But then, remembering that Luke would *not* be staying at the embassy for any appreciable time, he became a little calmer. "You will know your own business best. But really, I'd not pursue that particular friendship, if I were you. The man is uncanny. All the mystery and intrigue in this boring little city tied up in the one man—it's simply too much.

"Besides," he added, sliding the snuffbox back inside his waistcoat pocket, "the Levellers don't receive him. He's been defrocked, or excommunicated, or cast into outer darkness—whatever it is they do to punish their own kind. The charge, as I recall, was working hexes." He shook his head ominously. "For all that, he seems to have some sort of hold over them, or they over him. Perhaps I shouldn't say so, since you and I are hardly acquainted, but if I were you, I would stay strictly away from the fellow."

"Not at all. You can say anything you choose," Luke answered frostily. It seemed to be his day for receiving unsolicited advise. Oddly enough, he found himself resenting Lord Polyphant's contribution as he had not resented Raith's. In any case, he had never been one to allow others to choose his friends for him, and he had no intention of beginning to do so now.

16

Autumn breathed a last fluttering gasp in Luden, and winter came on with full force. Snow piled high on the red-tiled roofs and in the red-brick streets; it dusted coaches, sledges, and sedan-chairs; it frosted the statues and the bare black branches of all the trees in the public parks and gardens.

Meanwhile, Luke had taken a comfortable set of furnished rooms in a three-story house with a stepped gable roof, overlooking a frozen canal. He hired a cook, a coachman, and a brisk young footman to assist Perys, and leaving this skeleton staff to unpack his things and put the house in order, he sallied forth to explore the city.

This kept him amused for a fortnight, and when the novelty wore off he was more than ready to settle down by a sea-coal fire, with his books, his papers, and a bottle of port wine.

He had picked up some mildewed histories in one of the bookshops. The pages were badly foxed, and the quaint old lettering difficult to read, but leafing through one of these volumes, he was immediately struck by the use of so many different type-faces, which appeared on the page in an entirely random fashion.

Staring raptly down at the book, he felt his pulse begin to race. Someone had told him, once, that varying letter shapes were sometimes used to encrypt a cipher. Could the printer and the historian, working in concert, have concealed a series of secret messages inside this apparently innocent text? Of course there were several different types here, instead of just two, but perhaps—perhaps only two were used in the cryptogram itself? Perhaps the other letters, in the other types, ought to be regarded merely as blanks? Luke took a deep breath and released it slowly, certain he had hit on the most likely solution.

Somewhere, in one of the books he had collected since leaving Winterscar, he had the key to a famous version of the Bilateral Cipher. Luke opened the horsehide trunk and began tossing out books—until he found the one with the tattered blue cover. Laying both volumes open on a table by the fire, dredging up some blank sheets of paper, a pen, and some ink, he set eagerly to work. If the black-letter alphabet stood for "a" and the flourishing italic for "b"—

He was still busily deciphering, several days later, when the ambassador came by for an afternoon visit.

"My dear Mr. Guilian, *how* are you keeping yourself? I hope you are keeping yourself tolerably amused," said Lord Polyphant as he lifted the curiously long tails of his coat and accepted a seat by the fire. "For I have seen you nowhere, my dear sir, and nobody seems to know you. I hope you've not been making an absolute *hermit* of yourself?"

"Nothing of the sort; I have been nearly everywhere." Luke closed his books, made a pile of the scattered papers, and signaled Perys to bring in the tea-tray. "Everywhere that is, but in Polite Society. I have seen the university, and the Foundling Hospital, and there is an intriguing little coin shop by the Grand Canal—" The last sentence faded out unfinished, as it became evident the ambassador was not really listening.

"To each his own, Mr. Guilian," said Lord Polyphant in a failing voice. For all his gentle air of boredom, his prominent blue eyes were exploring the entire room, every nook and cranny, as though he were making an inventory of the furnishings and calculating their exact value.

"But I wonder if I might induce you to tear yourself away from these—peculiar amusements. I should tell you that your presence in Luden has aroused curiosity. People are beginning to wonder why you never accept their invitations."

"I beg your pardon. It was not to engage in fashionable dissipations that I came to Luden. And really, I don't see why it should be anyone's business how I choose to amuse myself."

The ambassador smiled seraphically, determined to maintain his good nature no matter what. "For all that, you really must show yourself. Luden is not like Tarnburgh, and Rijxland is not like Winterscar. It's positively not advisable to appear unsociable. I hope I needn't say more?"

"I'm not quite certain what you mean," Luke said stubbornly. "However, it's certainly not my intention to appear antisocial or ill-natured."

In any case, the process of deciphering was beginning to pall. While Luke's early efforts had been marked by a striking success and he had already uncovered a number of fragmentary sentences within the text, including some very famous names—two of the legendary founding fathers, and some early rulers of Rijxland and Herndyke— he had yet to come up with anything that made any real *sense*.

Going over to a desk by the window, Luke picked up a pile of cream-colored calling cards left behind by the various visitors to whom he had "not been at home" and brought them back to the table by the fire. "Perhaps you can advise me which of these visits I ought to return. Do I know these people? Did I meet them at the embassy? I can't for the life of me remember who any of them are."

The ambassador sorted through the cards swiftly, then put them aside with a languid air. "The Hoodjs, the Helzts, the Boijmans, and the Doux—you may visit any of these families, you should visit them all. The important thing is to be seen, which you *can* be in any of these houses." He leaned a little forward in his chair. "But enough about that. The reason I came to see you was to extend an invitation of my own."

He waited while Perys put out plates of currant buns and tiny iced pastries, then continued on as soon as the valet left the room. "I go, this afternoon, to Doctor Van Tulp's to meet with Lord Catts, the Minister of Trade. It has become quite fashionable to be seen there, you know, and I thought you might like to join me."

Lucius hesitated. Doctor Van Tulp was the eponymous founder of the model madhouse. Though the doctor had been dead for more than eighty years, his name and somewhat eccentric fame lingered on. Luke was, quite naturally, wild to see the place. Indeed, he had considered going there long before this, but an innate delicacy held him back.

On the other hand, he would have liked to catch a glimpse of the great man whose published speeches and letters were so familiar to him, and who, in happier days, had excited so much of his admiration. It occurred to him, now, that King Izaiah, having already been subjected to so very much, could not possibly be harmed—and who knew but that he might not even benefit?—by the presence of one sympathetic and respectful observer, among so many others animated solely by vulgar curiosity.

It seemed that all the world was determined to see and be seen at Doctor Van Tulp's—or at least all of the world that was idle and fashionable. When Luke and Lord Polyphant arrived, the long galleries were already crowded with the very cream of Luden Society, who had come to promenade the marble halls of the great institution, to gossip, flirt, eat nuts and gingerbread, and to ogle the poor lunatics.

Never in all his life had Luke seen such a gathering of oddly dressed people—such gowns, such swallow-tailed coats, such out-sized hoops, headdresses, jewels, and time-pieces—or the use of so much false hair and powder. Never before had he beheld such a mob of shabby peddlers and hawkers, selling everything from the afore-mentioned gingerbread to gloves and silver snuffboxes—or ob-served such an utter lack of decorum in their supposed betters. He had not been in the place a quarter of an hour when he began to ex-perience the disorienting impression that it was going to be ab-solutely impossible to distinguish the visitors from the inmates. A lanky gentleman in purple hair, and garments so curiously shrunken that his abbreviated vest and trousers actually failed to meet at his middle, turned out to be Lord Catts, the Minister of Trade. And a dignified old lady, in a grey silk gown and a high lace headdress, was identified in a pointed whisper as the Dowager Duchess of Flay, well past ninety and a long-time resident.

For himself, Lucius saw nothing in her style or behavior to indi-cate derangement—unless it might be an insistent attempt to sell him a card of pins. But much might be forgiven a nonagenarian. Far more embarrassing, to his way of thinking, were the dress and the antics of the visiting dandies and exquisites parading through the halls—in whose company, the violet-tinted hair and bright, ill-fit-ting garments of Lord Catts hardly appeared extravagant.

Luke's sneer of distaste became more pronounced as he and Lords Polyphant and Catts moved from gallery to corridor. If there was nothing on earth to match the common sense and sober indus-try of the ordinary Rijxlander, Luke was beginning to suspect that the more exalted classes came of another species entirely. As he ob-served the wild behavior of several young ladies in diaphanous gowns playing a noisy game of *catch-me-quick* between the marble pillars and miniature palm trees that lined the central corridor—as he listened to the inane shrieks of laughter issuing from a painted youth in striped stockings and a truly monstrous wig—as he watched the ambassador tottering about on the absurd eight-inch red heels of his fashionable shoes, or pulling out and consulting a pocket-watch the size of an onion—Luke began to wonder if something of King Izaiah's madness had not spread throughout the upper ranks of Luden Society.

While his two companions occupied themselves with a long and not entirely comprehensible conversation on an upcoming trade agreement, Lucius slipped off by himself. Soon, he was utterly absorbed in the bizarre workings of the great institution.

In one room, a pale young woman had been strapped to a chair, and a pair of grim-looking females were applying magnets to her bare feet. In another, a troop of old men in yellow linen nightshirts were alternately ducked in tubs of steaming hot and what *must* have been frigidly cold water, as Luke could see blocks of ice from the canals floating in every other tub. In a third room, he paused to watch while two young men, scarecrow thin, were attached to a vast and intricate contraption—a convoluted mass of copper pipes, glass vessels, and rapidly inflating and deflating leather bladders—which seemed to be pumping, by way of thin glass tubes, some sort of thick red fluid directly into their veins.

"Lamb's blood," said a soft voice behind him. Luke turned to see a silver-haired gentleman in a bottle-green coat regarding him with a gentle smile. "A revolutionary new treatment. The blood of animals—in this case, sheep—being uncorrupted by the vices, the passions, and the inordinate appetites of Men and Goblins, is believed to impart a soothing and altogether beneficial influence."

Luke's dark eyebrows twitched together. "Does this really work?"

"Indeed yes," said the old gentleman, his smile broadening. "As you may see for yourself by the peaceful expressions of these unfortunate men—who not very long ago showed all of the symptoms of Frenzy."

Luke continued to regard him doubtfully. "But afterwards, when they are removed from the apparatus?"

The old man stopped to pat one of the emaciated patients on a bony shoulder before answering Luke's question. "Those who do not die in the course of the treatment are usually cured by it." Seeing how Lucius frowned, he continued on: "But perhaps you consider the risk unacceptable? Yet you are a healthy young man. I wonder what you would think if you suffered from a malady which seized your limbs as in an iron vise and caused them to twitch uncontrollably; which caused you to screech and howl and pour forth obscenities; which robbed you not only of reason, but honor, dignity, manhood—of everything, in short, that makes life worth living. Would you not, then, think almost any risk acceptable, if it accompanied the reasonable hope of a full and permanent cure?"

"Yes," said Luke, his frown lifting. "Yes, I would." And he made a deep bow to show how very much obliged he was for the explanation.

His new acquaintance responded with a dignified bow of his own. "You show a sincere interest in our work, sir. I find that refreshing. All too often—but you have undoubtedly seen the sort of visitor we usually attract here. Perhaps, as you *are* so interested, you will permit me to show you through the asylum, and to explain to you just a little bit more of what it is we do here?"

Luke accepted eagerly. He had already decided this intriguing old fellow *must* be one of the senior physicians, and that opinion was strengthened during the next memorable hour, as he strolled through the institution with the genial old gentleman, before whom all doors opened, and for whom the healing arts appeared to hold no mysteries.

"It was once thought that Hysteria, which afflicts the tender sex by far the most frequently, was the result of a wandering uterus. This has since been proven the merest nonsense, and the disorder properly ascribed to a severe Ataxy and a consequent shattering of the animal spirits. As a result, we have finally discovered a rational treatment."

"And that is?"

"Fresh air and exercise, preferably on horseback. And daily doses of *steel syrup*—that is, of iron filings steeped in wine. I wonder my dear young sir—" The old gentleman paused, as though struck by a sudden inspiration. "There are a number of interesting volumes in my chambers upstairs, my records of some difficult cases. Perhaps you would care to examine them?"

"I would like that very much. But it occurs to me, sir, I still don't know to whom I am indebted—?"

The old gentleman inclined his head. "I beg your pardon. I thought that you knew. I am Titus Van Tulp, very much at your service."

At this, Luke felt his first twinge of doubt. "The—son of the founder?" That would at least explain the distinguishing attention which had greeted them on all sides. "Or perhaps—the nephew or grandson?"

"Nothing of the sort. I *am* the founder." The old gentleman made an expansive gesture. "All this has been my sole care and concern for considerably more than a hundred years."

It was then and only then that Luke finally realized just how completely he had been taken in.

He hesitated, torn between dismay and delight. Dismay, because it was humiliating to reflect how truly gullible he had been, and delight, because he had apparently spent the hour just past in company with the man who had once possessed perhaps *the* most brilliant mind of the century: King Izaiah of Rijxland.

* * *

King Izaiah had been given rooms on the top floor, up three long flights of increasingly steep and uneven stairs, right under the roof. Despite a remote location, these were luxurious chambers, if very much cluttered: with books and pipes, a pair of embroidered velvet slippers, any number of maps and globes, and the rare museum of curios and artifacts he had been allowed to bring to the madhouse with him.

"A petrified oyster," said the king, displaying for Luke's edification a very fine specimen. "And a phial of blood, said to have rained from the sky over the Isle of Finghyll."

There was also a vast collection of strange worms and insects; a giant's tooth, somewhat decayed; two brains, one Human and one Goblin, preserved in a greenish fluid; some dried fishes; and a number of bones, one said to be the rib of a triton. Nor were man-made curiosities lacking. There was the tusk of a mammoth exquisitely carved, and a set of ivory chessmen, so miniscule they were all kept inside a hollow cherry stone. There were trays full of coins and ancient military insignia that made Luke's fingers itch to acquire them. And there was an exceedingly fine chain and a tiny lock of iron, steel, and brass—so very, very small that a flea might wear them. As indeed (the king said) a flea had, when they belonged to the proprietor of a travelling flea circus.

In the Mad King, Luke was delighted to discover a kindred spirit. Even in his present state of mental infirmity, there were few matters on which he could not discourse at length, fluently, and with an impressive degree of familiarity. In the course of a long life he had been a sort of intellectual magpie, gathering together not only his cabinet of curiosities but also such diverse glittering nuggets of information as came his way.

Yet there were lapses into pure fancy as well. As when, in the midst of showing Luke a particularly fine telescope, he spoke of great cities encased in opalescent bubbles of steel and glass, endlessly circling the sun—first theorized and then discredited by ancient philosophers, though he claimed to have seen them himself on more than one occasion, with the help of a very strong lens.

And later on, explaining the disappearance of his emerald pocket-watch, he declared that no one else would be able to find it, as he had buried the watch fathoms deep in an iron chest under the sea, and set whales and narwhals to guard it.

"They want it very much, Marjote and the others, but I simply don't choose that they should have it." He lowered his voice to a confidential whisper. "An excellent chronometer actually set inside a single enormous gemstone—far too valuable—and the truth is, I trust no one."

He looked vaguely around the room, as though he had just missed something else, began alternately patting his waistcoat and the pockets in his coat.

"Is there something you want?" Luke asked politely.

"My spectacles," said Izaiah, on a rising note of distress. "I *do* want them, but they have been missing so long, I doubt I will ever find them." He lowered his voice again, adding with an angry look, "My doctors are always taking my things away, though they pretend otherwise."

Luke shook his head doubtfully. "Infamous if true," he heard himself saying, then wished he had held his tongue. There was no purpose to be served by distressing the old man, or contributing to an already lively sense of persecution.

Just then, the king gave a crow of delight and pointed at something behind Luke's back. Turning, Luke saw that a very pretty young girl had just entered the room. Apparently just in from a walk or a carriage ride, she wore an immense black velvet hat and carried with her a muff made of silky white fur.

As she stepped past the threshold, his first impressions were all of light, motion, and color: a little firefly of a girl in a gown of spangled blue satin, a riot of dark curls under the big feathered hat, a brilliant complexion, eyes of an indigo blue so dark and intense he had never seen anything like them before.

"Allow me to present," said the king, with a glowing look, "my eldest grandchild: the Grand Exalted Hereditary Duchess, recently come to earth from her palace on the moon, on the back of that fabulous bird, the Roc."

Who this enchanting creature could actually be, Luke did not know. The eldest offspring of the Princess Marjote was a boy of twelve or thirteen, the three princesses several years younger—and naturally, he did not believe any farrago of nonsense about lunar palaces or interplanetary travel.

But when the "Grand Exalted Hereditary Duchess" crossed the room, with a swaying of hoops and a sweep of her starry skirts, when she offered a tiny gloved hand in a *truly* regal gesture, he could not resist playing along. He responded with a bow and a flourish as he raised her hand to his lips.

"Sir," she said, "it is my pleasure."

"Madam," he replied in all sincerity, "it is entirely my own. I am her Grand Exalted Hereditary Grace's ever grateful and devoted perpetual servant."

She was as fashionably attired as anyone he had seen that day, but what had seemed like a bizarre extravagance in Lord Catts and Lord Polyphant, a vulgar singularity in the romping damsels and their dandified escorts, had been here refined to a charming originality, a delicate ingenuity. Certainly, nothing could be more dainty or tasteful than her perfumed gloves, or the pale blue flowers painted on the heels of her red leather shoes, or the little crimson heart-shaped beauty patch she wore high on one cheek.

And now that he saw her so close, Luke realized that he had at first mistaken her age, perhaps deceived by her tiny stature. He revised his estimate upward: say fifteen or sixteen at the very most.

Still much too young to interest a hardened bachelor of seven-and-twenty. Yet when she lowered those dark lashes against that flawless skin, for some reason his pulse gave a sudden unexpected bound.

"Now that she is here," said the king, observing their exchange of civilities with a benevolent smile, "I believe it is time that we all drank tea."

Though Luke had already shared tea and cakes with Lord Polyphant earlier, he was not about to decline this interesting invitation. He accepted at once, and they each found seats around an octagonal table. While the king pulled up one of the deep armchairs, Luke disposed himself on a dusty loveseat. As for the lady, she seated herself on a high stool in order to accommodate her spreading hoops, removed her gloves, unpinned her picturesque hat, and shook out her dusky curls.

As it developed, nobody's appetite was unduly taxed. Tea consisted of a very strong orange-flavored brandy—which the "Hereditary Duchess" served out in china teacups the size of walnut shells—and a plate of broken biscuits sprinkled with colored sugar. Yet looking back later, Luke would be firmly convinced that he had never spent a more enjoyable meal in his life. At the king's urging, the lady was encouraged to tell something of her "long and arduous journey from the Outer Planets."

Such adventures Luke had never before heard or imagined. She told of pirates lurking in the white ice caverns of the mountains of the moon; of the long, unrequited love of the Roc for the Phoenix, the passion that had moved him to appear at her funeral pyre with his brilliant feathers all stained black; of narrow escapes, thrilling rescues, and harrowing perils, which would have turned the hair of a less courageous damsel white with terror. These were, Luke believed, not the product of a deranged mind but of a remarkably ready facility of invention—for there could be no doubt that much of her story was concocted on the spot.

Similarly inspired, he tried by his comments and questions to match her for cleverness. At length, he found himself pleasantly weary, as though he had spent the entire afternoon at intense mental and physical activity. Weary or not, he was still so stimulated that he might have continued in the same way for hours.

Eventually, however, he became aware of the time, and bethought himself somewhat guiltily of Lord Polyphant, who must be wondering what had become of him.

"I am afraid I must tear myself away," he said, as the lady concluded a particularly breathless narrative.

"Yes, it is growing late," answered the King, leaning back in his chair and closing his eyes. Lucius felt a pang, wondering if he had selfishly encouraged the old man to over-exert himself. "Perhaps, my dear, you will escort our visitor out?"

"As you wish, Your Majesty," said the lady. She rose to her feet, pinned on her hat, and accepted the support of Luke's arm.

As they followed the crooked staircase down to the floor below, Luke felt as though he were leaving behind a rarefied world, one made up wholly of fancy and delight, and in leaving that world he was descending into a realm of grosser elements. The idea that he might never return there deeply oppressed him.

He shot a sidelong glance at his companion. She, too, seemed suddenly subdued, transformed all in an instant from the lunar princess to a perfectly ordinary, if still very attractive, young woman: older, sadder, and wiser than the delicate, whimsical creature she had been only moments before.

But who was she? Luke felt an urgent need to know. He had given his own name but had yet to learn hers. Perhaps she really *was* the king's granddaughter—the recent product of some past indiscretion—living with him, like the Princess Marjote and his legitimate grandchildren, at the asylum.

Certainly, when she spoke it was with all a granddaughter's respectful affection. "I must thank you for keeping His Majesty so well amused. It has been a long time since he last enjoyed himself quite so thoroughly." She gave a deep sigh. "Of course, the Crown Princess is very good. She sits with him often, and so do many of his old friends. But he is always so acutely aware of—of how much it grieves them to see him so sadly changed, that I can't help thinking their visits cause him quite as much pain as pleasure."

This lucid, sensitive analysis convinced Luke of one thing at least: whoever she was, she was not one of the inmates. "The truth is, I would like to call again. But would it be advisable?"

"Because you are so nearly connected with the King of Winterscar?" She considered carefully. "If King Izaiah were in full command of himself and affairs of state, I doubt a friendship would be permitted. But as things are—I think you may visit whenever you choose."

By now, they had reached the ground floor. Lucius looked around him with a dull eye, searching for the ambassador. The enchanted interlude was over, stale reality was about to engulf him. A voice called out his name, and he spun around. He saw Lord Catts and Lord Polyphant moving his way, and he raised a hand to acknowledge them.

But when he turned back to bid the lady good day, Luke discovered that she was already gone, had somehow slipped away without a word of farewell. And he was still staring, with a puzzled frown, at the place he had seen her last, when the ambassador and Lord Catts finally came up to him.

"Perhaps one of you gentlemen can tell me the name of that extraordinary young woman who was with me just now?"

Lord Polyphant and the Minister of Trade exchanged a significant glance; neither one seemed disposed to answer his question. At last, Lord Catts raised a perfumed handkerchief to his lips, rolled a bloodshot eye in Luke's direction. "But don't you know? That little beauty, that delectable article of virtue, is none other than the notorious Tremeur Brouillard, the king's whore!"

Luke felt as though all the wind had been knocked out of him, as though all the blood had drained from his heart.

"That pretty child?" he managed at last. "The king's mistress, Lord Flinx's protegée—of whom one hears so many indecent stories?"

"But of course," said Lord Catts, with an ugly leer. "Young in years but old in vice, or so the story goes. Did no one tell you? She is only *just* sixteen."

"Yes," said Luke, "I suppose that I did know." He still felt dazed and bewildered, he was beginning to feel angry and ill. "But for all that, I was expecting a very—different style of female."

17

ord Lieutenant Marzden of the City Guard lived in a large
house on the outskirts of town. Ten centuries ago, it had
been the home of some country squire, a handsome
manor house built of the native stone, with turrets and balconies,
courtyards and gardens, all surrounded by lawns, reflecting pools,
orchards, and fields. But in a thousand years the city had expanded
outward many times, licking up miles upon miles of the surrounding countryside, grinding the tiny villages and settlements between
her cannibal teeth and greedily digesting them. A thousand years of
rain and wind and city grit and smoke had left their mark. Now the
building was largely ruinous, and hemmed in close by slums and tenements.

Yet winter and summer the house presented a lively appearance.
As soon as any visitor passed the massive gate studded with square-
headed nails and entered the weed-infested courtyard, he found
himself in what appeared to be an armed camp. Young red-coated
guardsmen strode to and fro, talking, quarreling, boasting. From
daybreak until sunset, the yard resounded with the clash of their
swords—and sometimes into the night, as the bold young blades of
the City Guard conducted their mock battles by torchlight.

But there was a second entrance, less well known, where those with confidential information could come and go unobserved. An anonymous gate, an empty yard, a long stone staircase winding up to the top of the house—in this way, Lord Marzden's spies could enter his inner sanctum by a secret door.

And in this way, on one particular morning, a certain shabby figure slipped quietly into the house and surprised Jack Marzden at work at his desk.

Glancing up from a roll of papers he had been studying for the last half hour, Marzden gave a violent start. Recovering, he set aside his work, rose from his chair, and offered the young man a firm handshake across the desk.

"I'll swear you look worse every time I see you," he said with an amiable grin. The figure before him wore a dusty frieze coat of dubious antecedents, skin-tight trousers, a striped waistcoat, and a large shovel-brimmed hat, very much battered. "What is this fashion, young Blackheart? You resemble something—I hardly know what—something between a sweep and a grave-robber!"

"I'm pleased to hear it," Wilrowan replied cheerfully, as he accepted a chair. "You can scarcely imagine how much time and effort goes into achieving precisely that effect."

He tilted back the chair. "I have been putting my disreputable appearance to good use these last few days, in practically every tavern in the city. Investigating—a private matter with which I won't trouble you—and as I was passing by this place, I hit on the idea of paying you a visit."

"That's good of you, Will, particularly as you can see how little I have to occupy me." Marzden indicated, with a broad sweep of his hand, the mountain of papers piled on his desk. "But what's this I hear about you being arrested and cast like a common felon into Whitcomb Gaol? When I think of the nights my men and I chased you all through the city, only to have you elude us at last, I confess I was vastly diverted to learn you had finally been laid by the heels—and after you've grown so old and respectable, too!"

The Lord Lieutenant enjoyed a good long laugh at Wilrowan's expense, which Will was obliged to tolerate, no matter how much the incident still rankled. Afterwards, Marzden urged him to tell the whole story, which Will was ready enough to do. He wanted information and had learned long ago that the best way to get it was to assume the pretense of candor himself. He gave a full account of the duel and of his enforced visit to Whitcomb Gaol, but he said nothing about the theft of the Mountfalcon Jewel. It had been decided, over Wilrowan's protests, that Marzden should not be trusted with a secret of this magnitude.

"No one has seen or heard from Macquay since," Will concluded. "And I must admit it begins to look as though something has happened to him. I hope it won't prevent me from horsewhipping the fellow, which is what I fully intend."

"I am afraid you'll have to remain eternally frustrated in that respect. Rufus Macquay is dead and buried. He was killed in a quarrel at the Leviathan. There was some initial confusion about his identity, and it apparently took a day or two to clear that up, but it was certainly Macquay."

Wilrowan scowled at him. "And may I venture to inquire why you never sent word to his friends at the palace?"

"I didn't know it myself until an hour ago. There has been a good deal to occupy me since I returned to Hawkesbridge, and I've only just this morning found time to read the reports."

Marzden took a long-stemmed pipe out of a pocket in his coat, a leather bag out of a drawer in his desk, and proceeded to fill the bowl with a mixture of tobacco and mildly intoxicating herbs. Marzden was older than he looked, and it was but one of his many idiosyncrasies that he clung to the dress and the manners of a bygone era. He wore his thick chestnut hair loose over his shoulders and he never appeared in public without his scarlet cloak, bucket-topped boots, and a wide soft-brimmed hat with crimson feathers, the very image of a dashing guardsman—forty years back. In private, he smoked an old-fashioned clay pipe. "In any case, Will, I would have thought you of all people already knew."

"I? How should I know—unless you suspect me of murdering Macquay, which I can assure you I've not done. I most particularly wanted to speak to the man."

Marzden stopped with the pipe halfway to his mouth. "Perhaps I've been indiscreet. Never mind. It was of no real importance."

There was only the smallest of fires burning on the hearth, yet there was something in Marzden's glance that made Will feel suddenly hot and uncomfortable. "I think it must be of *some* importance. Pray disregard my feelings, Jack—if it *is* my feelings you fear to offend—and tell me exactly what you meant just now."

"Very well," said the Lord Lieutenant with a shrug. "And after all, on thinking a little further, I realize the circumstances were not so compromising." He handed Will one of the reports and indicated a paragraph he thought might be of interest.

"*A young woman of respectable appearance,*" Will read out loud, "*who was recognized by one of the officers and did eventually admit to being one Lilliana Brakeburn-Bla—*"

The report fell from Will's nerveless fingers onto the desk. "Fire and Damnation! What was my wife doing in a filthy hole like the Leviathan?" His mind reeled with possibilities, none of them anything a man and a husband might be expected to stomach.

"What brought her there to begin with, I can't tell you," said Marzden, rising from his desk and walking over to the fire. "But she seems to have been accompanied by Miss Allora Brakeburn, and the two of them were apparently engaged in nursing one—" (with a pair of pewter pipe-tongs, he extracted a coal and held it to the bowl of his pipe) "—Sir Bastian Josslyn-Mather, through a bout of Black Bile Fever."

Will racked his brain, tried to remember what Lili had said when they spoke together at Brakeburn. "She did say something about some devilish old fellow who had taken ill. Though she failed to mention the very small matter of a dead body. Perhaps she considered it beneath my notice—the gods only know *what* she thinks my life is here in Hawkesbridge."

He gave a bitter laugh. "Of course, I know who to thank for all this. I don't care if all the old men in the city came down with the Fever simultaneously, Miss Allora Brakeburn had no business taking Lili into that sink of whores and footpads! If she were not a woman—and an interfering busybody of an *old* woman at that— I'd be tempted to blow a hole right through her wicked old heart!"

"Yes, very likely," said Marzden, who had finally managed to light his pipe, and was filling the room with a faintly unpleasant smoke. Will himself had no use for hemp, nor did he care for the effect the weed produced in those of his friends who used it, but he was hardly in a position to say so.

Marzden returned to his seat behind the desk and continued to puff on his long-stemmed pipe. "One must naturally deplore the hidebound conventions which forbid a young man like yourself from challenging a woman of sixty or seventy—but you expose Lilliana to your own company, Will, and that is very nearly as bad as anyone she might meet at the Leviathan!"

Wilrowan was not inclined to allow it, his sense of humor slightly impaired under the circumstances. With an impatient gesture, he picked up the report again, read it all the way through, then went over it a second time. More than ever, he suspected a connection between his duel with Macquay and the disappearance of the Goblin artifact.

Looking up from the paper, Will cleared his throat. "Speaking of my quarrel with Rufus Macquay—would it be possible for me to question a few of your men? The recruits who arrested me? They may know something of his intentions."

"Macquay's intentions appear obvious enough, and hardly seem important now. However, I will send for the men in question. If you'll go about your mysterious business for the next few hours, and come back in the afternoon, you can speak to them then."

Will spent the rest of the morning prowling the streets of Hawkesbridge, trying to make sense of Lili's visit to the Leviathan. But the truth was: it *made* no sense. Absurd to suppose that if Lili had gone there to meet a man she would take Allora with her; equally ridiculous to suppose that a woman so fastidious would select the Leviathan for a romantic tryst. But if her visit to Hawkesbridge were perfectly innocent, then why not write to tell him she was coming, why keep it all a secret afterwards?

Will moved through the city—past the taverns, brothels, and almshouses of Black Nag Alley down by the Zule—past the thriving little shops of Whey Street and Bedstraw Lane—then uphill to the fashionable district around Tooley Square, with its wide clean streets and tall stone mansions struggling to remove themselves, by their reckless piling of story on story, above the damps and foul odors of the river.

He clenched his hands into tight fists, remembering that Macquay and Dionee had both seemed to warn him of—something, he was not sure what. Dionee had admitted she was only speculating, but Macquay had claimed some particular knowledge—and was it only coincidence that placed Sir Rufus and Lili both at the Leviathan the night he was murdered? Had she been there often before? Had Macquay seen her?

But *Lili* at a clandestine meeting with another man? Will felt a pain stab at his belly. A fine fool he would look playing the injured husband. A fine fool he was *going* to look when he hunted the other man down and slowly strangled the life right out of him.

Will shook a fist at the lowering sky; he raged and paced. But if Lili had fallen in love with somebody else, why go to such lengths to disguise it? They had made a most damnable bargain between them, and *he* had been enjoying the immunity it provided for years and years. Will stopped breathing quite so hard. The truth was, it was *all* completely unlike her: the place, the motive, the secrecy. Lili's image rose up in his mind to refute these sordid speculations: cool, ladylike, serene. If he could not trust her, then who in all this wicked world *could* he trust?

He marched into Marzden's sanctum in the mid-afternoon, still in an evil temper, and was greeted by the unwelcome intelligence that only one of the offending guardsmen was available to speak to him. "The others have all disappeared."

"Disappeared?" said Wilrowan, raising his eyebrows. It seemed to him that a great many things and people were disappearing lately. Or else turning up where they had no business to be. "Have you reason to suspect foul play?"

"No, why should I? What puzzles me is how such a promising young fellow as Nat Dagget fell in with that lot to begin with. But perhaps you can get more out of him than I did. You will find him waiting for you in the room at the end of the hall."

Will declared himself very much obliged, and leaving the Lord Lieutenant to his reports, bowed himself out of the room.

Shortly thereafter, he confronted Corporal Dagget, whom he immediately recognized as the sturdy youth who had appeared so cool-headed during his arrest. The corporal was not nearly so collected now. Seeing how uneasy he was, as he clicked his heels and stood at stiff attention, Wilrowan might have shown some pity—but on a day so full of disturbing revelations, Will was ready to take his revenge where and how he could.

Without any preamble, he began to fire questions. "Perhaps you will explain to me why your friends left Hawkesbridge so very suddenly?"

"Sir," said the youth, swallowing hard. "Captain Blackheart, there was nothing wonderful about that. They were all of them reluctant recruits, already singled out as potential trouble-makers, not any of them looking forward to long careers in the City Guard. And finding themselves in possession of ready money—"

"Ready money? So you *were* bribed?"

The corporal nodded miserably. "Sir, I was about to say. A—a gentleman asked us to watch the duel and interfere at need, and afterwards I learned that a considerable sum of money *had* changed hands. That made me wonder if his request was really so innocent as it seemed at first, but of course, by then, it was already too late."

Will was quick to pick up on his slight hesitation. "You paused before you said the word *gentleman*. Why was that?"

"He had the air of a gentleman, sir, and his appearance was respectable. But I began to think afterwards there was something queer about him, some—some subtle deformity, and that far from being a gentleman, he wasn't a Man at all. But there was a lady with him, a little, plump woman with very white hands and a soft voice, and she was *entirely* genteel."

Will paced a circle around the room, absorbing this information. The woman, whoever she was, did not interest him much, but the possible involvement of a Goblin did. He remembered the Wryneck that Blaise had seen at the duel. Of course, the whole idea of using such a creature in a scheme like this one was utterly fantastic—he had never met a Goblin yet who was not bound and determined to stay on the right side of the law. But supposing that you caught one in some slight misdemeanor, threatened him with prosecution which they all seemed to fear—say that you even waved a flame under his nose to frighten him further? It was likely under those circumstances the Goblin would do anything you asked. And even if he lost his nerve and tried to betray you later, who would take the word of a Goblin over that of a Man?

"And did this—person—or the lady with him, indicate why they were arranging matters in that particular curious fashion?"

Corporal Dagget hesitated. "Yes, sir," he answered at last. "The—the person said it was a duel between Sir Rufus Macquay and a man he had privately determined was a danger to the Crown, a man Sir Rufus and the king were unwilling to bring openly to account."

"And *I* was that man?" Will ground his teeth at such boundless effrontery. "And when you and your friends arrived at the duel, did I strike you as such a desperate character?"

"Captain Blackheart, you did. If you will pardon my saying so, when I first caught sight of you, you had the look of a man who was capable of anything. Neither I nor my friends had any idea we were doing something wrong." He gave Will a pleading look. "Though the circumstances were slightly irregular, we sincerely believed we were serving the Crown."

But that was too much for Wilrowan. "And do you imagine the Crown of Mountfalcon is in the habit of conducting its business in that disgraceful fashion? Duels tainted with magic. Goblins bribing guardsmen. A citizen of Hawkesbridge being hauled off to Whitcomb Gaol on trumped-up charges. What the custom may be in other places I can't say, but I assure you that neither King Rodaric nor any of his agents would ever stoop so low. And if you truly believe anything of the sort, I'd think you would be ashamed to wear that uniform!"

The young guardsman cringed visibly. All this time, he had been standing at rigid attention, not altering his stance by so much as a finger; now some of that tension relaxed—not as though he were relieved, but as if the courage had all drained out of him. "No doubt you are right: I don't deserve to wear these colors. Which more than likely I won't, as soon as you tell Lord Marzden everything I've told you."

Will would have liked nothing more than to tell Marzden. Were he in the Lord Lieutenant's place, not content with stripping the youth of his rank and scarlet uniform, it was altogether likely he would have sent the boy on his way with some stripes on his back as well. But then a dim memory surfaced, a fleeting glimpse of himself when he was much the same age as young Dagget and in serious trouble of his own. It did nothing to appease Will's wrath, but it suddenly made him feel weary, jaded, and old.

With a frustrated gesture, Wilrowan took another turn around the room. "You are perhaps aware that I was at one time an officer in the City Guard?"

"Captain Blackheart," the young man said earnestly, "I think that everyone in Hawkesbridge must be aware of your illustrious career. If my friends and I had believed for one moment that you were who you said you were, we would never—"

"Yes, quite so," said Will, clearing his throat. "My illustrious career." It had at least been recklessly heroic, which accounted in part for his later promotion to the Queen's Guard.

"I did not, however, begin that career in any admirable fashion. I had just been expelled from the university, was reluctant to go home and face my father, when Lord Marzden, who had reason to— to know my name and know something about me, decided to give me a chance at redemption, and offered me a commission. A commission I immediately put in peril, that I ought to have lost ten times over, had Marzden not been patient with me. Eventually, I rewarded his somewhat misplaced faith, if not by entirely mending my ways, at least by those distinguished actions you alluded to just now."

He frowned sternly at the younger man. "I don't mean to excuse your behavior, which has been truly reprehensible. And if one of my own men at the palace had done anything half so bad, you may believe he would have suffered for it. But the City Guard is—an organization where young men sometimes learn from their mistakes—where silk purses are not infrequently produced from sows' ears—and for that reason, I'm not altogether certain I wish to acquaint Lord Marzden with the full extent of your transgressions."

"You are very good, Captain Blackheart. But I intend to do that myself, just as soon as he is willing to see me."

"Very well. But I hold my tongue and give you the opportunity to make your confession—which *may* spare you the worst of Marzden's displeasure—on one condition only."

The corporal assumed once more a painfully stiff position. "I am aware, sir, that I owe you a great deal more than my confession. If there is anything I can do to right myself—"

"I am going to give you that opportunity as well, though I doubt you will thank me for it afterward," said Will, with a militant gleam in his eye. "Because every single hour you are not on duty—every single minute of the day that you can snatch—you are going to be searching this city, street by street, house by house, and if it should prove necessary, inch by inch, for the creature who paid you and your friends that bribe, and the woman who was with him."

Will left Marzden's headquarters in no better temper than he had arrived. Nearly two miles lay between him and the Volary, and the activities of the last three days, as he slouched from tavern to tavern gathering information, were beginning to tell on him. He had hardly paused for sleep or for rest during the last thirty-six hours, and during that time had consumed very little food and a great deal more bad liquor than he was accustomed to drink.

Looking up at the sky, he saw that the weather was threatening. There was a yellow glare in the east, and the air felt heavy with the promise of snow. Yet, exhausted as he was, Will knew there was not a coachman or a chair-bearer in the city who would accept a fare from such a dirty and disreputable figure. Accordingly, he set off on foot.

Two blocks later, he turned down a dark, seedy-looking alley which stank like a sewer, but appeared to offer a shortcut home. His mind still very much on the problem of the missing Jewel, he failed to notice how closely he was being followed. When he finally did hear stealthy footsteps almost at his back, he was surprised to realize he had been so careless.

He had barely enough time to draw a pistol out of his pocket, at the same time cocking it, before a rough hand clapped him on the shoulder. As quick as thought, Will half turned, leveled the long silver barrel of the pistol, and pulled the trigger. There was a flash and a loud explosion, and the hard hand on his shoulder suddenly lost its grip. His assailant doubled over, then went down in a kneeling position on the ground, a bloody hole the size of a fist in the middle of his stomach.

Catching sight of a movement at the edge of his vision, Will dodged just in time to avoid the full force of a blow that might otherwise have shattered his skull. The oak truncheon glanced off the side of his head, clipping his shoulder as it passed. The shock was tremendous. Reeling forward, Will saw steaks of light before his eyes. Then he was down in the mud and the slush, wrestling with a man very much larger and heavier than he was.

A pair of strong hands closed around his throat with bruising force; two large thumbs began to press on his windpipe. "You'll be dead in a minute, you don't lie still," said a harsh voice in his ear.

Will did not lie still; he continued to struggle. The world had dwindled to a wavering circle of light around the big man's heavy face when, inexplicably, the ruffian cried out, went limp, and relaxed his grip.

Lying there dazed and ill, it took Will several moments to recognize that what was pinning him down to that cold patch of ground was no living man but the crushing weight of a very large corpse. When this fact finally penetrated, he rolled the body off, and somehow managed to push himself up on both elbows.

As the mists cleared, Will realized that he was *still* not alone. A tall figure, standing about ten feet away, came slowly into focus. It was an exceedingly slim and straight figure in the maroon velvet and gold facings of the King's Guard, and it was engaged in the process of fastidiously cleaning the blood off a silver-hilted rapier with what appeared to be a fine lawn handkerchief.

"Nick Brakeburn," Will said hoarsely. "What are you doing here?"

"I beg your pardon," Lili's cousin replied, with a flash of even white teeth. "I would hate to think I had intruded on a private quarrel." He put away his sword, wadded up the bloody handkerchief in his fist, and extended the other hand to Wilrowan.

Will summoned up a weak, shaky grin of his own. Accepting the offered hand, he wobbled to his feet. "You don't intrude at all. By what trick of luck or the gods did you manage to happen along at just the right moment?"

Young Brakeburn lifted a broad shoulder under the wine-colored coat. "I saw you turn down this alley and I saw the two men follow you. As I didn't care for the look of the place or of them, I decided to watch what happened.

"Although, if you will pardon my saying so," he added, as he bent at the waist, picked up the fallen pistol, unfolded his long lean body, and handed the firearm back to Will, "you don't look like someone who has anything worth stealing—or was this a personal matter, after all?"

"I have no idea." Pocketing the pistol, Will prodded one of the bodies on the ground with the toe of his boot. "Since neither of these fellows appears to be capable of answering any questions, I suppose their motives must remain a mystery."

With an effort, he stooped and rescued his hat, which had fallen off during the struggle and was lying in a muddy puddle along with some fish heads, a rotting cabbage leaf, some potato peelings, and one or two other things better not identified. He put a hand to his aching head. Was it possible he had picked up some piece of information today that was far more valuable—and therefore far more dangerous—than he knew?

He turned over the smaller of the two bodies and bent to examine the face. The process made him wince with pain. "I'm not acquainted with either of these men. Are you?"

"No, I am not," said Nick, with evident distaste. "Leave them be, Wilrowan! You've gone most damnably pale, and I wouldn't be surprised if you have a concussion. Let me hail a chair and send you home—where, if you have any sense at all, you'll send for a doctor."

"Very well." Painfully assuming an upright posture, Will followed Nick out of the alley. He had to agree that there was nothing to be learned by lingering over the bodies, for what could those men have intended except to rob him? He had his ring, his pistol, and his pocket-watch, all worth stealing; these attacks were far from uncommon.

So why did he continue to harbor an uneasy feeling there was something out of the ordinary about this one?

18

ick hailed a chair and watched, with a solicitude very much in contrast to his usual brisk manner, as Will climbed inside. With a combination of bribes and threats, he convinced the chair-men to carry Wilrowan as far as the palace. A silver coin changed hands, and subsequently found its way into a dirty pocket.

"And for the love of Heaven, go straight to bed," Nick admonished. "I daresay you have a lump the size of an egg under that ginger thatch of yours."

"Thank you, Lieutenant," Will said dryly. "I'll attend to the matter at my earliest convenience."

Nick grinned and sketched a salute. Then he stepped back as the chair was lifted and the bearers set off at a brisk pace. Will leaned his head against the padded silk interior and closed his eyes for the entire journey.

By the time the chair-men let him off near the Volary, he was feeling a little revived, at least sufficiently so to make his way through the front gate and then through a maze of courtyards and rooms to the queen's apartments. He had, however, a villainous headache. Arriving outside Dionee's bedchamber, he was directed to the Music Room.

Over the last two weeks, while Will was plumbing the depths of Hawkesbridge society, Dionee had dined, danced, gone riding, attended the opera, the theater, and the ballet with the ambassadors from Kjellmark, Lichtenwald, Winterscar, Tholia, Montcieux, Chêneboix, and Rijxland—in short, with every foreign dignitary in Hawkesbridge that winter, except for Thaddeus Vault, the ambassador from Nordfjall. With a seemingly artless ingenuity that would have left a less experienced charmer breathless with admiration, she had conversed with each of these gentlemen on a variety of subjects, finally bringing the conversation around to her recent terrifying experience at the hands of robbers—all with an idea of gauging the ambassadors' reactions. She had left Lord Vault for last, when in fact he had been her first object, not wishing to appear to single him out. When Will arrived in the Music Room, he found her playing at cards at a round boulle table with that worthy gentleman.

The Music Room was vast and splendid—yet somehow oppressive. The walls were covered with a rich red brocade, the gold threads that made up the pattern growing a little tarnished; a crystal chandelier, too large for the room, hung down from the coffered gold ceiling. As neither the king nor the queen was musically inclined, this was no longer a room devoted to the performance of music. It had become, instead, a museum for queer old instruments: bombardes, armonicas, and zithers; violins carved with grotesques; virginals painted with landscapes; pandurinas, seven-stringed lira, and hurdy-gurdies; even (the pride of the collection) a glass pianoforte. When Dionee caught sight of Will, standing just inside the double doors with his disreputable hat in his hand, she rose from her seat in a flutter of violet silk, begged the ambassador to excuse her, and tripped lightly across the floor.

"Wilrowan," she said with mock severity. "You really ought to know better than to come here!" Officially, Will was in disgrace, still in command of Her Majesty's Guard but banished from the royal presence—supposedly because of his scandalous arrest, and for the bad luck of not being on hand to defend the queen when she was robbed, but actually as an excuse for his extended absence from the palace. Dionee lowered her voice. "What have you learned? Oh, please tell me you have discovered something, for I have accomplished nothing here."

There were lavender shadows under her eyes. Will knew that she had been wearing herself out with worry and guilt; for one moment, he considered telling some comforting half-truth. But then he hardened his heart. She was responsible for what had occurred, and who should suffer if not herself?

"Not a breath, not a whisper," he said with a shake of his head. "I did think your diamonds might be found, and I could wring information from the scoundrel who had fenced them—but they seem to have disappeared as effectively as the Chaos Machine." He made an impatient gesture. "Believe me, the sums I have offered and the places I have offered them, I ought to have heard *something*." Nor had the ravens been able to report even a snatch of incriminating conversation.

He looked over her shoulder and across the room, watching the ambassador, who had risen when the queen did, but had by now quietly resumed his seat at the table, where he was picking up the thin pieces of painted ivory and fanning them out in his hand. "He looks ill at ease, and that's not like him. He's the most polished man I know. He watches us, too, though he pretends only to be counting the pips in his hand."

Indeed, Lord Vault's scrutiny appeared to be more than ordinary curiosity; there was a strained intensity to his sidelong glances.

Dionee sighed. "He has been playing very badly all afternoon. And when I spoke of being robbed—" She stopped and stared at Will. "My dear, is that blood?"

"But not my own. Pray, don't regard it. You were about to say—?"

"I was about to say——" Dionee interrupted herself again. "Will, you have gone all white around the mouth. What have you been doing to yourself?"

"It is all part of an ingenious disguise." He made another impatient gesture. "You were saying that when you spoke to Lord Vault about being robbed——?"

"Oh, but they *all* ask such searching questions. The ambassadors from everywhere. Of course, they may only be concerned for their own safety, thinking the footpads have grown so bold."

Wilrowan experienced an uneasy twinge. There was something very wrong here: the thieves of Hawkesbridge so ignorant, the ambassadors so interested. "I wonder if everything is quite as it ought to be in Chêneboix, Nordfjall, Winterscar, and those other places? I wonder if Rodaric is the only one who is missing something of inestimable value."

Dionee opened her eyes very wide. "Please don't say that; you will give me nightmares. The king has people in all those places; if there were really anything wrong, surely we would have heard *something*?"

"Perhaps. Yes, we must have done. *They* all know something is amiss *here*, even if they don't know what."

When Will opened the door to his chilly attic room, he was surprised to see that somebody else had already been in to light the candles. He hesitated in the corridor, sniffing the air for perfume. There was a certain Letitia Steerpike, the boldest and most predatory of Dionee's women, who had taken to paying him unexpected visits, despite the cool reception he always gave her. There *was* a faint scent, but of neroli rather than jasmine, and as Will entered the room, a figure gorgeously attired in plum-colored velvet and silver lacings rose slowly from a chair and favored him with a long hard look through a jeweled eyeglass.

"I had almost given you up for dead. But I see you are strong of wind and of limb—it is only your memory that suffers."

Will responded with a sheepish grin. "You are undoubtedly going to tell me I've forgotten some engagement. I beg your pardon, Blaise, but whatever it was has slipped my mind."

Trefallon dismissed his apology with a graceful gesture of one white hand. "We were to hire a carriage and visit my family at Crowsmeare. Don't let it trouble you, I beg you. No doubt whatever appointment you had in the stews was far more pressing."

Will groaned, tossed his hat on the floor, and collapsed into a chair. "And you've wasted the entire afternoon waiting here for me to return and explain myself."

The worst of all this secrecy was that Will had not been allowed to tell Blaise about the missing Jewel. *"I have nothing against young Trefallon,"* the king had said. *"But I don't see how he can possibly be of use in recovering the Chaos Machine."* Lacking any explanation, Will could only imagine what his friend must make of his present behavior.

"I think I'd rather feed than revile you, Wilrowan. I don't know what you have been doing to yourself, but you have a certain lean and wolfish look that I find altogether distressing. Come with me to the Imp and Bottle, and I will buy you supper."

Will considered this offer. He wanted his bed almost as much as he wanted his supper. And while a meal at an inn like the Imp—famous for its ale and for immense sea-pies stuffed with shad, haddock, cod, salmon, sturgeon, and lampreys between thin layers of pastry—would be far superior to anything he might find here at the barracks, he could hardly put in an appearance as he was now. "Oh, very well," he said at last. "It's very good of you, Blaise. I'll ring for Young Swallow and try not to keep you waiting too long."

He crossed the room and gave a hard pull on the velvet bellrope, then he shrugged out of his coat and tossed it over a chair. When he looked back up, Blaise was watching him with an expression of intense concern on his face. "What is it now?"

"You're bleeding. Fiend seize you, Wilrowan, didn't you even notice?"

Will looked down at his right sleeve, where he had knotted a strip of dirty muslin some twelve hours earlier. There was a fresh red stain. "Oh—did that start again? But I expect it's already stopped; it was never more than a scratch. I was in a knife fight last night."

"You were—in—a knife fight?" It was evident from Trefallon's voice that he did not believe a word of it. "My dear Blackheart, since *when* do you carry a knife?"

"I will after this. I was forced to borrow some damned clumsy thing from somebody else. Please don't concern yourself on my account. It was done for a wager, and no serious harm done on either side." He did not like to mention the scuffle in the alley, which had probably started the bleeding again. If Blaise knew, he would undoubtedly side with Nick and call in some cursed saw-bones.

Resuming his seat, Will was still struggling out of his high boots when Blaise picked up a folded piece of paper from a table by the door and examined it with his glass. "What is this? It looks to be of some importance."

Will put out a hand to take the letter, turned it over to look at the seal. The thick red wax was imprinted with Rodaric's cypher. "I wonder how long it's been waiting." He broke the seal, unfolded the heavy sheet of embossed paper, and read the contents with little enthusiasm.

It was a request to attend the king—not in his own apartments at the palace, but at the home of one of the two Malachim professors the chancellor had recommended. To arrange a meeting had been far more difficult than either Wilrowan or the king had imagined, as both men were out of town. Now it appeared that one or both of them had finally returned.

Will's fingers closed around the letter, crumpling the paper.

Weary and out of sorts, he had no desire to spend what remained of the day in the dry, repressive company of two Hawkesbridge dons. Even under the best of circumstances, it was a meeting he would have given worlds to avoid.

But unfobbing his pocket-watch, flipping open the cover and taking note of the hour, he saw the time was just after six. Rodaric was expecting him to appear between five and eight.

"I'm sorry, Blaise, but it looks like I've been invited to a damned supper party at the university!" He picked up one of his boots, knocked it against the floor to remove some dried mud from the heel, and pulled it back on again.

"But Will—no really, Wilrowan! Surely you don't intend to go dressed as you are?"

"There is no time to change," said Will, pulling on the other boot, shrugging back into his coat, catching up his shovel-brimmed hat as he headed toward the door. A gleam of malicious pleasure came into his eyes. "I'm afraid the reverend professors will just have to take me the way I am." Though he did pause on the threshold to remove the silver intaglio ring from his right hand and slip it into his coat pocket.

19

ilrowan rode across town in a rattling hack. The threat of snow had not been in vain, and small hard flakes came blowing in on a cold wind and beat against the bull's-eye windowpanes of the coach.

The University of Hawkesbridge, that ancient and venerable seat of learning, was a vast uncharted maze of libraries, dormitories, lecture halls, theaters, laboratories, cloisters, chapels, and groves, occupying six square miles on the eastern bank of the river. It was divided into thirteen colleges—one, it was said, for every month of the year. There was stately Cornelius, with its starry domes and golden spires, its schools of Mathematics, Astronomy, and Navigation. Julian, with its high stone walls, shady walks, and mysterious enclosures, where the young men flocked to learn Law and Rhetoric. Manasseh, with its Physick Garden and great Hall of Surgeons; and Galerius of the famous Museum of Natural History. There was Jacinth, devoted to the study of Music and to the making of musical instruments; and grim old Sacrifice, with its entire faculty made up of Levellers. Nôdier, Augustus, Flamel, and Gemini—fantastical in their architecture, rich in their history, their learning, and traditions—Hathor and Nicodemus—like so many cities of dreams floating on the river. But the most ancient of these, the most worthy of veneration, was Malachim of the Magicians.

When Will disembarked near his old college and paid off the driver, the hands on the dial in the great Malachim obelisk clock-tower indicated a quarter to seven. If he felt any emotion at returning once more to those sacred precincts, he took pains to conceal it.

The narrow old houses, mantled in ivy, were shuttered and silent, nearly identical, virtually anonymous. Yet he had no difficulty picking out the right place: Rodaric's gilded coach was pulled up outside, and a company of guardsmen in maroon-and-gold uniforms were lounging on the steps.

The coachman had uncoupled two of the horses and was walking them up and down the gas-lit street. Will greeted him with a curt nod, climbed the steps, brushed past the guards with only the bare indication of a salute, and raised his fist to the oak door panels. He announced himself to the ancient servant in rusty black livery who answered his knock: "Wilrowan Krogan-Blackheart," and walked right in without waiting to be invited.

The old man accepted this invasion with equanimity, stepping aside to make room for Will in the hall. "You are expected, Captain Blackheart. Allow me to show you the way."

Feeling somewhat chastened by this display of civility, Will followed him up a flight of stairs and into a large drafty chamber. As he crossed the threshold, Will groaned inwardly; it was all too evident he had missed his supper. This was no dining room, but a magician's laboratory, with a mosaic floor set with mystic diagrams—sunbursts, calipers, snakes, and keys—and a vaulted ceiling painted with planets, constellations, and wandering comets. Rodaric and two old gentlemen instantly identifiable as Hawkesbridge professors, by their full-bottomed wigs and long, plain coats, were seated in tall leather armchairs drawn up before a large fireplace flanked by black marble sphinxes.

216 ᴅ· TERESA EDGERTON

Will swept off his battered hat at arm's length and made a flourishing bow. Reaction to his appearance, by at least one of those present, was all that he could have wished: the stouter of the two old
gentlemen stiffened and glared. Yet the other professor merely nodded politely, and Rodaric gave a deep, half-humorous sigh, and
rolled his eyes expressively.

"I must apologize for Captain Blackheart, who has adopted this
disguise at my request, in order to prosecute certain inquiries into
the disappearance of the item we were just discussing. Allow me to
present you, Wilrowan, to our host: Professor Octavio Prenderby-
Fox, Doctor of Magic."

Will made a slight bow. "I had the honor of attending Doctor
Fox's lectures on several occasions, though I scarcely expect he remembers me. I was hardly one of his most promising students."

"On the contrary," said Professor Fox, with an unexpected twinkle. "I remember you, Wilrowan Blackheart, very well. The papers
you wrote contained some very interesting ideas. Your conclusions
were entirely faulty, of course, founded as they were on inadequate
preparation and incorrect premises, but you displayed a certain ingenuity in reaching them. I wish you had been able to stay with us
longer—but the chancellor, as I recall, had a different opinion." He
gestured toward the other old gentleman. "You are not, I think, acquainted with Sir Frederic Tregaron-Marlowe, who has made an ex-
tensive study of the Maglore and their sorcery."

As Sir Frederic did no more than return Will's bow with a chilly inclination of his head, a momentary silence fell over the room. A silence
that ended when Rodaric cleared his throat. "Take a seat, Wilrowan.
No, not there. Your work for the day is done, and there is no need to
skulk in the shadows."

With a shrug, Will cast himself down into an empty armchair
and assumed a negligent pose. Doctor Fox offered him port, which
he declined, though he did accept a cup of weak tea and a thin slice

of plum cake. The formalities satisfied and the servant dismissed, Rodaric immediately addressed the subject on everyone's mind.

"You will be pleased, Wilrowan, to hear that Sir Frederic is convinced the Chaos Machine can't have gone far. You will oblige me, Sir Frederic, by explaining to Captain Blackheart what you were just telling me."

Will and Marlowe exchanged unfriendly glances. He and Sir Frederic had never met, yet Will had an idea the other man knew him, if only by reputation. It seemed as if he could go nowhere, lately, and do nothing, without tripping over reminders of his past misdeeds.

"If Your Majesty desires it," Sir Frederic was saying, "of course I will acquaint this gentlemen with all the particulars of our conversation. Though if you will permit me to say so, in a matter so delicate, so——"

"Thank you," said Rodaric firmly, "but any such caution is entirely unnecessary. Captain Blackheart enjoys my complete confidence in this, as indeed in all matters, and you may speak as freely before him as you would before me." And under the king's cool and steady gaze, Sir Frederic resigned himself to speak, just as Will resigned himself to listen.

"You are no doubt familiar," said Marlowe, "with the theory of Universal Magnetism. I am speaking of a subtle spirit, an astral vapor, which penetrates even the hardest bodies. Through the activity of this spirit, bodies are attracted one to another; by the action of this spirit, electrical bodies may operate at even the remotest distance.

"The influence of this magnetism is to be found everywhere, sometimes creating magnetic currents or rays that exert a force so powerful it can actually be detected by particularly sensitive magicians. Moreover, there are different species of magnetism: of one sort in animals, another in plants, another in metals, and so on and so forth. Man himself is but a miniature of the earth, possessing his own magnetic poles that attract and repel. His very thoughts may be regarded as magnetic emanations, which—"

"As you have already suggested," Will interjected impatiently, "I am familiar with the principle." Though he expected Sir Frederic would eventually get around to revealing something of importance, he was not prepared to listen to an entire lecture on elementary magical theory. "Perhaps you will tell me how all this relates to the Goblin Jewels—and most particularly to the one that is missing."

Sir Frederic bridled, apparently unaccustomed to being interrupted in the full flow of his eloquence. He looked to the king as though expecting him to issue some sharp reprimand. But Rodaric merely nodded encouragingly, and Sir Frederic was forced to continue.

"The ancient Maglore were creatures of extreme ingenuity. Among their most notable inventions were artificial gemstones, closely resembling their natural counterparts but different in one important way: the Maglore gems could be used to absorb and channel the Universal Magnetism. These gems, occasionally carved intaglio, were set into rings, necklaces, and brooches, and became what we may term the Lesser Goblin Jewels. They were employed in a number of interesting ways—most frequently as a means of projecting the thoughts of one individual into the mind of another."

As Marlowe said this, Wilrowan absent-mindedly put his hand in his coat pocket, searching for his grandmother's ring.

"But it is not of the Lesser Jewels that I mean to speak," Sir Frederic continued. "The Maglore also excelled at inventing miniature mechanisms of remarkable complexity, which came to be known as *Philosophic Engines*. Originally, they regarded these devices as mere toys, but as their makers waxed more and more ingenious, the engines themselves became more and more powerful. When someone conceived the idea of incorporating into their design such artificial gemstones as I mentioned earlier, the Great Jewels came to be made, and marvels hitherto unsuspected suddenly became possible."

While Marlowe continued to speak, Will glanced listlessly around him. Two long walnut tables occupied the center of the room, and the walls were lined with shelves and cabinets filled with the books and magical artifacts which were the lifetime study of the academic magician. Without thinking what he was doing, Wilrowan put down his teacup, left his chair, and began to wander around the room, examining some of the more interesting objects.

There were scrolls of white snakeskin covered with spells written out in vermillion letters, and marble tablets inscribed with gold. In a glass vessel, Will discovered an aborted mandrake just developing the distinguishing features of an infant Wryneck. Displayed on both long tables he saw golden triangles, divining rods, magic lamps, and a number of curious old talismans stamped with ankhs, solar disks, and ram-headed deities. The Malachim professors examined these objects and noted their qualities in obsessive detail, wrote long monographs on the magical principles each one embodied, but to actually *use* magic on a frequent basis was deemed far too dangerous. In the sterile academic world they inhabited, Theory was everything and Practice was only a way of demonstrating what had already been "proven" by other methods.

"I simplify, of course, rather than try your patience with irrelevant details," Marlowe concluded with heavy irony. "I trust I have not been obscure."

But Will had been listening far more carefully than it might have appeared. He looked up from his inspection of some soap-stone idols. "You said that the Lesser Jewels were used for the projection of thoughts. I suppose you might say, to impose the will of the magician. But not so with the Greater Jewels?"

"With the Great Jewels, the will of the magician is imposed on the mechanism itself. That is how the engine, so remarkably delicate,

is constantly adjusted and attuned." Sir Frederic smiled compla-
cently, warming to his subject. "But more is required than an understanding of the principles involved; these adjustments require a
species of magical sympathy, which can only be established under
the guidance and control of one who is already perfectly attuned to
the device in question. Only our rulers and their nearest heirs are
trained in this way, and each knows only enough of the rudiments of
magic to make use of the Jewel that is in his keeping."

"Do you mean," said Rodaric, "what I have long suspected, that
with greater knowledge it might be possible for someone —say myself or any other ruler you might care to name—to exercise his skill
on one of these little jeweled engines other than his own?"

"He might be rash enough to suppose he could, should a second
engine fall into his hands, but his chances of failure would be very
great, lacking the requisite sympathy. And a failed attempt would
have devastating consequences. That is why colleges like Malachim
are forbidden by law to admit young men of royal blood, and our
rulers are so strongly cautioned against including magicians among
their nearest friends and advisors."

Will raised his eyebrows. "Then it is just as well my days at
Malachim College were so mercifully brief. Had I gone on to take
my degree in Magic, I would never have been permitted my present
commission."

There was another uncomfortable silence, until Sir Frederic
cleared his throat. "As you say. Situated as you are—as the king assures us—so completely in the Royal Confidence, even for you to
form friendships with trained magicians might be viewed as potentially dangerous."

Wilrowan smiled to himself, thinking of those secret apartments
where "Wilobie Culpepper" conducted experiments in alchemy
which sometimes veered dangerously close to experiments in
magic.

Professor Marlowe shifted his attention back to the king. "But we digress. I spoke, a while since, of the Universal Magnetism. Though it exists everywhere, there are exceedingly subtle variations in the magnetism as one travels from place to place, according to the species of metals which lie under the ground and a variety of other factors. Through long proximity, these Philosophic Engines have become attuned. To suddenly remove one of them at any great distance from the site it has occupied for more than a millennium would cause an abrupt repolarization of the internal gemstones, and consequently a massive disruption in the nearby magnetic currents."

"And you were about to explain," said Rodaric, "when Captain Blackheart came in, what was likely to result from such a disruption."

"It might be anything," Doctor Fox said, joining the discussion for the first time. "As the influence of magnetism is universal and as living creatures are most particularly affected—for the fluid of which we speak penetrates the nerves and influences them directly—so a disturbance in the magnetic currents might become apparent in many ways: civil unrest, natural disaster, outbreaks of disease, madness in animals, even accidental mishaps, such as fires and explosions.

"The larger events, such as floods and earthquakes, would tend to occur in the immediate vicinity of the Jewel itself, and the minor mishaps spread out to encompass an area of eighty, ninety, perhaps even a hundred miles. For this reason, if anyone were to rapidly transport the Mountfalcon Jewel out of the country, he would leave so clear a trail of disasters both large and small in his wake, it would be possible to chart his course and possibly overtake him. As no such wave of destruction has appeared, we assume the Chaos Machine is still in the country, or only a very few miles beyond her borders."

Rodaric considered that. "You suspect one of our neighboring monarchs of plotting this theft?"

"That would not necessarily follow," said Sir Frederic. "Even if the Jewel is now just over the border, we have no assurance it will not be removed even further at some later time. Indeed, if I were secretly moving one of these devices, I would make the journey in short stages with lengthy rests in between."

"To what end?"

"Even under ordinary circumstances, fires, floods, and the like do occur, and if one were to plot them on a map, no recognizable pattern would develop. And so, by moving the Jewel gradually over a considerable period of time, I would not only hope to lessen the disruption, but also hope these more commonplace disasters would serve to camouflage the progress of the Jewel from country to country across the continent."

Rodaric frowned. "I hardly see how any of this works to our advantage, if the thieves are careful. Even if the Chaos Machine remains somewhere this side of the border, that is still a considerable territory for us to search, and how are we to find it, much less recover it?"

"No," said Will, "it does work to our advantage. If those who have taken the Jewel are forced to pause often along the way, that allows more time for mistakes, accidents, betrayals—any number of circumstances that might provide a clue to their whereabouts."

"One such clue—" Sir Frederic cleared his throat again. "This is only theoretical, for nothing of the sort has ever happened before. But when the Chaos Machine travels so far from its original location that it ceases to act on its original object—which is to say, the pumps and the other machinery in the iron and tin mines—it may begin to react on other machinery instead."

"The principle question at this time," said Professor Fox, "is how many people to involve in the search. You will need to have eyes and ears everywhere, Your Majesty, both in Mountfalcon and abroad."

"I have a modest system of spies already in place. Most of them dating back to my father's or even my grandfather's time, many of whom I've never even heard from."

"Then pardon me for asking," said Professor Fox, "but do you think it quite advisable to tell these agents—many of them not even personally known to you—that one of the Goblin Jewels is missing?"

Rodaric considered. "I suppose we must tell them that *something* of value was stolen, but I think we may conceal from them what that something actually is. We will say—I hardly know what. No doubt a suitable story will occur to one of us."

Several minutes passed while everyone thought. A log collapsed on the grate in a shower of sparks. A carriage rattled by in the street outside. An idea occurred to Will, which brought a gleam of unholy amusement into his eyes.

"Let us say that the learned professors of Malachim College, in a moment of indiscretion, sought to create a Philosophic Engine of their own, and that this mechanism, recently completed, has mysteriously gone missing."

Sir Frederic stiffened at this suggestion and even Professor Fox looked troubled and shook his head.

But Will continued on, much enamored of his own idea. "It should be something exceedingly dangerous of course, a small but potent engine of destruction, which Your Majesty seeks to recover before it falls into the wrong hands." He thought a few moments longer. "In this way, we may even describe the effects that will reveal its presence."

Rodaric could not repress a smile. "Ingenious," he said. "Though I'd prefer not to slander these excellent gentlemen."

But after an hour spent discussing alternative schemes and rejecting all of them, even Sir Frederic was forced to admit that no other story would fit the situation quite so well.

"It seems we must sacrifice ourselves, my dear Octavio, for the general good," he said with a sigh. He bowed to the king. "Very well,

Your Majesty, we will not object if you adopt this fantastic story of Captain Blackheart's. Let it never be said that a Marlowe hung back when called on to serve his country."

As it was well past eight, the king soon excused himself. Picking up his hat and his ebony walking-stick, motioning Will to follow, he left the room, and proceeded down the broad staircase. But he stopped at the bottom and allowed Wilrowan to catch up to him.

"You will accompany me in the coach," he said quietly. "I have something to say that is for your ears only."

Conscious he had not conducted himself very well up above, Will followed the king out into the blowing snow and then into the coach, flinging himself down on the opposite seat. "I suppose I have offended."

"You haven't offended *me*," Rodaric said calmly. "And I received the impression that you did not offend Professor Fox." He settled himself more comfortably against the green velvet cushions. "But you certainly made an extraordinary effort to annoy Sir Frederic. I wonder why?"

Will shrugged. He was always at his worst when asked to explain himself, since even he was not always perfectly sure of his own motives. "Sir Frederic seemed to expect it."

"And you, of course, were loath to disappoint him." Rodaric shook his head. "That was good of you, Will, though I suspect that Marlowe scarcely appreciated it."

Outside the coach they could hear the driver hitching up the horses. Inside the coach there was a long, moody silence, broken at last by Rodaric. "Did it distress you so much, being expelled from the university?"

"No." Will shifted his position, looked out the window at the falling snowflakes. "Yes. It wasn't for any of the reasons that you might think, not for rioting, whoring, or public drunkenness."

"It could hardly have been the latter," said Rodaric, as the coach finally rumbled into motion.

"They would have forgiven any of those things—which I knew very well. It was for the thing that Fox said: 'incorrect premises and faulty conclusions.' They said I was infecting the other students." Will gritted his teeth. "Let me not do those excellent old gentlemen a grave injustice. They were prepared to be generous, they said they would give me another chance, if I only consented to admit my errors. I would not—could not do it—and there was an end to my days at Malachim College."

"So you sacrificed your prospects for the sake of a principle. However unwise, it was a splendid thing to do. I believe that I am genuinely impressed."

The coach turned a corner. Will continued to gaze out the window, watching the blurred prospect of gas flares and whirling snowflakes as they passed by. "You shouldn't be impressed; I *was* in error. My methods were imprecise, my thinking unclear, and as a result I sacrificed my 'prospects' for the sake of a stupid mistake."

"The fact remains that you were willing to suffer for what you imagined to be the Truth. I feel that I have misjudged you, Wilrowan."

Will twitched uncomfortably, more used to hearing ill of himself than the reverse. Seeing this, Rodaric laughed. But then, remembering what he had originally meant to say, he grew serious again.

"Regarding the Chaos Machine: as I cannot leave the city, you must be the one to pursue any trail my spies or our Malachim friends may chance to uncover. I could not trust anyone else. No, Will, spare me your blushes. You seem to have been chosen for this particular task, but not by me. Let us say that Providence has singled you out." He considered for a moment. "For all that, I don't mean that you should do everything alone, or attempt to be in several places at once. Choose three men, three trustworthy men from the palace guard—you may take any of mine you like—and tell them this tale we have concocted today. They will help you to expand your inquiries beyond the city proper; if a longer journey should be necessary, they can accompany you."

Wilrowan was forced to think. With his lieutenants dead, his choices were limited. He named two of his own men and Nick Brakeburn, and the king gave his approval at once.

"I am sorry if this affects any of your plans, but I wish to be apprised of your whereabouts at all times. Moreover, you must maintain yourself ready to depart the city immediately, should any such leads materialize."

Will nodded gloomily, thinking of Lili's impending visit in the spring. He could hardly cry off, now that he had invited her, and it was going to be embarrassing, once he had Lili in Hawkesbridge, if he had to go running off on a series of unexplained wild-goose chases. The revelations of the day had only served to lend a sense of urgency to the plan he had conceived so impulsively at Brakeburn.

Still, she would not arrive in Hawkesbridge for nine more weeks, and it was even possible the Chaos Machine would be safely back with Rodaric's other treasures long before that. For now, at least, he allowed himself to hope.

So he mustered up a weary smile, tried to look as though he actually enjoyed the prospect of chasing after the damned Jewel on a moment's notice. After all, he had his reputation as a scapegrace adventurer to maintain. "I am naturally at Your Majesty's disposal. In this as in all things."

Book Two

pring had finally arrived in the north, and the skies over Tarnburgh were filled from dawn to dusk with the angular black shadows of migrating waterfowl. At twilight, they settled on the mud
flats outside the city, where the snow-melt created acres of marshland. Even
in the heart of town, one could hear their incessant mournful honking.

On the high peaks to the north and east, the snow never melted—except
during an eruption, when the slopes ran with rivers of liquid fire. But the
mountains were slumbering now, and their flanks were a dazzling white, uncomfortable to look at in the cold spring sunlight. Though days were long,
the air remained biting sharp; at Lindenhoff, coal fires burned in all of the
public rooms.

In those gay, gilded over-heated salons, a semblance of courtly life was returning after a prolonged period of mourning. It began with card parties,
where ladies in flowered silks and quilted satins sat up late playing Whisk,
Ruff, and Honors; and gentlemen in gold-embroidered waistcoats staked
modest fortunes on the fall of a pair of silver dice. Then a gambling fever took
hold, and everyone wagered on everything, from spider races to the probable
color of a newborn foal in the king's stables. There followed a passion for
practical jokes—though of the prettiest, most civilized kind. Eggshells were
filled with confetti and sweet perfumes, then cast by pranksters into crowded
rooms, showering the occupants with tiny pellets of pastel plaster and the

scent of roses. Colored sugar-water replaced brandy in palace decanters, and cross-dressing, combined with a fashion for black velvet masks, yielded many a humorous incident of sexual confusion.

There were midnight picnics by torchlight in the palace gardens by the marble fish ponds. In that northern climate, it was impossible for goldfish to survive under ordinary conditions, so the ponds were heated by a constant supply of the mineral-rich thermal waters, which were blended with the icy snow-melt that came down from the mountains in crystal streams. There was something in the resulting tepid mixture that affected the fish, made them grow to an enormous size, assume strange shapes, and burn through the water like comets in rare and vivid colors: blood-orange, cerulean, magenta, and a peculiarly glowing shade of yellow. In such an inspiring setting, under a silvery arctic moon, was it any wonder that fancy waxed eloquent, and daily the court produced more and more fantastic conceits?

Next came a rage for fortunetelling. Madame Zaphir, the Ouph seeress, who had been relegated to the kitchens a few months earlier to entertain the scullions, was promoted to the drawing room, where she read the white palms of duchesses and examined the dregs at the bottoms of porcelain teacups as fragile as flowers.

Was there, in all of this, no presentiment of disaster? No uneasy sense that something old and wicked and inimical to Man had found its way inside Lindenhoff? If there was, it went unacknowledged. The card parties continued, and the salons were animated night and day by the brittle music of harpsichords and the murmur of discreet laughter.

20

𝕴n the very tallest of the Lindenhoff towers—in a suite of tiny, airless rooms—a dutiful Ys spent much of that spring meeting twice a week with Lord Wittlesbeck, the Master of Ceremonies, there to be instructed in matters of protocol and court etiquette.

Not for Ys the card parties and the light flirtation. She would be queen, and it was up to her to learn the almost dizzying intricacies of a highly ritualistic way of life. "You will," said Lord Wittlesbeck, "carry on your shoulders the weight of a thousand-year-old tradition."

It was a tradition, apparently, that could make even a simple act like drinking afternoon tea as elaborate a ceremony as a coronation.

"Always at the same hour. There can be no room for deviation. The teapot shaped like a silver lion. The macaroons and the almond biscuits arranged on the plate in a rayed pattern. You lift your cup *so*, with the handle between your thumb and middle finger, take the smallest possible sip—"

"But what if I am thirsty?" she interrupted impatiently. "And if I don't want *tea* at all? What if I prefer chocolate, or cinnamon-water, or even sherry?"

"No doubt there will be suitable occasions for indulging those tastes. But not at afternoon tea. Now *as* I was saying, mademoiselle: You will have precisely twenty minutes, after which time you exit the room through the south door, and proceed, with a slow and stately gait, to the west balcony, where—"

As Doctor Purcell had predicted, Ys was dismayed. When she was queen, she was rapidly discovering, her time would no longer be her own. It had all been assigned and parcelled out, restricted by ritual, ordered by custom. At last, she was moved to protest. "But is this how King Jarred lives his life? I don't believe it! Surely the *king* does not live a virtual prisoner in his own palace."

"Indeed he does," said Lord Wittlesbeck primly. "Except for a few hours he spends each evening with his old tutor, an occasional visit to an old friend, that is substantially how he *does* live his life. Though for him, of course, having been born to it, it is all as natural as breathing."

Ys was incredulous, but she was also determined. If Jarred could, she could. She was a hundred times more royal than he was. After all, *her* ancestors had ruled the earth for five thousand years, while his—what were they? They were less than the lackeys that waited on him now.

Yet the hours were long and her heart was weary in those stifling little rooms, crowded with books and rolls of parchment, with maps and diaries and documents so old as to be practically primeval, with chests and cabinets bursting with regalia—most of it pinchbeck and paste, for real jewels were so common at Lindenhoff that only stage props could possibly be magnificent enough for state occasions—and over it all lay the dust, dust, dust.

For these were the Lindenhoff Archives, where the records of births, deaths, marriages, coronations, and christenings had been kept for more than a thousand years. On the walls, between the inevitable golden cupids and arabesques, crowded an immense collection of dim oil paintings in gilded frames, Jarred's ancestors and not a few of her own—dating back to the days when Lindenhoff was a summer palace of the Maglore Empress.

As for Lord Wittlesbeck, he was a little old man, very quick, light, and active, exquisitely attired on all occasions. His fluttering movements, his thin painted eyebrows, the two exceedingly high points of his white wig, lent him a perpetually startled appearance—or perhaps that was only owing to Ys, whose sharp tongue and uncooperative spirit might well keep him in a constant fever of agitation.

When Lord Wittlesbeck recited in his high quivering voice the details of endless court ceremonies— when Ys leafed through the thick old books he placed before her, learning by heart the Order of Precedence, the Order of March—when she listened with growing dismay and contempt to Lord Wittlesbeck's hoary old tales of ambitious courtiers and their social-climbing wives—a claustrophobic panic set in.

Sometimes, Ys closed her eyes and tried not to listen, but the old man continued to buzz in her ear like a particularly annoying gnat, and some of what he said inevitably penetrated.

Even to dress in the morning was going to take hours, as there would be separate women appointed to hand over her shift—her petticoats—her garters—her stockings—each one fiercely protective of her hereditary "privilege."

"Feuds have begun," said Lord Wittlesbeck, "and have lasted for generations, over a single encroachment—a glove in the hands of the wrong noblewoman, a countess who had the temerity to usurp the duties of a royal duchess—and it will be up to you to make certain that nothing of the sort happens again."

"*I?*" said Ys, her eyes flying open. "I look after the whole quarrelsome brood like— like a school-mistress or a nursemaid? Surely *they* will be there to look after *me*?"

"They will be there to enhance your status," replied the Master of Ceremonies, with a lift of his insignificant small nose. "And to enhance their own. Your comfort, your convenience will not matter to them at all—as, indeed, it should not matter to you. You will learn, mademoiselle, that superior minds are above such trifling considerations. Heat, cold, hunger, boredom, thirst—these things are but transitory. But beauty, elegance, the continuation of an ancient tradition—these endure."

Ys stared at him, her eyes growing wide with disbelief. It seemed to her these petty Human monarchs had arranged everything the wrong way around. Yet when she looked at those portraits of the Maglore Empresses up on the wall—when she saw them, with their still pale faces and their cold dark eyes, prisoners inside their stiff, bejeweled, old-fashioned gowns and their monstrous yellow cartwheel ruffs—it seemed as though they must have suffered, too. Why had they done so?

Madame would say that they did what they did for pride, for dignity, above all for Power. But what was the use of Power, Ys wondered, unless it allowed you to make *other* people uncomfortable, to suit your personal convenience?

The discovery of a nest of rats in the Archives eventually drove Ys and Lord Wittlesbeck to a lower chamber, this one more open and airy, and a series of lessons on dancing and deportment.

Yet Ys was no happier now than she had been before. She listened with a mutinous heart and a resentful spirit, as the fussy little man instructed her in the art of the perfect graceful curtsy.

"No, no, no, mademoiselle! The wrists must be held exactly *so*. And as one rises, the head must dip just the slightest—*Mademoiselle Debrûle* are you attending to me at all?"

"No," said Ys, rising straight up. "I am *not* attending."

The skill in question was one she believed she had already mastered. Even Madame Solange, that harshest of critics, had agreed that she did it very prettily. But now it appeared, all these months later, her previous training was quite inadequate. There was not one *single* form of obeisance she was expected to learn. There were *three* basic styles—the nod, the bow, the deep genuflection—and dozens of different variations, each one precisely calculated to the relative ages and titles of the parties involved.

Ys smoothed out the skirts of her new silk gown, made a slight adjustment to the old and valuable rose-point lace fichu covering her shoulders. "When I am King Jarred's queen, everyone will bow and curtsy to *me*. When that day comes, there will be nothing for me to do but respond with a regal inclination of my head."

Lord Wittlesbeck cleared his throat, rocked back on the heels of his tiny pumps, regarded her sternly. "Mademoiselle, there will be a period between the day when your betrothal is officially announced and the day you are wed. During that time, it will be up to you to set an example for others to follow later.

"I know nothing of the customs in Château-Rouge—or in any of the other places mademoiselle may have graced with her presence— but if you will heed my advice, you will pattern your behavior after King Jarred's, which is always impeccable."

Ys bit her lip. She was growing heartily sick of hearing King Jarred's perfections endlessly extolled, and she wondered what she could have possibly done to deserve such a noble *bore* for her future husband.

The lesson over, Ys gathered up her fan, her gloves, her cloak, and pinned on her big, black velvet hat. She left the room in a rush, almost colliding with the king's uncle in the corridor outside.

"Lord Hugo Sackville," she said, with a cold, perfunctory nod, her lessons in courtesy apparently forgotten.

The stout old gentleman leered at her. "Mademoiselle Debrûle. You seem to be quite a fixture at Lindenhoff these days. If I may say so, you are looking particularly delightful this afternoon; I do not think I have seen that gown before."

Ys felt her stomach turn over in disgust. She knew what he was thinking: that she was Jarred's mistress, that her lovely new things had been his gifts, his *payment* for services rendered.

"You may recall, Lord Hugo, that I am but recently out of mourning." And she swept on past him, before he could detain her a moment longer. As much as she disliked them all, as much as she despised every Human in the palace—from the scullions down in the kitchen all the way up to Jarred himself—she held a special contempt for this aging lecher.

She ran down three flights of stairs and climbed into the open carriage that was waiting for her down in the courtyard. She told the Ouph coachman to go slowly, as her head was aching. This was not strictly true: she felt light-headed and more than a little queasy after so many hours in that stifling salon, but it was her back and her legs that ached, a nagging pain that had been with her for days. Yet she was not inclined to confide such intimate details to a mere coachman, so she pleaded a headache. The barouche went out though the palace gate at a slow and stately pace.

Ys closed her eyes, leaned her head back against the padded seat. How she would make them pay—for all the discomforts, all the indignities! *Her* elegant mind was not above considering these "trifling" matters, and she fully intended to be revenged when the time was right.

The carriage swayed as it turned a corner. Feeling somewhat revived by the cold air, Ys opened her eyes and glanced around her. The barouche was crossing a neat little brick-paved square at the center of town. A movement caught her eye, caused her to turn her head. An exceedingly handsome youth in a striped satin waistcoat and a large snowy neckcloth was bowing in her direction. Recognizing him at once, Ys felt a sudden stir of excitement and instructed the driver to pull up his horses immediately.

As the barouche rattled to a halt, the good-looking youngster moved to intercept it. With one hand on the door, he smiled up at Ys. "If the lady permits?"

"Yes, of course," said Ys, suddenly breathless. "Come with me, Zmaj. I've had the most deadly afternoon! It is time that I had some amusing company."

Zmaj opened the door, ascended gracefully, and sat down on the seat beside her. He had lived for a time at the mansion with Ys and Madame, but he was lodged now in rented rooms. It had been almost a month since his last visit, not since Ys abandoned the blacks and greys and whites of half-mourning. With a lift of one dark eyebrow, he took her in: the dashing hat, the dainty gloves embroidered with seed-pearls, the new and elaborate way that she had of wearing her bright golden curls.

Though she had bitterly resented a similar scrutiny on the part of Lord Hugo, she felt a thrill of pleasure at the frank admiration in the Maglore youth's gaze.

Perhaps because Zmaj was so beautiful himself. His skin was so white as to be nearly transparent, his features were chiseled—the shape of his mouth was particularly enchanting—the dark hair curled at the nape of his neck, where it was caught back and held by an immense black bow. Yet for all his prettiness, he was tall and well-made, and whatever he happened to be doing—whether it was walking, or dancing, or sitting, or especially making love—he did with a muscular grace that was peculiarly his own.

But perhaps, Ys cautioned herself as the carriage moved on, she was so enamored just because Zmaj, and his brother Jmel, and his cousin Izek, were the only young Maglore she had ever met.

"Beautiful, but of limited intelligence." That was how Madame Solange described the three boys. "Like too many of our kind they lack certain qualities, qualities which I have labored mightily to instill in you." Ys put a hand to her brow. She was tired of carrying Madame's ideas,

238 ☽· TERESA EDGERTON

Madame's pronouncements, even Madame's voice inside of her head wherever she went.

She tried to make light conversation as the carriage left the town and started down the shady country road leading to the mansion. Though it was Ys who spoke and Zmaj who sat back with a satisfied smile, playing with his coral and tortoise-shell watch fobs, the journey passed swiftly. Just outside the gates, the barouche stopped, and Zmaj descended. He handed Ys down, dismissed the driver with a casual wave, then offered her an arm and escorted her into the house.

They paused in the vaulted entry hall, where Ys hesitated. For some reason, Madame was now discouraging his visits—though an affair between him and Ys had clearly been part of her plan from the very beginning.

Thinking of how prettily Zmaj made love, Ys made up her mind to defy her governess. With a blush and a rapidly beating heart, she offered him her hand, a gesture that might have meant dismissal as easily as invitation. But Zmaj being Zmaj—and every bit as aware of his own beauty as she was—he needed no more encouragement than that.

With careless gallantry, he raised her hand to his lips, kissed first the palm, then the place on her wrist where the blood raced so swiftly beneath the skin. He was just leaning over to kiss the pulse-point at the base of her throat— But a door burst open somewhere above, there were hurried footsteps, and Madame Solange swept majestically down the carved oak staircase, with Ys's Aunt Sophie trailing three steps behind.

Though Zmaj had jumped back at the first opening of the door, though he and Ys were standing decorously at opposite ends of the hall, with a vast stretch of black-and-white floor between them by the time she reached the foot of the stairs, it took Madame but a single comprehensive glance to assess the situation.

"That will do, Zmaj." Her dark eyes moved from one flushed and excited face to the other. "It was good of you to escort Her Highness home, but your presence here is no longer required." And the Maglore youth, without demure, bowed to each of the ladies in turn and quietly left the house.

He was of Imperial Blood, just as Ys was herself. So why, she wondered resentfully, did he allow Madame to speak to him so? *He* was not the one who had spent his entire life under her thumb.

But they all obeyed Madame: Lord Vif, Aunt Sophie, Zmaj and Jmel, and all the other Maglore who had joined them in Tarnburgh—quite as though it were Madame Solange who was the Empress-born, instead of Ys. *"They like taking orders,"* said that intrusive voice in her mind. *"It spares them from thinking too far ahead for themselves."*

"As for you——" It was the real Madame Solange speaking now, in her hard, impatient voice. "You may go upstairs and wait for me there. I have things to say to you, things that are not for the servants to hear or know about."

Ys paused at the foot of the oak staircase. For a moment, she considered what it might cost her if she refused. But then she shrugged. Whatever it was that Madame had to say, there was no point in putting it off. Without a word, she turned on her heel, set one small foot on the first step, and then headed slowly up the stairs.

21

Ys had taken a seat by one of the diamond-paned casement windows in her little sitting room. She had picked up a book and was leafing through the pages, when the door flew open, and in came Madame Solange in a typical rush, followed a moment later by the small plump figure of Aunt Sophie.

"No, keep your seat," Madame said sharply, as the girl made to rise. "Remember who you are, what you are destined to become."

Remembering exactly who she was, Ys rose defiantly to her feet. But then—finding Madame's indignant gaze too much to bear—she merely put down the book and changed her place by the window for a chair on the other side of the room.

Madame's chest heaved inside her burgundy velvet gown; her eyes burned. Like Ys, she was dressed in accordance with her new rôle; strings of pearls were twined in her rich dark hair; the long bodice of her wine-colored gown was trimmed with yards of gold galloon. "You are a very wicked and willful——" she was beginning, when Sophie interrupted her.

"Val, dear, you can't command her to remember her dignity in one breath, and then scold her like a naughty little girl in the next. And really, you know, she does it all very well. You have been with her from the very beginning, have seen her change so gradually—I daresay you are hardly aware that she *has* changed. But I can't tell you how impressed I was when I arrived two days ago." Sophie smiled her gentle, conciliating smile. "Impressed by what you, more than anyone, have accomplished here. She *looks* every inch the Queen of Winterscar and she has so many pretty airs and graces—"

"Unfortunately," said Madame Solange, between her teeth, "the *King* of Winterscar does not appear to think so. Two long months ago, Sophie, he all but pledged to marry her, right here in this very room, yet still the arrangement remains a secret one. I begin to fear that he has no intention of marrying her at all."

Madame moved about the room with her usual impatient step, and (also as usual) the room with its vaulted ceiling and high casements, the entire house with its dozens of rooms and passageways, seemed scarcely adequate to contain her energy. "This girl's failure to secure her position is all the more pitiable, because there is no other female claiming his attention."

"But I do have a rival," Ys protested. She struck what she thought was a demure pose, hands folded, eyes lowered, but her voice was dripping with spite. "The peerless Zelene, so perfect, so flawless, so pure—I can't begin to tell you how difficult it is measuring up to a dead woman."

Madame regarded her with unconcealed contempt. "I *might* believe you were at some disadvantage, were you not in possession of your mother's necklace. Surely that is an advantage that no other woman, living or dead, can hope to match. Though I must say," she added with a cruel smile, "you have been very clumsy in the way that you use it!"

Instinctively, Ys put her hand to her throat, where the double string of stones rested. Even when they were not there, when she was in her bath, or when she took them off before going to bed at night, she could still feel their ominous weight pressing against her flesh. And she was learning to hate the necklace, which more and more seemed to her a poisonous thing, a deadly thing that it was dangerous even to use.

"Until now, you have only been able to arouse and intrigue him, to mesmerize and bedaze his mind. But that's not enough. You are attracting and repulsing him at the same time, which means that your spell remains imperfect. It wouldn't be necessary to blind him with headaches or play tricks with his memory, if your hold on him was complete."

"Now Valentine," said Aunt Sophie, taking one thin, nervous hand between both of hers, speaking in her most soothing voice, "she is still very young. Ys has nothing to match Chimena's experience."

Madame suffered her touch with uncharacteristic patience— though her nostrils flared, and her free hand clenched, and opened, and closed tight again. "Experience means very little. Chimena knew how to do these things instinctively. It almost seemed that the necklace was made for her and she was made for the necklace. Ys is Chimena's daughter, and if she is not so apt for these things as Chimena was, there should still be enough of the mother in the child to teach her the proper use of the stones."

With a sudden movement, Madame waved Sophie away and rounded on Ys with a glance of concentrated venom. "This girl knows very well there is only one way to make Jarred of Winterscar utterly her slave. She must take him into bed with her, demonstrate some of the darker pleasures the necklace can offer—no, Ys, spare me your blushes. You are not the innocent you were three months ago. At least—not if you have been doing your duty with that boy who just left, and with the others."

Ys sat frowning down at her tiny feet, so that no one could see the burning color rise up in her face. "I have been doing—what is required—with Zmaj."

"But not with Jmel? Not with Izek?"

"I have been doing what is required." Ys raised her head with a flash of defiance that ignited and died before the sentence was finished. "Why should it matter which one I have chosen to father my child?"

"It matters," said Madame. Her handsome face had grown harder with the years, the dark eyes brighter, the red lips thinner. It often seemed that her brittle control over her outsize emotions must snap at any moment, but it never had.

"You are not to single out any one of those boys. To do so would give him an inflated idea of his own importance. When you conceive, I want no one to know which one of the three is really responsible."

Madame began to pace as she spoke. The high heels of her satin slippers made sharp little sounds as they hit the hardwood floor. "We don't want any jealous scenes enacted before the king. Which we will have, if Zmaj is encouraged to believe that he has an exclusive claim on you. You don't know these Maglore youths as I do. With all their posturing, their suicidal passion for duelling—it's a wonder our race has survived. And there will be no time to waste on placating Zmaj. You must devote yourself to entrapping King Jarred."

Her brilliant gaze wandered again to Chimena's necklace; she lowered her husky voice almost to a whisper. "You must bewitch him—you must seduce him."

"But I don't want to seduce Jarred," Ys protested. "And why should I? He can't father my children."

"No. But he must believe that he can. He must, when the time is right, believe that he has."

"But not just yet. Even if I conceived tomorrow—I could easily put off marrying Jarred for another six months." Ys left her seat, wandered across the room, and stopped before a large looking-glass in a silver frame, where she was caught and held fascinated by her own reflection.

As with all the other mirrors in the house, the surface had been painted by a Padfoot sorcerer with a spell of confusion, meant to put any Human who entered the room at a distinct disadvantage, a spell to which the Maglore were entirely immune. Again like every other mirror in the house, the frame was ancient; the old dark silver had been cast in an elaborate design of skulls and imps, hearts, and lizards. It made an interesting contrast to her own gilded prettiness.

Pinning a stray curl back into place, Ys was pleased to note that her face was still flawless: the delicate skin firm, the clean-cut bone structure only a little more prominent than it had been ten years ago. By Human standards she looked perhaps seventeen—though in fact she was more than twice that age. As with all her race, she knew that from this point on she would age more and more slowly, until the first deep lines began to appear at or about the age of two hundred. After which, if she chose to live, she would deteriorate faster and faster, and in the space of a few short decades grow so withered and haggard that even her closest friends would fail to recognize her. But many of the Maglore, unwilling to face that rapid descent into old age, chose suicide instead, and made away with themselves, discreetly and quietly, while youth and beauty still remained. Even those who could withstand a few wrinkles, a few grey hairs, rarely waited for a natural death to claim them. All but a very few poisoned themselves with salt, or else swallowed ground glass, before the process of decay was far advanced.

But I may decide that I don't want to do it. The thought came unbidden, rendering Ys almost breathless with her own daring. *I may decide to be like the great Sophronispa, live to three hundred and die in my bed.*

It was a bold idea, not only because it defied custom, but because it involved thinking so many years ahead. Which proved that she *was* more like Madame Solange than she was like the others. *And perhaps someday I shall even surpass her.*

"And what do you suppose you would accomplish by waiting six months? There is more at stake here than whether or not Jarred imagines he has fathered your child." As Madame spoke she crossed the room and came up behind Ys; their eyes met inside the mirror, between the imps, hearts, and skulls. For a moment, Ys froze, wondering if her governess had guessed what she was thinking.

"And once you have married him, you may have to live with him for months or even years. You'd best learn not to be so squeamish where he is concerned. I really don't know why you *should* be squeamish. Surely his appearance is not repulsive?"

"His appearance, no." Ys came back to life with a shudder. "But you've never made love, you've never been mauled by one of these Human creatures. His hands are so hot, and his lips and tongue taste of salt; I grow dizzy and nauseated whenever he kisses me."

Sophie interceded again. "Val, you have only succeeded in frightening poor Ys. Let us leave her alone to think things out for herself. I am sure if we give her the opportunity, she will eventually see how——needful it is that she should do exactly as you say."

Turning away from Ys and the mirror, Madame made a wide, dismissive gesture. "I am weary of trying to reason with her. Either she will do as she is told because she knows it is right——or else I'll be forced to resort to sterner measures."

The Grant was by far the oldest Goblin in the neighborhood. He had been dispensing his quaint old-fashioned cures from a dank basement shop on the outskirts of Tarnburgh for much, much longer than anyone could remember. The skull of a cat was nailed up over his door, and though the faded sign below read: *APOTHECARY * Pills * Potions * Powders & Unguents*, he was the only physician to whom the Padfoots and the Ouphs had access. And indeed, so vast was his knowledge, so practical his advice on every occasion, they wanted no other.

One chilly spring morning, he ushered a visitor into a dark little room at the back of his shop—the room he reserved for his private consultations—and he bade her be seated on a high stool. She was a very young lady, very well dressed, but the Goblin was not deceived. Like all of the Grants and Wrynecks, he possessed a singularly penetrating eye. He possessed, too, information that few Men shared: he not only knew what to look for, he knew there was reason to look.

He took a seat for himself on an elaborately carved sandlewood chair. Lighting a stub of candle inside a green glass bottle, setting it down on the damp stone floor near his feet, he listened most attentively while she described her symptoms: the backache, the nausea, the dizziness.

When Ys had finished, he nodded his head wisely. "I should say, madam, that you are certainly increasing. Pray accept my congratulations. However, you may not wish to announce the fact—to the father or any other interested party—for some little time."

"But why not?" Ys gave him an uneasy glance across the room. There was something about the place that made her skin prickle: dusty bunches of herbs hung drying from the low beamed ceiling; the air was very close and filled with complex odors.

At the same time, she felt a glow of excitement. Madame had told her the Maglore were notoriously infertile, had declared it would take a great many attempts with many different lovers before she conceived, and yet she had accomplished it in three short months.

"I am sorry to say that nine times out of ten nothing comes of this. Excuse me for being so frank, but I must suppose that like most—young ladies, you have been denied certain details regarding conception. No doubt you believe it occurs in Goblins much as it does in Men and the lower animals—but nothing could be farther from the truth!" The Goblin rubbed his hard old hands together as he spoke. "What is growing inside you now is nothing more than a vegetable mass, highly dissimilar to a Human infant. This thing has life, it grows, but it has not yet been—animated—it has not yet quickened. That must occur at a later stage, with another insemination. If and when it does quicken, the fifteen months gestation will truly begin."

Ys felt crushed, and also confused. She struggled to make sense of what he had just told her. "You said—another insemination. But then—is it possible for my child to have *two* fathers?"

The Grant rose from his seat, hobbled across the room to a tall bookshelf, where he took down a large speckled volume bound in toad-skin. "It is *entirely* possible for the child you carry to have two fathers. The principle of Telegony is well-established in the Goblin races—at least among those who bear their children in the usual way.

"Indeed," he added, gesturing toward a large wooden vat near the back of the room, where he appeared to be growing some infant mandrakes, "many believe that it is even to the child's advantage to have more than one father, citing the defects of creatures like myself as evidence that a multiple parentage is eminently desirable."

Ys felt her spirits sink even further. It was possible, then, that Madame was right, that it was actually her duty to take several lovers. She shuddered inwardly—she was in love with Zmaj, and the idea of sleeping with anyone else was simply distasteful.

"But Grants and Wrynecks—they don't have *mothers*." Ys brightened at the thought. "Surely that is why they are less than perfect."

As the Grant returned to his seat, carrying the book with him, the odd articulations of his long limbs were very evident. "As you say." He eased himself down into the low chair again. "While the Padfoots and the Ouphs, enjoying all the supposed benefits of two or more parents, remain inferior. It seems evident that physical beauty is inherited from the mother, and that all other gifts—of intellect, stamina, courage, and so forth—are purely a matter of chance."

Ys felt a rush of relief. "So, if I desire there should be *one* father, one father only?"

"I do not think your child would suffer." The Grant opened the book and began leafing through the pages, which exhaled a strong odor of mildew into the room. "I am firmly convinced that two parents are quite as good as three—and perhaps even better. It is possible, you know, to carry a good thing to excess."

Ys sat staring down at her locked hands for a long time. There was another question that she wanted to ask, but she was finding it extremely difficult. "Is it—is it even remotely possible—that a Human male, if he were included in the process—might play some part in fathering my child?"

A faint smile appeared on the Grant's withered face. "Again you will pardon me for being so frank. You had as well ask if an oak or a rose or a cabbage could impregnate you. Indeed, the chances are slightly better. The organization of the Human animal bears no resemblance to that of a Goblin, whereas a cabbage—"

Turning the volume over, he held it open so that Ys might see the curious old woodcut: *The Anatomy of the Gobline in Cross-Section*. The internal organs *did* bear a certain resemblance to tough old roots, and the child curled up inside the womb appeared to be wrapped in broad, fibrous leaves.

"I should warn you, however, that if you plan to be intimate with a Human male just at this time, there is some slight risk to you and your child."

Ys drew in her breath sharply. Did Madame know? Did she even care? Most likely she *did* know and had dismissed the risk as inconsequential—since it was a risk to Ys and not to herself.

"For which reason," the old Grant continued, as he closed the book, "I would recommend the following precautions—"

With glowing cheeks and a bounding heartbeat, Ys listened carefully to what he proceeded to tell her. It was nasty, it was humiliating—but it was also, she realized, going to be necessary. "Yes," she said breathlessly, when it was finally over, when he had described in full all the degrading details. "I quite comprehend what I must do. But do you tell me he will not know the difference?"

The Grant considered. "That will depend, in part, on whether or not he has a wide experience of the female sex."

Ys began to breathe more naturally. "I think he has not. He is widely known as a man of delicate principles and—and temperate habits." And she hoped, desperately, that this was true, that the boring Jarred was just as noble and upright as everyone thought him.

"Then I do not foresee a problem. And even if he does notice something, he will hardly know what to make of it."

Half an hour later, Ys left the apothecary shop with a small package wrapped up in brown paper and sealed with red wax tucked into the bodice of her gown. As she climbed the short flight of steps to the street, as she entered the hackney coach she had left waiting outside, she was feeling particularly pleased with herself.

Nevertheless, she decided, there was no great hurry to take Jarred of the hot hands and the tedious principles into her bed. *That can wait until my child quickens. And Madame can do and say what she likes in the meantime.*

22

*L*ili woke in the middle of the night to a flicker of golden candlelight and her great-aunt's voice urging her to exert herself. "A message has come. Arise and dress at once."

With an effort—for her limbs felt heavy and her mind was still drugged with sleep—Lili sat up. Though the hour was late, Allora stood by the bed fully clothed, with a waxen taper burning in her hand. "Is somebody ill?"

"Not ill, no. But certain arrangements have been made, and it would be awkward to remake them." Allora spoke in a low, urgent voice. "If we wait until your father wakes, until the whole house is stirring, there could be a delay. Make haste, Lilliana."

Reluctantly, Lili left her warm bed, put her bare feet down on the icy floor. "Before Papa wakes? But we can't take the—"

"Our friends have sent the same coach and driver that we used before. Dress now, and we'll speak of this later. It would be shocking to keep the horses standing on a night like this."

"Yes, very well." Lili crossed the floor to the wash-stand, tipped cold water into the basin. While she washed her hands and face, drew a comb through her tangled chestnut curls, her aunt played lady's maid, laying out clothes on the bed.

With Allora's assistance, Lili dressed swiftly, then followed the old woman downstairs to the waiting coach. As soon as they took their seats inside and closed the door, the berlin lurched into motion.

Lili swallowed hard. This early rising, followed by what promised to be a long ride on an empty stomach—already she felt queasy. "You promised to explain."

"So I did." Allora was busy for a moment, lighting a brass lantern and placing it on the floor at her feet. She drew the black moiré silk curtains over the windows, shutting out the light of the carriage lamps. "Something has happened. Although we are not yet certain, you *may* be called on to play an important rôle. For that reason, you are to enter into your full initiation as a Specularii magician tonight."

"Tonight?" Lili frowned at her aunt across the coach. "But—do you think I am ready?"

"My dear child, you are far, far beyond what I was when I was first initiated. We have only delayed this long because I, as your preceptor, hoped you might eventually come to this with heart and loyalties less divided than they are now."

Which of course meant Wilrowan, Lili thought miserably as she settled back in her seat. All of Allora's doubts, all of her fears for Lili's future, always revolved around Will. That was why Lili had yet to mention his plan, to tell her aunt she had agreed to visit him in the spring. Keeping the truth from Allora was a new and uncomfortable thing—though she was certainly practiced enough at lying to Will.

A life of conscious duplicity, that's what I lead, Lili thought guiltily, as she slid her icy cold hands into her squirrel-skin muff.

Even in a marriage of convenience, there ought to be trust between a husband and wife. Yet the secrets kept piling up like a wall between them. More than a month had passed since Will's hasty departure, and not a word of explanation had arrived, though he had

sent her a bottle of scent and a pretty ivory fan. It was an apology
for something, as she was able to gather from his nearly illegible
note, but an apology for what? It was not like Will to makes excuses
for his infidelities.

She remembered one of his most notorious misdeeds, in his days
as a City Guardsman: how he had dressed up as a highwayman and
abducted one of his mistresses out of her own carriage, right under
the nose of her rich and elderly spouse. And how the scheme had
succeeded, allowing Will to spend a few days alone with the lady—
except that he was later found out, when one of the footmen identified him. The scandal had been enormous. Yet Will had arrived one
day at Brakeburn Hall, long before the talk died down, and never a
shamefaced look or a hint of contrition.

Well, why should there be? Wilrowan had never deceived her
about the life he led, had never pretended he would allow their marriage to curtail his amusements. And still Lili had consented to be his
wife. She sighed and closed her eyes, picturing in her mind that day
more than six years ago.

*"I begin to think perhaps I should marry you, Mr. Blackheart," Lili had
said. "Indeed, my father assures me I must either do so, or else resign myself to
utter disgrace. But you——can you really bear the idea of marrying so young?"*

*"So young?" Will laughed softly. "I am, I believe, some twelve or
thirteen months older than you are. If you can sustain the shock of so early
a marriage, I feel tolerably certain I can do the same."*

*"But I am a woman," she answered with a faint smile. "Girls do sometimes
marry at my age or a little older. Though indeed, I've often wondered if I
would marry at all. That is, I wondered if I would have the opportunity. You
understand, I have no objection to the idea of matrimony, and have often
thought I should like to be the mother of a large family. But for you——you
are still a student. I don't see how a wife could possibly add to your comfort;
on the contrary, I think she would prove a dreadful inconvenience."*

"Believe me, Miss Brakeburn, despite any chivalrous inclinations I might have—based on the insupportable position I seem to have placed you in—I couldn't possibly be induced to sue for your hand if I thought you would inconvenience me in any way. I'm not in the habit of allowing myself to be inconvenienced, and I have no intention, after we are married, of altering my behavior in the least."

Lili drew in her breath. "That's honest, anyway!"

"It's as well to be honest," said Will, little suspecting the irony, for he and Lili were both very far at that time from guessing Lord Brakeburn's deception. "It could hardly lead to your happiness or my own if our marriage were based on a lie.

"I don't mean," he added earnestly, "that I would treat you with anything less than respect, or allow others to regard you as a scorned or neglected wife. It's not possible for us to live together now, but I would visit you, you would visit me—as soon as I move into quarters where you could visit. And I would certainly hope our—meetings would be friendly enough that a family would eventually result."

He took her hand in both of his and clasped it warmly. "I believe you are, in all respects, exactly the sort of woman I would wish to be the mother of my children. Much better than I deserve, really. And though the idea of marrying, just at this time, was not immediately appealing, I can assure you our situation is one to which I am now entirely reconciled—providing, that is, you do me the honor of becoming my wife."

Lili sighed. "I wish my Aunt Allora were here to advise me." All the stress and all the pressure of the last few days was beginning to tell on her. She was tired of listening to Lord Brakeburn rant, and she had not slept at all the night before. If she said "yes" now, it would all be settled and she could be comfortable again.

"Then yes, Mr. Blackheart," Lili had finally agreed. "Yes, I will marry you."

There was a dip in the road and a violent jolt of the coach, bringing Lili back to a sudden sense of her present surroundings. Had she been sleeping? Or merely absorbed in memories of the past? How long had it been since they left home? It felt like hours.

She reached out to move aside one of the black moiré curtains, hoping to recognize some landmark, but Allora stopped her. "No, child, leave it be."

So—she was not to know where she was going. Once again Lili was uncomfortably reminded that the interior of the berlin, lined as it was with black leather, curtained in black silk, bore an unfortunate resemblance to the interior of a coffin. She suddenly felt oppressed, as though the walls were too close and the coach too full of shadows.

"You are very quiet, Lilliana. And you appear—melancholy. Do not tell me you have wasted this journey thinking about that graceless husband of yours!"

"And if I have? Isn't this an appropriate time for me to be thinking over my entire life up until now?"

Allora opened her mouth to speak, but how she might have answered was to remain a mystery. Just then the berlin rattled to a halt, and both women sat up very straight, exchanging a glance of bright expectation. There came a sound of voices outside: two deep ones, unknown to Lili, and the voice of the driver.

"We have arrived." Allora began to gather up her things: her muff, her cane, her gloves, the lantern. She gave Lili a keen look across the coach. "You will not mind if I abandon you for a time?" Lili shook her head.

"Then stay here until someone calls you." Even as she spoke these last few words, the old woman pushed the door open and slipped through the gap. Closing the door sharply behind her, she left Lili to wait alone in the dark.

As Allora disappeared from sight, Lili heard a spirited discussion start up outside the coach. More than once, she thought she heard her aunt raise her voice as if in protest, but it was impossible to distinguish any of the words. At last the sounds of debate fell to a dull murmur.

She was just nodding off to sleep when the door flew open, and a glare of torchlight dazzled her eyes. "Come, Lilliana, your hour is approaching."

Wide awake now, Lili obediently stepped out into the torchlight. Shivering a little in the pre-dawn chill, she wrapped her cloak more closely around her.

She saw that the berlin had stopped at the edge of a broad grassy field, surrounded on three sides by shrubs and willows. Behind the trees, only partially concealed by them, was the faint outline of a large country house, and somewhere off in the darkness Lili thought she heard the sound of running water. About thirty feet to her right, there was a white marble folly, shining ghostly pale in the faint moonlight.

At first, she had difficulty finding her aunt. Allora had retreated to a short distance, and when Lili finally located her she was standing encircled by five mysterious figures. Concealed behind masks of beaten gold, hidden under long white wigs and black satin dominos, each unknown magician held a lighted torch in one black-gloved hand.

Lili went suddenly weak in the knees. Up until now, she had either been dozing or thinking of Will, but these ominous disguises of jackels, lions, and rams, this evidence of deliberate mystification, finally impressed her with the serious nature of her strange journey, of the wonderful and possibly terrible events that were about to unfold.

"You may approach, Lilliana."

As she advanced, the circle opened up and Allora reached out, drawing Lili into the center with her. As the entire group began to move in the direction of the folly, Lili looked down at her great-aunt, surprised by the old woman's unusual agitation, by the nervous clasping and unclasping of one thin hand on the ivory head of her cane.

"Aunt, are you well?"

"I am perfectly well. It is only—"Allora hesitated. "It is only, dear child, that they mean to initiate you at a higher level than I had anticipated. This means the tests you must pass will be a little more difficult, a little more dangerous—but there is not a doubt in my mind that you will meet the challenge."

By now they had entered the confines of the folly, were moving within a broken circle of cracked marble columns. At the center of the "ruin" a great white slab had been pried up out of the ground and moved to one side, leaving a deep gash in the earth. As Lili drew nearer, she saw that a circular staircase of white stone had been built into the sides of the pit, a stair which appeared to lead down and down, into the depths below.

Quite suddenly, Allora was no longer there at her side. At the same moment, the masked figures at the front and to both sides of Lili disappeared as well. Slightly dazed by this abrupt defection, wondering how they had all contrived to move away so quickly, Lili stood alone among the marble pillars. Alone, until a quiet voice commanded her to turn around, and doing so, she found herself facing a single masked man.

He was disguised as the rest were, yet there was something familiar about the dark grey eyes behind the sinister golden mask, about the thin straight figure under the black satin cloak. When he spoke again, she knew his voice.

It was Sir Bastian Mather, only just recovered from his long illness, and still, for all that he held himself so carefully erect, bound to be very weak. Lili felt a rush of gratitude, knowing what it must have cost the old gentleman to be there with her on this important night.

"Lilliana," he said quietly, "this is a solemn moment. You face a tremendous ordeal, one from which you cannot possibly emerge unchanged. I would be deceiving you if I did not tell you there is considerable danger, and that none of us—no, not even your aunt—can or will aid you at your moment of greatest peril. I have also to tell you that not all who enter the Temple of the Mysteries survive the experience. Yet even so far as you have come to arrive at this moment, you have still a choice. Will you decide to go immediately from this place, or will you hazard your life by entering the underground temple?"

"Sir, you tell me nothing that I have not known for years," Lili answered steadily. But hearing the familiar cautions spoken in this strange place, her peril seemed far more real than it ever had before.

She felt her mouth go dry. Well—and so she might die here. She might also die another day of a perfectly ordinary accident or a perfectly ordinary complaint. At least if she died tonight, it would not be for some trivial cause.

"I will not lie to you," she went on, "and say that I am not afraid—I believe I am terrified. But for all that, I am no less prepared, no less eager to confront this danger."

"Then, as you are resolved—you have already taken various oaths of silence, and if you survive your ordeal tonight you will be called on to make a most solemn vow. But in the meantime, I would ask you to swear again: If, for any reason, you should walk away from this place not as a Specularii magician, you will still preserve perfect secrecy in regard to the events of this night."

He held out his gloved right hand, the palm facing her, and Lili put her own palm to it. She knew the ritual; it had been enacted and reenacted at every stage of her training. "I do so swear, by the blood of the last Maglore Empress, by the glorious deaths of all those who were martyred in the cause of Human freedom, by the deeds of those who struggled for knowledge in the dark years of our ignorance."

Sir Bastian stepped aside and gestured toward the gleaming white staircase leading down into the earth. "The way is before you, Lilliana. I wish you good fortune on your journey."

By the second turning of the stairs, the light had entirely disappeared. Lili was forced to feel her way cautiously, one step at a time, her fingers brushing against the rough earthen wall.

Down and still down she went, circle upon circle, until at last there came a time when there were no more stairs, when there was no wall to guide her—there was only a vast darkness, stretching out endlessly on three sides, leaving Lili with no idea which direction she was expected to move.

Then an invisible hand reached out and took one of hers in a firm, masculine clasp.

"Don't be alarmed, Mrs. Blackheart. I have been sent here to guide your steps for a time." The voice was deep and sonorous, completely unfamiliar.

"I—do not know you, sir?"

"We have never met. Nor will you be permitted to see my face or learn my name until after the ceremony. Nevertheless, I hope you will trust me and follow my instructions."

Lili nodded, without thinking how useless the gesture was in total darkness. "I have been brought here, sir, by those I trust. I'm perfectly willing to place myself in your hands."

His grip tightened ever so slightly, and she felt herself being pulled gently forward. "Then permit me to lead the way. Do not fear that you will stumble; I will warn you of anything that might trip you up."

Some ten or twelve steps later, they entered a narrow passageway. Lili's skirts brushed up against something on the left-hand side;

her unknown escort moved closer on the right. "Pardon me, if I am about to tell you things you already know, to ask you questions you have already answered. I can assure you that none of this is done in vain, that there is a purpose in everything."

"Yes, sir," Lili answered calmly. These repetitions had been a feature of her magical education from the beginning; she understood that those who instructed her were required to test her resolve again and again.

"I will begin by acquainting you with the history of the Specularii—but Mrs. Blackheart, I caution you now to watch your step. We are about to descend another long staircase and the steps are treacherous."

As he spoke, Lili felt a damp chill rise up through the soles of her shoes; a strong odor of wet earth assaulted her nostrils. The steps, however, were broad and shallow if a little slick. By moving slowly and carefully she was able to descend safely, at the same time listening attentively to what he was telling her.

"In the last evil years of the Maglore Empire, many secret societies came into being. Their purpose was the education and advancement of the Human race, which until that time had not only been slaves but had been kept by their Goblin masters in a state of the most abject and degrading ignorance. How the founders of those secret societies—of which some hold the Specularii to be the most ancient—were first able to acquire the knowledge they would subsequently pass on to others—what shifts they were forced into, what dangers they were required to face, in order to gain even such simple skills as every schoolroom child is taught today—all that is a story for another time. It is enough to say that had they been discovered, had there been even a suspicion of what they were about, they would have been punished with a swift but terrible death."

By now, Lili and her escort had reached the foot of the second staircase; she thought they must be at a level far below that of any ordinary cellar. Setting off at a brisker pace, they moved down what felt like another narrow passage.

From time to time, a breath of colder or of warmer air told Lili she was passing an intersecting corridor, either ascending or descending. From time to time, she and her escort turned into one of these intersecting corridors, and she felt the floor rise up or tilt downward beneath her feet. She began to marvel at the size and the complexity of what seemed to her a great maze under the earth.

All this time, the deep voice continued to speak in her ear: "The complete overthrow of the Maglore Empire became the ultimate goal of these secret societies, yet they bided their time. The Empress Sophronispa had ruled for nearly three hundred years and was generally regarded as having long outlived her allotted life-span—for she had not suicided at the usual age and lived on to a state of advanced decrepitude. Indeed, her nearest relations, her logical heirs, had all reached the Age of Suicide and effectively removed themselves. By the time Sophronispa finally died of natural causes, there was considerable uncertainty about who would succeed her. In the confusion that followed, Humanity recognized an opportunity that had not existed in five thousand years. The result was revolt and mass insurrection.

"In the years of revolution and reform that followed, the Specularii took an open and active part. Many of the precepts we live by today originated in debates inside Specularii lodges. Yet after almost a century of recognized service to Mankind, it was decided the time had come to play a less prominent rôle and to assume once more the cloak of secrecy."

Lili felt a slight pressure on her arm, turning her gently to the left. It felt increasingly strange to be walking so close to this unknown man. There was something curiously intimate in the touch of his hand, the sound of his voice speaking in the darkness. And despite—or perhaps *because* of the fact she could not see him, Lili was keenly aware of his physical presence. In the absence of sight, her other senses had become wonderfully sharp. By the direction of his voice, she knew he must be very tall; because his hand was so large and firm, she imagined he must be powerfully built. He did not wear scent as many men did, but there *was* a distinct aroma, as of ink and chalk, lye soap and tallow candles.

"There were two principal reasons why the Specularii magicians chose to shroud themselves in secrecy. Our vast influence terrified us. We had been instrumental in bringing down one Empire and creating a new civilization in its place; we foresaw a time when that new civilization might mirror the old one, with ourselves as the new Maglore. Only by operating outside the structure of power, only by humbling ourselves and accepting the limitations of operating in obscurity, could we hope to keep our motives pure.

"And though it was widely believed the Maglore had all been exterminated, there were those among us who believed otherwise. The Maglore were too cunning, too wise in the ways of dark sorcery, and of course, they too nearly resembled Men. Some few of them must have escaped the general slaughter, some few of them must still exist, either hidden away completely or else passing themselves off as Men and Women. And if they did exist, the time must eventually come when they would attempt to rise again in power. Their first act in doing so would undoubtedly be a concerted effort to destroy those who had so nearly destroyed them. As visible as we were at the time, we felt we made too easy a target. And so—as the Maglore were hidden, we too would be hidden. What they could accomplish by secrecy, subtlety, disguise, we could accomplish by the same means.

"I think, Mrs. Blackheart, by this time you must be very weary of hearing me speak."

"Not at all," said Lili. "I find what you tell me most illuminating."

"Nevertheless, I will attempt to be more concise." They had

turned into another corridor, where Lili could hear the roar and hurry of some subterranean river not far in the distance.

"Over the years, we acquired another purpose. Our civilization was stagnating. No more than anyone else did we desire rapid change, the destruction of the delicate balance we had helped to create. But rational change, gradual change—this we felt was essential. As Society was so resistant to new ideas, so cruel to free-thinkers, *we* must be kind to them. We became the secret guardians to all men of great ideas and noble purposes. Wherever such men are known to exist, there are Specularii near at hand to guide and protect them, though they seldom if ever suspect our presence. Alas, we cannot always protect them from the harsh chances of this world. In the case of the King of Rijxland, for instance, we could not prevent his descent into madness. I might recite to you a long list of our successes and failures, but I trust I have already said enough for you to understand the goals of our society."

"Indeed, sir, you have," said Lili. "And more clearly than they have ever been explained before."

His grip on her hand tightened. "Do you find that you are still determined to dedicate the rest of your life to serving those very goals and purposes?"

"I am more determined than ever."

"It is well," he said, bringing their progress to a sudden halt, "for we have reached the first stage of your ordeal." He released her hand. "If you will turn to your right, you will discover a niche in the wall. Inside that niche is a drinking vessel. Before we proceed any further, you must pick up that vessel and drink the contents."

Lili turned and groped in the darkness; her hands brushed against cold stone, then found emptiness. A moment later, her fingers closed around the stem of a cold metal goblet. As she lifted the cup to her lips, she could not resist taking a cautious sniff.

Wine, she decided, but also something more. The draught was

bitter and slightly salty. No sooner had she swallowed it than a queer drowsy warmth began to spread through her veins. She put down the cup, turned, reached for the hand of her guide. But as their fingers touched, Lili gasped and drew back.

That brief contact had caused a thrill to pass through her like a shock, *a shock that made her aware of every inch of her own skin, of every nerve-ending.* At the same time, she had been intensely aware of him, his powerful body, his masculine solidity—aware, too, that he had shared in everything she was feeling. She knew if she allowed herself to touch him again, it would be an act more intimate than anything she had ever shared with Wilrowan.

"You have nothing to fear, Mrs. Blackheart. I am aware of your present condition and will not take advantage. It is necessary for me to hold your hand a little longer, but I can assure you there will be nothing worse than that between us."

Lili swallowed hard. This was very like the moment when she had been obliged to trust Sir Bastian and go up to his room at the tavern.

"I beg your pardon. I was merely—startled." She forced herself to take his hand again. This time the shock was less, but her pulse leaped, the sweat started out on her skin, and it seemed as though she could not possibly get enough air into her lungs.

"Breathe as I breathe," he said. "Do not be afraid. Match your breaths to mine, and regulate your pulse in the same way." He adjusted her grip so her fingers were wrapped around his wrist, so she could feel the ebb and flow of blood under his skin. "You have done this thing many times before."

Yes, she had done it, when her patients were weak, when their spirits were failing, in order to keep them alive. But never before with a strong and virile man, standing in the dark. Yet, if she did not do this, she knew she was the one who was going to be sick, who was about to fall into a deadly swoon. Reluctantly, she did as he told her. Focusing her mind, she took a long, slow, deep breath. *She drew in the* pneuma, *which was the breath of the cosmos, and sent it coursing through her body to purify the blood.*

"If you are feeling better now, we will proceed." He did not wait for Lili to answer; linked as they were, he knew as well as she did that the effects of whatever drug or poison had been in the cup were under control.

As Lili and her escort moved down the corridor, the sound and scent of running water increased. A moment later, their footsteps rang hollow over wooden planks; she realized they were crossing a bridge over the underground river.

When they stopped on the other side, he spoke in her ear. "We are now entering the innermost regions of the Temple of Mysteries. From this point on, there is no turning back. I urge you, Lilliana, to follow my directions exactly." He spoke roughly, hoarsely. Nor did Lili fail to notice how he had abandoned the polite "Mrs. Blackheart" for her given name.

She thought that he must be trying to frighten her, that it was another test. She forced herself to answer confidently. "I have followed your instructions so far, sir. I am happy to continue doing so."

"That is just as well," he said, leading her forward again. "For I tell you now that your very life depends on it."

23

It seemed to Lili that she must have been walking for many miles. Thanks to the draught she had swallowed, the exalting warmth running through her veins, she was far from weary, but the time she had spent under the ground seemed to stretch back days, weeks, even years, into some immeasurable past.

"Here I take leave of you," said her escort, coming to a halt. "But I will tell you what you must do and you must listen very carefully. A wrong step or a wrong turn could be fatal. Twelve steps from the place where we stand, this corridor opens on another. You will take the right-hand turning and proceed for thirty paces more. At that time you will find yourself at the junction of two corridors. Turn to your left and walk for one hundred and thirteen paces, counting the numbers backward. Can you tell these instructions back to me?"

"I believe I can," said Lili, and repeated them as she remembered them.

"Very good," said her invisible guide. "When you have done all this, you will find yourself facing a door. Knock three times on that door and wait for an answer."

Suddenly, his hand was no longer there; Lili could hear his rapid footsteps moving away. She felt oddly bereft, though she had known him such a very short time. She wondered who he was, if they would ever meet again.

Lili turned her thoughts back to the task at hand. She must remember the numbers: 12, 30, 113. Was there some sort of significance? No, she must not think about that, she must concentrate on what she must do, mind her steps very carefully, as she had been warned that a false one might prove fatal.

She took twelve slow, measured paces, turned to her right, and began to count again. After another thirty steps, a draft of cold air indicated she had reached the cross corridor. Turning away from the draft, she started to count backward, starting at one hundred and thirteen.

As she moved slowly forward, a great wind came sweeping down the dark passage, nearly knocking her off her feet. The wind became a tempest, shrieking and tearing at her clothes, swirling around her on all sides, until she felt that she stood at the heart of a hurricane. It became more and more difficult for Lili to concentrate, harder and harder not to lose count. But she was determined. The Centrifugal Wind continued to roar in her ears, to buffet her on all sides.

"Three, two, one," she shouted above the blast. There was a sudden silence; the tempest died away. Lili realized that she was drenched in cold sweat and her hands were trembling.

Reaching out with her left hand, she felt the grain of a rough wooden panel. Raising her fist, she rapped three times. There was no answer at first, except that a dim light began to grow in the inky blackness behind her, as if someone slowly uncovered a dark lantern.

<*Look back the way that you have come.*> The words seemed to create themselves out of the increasingly bright air; they had no apparent source, though somehow Lili had the impression of a woman's voice, high and sweet.

Obediently, she turned, gave a gasp of surprise. She was not in an underground tunnel, but in a vast cavern. Two short steps from the place where she stood there was a wide chasm, a deep cleft in the floor of the cave, cutting straight across the path she had just travelled.

And the depths were unfathomable. Had she fallen, she might well be falling still.

I should *have fallen,* thought Lili. It would have been impossible for her to step across so great a distance. But how on earth had she managed to reach this place without walking on—nothing? The question was still burning in her brain when the light went suddenly out, leaving Lili once more in impenetrable darkness.

The disembodied voice spoke again. <*Lilliana.*> Lili turned away from the chasm. <*That is right, Lilliana. The door is before you. Do not hesitate to enter the Inner Sanctum.*>

Lili reached out with both hands, searching for a knob or a handle. When she found neither, she pushed on the wooden panel, first lightly, then with all her strength. The door would not budge.

<*Why do you wait?*>

"I wait because the door will not open."

<*That is no reason. If the door will not open to let you pass, you must simply pass through the door.*>

"I—but how am I to do that?" Lili was willing, but uncertain how to proceed.

<*You have just walked unaided across a great gulf of air, escaping what should have been certain death. You must not ask how to pass through solid wood, you must simply do it.*>

"Yes, I see." And it was true. Though later Lili would search her mind in vain for the means to accomplish this, for now the way seemed perfectly clear. Squaring her shoulders and stepping confidently forward, she moved right through the oak panel and into the chamber beyond.

*   *   *

She stood inside a great eight-sided tomb. In niches all around the vault there were iron torches, each one producing a blue flame, each one filling the air with a thick, faintly sweet odor. Was it naphtha? Lili wondered. The walls were covered with inscriptions, and a long line of empty marble catafalques stretched before her—empty, that is, except for one, where a body lay on the white marble slab draped in a veil of thin yellow silk. With a deep sense of dread weighting her footsteps, Lili moved in that direction.

With trembling hands, she raised the veil, half expecting to see her own face. It was not her own face, it was Wilrowan's: cold, still, and pale. She let out a cry of pure horror, and shrank back, covering her eyes with her hands.

But it is only a wax effigy—it must be. Again Lili forced herself to look. The face changed—it melted and reformed itself in another likeness: Lili's father. Then, in swift succession, it became Allora—Sir Bastian—Dionee—Lili's cousin Nick.

Was this a vision, a premonition? Were all these people soon to die? *No, it can't be,* something inside her insisted stubbornly. *But it may be a sign for me to interpret. What does it mean?*

"I must let the past bury the past. I must be prepared to enter into a new life."

<That is correct,> said the same sweet voice that had spoken outside the door. <And as you have gained that much wisdom, Lilliana—answer me now and answer me truly: Through what four agencies does the Creator manifest the Universe?>

Taken for a moment by surprise, Lili hesitated. Then she remembered the lessons that Allora had taught her. "Through Spirit, Matter, Motion, and Rest."

<And what is Time's Trinity?>

"Past, Present, and Future," Lili recited. "But there is a fourth mystery that will only be revealed in the Final Days."

<*Of what four elements does the body consist? Of how many elements the soul?*>

Lili began to feel more confident. "The body is made of four elements: Spirit, Flesh, Bone, and Humor. The soul is made up of three: Passion, Desire, and Reason."

There were more questions, growing more and more difficult, until at last, after a long pause:

<*Pass on to the next stage*> said the voice, and part of one wall seemed to melt away, letting in a sudden blaze of yellow firelight.

There must be some mistake, thought Lili, as she stumbled through the gap in the wall and into the brilliant chamber beyond. It was an ordinary room, lit by dozens of candles— at least, it seemed like an ordinary room, until one remembered that it was not located in an ordinary house upon the earth, but was situated hundreds of feet under the ground. There were several chairs and tables, a sofa upholstered in crimson velvet, a painted screen. Occupying that room, gathered in sociable-looking groups by the sofa and the fireplace, were a number of perfectly ordinary-looking people.

Lili blinked. It was like blundering into some formal gathering without an invitation. It was like—it was *very* like a dinner party, or some equally mundane occasion.

Whatever the occasion, it seemed that Lili was the guest of honor. Her Aunt Allora detached herself from one of the groups, and everyone else turned in Lili's direction with smiles and greetings. "You have done well to come so far," said Allora, standing on tiptoe to brush a kiss on Lili's cheek. "You have passed through even greater dangers than you know, and the best part is yet before you.

"But in the meantime," she added, "allow me to present—" and Allora went on to name a great many names. Feeling very much as though she had wandered into some bizarre dream, Lili caught only a few. "—Sir Bastian, you already know. But you will be pleased to be made acquainted, I know—with Miss Chloe Hunt, Mr. Horace Powers-Payne—and especially Sir Frederic Tregaron-Marlowe."

Sir Frederic was a stern, stout, professorial old gentleman, who bowed coldly. "Doubtless, Mrs. Blackheart, you have many questions, but the time for you to ask or for us to answer them is not yet. Doubtless, too, you are famished, and that will be attended to shortly. For now, we congratulate you on your courage."

There was a flutter of excitement among the younger women. Moving across the room, Sir Frederic lifted a purple velvet drapery along one wall, revealing an open door on the other side. "I will leave you, now, in the hands of these young ladies. Under Miss Hunt's direction, they will prepare you for the ceremony. We will meet again presently." He stepped through the door, and Allora and all of the men followed him out of the room.

The young women swarmed around Lili, exclaiming how tired she looked, offering to help her to bathe, to dress before the ceremony. *But how very odd—they are treating me just like a bride,* she thought, remembering a young cousin's wedding two years before.

Still feeling dazed, she yielded to their ministrations. Chatting among themselves, they removed her cloak, her muff, and her shoes. Miss Chloe Hunt was the one who unhooked her gown. Someone moved the painted screen and a large marble bathtub was waiting on the other side. Lili blushed at the thought of bathing before so many people, but the young ladies were determined. Before she knew it, they had stripped off her clothes, were ruthlessly pulling the hairpins out of her hair —then she was dressed in a coarse linen bathing gown, and seated in the water.

The water was tepid, but rose petals floated on the surface, and someone handed her an enormous wedge of rose-scented soap. Lili would have been glad to sit and soak after she bathed, but the others were already urging her out of the water, admonishing her to make haste, make haste—

She climbed out of the tub, dried herself under the gown with a thick white towel. She had little time to inspect the fresh garments she was expected to put on, because her attendants were already hurrying her into them.

But when they had finished dressing her, Miss Hunt took Lili by the hand, leading her over to a long mirror. Lili stared into the glass, pleased and amazed at her own reflection. *How nice I look. If Wilrowan could see me—*

The dress was made of ivory silk, very old and fragile, embroidered all over with silver threads; it fit so well that it might have been made for her. The full skirt divided in front to show a petticoat made of creamy brocade, and there were puffed sleeves ending just above the elbow in ruffles of antique lace. No corset had been provided, but the low-cut bodice was heavily boned and it laced in front with silver ribbons.

"Now you must eat and drink to give yourself strength," said a thin blonde girl. She brought Lili a six-sided brass plate filled with tiny cakes, and a golden goblet on a short stem set with rough emeralds.

Lili took one of the cakes, ate a few bites, then realized she was not really hungry. Yet she forced herself to eat the rest. Her hands were beginning to shake with exhaustion, and she could only hope the cakes, and whatever the cup contained, would provide the strength she needed. She raised the goblet and tasted the contents.

It was not the same potion as before, but it was equally efficacious. The blood raced in her veins. Lili felt light-headed and yet strangely alert at the same time.

As the goblet was carried away, Miss Hunt stepped forward and draped a gauzy veil over Lili's head and shoulders. "I am to remind you that it is necessary to give oneself entirely to the mysteries; it is an act of surrender, like the act of love.

"But I need not explain that to *you*," she added with an arch smile. "You are a married woman and must know what I mean."

But I don't *know,* thought Lili. As one in a dream, she moved past the purple drapery, through the open door, and up a long, white, circular staircase, like the inside of a nautilus shell. For all the nights she and Wilrowan had spent together, Lili had never once lost herself in the act or in him. She had always been too self-conscious, too guarded, and whenever she seemed in danger of feeling too much, she had panicked and drawn back.

At the top of the stairs there was a long gallery paved in a dark marble glowing with mysterious patterns. "Surrender"—the word echoed at the back of her mind as Lili moved down the gallery. Was that what had been missing all of these years? Was it her failure to give herself up, to exist entirely in the moment and in the experience, was that the reason she always felt dissatisfied after—why Will looked elsewhere for his amusement? Yet if she had ever gone to him with her heart pounding as it was now, with the drugged wine singing in her veins, it might have been very different.

By now, she was nearing a pair of immense bronze doors: doors etched in silver with numbers, symbols, and ancient pictographs. At her approach, the doors swung slowly open.

When she entered the vaulted chamber on the other side, there was a faint sounding of hidden trumpets and brassy cymbals. A crowd of well-dressed people had assembled within, forming an aisle down the center of the room. As Lili drew near, Sir Bastian stepped away from the rest and made her a very pretty bow.

"My child, I have the honor to act in place of your father." He had obviously dressed with special care: his long white hair was brushed back from his forehead, and he wore a scarlet coat, very full about the skirts, with bunches of black ribbon on the shoulders. Taking her arm, he led her gently down the aisle. "This is a great occasion, and one on which all of your friends must share in your happiness."

It was beginning to feel more and more like it *was* a wedding. Except that no one, least of all Lili herself, had been happy on her real wedding day. She blushed as she had not blushed on that other occasion—although, mindful of the solemnity of this one, she tried not to smile.

On a stepped black marble dais before an altar of glass stood a tall, broad-shouldered man in purple robes and a mask like the head of a great golden falcon, awaiting the "bride" and her "father."

"Who presents this woman in the Temple of the Mysteries?" he intoned, in a deep, sonorous voice.

"I do," said Sir Bastian, stopping before the first step. "And for these reasons: That she has proved herself to be a woman of the highest character and remarkable talents. That she has made a conscientious study of the healing and the magical arts. That she has allowed herself to be unmade and reborn in the dark womb of the world, swallowed deadly poison without being harmed by it, successfully passed the tests of air and solid matter, and been renewed by water."

"Then approach, Lilliana, and kneel before the altar."

With Sir Bastian's guidance, Lili climbed to the second step and sank slowly to her knees. This done, the old gentleman released her arm and moved away.

"Lilliana Brakeburn-Blackheart, I ask you for the last time," said the man in the falcon mask. "And I charge you to examine your conscience thoroughly before you answer. Do you come here solely of your own will, under no constraint, under no persuasion? Do you make your vows and join this ancient brotherhood with a full and grateful and joyous heart?"

After a brief pause, Lili replied. "Sir, I do."

A bright column of fire sprang up on the altar. "Do you dare stand the test of fire? Will you place your hand unprotected in the flame?"

"I will." Steeling herself, Lili stretched out one hand to the spot where the fire seemed to burn the hottest. There was no pain, no sensation at all. And when, after another moment, she withdrew her hand, there was no redness or other mark of the flame to be seen on her skin.

The tall man seemed to smile behind his mask. "You have a powerful will. Now, Lilliana, you must speak the words after me, exactly as I say them to you."

With his next words, his voice seemed to grow physically bigger as it grew louder, to expand until it filled the whole room like a palpable presence: "*I am the Bride of the Universe, the Handmaiden of Nature, and Sister of the Four Elements.*"

"I am the Bride of the Universe," Lili echoed softly, "the Handmaiden of Nature, and Sister of the Four Elements."

"*I am the earth, I am a star, I am a spirit. I partake of the nature of all things, for I am one with the World's Soul.*"

"I am the earth, I am a star, I am a spirit. I partake of the nature of all things, for I am one with the World's Soul."

"*By the stone generated by the fire, by the water that burns, by the salt that transforms all things out of their own nature, I do give myself, my flesh, my bones, my soul, my spirit, unreservedly, in the sure knowledge that as I give so I shall receive in tenfold measure.*"

"By the stone generated by the fire, by the water that burns, by the salt that transforms all things out of their own nature, I do give myself, my flesh, my bones, my soul, my spirit, unreservedly, in the sure knowledge that as I give so I shall receive in tenfold measure."

"*I offer myself as a vessel for the mysteries.*"

"I offer myself as a vessel for the mysteries."

There was a long silence, broken at last when Sir Bastian reappeared and offered her a copper bowl to sip from. "Drink deeply, Lilliana. You will find this draught far sweeter than the two before."

It *was* sweet, and when Lili had drained the last drop, it left her with an intense thirst for more.

"*I permit myself to be impregnated with the seed of things not yet seen or contemplated,"* intoned the man in the mask. *"I die a thousand deaths and I am reborn to live a thousand lives."*

"I permit myself to be impregnated with the seed of things not yet seen or contemplated." Something was growing inside of Lili, something so great, so immense, it threatened to split her apart from her breastbone to the base of her spine. She felt suddenly weak and giddy, but she continued to force out the words. "I die a thousand deaths and I am reborn to live a thousand lives."

"Your bridegroom comes to claim you, Lilliana," said a soft voice, and before her astonished eyes, a dark hole was ripped in the cosmos and something reached out and drew her through the gap.

She stood at the apex of a whirling world, watching stars and planets dance in the void. Suns exploded, shooting sparks like fireworks in the night. Chaos spun in the heavens like a pinwheel. Lili had neither the power nor the will to resist. She surrendered herself utterly to the mysteries.

E audaimanté, high in the southern mountains, was a tiny walled city on the shores of a beautiful sky-blue lake, almost unknown to history. Had she not possessed an equable climate, and a pretty little marketplace with pointed arches, an ancient hot spring of proven virtue, she might have remained equally unknown to the fashionable world. As it was, she enjoyed a certain reputation. The sick and the weary, the old and the jaded, were accustomed to visit her winter and summer, to drink her bitter magnetic waters, to soak in her steaming baths, and to sample her other (exceedingly sedate) pleasures.

Placid—dignified—matronly—all this she certainly was, but she was a fashionable matron, addicted to dress, gossip, and slow promenades in the afternoon. As such, she had more than her share of mantua-makers, jewelers, perfumers, and makers of other luxury goods. From the moment any visitor entered through her southern gate—passing between the twin towers and under the painted arms of the city—it was plain to be seen that her crooked streets were lined with shops selling pastry, snuff, gold braid, lace, and silk stockings.

But she had her darker side as well. With the invalids came the medical men—many of them highly questionable. In a single neighborhood there were over two dozen barbers, empirics, midwives, corn-cutters, bone-setters, and urinarians. Outside the baths, quacks hawked their patent nostrums— good for everything from wind in the blood, to flying gout, moon pall, gravel, and rising lights. Inside the lecture halls, more scientific practitioners spoke wisely of "insensible perspiration," and "imperfectly concocted humors." And in tiny shops throughout the town, apothecaries prescribed such recognized remedies as snail-shells, soap, snakeroot, brandy, mint-water, and spittle.

If those who suffered from disease or ennui attracted the medical men— qualified and otherwise—rich old widows and their gullible sons and daughters attracted confidence men of another sort. With excellent manners, easy address, and a velvet coat, one might go far in Eaudaimanté.

In fact, the shadier sorts almost invariably went so far as the north end of town, where, in a certain tall house, a certain old lady with a formidable reputation was known to buy information—

24

$\mathfrak{I}$t was a narrow house, six stories high, squeezed in among
other houses on a short cul-de-sac ending in a graveyard. Like
all the other houses on the street, this one presented a forbidding face to the world: the windows shuttered, the dark wood of the
front door banded in iron, the thirteen steps leading up to that door
high and steep.

Rumor had it there was a glassed-in garden behind, a conserva-
tory where the lady of the house cultivated a remarkable collection
of plants as exotic as they were poisonous. But, as visitors who had
stayed in the house stoutly maintained that the Dowager Lady Krogan grew nothing more unusual than foxglove, cultivated nothing
more dangerous than fly-agaric, it was possible that rumor lied.

To this mansion of sinister reputation, one day, came Blaise Trefallon in a borrowed carriage. He appeared to be confident of gaining admittance, for he dismissed the driver before he even knocked.

That confidence was justified. No sooner had he tapped on the
door, no sooner had the servant who answered taken in his elegant
figure, than he was ushered inside. Nor was he obliged to linger long
in the entry hall. Within minutes of sending up his card, Blaise was
escorted upstairs and into the dowager's sitting room.

Lady Krogan did not rise to meet him. Sitting up very straight in a high-backed chair without a cushion to support her, she presented a formidable picture in her black satin weeds. Though her white hair was thinning, and the body which housed her indomitable spirit had grown lean and enfeebled, Wilrowan's grandmother remained an exceedingly handsome old woman. As her visitor entered the room she extended a very white—and still very smooth—blue-veined aristocratic hand in greeting.

"Mr. Trefallon. You are very prompt in gratifying my request. Dare I hope you have come for an extended visit?"

"An afternoon call only," said Blaise, tucking his lace-edged tricorn under one arm, achieving a highly creditable bow. "I hope I have better manners than to foist myself on you as a house-guest, when no such invitation was mentioned in your letter."

Lady Krogan sniffed audibly. "My resources are not contemptible, young man, and my household sufficiently well managed. I am able to accommodate unexpected guests with very little trouble."

She waved him toward a chair to the left of her own, waited until he was seated before going on. "I believe I told you, once, that you might stay with me here whenever you chose."

"You were so gracious as to extend that invitation—two or three years ago." Blaise hid a slight irritation behind his blandest and most polished manner. He had forgotten how like fencing it was to hold even the simplest conversation with this fierce old lady.

"Now that you *are* here, perhaps you will tell me something of my grandson. He is a poor correspondent, as perhaps you know, and his letters to me are extremely sketchy."

Trefallon took out a delicate cambric handkerchief and carefully polished his jeweled eyeglass. Examining the result, apparently dissatisfied, he blew off an almost invisible speck of dust. There was something he was very much inclined to say, but a gentlemanly restraint urged him not to say it.

At last, he cleared his throat. "I believe there is something we should establish at the outset. Three years ago, you asked if I might find it convenient to write to you here from time to time, in order to assure you of Will's well-being. This trifling favor I was pleased to grant you, as I might have done the same for any female relation of *any* of my friends. However——" He abandoned his show of diffidence and looked her straight in the eye. "However, I must make it very clear to you, Lady Krogan, that I am not and never shall be one of your spies."

The dowager glared at him. "Spies, Mr. Trefallon? You seem to have mistaken me for somebody else. The days when I resided in the courts of power are long past. That being so, what reason could I possibly have for the employment of *spies*?"

"I beg your pardon if the term offends you." Blaise suffered her displeasure with apparent composure. "But for all that, it is widely acknowledged that considering your family history, considering your patronage of half the shady characters on the continent, considering your—we will call them hobbies, for lack of a better word—it is hardly possible that you would live here unmolested, were it not for the fact that you possess information likely to prove damaging to half the royal houses in existence."

Lady Krogan smiled. Perhaps she appreciated the fact he could not be intimidated, or perhaps by doing so she meant to disarm him. He was not disarmed. She had been known, in her time, as a woman who used both her beauty and her wit as potent weapons—even at her advanced age, he suspected, they were still sharp enough to cut. "Mr. Trefallon, I will confide in you. I hope you are suitably flattered, because generally speaking I am not of a confiding disposition."

The dowager reached out, pulled a tall embroidery stand up to her chair, took out a needle, and began to thread it. "I have led a long and a very interesting life. Do not felicitate me. An interesting life is not always to be envied. As a young girl, I had the misfortune to see a great many members of my family imprisoned or executed. Indeed, on my sixteenth birthday, I was arrested myself on charges so vague and mysterious I do not understand them even now. I spent the next two years in the vilest hole of a prison you can possibly imagine, awaiting my trial. But I happened—and this was entirely by chance—to know something that a certain powerful person wished to keep secret. Had I ever come to trial, I would have told what I knew. I could hardly do otherwise, being under oath. Because of this, I never *did* come to trial, and my arrest eventually became an embarrassment to those who had arranged it. When public opinion finally shifted, when the persecution of my family came to an end, I was the very first one to be released from prison. This entire experience, as you may imagine, taught me a valuable lesson: It is far better to know things, even if that knowledge should prove to be dangerous, than to live in ignorance."

The silver needle flickered in her hand. "You mentioned, a moment ago, my hobbies. I can assure you they do not include gratuitous interference in other people's lives. Equally, I am determined that others shall not interfere in *my* life, nor in the lives of my children or grandchildren. So I prepare myself to discourage interference." She smiled at him fiercely over her embroidery. "Let us just say—I do have my little ways of learning things, and I contrive to remain tolerably well informed for an elderly widow who spends ten months out of every year in an obscure watering place principally inhabited by fops and invalids!

"But allowing that you are not to be regarded in the same light as some of my other sources of information—what then, Mr. Trefallon?"

Blaise sat thoughtfully twirling his eyeglass at the end of its satin ribbon. "Lady Krogan, not even to oblige you, not even to set your mind at rest, would I ever tell you anything that Will said to me in confidence. And naturally I feel a very similar reluctance to speak to you of matters that Wilrowan has not even chosen to confide to *me*, his closest friend."

The silver needle ceased to move; Lady Krogan leaned forward in her chair. "Well, perhaps I can make it easier for you to ignore your— really quite admirable—scruples. What can you tell me about Wilobie Culpepper?"

Trefallon dropped his eyeglass. "You know about Culpepper? But that—" Recovering swiftly from his surprise, he laughed and shook his head. "Lady Krogan, that is just nothing. It was a hoax of Will's when we were students. He set out to establish a false identity, to see how many people he might fool. A great many people *were* fooled, but once he realized his joke had succeeded, he typically lost interest and very soon abandoned it."

"And what if I told you that Mr. Culpepper had been recalled from obscurity, that he is, at this time, quite active in and around the city of Hawkesbridge? What would you say to that, Mr. Trefallon?"

Blaise took up his jeweled eyeglass, began to play with it again. "I would say that your information is better than my own. And that there is probably very little I could tell you about Will—or about Willie Culpepper—that you don't know already."

Lady Krogan took up her needle and set several more stitches. "That is entirely likely. Yet I think the information I have may be seriously flawed, coming as it does from those not intimately acquainted with my grandson. I had hoped that you might help me to put a more accurate interpretation on things that I already know."

Abruptly, Blaise abandoned all attempts at concealment. They seemed, in any case, to be remarkably futile. "I've had an idea for a long time that there was something seriously amiss with Will. Some secret grief, some sickness or trouble —which makes him do reckless things, which makes him court his own destruction. But in the last few months I've seen him behave in a way that is far beyond anything I had ever seen before."

Rising from his seat, Trefallon began to pace the floor. "He attends but rarely to his duties at the Volary—how Dionee continues to tolerate this, I really don't know—and he seems to spend at least twenty hours a day in the very worst company possible. Naturally, I fear for his health, since he rarely sleeps, but it's much worse than that."

Lady Krogan tied off her thread in a knot, then picked up a pair of silver scissors and snipped it off. "In what way worse?"

"Will's principle failings have always been his love of danger and an almost insatiable sexual appetite. But as for any other vices: he has always practiced them in strictest moderation or not at all. Yet, in the fortnight before I quit Hawkesbridge, he would have gambled away a fortune had the luck not remained so remarkably even, and though I have known him from a boy I have never seen him consume such quantities of wine and spirits as he has recently. Moreover, he frequents opium dens and—and worse places besides. And what is particularly inexplicable, he's been taking Nick Brakeburn with him, on these expeditions into the stews." Blaise threw himself down in a chair by the fireplace. "Whatever anyone might say about Will, he has never been a—a corrupter of youth, or a despoiler of maidens, and so I consider his recent behavior completely unlike him."

In the act of measuring out a new length of silk thread, Lady Krogan paused. "I admit what you tell me is most disquieting. Well, Mr. Trefallon, is there anything more?"

"Surely all this is more than enough. And the timing, of course, is so particularly bad. Because why would Will choose to behave so disgracefully, now of all times?"

Lady Krogan leaned forward over her needlework. "You speak as though this were a time of particular significance."

"It is partly because Will has invited Lili to visit him; she is supposed to arrive in about a month. He is looking forward to her visit with such painful intensity—and yet at the same time dreading it—

I have an idea he intends something more than an ordinary visit. But I ask you, what will Lili think—and say and do—when she arrives in Hawkesbridge only to find her young cousin absolutely *wallowing* in dissipation, and learns that Will is the one who is leading him astray?"

"That is a problem indeed," the Dowager admitted.

"But there is more. And if you have not heard this already—though I expect you have—let me be the first to felicitate you." Blaise stood up, made a quick bow, and resumed his seat. "It has recently been announced that the queen is in an interesting condition. And I simply don't understand why Will should go out of his way to distress Dionee at a time like this!"

The dowager sat frowning down at the emerging pattern on her embroidery frame. "And *is* my step-granddaughter distressed?"

"She is distressed about something. I couldn't positively say that Wilrowan is the cause. And while I understand that she might well grow faint and ill, on account of her condition, is it natural she should also be so nervous and ill-tempered?"

The dowager shook her head. "Not so soon. No, not so soon." One white hand strayed to the ambergris necklace at her throat. She passed the dark, rose-cut beads slowly between her fingers as she sat considering the facts for several minutes. "But putting aside our concern for Dionee, to what—if anything—do you ascribe Wilrowan's remarkable behavior?"

"I think that it has something to do with Lili. From things he has said, things he has let slip, I think Will has recently learned something that has—broken his heart, broken his spirit—" Trefallon shrugged. "I don't know what it has done, but it has certainly changed him."

"Do you think that Lilliana has taken a lover?"

"No." Blaise shook his head emphatically. "And pardon me, Lady Krogan, but I think you are playing with me. I do *not* think that Lili has taken a lover—and neither do you. If that were the case and Will suspected it, Wilrowan would simply have called the fellow out—put a bullet through him, cut him to pieces—and that would be an end to it."

"But supposing," said Wilrowan's grandmother, "my grandson did not know, or was not certain, who Lili's lover might be?"

Trefallon shook his head again. "If he did not know, or was not certain, that would hardly prevent him from murdering half the young men of her acquaintance. As no such slaughter has occurred, I think we can safely acquit Lilliana of adultery."

"And yet you still think my grandson suffers from a broken heart?" the dowager persisted.

"I do. It may be however, that he was wounded long ago, and this recent injury, whatever it is, has only started the bleeding again."

The old woman sat quietly over her work for several minutes, setting stitch after stitch, apparently deep in thought. "Well, Mr. Trefallon," she said at last. "I think you are right. It has always seemed to me that Will *does* care for Lilliana, more than he admits, and that there was something or someone coming between them. Out of respect for his feelings, I thought it best not to inquire too closely, but it may be time to discard that policy."

Lady Krogan gave Trefallon one of her sharp, dangerous smiles. "It might be to my grandson's advantage, for instance, if I were to learn just how Lilliana spends her time at Brakeburn—particularly during the long weeks and months between Wilrowan's visits."

25

One Mr. Silas Gant kept a discreet gaming-house down by the River Zule. In three luxurious rooms, it was possible to find games of chance in progress at any time of the day or night—possible, when the fever burned very hot, to find gentle-men in satin coats and powdered wigs, or in the raffish togs of the "palace" set, thoroughly engrossed in the mysteries of Hazard, Faro, and Deep Basset, for twenty or even thirty hours at a sitting.

But to enter these rooms, which were located at the top of the house, it was necessary to ascend many long flights of ill-lit stairs, climbing past a fencing school and an academy of music along the way, to pass muster with the keen-eyed lookout loitering on a land-ing below, and to slip a coin into the calloused palm of the daunting individual who answered the door at the top.

The visitor seeking admittance, on this particular day, was a *very* young gentleman in the scarlet uniform of the City Guard. But the lookout suffered him to pass without demure, and the hulking porter was more than willing to accept his offering of silver. At length, the young officer was ushered into a very bright room en-tirely draped in crimson satin, with crystal chandeliers hanging from the ceiling.

Large as it was, the chamber was still very crowded, and the visitor was several minutes locating his quarry—slumped in a wingchair with a much-battered hat drawn over his eyes, either sodden with drink, or dozing after a long spell at the tables.

With a determined stride, the youth crossed the room. He bent low to speak in the sleeper's ear. "Captain Blackheart! Sir—if you please!" Will yawned and stretched, pushed back the old black hat, and stared muzzily up at a half-familiar face. "Captain Blackheart, I don't know if you remember me, but—"

"Young Dagget, isn't it?" said Will with another yawn. "It *is* still Corporal Dagget?"

"Yes, sir. Thanks to your forbearance it is. Sir, I have something to report but—if you don't mind my asking, are you drunk or merely exhausted?"

"A little of both, I think," said Will, rubbing his eyes. He had come straight to Gant's place after a flying visit to one of the mining towns, following up what now appeared to be a false clue as to the whereabouts of the Chaos Machine. "Something to re— Shades of Darkness! Have you found the Wryneck? Then wait just a moment."

Will reached into one of his pockets and drew out a stag-horn flask with a silver stopper. He pulled out the stopper, took a long pull, then laughed at the corporal's grimace of distaste. "A tonic given to me by my grandmother. Quite harmless, I can assure you." As Dagget either did not know or had forgotten the name of Captain Blackheart's grandmother, his face relaxed.

"It will clear my head for about fifteen minutes," Will added, as he returned the flask to his coat pocket. "I urge you to say what you have to say with as little preamble as possible."

"Sir, I have located not only the Goblin but the lady who was with him. Only, they aren't in Hawkesbridge, or anywhere near it. I found them in Chetterly, near the Chêneboix border."

Will put a hand to his forehead. Lady Krogan's potion might

serve to dissipate some of the mists, but it did nothing to banish a raging headache. "You're damnably thorough, anyway. But what led you so far afield as Chetterly?"

Young Dagget blushed. "Sir, I went into the mountains for personal reasons. My family—but you don't care to hear about that. Encountering the Goblin was the last thing I expected, but I've been in the habit of scanning faces wherever I go. Fortunately, he didn't see me, and I was able to dog his footsteps for quite some time. I took particular note of a house he entered, and a man who lives in the neighborhood told me he goes there *often*, and sometimes takes the lady with him."

Wilrowan scowled. "You followed the Wryneck but didn't arrest him?"

"Captain Blackheart, how could I? I have no authority to make an arrest outside the city, and it's not as though he was doing anything illegal when I saw him in Chetterly. Without a warrant—"

"Quite right." Putting his hands on the arms of his chair, Will levered himself to his feet. "Now that I think of it, you did just what you should have done. Particularly in coming directly to me. You did come directly?" Dagget nodded. "It happens I *can* make an arrest anywhere in the realm, with or without a warrant, if I have reason to suspect a plot against the queen."

The corporal was looking vaguely offended. "Sir, on what charge? Surely this was a plot against your own safety, and as such—"

"You needn't trouble yourself about that."

Leading the way out of the gaming rooms and down the stairs, Will gave his companion a sidelong glance. He seemed to remember lecturing young Dagget at their last meeting, on the methods and integrity expected of those who served the Crown—no wonder, then, if the corporal was shocked at what must appear an abuse of Wilrowan's position, in pursuit of a private vendetta. This was unfortunate, but it could not be helped. The story of the Hawkesbridge professors and their infernal engine would not suit the present circumstances, nor was Will about to devise a whole new tale for the corporal's benefit.

"You will accompany me back to Chetterly and point out the house," he said firmly. "Then, if the Wryneck appears, you will assist me in making an arrest."

Nick Brakeburn had been left behind in the mining town, just to make certain there was nothing more to be learned, and Gilpin and Odgers—the other two men that Rodaric had approved to assist in the search—were out of the city as well. To recall them might take several days.

"Sir, I—"

"Moreover, you will take my word that this action is perfectly appropriate on my part. Is this *understood*, Corporal Dagget?"

The corporal saluted. "Yes, sir."

"Very good," said Will. "I'll go to the palace, pack up my things, and send word to Marzden to extend your leave. You, in the meantime, will go to a posting house, hire a carriage, and meet me at the North Gate in about two hours."

Chetterly was a drowsy little town in a mountain valley, the kind of place that seemed perfectly content to daydream the years and the centuries away, sleepily regarding its own reflection on the slow-moving waters of the Zule.

By the time Corporal Dagget drove his post chaise into the stableyard of the only inn, two days later, Will felt considerably refreshed after a sleep of about twenty hours, and he had taken advantage of a stop earlier that day to wash up and change his appearance. As he swung down from the carriage, Will looked a different person, in a severe brown coat of military cut, biscuit-colored small clothes, and well-polished boots, his auburn hair liberally powdered to disguise the color.

When the horses were stabled and a room had been engaged for the night, Will and Dagget took a brisk walk though the town, starting at the town square, eventually arriving outside the house where the Wryneck was known to visit.

It was a typical cottage, white-washed stone with a slate roof, with windows curtained in chintz and shutters painted green, and evidence of a tiny walled garden behind.

"Will we question the people who live inside?" the corporal asked.

"That would only serve to alert the Goblin. No, I want to arrest him, but to do it discreetly. Then we can take him off to some private spot, and squeeze the information out of him at our leisure."

Young Dagget was frowning. No telling what he imagined Will meant by "squeezing" the information out of the Goblin—nor had Wilrowan failed to notice that the corporal's speech was larded with fewer "sirs" and "Captain Blackhearts" than it had been formerly.

Once more, Will cursed the need for so much secrecy. In fact, he had a warrant from the king tucked inside his waistcoat, which granted him extremely sweeping powers. It might have eased the corporal's conscience had he known, but Will had been cautioned against showing the paper to anyone, until and unless it became absolutely necessary.

"You have grown very nice," he said sharply, "for a man who not three months since was accepting bribes."

Dagget flushed to the roots of his hair. "I believe I told you—sir—that on that occasion I believed I was serving the Crown."

"As you may also believe it now," Will answered coldly. "And on immeasurably better authority."

Leaving Dagget to his own thoughts, he began to study every detail of their surroundings. The street was a narrow one and not very long, ending at a mossy stone wall at least twelve feet high. The buildings opposite the cottage were neat little shops, with upper stories given over to lodgings.

"We need to keep an eye on this house at all times, but without drawing attention. Perhaps we should begin by renting a room across the way. We will say—we will say we are planning to stay for a least a fortnight and therefore don't wish to remain at the inn."

But now Dagget was shaking his head.

"Well, Corporal?"

The youth hesitated. "It is a good plan, sir. I don't dispute that. But I—some of the people here know me; they know that my father lives not seven miles from this very spot."

"Yes, I see," said Will. "I'll make inquiries about a room, while you wait here and try not to be seen."

So Wilrowan set out purposefully in search of temporary lodgings. The shop directly opposite belonged to a tailor and would have been ideal, with its broad upper windows facing the street, but the tailor and his family occupied the entire top floor and the attic as well, and could not be coaxed into letting out a room. A chandler, a cooper, and several others were equally reluctant to oblige. In the end, Will was forced to settle for a two-room lodging several houses down on the wrong side of the street.

A day and a half of watching, turn and turn about with young Dagget—a day and a half during which Will grew increasingly impatient, as the only Goblins to appear were two Ouphs and a Padfoot with business in the neighborhood—and finally he was rewarded by the sight of a stoop-shouldered figure moving down the lane in the faded light of late afternoon.

Will hailed the corporal out of the other room, where he had been taking a nap, and Dagget arrived just in time to hang out the window and catch a glimpse of the blue-coated Goblin as he entered the cottage. "Yes, sir, that is certainly him."

Will glanced at the sky, then took out his watch. "It should be dark in another hour. Really, this could hardly be better. If the Wryneck stays with his friends that long, we can follow him home when he decides to leave, and overpower him in the dark."

He felt a tensing of muscles, an intoxicating rush of blood to his head, now the time for action had finally arrived. Speaking over his shoulder to Dagget, he armed himself and headed for the door. "For the love of heaven, Corporal, don't you forget to bring the rope."

But once Will and Dagget were down in the street, they were forced to loiter in the shadows for the next two hours, until the door of the house finally opened and an angular figure appeared briefly silhouetted against the light, then stepped out onto the narrow lane.

Will drew a long hissing breath. "This street is not so dim as I would like." Though these village streets lacked gas-lights or flares, several of the shopkeepers hung lanterns outside their doors. "The next street may be darker. If it is—we'll take him as soon as he turns the corner."

Dagget whispered his assent, and they both moved stealthily after the shambling figure of the Goblin. The next street was dark, and deserted as well, and their quarry seemed quite unaware he was being followed. Will caught up in a few swift strides, took the Goblin roughly by the arm, and thrust the barrel of a silver pistol into his side.

"You, sir, will make no outcry nor any attempt to escape. Not if you value your miserable life." The Goblin stood passively. "Corporal, tie his hands behind him, and make very certain that the knots are tight."

No sooner were the words out of Will's mouth than there came two loud cracks of gunfire. At the first, Dagget cried out and collapsed to the ground; the second whizzed past Will's head, so close he could feel the wind of its passage fanning his cheek.

Acting instinctively, Wilrowan wrenched the prisoner around to cover him. He peered into the shadows, looking to see who had fired the shots, but the street appeared empty.

"Corporal Dagget?" A faint moan answered him. Will drove the muzzle of his pistol a little deeper into the Goblin's side. "How many men—Goblins—are there?"

Before the prisoner could answer, there was another crack of gunfire, and the Goblin grunted and doubled over. Despite Will's attempts to keep him up, he began to slide heavily down toward the pavement.

"Damn!" said Will, abandoning the effort, letting him go, and throwing himself down flat on the hard cobblestones. He found one of the Goblin's wrists and felt for a pulse. There was not so much as a flutter, the flesh was as cold as ice. As the creature was obviously dead, Will crawled over to see to Dagget.

The corporal, he was relieved to discover, was still breathing, though he had a very large hole in one shoulder which was bleeding copiously. By now, doors were flying open and people were pouring out of the shops and into the street. Will hesitated, not liking to desert his comrade.

Yet neither he nor Dagget was of any account when weighed against the greater significance of the Mountfalcon Jewel. Realizing this, Will abandoned the corporal to the care of the emerging shopkeepers. Springing to his feet, pulling another pistol out of his pocket, he took off in pursuit of the two dark figures just disappearing around a corner.

Being lightly built and fleet of foot, he gained on them rapidly. When one of the two crossed a patch of yellow lantern-light, Will stopped, aimed, and fired, then dodged into a recessed doorway to avoid being shot in return. He thought he had winged the fellow, but when he looked cautiously around the corner of the recess, he saw that both figures were still moving.

There was a stamping of horses and a rattle of wheels as a carriage came rolling out of nowhere, stopped just long enough for the two who were fleeing to leap inside, then went careering around the corner and out of Will's sight.

In the meantime, he had managed to get off another shot and hit the driver, but the carriage continued on—as evidenced by shouts and screams on the other street where the gathering crowd was forced to scatter. By the time Will rounded the corner himself, the carriage was already out of sight.

Three men stood over the place where Dagget still lay crumpled and bleeding on the cobblestones. A fourth man knelt beside him, with a brass lantern in hand. Will concealed both pistols inside his coat and hurried over to take charge. "Is he still alive?"

"Aye, just barely." The man with the lantern put down his light, drew out a handkerchief and wadded it up, making shift to cover the wound in Dagget's shoulder. "We'll need better than this, though."

"Someone should send for a surgeon." Will pulled off his coat, removed his neckcloth, was just about to kneel and offer his assistance, when one of the other men took a step in his direction, removing a stout-looking club from a chain at his waist. Will knew at once that he and Dagget were in the capable hands of the citizen Watch.

"Already sent for," said the man with the truncheon. "But if you please, sir, 'tis a very bad business, and there be a good many questions you maybe ought to answer—"

"As you say." Will handed his neckcloth to the man beside Dagget. Reaching inside his waistcoat, he pulled out the warrant and passed it over to the other burly watchman. The time for showing his credentials had clearly arrived.

"This *is* a very bad business. But I am Captain Wilrowan Blackheart, and as you no doubt recognize the king's seal and signature on this document, you'll do me the favor of following my orders *now* and asking your questions later. Is there some house nearby where we can take Corporal Dagget and the body of the Wryneck?"

One of the spectators stepped forward to offer his house. Will accepted the offer gladly, and Dagget was very carefully lifted by four men, carried inside, and gently laid out on a table to await the surgeon. Meanwhile, the Goblin was wrapped in a ragged sheet and deposited unceremoniously on the floor.

As Dagget appeared to be in reasonably good hands, Will turned to the two watchmen. "I'll want you both to assist in the search of a house on the next street. I doubt there is anyone there—but it's just possible, in their haste to be gone, they left something of interest behind."

After half an hour, the search turned up nothing more revealing than some clothes, some broken crockery, and some scattered household goods—nothing, that is, until one of the watchmen crouched down to look under a table in one of the bedchambers and discovered, much to his surprise, an odd-looking map nailed to the underside. Detaching the parchment carefully, for it was crumbling at the edges, he brought it to Will.

Wilrowan inspected the map with growing interest. That someone had gone to so much trouble to conceal it was naturally suggestive. The question was: How long had it been there? It was very old and extremely brittle; it was possible, therefore, that the map had been nailed to the bottom of the table months, even years ago, and that neither the Goblin nor his confederates knew anything about it. But Will thought otherwise.

The map was largely scribbled over with unfamiliar symbols done in brown ink, and the names of several countries had either been underlined or circled in red. Underlined were Rijxland, Lichtenwald, Catwitsen, Finghyll, and Château-Rouge. Circled were Herndyke, Nordfjall, Mountfalcon, Kjellmark, Winterscar, Tölmarch, and Tholia.

Looking over the map, he noticed that Nordfjall and Mountfalcon had *both* been marked with a red circle. Did this indicate a connection between them? After all, it had been Thaddeus Vault, the archduke's ambassador, who had encouraged Dionee—

But no, Will suddenly recalled, Lord Vault had not asked to *see* the Jewel, he had only asked *about* it. It was Rufus Macquay who had done all the rest.

A whole new story began to take shape in Wilrowan's mind. He had wondered at one point if all was well elsewhere, and suppose it was not? Suppose—suppose that a Jewel was missing in Nordfjall, too. That the archduke, suspecting a widespread plot, wanting to know how far the trouble had spread, assigned such men as Thaddeus Vault to find that out? Suppose that the ambassador had only meant to learn if the Chaos Machine was still where it ought to be in Rodaric's treasure room? In that case, it was easy to imagine the Nordfjaller's horror at the embassy fête, when he learned that Dionee had taken the Jewel from its place of safety and—

Will shook his head, brought this train of speculation to a sudden halt. He had been building an elaborate edifice of suppositions on a somewhat doubtful foundation. It would be up to the king to pursue these questions, as it would also be up to Rodaric (and the Malachim professors) to examine the map for clues.

Rolling the parchment up in a tight cylinder, Will slipped it inside his waistcoat for safe-keeping, and went back to the shop where he had left Corporal Dagget.

But Dagget was now in the hands of the surgeon. Rather than distract the doctor at his work, Will decided it was time to examine the body of the Goblin. Taking up a lighted candle, he knelt on the floor beside the corpse, lifted the sheet which covered the face— and experienced a profound shock.

This was not the Wryneck the corporal had identified, the one they had both seen entering the cottage. In the ill-lit street, it had not been possible to tell the difference, but here in the lighted shop, it was all too evident: *that* Goblin had not been scarred as this fellow was from cheekbone to chin, with a long white line, slightly jagged across the jaw.

Was this even a Goblin? He remembered that someone once told him it was very difficult to kill a Goblin by shooting or stabbing him. You had to strike again and again, or else hit the spine, or else shatter one of the brittle bones, which might then do additional damage.

Will felt a sinking sensation in the region of his stomach. Having been so far mistaken, might he also have contributed to the death of an innocent decoy? Of course, there had been the angular figure, the odd way of walking. Will remembered, too, how the skin had been cold when the body was still only moments dead. Feeling behind the neck for some sign of a hump, he was dismayed to find none. But raising an arm and flexing the wrist and elbow, he was struck by the way that both joints moved. Could this be the body of a Grant?

Calling for a pair of scissors, Will snipped off a lock of dry, straw-colored hair, and held it next to the flame of his candle. It caught instantly, literally disappearing in a flash of smoke and fire. So perhaps the ball *had* hit the spine. His question answered, he prudently removed the uncovered candlestick to a safer distance.

Will stripped off the sheet and made a swift but thorough search of the Goblin's clothing. Nothing of significance turned up, unless one counted a watch, a key, a pewter snuffbox, a handful of brass coins, and a red cotton handkerchief. Will deposited them all in an inner pocket of his coat. Though of little apparent worth, he would take them to Rodaric and the two professors.

By now, the surgeon had finished with Dagget. When Will approached him, he had already washed and dried his hands, and was just slipping back into his coat.

"The wound is very deep and there was a dangerous loss of blood. While there is no fever yet, if one should develop—" The doctor shrugged, indicating that the outcome was out of his hands. "For now, you should put him to bed and keep him very warm. If he survives the night, I'll visit him again in the morning."

Will cursed softly under his breath. Somewhere he had made a mistake, had allowed himself and Dagget to be noticed by the Goblin and his confederates, and instead of suffering for that mistake himself, it was the corporal who had paid the price. "His name is Nathaniel Dagget. His family live somewhere nearby."

"He has already been recognized." The surgeon picked up a bamboo cane and a soft hat. "As I am slightly acquainted with the father, I am now on my way to acquaint him with his son's misfortune."

He was turning to go but Wilrowan stopped him. "Is he awake? Am I allowed to speak with him?"

The doctor subjected him to a long speculative look before he replied. Will was suddenly aware that his coat was dirty, his garments askew, and there was a great deal of blood both Human and Goblin on his hands. In spite of this, the surgeon nodded. "He is sometimes conscious, sometimes not. You may speak to him briefly, providing you do not say anything likely to disturb him."

"Thank you," said Will, humbly. "I think he will want to hear what I have to tell him."

He found Dagget lying with his eyes open and his face white and strained. "Captain—Blackheart." The words came faintly. "Did—did the Wryneck—escape us?"

Will bent down and spoke very quietly and calmly in the young man's ear. "You are not to concern yourself about any of that. I have matters very well in hand." He drew out the warrant, held it up so the youth could see both the signature and the big wax seal. No matter what Rodaric had to say about maintaining secrecy, Will would be *damned* if he allowed this boy to suffer, and perhaps to die, believing he had sacrificed himself for nothing.

He lowered his voice further, so that only Dagget could hear him. "You have aided me in a very vital and secret matter, and have rendered your country a very signal service. When I return to

Hawkesbridge, I am going to call on the Lord Lieutenant and instruct him to expunge all mention of our misunderstanding last winter from your record."

Dagget tried to smile. "You are very good. I'm afraid I— wasn't—cooperative. I should have—trusted you, sir."

Will shook his head. "Your doubts and your questions were understandable. I commend you for being so cautious." Continuing to look down on that pale suffering face, he could not help offering a further word of comfort. "You are going to make a very fine officer. And in a few more years, if you decide you would like to serve in one of our elite companies, we'll see what might be done about obtaining you a commission."

26

Though Will spent a long, anxious night on the corporal's behalf, by the time the surgeon stopped in the next morning, the patient looked like he would survive. It was with a sense of relief that Wilrowan left Dagget in the capable hands of the mother and sister who had arrived with the dawn, and set about organizing a search of the town, the valley, and the surrounding mountains. He still hoped to pick up the trail of the surviving Goblin and his confederates.

But two days later, Will was forced to admit that those he was hunting had disappeared without a trace. Moreover, there was still the matter of the map, which ought to be taken to Hawkesbridge as swiftly as possible. Leaving the local constabulary to continue the search, he made arrangements for the return of the hired chaise, bought himself a horse, and left Chetterly during the night.

He arrived in Hawkesbridge after a swift and exhausting journey and went straight to the palace, where he turned over his findings to the king. Then he was free for the first time in many weeks to devote himself to his own business.

This he was glad to do for the next several days, until the summons he expected from Rodaric finally arrived.

*   *   *

The king was alone in his panelled study, when Wilrowan
marched in a little after noon, clicked his heels, and snapped one
hand to his brow in a smart salute. In proper uniform, his red hair
tied back in a neat military braid, Will carried a three-cornered hat
tucked under one arm. Rodaric acknowledged his salute with an abstracted nod, then went back to studying the map, spread out on the
desk in front of him.

Will remained standing at stiff attention until the King looked up
again, and waved him toward a chair. "I have had some disturbing
news."

Very carefully placing his cockaded hat on a corner of the desk,
Will took the seat indicated. "Nordfjall?" he asked.

The king nodded solemnly. "Yes. Taking into account your
guesses based on the map, I immediately wrote to Thaddeus Vault.
You can imagine my displeasure when he did not reply immediately.
I was about to write again, changing my original invitation to a more
peremptory command—when I received this most interesting letter."

He reached into a pocket of his corded silk coat, drew out a
folded piece of paper, and handed it to Will. "Lord Vault wrote that
he had something important to communicate to *me*, but had been
waiting several months for the archduke's permission to share what
he knew. The archduke's letter being delayed along the road by winter storms, it was only yesterday that he finally received it."

Leaning back in his chair, Rodaric spread his hands, as though
what followed must be obvious. "We were closeted together for
about three hours. I'll spare you the preliminary courtesies that
passed between us and tell you at once: the Jewel of Nordfjall is
missing. It disappeared as the result of a plot of considerable artifice
and ingenuity, but I will spare you those details, as well, and only tell
you that all this occurred a full four months before the Chaos Ma-

chine was taken. Having established that ordinary thieves were not responsible—fearing a plot of the sort that we fear also—the archduke put all his ambassadors secretly to work gathering information."

"My guesses were good, then?" Having been too busy listening to examine the letter, Will now passed it back unread.

"Your guesses were extremely good. It all fell out very much as you thought: a well-meaning inquiry on the part of Lord Vault, and Macquay was there to take advantage of the situation."

Rodaric sighed and shook his head. "It all sounds so fortuitous. How long Sir Rufus may have waited for just such an opportunity— what he and his confederates would have done to *create* such an opportunity, had Dionee proved wiser—we will never know. Unfortunately, she fell in with Macquay's plans all too easily."

Pocketing the letter, Rodaric sat back again in his chair. "The day after the queen was robbed, Lord Vault wrote to Nordfjall. But the archduke's reply, so long delayed, contained rather more than Vault had expected. It conveyed information which takes on a truly *ominous* significance, in the light of what you brought back from Chetterly."

There was a long pause, during which the king sat gazing down at the map again, apparently lost in thought. "And that would be—" Will prompted him.

Rodaric glanced up again. "The archduke knows for a fact that the Tholian Jewel is also missing. He has been in communication with King Alejandro. In addition, the Prince of Lichtenwald has closed his borders, and the northern region of Tölmarch has recently been swept by a series of natural disasters—the archduke conjectures that either the Jewels have been stolen from both of those places, or that some of the missing devices are passing through those countries, causing a serious disruption. Finally, he forwards disturbing if ambiguous news out of Rijxland and Winterscar."

Unable to contain himself, Will sprang up from his seat. "But the names of all those places you mention have been circled or underlined on the map!"

Will eyed the parchment and its strange notations. Were *all* the countries indicated threatened? He thought the map must contain a great deal of vital information, if only they could find the way to decipher it.

"But a plot so vast—" His mind boggled at the very thought. In spite of everything, up until now he had only allowed himself to think in terms of two, perhaps three, neighboring realms. That there might be as many as a dozen involved— "The very idea is monstrous. But *whose* plot? Just who is it that entertains such obscene Ambitions? Are they Men or are they Goblins?"

"They appear to be both, but in the main they are Men. At least they were Men in Nordfjall and Tholia." Under the circumstances, Rodaric sounded remarkably cool. Yet his face was white and a large vein was throbbing in his neck.

"Who is ultimately responsible, we may not know until he believes we are all too feeble to move against him. Indeed, why should he reveal himself too soon? If he waits—until our mines collapse, until volcanoes erupt in Winterscar, until earthquakes rock the foundations of Finghyll and the sea reclaims it—until we suffer all that we *must* suffer without the remarkable devices on which we depend for so much—then he will have very little to fear from any of us."

But Will was shaking his head. "He may not have anything to fear from any of *us*, but there are a hundred kingdoms, duchies, and principalities. If a dozen nations are threatened in this way, then surely the rest—"

Rodaric stopped him with an abrupt motion of one hand. "*What* will the rest do? Will they ignore everything they have ever been taught to believe and form an alliance against this menace—whoever or whatever it is? Or will they be paralyzed by doubt into doing nothing? We really can't know what they will do. As a Society, we have been forbidden to even think what ought to be done in the face of a threat like this one—as though the thinking might make something happen. And those who *have* thought, those who *have* dared to speculate, have all been punished!"

Will nodded glumly, remembering his student friends who had been disgraced and expelled—recalling that he, too, had been sent away from the university for nothing more nor less than incorrect thinking.

"You said once, that our ancestors had been naïve in setting up their scheme to protect the Jewels. It seems to me that they were actually unpardonably foolish and vain, thinking they could foresee and plan for everything that might possibly occur. We are paying for that vanity now.

"Because whether this plot succeeds or fails, I do know one thing," the king continued grimly. "If the Jewels that are already missing are not recovered, if the Jewels in Rijxland, Finghyll, Château-Rouge, and the rest should also disappear, if all that power should come into the hands of one man or one woman, the world will be changed forever—and just as certainly, this Kingdom of Mountfalcon as we have known it will no longer exist!"

Wilrowan put his hands to his temples, which were suddenly pounding. "Who—no, that's not what I want to ask. Will you be warning them in Rijxland, Finghyll, and those other places on the map? Will you be taking them into your confidence? Surely the time for so much secrecy is past!"

"I will warn them, yes. I can't in good conscience do anything less—yet I can't be certain I should do anything more. Because the need for secrecy has only increased. I dare not risk starting a panic. If the people knew of this, some would start seeing plots where they don't even exist. The persecution of the Rowans would be nothing beside it! It would be like the end of the Empire all over again, except this time we would be hunting and murdering our own kind."

Rodaric sat staring bleakly ahead of him, as though he were contemplating the direst prospects that the future offered. "And that's not taking into account the inevitable slaughter of hundreds, perhaps thousands, of perfectly innocent Padfoots and Ouphs if anyone begins to suspect there are Goblins behind this."

"Shades!" breathed Wilrowan. The Padfoots and Ouphs were such small creatures—so easily recognized, so difficult to disguise—who had only a few harmless magics with which to protect themselves and a dreadful vulnerability to fire and salt. They were obvious scapegoats.

"I must admit," said the king, "I have never felt any love for my Goblin subjects. Yet such as they are, they are my people; such as I am, I have a duty to protect them." His grey eyes became suddenly fierce; one hand clenched into a fist and crashed down on his desk. "I will not have them brutalized, I will not have them hunted, terrorized, butchered—not if I have to shed my *own* blood to prevent it!"

He pushed back his chair, rose to his feet, and began pacing the floor with a swift, impatient step. "But there are any number of reasons for maintaining secrecy. Because in the light of all this, who can we trust? A notation on this map is no guarantee of anyone's innocence. You may have been *intended* to find it. And even if we could trust every single one of my fellow monarchs, can the same be said of everyone close to them? Indeed, how *could* so many of the Jewels disappear without considerable treachery in high places?"

"It seems to me," said Will, watching his restless movements around the room, "that the people responsible for this monstrous situation are hoping to create exactly this kind of mistrust. In refusing to share everything we know, we are behaving exactly as they would wish."

"I don't dispute that. And yet, knowing I have already been betrayed—even by someone I regarded so little as Macquay—knowing there may have been others even closer to me involved — I find myself looking at my own friends, my own advisors, and I do not like what I see. Consider, for instance, your friend Jack Marzden."

Will shook his head, folded his arms across the front of his green coat. "Marzden was not even in Hawkesbridge, not even in the country, when the Chaos Machine was taken."

"Precisely. And what an amazing number of important things just happened to occur while the Lord Lieutenant was so conveniently out of the way. Your duel and arrest. The theft of the Jewel. The murder of Macquay. This all makes me think I must have been mad to entrust this city to a man with so many vices!"

Will uncrossed his arms, stood up a little straighter. "Are we speaking of Jack now—or is this meant for me?" He had never imagined that Rodaric was aware that Marzden smoked hemp—or that he knew of certain vast sums the Lord Lieutenant had gambled away in houses like Silas Gant's.

The king collapsed in his chair. "We are speaking of Marzden. And yet I don't really mean to accuse him of anything. There has never been any hint of corruption in the City Guard. So long as that remains true, Lord Marzden may be sure of retaining his position— but that doesn't mean I would ever trust him with a secret as important as this one!"

Standing with his legs spread apart, his hands on his hips, Will scowled darkly. "I wonder," he murmured, "that you are willing to trust *me*, since I also have—vices."

"But not the same ones." Rodaric's lips curled ever so slightly. "And the ones that you do have are conducted so openly—one might even say brazenly—you are virtually impervious to blackmail. Rather more to the point," he added, with a shrug and a lift of one dark eyebrow, "you were admitted into this secret before I realized that you were even there!"

The eyebrow came down. Suddenly, Rodaric was very much in

earnest. "I wonder, Wilrowan, why you insist on thinking that I dislike you? If I did not trust you implicitly, if I had no high opinion of your courage, your loyalty, your devotion to the queen, is it likely, do you think, that I would have given you command of the men who guard her—no matter how Dionee begged me to do so?"

Will looked down as his feet. It was a new idea, and not a welcome one, that any trouble between him and the king might have been the result of his own intolerance rather than Rodaric's.

"Wilrowan," said the king quietly, "I know it does sometimes suit Dionee's purposes to play us one against the other, but I wonder if we would not be very much wiser if we refused to oblige her?"

Will clasped his hands behind him, over the silver buttons at the back of his coat. He continued to study the toes of his well-polished boots. "You make me ashamed, sir."

"Do not be ashamed. If there has been any misunderstanding between us in the past, the blame must be mine as well as yours. Let us simply resolve to do better in the future and leave it at that."

Rodaric cleared his throat. "Although, now you are feeling somewhat chastened, I may take advantage of this softer mood, by giving you new orders." Will glanced up. "The Chaos Machine has passed out of the country. I felt it go.

"No," he added, at Will's hopeful look, "I can't say where it is now. It is just that the sympathy which existed before—is no longer there. It seems likely the Jewel is in Chêneboix, since the conspirators were seen so near our eastern border. But they might have passed the device on to others weeks ago, and it might have gone north—south—west—I simply can't tell. I only know that the Chaos Machine is out of our reach. This being so, we can only await further events. In the meantime, I want you to stay very close to the queen."

Wilrowan stiffened; his eyes dilated. "Is the queen in danger?"

"The queen is in danger of doing herself some grave injury. You are aware of her condition. This is not a time for—for what one can only characterize as madcap and reckless behavior in a woman four months gone with child. This is a time for moderation in all things."

Will shook his head, gave a small bitter laugh. "But did you ever really think that when the time came she would—moderate her behavior? If so, I must say, you were doomed to disappointment from the very beginning."

"I did *not* think that Dionee would change her ways merely because she was carrying my child. But is it like her, Wilrowan, to take long, exhausting rides into the country? To play raucous, romping, childish games on the grand staircase? To drink so much wine that she becomes tipsy?"

"No," said Will, emphatically, "no, it is not like her! But do you actually tell me she is doing any—*all* of those things?"

"I do tell you," said the king, "though with infinite pain and regret."

Will blew out a long breath. It seemed that quite a lot had been happening while he was in the mining towns, when he was in Chetterly—even in the last few days, while he was searching the city for a suitable house to rent for Lili. "And what has been done to prevent her from behaving in such a reckless manner?"

"I have tried to caution her, others have tried as well. She does not listen. I might, of course, enforce her obedience, but that is something I'm reluctant to do, seeing that she is so desperately unhappy already."

Will cocked his head. "You think that is the cause: desperate unhappiness? I must say, that would be my first guess as well. You think she continues to reproach herself for the loss of the Jewel?"

"Yes. And also, I think she suffers from an enormous dread of the future. At a time when she ought to be looking ahead with joy to the birth of her child, she can only see a world full of terrifying possibilities. It is to avoid thinking of these things that she has become so bent on diversion."

"And I am to keep her amused?" said Will, leaning forward and putting the heels of his hands on the desk. "Or am I to scold and to lecture her into more seemly behavior?"

"You are to do both. Or to do neither. You must do anything you deem likely to be effective."

The king shook his head sadly. "I have never understood why that is, but she never seems to take offense at anything you say, no matter how roughly you speak to her. Yet I have only to make the mildest criticism, and she either bursts into tears or flies into a fit of pique."

"It is only that when *you* criticize her she begins to fear that you love her the less. And that my love, which is a brother's love, is not nearly so vital to her."

"I believe you are being kind," said the king, with a wistful smile. "And for that I thank you. But I am less concerned with my own heart-burnings than I am for Dionee and the child. And of course, she must *not* know anything of the other matters we have discussed here today. As distressing as her present uncertainty must be, were she even to learn the half of what you and I know now——"

"It doesn't bear thinking about." The very thought of how frantic Dionee might become, how wildly self-destructive if she began to guess the truth, was enough to make Will feel queasy himself. "Though in the end, she may learn it all in spite of us—particularly if things go from bad to worse."

"I have thought of that, too. But I am asking you to shield her from the truth as long as possible. I know this comes at a bad time for you, when you expect Lilliana within the fortnight. But I hope that Lili will understand and not feel neglected. And of course, you may feel free to bring her to visit me at any time."

"Thank you," said Will, frowning slightly. The offer was kindly meant, but he thought that Lili would be bored to tears, having no taste for life at court. He had intended something very different: to devote himself entirely to Lili's amusement, to do whatever pleased *her*, whether that meant walks and rides and picnics, romantic suppers, or nights at the theater. All of that was impossible now, if he must always be dancing attendance on Dionee.

Rodaric seemed to guess something of this without being told. "I have a high regard for Lilliana. If she grows weary of the usual amusements here—of gossip, flirtation, and politics—perhaps she would like to make use of my library, or engage in some other rational pastime. I would welcome her company." He saw that Will continued to frown. "Still, I realize this is not like anything you have planned. I would not ask you to sacrifice those plans, if it weren't absolutely necessary. I know what your efforts have been these last months. I wish it was possible to ask less of you now."

"I understand," said Wilrowan. He was beginning to feel a grim inevitability, an exorable trend to events, which seemed to doom all his efforts toward a reconciliation with Lili. But the child that Dionee was carrying would be heir to the throne and so must be doubly precious to all of them. Will stood up straight again, saluted smartly. "It will be my honor to attend on the queen."

"Thank you, Wilrowan. You'll not find me ungrateful or ungenerous, that I can promise. If we can bring this all to a favorable conclusion, there is very little you might ask that I would be unwilling to grant.

"Supposing that is," Rodaric added with a sigh, "that five months from now when the child is born, I am in any position to reward anyone for anything."

27

It was high summer in Winterscar, the season of endless light. The cafés and coffee-houses never closed, the theaters staged operas and dramas beginning at midnight, and the streets of Tarnburgh were filled twenty-two hours a day with a rumble of carriages and a passing of sedan chairs, and with light-hearted, light-headed, light-footed parties of revelers in thin summer satins and tissues and muslins, going from dinners to the theater to balls on foot—for who could sleep when the air was so soft and bright?

Even when the sun dipped briefly below the horizon it was hard to rest, knowing the full light of day would return so soon. Better to nap in the hot afternoons, when heat and the physical toll of so much gaiety combined to make one deliciously drowsy. People stayed in-doors during the brief twilight, but they left all the torches and the lamps burning.

The sunset hush was just settling over the city, the clamor of passing carriages outside had died away, when King Jarred walked through his candlelit palace, deep in thought.

In the anteroom to his bedchamber, he found his two pages sprawled on the floor, playing with a set of ivory spillikins. At the king's approach, the two boys abandoned the game and sprang to their feet. Their white wigs were askew, the knees of their blue satin breeches wrinkled and dirty, and they hung their heads, whether ashamed at being caught at such a babyish pastime, or because it was long past their bedtime, he could not be certain. It occurred to Jarred that he ought to say something, as he was responsible for them.

"We will play cards," he decided at last, remembering that Zelene had sometimes done so with her own pages. "It is—a more gentlemanly occupation."

The boys were pleased, though perhaps a little surprised. They brought out the cards and pulled up chairs to a table by a latticed window, where the moonlight came in. Jarred played with them for the next hour, *Beggar My Neighbor* and *My Bird Sings*, until the sunrise, when Doctor Purcell arrived.

"You sent for me earlier, I know." The old man looked apologetic as he made his bow.

"It was nothing urgent. I told them not to disturb you if you were resting. But now you *are* here, you may congratulate me. I seem to have extricated myself from that little difficulty we discussed before."

"Extricated?" said the philosopher. "Do you mean the young lady?"

Jarred sent the pages away; it was long past time that he did so anyway. "I followed your advice to the letter," he told Purcell, once they were alone together. "Well, you know that I did. Mademoiselle and her family fairly haunted Lindenhoff."

"So I recall," said Purcell. "And the result?"

"She is apparently convinced that being my queen would be simply unbearable." Jarred picked up the cards and shuffled through them absently. The deck was a fanciful one: the suits were hearts, roses, rubies, and poniards. "Because—while I never spoke of our future together after that first time, I did—rather make love to her.

Nothing serious, just a few kisses, which I have to say she disliked amazingly."

He smiled ruefully, remembering what a chilly reception his kisses had received. He could smile now, though he had hardly been inclined to do so at the time. But it often seemed to Jarred that when he was with her and when they were apart he was two different persons. "And when I realized exactly how she felt about it, it came to me that if I pretended to be very stupid—if I kept on imposing in that particular way, it might serve to foster her aversion to me."

"And did it?"

Jarred dealt himself the Queen of Hearts. Amused by the fancy, he ran through the pack until he came to the Knave of Poniards. "Unflattering as all this is to my self-esteem, I must admit it has succeeded admirably. Even better, she has fallen in love with her handsome young cousin, just as you predicted."

Purcell walked over to the marble fireplace at one end of the room, examined his reflection in a gilded mirror over the mantle. "Jmel, Your Majesty—or Zmaj? I confess I have trouble telling those young men apart." The doctor made a slight adjustment to his neckcloth. He had dressed in haste on receiving the king's summons.

"Zmaj. I should tell you, Francis, that I haven't been near the Debrûle mansion for several weeks, and Mademoiselle has been missing her lessons with Lord Wittlesbeck in the archives. Naturally, I suspected the truth. And when I encountered the young lady in town with Zmaj today—when they both looked so startled and guilty—I knew for certain that our plan had succeeded."

And if his relief had been mixed with jealousy—it had still been relief. Relief that this pastel fantasy of a palace would remain his exclusive domain, that the comforting old rituals, seldom altered, would remain intact. Relief, above all, that there would be no more intrusions by the dark-eyed little foreign beauty and her bizarre relations.

"This is all very satisfactory," said the philosopher. "And you may congratulate yourself that no announcement has been made, that you did not write to any of your relations warning them to *expect* an announcement." He turned and looked expectantly at the king. "But when do you intend to discuss this with the young lady?"

Jarred put down the cards. "I will visit Mademoiselle the day after tomorrow. After I saw her in town, she sent me a letter asking me to call, suggesting that I come on either the sixth or the tenth, when her aunt will be out of the house. I believe, Francis, that I am about to be asked to grant her her freedom. Naturally, I mean to oblige." He knew there was still some danger of fanning the embers of his cooling passion back into flame, but a final interview seemed to be required.

"On the sixth, Your Majesty? But are you not engaged to visit your cousin, Lady Serena, at Ravenhurst that day?"

"My heavens, yes," said the king, slapping his forehead. "Now, how did I come to forget!"

He folded his hands and rested his chin on them. "Though I must admit, while I have always considered poor old Cousin Serena the greatest bore in nature, compared to an afternoon call at the De-brûles', with the aunt pretending to be so amiable and Zmaj looking daggers at me—"

Despite the growing light outside, it was still very dim in the room; several of the spermaceti candles had burned down. Purcell was in the act of relighting two of them under the mirror, when the king startled him with a sudden peremptory command. "No, don't do that!"

The doctor jerked and turned around. The king laughed uneasily. "I do beg your pardon, Francis. I can't imagine what made me speak so sharply. But let that be. There is light enough already, and the truth is, I find that any sort of—glare—gives me a headache."

Purcell moved forward, took out a pair of his spectacles from a

coat pocket, and placed them on the end of his nose. "Is there something amiss with your eyes, sir?" He peered intently into the king's
face.

"I expect it is only the time of the year. I'll be myself in another
few weeks," said Jarred. Then he wondered why he had not simply
stated the truth: It had nothing to do with the light in the sky, it had
everything to do with bright lights shining on mirrors and other re-
flective surfaces.

But there were many things he hid from Purcell: his frequent
confusion and lapses of memory, the way that Mademoiselle Ys alternately attracted and repelled him.

"At least," he said out loud, "there will be no more saltless feasts
at the Debrûles'." He had finally discovered the reason why meals
there were always so tasteless: it was a general deficiency of seasoning and a specific lack of salt.

"Feasts without salt?" Purcell had been in the act of removing his
spectacles, but now he put them back on and regarded the king with
a puzzled frown. "I was not aware that there were any invalids living
with the Debrûles."

It was true that many physicians advised their patients against
salting their food. The reasoning was: as salt was deadly poison to
Goblins, it could not be entirely wholesome for Men. Accordingly,
children, old people, and invalids were often warned against
overindulgence—or any indulgence at all. But that healthy adults
should shun the seasoning was highly unusual.

"Mademoiselle has a delicate constitution. Not precisely sickly,
but highly susceptible. So, Madame Debrûle has engaged a chef who
cooks without salt, and the rest of the kitchen staff, if you will believe me, appears to be made up entirely of Ouphs!" Thinking of
this, Jarred shuddered. Of course, everyone *had* things of Goblin
manufacture—but to actually trust them with the preparation of
food? It seemed just a little unsafe.

"You will be going to Ravenhurst, then?"

The king nodded. "I'll tell young Faison." Mr. Faison was his personal secretary, an active and enthusiastic youth with his eye on a cabinet post some years in the future. "He can make my excuses to the young lady, and also write a letter to Cousin Serena, reminding her to expect me. Her memory is not what it was."

But two days later, a little after noon, the king and the philosopher met in the courtyard between the clock-tower and the stables, just as Jarred was preparing to enter his summer carriage.

"My dear Francis," said the king airily, pausing beside the barouche to pull on a pair of tan gloves, "why do you frown? Is it the startling shade of my coat? Or the coquelicot ribbons on my walking-stick, which I must admit are a little gay?"

"Not at all," said Purcell. Though he *had* noticed that the king wore his dark hair unpowdered, that there was a lightness and a lack of formality about his attire unlikely to find favor in the eyes of such an exacting old woman as Lady Serena. "I am pleased to see that you are finally wearing colors. It merely occurred to me that you are leaving rather late, if you intend to reach Ravenhurst in time for supper."

"Ah," said Jarred. A lackey opened the door of the carriage, and the king climbed inside. "There has been a foolish mixup—a slip of the tongue on my part. Mr. Faison *assures* me I told him today for the Debrûles and the tenth for Cousin Serena. I only learned of the mistake this morning."

He laughed uneasily. "I can't think how I came to do anything quite so stupid. But after all, it has worked out much for the best. The sooner I break with Mademoiselle, the better for all concerned."

"Indeed, Your Majesty, I quite agree. And I felicitate you, sir, on the cancellation of your impending nuptials."

*　　*　　*

The king found Ys waiting for him in the parlor, the room with too many mirrors. Madame Debrûle had *not* gone out, though she had retired to her room with some minor complaint and would not be able to receive him.

Mademoiselle looked ill herself, her face flushed and her lips very white. Either she was sick, Jarred decided, as he strode into the room and caught sight of her sitting on a chair by the window, or she was in a violent passion. Then he realized that she was all in black again, swathed in yards of heavy bombazine despite the heat, and wearing black gloves as well. Perhaps that was why she looked so feverish.

"I beg your pardon," he said, as she jumped up from her seat, sank gracefully down in a low curtsy. "I hope I've not come at an awkward moment. Mademoiselle, have you suffered another loss?"

"Yes," she replied in a low stifled voice, as she accepted his hand and allowed him to raise her. "It was my Cousin Izek. Do you remember him, Your Majesty? I think that you saw him only once or twice."

Jarred tried to dredge up some memory of the young man's face. "Izek. The thin boy with the romantic duelling scar. Were you very close?"

Ys shook her head. "But it was so very sudden. They say he ate something that violently disagreed with him." She shuddered from head to foot, as though that stifling room had suddenly turned much too cold. "My Aunt Valentine says it should be a lesson to us all."

Jarred was confused, and not because of the mirrors on the wall. He was learning to avoid looking directly at them, to slide his gaze around the edges without appearing to do so. "I don't quite—you did say that it was food poisoning? I fail to see what your aunt—"

Ys gave a bitter laugh. "She says that life is short and full of dangerous chances. That we are not to look to future happiness, but to take what we want today!"

"Yes, I see. It seems a rather harsh thing to say, under the circumstances, and yet——" He felt a sudden desire to confide in the girl. "And yet, I can't say that she is wrong. Zelene and I, we had so many plans for the future. And all the time we were making those plans, there was a weakness inside her. We never knew, no one ever guessed, until one day she just stopped breathing."

All the while that he spoke, Ys was gazing up at him, her eyes wide, her lips even whiter than they had been before. He did not know if it was sympathy or shock. "It could happen to any of us, just that way, to just stop breathing. Particularly in *this* house." The king was surprised by the sudden flash of resolution in her eyes. "But it will not happen to me, and it will not happen to anyone that I love."

Her hands went to the necklace at her throat, fingering the crystal pendant. Seeing her do so, Jarred felt the blood grow thick in his veins, his heart leap inside his chest. Ys was staring at him with what could only be described as a calculating look.

"It is very convenient that you came here today. Convenient— but I wonder if it was precisely fortunate for either of us?"

There was darkness and there was confusion. When Jarred finally came back to himself again, he found that he was lying in semidarkness on a large four-poster bed in a strange room.

Listlessly, he moved his head on the padded bolster to look around him. The windows were heavily curtained, and there was only one candle, burned almost to the socket, on a table by the door. When he raised himself up on his elbows to get a better look, he caught a faint, ghostly reflection of himself in another one of the long mirrors.

A wave of dizziness forced him to lie back again. Though it passed, he still felt weak and drained. How had he come here? He had a vague recollection of cold kisses in the dark, a faint, teasing memory of a necklace of pearls sliding across bare skin, winding around a pair of wrists and holding them together, then—

He felt himself go first hot and then cold, as the rest came flooding back into his memory: *The passion that melted his bones, that burned along every nerve in his body. The dark craving that seemed to grow greater the more that he strove to satisfy it.* He had been dreaming, of course, but what a remarkable dream!

Gradually, he realized that he was not alone, that a slender figure in a black dress was sitting on a chair near the foot of the bed. "What has happened to me?"

"You have been ill, Your Majesty, but you are better now," said a soft, tremulous voice.

Jarred continued to lie there a little longer, staring at nothing, until it suddenly occurred to him, by the quick catch of her breathing, that Ys was crying. "You are unhappy," he said. Somehow, he felt responsible. "Is it something I have said or done?"

"Then you—don't remember? Oh, sir, what will become of me if you do not honor any of your promises, if you didn't mean *anything* that you said to me? Have I ruined myself forever?"

So, it had not been a dream: the kisses, the perversely pleasing pain, it had all been real. He struggled to sit up, but he was still too dizzy. He could only lie there and listen to her weep, so bitterly, it made his heart hurt to hear her.

She gave a wrenching sob. "Perhaps it was my fault. I must have led you to think—but after all, we have been secretly engaged for almost four months. Was I wrong to let it happen this way?"

That was too much for him. "No. No, you have not ruined yourself, Mademoiselle. Believe me, I have nothing but respect and the deepest affection for you. And as you say—we are going to be married."

Jarred closed his eyes. The words were spoken; he could never take them back again. What troubled him more than anything was how little he regretted saying them.

28

Throughout the city, in all the fashionable salons and coffee-houses, the king's astonishing betrothal—not yet officially announced but an open secret—was endlessly discussed. Silk-clad ladies whispered of it behind lace fans; dandies spoke of it over glasses of iced licorice-water in the cafés. The gossip circulated with the newspapers and the port in all of the clubs, was served up on silver trays and on painted porcelain plates along with afternoon tea. At supper parties, the scandal lent a subtle spice to every dish.

"Imagine," said the women, "a mere nobody!"

"Imagine," the gentlemen replied, "a beauty, of course, but just a trifle under-bred, wouldn't you say?"

At Lindenhoff, however, the matter was discussed tensely and behind closed doors. After several days of rampant speculation, Jarred called together his councilors, his government ministers, and a handful of ranking courtiers. Closeted with them in his trompe l'oeil council chamber, he announced his intentions formally.

As he expected, the news was greeted with shock and dismay, followed by voluble and vigorous protests. He listened carefully to all that was said, but could not be shaken; he believed he was acting according to principle and was determined to do the right thing.

"But, Your Majesty, so little is known of the young lady," said the Prime Minister. In that room without windows, he looked flushed and over-heated in his fine clothes. "Aside from the fact that *nothing* is known."

"What you need to know—the most significant thing—is that I have already pledged my honor. Also, that her birth is sufficient, her breeding impeccable, and her reputation without any blemish."

"No doubt the young lady is virtuous enough. But she is generally regarded as highly eccentric." This was the President of the Winterscar Senate. "The way she surrounds herself with Goblin servants—and have you considered, sir, the reaction among your *own* servants if she brings the creatures with her to Lindenhoff?"

Jarred felt his self-control slipping away. The debate had already been going on for hours; every conceivable argument had been advanced and refuted again and again.

His fingers curled around the arms of his white-and-gold chair. "It was not to discuss my servants that I called you together. Nor do I require your permission to wed—though I confess I had hoped to obtain your blessing."

"And your heir?" said the president. "Have you notified Lord Rupert? Surely this must come as a great surprise, and even—I beg your pardon—a grave disappointment."

"It could hardly be that," Jarred answered coldly. "Being my father's cousin and of my father's generation rather than my own, Rupert could scarcely expect me to predecease him."

The president stepped back, took out a silk handkerchief and mopped his brow, but another official stepped forward to take his place. "Sir, I never thought it would ever be necessary to remind the king of his duty. Your edicts have always been so reasonable, your judgements so fair, no one could ever accuse you of caprice or indifference when it comes to the welfare of your people. But you have another responsibility, which ought not to be treated lightly, to provide the nation with a suitable successor to the gracious and lovely—"

Jarred rose from his chair, brought to his feet by a surge of indignation. "We will not speak of my late queen. Only *I* know what she was, what this nation lost—"The thought of any woman replacing Zelene was like a dagger through his heart.

With an effort he collected himself. Returning to his seat, he continued more quietly. "I don't forget my duty to my people. The truth is, I am thinking of them every moment. You mentioned, just now, my edicts. If my word is not good, if my signature means nothing, then how can anyone regard anything I do sign as carrying the full force of law?"

There was a stunned silence throughout the room, broken at last by Lord Hugo Sackville. "Your—signature—Your Majesty?" said the king's uncle. "Do you tell us, sir, that you have already signed a marriage contract?"

"I have. Yesterday afternoon, in the presence of a notary."

There were chagrined faces throughout the room. Many looked as though they would have liked to protest further but did not know how. Indeed, there was nothing anyone *could* say. A notarized contract was legally binding and could not be set aside without significantly altering a code of laws that had remained constant in all its essentials for more than a millennium.

With a profound sense of relief, Jarred watched them file out of the room, and then sent for his Master of Ceremonies.

Lord Wittlesbeck came in looking self-important. During the months he had tutored Ys, the old man had grown—if not precisely fond of his pupil, at least to regard himself as her sponsor and Mademoiselle as his own creation. As might be expected, he was in his element planning the ceremony.

"You may leave it all to me, Your Majesty. I will attend to everything. A golden carriage—a thousand white doves released from the palace courtyard—no detail will be neglected."

322 ᗡ· TERESA EDGERTON

"A second marriage," Jarred reminded him. After so many hours of heated debate, he was feeling jaded and a trifle ill. "And at my age, I wouldn't like to be made—ridiculous. There must be pageantry, of course, we must observe every tradition, but we should also show restraint."

"You are not yet thirty," said the Master of Ceremonies, with an indulgent smile. Then, seeing how the king compressed his lips into a hard line, he added hastily: "Of course, Your Majesty, it shall be as you wish. No doubt there are suitable precedents, some-where in the archives, for a—restrained second marriage, and I will locate them. Now, as to the dinner when you make the official announcement?"

"As soon as possible." Jarred felt a strong sense of urgency, quite inexplicable. After dreading this marriage for so long, the thought of any further delay was suddenly insupportable. "How long will it take for you to make the appropriate arrangements?"

Lord Wittlesbeck considered briefly. "We could not accomplish it in less than ten days. A fortnight would be even better."

The king jerked his head from side to side. "As soon as possible," he repeated firmly. "After such a long secret engagement, you must understand how impatient I am to claim my bride."

"Of course," said Lord Wittlesbeck, bowing so low that the high points of his powdered wig almost touched the floor. "In ten days, Your Majesty. I will speak to your major-domo and we will begin preparations for the betrothal dinner at once."

On the night of the banquet, Ys was dressed and coiffed with spe-cial care. Her gown had been prepared many months in advance and stored since then in a great oak chest, along with sachets to keep it sweet. When the Ouph maid-servant opened the lid and drew out the gown, the scent of lavender filled the room. Made of white satin and yards of gauze, the dress was ruched, pleated, flounced, adorned with ribbons and rows of lace—the very essence of fashion. Ys had never seen anything nearly so beautiful.

As the maid-servant laced her up, as she slipped her feet into a pair of pretty red shoes with diamond buckles, Ys struggled to master a sudden attack of nerves. This, after all, was her moment of triumph. There would be no sneaking about in tattered sealskin cloaks, no surreptitious entry by the back gate. She would enter the palace openly, on the arm of Lord Vif, and the king himself would come to greet her.

Down in the first-floor parlor, she found Madame and the other Maglore practically delirious, certain that the time was drawing near when everything they had lost would be restored to them. Ys was excited, too, but for a different reason. Tucked into the front of her bodice, between her whalebone corset and the fashionable ruched satin, was a tiny glass phial containing a deadly poison. As she left the house and climbed into her coach, she felt a queer fluttering sensation in the region of her heart.

She tried to calm herself, sitting in the coach with her hands knotted so tightly in her lap that the knuckles turned white, hoping that no one would see how her whole body shook with anticipation.

She glanced at Madame across the carriage. Her former governess looked uncommonly smug. *How surprised she is going to be,* Ys thought. *Let us hope that she profits by it. She may have frightened me in the past—made me do her bidding in all things—but she will never do so again. Before this evening is over, she will understand that I am a force to be reckoned with!*

By the time the carriage stopped at the foot of the palace steps, her heart was beating so hard, Ys marveled that Madame and the rest could not hear it.

The evening was wearing on and the banquet was almost over, but the room was abuzz with anticipation. Everyone knew that when the clock struck midnight the king would make his unpopular announcement.

Though all the windows were standing open, the room was warm. It was nearly eleven o'clock and the light outside had scarcely faded. Jarred turned away from his conversation with Lord Rupert, and he signaled to his uncle across the room. With an apology to the lady seated beside him, Lord Hugo left his seat and hurried over to speak to the king.

There was a sheen of perspiration on Jarred's brow, and he laughed often. Lord Hugo had never seen his nephew in such an exalted mood, not even at his first marriage. Odder still was a restless, unsteady movement of the king's eyes, particularly whenever his gaze chanced to cross that of his bride-to-be.

I have seen old men make fools of themselves over pretty faces, thought Hugo. *And striplings, too. But I never imagined that a man of Jarred's years and temperament would be susceptible.*

"More wine," said Jarred, with a broad, sweeping gesture.

Lord Hugo signaled to a passing footman, and the lackey brought over a wrought-silver flagon with a mermaid handle, enriched with enamel and precious stones, which was always used on state occasions. Hugo sniffed at the wine, poured a little into the silver thimble cup that accompanied the flagon, and made a great show of tasting it. Finding it good, he served his nephew with elaborate formality.

"Drink with me," Jarred demanded, raising his crystal goblet. Momentarily startled, Hugo swiftly recovered and bowed his assent. This peremptory order was *not* according to form, and certainly unusual for Jarred, who was the soul of courtesy. The stout old gentleman trudged across the room, picked up a crystal wine-glass from his place at the table, made a half bow to Mademoiselle Debrûle who was seated nearby, and then returned to the king.

"I propose a toast: To youth and beauty. May they never fade." As

Jarred lifted his goblet to his lips, Lord Hugo raised his own cup and drank deeply. Two minutes later—his face suffused with blood, his eyes bulging, and one hand clutching his throat—he fell forward on the table, scattering the silver and shattering the glassware.

The royal physician sprang from his seat next to Doctor Purcell and bustled across the room. But by the time he had loosened his patient's neckcloth, by the time he put two fingers on the old man's throat, feeling for a pulse, Lord Hugo Sackville was already dead.

In his bedroom later that night, a shocked and grief-stricken Jarred dismissed the physician and all of his servants, and spoke privately with his Master of Ceremonies.

"Am I to assume," said Lord Wittlesbeck, "that since this tragedy prevented you from making the expected announcement, no such announcement may be expected in the near future?"

White-faced and haggard in his gold brocade dressing-gown, Jarred threw himself down on his bed. "If I am to exist in a state of perpetual bereavement, and be forever putting things off—" With a nervous gesture, he lifted the damp hair off of his forehead. "What am I saying? Of course, you are right. Out of respect for my uncle's memory, we will delay the announcement until the end of summer."

Lord Wittlesbeck was unable to conceal his surprise. "So soon? But I need not tell you that the traditional period of mourning for so near a relation—"

"—is a good deal longer than I am willing to wait!" Jarred gave a short, bitter laugh, embarrassed by his own behavior. It was hard to believe that an hour of lovemaking could enslave a man so completely: rob him of every natural feeling, make him an object of revulsion and wonder to himself, a stranger to all who knew him. But so it was.

"The announcement at the end of the summer, and the wedding as soon after that as we can decently arrange it," said the king. "I mean to be married before winter sets in."

29

The rain poured down in sheets and the sky was a dismal grey overhead, as a cumbersome old coach painted with a gentleman's arms splashed through the mud on the road to Hawkesbridge.

Inside, Sir Bastian Mather glanced across at his young companion, who was trying to keep up a brave front but had only succeeded, so far, in looking cold and miserable. The lumbering vehicle was only Lord Brakeburn's second-best coach, which leaked, and creaked, and was generally wretched—as Sir Bastian and Lili had learned as soon as the rain came down. But the selfish Lord Brakeburn had considered it good enough for his daughter's journey to Hawkesbridge.

Sir Bastian smiled encouragingly. "Captain Blackheart is expecting you to arrive today?"

"He has rented a very fine house near the Volary, and he has written to say that he'll wait for me there. But knowing Wilrowan, how impatient he is, I would hardly be surprised if he rode out to meet us."

Sir Bastian frowned under his soft black hat. "Then I must stop off at Wellburn and travel by post from there. It is far better if Captain Blackheart and I never meet in your company. We don't want him to suspect that you are visiting the city for a double purpose."

Lili moved her fingers inside her fox-fur muff. They were cold and stiff. "It seems—it seems a great inconvenience to travel by post in such dirty weather. And why should Will think anything if he sees us together?"

"He would not think anything at first. But he may meet me later, when I am staying at Marlowe's, and there is no telling what he might think then."

Lili drew a deep breath. "Of course. How stupid of me not to realize." She laughed softly at her own mistake. "*That* is why Will left Brakeburn in such a hurry. He is searching for the Chaos Machine, the same as we are!"

"He was—while it still seemed possible the Jewel was in Mount-falcon." The coach hit a series of ruts, and the old gentleman raised his voice in order to be heard over the rattling of the windows, the creaking of the ancient panels. Among its other deficiencies, the coach lacked springs and was hung on leather straps. "But having returned to his ordinary duties guarding the queen, he is unlikely to present a problem—or to guess what you are doing in Hawkes-bridge yourself."

Lili felt a sharp twinge of guilt. "Sir Bastian, I don't know what Aunt Allora has said to you, but Wilrowan is not a bad man. And if the king and queen are willing to put their faith in him, I don't see why we can't do the same."

"I am far from doubting young Blackheart's good intentions. I am sure, Lilliana, you would never bestow your friendship on a truly wicked man. But it is his lack of discretion and self-regulation that could be absolutely fatal in this delicate matter."

"Perhaps," said Lili, still feeling troubled. Her teeth rattled as the coach passed over a large bump. "But it seems very odd to be working at cross-purposes with my own husband." She sat staring out the

328 ⟁· TERESA EDGERTON

window, watching the wet grey countryside passing by. There was a certain irony in the fact that everyone kept saying she should not trust Will—who, whatever he had done, had never lied to her—while assuring her all along that it was perfectly proper to go on deceiving *him*.

"Lilliana," said Sir Bastian, drawing her attention back from the window, "I understand this is going to be exceedingly awkward, that you will often feel torn by conflicting loyalties. It cannot be helped. You must simply regard this as another test."

"Yes," said Lili softly. "Another test." But that put her in mind of something which had been troubling her for quite some time.

"Sir, perhaps it's not proper that I should ask this. But during my initiation, when I was in the underground temple, did I really do all those remarkable things? Or was it merely that the drugs in the wine made me *think* I was doing them?"

Sir Bastian smiled at her across the coach. "Did you walk on air, pass through solid wood, place your hand in the heart of a flame and emerge unscathed, drink deadly poison and survive?"

"Yes. Though I expect the poison was real enough. At least there I had my training as a healer to aid me."

"Everything was exactly as you perceived it. You were in a state of extraordinary mental excitement and your powers were very great. But I would not, if I were you, attempt to do any of those things under *other* circumstances. The least distraction, even a momentary twinge of self-doubt, would cause you to fail, and that failure could cause your death."

Lili sat up a little straighter in the leather seat, studied her companion with greater interest, realizing that he, too, had passed the very same tests.

He guessed what she was thinking. "Yes, my child, I have walked on air, done all of those things and many more besides. But never again after the first time. To try to do so, merely to prove that I still could, would be exalting myself beyond what is right."

Lili hesitated. "But then—I am not wrong in supposing that my initiation changed me? I feel as though all my senses have sharpened, as though I am more *aware* of things." She stroked the squirrel-skin lap robe, which Sir Bastian had spread across her skirts earlier. "The way the fur feels under my fingers, the scent of wood smoke when we pass by a farmhouse." She gave a deep sigh. "Even the dampness and discomfort of this interminable ride."

"You are not wrong. The entire ordeal was meant to refine and sharpen your abilities, as well as to test you. And believe me, Lilliana, you are going to need all of the strength and the courage you demonstrated that night." Drawing his hands out of his coat pockets, he leaned forward, caught up her hands in a warm, reassuring clasp, and spoke to her very earnestly. "Do you remember the moment of ecstatic surrender to magic and mystery? From this day on, you will be called on to surrender again and again, though never again in such a thrilling fashion, and never to be so pleasantly rewarded.

"More often than not," he added, releasing his hold on her, "the only reward will be the necessity for further sacrifice. Do you think you can bear it? I must warn you that the tests you passed at your initiation were comparatively easy ones."

Lili thought about that for a long time, sitting with her head bowed and her hands inside the fox-fur muff. "I will bear it, sir," she answered at last, "because I must."

The coach finally creaked to a halt outside the rented house in Hawkesbridge. Sir Bastian had stopped off at Wellburn as planned, and the last ten miles of the journey had been lonely and disheartening. Lili was glad to be home, even if home was this strange tall house on a narrow, climbing street, in an unfamiliar part of the town.

But when Will came out on the steps to meet her and escort her inside, when his face lit up at the sight of her and her heart gave an unexpected leap at the sight of him, she realized, with a pang, that the task before her was going to be harder than she had imagined.

Will looked very well in his green uniform: trim and active, disturbingly masculine. As he pressed a kiss into the palm of her hand, as he kissed each of her fingers in turn, Lili felt her knees begin to tremble under her skirts.

"I have missed you," he said under his breath. "And you look like a breath of spring though the weather's so foul!"

They paused inside a crowded entry hall, at the foot of a rosewood staircase gleaming with wax. Though they were surrounded by servants, Wilrowan slid a strong arm around Lili's waist and planted a kiss firmly on her lips.

Oh dear, thought Lili, much too keenly aware of his lean, hard body, wonderfully and terribly aware of the taste of his mouth as it touched hers. The change inside her, the new way of *noticing* things was affecting her in a wholly unexpected way.

To cover her confusion, she looked around her. "It—it appears to be a charming house."

Will laughed and released his hold on her waist, though he still retained his grip on her hand.

"I trust," he said, leading her up four short steps and into the next room, "that I know your tastes. But if you find you don't like it, if you think there are too many stairs, we will look for another house. I want you to be happy and make a long visit." Then, inexplicably, his face clouded. "Unfortunately, I won't be here as much as I hoped."

"No?" It was ridiculous, Lili knew, to feel so disappointed. "I thought—"

"I asked for leave and I expected to receive it. At the time we first agreed on this visit, there was no reason I knew why I shouldn't get it. But things have changed. I am needed elsewhere and can't be spared."

Lili felt her stomach twist into a hard knot. Did Will know something about the missing Jewel that she and the Specularii did not? If so, in addition to deceiving him, she was going to be expected to spy on him as well. "Something—something has come up?"

"It is only that the queen is so delicate. She must be shielded from every shock, spared every discomfort and inconvenience. Of course, much of this falls on me."

"Of course," said Lili, in a doubtful voice. Though she did wonder why Will, of all people, should nursemaid Dionee. "At least, I suppose it must, since you say so."

They sat down together on a tapestry-work sofa. "Lili," he said, pressing her hand, "if you want to go home and try this again in the autumn, I will understand. But I really must tell you: I am excessively glad to see you."

Lili wished fervently that she might believe that. Yet she had come too far to turn back now. "I don't think that I will go home. I believe I can keep myself—tolerably well amused when you're not with me. I'm accustomed to making the effort, at least."

She saw Will cringe at the unintended bitterness in her voice. "This wasn't how I——" He stopped and shook his head. "There is no use in making excuses, and very little time for it, anyway. I return to the Volary within the hour. If you would like to come with me, you are welcome to do so, though I should think after such a long day——"

But would *I be welcome?* she wondered. Despite the warmth of his greeting, despite that moment in the hall, Lili found herself doubting that Will really wanted her. And it was true enough what he implied: she was tired and dirty and cold, after two days of travel in filthy weather, after a miserable night spent at a drafty inn. While she had business of her own at the Volary, that business could wait. "No thank you," she said, with a weary shake of her head. "I think I had rather stay here by the fire and go to bed early."

*   *   *

It was a strange old house, as Lili discovered the next morning, when she set out to explore it immediately after breakfast. Built halfway up the side of a hill, it was made up of no less than thirteen different levels—one it would seem for each of its major rooms. As a result, she could not go *anywhere* without first going up, or else going down, at least four or five steps—though there was also, of course, the great rosewood staircase which began in the entry hall and led all the way up, for five long flights, to the very top of the house.

Up under the eaves, she eventually discovered a tiny sitting room, evidently meant for her own use. It was an odd little room, all angles and nooks, a sort of after-thought tucked away in a corner, but it was very prettily and curiously furnished—with lacquer cabinets and teakwood chairs, and an ostrich egg in a golden stand up on the mantle—and it boasted as well a tall dormer window where the roof peaked, which offered a breathtaking view of the city below.

Drawn to that view from the very moment she walked in, Lili was still sitting, an hour or two later, curled up on the window-seat, gazing down and down at a jumbled vista of slates, tiles, gables, chimneys, cats, and rusty iron stove pipes, when the butler came in and announced Trefallon.

Abandoning her vantage point, she rose immediately and awkwardly to her feet, trying to think what her rôle as hostess must be. It was one she had never been called on to play before, as Allora always did the honors at Brakeburn Hall.

"You will forgive me, I hope, for such a late visit," said Blaise, bowing over the hand she belatedly offered him. His breath came quickly after his climb, but he looked cool and elegant, the very picture of a worldly young gentleman.

Taking in the magnificence of a deer-colored coat and embroidered waistcoat, an intricate neckcloth with a dragonfly stickpin, the

diamond and topaz rings that he wore on his very white hands, Lili
was astonished and just a bit daunted. As their previous meetings had
all taken place in the country, she had never imagined that Will's best
friend cut such a fashionable figure in the city. "Not at all," she managed to reply. "Will you take a seat—Mr. Trefallon?"

He tilted his head, raised a shapely eyebrow. "With the greatest
of pleasure—my dear Mrs. Blackheart. But the last time we met it
was 'Blaise' and 'Lili.' May I venture to ask what has changed in the
meantime?"

In spite of her embarrassment she found herself laughing at his
quizzical expression. "Of course," she said, with a rueful shake of her
head. "How very stupid of me to forget."

They each took a seat on a teakwood chair and were easier after
that, conversing amiably on a number of subjects—though she did
experience some *slight* difficulty keeping her countenance when
Blaise reached into a coat pocket, took out a tiny brisé fan, and
began to wave it gently in front of him.

"No doubt," he said, giving her an arch look over the tortoise-
shell sticks, "you are stunned by my splendor. The merest affecta-
tion, I do assure you—I can be quite a sensible companion when I
put my mind to it."

"So I have heard," said Lili, with an answering twinkle. "Will always says——"

"Don't, I beg you, believe a word of it. If you believe Wilrowan,
you'll think me the dullest dog in the city." Grown suddenly sober, he
closed his fan with a decisive snap. "And the truth is I have come here
to offer myself as your escort. I would be perfectly enchanted to take
you—well, to take you practically anywhere you'd like to go."

Lili felt her heart sink. Despite her best efforts, her smile
dimmed. "Did Wilrowan send you here to look after me, Blaise?"
And she wondered how she could possibly bear it if Will came to regard her only as a burden to pass off on others.

"Not in the least!" said Trefallon, with a very convincing show of surprise. "I volunteered. No, honestly, Lili, I am your most obliged and obedient servant. I hope you don't mind?"

She forced herself to answer brightly. "How could I mind? And I suppose——" She looked down at her hands, which she was surprised to discover were clenched in her lap. "I suppose since you *are* Wilrowan's closest friend, no one would think anything of it?"

"No one will think anything if we are occasionally seen together," Blaise reassured her. "It is quite the mode for young married ladies to choose their own escorts." As he pocketed the fan, his manner became coaxing. "Now where may I take you tomorrow? The theater? The opera? The Royal Exchange?"

Lili noticed that he did not propose a visit to the Volary, to pay her respects to Dionee. Had the omission been calculated? "Wherever you please, sir. You will know better than I do what is really worth seeing."

She hesitated, not wishing to impose on his good nature. "But I do have one suggestion. You must be acquainted with my Cousin Nick——with Lieutenant Kestrel Brakeburn?"

"Of course," said Blaise, rising smoothly to his feet as an indication that his visit was over. "I will try to bring Nick with me tomorrow——if he is not on duty or otherwise engaged. No doubt we will make a very pleasant party."

Lili was forced to agree. Though she could not help wondering why he——or Wilrowan——was taking such pains to keep her amused and away from the palace.

Will did not reappear until two evenings later. The weather had cleared, and Lili spent the entire day with Blaise and Nick, riding about in an open carriage, visiting a park, a museum, and the Royal Exchange. But she had dined alone, and feeling weary and dull after such a full day, she decided to retire early.

She was sitting at her dressing table, already down to her green linen stays and starched muslin petticoat, brushing out her chestnut curls, when the door flew open. Expecting the abigail that Will had engaged, Lili was just turning to dismiss the girl—when in strolled Wilrowan himself.

The hairbrush slipped out of her hands, falling to the table with a loud clatter. At Brakeburn Hall, Will had never appeared while she was still undressing; at Brakeburn Hall he had too much delicacy to ever intrude in this extraordinary fashion.

But this is Will's *house,* she suddenly realized. It was Wilrowan's house, they were his servants, and the big oak bed with the heavy red velvet curtains, that was his bed—at least for the next two months. Inexplicably, Lili felt herself at a great disadvantage.

Will closed the door softly behind him. "I trust," he said, with a faint touch of sarcasm, "that Trefallon has been keeping you suitably amused?"

"Why, yes," said Lili, wondering why on earth he should sound so put out, when *he* was the one who had asked Blaise to escort her. "Blaise Trefallon—and my cousin Nick."

Crossing the room, Will took one of her hands between his thumb and forefinger, brushed the lightest of kisses across the back. The sensation was so intense, her reaction was so surprising, it was all that Lili could do to maintain her composure. "I stopped in briefly this afternoon, only to learn that you had gone out."

With an effort, she collected herself. "Oh, dear. If I had known you were coming, I would have—" She heard herself give a light, affected laugh. "But really, there was no particular reason for me to expect you, was there?"

"No reason in the world," he replied, dropping her hand and taking a step backward. "Except that husbands do, occasionally, spend an afternoon with their wives. But the fact is, I was only here to deliver a message from Rodaric. He wishes to see you tomorrow af-

ternoon." Again there was that touch of irony. "I trust you don't already have some more pressing engagement?"

"If I have," said Lili, goaded by his unpleasant manner, "then I
must try to get out of it, mustn't I!" She picked up her hairbrush
again, and ran it through her curls. "A summons from the king
should not be refused."

"As you say—it would be impolitic." He had been watching her
lips intently while she spoke; now his eyes moved slowly down the
entire length of her body, in an insolent way that made Lili long to
slap him. "May I claim the privilege of escorting you tomorrow?"

She took such a vicious pull at her hair that the tears started up
in her eyes. "Of course. I can be ready by eleven, if that is what
you—" But she stopped in mid-sentence, with the brush in the air.
"Wilrowan, are—are you going so soon?"

He paused with his hand on the door. "What do you take me for?"
he said under his breath. "Am I really capable of such crude behavior? To neglect you for two whole days, yet expect to spend the
night?"

You can stay if you choose, thought Lili, blinking back the tears, but
she was much too proud to say the words out loud. "You must do—
you must do whatever pleases you," she heard herself saying instead.
"As Heaven's my witness, you always have!"

There was a spark in his eyes, a moment of hesitation, which
made Lili think—which made Lili hope—he was going to stay in
spite of her. That he was going to stay *to* spite her, if that made any
sense. And while the consequences of that could hardly be pleasant,
they might be—interesting.

But the light in his eyes died; his face became suddenly very cold.
"On that note, madam, I will take my leave." And before she could
say anything more, he was out of the room, shutting the door very
quietly behind him.

30

After a restless night, Lili rose at eight and drifted downstairs to breakfast. As she sipped her morning tea, as she buttered a crumbling caraway scone and set it aside untasted, she suddenly remembered that today was the day she would go to the Volary. Her heart gave a sudden bound. A delicate task lay before her; was it possible she could succeed on her very first visit?

One of the footmen came into the room, and announced that a gentleman had called. "A gentleman? At this hour?"

"A Sir Bastian Josslyn-Mather, madam. I told him—"

"No, no, show him in at once." And Lili spent the next few minutes wondering what this unexpected visit could possibly mean, until the old gentleman himself appeared at the door of her dining parlor, hat in hand.

"Do not rise," he insisted. "And do not look so anxious, either. There is nothing seriously amiss. But as there is something I most particularly wished to discuss, I took the chance that Captain Blackheart would be out."

"If I am not to rise, then you must take a seat and allow me to pour you a cup of tea," said Lili, lifting the flowered teapot. "But, sir, did you *know* where I am going this afternoon?"

Sir Bastian pulled up one of the walnut side-chairs and sat down facing her. "To the palace, Lilliana? That is excellent news. But not, I am afraid, the news that brings me here. If indeed it may be called news at all. The matter may be important, or again it may not." He cleared his throat, looked faintly uncomfortable. "I saw Captain Blackheart at the theater last night. Not to speak to, of course. He was there with—he was there with the queen and a very large party, and someone was kind enough to point him out."

Lili wondered about that momentary hesitation. Who *had* Will been with that Sir Bastian was reluctant to mention? She remembered that one of Wilrowan's most notorious romances had been with a certain Mrs. Sidmouth, a tragedian. While it was unlikely the liaison had lasted for more than two years, it was also unlikely that Will had lost his taste for actresses.

"—with the queen on the terrace afterwards," Sir Bastian had continued on, while Lili's thoughts were elsewhere, "he wears a ring on his right hand, a smoke-colored stone, carved intaglio, in a silver setting. No doubt you know it?"

"Yes, of course," Lili answered, with a puzzled little frown.

"It is of Goblin manufacture?"

"It's so very old, it could hardly be anything else." Lili lifted her cup and took a sip. "It came to Will from his grandmother, two or three years ago."

"Ah," said Sir Bastian, looking satisfied. "Then I was correct in thinking I had seen it before."

Lili put down her teacup. "Do you *know* Lady Krogan?"

The old gentleman smiled. "My dear, it would not be possible to live as long as I have, and to see so much of the world, and *not* at some point meet Odile Krogan. The reason I marked the ring when I saw her wearing it—she was Miss Odilia Rowan at the time—was because I had seen and handled similar stones before." He leaned forward. "Are you quite, quite certain that Captain

Blackheart knows nothing of your secret activities these last several years?"

Lili gave a tiny jerk and spilled her tea. "Does he know I have been training as a Specularii magician?" She righted her teacup, picked up an embroidered napkin, and began to mop up the spill. "So far as I know, he is unaware the Specularii even exist. Why do you ask?"

"Perhaps I am wrong, then. These stones are not always used for reading the minds of other people."

Lili stopped and stared at him, with the tea-stained linen still in her hand. "Sir Bastian, are you saying that—that Will might have been invading my thoughts all of these years? But that is incredible!" Shaking her head, she began mopping up tea again. "Will did study magic at the university, but he completely lost interest when he left."

"You will know best. Yet I think you ought to be cautious anyway. You must guard your thoughts whenever your husband is near. There is no harm in being careful."

But Lili was no longer listening. She sat with burning cheeks, thinking of all the things that she would rather *die* than reveal to Wilrowan. Last night—what if he had known that she wanted him to stay? What if he had known, and still he left, to meet some actress at the playhouse?

And if he did, Lili wondered bleakly, *how could I ever, ever face him again?*

Will appeared that afternoon in a conciliating mood. With one of those startling changes of front for which he was so justly famous, he was all smiles, charm, and easy conversation as he escorted Lilliana to the Volary. Despite Sir Bastian and his disturbing theories, she found she was still capable of enjoying Wilrowan's company.

The king received her in his study. If Lili was shy at first, Rodaric soon disarmed her with his forthright, sensible manner. They spent a pleasant afternoon, during which he allowed her to examine his collection of ancient manuscripts, and they discussed a number of books they had both read. The visit was apparently a success; she was invited back for the next day, to play chess with the king.

Much to Lili's surprise, Will reappeared in time to escort her home. Hailing a chair, helping her to climb inside, making every effort to secure her comfort, he walked alongside as she was carried back to the house. He stayed for supper, making agreeable conversation all the while, and it was only much later, when she realized that he was spending the night, that Sir Bastian's words came rushing back into Lili's mind. Then she grew flustered, excused herself early, and ran upstairs to her bedroom to cool her cheeks in privacy.

She was already in her nightgown, just climbing into bed, when she heard Wilrowan moving around in the adjoining dressing room. She sat bolt upright against the pillows, pulling the crimson counterpane up to her chest and trying to regulate her wildly beating heart. For once, her Specularii training was no help at all.

After a few minutes, the connecting door opened and Will walked into the room, barefoot, stripped down to his linen drawers and shirt, carrying a lighted candle in one hand. He put the candlestick carefully down on a table and seated himself on the edge of the bed.

Lili had always felt safe in her big white bed at Brakeburn Hall, safe in her long-sleeved nightdress that covered everything. *But if Will knew everything that I was thinking,* she thought in a panic, *if he always knew everything that I was feeling—I was worse than naked the whole time!*

"So," he said softly, as she caught her breath sharply and averted her eyes, "it seems that I am *not* forgiven. I must admit that is disappointing. I thought we were getting along so well."

Lili gave an uneasy little laugh. "I suppose it depends on what you have done that needs forgiving. I can—I can hardly forgive something I don't even know about."

He shook his head slowly. "Not a thing, I swear to you. Not a blessed thing in a long, long time. I wish you wouldn't listen to what others say of me. If you want to know something, you have only to ask. I may be a scoundrel—a rogue—anything you like, but I would never lie to you."

Lili cringed inwardly. There *was* a liar in this room, and she knew who it was, even if he did not. She swallowed hard, tried to relax, but found that she could not.

And as Will bent over to kiss her gently on the mouth, as she felt herself go suddenly stiff and cold under the covers, Lili knew that it was going to be another dissatisfying night for both of them.

In the weeks that followed, Lili visited the Volary often. At Dionee's invitation, she attended two card-playing evenings, and a third devoted to dancing, held in the Music Room under the oppressive gold ceiling and the great chandelier. On each of these occasions, it seemed to Lili that Will was less occupied attending the queen than he was with some of the women attending her.

Almost on sight, Lili conceived an aversion to a certain Lady Steerpike and a Maria Ascham, as both of these ladies were far too caressing, *much* too familiar in their manner toward Wilrowan. Letitia Steerpike was handsome and hard-looking, her lips very red, her eyes very bright, and her bosom very bare in her low-cut gowns. As for Maria Ascham, she was the woman that Will had "kidnapped" all those years ago.

Thanks to Blaise, who danced with Lili twice, the informal ball was not a complete disaster, but her one dance with Will was silent and hostile, simply because she had seen him in whispered conversation with Letitia Steerpike only moments before.

Why did he invite me to Hawkesbridge only to humiliate me? Lili asked herself, all through the dance. She felt hot and miserable in her splendid new gown. The dress—made of peacock satin with three rows of lace—had made her feel elegant when she first put it on, but how had she imagined she could ever compete with the far more mature, and certainly more blatant, charms of a Letty Steerpike?

That the Steerpike creature's interest in Will was considerably more marked than his in her was not much comfort. Even Wilrowan would not be so shameless as to flaunt his mistress in the presence of his wife.

He is such an accomplished flirt! thought Lili, as they walked through the complicated figures of the dance. A slight squeeze when their hands touched, a light brushing of fingers as he passed on her left—oh, he knew all the tricks, that much was certain. Had she not been so well-acquainted with her wayward husband, she might have been fooled into thinking that it actually *meant* something.

But if Lili was learning to dread Dionee's evenings, she did look forward to her afternoon visits with the king, where the mix of books and tea, chess and conversation, was exactly to her taste.

One afternoon, during a visit to his library, he offered to show her some of the rarer items inside the Treasure Room. Lili felt a stir of excitement; the chance she had been waiting for had finally arrived. It was only with difficulty that she hid her elation.

Leaving the building through an arched doorway, Lili and the king followed a meandering stone path across a vivid green lawn. Somewhere in the distance, a bird or a monkey shrieked, a great cat roared. Passing down an avenue of budding fruit trees, Rodaric led the way up a short flight of mossy brick steps, through another door, and into the dim, chilly vastness that was the museum wing.

Moving from one drafty chamber to the next, he paused briefly in a long torchlit gallery to show Lili a collection of full-length portraits done in oils. "My earliest ancestors," said Rodaric, with a motion of his hand. "I should say: the earliest kings and queens of Mountfalcon. One knows so little of one's family history before the Fall of the Empire, but I believe we had some employment in the southern tin mines."

Yet these were no portraits of men and women contemplating their humble origins. There were dignified men in pouter-pigeon doublets stuffed with bombast; more dashing ancestors decked out in love-locks, slashes and ribbons; amorous young women in bare-shouldered wasp-waisted velvet gowns—and one small grey-eyed boy, closely resembling Rodaric himself, though by the cut of his coat and the length of his loose flowing hair, he had probably been dust for centuries.

Then it was out of the gallery and into a long corridor, where the king proceeded to point out some of the choicer curiosities for which the Volary was famous: some newts, frogs, lizards, and serpents put up in pickle; a corn-mill in a bottle, that moved without wind, water, or clockwork; the skeleton of a whale; a dried cockatrice and a necklace of tears; and an immense great-grandfather clock, towering (so Lili discovered by craning her neck) a full two stories high inside a stairwell.

Ascending those very same stairs, Lili and the king finally reached the corridor just outside the Treasure Room. Two guards in maroon-and-gold stood at stiff attention before a massive door; at Rodaric's approach, they saluted smartly and stepped aside.

The king reached inside a pocket in his waistcoat and drew out a large and ornate silver key, which he proceeded to fit into the lock. As the heavy oak door with its five bars of iron swung slowly open, Rodaric sent one of the guards in to light the candles, then he beckoned to Lili to follow him in.

Once inside, Lili glanced around her in wonder and delight. There was so much color, so much beauty—it was like entering a private universe, a miniature cosmos, exquisitely painted.

The walls were all covered with allegorical frescoes, depicting the four seasons—the elements—and the arts and sciences. Ancient gods and goddesses sported overhead, in a cloudless sky of purest blue, while the golden chariots of the sun, the moon, and the thir-

344 ᗄ· TERESA EDGERTON

teen planets chased each other in endless circles across the painted firmament. At Lili's feet, a beautifully inlaid mosaic tile floor depicted the depths of the ocean, with glowing fishes, colorful seaweeds, and deep-sea monsters swimming about with their mouths wide open.

Walking a few steps ahead of her, Rodaric touched an unseen spring on one of the frescoed wall panels. A door slid open, exposing the secret cabinet behind. "As you will see," said the king, moving on to another place and opening up a second section of wall, "the objects inside each represent absolute mastery of the various arts: metallurgy, lapidary, clockwork, bookbinding——" He went on to open another, and yet another hidden cupboard.

On velvet cushions inside these cabinets the Royal Treasures fairly dazzled Lili's eye, with the gleam of silver and gold, the flash and glitter of precious stones.

Rodaric watched her reaction with a faint smile. "Yes, it is a monstrous display of vanity and avarice. You must remember, however, that my family has been collecting these things for fifteen hundred years."

"But I think it's perfectly beautiful," murmured Lili, impressed in spite of herself, as much by the craftsmanship as by the costly materials. "Though perhaps I *would* be embarrassed if it was all mine."

"Fortunately, very little of it actually *is* mine, which removes some of the embarrassment. I hold most of this in trust for my heirs, and for the people of Mountfalcon."

Continuing around the room, Lili felt a tingle across her skin. It was the result of the currents of force drawn to this place over many years by the presence of the Goblin engine. Now that the Chaos Machine was gone, the effect would eventually dissipate as the magnetic rays were attracted elsewhere, but for now it was still very strong, at least to someone as sensitive as she was.

"The Orb of Mountfalcon," said the king, opening one of the cabinets and indicating a golden globe of the earth, about the size of an apple. Tiny gemstones sparkled at the poles and around the equator.

Though Lili knew that the Orb was only a decoy, she could hardly say so. Believing her interest genuine, Rodaric took out the globe and opened it up, displaying the intricate clockwork mechanism inside. As she watched the small wheels spin, the various movements of the delicate machinery, Lili thought it was all so cunningly made, it was a great pity that it *did* nothing.

On the same shelf where the Orb had been resting, there was an empty cushion. When Lili bent down to peer at the red velvet pillow intently, the tingling sensation was stronger than ever. "And what was here?"

"Nothing of great importance," said Rodaric with a shrug. Only because she knew the truth and was watching him did Lili see that sudden tightening of muscles which belied his casual reply. "A little jeweled orrery."

So this was the very spot where the Chaos Machine had rested. Around Lili, the magnetic forces seemed to coalesce like a tiny thunderstorm.

Concentrating her will, she forced all of the air out of her lungs in one long breath. The room began to grow grey, the walls to close rapidly in around her. As her knees buckled, she heard the king say her name, felt him reach out and grasp her by the waist.

Then the world went black, and Lili went limp in Rodaric's arms.

When Lili came back to herself, she was seated on a low marble bench in the corridor outside the Treasure Room. The king was kneeling at her feet and vigorously chafing her wrists, while the two guards hovered behind him.

As her eyes fluttered open, Rodaric gave an audible sigh of relief. He turned to the guards and waved them away. "For the love of Heaven, one of you go at once and fetch Captain Blackheart."

The taller of the two guards saluted and hurried off; the other took up his position again by the door, leaving Lili alone with the king at the other end of the corridor.

"I beg your pardon. I can't think what made me do anything quite so—foolish."

"Not at all," said Rodaric, taking her wrist and stroking it more gently this time. "I am the one who should apologize. The room needs airing. I should never have taken you inside."

Lili flushed guiltily. Her swoon had been authentic enough, but it had not been the fault of the stale air. It was the sort of trick she despised, feigning the sort of feminine weakness she hated even more, but it had been necessary in order to initiate that brief yet intimate contact with the king. During the moment before she lost consciousness completely, when she was in his arms at the heart of the magnetic storm, something had passed between them, unnoticed by him but not by her.

Images had crowded into her mind: *the Chaos Machine and its delicate internal workings, the dizzying labyrinthine complexity of the Mountfalcon mines.* For the moment, it was all a muddle; there had been so much received in a single instant, so much to remember, so much to be mentally sorted out, when she had the leisure and privacy to do so. But Lili knew that when she had done so, she would know the Goblin device every bit as well as Rodaric knew it himself. More than that, she was now attuned to the exact vibration that would announce the presence of the Chaos Machine—if and when she ever came within its orbit of influence.

"I am feeling much better now."

She tried to rise to her feet, but found it impossible, so long as Rodaric continued to hold her gently in place. "You will stay where you are until I tell you otherwise," he insisted. "I see that you have regained your usual charming color, and that is a very good sign, but until—"

He stopped speaking, when a familiar impatient step sounded in the corridor behind him. As Rodaric turned, Lili looked up at the same time, and saw Will just arriving—and not best pleased, it would seem, by the sight of his wife all but reclining in the king's arms.

"Wilrowan," Rodaric said calmly. "You arrive in good time. Lili has been a little unwell. I think that you should see her back home."

Wilrowan glared at them both. His nostrils flared and his mouth compressed in a thin, hard line. His lips barely moved as he spoke. "I think you must be right, Your Majesty. It is past time that I took my wife home."

31

*L*ord Polyphant was entertaining visitors, when Lucius Guilian suddenly appeared in the ambassador's salon, as though he had been impelled by the force of a cannon.

Outside, it was a white winter afternoon. Inside, Lord Polyphant and his guests had gathered in a room with two large fireplaces, where they were blunting their sharp winter appetites with caviar, plovers' eggs, and champagne. But conversations were beginning to lag, people were starting to make their excuses and drift away, when Luke's precipitous entrance provided a much needed spark of interest.

Lord Polyphant rose slowly from his seat by one of the fires, smiling his false sweet smile. "Mr. Guilian, what a pleasure to see you. I trust you are acquainted with—" he turned and gestured toward the various gentlemen who made up a group around him "—Lord Catts, Lord Hoodj, Mr. Varian Dou, and of course, Lord Flinx."

Luke, who had entered with such energy, went suddenly very still. It was—as one of those present would later describe it—like watching ice freeze. His back stiffened, his jaw clenched so tightly the teeth rattled, his usually expressive dark eyes turned as cold and as hard as stones. It almost seemed as though something would shatter, as very slowly, and very stiffly, Luke made the very smallest of bows in the direction of Lord Flinx. "I don't believe I've had the—pleasure."

The king's nephew looked nothing like rumor had painted him. In that gaudy assembly—among those improbable wigs, those exaggerated coattails, hoops, and stilt-heeled slippers—he was as soberly and modestly dressed as a Pantheist clergyman. A middle-aged man, with light hair unpowdered and neatly clubbed at the back, he had a soft air of gentility utterly at odds with his vile reputation.

"Yet I feel as though I know you, Mr. Guilian. My little niece is full of your praises. She is always repeating the clever things that her new friend 'Lucius' says and does."

Behind his frozen smile, Luke began to feel ill. As though Lord Flinx were an ordinary doting uncle. As though his niece were an ordinary schoolroom miss.

"Perhaps you have not yet heard," put in Lord Polyphant. "Lord Flinx has just been appointed the new Prime Minister."

Again that very smallest and stiffest of bows. "I congratulate you, sir," said Luke, forcing out the words. "No doubt this is your reward for the truly—extraordinary sacrifices you have made on behalf of your country."

Lord Flinx smiled urbanely. "But I understand that you, also, are to be felicitated. No doubt there is great rejoicing in Winterscar."

At this, Luke swiveled to address the ambassador. "It is on that very matter, Lord Polyphant, that I desire to speak with you. If you will be so good, I would like a few moments of your time—alone."

"With the greatest pleasure in the world," said the ambassador, continuing to smile sweetly. "We can speak privately in the next room."

When Lord Polyphant and Luke were alone in the embassy library, the ambassador's smile faded. "Need I tell you, Mr. Guilian, that was not very wise?"

"That may well be," Luke retorted. "But if you value my friend-ship, you will not make a habit of presenting me to men who would never be acknowledged or received in Winterscar."

Lord Polyphant cocked his head to one side. "May I remind you that this is not Winterscar, that this same Lord Flinx is a very pow-erful man? He is, I might add, the very pink of gentility. I think that you listen to too much gossip."

"Gossip?" Though he had not been invited to sit, Luke flung him-self down on one of the lyre-back chairs. "I don't listen to gossip at all. But when a man is paragraphed in the newspapers of every na-tion on the continent, when his name may be heard in scurrilous bal-lads sung on the streets in places as far away as Vordheim in Kjellmark—" Luke's teeth came together with an audible click. "You are correct, Lord Polyphant, this is not Tarnburgh and this is not Winterscar. It is a nation run by madmen and hypocrites. Unfortu-nately, they would be much better off were they ruled by the mad-men solely, and dispensed with the hypocrites altogether!"

The ambassador regarded him with mild amazement. By now he was accustomed to Luke's vehemence, knew him to be a man who might wax eloquent on a variety of subjects, from the trivial to the profound, yet he had never seen him display anything resembling such furious indignation.

"Such heat, Mr. Guilian. One might almost think you had a per-sonal grudge."

Luke glared. He opened his mouth as though he would speak, but the ambassador made haste to change the subject. "Yet I believe you meant to speak of events back home in Winterscar."

This was not so happy a switch as Lord Polyphant might have wished. Lucius reached into his coat, pulled out a piece of paper, very much tattered and water-stained. "This came this morning. A letter from my old tutor, Doctor Purcell, in which he describes the ceremonies and festivities surrounding the royal nuptials in Tarnburgh——three full months ago. The letter was delayed along the way by storms in the north.

"What I wish to know," he went on, with a savage gleam in his eye, "is why it is that since *you* knew, since *Lord Flinx* knew, since seemingly *everyone in the world* knew but me, you never bothered to mention the fact that my cousin the king was so recently married?"

Lord Polyphant shrugged. "The news is but a day old here. Indeed, it was I who told Lord Flinx, not a quarter of an hour ago. Other letters than your Doctor Purcell's were delayed by the weather."

"Quite possibly true. But according to this letter, the *betrothal* had been officially announced during the month of Oragia, when communications are very swift. So why was this not the very first thing that anyone mentioned when I arrived in Luden eight long weeks ago?"

The ambassador fingered a pair of ridiculously ornate scissor eyeglasses, which he wore on a scarlet ribbon around his neck. "But do you mean to tell me, Mr. Guilian, that you were actually ignorant of the king's *betrothal?*"

"I spent most of the summer and early autumn in the Phelegra Montes. I did hear rumors while I was passing through Lichtenwald. I dismissed them as gossip——which, as I told you, I never listen to."

"Then perhaps you should have done, that one time. I thought—— everyone thought——when you appeared so reticent on the subject, that it would be tactless to mention a union of which you so obviously disapproved."

Luke's dark eyebrows came suddenly together. "I disapprove? Why should *I* disapprove? I know nothing about the young lady myself——that is, about Her Majesty, the new Queen of Winterscar. I met her only once. Is there any reason that I *might* disapprove, something I don't even know about?"

Lord Polyphant hesitated; something flickered behind his eyes.

"It was only your seeming reluctance to discuss the match. Speaking for myself, I naturally assumed King Jarred had written to tell you himself."

Luke frowned thoughtfully. It *was* very puzzling, even disquieting, that Jarred had never done so. But he was not about to mention his misgivings to Polyphant, whose discretion he could not rely on.

The air on the street seemed cleaner, the winter landscape of snow-covered roofs and frozen canals a better and purer place, after the perfumed decadence of the ambassador's salon. Luke leaned up against an iron lamp post and took several deep, restoring breaths of the crisp air.

As usual, the street was filled with a hustle and bustle of tradesmen hawking their wares, with a great coming and going of carriages, wagons, and horse-drawn sledges. Knife-grinders, pie-men, and bustling housewives; country bumpkins carrying baskets of eggs, turnips, hickory nuts and chestnuts over their arms; all of these passed by on foot, while stout old merchants and their even stouter wives went bouncing by in rattling dog-carts. Over on one of the canals, Luke spied a group of children whisking about the ice on skates made of bone and steel.

He took a final deep breath, and then set out walking at a brisk pace. On an impulse, he headed in the direction of Doctor Van Tulp's.

It was a fine day, as sunny as it was cold, and if the streets were a bit slick, there were footpaths and wooden sidewalks most of the way. Within half an hour, Lucius was at the wrought-iron gates of the great institution. He nodded to the porter, who by this time knew him very well by sight, paid a penny for a ticket, and was immediately admitted inside.

In their private world at the top of the house, Izaiah and Tremeur were working on their map. It was a vast project, one that took up most of the floor, and had already occupied a week of their time. The map was made of six soft calf-skins, beautifully tanned and sewn together, offering a fair smooth surface for the king and his "duchess" to sketch in a fanciful representation of an imaginary continent in charcoal and chalk.

Luke was surprised by the progress they had made since his last visit: the southern half of the continent was finished and all made permanent in black and scarlet ink. Now the lady was very busily chalking in a large portion of the north, while the old man sat on a stool and offered suggestions.

The map was a remarkable portrait, not only representing the physical features, but also the cities, palaces, and the native flora and fauna of the lunar landscape. Though the interior was fanciful—with fire swamps, impossibly high mountains, and floating cities—though the coastline was jagged and unnaturally angular, it was possible to perceive in the overall outline a certain resemblance to terrestrial maps.

Staring down at what the king and the girl had created, Luke knew he was seeing something far more profound than the wild inventions of a mad old gentleman and his fey young companion. The king who had seen his reforms balked again and again by smaller, less far-seeing men, was mapping out a world of his own—a world of the mind where he reigned supreme, where he and his charming little consort in fancy could have everything exactly as they wanted it to be.

The lady was kneeling down on the map in a delightful confusion of flowered satin, lacy petticoats, and whalebone hoops, but at Luke's approach, she sprang to her feet and dropped him a very pretty curtsy.

"Well, General Zabulon," she said, with a whimsically haughty lift of her eyebrows. "We had begun to think you were never returning to us, that the squids and the cuttlefish had finished you off."

Luke clicked his heels and saluted. "General Zabulon" was the name she had given him, part of the endless adventure that occupied much of her time. The general, he remembered, had last been seen sailing off in a silver galleon, in search of sunken gold. "Indeed, Your Grace, the cuttlefish and the purple octopi all grow very fierce in this weather, but I found I was able to fight them off."

The king nodded approvingly. He seemed to take special delight in tales of the sea and of buried treasure, so his duchess humored him with as many such stories as her fertile invention was able to provide. "And the tides?" he asked, on a slightly querulous note.

Luke knew the answer that Izaiah wanted. "The tides, sir, could hardly be lower, and the dikes still hold." The king was always agitated when the sea ran high. Was he thinking, Luke wondered, of the Maglore engine, the Silver Nef, now in the keeping of the Princess Marjote?

The duchess left her place in the middle of the map, being very careful about the placement of her tiny feet along the way, in order to avoid smearing her handiwork. Under the skirts of her lacy petticoat, Lucius caught a glimpse of rose-colored stockings. Stepping lightly onto the floor, she extended a soft white hand. Feigning a casual gallantry he was very far from feeling, Luke brushed his lips across the tips of her fingers and reluctantly released it.

"We have needed you sadly," she said, indicating with a motion the map on the floor. "We are baffled by the arctic climate, and have no idea how we ought to go on. We thought if you told us some stories of your northern countries—"

"I have never been in Nordfjall," said Luke, still reeling from that moment of contact, "and only for a short time in Kjellmark or Lichtenwald, but nothing would give me greater pleasure than to tell you something of my home in Winterscar."

"Then do so," she replied, with an imperious wave of her hand. Moving carefully around the edge of the calf-skin, she knelt down near the polar regions to resume her drawing, this time according to Luke's directions.

So he tried to describe the wild, stark beauty of his native land: the icy glaciers, the rocky moraines, the terrible fissures ripped in the earth, where it was actually possible to see the volcanic fires burning down in the depths. He spoke of dark blue lakes, so cold and so pure, and of boiling hot springs; of the River Scar which tumbled down from the mountains and continued along its course for hundreds of miles through dangerous rapids; and of bears, wolves, and shaggy white boars lurking in the pine woods. "Perhaps it was for contrast with the rugged landscape, the dangerous wilderness to be seen on every side, that the Goblins, when they built the great city of Tarnburgh, chose to make everything so dainty, so exquisite."

The duchess stopped drawing volcanoes and ice-caverns. She gazed up at Luke, her violet eyes sparkling. "Are the cities of Winterscar truly as people describe them? Are they really like something out of a fairy tale?"

He knelt down beside her. "Tarnburgh is ten times a fairy tale. It is like an expensive toy, a beautiful little clockwork city. And life there can be so elegant, so mannered, so utterly humane, that it's sometimes hard to believe that pain or suffering or cruelty could possibly exist anywhere in the world."

She was watching his face intently as he ended this speech. "And is that why you first set out on your travels? To see for yourself if these things were true?"

Luke smiled ruefully; he shook his head. "A single visit to the Goblin Quarter in Tarnburgh was enough to teach me the truth. Though I must admit, even the very worst parts of Tarnburgh have nothing to compare with the dirt and wickedness and misery I have since seen elsewhere."

She gave a deep sigh. They were kneeling so close together there on the floor, Luke could feel her breath on his face. She smelled of soap, and gingerbread, and attar of roses. Inhaling that scent—looking into her pretty, innocent, whimsical little face—he could not at that moment believe any of the vile stories attached to her name.

Even when he was away from her, even when he was far removed from the spell of her beauty and her wit and her originality, Luke was convinced she could not possibly be the king's mistress. There was something in the way that Izaiah looked at her, something in the way that she spoke to him, that made the idea unthinkable. In this, at least, she must be the victim of evil-minded gossip—of the uncle who was willing to let people believe that terrible, incestuous thing about her, merely because it suited some purpose of his own.

Of the other things—things that were said about her disreputable past, of the many men she had slept with and the shocking details and circumstances under which she had done so—when he was not actually with her, Luke was not so certain whether he believed them or not.

But one thing he knew, one thing remained unshakeable in his mind: whatever the sins of one Tremeur Brouillard—whatever she might have done, or suffered to have done to her—those sins had nothing to do with that sparkling little creature, the "Grand Exalted Hereditary Duchess," who lived with the king in these enchanted rooms.

There was a short moment of slightly embarrassed silence between them. Then she blushed and looked away, went back to sketching her map. "You must be very eager, I think, to go back home."

"Sometimes I do want to go home. But I promised myself that I would not return for a very long time. There is still so much that I want to learn."

While they had been speaking, the king had temporarily lost interest in the map. He had wandered off to another part of the room, where he was studying a seashell under a magnifying glass.

Finding himself in this rare private moment with the object of so many confused emotions, so many tortured speculations, Luke suddenly blurted out: "Is Lord Flinx your father?"

Her face turned pink, she caught her breath. For a moment it seemed the pleasant illusion must shatter, that the temptress of the street ballads and the scurrilous stories was about to become a palpable presence in the room.

But then the girl at Luke's side went back to her map, began sketching in wolves and shaggy white boars at the foot of a range of active volcanoes. "Do you know, General Zabulon, I really can't say. He has certainly told me so, again and again, but he is such an unconscionable liar, it is difficult for me to trust anything he says."

The scarlet woman retreated even further, and Lucius was more than happy to see her go. "On the whole," said the Grand Exalted Hereditary Duchess, with a shake of her pretty dark curls, "I think I would rather be the Princess from the Moon than anyone's daughter at all!"

*J*t was a strange and changeable spring in Hawkesbridge. One never knew, when one left the house, what the weather would be like, so cloaks, top-boots, and oiled-linen umbrellas continued to be seen on the city streets.

Yet there were signs of the season, too. Ravens built nests in the eaves of old houses and in broken-down chimneys; light pleasure boats with awnings of red, blue, and green began to appear on the slow-moving waters of the Zule. As in other years, mountebanks, vagabonds, and readers of "fortune's urns" started drifting in from the surrounding countryside. They strung up their rope-walks in Tooley Square, they danced on their hands and sang ballads on practically every street corner. Some even had the temerity to set up their peep-shows within the precincts of the university.

If the wandering folk looked dustier, more ragged and foot-sore than before, they compensated by bringing with them more fantastic stories. They spoke of a world in turmoil: pirates on the coast, whole cities aflame in the north, bloody rebellion on the isle of Finghyll.

Some who listened to these tales were vastly disturbed, many more dismissed them as mere inventions. "Travellers," they said, "will always exaggerate."

So, for the most part, life went on as usual. Attics and lumber-rooms were turned out in a flurry of spring cleaning; peddlars hawked nosegays, nightingales, and maple-sugar sweetmeats outside the Volary; children were dosed with mineral salts, brimstone, and treacle.

Only the Goblins appeared to be truly uneasy. They went about the city on their usual business, more silent, more unobtrusive than ever before. As the days passed, they were seen less and less. When they were seen, they hurried on past with their eyes on the ground, and no longer answered when anyone spoke to them.

32

It was a changeable spring for Lili and Will as well. Since that day at the Volary, when he had walked in on her and Rodaric in what he apparently considered suspicious circumstances, Will had only paid her a single afternoon visit, only two times in ten days had he spent the night. With her task at the palace complete, Lili was beginning to consider a return to Brakeburn Hall.

She was dressing to go to the opera one evening, when Will lounged in. He had an odd, unsettled look about him that she did not trust. "Another evening with Blaise Trefallon?" Sitting down at her dressing table, he watched her put on a pair of long silk gloves. "It would seem the two of you have become inseparable."

Lili silently fastened the pearl buttons at her wrists. She had not seen Blaise in almost a week; she did not think, however, that Will was entitled to an explanation, and she held her peace.

Wilrowan sighed. "Lili," he said, with an appealing look, "have I truly offended past all redemption?"

For a moment, she hesitated. It was wearisome playing the rôle of the injured wife. "I hardly know what you mean. If you would like to join us, it is not a large party, and naturally Blaise has rented a box."

"I would be happy to join you. But I have only an hour's leave from the palace. Dionee is—nervous and fretful today. But I think she intends to make it an early night; perhaps I will meet you later."

As Lili moved around the room, Will began idly examining the bottles and jars on her dressing table. "What is this, please?" he asked very suddenly.

Lili stopped in the act of picking up her velvet cloak. When she saw what he was holding, she gave an embarrassed laugh. "It's ceruse, Wilrowan. Don't you approve?"

"Approve? Why should I approve you dabbling your face with purest poison? It's not like you, Lili, to be so vain."

She put down her cloak. "Almost everyone wears it," she answered defensively. "I know what white lead does to the skin, but I thought if I only used a very lit—" Lili broke off, shaking her head. "You are right. I can't think why I bought it," she said in a mortified voice. "But, as you can see, I'm not wearing it now."

"Yes, I *can* see. Believe me when I say you are better without it. Rouge if you must—though why you should want to, I really don't know, when you already have such a 'charming color' as someone once said—but don't, I beg you, take up ceruse. You will only be spoiling what nature has already done exceedingly well."

Lili felt her heart begin to pound. This was a very different Will than she had seen in weeks. As she moved past him, he caught up her hand, and lifted it quickly to his lips. Even through her gloves, she felt the heat of that kiss.

He left the chair, made her sit down in his place, turning her by the shoulders until she faced the mirror. "This new way of dressing your hair is lovely, but never use anything more than the lightest coating of powder, as you have it now. And if you use patches, remember they are only there to call attention to your very best feature."

"Which is?" said Lili, hardly daring to breathe.

Wilrowan laughed. "Fishing for compliments?" he asked, with a teasing smile.

"I suppose one might have a *best* feature without actually having any *good* features."

"Very true. But—happily—not true here." He pretended to examine her reflection in the glass. "The best feature is undoubtedly the eyes, for their shape and color." He opened one of the little patch-boxes, took out a tiny piece of black silk, showed her how to affix the glue, and placed it on one cheek, just under her eye.

Lili smiled tremulously. This was all very charming—and however oddly he had looked at her before, she knew very well this amorous gleam in his eyes. As Will leaned closer to examine his handiwork they were almost kissing. Lili closed her eyes, waited for the kiss to become real—

Just then, one of the servants knocked on the door. Will jumped back. Folding his arms, he gave her another enigmatic glance. "I suppose that Mr. Trefallon has arrived to escort you."

Lili bit her lip, thinking how close she had come to making a fool of herself, merely because Will had suddenly decided to play at lovemaking. She picked up her fan and rose to her feet in a rustle of petticoats. "It would be rude of me to keep Blaise waiting."

Will unfolded his arms and preceded her across the room. "As you say," he agreed, as he obligingly opened the door, "it is always rude to keep a gentleman waiting."

At the grand, gilded twelve-tiered Opera House down by the river, the singing that night was particularly superb. But as the evening progressed, as the music soared and the drama of the story gradually unfolded, Lili became increasingly abstracted.

Perhaps it was the violent, romantic, improbable plot. There were features about it that were oddly familiar—at least to anyone who had the misfortune to follow Wilrowan's career. One had to admit, there was a certain Grand Opera quality to all his affairs—or to the ones that Lili knew about, anyway. *It is all just playacting. Men always say their casual affairs mean very little; with Will, I suppose, it is actually true.*

In the interval between acts, Lili grew pensive.

"You are bored," said Trefallon, hitching his chair a little closer, leaning over to speak in her ear. "Would you like to go home?"

"No, of course not," she said, still hoping that Will would arrive to join them. She searched her mind for a suitable topic of conversation, and her eyes chanced to fall on a frivolous something that Trefallon held in his hand. "What a droll little fan! I have never seen anything quite like it before."

"It is a puzzle fan." Blaise spread out the sticks to give her a better look. "The pictures, you see, are meant to form a rebus and spell out riddles or other conceits." He leaned closer still and spoke softly behind the painted leaf. "Sometimes the answers are a little naughty."

"My goodness," she said, pretending to an interest she did not feel. "Must I work it all out for myself, or will you tell me what these pictures mean?"

"With the greatest of pleasure." As Blaise launched into a detailed explanation, Lili was not really listening; she was thinking instead about another fan, the one that Will sent her all those weeks ago. Had that fan—Lili caught her breath at the thought—had that fan contained some secret message, something sentimental, which she had simply been too ignorant to decipher at the time?

But the pleasant fancy forming in her head was almost instantly dashed. Looking across the house to the seventh tier, she chanced to spot Wilrowan amidst the gilded extravagance of the Royal Box—with that creature Letitia Steerpike hanging right over his shoulder. Playacting or not, it made her blood boil.

As Lili spotted Will, he saw her. For a moment, he actually looked pleased; then his body went rigid and his face deadly pale, at the sight of his wife and Blaise Trefallon, conversing with their heads so close together.

Wilrowan arrived in the box a few minutes later: very stiff, very military, very correct, in his green uniform. He bowed to the company, said a few polite words to Trefallon's friends who were sharing the box.

Without sparing a glance for Lili, he fastened his outraged gaze on her escort. "If it is all the same to you, Trefallon, I will relieve you of my wife's company. There are one or two matters that I wish to discuss with her."

Far from taking offense at Will's insolent tone, Blaise only laughed. He rose to his feet and made a flourishing bow. "You need not go if you would rather not," he said to Lili, over his shoulder. "Even Wilrowan has more sense of propriety than to carry you off by force from the Opera House.

In a daze of anger and humiliation, Lili rose slowly to her feet. Her brain felt congested with a sudden flow of blood, and it was difficult to think. "Thank you, Blaise," she heard herself saying. "But it happens there are a number of things that *I* wish to say to Captain Blackheart, and I hardly think this is the place for me to say them."

Will stepped aside. He held open the velvet curtain at the back of the box, and Lili went through, with her head held high. She kept right on going across the mezzanine, and was halfway down the second flight of red-carpeted stairs leading to the ground floor, when Wilrowan finally came even with her. Reaching out, he took her—more roughly than he might have intended—by her upper arm.

"I thought," said Will, "that you were going to see the tragedy at Sadler's Theater."

"Did you?" answered Lili, feigning a puzzled frown. "I know that

I never said so. I expect you merely jumped to that conclusion—
wishing, no doubt, to have the Opera House all to yourself!"

"Very well, madam, I *assumed* as much, since you had already
been to the ballet, and Trefallon has never been one to haunt the
opera."

"But *I* like the opera. Or at least—I thought I would like to see
it, and Blaise very kindly offered to escort me. I admit to being
under a misapprehension myself. You did say that you and the queen
were planning an evening at the Volary?"

Wilrowan shrugged. "Dionee is a creature of impulse. She decided on the opera at the last minute."

As they continued on down the stairs, his grip on her arm tightened painfully. "If I had known you were here, I would have—I
would have sought you out earlier."

But Lili had noted that slight hesitation. "What I suppose you
were really going to say," she retorted, "was if you had known I was
going to be here, you would not have been comporting yourself so
disgracefully with Letitia Steerpike!"

Will spoke through his teeth. "As you—had you known that *I*
was going to be present—might have restrained yourself from
such—intimate conversation with Blaise Trefallon?"

Lili felt a swell of indignation. By now, they had reached the ground
floor. They swept on past the golden pillars and the immense pier
glasses leading to the door, still arguing. "I think it's absolutely incredible," she hissed, "that *you* should be lecturing *me* on decent behavior!"

"Do you?" said Will with a sneer. "As I think it equally incredible
that *you* should pretend to care what I do, after all these years of
supreme indifference!"

It was not a pleasant ride home. Lili sat very stiff on her seat in
the hackney coach, and Wilrowan glared at her the whole way. These
past weeks, he had been prey to one stormy emotion after the

other—anger, jealousy, guilt, despair—and he was feeling a mixture of all of them now.

His heart swelled at the very sight of her, sitting there trying to look so prim and injured, when he knew very well he had *finally* shaken her out of that sweet, everlasting, infuriating complacency. The pulse pounded in his temples as he eyed her narrowly across the coach. Say what you might about the court beauties, there was not another woman in Hawkesbridge who had such skin, such eyes, such a damnably kissable mouth. And when he thought of the times when it had seemed she was about to catch fire, when it had almost, almost seemed she was about to respond—there was passion slumbering somewhere inside of Lili, and he would be *damned* if he allowed any other man to be the one to awaken it.

The hackney lumbered to a halt. One of the servants came out of the house and threw open the coach door. Will climbed out first, brushed off his green coat, and straightened his neckcloth. Then, scrupulously polite, he reached up to help Lili as she descended. Her gloved hand rested briefly in his and a glance passed between them, but she was up the stairs and inside the house before he had time to utter a single word.

Will ground his teeth. It was the final insult, the very last one he was prepared to endure. *By the gods, I'll have you tonight,* he vowed in his rage. *And I'm not about to settle for only half of you either!*

Lili was in her bedchamber—had already handed her fan to the abigail, was in the process of removing her velvet cloak—when the door flew open and Will walked in, already divested of his coat and his boots.

She had known, of course, that he would arrive eventually, but not so soon. She swept a hand across her eyes. The anger that had fueled her earlier had all been consumed, leaving her tired and depressed. "If you don't mind, Wilrowan, I'd like a few minutes longer." The cloak dropped from her shoulders to the floor, and the abigail silently picked it up and folded it over one arm.

Will continued to stand there in his shirt-sleeves and his stocking feet, holding the door open. "Send the girl away. You are not a child; you can undress yourself. Or at need, I will help you myself."

Lili blinked at him, this was so unexpected. The abigail quickly left the room without even waiting for Lili to send her away, and Will closed the door firmly behind her.

He leaned up against the door frame. "Pray don't allow me to hinder you, madam. Go on as you would if I were not even here."

Lili swallowed hard. What on earth had gotten into him? They had been married for almost seven years, and always he had treated her with gentleness and respect. She felt her anger revive. What did he expect of her now—that she would *flaunt* herself like one of his hussies from the palace?

She took in a long angry breath, remembering how the Steerpike creature had looked at her earlier: those mocking eyes, those painted lips, and that superior smile—as though she knew something that Lili did not. *But I do know,* thought Lili, *and I could do it, too. Make him burn as he burns when he looks at those others, make him sick with wanting me.*

Hardly believing what she was doing, Lili pulled off one glove and then the other, holding the embroidered and scented silk for a long moment, before she let it slide out of her fingers and down to the floor. Still more slowly, she took the hairpins out of her hair, dropping them one by one at her feet. When they were all gone, she shook out her hair, until the powdered and perfumed curls fell over her shoulders.

Well why not? she thought defiantly. *I may not be able to hold him forever, but I could certainly keep him interested for a single night. There is hardly a woman in Hawkesbridge who hasn't had Will for a single night. And none of those women can do what I can: make his skin shiver, his heartbeat match mine, touch him in ways he could scarcely imagine.*

Lili felt her blood run hot as she unhooked the back of her gown, shrugged it off her shoulders, then pulled it over her head and cast it aside, so that it lay in a shimmer of brocade satin on the floor.

She saw his nostrils flare, his lips compress; all of the color drained from his face, but Will said nothing.

With trembling fingers she unhooked the waist of her satin petticoat, unfastened the hoopskirt she wore underneath. Petticoat and hoops collapsed to the floor, and Lili stepped away in her linen chemise and pearl-edged corset.

Wilrowan continued to lounge against the door, slender and graceful, but quivering with tension. His auburn hair seemed to flame against the unnatural whiteness of his skin. Could he feel it yet? She could hardly breathe herself—were they breathing together?

This was not what the healing magic was for. Lili knew what she was doing was very wrong—but she did not care. She had endured too much over the years, was feeling too much now. Modesty, dignity, pride, none of it mattered. Lili knew that she was going to do this, and damn the consequences.

Slowly, she lifted one foot, removed the right shoe, a pretty thing with a satin rosette, and tossed it aside. Lifting her other foot, she slipped off the second shoe.

Better not to think past the moment, to spare no thought for what she might feel in the morning. She sat down on the side of the crimson bed, lifted the hem of her chemise over her knees, slid off first a ruffled garter then a white silk stocking, repeated the process on the other side.

Lili knew that she had Will now. His lips were trembling, his breath came and went along with her own. She felt a surge of triumph, of power, as she began to unhook her embroidered satin stays. As the stiff buckram at the front parted, he made a sound deep in his throat.

Before she knew it, he was across the room, on the bed beside her, bearing her down with his weight. He pulled at the drawstring on her chemise, pushed the linen aside with one hand. That hand, like fire, cupped her breast.

No, thought Lili, on a sudden surge of panic. He would know what she was feeling, he would know too much. She felt weak, giddy—giddier still when he bent his head, when she felt his mouth, his tongue, moving across bare skin. When she made an inarticulate sound of protest, Will drew back a little, breathing hard.

She could feel his warm breath on her breast as he spoke. "I intend to taste every inch of your skin."

And I am the one who is going to burn like a torch, thought Lili, somewhere between panic and pleasure. Then she cast away pride, abandoned all sense of shame, and simply gave herself up to whatever was going to happen next.

33

Mid-morning found Will and Lili at the breakfast table. The previous night had been a revelation of more than physical passion, and the tea, toast, baked apples, and chocolate were consumed in a self-conscious atmosphere of sidelong glances, and only half-concealed smiles. Lili—in a striped satin dressing gown—pretended to be reading a letter from her Aunt Allora, and Will—as yet unshaven—was doing justice to the toast and baked apples, though it appeared doubtful he tasted a single bite.

In the middle of the meal, there came a sudden and unexpected loud tapping at one of the casements. Lili glanced up from her letter. Something large and black was fluttering outside the window, rattling its beak against the panes of glass.

"How odd. It almost looks as though that bird is trying to get in."

Will was staring at the window, too. The raven was not only trying to get in, it was holding something small and brightly colored in its beak. He rose slowly to his feet, still keeping his eyes on the window. "There is a chill in this room, my sweet love. I'll go upstairs and fetch you a shawl."

Lili was obviously moved by his tender solicitude. "No, Will—

really. Or, if you insist, we can ring for—" But he was already across the room and out the door before she could finish the sentence.

He ran up four flights in his stocking-feet, taking them two steps at a time. He flung open the bedchamber door and stepped inside, swept a quick glance around to make certain none of the servants were present—then he was across the room in three long strides, unfastening one of the windows.

The raven heard the creak of the opening casement. Abandoning its attempts on the dining-parlor below, it came fluttering up to the bedchamber window and landed on the wooden sill. <*I have news, news, news.*>

The words beat against Will's mind as the raven's beak had beat against the window panes. And in that beak he saw the tell-tale scrap of scarlet ribbon, a prearranged token.

<*Then come in, damn you, and tell me what you know. It had better be something very good to excuse such an abominable lack of discretion. What Lili must be thinking now!*>

The raven jumped from the window ledge to the floor. Will went down on one knee, put out a hand to touch the glossy black head of the bird. It was easier to communicate if they were actually in contact.

<*Two travelers stopping at the Imp and Bottle. I heard them discuss a town in Chêneboix. Strange things happen. A grist mill and a paper mill are behaving oddly, though no one can find anything wrong with the machinery. At midnight on the twenty-third, the needles on every compass in the town spun madly around for a quarter of an hour. You said to watch for such signs as these. Have I done well?*>

Will took a long breath and let it out slowly. This was very good news; yet, with his mind still full of Lili and the night before, he could not help thinking it could hardly have come at a worse time. <*You have done very well. That is—if you can tell me the name of the town in question.*>

<*Fermouline.*> The raven dipped its head, dropped the bit of scarlet ribbon on the planked floor. <*On the River Ousel. At the Chêneboix and Bridemoor border.*>

Lili had put aside Allora's letter and was drinking her chocolate when Will returned without her shawl. He had finished dressing in a tearing hurry, was just shrugging into his coat as he crossed the threshold. His boots clattered on the floor as he crossed the room and dropped a quick, apologetic kiss on her hair.

"The stupidest thing. A message came from the Volary while we were eating breakfast, and some fool of a footman took it upstairs and left it in my dressing room. It appears urgent, so I *have* to go. This morning of all mornings—when I would have given the world to stay with you here."

"Yes, I see," said Lili, with a puzzled frown. "Though I never heard a knock at the—" She gave a tiny gasp as Will pulled her up to her feet, caught her in his arms, and stopped her from speaking with a hard kiss on the mouth.

It was a somewhat prickly kiss, as he was still unshaven, but Lili was happy to participate anyway. Unfortunately, it ended too soon. Will spoke in her ear, still holding her tightly around the waist. "I may have to leave the city today, for—for what might be a considerable time. I swear to you, I would never go if it was anything less than vitally important—not after last night. There are still so many things that I need to say to you."

The breath-taking embrace was suddenly removed, and Will's boots went clattering across the room, before Lili had time to recover.

But he stopped with one hand on the door, and said with a last pleading glance: "Promise me you won't go anywhere, until I've had the chance to stop back and say good-bye. If I have to move Heaven and earth, I'll try to be back within the next two hours."

*   *   *

Will had only been gone a few minutes when Lili's mind began to work again. An urgent summons from the king—had it not been a *secret* message, Will would have explained it. She felt her heart leap as she realized what that message might be. Acting with sudden decision, she left the room, started up the rosewood staircase. If the king had sent for Sir Frederic and his friend Doctor Fox when he sent for Wilrowan, she ought to be hearing from Sir Bastian very soon.

But Lili had ample time to dress before news finally arrived. It came in the form of a note carried upstairs by one of the footmen. Tearing it open, she scanned it quickly. The message was brief: *"Be prepared to leave Hawkesbridge at once. I will make the other arrangements."*

She sat on her bed staring down at the words. Leave Hawkesbridge at once? Well, of course—the Specularii wanted her to arrive wherever she was going and do whatever had to be done, before Will came along on the same business, and spoiled everything with his *"lack of discretion and self-regulation."*

Lili closed her eyes, tried to shut out the picture, so clear in her mind, of Will's face on the pillow beside her, so open, so vulnerable, so full of emotion. *We could do this together, Wilrowan and I,* something inside her protested. But no, the decision had already been made— and though not by her, at least it was a decision she had agreed to honor.

"Don't go anywhere— if I have to move Heaven and earth, I'll try to be back within two hours." Will's parting words seemed to echo in the room. Two hours did not leave her much time to get ready, and he might be back even before that. Putting the note aside, Lili sprang to her feet.

She dashed off a quick reply to Sir Bastian, asking him to come for her within the next hour. Then she set about packing as many of her clothes as she could fit into a single trunk.

But he asked me to wait for him. How can I do this—after such a night? It was an inward cry of anguish, as Lili stood before a mirror in the downstairs hall, tying the ribbons of her chipstraw hat under her chin. But she knew the answer even as she asked the question. Something important was afoot, something that might affect the future of Mountfalcon, the future of the whole world—and the Specularii were depending on her and her talents.

And it had been a wonderful, a remarkable night, but it had only been one out of six years, seven years of nights. How could she know if it really meant as much to Wilrowan as it meant to her?

Once she had instructed a footman to carry her trunk to the foot of the stairs, there was nothing left to be done but to go into the sitting room and compose a letter to Will. She hesitated with the quill in her hand, not knowing what she would say. The obvious thing was to invent some story, some plausible excuse, to say that Papa or Aunt Allora had taken ill, that she was needed back home at Brakeburn. Yet she found she could not lie to him, this of all mornings. Besides, it was entirely possible their paths might eventually cross. If so, he would realize she had deceived him, and never be able to trust her again.

While Lili was still agonizing over her letter, there came the rumble of a heavy coach pulling up outside. She put down the pen, stole a quick look out through a window. It was, as she had expected, the black berlin.

With a heavy heart, she returned to the table, to her pen and paper. Dipping the quill into the inkwell, she scribbled a few quick words. Then she folded the paper, wrote Will's name very clearly on the outside, and handed the letter to one of the servants, to be delivered the moment Wilrowan arrived.

Inside the berlin with Sir Bastian, Lili settled her hat, smoothed out her skirts, and tried to compose herself for the journey ahead. "I take it we are going in search of the Mountfalcon Jewel?"

"Yes, Lilliana. Your hour has truly arrived. No one but you, with your peculiar divining abilities, could hope to succeed at this important task."

"But—I suppose we are not going out to look at random?"

"We are going to Fermouline in Chêneboix. Whether we go on from there remains to be seen."

As the berlin rumbled toward the city gate, the old gentleman explained how the king had just received news of such curious behavior on the part of the mills and compasses. "It is a part of the world that had already attracted our attention before—not only because two of the conspirators involved in the theft were traced to Chetterly near the Chêneboix border, but because we had already received word of a fire, a riot, and a serious outbreak of disease, all within a twenty-mile radius of Fermouline. If the Chaos Machine is not in that city at this very moment, then I suspect it has recently passed through."

He glanced across at Lili. "But you are the one who has established an affinity for the Jewel. When we arrive at our destination, *you* must be the one to tell *me* if the Chaos Machine is still in the vicinity."

Lili sat staring down at the muddy toes of her shoes; in her haste, she had walked right through a puddle to reach the coach. "I left Hawkesbridge so suddenly; there can be little doubt that people will talk. I don't want Papa and Aunt Allora to worry."

"You need not concern yourself about that. A message in cipher has already been sent to your aunt, telling her everything." His glance sharpened. "What excuse, may I ask, did you leave Captain Blackheart?"

Lili tried to remember, attempted to call up that hurried letter in her mind. "I told him—very little. I could hardly tell him where I was going, even had I wanted to. And I certainly didn't mention my reasons for going."

"That is what I would have expected. If we should chance to

meet your husband later, you must continue to tell him as little as possible. In fact," Sir Bastian added, "it would be far better if we never stopped to make any explanation at all."

Blaise Trefallon was still in bed when Wilrowan burst into his rented lodgings. He had spent most of the night after the opera gaming at Silas Gant's, returning to his chambers a little after sunrise. He had slept for several hours, was just sitting up in bed and beginning to think about breakfast, when the door of his room flew open and Will strode in, dressed for travel in jack-boots, doeskin trousers, and a long drab coat, nervously flicking a silver-handled riding crop in one white-knuckled hand.

"Trefallon," he demanded without any preamble, "what have you done with my wife?"

Blaise rubbed the sleep from his eyes, and gave a gaping yawn. He was never at his best in the morning, before he spent that first crucial hour with his barber and valet. "I beg your pardon? What do you *suppose* I've done with your wife?"

Will waved a clenched fist. "Lili has disappeared. She rode off in a black berlin, taking a trunk full of clothes with her. The servants tell me they are certain there was a gentleman with her, but no one caught a glimpse of his face. As there is no other man I can even imagine Lili eloping with, I come to you and I ask again: What— have—you—done—with—my wife?"

Blaise threw back the covers and rose to his feet. He was a very different Trefallon, just now, from the elegant creature of the court and the drawing room, from the rakish habitué of the taverns and the gaming hells. Nevertheless, standing there in his night-shirt, with his fair hair disheveled, he was able to assume a certain amount of hauteur as he raised one arched eyebrow and asked:

"It does not occur to you, Wilrowan, that if I had eloped with *anyone*, I would not be here speaking with you now?"

"It occurs to me," said Will, looking very white around the mouth, "that you might have taken her away and left her—somewhere—and doubled back here to allay my suspicions."

"I see," said Trefallon, his chin going up and a belligerent look coming into his eye. "You burst into my room at this ungodly hour, and inform me, firstly, that I am a vile seducer and have stolen your wife, and secondly, that I am undoubtedly a coward and a sneak."

It might be difficult for a man to stand on his dignity while barefoot and in dire need of a shave, but Blaise was succeeding admirably. "I take leave to inform you, Captain Blackheart, that if I had any designs on your wife, I would never think of ruining her with an elopement. Instead, I would take the more honorable course of putting a sword or a bullet through your *bastard* heart, and then marrying your widow. I do trust I have made myself perfectly clear?"

Will made a mighty effort and swallowed his wrath. "I suppose that I owe you an apology," he said, in a stifled voice.

"I should very well think that you do. But pray don't offer one if it's too much trouble. I had just as soon meet you as not, considering your insufferable—" Blaise stopped himself and stared at his friend, suddenly struck by Will's tragic demeanor. "You really mean this! You sincerely believe that Lili has done this."

"Yes," said Will, collapsing in a chair. "And please don't tell me how richly I deserve it. I know that as well as you do, and it only makes everything infinitely worse."

"Yes," said Blaise, reaching for the pair of nankeen breeches he had thrown over a chair a few hours earlier, beginning to put them on. "I feel certain it must. But this is ghastly, Will. Do you tell me she left without any explanation?"

Will shook his head bleakly. "An apology but no explanation. I have to get her back, Blaise. The truth is—I don't think I can possibly live without her."

Trefallon examined him thoughtfully. "I must confess, I've sus-pected something of the sort. How long have *you* known?" He pulled off his night-shirt and tossed it on the bed.

"That I love Lili?" Will gave a bitter laugh. "I can't say how long. Almost from the very beginning, I think."

Blaise shook his head in exasperation. "Sometimes I despair of you." He crossed the room, opened a drawer, and pulled out a clean shirt. "If this is true, then why on earth did you never tell *Lili?*"

Will bent the riding crop in his hands until it seemed it must snap. "Because I was a coward. Even in so short a time, I had already— transgressed a dozen times, and I was afraid she would never be able to love me in return."

At this point, Blaise surprised him with a shout of laughter. "My dear Blackheart, are you absolutely blind? If there is one thing I know, one thing I have become utterly certain of this last month, it's that Lili loves you. I find it hard to believe she has really run off with another man. Besides, who would she go with? She doesn't really *know* any men but you and me and Nick and Rodaric, and you surely don't suspect either of them."

"And, oh yes," he added, as he went on dressing, "that civil old gentleman I saw her walking with, one day by the river."

"Civil old gentleman?" Will's eyebrows drew sharply together.

Blaise waved a hand. "I forget his name, if she ever mentioned it. Well past seventy and exceedingly avuncular. Besides, they were very well chaperoned, and by no less a personage than Sir Frederic Tregaron-Marlowe."

This news had the unexpected effect of galvanizing Will. He had been sitting slumped and dejected in his chair; now he jerked erect. "Sir Frederic *Marlowe?*"

"Why yes," Blaise answered coolly, as he knotted his fringed neckcloth. "Did you ever attend any of his lectures? I did, and he was the most prolix old— Why do you look at me that way? Undoubtedly Marlowe and the other man were friends of Miss Brakeburn, paying a duty call on her great-niece."

Will settled back into his chair. "Of course."

"I feel very certain," Trefallon went on, "that if Lili is truly gone, she must be going home to Brakeburn Hall, to nurse her wounded feelings."

"But why?" said Will, continuing to look both ill and bewildered. "Last night—I thought—I swear to you, Blaise, everything was different. And if she was only going home, why didn't she say so in her letter?"

Blaise shrugged. "I don't pretend to know what happened between the two of you last night. But I do know what Lili has been feeling this last month." He pulled back his hair and tied it up at the nape of his neck with a brown silk ribbon. "If she didn't write to say she was going to Brakeburn, it was probably because she thought it might sound like an invitation to follow her. She does have some pride, you know. And you have treated her abominably."

"I don't dispute that," said Will, wearily. "But not, I tell you, last night. I told her everything I had been feeling for so many years and we—we settled everything between us."

Blaise looked across at him with pitying eyes. "Then why, Wilrowan, is Lili gone today?"

Will spread his hands. "I don't know. I don't know. And that is the very thing that stabs at my heart! It may be—I can hardly say—but it may be that she didn't believe anything I said."

"Well then, it is clearly up to you to find her and convince her that you were entirely in earnest. If you follow her all the way to Brakeburn Hall, that should make a good beginning."

Will threw down the whip, sprang to his feet, and began to pace a circle around the room. "But that is the worst of it. I can't go to Lili—at Brakeburn or anywhere else. I am leaving the city on urgent business. I can't tell you where and I can't tell you why. But if Lili should come back to Hawkesbridge for any reason——" He stopped and gave Trefallon a pleading glance. "If she should write to you and tell you her whereabouts—tell her—tell her——"

"I'll tell her how you looked and what you said," Blaise answered soothingly. "I'll do everything in my power to persuade her to stay here and wait for your return."

Will paid a quick visit to his secret rooms at the wigmaker's house, where he retrieved a number of odd little bottles and curious potions, and dropped them into a coat pocket. Then it was back to the palace, where he learned that Young Swallow had already packed up his things in a small wooden chest and two portmanteaux.

"Send them by the mail coach to meet me at the Cinque d'Or in Fermouline." Will had previously arranged to meet Nick and his other two men at the same inn. They were travelling separately to avoid attracting attention.

Arming himself with pistols, powder-horn, shot, and a silver-hilted rapier on a red silk baldric, he caught up the shovel-brim hat and a pair of pigskin gauntlets, and headed for the door.

Will's next stop was the king's apartments, where Rodaric gave him a warrant they had discussed earlier—one with such broad and sweeping powers that it virtually amounted to a carte blanche. It would lose some of its force once he crossed the border, but it would still carry considerable weight in Chêneboix, Bridemoor, and Montagne-du-Soliel, according to recent treaties signed with those nations.

"Short of murder, arson, or highway robbery," said Rodaric, as he handed the paper over, "it ought to clear you of practically anything in any of those places. But be careful how you use it and to whom you show it."

Will nodded, slipped the warrant into an inside pocket, and then went upstairs to exchange a final word with the queen.

He found her alone in her pretty bedchamber, where the song-birds in their silver cages were ominously silent. When Will came in, his riding coat flapping around him, Dionee turned a haggard face to greet him. Ever since Rodaric had informed her earlier that day that the Chaos Machine had perhaps been located, she had been alternately filled with transports of joy and the most agitating apprehension.

"You will bring it back. Promise that you will bring it back," she whispered, as Wilrowan cast himself down kneeling at her feet. The look on her face terrified him.

"I promise," he said, taking both of her hands and kissing them repeatedly, "that whatever happens I won't come back without the Mountfalcon Jewel. This waiting about for information has gone on too long. If I don't find the Chaos Machine in Fermouline, I will keep on searching until I do."

He rode out through the Volary gate on the same grey mare that had carried him to Brakeburn Hall earlier that year, and he could only regret that a visit to Lili at Brakeburn was not his goal today.

But riding through the mountains, many hours later and close to midnight, Will began to entertain second thoughts. Travelling down the pass linking Hawkesbridge to the plains of Chêneboix and Bridemoor, torturing himself with thoughts of Lili all along the way, he finally came to realize that the purpose of his journey, no matter how vital, was never going to receive his full attention until and unless he made some final attempt to find and speak to his wife.

Brakeburn Hall and the village of Fernbrake were located several hours to the north, Fermouline many miles more to the northeast. While Brakeburn was not on his way, neither was it so far afield that a flying visit would cost him more than eight or ten hours. He could make up some of that time later by changing horses, by riding through the following night, as he was riding through this one.

Will made his decision. When he came out of the mountains, he and the tired mare headed north. It was a clear night and the moon was waxing near to full, the road was familiar, and he had no difficulty finding his way.

He arrived at Brakeburn Hall, dirty and exhausted, an hour after daybreak. He left the mare in the capable hands of the head groom, and surprised Miss Allora Brakeburn just as she was sitting down to her breakfast.

"I want to see Lili," he demanded at once.

"She is not here," said Allora, glaring at him over the willow-pattern teapot. "Nor is there any reason for you to prolong your visit—which I trust will be brief. She may not return for a very long time."

Will ground his teeth audibly. "From which I take it," he said, in a tight voice, "that you know where she is but have no intention of telling me."

"You are perfectly correct, I have no such intention," Allora answered primly. "It is for Lili to notify you of her whereabouts, if she wishes you to know them." She picked up her napkin and spread it across her lap. "You may close that door behind you on your way out."

Will's hands began to itch, as he considered, for a moment, what pleasure might be gained by choking the information out of her—were she thirty years younger and a man.

But there was no use thinking of that; her age and her sex protected her. There was no way he could force her to tell him anything. Not any more than if she were his own—

At that thought, a dangerous gleam came into his eye. "Miss Brakeburn. Never, in all the years I have known you, have you ever let pass a single opportunity to do me an ill turn. But the truth is, I have finally run out of patience, and I will *not* brook your meddling interference in my marriage any more."

Allora appeared unmoved. "And what," she said tartly, "do you intend to do? Will you call me out, brave Captain Blackheart? Would you mishandle a weak old woman?"

"Not at all," said Will, as he turned to leave the room. "I intend to fight fire with fire."

From the dining room he went immediately into his father-in-law's study. Finding the room unoccupied, he went to the desk, cut himself a pen, and wrote out a quick but comprehensive letter on one side of a sheet of paper. Signing, blotting, and folding this missive, Will sealed it with Lord Brakeburn's wax and his own intaglio ring, then added the direction in a bold hand.

For a moment, he toyed with the idea of giving this message to one of the Brakeburn lackeys to post, but he rejected the notion almost immediately. He was going to have to stop in Fernbrake anyway, to get a fresh horse and to eat a quick meal. It would be easy enough, if he offered sufficient money, to find somebody there who was willing to carry the letter as far as Eaudaimanté.

34

inter had come again, all too soon, and the streets of Tarnburgh were drifted with snow, the pointed rooftops frosted with ice. At Lindenhoff, the nuptials of the king were celebrated with due solemnity. The death of Lord Hugo Sackville less than four months before—and his bad taste in actually collapsing and dying at the betrothal dinner—cast a shade over the proceedings. The visits, the balls, and the other events leading up to the wedding, were brief and colorless affairs.

The day itself dawned clear but cold, and the wedding party went to church in ermine and sables. In a quiet ceremony, attended by no more than two hundred guests, the bride in grey and the groom in black, each spoke the vows in a subdued voice, and the thing was done.

There was a cold supper afterward, which five hundred people attended. The food and the wine were excellent, and so was the music—provided by zither, violins, and virginal—but the guests looked strained and uneasy under their rouge and powder.

Perhaps it was because they had been forced to make their way through the sullen crowds gathered outside the palace. For nearly half a mile the mob filled the streets around Lindenhoff: carpenters,

384 R• TERESA EDGERTON

bricklayers, and iron-founders; coopers, weavers, gunsmiths, and glaziers; members of every conceivable trade, all jostling each other in their efforts to gain a place near the palace gate. They were taking advantage of the declared holiday to express their contempt for the king's foreign bride. This was a new and unwelcome experience for Jarred, who had always before known the love of his people; he believed, however, that time would reconcile them to his marriage.

Had he listened to the rumors circulating in the streets, had someone handed him one of the newly inked broadsheets being passed around, he might have thought otherwise. The masses were whispering that Ys was closely connected with some foreign house of royalty—which would make her marriage to Jarred illegal. The handbills, on the other hand, satirized the sharp-faced bride and her questionable antecedents: she was the daughter of pirates—a trollop risen from the stews with the aid of some nameless wealthy protector—a lady's maid who had murdered her employer and usurped her identity. As yet, no one suspected the truth, which would have been rejected as too fantastic by even the most rabid of the gossip-mongers.

Meanwhile, at the wedding supper, the fashionable guests ate, drank, danced, and made half-hearted attempts at flirtation, to the wailing accompaniment of the violins. Toasts were made, appointments within the new queen's household announced, then Jarred and Ys climbed into a gilded sleigh behind six white horses, and were carried off to a house in the country for a brief honeymoon. A large group of servants followed behind in a carriage.

When the newlyweds returned to Tarnburgh a fortnight later, Madame Solange was one of the first to call at Lindenhoff to pay her respects to the royal bride. Ys received her former governess in a suite of sumptuous redecorated rooms, which had been plastered, painted, and gilded during the honeymoon.

"You seem very pleased with yourself," said Madame, looking Ys over.

Ys was flushed and excited, enjoying all of the fuss and attention, this first day back at the palace. If the wedding trip had been like one prolonged nightmare, she had already pushed the memory of that to the back of her mind. And like a true Maglore, she was much too absorbed in the present moment to give more than a passing thought to the future.

"Of course I am pleased. Why should I not be—with all this around me." As she spoke, Ys played with a pair of dainty gold filigree bracelets, which Jarred had given her just that morning.

"That is all very well," Madame retorted, "so long as you don't forget how you came to be here. So long as you don't forget how vital my aid and council will be in *keeping* you here." Though Madame looked regal in lynx and black velvet, her voice was bitter, her manner dissatisfied. "I must say, when you tried to take charge of things for yourself, you bungled them badly. The death of Lord Hugo—such deplorable timing."

"But you were the one who wanted him dead," Ys replied, with an edge to her voice. "You are the one who said they must all be disposed of one way or the other: all of Jarred's relations, all of his friends and most trusted servants. Think how it would have looked if they had started dropping off *after* the wedding. And I think that I managed it beautifully," she added smugly. "Just because it came at what seemed like a bad time for *me*, no one will suspect I had any hand in Lord Hugo's death."

"No one suspects *as yet*; you may not have covered your tracks so well as you think."

But Ys thought otherwise. In fact, she had chosen the timing of Lord Hugo's death very carefully. Firstly, of course, she had meant to impress Madame, who had poisoned Izek as a warning to Ys that she had best stop shilly-shallying when it came to the king, or Zmaj would be the next one to die. So Ys had determined to send a message of her own: *I can be ruthless, too.* Secondly, the delay had spared her many long weeks with a husband whose attentions made her physically ill.

Thinking of this, her mood dimmed. Her child had not quickened—or else her symptoms had been deceptive, and she had never conceived at all. Either way, it seemed she was no more fertile than the rest of her kind.

Echoing her thoughts, Madame said: "It could take months, even years, before you conceive. Until you can announce the impending birth of an heir, our plans for Jarred must be held in abeyance. As for those others—a death here, a high-placed official discredited there, a trusted servant dismissed with a bad character—there is more than one way to accomplish our ends, and now that you are actually inside Lindenhoff, your opportunities will be that much greater."

Ys sighed and wandered across the room to one of the high arched windows, where she stood looking down at the gardens below. A brief thaw followed by a sudden drop in temperature had encased each separate branch, twig, thorn, and trunk in a transparent coating of ice. The palace gardens looked like something created by a master craftsman out of spun glass. It was all very pretty, but Ys found it depressing. After almost a year in Tarnburgh she was learning to hate this northern climate: the short, bright, intense summers; the early onset of winter. The prospect of living in such a horrible place for the rest of her life was a hateful one.

Nor did she relish the idea of months, even years, as Jarred's wife.

Ys fingered the white stones encircling her throat. While exploring the properties of the necklace, she had learned to induce an intense and unhealthy state of excitement, bordering on delirium. There was an ugly fascination to observing Jarred in the grip of her spell, and he was always abjectly eager to please her afterward. It also exacted such a pitiless physical toll, she believed it might, if prolonged, lead to apoplexy or heart failure. Indeed, the temptation to kill him grew stronger and stronger. She had already brought him dangerously close to the edge several times during their honeymoon.

Ys turned away from the window, tried to rally her failing spirits. By remaining barren, she extended her idyll with Zmaj, protected her lover from Madame Solange. Having been so reckless as to dispense with Izek, Madame would not be so profligate with Zmaj and Jmel. Not unless she could dredge up another youth of Imperial Maglore blood—and so far as Ys knew, there were none living.

Nevertheless, it was clear that Madame intended to keep the upper hand. "Don't allow all the comforts and flattery of your present position to go to your head," she said sharply, as she arranged her furs and prepared to depart. "There is still a great deal of work to be done—and a single misstep could cost you a good deal more than you seem to realize."

Jarred's first act on returning home was to send for Doctor Purcell. He received the old man in the trompe l'oeil council chamber, with its dozens of imaginary painted doors and windows, its pedimented arches leading absolutely nowhere. In the council chamber, they could speak alone without fear of interruption.

Purcell could not help noticing how pale and thin the king had grown in two short weeks, how his hand shook as he motioned the philosopher to take a seat beside him, in Zelene's old chair. "Have you been ill, sir?" he asked bluntly.

"Ill? But why should you ask?" Jarred smiled, but the smile did not extend to his eyes. "The truth is, I've never felt better in my life. If I don't look entirely myself, no doubt it is simply the result of too much pleasure. Now that I am home, I will slow the pace." The smile became a half-humorous grimace. "Really, what choice do I have? There is far too much to occupy me here, to allow much time for— dissipation."

Doctor Purcell adjusted his spectacles and continued to stare at him with troubled eyes. "Dissipation, Your Majesty?"

The king moved uneasily in his gilded chair. "My wife has strange tastes for one so young. And I have learned, Francis, that I am not the man I always thought I was. There is a dark side that seems to crave the most exotic pleasures." He rubbed one wrist as he spoke. "All of my life, I have made every effort to avoid giving or receiving pain. Yet, there is a thrill that passes along the nerves—"

Jarred gave a short, false laugh, and blushed to the roots of his hair. "But really, I don't know why I should say any of this to you. I do beg your pardon." He passed a hand over his eyes. "It was an interesting diversion, but I assure you, I *assure* you, it is all in the past."

"So I must hope," said the old man. "If these exotic pleasures of which you speak leave you looking so weak and depleted."

35

ﾟinter had nearly lost her grip on Luden. Though the wind from the sea was still tinged with ice, the sun shone all day long, and the marshes beyond the city turned grey and hazy. The city itself was undergoing a swift transformation. The red-brick streets had been swept clear of snow; skating parties on the Grand Canal had been declared too dangerous; in every garden there was the *drip-drip-drip* of icicles melting off of wych-elms and horse chestnuts.

Luke had grown restless with the changing season. He set out one morning from his rented rooms, with no clear idea where he meant to go. He had not proceeded more than twenty yards from the house, when he heard someone call out his name.

"Mr. Guilian. A moment, if you please, sir." At the sound of that pleasantly modulated voice, Luke stopped and turned. Spotting a vaguely familiar figure striding in his direction, he politely waited for the man to catch up.

Mr. Varian Dou was a fresh-faced member of the Rijxlander parliament, three or four years younger than Luke was himself, with a calm and sensible air about him. Being but slightly acquainted, Lucius thought well of young Mr. Dou—when he chanced to think of him at all.

He and Luke exchanged civil bows, and fell into step together. "I could not help noticing, the last time we met, that you do not seem to approve of Lord Flinx."

"Pardon me. As Lord Polyphant was kind enough to remind me, I don't even live here. It is not for me to either approve or disapprove of your new Prime Minister."

The Rijxlander laughed. "Or at least not for you to express that disapproval quite so openly. Though I must confess, I don't care very much for the fellow myself. When he smiles that soft smile of his, my skin crawls."

Luke eyed him narrowly, suddenly remembering that this Varian Dou was said to be a protegé of the Crown Princess, and therefore strongly allied with the opposition party. "And yet," said Luke slowly, as they turned a corner and crossed over one of the arched bridges, "you appear to be on the friendliest terms with him."

Mr. Dou made a wry face. "When one chooses to pursue a public career, one learns to tolerate certain people—no matter how much one may secretly despise them."

"That is unfortunate for *you*. As a private gentleman, I may choose my friends with much greater care."

Mr. Dou cleared his throat loudly. "And yet, Mr. Guilian, though you do lead the life of a private gentleman in Luden, everyone knows you are a man of consequence back in Winterscar." He looked down at his feet. "As you say, you don't even live here; what Lord Flinx thinks of you can scarcely be more important than what you think of him. At the same time, it would not be advisable for you to offend quite so many *other* people as you seem intent on doing."

Luke came to a sudden halt, and his companion stopped, too. "I was not aware that I had offended anyone. My manners may not be the best, my opinions a little too decided, but—"

Mr. Dou was vigorously shaking his head. "No, no, your manners are excellent, and your opinions are regarded as highly amusing. Perhaps I should not have said 'offended.' I meant to say that you should not scandalize so many people by such marked attentions to——a certain young woman."

Luke felt a muscle begin to twitch in his cheek. "Mr. Dou, is it your intention to offend *me*? Because I really must tell you, that while I may lack friends here in Luden, I think I could manage to name the requisite two if——"

"No, no, Mr. Guilian, I assure you, I assure you." Mr. Dou was turning very red in the face. "This is meant as the friendliest warning imaginable. But of course, you are right. We are barely acquainted. In my zeal to perform a good office, I have over-stepped myself. I do most sincerely apologize."

Luke's quick temper cooled off, almost as suddenly as it had flared up. He was not really interested in challenging this Varian Dou, or anyone else. He was wretched with the small sword, worse with a pistol, and only moderately accomplished with the rapier. A barbed wit and a poisonous tongue had always been his weapons of choice. "No doubt I misunderstood you. There is really no need for an apology." They started to walk again. "Indeed, sir, as you are inclined to be frank with me, I wish you would explain something that troubles me very much."

"With the greatest pleasure in the world," said Mr. Dou, who seemed to think he had enjoyed a more fortunate escape than he actually had.

"Then tell me why a man like Lord Flinx is not only tolerated but fawned on and courted, while the young lady you mentioned is openly scorned. I have seen people turn their backs when they see her approaching on the street, and when the Princess Marjote visits her father, she maintains an elaborate——and I must say highly inconvenient——pretense that the lady doesn't even exist. If this is not hypocrisy, I wish you would tell me exactly what it is."

Mr. Dou looked puzzled by the question. "Things can not be so very different in Winterscar than they are here. Surely even in the north, a man is given a certain latitude in these matters, while a woman who openly strays from the path of virtue—"

"But not," Luke interrupted impatiently, "when the woman is—or is said to be—the mistress of a powerful man. Such women are usually courted and flattered. And if everyone here finds their sensibilities shattered, as they might well be—on account of this lady's age, on account of the possible tie of blood between her and the king—then why is the liaison allowed to continue? Had the king his sanity, his freedom, who should stop him? But situated as he is, it seems to me that a word from the Crown Princess ought to be enough. In any case, I wonder the princess failed to intervene at the very beginning, considering the young woman may be related to *her* as well."

"But surely you understand that Mademoiselle already ceased to exist for women like the princess, long before she came to the king's attention. And as to her youth—" Mr. Dou shrugged. "Other, more suitable women, had already been introduced, but the king showed no interest until they brought him Tremeur Brouillard."

For a second time, Luke stopped in his tracks. The morals of these people vastly offended him. "Other women were *introduced*? Do you mean to tell me they actually paraded an assortment of doxies before that sick old man? A grieving widower, too, whose feelings ought to have been respected."

"But it is precisely because of King Izaiah's condition that a woman was necessary. His physicians—" Mr. Dou wrinkled his brow. "I do not perfectly understand the medical terms involved, but it has something to do with an imbalance of the male and female principles within the four humors, causing the seed to putrefy inside of him. So it was decided that he ought to ej—" Mr. Dou stopped and threw up a hand, as Luke was beginning to look dangerous again. "Well, I will leave it to you to imagine what the king is supposed to do on a daily basis, and whether you consider the treatment rational."

"Rational? Under the circumstances, I consider it absolutely dis-

gust——" Luke bit back the words. This entire conversation made him
sick and enraged, but Varian Dou was telling him things that nobody
else had been willing to discuss before.

"But do you really believe this——treatment——has been literally followed? That the young lady is anything more than King Izaiah's nursemaid, playfellow, and friend? That he ever approaches or even addresses
her in anything but the most delicate and respectful manner?"

Mr. Dou was blushing furiously. "Sir, I see that you find the subject a very painful one. I am sorry I ever instigated this really quite
distressing conversation. But having gone so far, I feel I must go a bit
further. Even if what you believe is true, the young woman had
hardly a spotless reputation before. I could introduce you to several
men who could tell you that they enjoyed her favors when she was
yet at a very tender age. I could——"

Now it was Luke's turn to throw up his hand. "I thank you, no. Men
who prey on children sickened me. As for anyone who would buy the favors of a mere child and boast of it afterward——worse, openly meet
and acknowledge the uncle responsible for arranging the whole vile
transaction——I believe I can do very well without their acquaintance!"

In his heat, Lucius had raised his voice far more than he intended.
Passersby were staring at him, some with curiosity, others with approval. These were not, however, sentiments he had really meant to
submit for public inspection, so he lowered his voice. "I thank you,
sir, for answering my questions. Now if you will permit me, I'll bid
you good day!"

He was turning to go, but Mr. Dou stopped him with a light
touch on the arm. "Pardon me, Mr. Guilian. But I think I have said
far too much——and yet at the same time, far too little. For we have
not yet come to the thing I wished to say at the very beginning."

"Well?" Luke said sharply. He was heartily wishing by now that
the whole conversation had never taken place. Even *his* curiosity had
its limits, and these had been surpassed some time ago.

Mr. Dou hesitated. "Now that we come to it, I wonder if—but there is no going back. Everything you say convinces me that you have formed a strong, one might even say a *dangerous* attachment. But I ask you to consider: even were the young woman a complete innocent and in need of rescue, whatever chivalrous inclinations she might inspire, whatever desire you may have to make amends for all she has suffered, *you* can't save her.

"You are the King of Winterscar's cousin, and she is—perhaps— the great-niece of King Izaiah. It is barely acceptable for you to know her, and as to anything rash or romantic that you might contemplate: That could only spell ruin for both of you!"

For three days, Luke brooded over his conversation with Varian Dou. On the fourth day his natural curiosity—that overwhelming inclination to ferret out the solution to any puzzle, which had already sent him travelling across so many miles—overcame his reluctance to learn more of this matter in which his feelings were already so painfully involved. Having finally made up his mind to learn the truth at all costs, he decided that a visit to his oldest friend in Rijxland was long overdue.

Changing his coat, he snatched up his hat and a lacquer walking-stick, and set out on foot. He was somewhat reluctant to present himself at the house of the Crown Princess, where he had never been invited, but much to his relief, he soon discovered that no such intrusion was going to be necessary. Strolling down the street in the direction of the asylum, he met the five young children of the Princess Marjote out taking a walk, with the lean, long-legged figure of their tutor and bodyguard pacing behind them.

Lucius could not help smiling at the picture they presented: the royal children, so stolid and ordinary, and their grim Anti-demonist preceptor. As Luke watched, the smallest one stumbled and the Leveller swooped down like a great black crow, scooped her up in his strong arms, and continued on without breaking step, with the rosy-faced little girl perched comfortably, if somewhat incongruously, on his broad shoulder.

"My dear Raith, how extremely fortuitous," said Luke, stifling his amusement. "You are the very man that I wanted to see."

"It is a pleasure to see you also." With his usual meticulous courtesy, Raith proceeded to present Luke to his charges, one by one. When the whole party began to move forward again, Lucius fell into step at the Leveller's side.

"There is something I particularly wanted to ask you. But as the matter is—somewhat confidential—I suppose we should put it off for another time."

"You need not worry that anything you say will be repeated." The schoolmaster gestured toward the child on his shoulder, then indicated the older ones, who had gone ten paces ahead. "This one does not yet speak—and as you can see, the others are engaged in their own conversation."

"Well then—" said Luke, after a momentary hesitation. "I have been told, Raith, that if a man wants information he should come to you."

The Leveller smiled. "Mr. Guilian, you surprise me. I thought we were agreed, a long time ago, that I was simply too conspicuous for a secret agent."

"But not for a master of spies. What does it matter how conspicuous you are in yourself, if you are the one who sends out the agents, who organizes their movements, and collects their information?"

Raith continued to look amused. "Let us pretend, for the sake of discussion, that what you have guessed is true. What then?"

Luke took a deep breath and let it out slowly. "Then I would ask you to tell me everything you know about a certain young lady. I think you can guess who I mean."

The smile faded, the dark eyes grew sober. "I believe that I knew, soon after I met you, that you and she were likely to discover a meeting of minds."

"Yet you said nothing of that—nothing that I remember—when we spoke of her before." As they walked, Luke slashed at the air with his lacquer walking-stick.

"After all," said Raith, "I knew that even the most innocent friendship might seriously threaten your peace of mind. I also knew that any warning I might give would only serve to pique your interest."

By now, they had reached one of the parks in which the city abounded, and the young prince and his sisters moved further ahead. The ground was still bare and the trees leafless, but there were bronze statues, a three-tiered fountain, and a boxwood maze for the children to explore.

"I am tempted, Mr. Guilian, to tell you a story. Not, I hasten to add, one I received through any mysterious agency, but one that was told to me by Mademoiselle Brouillard herself."

"One of her fairy tales?"

"Perhaps. I will leave you to determine that for yourself. It certainly begins like a fairy story. Once upon a time, there was a young girl, who lived with her father—"

"Yes, I know," said Luke, with a look of disgust. "She lived in a palace on the moon."

The Leveller shook his head. "Not at all. She lived, I was about to say, in Montcieux. She was a perfectly ordinary little girl, no more vicious—or virtuous—in her habits than our young princess here. Unfortunately, her mother was dead and her father was addicted to the vice of gambling. He had a habit of borrowing money to pay off his debts, then losing that money and borrowing still more. When he died, his debts were considerable, and there was nothing left for his daughter to live on. She was, by then, some twelve years of age and beginning to show some promise of beauty. Some of her father's friends—they were very bad men, I regret to say—came to her with offers of protection, on such terms that, even so young as she was, she knew better than to accept. But there was another man, who said he had been married many years before to the girl's young aunt who died soon after the marriage. He seemed—more respectable than any of the others who had approached her before, so she accepted his invitation and went to live in his house."

They stopped by the fountain, where Luke leaned on his stick, staring moodily down into the pool at the base. A thin coating of ice covered the water, and the surface was broken by a thousand tiny, intersecting lines. "But it was not a safe house for a young girl to live in," he said in a flat voice.

"At first it appeared to be. The girl was inexperienced, and it was a long time before she was capable of understanding what sort of man her supposed uncle was. Even then—no one had offered her any insult, and she had no other place to go. But when she was a year or two older, and the promise of beauty had been fulfilled, the uncle asked her to play hostess at his dinner parties, to entertain his guests, and—you can guess the rest. Of course, she refused."

"Until he threatened to throw her out into the streets to make her own way?" Luke's fingers on the head of the walking-stick clenched and unclenched.

"He did threaten, but the girl stood firm, even when he tried to assert his authority by claiming she was his natural daughter. She said she would rather starve in the gutter; she said she would rather die. So he cast her out, and she spent two weeks living on the streets, begging for her bread in the dead of winter, fending off the violent approaches of the men that she met there. At the end of a fortnight, she decided there were worse fates than death or dishonor, and she returned to her uncle's house."

Luke glanced up at him. "You sound sympathetic." His own sympathies were most thoroughly engaged, but he had expected something quite different from Raith. "Surely you, with your high moral standards—"

"You forget," said Raith, "that I know too well what it is to be young and friendless, entirely dependent on the kindness of strangers. Had I not been taken in by good people, what should *I* be now?"

The five children had left the fountain and moved on to the box-wood maze, so Raith and Luke moved on, too. "That Mademoiselle Brouillard resisted evil so long as she did, I think remarkable. Yet sin is sin. Someday, she will be called to account before a wiser judge than I am. He will know how far to condemn her—I do not."

There was a long pause. "But do you think—do you think she is leading that sort of life now? That she is, as they say, the king's mistress?"

"Mr. Guilian, I do not think anything of the sort. The girl and King Izaiah are like two children together. I am happy to think that she has, for a time, been allowed to reclaim some part of that child-hood she lost too soon. I do *not* like to think what will become of her, should she ever be forced to return to her old way of life."

Luke winced inwardly, for that was another question he had avoided thinking about. "Surely so long as she remains with the king she is safe, surely so long as she enjoys his protection—"

"I think that you cannot have visited the asylum in some time. We hear that the king's condition continues to deteriorate. He has good days and bad days, but the bad days come with increasing frequency, and his dementia has taken a frightening turn."

Luke felt his heart sink. "But this is terrible. I mean, it's a terri-ble thing in itself, that excellent old gentleman losing his way—but what becomes of Tremeur if the king turns dangerous to himself and others?"

"That," said the Leveller, "remains to be seen. But I cannot help thinking the results would be disastrous—for Mademoiselle cer-tainly, and possibly for the rest of us."

36

Spring came to Luden. The ice broke on the canals, the brackish water warmed, and for many weeks it was impossible to smell anything but canal anywhere in the town. Gradually, however, noses adjusted.

Luke was occupied, just at that time, exploring graveyards. His deciphering of books at home had given rise to the notion that additional messages might be hidden, in the form of anagrams, on tombs and cenotaphs throughout the city. Unfortunately, he had no idea *which* tombs and inscriptions might be involved, so he had set out to copy every potentially interesting epitaph he happened to find.

He was kneeling, one day, in a Proto-deist cemetery, in the bright new grass at the foot of a tilted gravestone, scribbling in a leather pocket-book. When he chanced to look up, he discovered, much to his surprise, a small female in a long scarlet cloak and a broad straw hat liberally embellished with feathers and satin butterflies, regarding him pensively from a low marble monument.

"Tremeur," he said, rising quickly to his feet, brushing off his knees. He had never addressed her by her name before—it was always "Duchess" or "Your Hereditary Grace"—but the word seemed to slip out naturally.

"Did I disturb you? I am very sorry. I didn't mean to."

"No, no," he said. "I——I have been meaning to call on you, but this nonsense of mine, I'm afraid it distracted me."

Her face was unusually pale under the brim of her straw hat; the ostrich plumes quivered in the breeze. "Please don't think that you need to explain. I do understand. You have heard too much about me and my scandalous past."

Luke drew in his breath sharply. Somehow, he had never thought she might view his prolonged absence in that particular light. "You are entirely wrong. I *care* too much about you. And I flatter myself that you are beginning to care for me——a situation which can only lead to pain for both of us." He slid his pencil and his book into a coat pocket, took two short steps in her direction. "Were it not for that and that alone! But you must know if you know me at all, that I care very little for what other people think."

Her face lit momentarily. Yet the smile was fleeting and her violet eyes soon went dark again. "I should have known, Luke, that your reasons for doing *anything* would not be the ordinary ones."

For his part, Luke gave a mirthless laugh. "I wish I *were* an ordinary man, and not the King of Winterscar's foster-brother. If I were, believe me, I would know what to do." But then, remembering what the Leveller had told him, he added very quickly: "King Izaiah——how is he now? I heard he was not very well."

"He is so very, very far from well, he sometimes frightens me." As Tremeur slipped down from her marble perch, Luke was struck anew by her tiny size.

And when he thought of all the ambitious would-be brides, the scheming mothers, who had laid their traps for him over the years—— not because of any personal attractions he might possess, but for the sake of his fortune and his birth——it was bitter, bitter irony to reflect how his fancy had chanced to alight on this pretty, wounded, delicate little female.

"Luke, he doesn't even know me. Whatever games we used to play at, whatever titles he gave me in fancy, there was always a—a kind of recognition between us. But now he acts as though I were a stranger. And even worse than that—"

"Yes?" Luke prompted, as she continued to hesitate.

She lowered her voice, averted her face. "They all blame *me*, the doctors and the rest. They say the most horrible things. That he would be well if I—if I pleased him better. And they want to know how many times a day—how many times we—"

"Intolerable!" Luke reached out impulsively; his hand hovered for a moment in the air, then he clenched it into a fist and brought it back to his side. "It's bad enough they are willing to use you as they *think* they have, but that you should also be subjected to their gross speculations, their intrusive questions!" He struggled to master his outrage and revulsion. "I have no right to tell you what you should do, but I think you should leave the asylum at once."

She slipped out of his reach, retreated to the other side of the monument, putting the low square block of white marble between them. "If I left the madhouse, if I left Luden, Lord Flinx would only send men to bring me back. As my legal guardian, he has that right."

"But why? I have never understood. King Izaiah is a sick old man, utterly powerless. What does Lord Flinx gain by keeping you near him?"

Tremeur made a deprecating gesture with a small gloved hand. "Izaiah is powerless. I am powerless. But another woman close to the king might do much. A respectable woman from an ambitious family. She could even claim to be the king's wife—which I never can be. It's bad enough for my uncle with the princess opposing him, but if a third party arose, who knows which faction would win in the end?"

"Then why not find such a woman himself, and put her in your place? I suppose that's not beyond your uncle's ability," Luke said with a sneer. "Or beneath his morals?"

"But would another woman be his creature and his tool in the same way I am? He could never trust her, as he trusts me, having no such power over her. Besides," she added with a sad little smile, "I am the companion the king prefers, and I can be useful in a hundred small ways."

A faint blush was rising beneath her skin. "A spy of his own, living in the madhouse, do you not see the value? The most important people gather there to discuss their affairs. They speak very freely before the inmates, and the inmates, in turn, speak freely to me. Though perhaps," she added, with a touch of defiance, "I pass less of this on to Lord Flinx than I might. Perhaps I know things I don't choose to tell him!"

Though they were alone in the graveyard, she lowered her voice even further. "Just before the king was moved to the madhouse, a number of things disappeared from the palace, and it's thought that Izaiah hid them away. You have heard him speak of his emerald pocket-watch? It's true what he says, that the princess and Lord Flinx are simply wild to recover it. I can't even guess why they regard it so highly. But Marjote's people tore up her father's rooms as soon as he left them. They dug in the palace gardens all summer long, and during the winter pulled up the floors. *That's* why nobody lives there."

She stood staring down at the short green grass at her feet, with a small, perplexed frown growing between her eyes. "If I could—if I was willing to betray him, perhaps I could use the watch to bargain my way out of the madhouse. I never thought to do so before, because I was happy to stay there. But now—the way that the king looks at me sometimes, it makes me uncomfortable."

Luke stiffened. "Do you have any reason to fear he might harm you?"

"I don't know. I honestly don't know what he might do." She looked up at Luke with a wistful smile. "And I was so happy. It was like living in a pleasant dream. Sometimes I think I would do any desperate thing, rather than abandon that dream and live in the world again."

Luke felt a chill. Forgetting his resolution not to touch her, he reached out across the monument, took one of her hands in both of his, and clasped it tightly. Even through the white kidskin glove, he could feel a shiver pass over her skin, an instinctive shrinking of the slight hand with its tiny bird-like bones.

"Promise me this: If at any time you begin to believe that you are *not* safe, send me a message at once. I will—I really don't know what I can do, but I will come to you and we will think of something."

A message arrived at his house on the canal the very next day, just as Luke was settling down by a comfortable fire after a long, cold walk. The spry young footman came in with a letter on a chased silver salver. Recognizing the writing at once, Luke snatched it up, broke open the seal, and read through it quickly.

He threw the letter into the fire, then rang the bell for Perys. "My coat, if you please. I am going back out again."

Out on the street, he signaled a passing hack, and instructed the driver to take him to the madhouse with all possible haste. Ten minutes later, he was striding purposefully through the marble corridors, nodding curtly to everyone he met along the way.

He took the steps up to the attic two at a time, but paused outside the king's rooms, in order to regain his composure. The door flew open just as he was raising his fist to knock. One of the doctors stood on the threshold, blocking his view of the room beyond.

"Mademoiselle Brouillard?"

"I believe you will find her walking in the gardens. The king is not well," said the physician. "He will not be allowed any outside visitors until his condition improves."

Luke turned away with a sharp sense of misgiving. If Izaiah had deteriorated so far that his doctors were hiding him from the public—

Down in the gardens, he found Tremeur, very simply and soberly dressed, pacing a stone-flagged walk with a dejected air. At the sight of Luke, she brightened, and came to meet him with both hands outstretched.

"What has happened?" he asked, taking her hands and pressing them to his heart. "You haven't—you haven't suffered any insult, from the king or anyone else?"

"An insult? Is it possible to insult a woman like me?" He felt her tremble in his eager clasp. "Yet it was unpleasant enough, for all that. He kissed me, Luke, not as grandfather kisses his granddaughter, but as a man kisses a woman. And when I tried to pull away, he squeezed me so hard, I could scarcely breathe. A moment later, he seemed to come back to himself, but I can't help fearing the next time it happens, I won't be so fortunate!"

Luke stood staring blindly before him, his mind reeling with all of the sickening possibilities. It had only been a kiss this time, but what would it be another day? And no one would try to help her, no one would intervene. The girl was nothing to the king's doctors—nothing but a plaything for the old man, to be used or misused as part of his so-called cure—and it was more than likely the doctors themselves had encouraged his outrageous behavior.

Luke came to a sudden, a dangerous decision. If he was ever going to retain even a shred of self-respect, it was for him to step in and take decisive action. "There will *be* no next time. You will leave this place today and never come back."

Tremeur made a small noise in her throat. "You know I can never leave. If I tried, Lord Flinx—"

"Lord Flinx can do nothing if you disappear. If you travel far and you travel fast, then fade completely out of sight in some foreign city."

"But how—how could I?" she faltered. "A woman travelling alone, with no money, no friends to go to? Even if I disappeared as you say, how would I live? I only know the one way to—"

"You won't be travelling alone. And I can assure you: I have money enough to take us both a very long way and to keep us in comfort for a very long time." He felt her recoil. "No, don't think that. My intentions are honorable. We will be married as soon as we cross the border."

Her face worked; she looked as though she would burst into tears. "Luke, Luke, this is very noble—but you must know that we can do no such thing."

"We would marry, of course, under assumed names. I suppose—I suppose we would have to lie about your age, which won't be so easy, but you can generally make people believe anything you wish, if you offer them money."

All the time he was speaking, she was shaking her head. "But only imagine the consequences if they found us out!"

"Why should anyone find out? We have only to go where no one knows us. In Château-Rouge, in Tholia, why should anyone suspect that we are who we are?"

There was a clatter of high-heeled shoes on flagstones, and a murmur of approaching voices. Luke glanced quickly around him, searching for some private corner on the madhouse grounds, where they could go on speaking without being seen or overheard. Keeping his hold on both of her hands, he pulled Tremeur down an overgrown pathway, through a gap in a privet hedge, and into the shade of an ancient lime tree.

She lowered her voice to a loud whisper. "You can't keep us forever on what you bring with us. You would be cutting yourself off from your family, your friends, whatever fortune you possess—"

"I could take a position—as a tutor, perhaps, or a gentleman's secretary." But he felt a pang as he said the words. The prospect of working was not a pleasant one, yet it was a hundred times better than the alternative. He forced a smile. "It might be amusing to earn my keep."

His smile did not deceive her. "Would it be amusing—two years, three years, ten years in the future? Luke, it is too much. I could never allow you to make such a sacrifice. Besides, think what I am," she said, as his grip on her hands tightened. "Think what I have been. A ruined woman, an adventuress whose name—"

"You would have a new name. A new name and a new life. No one would know anything about your past."

"*You* would know." She snatched her hands away, and held them behind her. "Can you honestly tell me it means nothing? And even if you are prepared to overlook it now—can you honestly say it would mean nothing in the future? Some day when it all came home to you, all you had sacrificed, all you had lost for my sake and my sake alone! Would you not hate me then—would I not hate myself? Can't you see that what you propose is impossible!"

"Very well," he said, "you leave me no choice. There is but one course open to me." He wheeled about, and headed toward the gate.

There was something so wild, so violent in the way he spoke that Tremeur cried out. Lifting the hem of her skirt, she ran after him, reached out and took hold of his arm in order to restrain him. "What do you mean? What are you going to do? Is it something dangerous?"

"I am going to challenge Lord Flinx to a duel. I am going to kill him; I have wanted to do so for long enough. And then you would be free of his pernicious influence."

"No, no," she said, continuing to hang on his brocade sleeve, but with both hands now. "You can't—you mustn't do that."

"Can't?" he said, raising one dark eyebrow. "I admit I am not an experienced duellist, but neither is Lord Flinx, so far as I know."

"But if you *did* kill him. Don't you understand what they would do to you?" She shook his arm as she spoke. "I don't doubt he would meet you, his pride is so great. But you can't fight a duel with the Prime Minister, it's against the law. You would never escape hanging—never!"

Luke gave a reckless laugh, pretending to a confidence he did not feel. "That remains to be seen. I am willing to take my chances. It is true I would rather elope with you, but as you have refused me, what else can I do to keep you safe?"

Tears were coursing down her face. "Luke, I will do whatever you say. I will be your wife, or your mistress—or whatever you wish. Only say you won't do anything so foolish!"

He scanned her face, wondering if he could trust in a promise so reluctantly given. "Then be ready to leave at sunset this evening, when I will come to the gate in a post chaise. It should take me that long to make the arrangements—to concoct some story for Perys and the rest." He thought for a moment. "I will say I am off to Herndyke to continue my researches, that I plan to be gone for at least a fortnight. If I pack up my things and drive out of the city openly, no one will think anything amiss. Then I will double back. But for you—I am afraid it won't be possible for you to bring much with you. No matter. I will buy you new things, when we are safely out of Rijxland."

She nodded her head, blinking back tears. "What I absolutely need, I will carry with me. But Luke, you haven't promised yet, that you won't do anything foolish when it comes to my uncle."

Lucius gently detached himself from her desperate clasp. "I promise not to challenge him while we are here in Rijxland. But if he has the poor judgement to pursue us elsewhere, to places where his position as Prime Minister gains him no special privileges—I won't be responsible for what happens then!"

Luke paid a flying visit to the bank where he had first presented letters of credit on reaching Luden. There was some chance that word of this visit would soon get out, but that was a risk he would have to take. By tomorrow or the next day, it might not be possible to make use of his credit again. Fortunately, the banker seemed to think nothing of handing over a very large sum, in banknotes and gold, to a gentleman with such impeccable credentials.

Then it was back to his lodgings to pack up some bags and a trunk—to take any less would scandalize Perys and arouse his suspicions. As it was, Luke had considerable difficulty convincing his valet to stay behind: "To keep an eye on the others, and the household running smoothly."

"That's all very well," said Perys. "But Master Luke, if you change your mind and decide to stay in Herndyke for more than a week or two—you *will* send for me?"

"Of course," lied Luke, a lump rising in his throat as he spoke. He was just beginning to realize that he would never see Perys again— no small matter, since the man had been with him since his sixteenth birthday. It would be difficult, he supposed, but not impossible, to survive without a man-servant—but what was going to become of Perys himself, abandoned by his master in a foreign land?

Luke took out a crumpled banknote, smoothed it out, and pressed it into the valet's reluctant hand. "If anything should happen to me while I am gone, this will buy you a passage back home. Go to Jarred or to Doctor Purcell; I know they will find you an excellent position."

"Master Luke, don't say such things," said Perys, visibly distressed. "Oh sir, it doesn't bear thinking about."

Half an hour later, the post chaise was at the door, and Lucius was dressed for travel in top-boots and riding coat. Perys and the footman were carrying out the last two bags, when a most unwelcome visitor arrived. Luke came to a sudden stop at the foot of the stairs, as the trim, gentlemanly figure of Lord Flinx appeared in the doorway.

Luke bowed stiffly, and the Prime Minister did the same. "So it is true the rumor I heard, that you are leaving Luden."

"For a fortnight only," Luke answered coldly. "Had you any particular business with me in the meantime?"

"Only this," said Lord Flinx, with his gentle smile. "That you might wish to consider not returning so soon. Indeed, you might be wise to extend your visit to Herndyke—indefinitely."

Luke felt a sudden rush of relief. Lord Flinx had not guessed his reasons for going; knowing that matters were soon to reach a crisis between Tremeur and the king, he simply wanted Lucius out of the way. And it would not be wise, Luke decided, to seem to yield to his wishes too easily. "I thank you, Lord Flinx, for your concern. But for all that, I intend to come back again. I am leaving so much behind me, you see."

The Prime Minister shrugged, pretending to misunderstand him. "But it is not too late to order your servants to pack up your things and follow after you. Really, Mr. Guilian, I would advise it. If you return to Luden, I will very probably have you arrested."

Lucius blinked at him. Of all the things that Lord Flinx might have said, he had never remotely expected anything like this. "Arrested? On what possible charge?"

"For debauching my niece, who is not yet of age." Lord Flinx appeared quite unaware of the irony. "I hardly know what may be permissible in Winterscar, but there are laws in Rijxland protecting young girls."

"Debauching your niece!" Luke gave a short, incredulous laugh. "When she has been living openly with King Izaiah for over a year? You must be jesting!"

"On the contrary. Just how serious I am, you will learn to your cost, if you do not give Luden and Mademoiselle a very wide berth."

His blood boiling, Luke stripped off his gloves, actually had one gripped in his hand, ready to administer the deadly insult from which there could be no going back—when he remembered his promise to Tremeur.

With an effort, he swallowed his wrath. "As you can see, Lord Flinx, I am just on my way out," he said coolly. "When I return to Luden, I will do myself the honor of calling on you, and we can discuss the matter then."

"You will find me at home," said the Prime Minister, with a sneer and a nod of his head. "Though perhaps in the meantime you will grow wiser." Turning on his heel he left the house without another word.

But Luke stood looking after him for several minutes. "It's possible I *will* grow wiser," he said under his breath. He generally did think better of these impulsive actions. Though by the time he had the leisure to think about this one, he would be in far too deep to consider turning back.

Book Three

ermouline on the River Ousel: she was a town of mazes, of courts within courts, alleys behind alleys, a town where every turn, every byway, every stair, every gate, seemed to lead deeper and deeper into the heart of confusion.

Where Hawkesbridge had been building up for more than a thousand years, the residents of this city in Chêneboix had been digging down, burrowing under, adding on, subdividing, building in back-yards, on commons, sometimes even encroaching on the already narrow lanes and byways, in an effort to utilize every square foot of space available. Laws had been passed over the centuries forbidding this practice, but like many such laws, they failed of their intent. All they accomplished was to render title to the shops, stalls, and houses extremely questionable, which in turn led to careless building, the use of cheap materials. Why would a man waste money constructing a house that would last for decades, when he might be required to raze it at any moment? So the buildings were shoddy. As they aged, half-hearted attempts were made to shore them up: with beams, crimps, bars, and the like, bearing walls added on at odd angles, and a hundred other shifts and expedients that only made the town uglier, crazier, more crowded than she had been before.

This was especially true down by the river, near the saw-mill, the brewery, the sugar-baking houses, and other manufactories, where the workers lived crowded—sometimes five or six families to a house—inside a great warren of shacks, tenements, and subterranean hovels.

Even in the better parts of the town, where the streets were clean, the houses well-built, the parlors sunny, there was not much elbow-room. If there were lanes too narrow to admit a carriage—no matter, it only made work for the chair-men. Gardens were practically unknown—but a flower in a pot was as good any day (said the doughty citizens) as an entire plot. They had adjusted to their crowded conditions, and even seemed to thrive on them. It was said that when a resident of Fermouline had to go elsewhere, the wide open spaces oppressed them. It was certain, anyway, that visits to the surrounding countryside were extremely rare. What had begun as expedience had become a necessity. Noise, smells, the constant press of humanity, had become as vital to her people as the unwholesome air that they breathed.

37

one of the clocks in the town kept the right time. That was one of the first things that Will noticed when he rode into Fermouline on the big buckskin gelding he had purchased in Fernbrake. Pausing in a square fronted by no less than three churches—each with its own dial prominently displayed—Wilrowan reached into a pocket of his long coat, pulled out his own timepiece, and flipped open the cover. His watch said noon, the church dials read *one*, *two*, and *half past three*, respectively. Judging by the position of the sun directly overhead, his watch was as accurate as ever.

Weaving a path through the complex pattern of streets, stopping every now and again to ask for directions, Will came at last to the Cinque d'Or, a rambling triple-galleried structure with a slate roof and a half-dozen chimneys, built on a stretch of rising ground about a mile from the Ousel. Entering the innyard through a sooty brick archway, Will dismounted, turned over the gelding to one of the hostlers, and asked for the landlord.

Having located the proprietor in the steamy coffee-room, and engaged a room on the top floor, he then headed for the comparative quiet of the taproom, where he found Nick Brakeburn and Cor-

poral Gilpin awaiting him. Will hooked a ladder-back chair in passing, and pulled it up to their table. Then he sat down, and received
their report. They had taken a room at the nearby Rouge-Croix, according to his instructions. They had been in town since the night
before but had so far seen nothing worth mentioning, unless it might
be: "A certain universal tension, a sense of unease," said Nick.
"Whether it's the result of the proximity of the professors' infernal
engine, I really can't say, but you have only to look at the faces of the
people you meet in the streets to see they are disturbed about *something*."

Will nodded his agreement. Strained faces and generally skittish
behavior on the part of the Fermouline citizens had been another
thing he noticed on coming into town. "And Lieutenant Odgers?"

Odgers had yet to be heard from, but as he and Nick had travelled together most of the way and only parted some thirty miles
back, it was likely that he would appear shortly.

With the arrival of his baggage, Wilrowan went upstairs to
change his clothes. He explored the town until sunset, getting his
bearings, then returned to the inn, where a message from Odgers
awaited him. The lieutenant had engaged a room on one of the lower
floors. He had entered the town on one of the barges that plied the
river; there had been some problem with the mechanism that emp-
tied and filled the locks and made travel against the current possible,
hence his late arrival. He extended his apologies, but thought the
captain might be interested in the cause of the delay. Will *was* interested—as he must be interested in anything that involved pumps or
similar machinery—but he was also exhausted, and put off a visit to
the locks until morning.

Going to bed that evening, he had the oddest and yet the most
distinct impression that Lili was somewhere quite close, and that she
was thinking about him. But that, he knew, was absurd. Climbing in
between the threadbare sheets, Will dismissed the impression as

wishful thinking. He closed his eyes and almost immediately fell into a deep, troubled sleep, dreaming of gears, wheels, pumps, and spinning compass needles all night long.

His first action, once he was dressed the next morning, was to unroll a large map he had purchased the afternoon before, and tack it up on one wall. Then it was down to the coffee-room, where he ate a quick breakfast of kidneys, bacon, toast, and sardines, in company with Nick and the other two men.

By mid-afternoon, Will had made his first discovery: his watch was running backwards. This he remedied with the purchase of a pocket sun-dial in a shagreen case.

During the following six days—as he received reports from his men, as he went out himself on long forays, gathering information—Wilrowan made many marks on his map. Nothing escaped his interest: fires, brawls, carriage accidents, broken machinery. By the end of that first week, he found that his notations were largely concentrated in a single section of the town: a square mile of shops and small manufactories down by the river. The neighborhood looked peaceful enough when strolling through the streets, or when observed from a boat on the Ousel, but that was deceptive. In fact, it was much too quiet. A busy paper mill and a large factory where felt had been made for sale to hatters had both closed down, with a consequent decrease in traffic. Yet behind the innocent facades of the shops and mills there had occurred a murder, a suicide, and three fatal accidents involving machinery, all within the last few weeks.

Remembering what Doctor Fox had said about the malign effects of magnetism on the Human nervous system, Will concentrated his personal efforts on this one neighborhood.

For another week, nothing happened. In a variety of disreputable disguises, he haunted the district, while his first excitement gradually turned to impatience, and then to boredom. Then one day, lounging outside an ironworks and trying to look inconspicuous, Will's disinterested glance fell on a ragged-looking guardsman, who happened to be engaged in earnest conversation with a small, fair-skinned female in a flowered silk gown and a frivolous hat. It was only as the two parted company, heading off in opposite directions, that Will recognized something in the way the guardsman walked. He was a Wryneck—no, he was *the* Wryneck—and the female probably the very same woman that young Dagget had seen with the Goblin in Hawkesbridge.

For a moment, Wilrowan hesitated, not knowing which one he ought to follow. But just as she was whisking around a corner, he decided on the woman.

That she was Human, he had no doubt: She was too tall and too perfectly formed for an Ouph or Padfoot, too small and too indisputably female for a Wryneck or Grant. It seemed to him that the Goblins in this conspiracy had been treated as though they were expendable; the woman, therefore, would make a more valuable prisoner.

Pretending to a nonchalance he was very far from feeling, Will slouched after her. Rounding the corner, he had no difficulty spotting her as she moved down a narrow lane between stalls selling baskets, hares, turkeys, guinea-fowl, cabbages, and second-hand clothes—though by now she was so far ahead that he was forced to quicken his pace to avoid losing sight of her again.

For the next several hours she led him a merry chase through the town: on foot, by sedan-chair, then on foot again. She seemed to know the city well and to be intent on some object. She never hesitated or paused to consult a single sign-post, but continued resolutely on through the maze of streets and courts and alleys, at a steady, tireless pace, moving from the fish market, to the fashionable quarter, to a district of small cafes and discreet rooming-houses, then back to the factories and grog-shops near the river, only stopping when the traffic of coaches and wagons forced her to do so, only looking back when some other pedestrian brushed past her, or her hat blew off in a gust of wind. Not wishing to be seen following her, Will dodged around corners, watched her from doorways, and generally exhausted himself in the pursuit.

To his frustration, she never entered any house or shop, nor paused to speak to anyone after she abandoned her sedan-chair. Since it was unlikely she carried the Chaos Machine with her, he had hoped to discover where she was staying and where she visited, before he made any attempt to apprehend her. But as the day wore on, he began to doubt the wisdom of this plan. If he put off arresting her, he ran the risk of losing her entirely.

She led him down to a dock by the river, where she boarded a public ferry, heading for Chalkford in Bridemoor, on the opposite bank. The ferry was preparing to cast off as she boarded. Will shouldered his way through the heavy crowd on the dock, searched frantically through his pockets for the necessary fare, which he handed over to the man who guarded the wooden turnstile—and then watched the boat slip away from its moorings while he was still on the wrong side of the barrier. Once through, he took several running steps, then gathered himself for a long leap across the ever-widening expanse of churning water.

He landed on the deck with a loud thud and turned his ankle painfully in doing so. He steadied himself, then looked around him. Behind him, one of the boatmen was just fastening a gate across the gap in the railing.

The broad deck was crowded. The other passengers had all scrambled aside when Wilrowan landed; now, they resumed their former places, blocking his view. Not being able to locate his quarry, he feared for a moment he had made a mistake. Then a stout gentleman in a mole-skin waistcoat stepped out of his way, and he spotted the woman, just sitting down on a bench.

Limping slightly, Wilrowan stationed himself by the railing, where he could observe her movements for the rest of the trip. In doing so, he was able to study the pretty, somewhat round face under the beribboned hat. How old was she? It was impossible to tell. Her skin was smooth and unlined, her eyes clear, yet he somehow thought she was not so young as she appeared at first glance.

And how had this demure little woman, sitting there so primly in her flowered silk, with her white-gloved hands folded in her lap, ever come to be involved in such an infamous plot? Had he made the wrong choice outside the iron-works? But Dagget had described the Wryneck's companion as entirely genteel, and she certainly fit that description.

The river was broad between Fermouline and Chalkford, and it took almost an hour for the ferry to cross. The sun was setting, streaking the water with a reflected glory of crimson and gold, when the boat finally docked and everyone disembarked. Moving across the boardwalk, the woman dropped a small beaded purse. Without thinking what he was doing, Will stooped to pick it up and hand it back to her. As they stood face-to-face, a curiously intent expression appeared briefly in her eyes.

Though she thanked him politely and turned away with a fine show of disinterest, Will cursed himself for a fool. He was lightly disguised—his chin unshaven, his hat worn low on his brow, his auburn hair rubbed with soot to darken the color—but he had no way of knowing how well she knew him. If she *had* recognized him, there was no point allowing her to go any further; she would not venture anywhere near the Chaos Machine while he was following her.

Will pulled out a pistol from his coat pocket, made certain it was loaded and primed, and hurried after her. She was twenty feet ahead of him, crossing a wide boulevard, when a sudden surge of foot and horse traffic came between them. The streets of Chalkford were busy; though he kept her straight little back and her brightly colored silk gown in sight for another quarter of an hour, he could not catch up to her. Then she turned down a narrow passageway between two buildings, and by the time Will rounded the corner she was nowhere to be seen.

He stood staring around him in stunned disbelief. There were no visible doorways opening on this alley and no ground floor windows, just a long line of weather-stained brick walls, the backs of shops and houses. Yet there was no place for the woman to hide herself, either. The only outlet was at least two hundred yards further on, and there had been no time for her to sprint even half that distance.

Had she used some Goblin magic to disappear? Perhaps a Padfoot cloak of invisibility? Such garments, he knew, were sometimes very light, woven of stuff so fine that she might have carried the cloak in the very same jet-beaded purse he had obligingly handed her. If that was so, he would never find her now.

For all that, he spent the next four hours searching the surrounding streets, first in the gathering dusk, and then by lamplight. At midnight, he gave it up. Berating himself for botching the thing so badly, he headed back toward the river and the ferry.

The afternoon sun was beating down. Lili was tired, dirty, and hot, inside her heavy bombazine gown, under the black net veil of a widow's bonnet. Lifting her hem in order to examine the scuffed toes of her black leather shoes, she shook her head in disgust. The soles were crusted with the curiously adhesive and corrosive mud that characterized Fermouline. People said it was made up in equal parts of dirt, Human waste, and metal particles struck from the wheels of the carts and carriages which made up the constant traffic. Whatever its origin, it stank to high heaven. To make matters worse, her shoes pinched. Though they had seemed to fit well enough back in Hawkesbridge, in Hawkesbridge she had never been obliged to spend so many long hours on her feet, to travel so many long miles of cobblestone and brick.

Lili looked around her for a shady spot to sit and rest. There was no place to sit—and perhaps, after all, it was time to move on to a new location. She had already been up and down this street twice, in and out of a score of shops, all without any success.

Rounding a corner, she found herself suddenly face-to-face with her cousin Nick. In her surprise, she almost spoke his name out loud. With a pounding heart she waited for him to speak, but he merely nodded politely and stepped aside, allowing her to pass. Thank goodness she was wearing the veil! Were it not for that, he would have known her in an instant.

Lili leaned up against a dirty brick wall. What was Nick *doing* here anyway? Had he come with Wilrowan? Several times during the last two weeks, she had been forced to dodge around corners or to hide in doorways as Will walked past. She had been on the lookout for *him* from the very beginning, knowing he must soon arrive on the scene, congratulating herself that *there* she had the advantage at least. But with Nick in town, too, her chances of discovery were doubled.

But this is ridiculous! she thought. *I should be concentrating on the Chaos Machine and the people who took it, not on hiding myself from my own husband and my favorite cousin.*

Indeed, her entire visit to Fermouline was beginning to assume the appearance of one long farce: the intrigue, the disguises, the elaborate game of seek-and-find, played on so many different levels—and all for what? She was no closer now to finding the Mountfalcon Jewel than she had been a fortnight ago, when she first came into the town.

It was late afternoon when Lili finally turned her weary steps toward the neat stone house on the east side of town where she and Sir Bastian were staying. The people who lived there were Specularii—or at least they had been, many years before. Now they were well past eighty, a quiet old couple, not very interested in Lili or her quest, but kind and hospitable. Staying with them was far more convenient than staying at an inn, and more respectable, too.

Not, she told herself, that it would matter a jot to Wilrowan. If he had any idea she was here with another man, no matter how elderly, Will simply would not care how many decent old people there were in the house. He would make no end of a fuss.

Or he would, Lili thought drearily, *if he hasn't washed his hands of me entirely by now.*

She found her mentor waiting for her at the house, in the sunny front parlor. There must have been something in the way that she walked, some sign of discouragement. "We are no closer today to finding the Jewel?" Sir Bastian asked.

Lili shook her head. "Several times I have seemed to be so close, I could actually sense the tiny machinery—the little gears and wheels moving, the magnetic lines of force—but the sensation always faded."

She sat down in a massive oak chair, gave a weary little sigh. "Yesterday, just at nightfall, it was stronger than ever. I was sure I had found the place where the Chaos Machine was hidden: a little basement shop where they sell pins and ribbons. But when I went back this morning, when I found a pretext to go inside, there was only a sense of—emptiness—a sense of loss. But how can you *lose* something you never had?"

Sir Bastian considered her words very carefully. "Had you felt that emptiness, that loss, before?"

"Never. It was very odd. I went up and down the street, but the feeling I had last night never returned. I think—I think that the Jewel was moved during the night. I believe it is no longer here in the town."

"And where do you think it has gone?"

Lili put a hand to her head. "North. I can't say why, but I feel a pull to the north."

Sir Bastian reached into his waistcoat pocket, pulled out a length of fine silver chain. At the end of the chain was a tiny pendulum shaped like a scythe. Wrapping several inches of chain around his fist, he held the pendulum suspended about eighteen inches from his body and closed his eyes, the better to concentrate.

For several minutes, nothing happened, then the silver scythe began to move: first slowly, then with increasing motion, until it was swinging violently from side to side. The hand that held the chain began to tremble and then to twitch, and a strong vibration seemed to pass up the entire arm.

Sir Bastian opened his eyes. "There is certainly a strong disruption in the magnetic currents to the north." When he gathered up the chain and the pendulum into his fist, the vibration in his hand and arm abruptly ceased. "How quickly can you pack up your things?"

Lili took a deep breath and let it out slowly. "I never really unpacked. Except for a few small items and the clothes on my back, everything remains in my trunk. I can be ready to travel in a matter of minutes."

"It will take longer than that to prepare the coach and hitch up the horses," said the old gentleman, sliding the pendulum back into his pocket. "And my dear child, you look exhausted and hungry. I will instruct the cook to pack us a basket—a complete cold supper we can eat in the coach. There is no telling when or where we will be stopping next."

Three-quarters of an hour later they were in the berlin, rattling through the city streets. As tired as she was, Lili felt a surge of elation. It was something to be moving again, to have a sense of purpose, after the last two discouraging weeks.

They reached the river, where the driver negotiated with one of the ferrymen to carry the berlin across. A bargain was struck, the horses were led on board, and the flat-bottomed boat cast off. Sitting on the seat opposite Sir Bastian, with the copper-and-crystal divining rod in her hand, Lili felt certain it would not take very long to overtake the Chaos Machine now that it was moving, now that the magnetic disruption was so very strong.

But on dry land again, a mile beyond Chalkford, she was suddenly overcome by a wave of sickness. Her stomach lurched, her pulses pounded. A cold hand seemed to take a hold of her heart and squeeze and squeeze until she was dizzy with the pain. Bringing all of her healer's training to the task, she tried to overcome it. But the sickness did not go away. With every yard that the coach travelled, her physical distress grew more and more intense. Finally, Lili could bear it no longer.

"Sir Bastian, we have to go back. We have to go back to Fermouline at once."

The old gentleman gave her a startled glance. "You are pale, my dear, and you appear agitated. What has happened? Has the Jewel returned to the city?"

Lili shook her head, swallowed hard to keep down the rising nausea. "No, no, the Chaos Machine is still moving north. But we have to go—we have to turn back anyway. I can't tell you why I know this, but I think that Wilrowan is dying!"

38

ill sat in the taproom at the Cinque d'Or, staring into a tankard of bitter ale. The room was dim and the ceiling low; a pall of smoke hung heavy on the air. Somewhere, a door opened. Candles flickered in the sudden draft and boot-heels clattered on the scarred plank floor. But Wilrowan remained oblivious to his surroundings. Ever since the night before, when the woman had eluded him, he had been cudgeling his brain, trying to come up with some scheme for discovering her whereabouts. She would be on her guard now, unlikely to return to that part of the town where he had seen her before, yet there must be *some* way of smoking her out—

Will took another drink of the thick, muddy brew. It was probably the worst he had ever tasted—the specialty of the house, he was told, a concoction known as *Cock Ale*, made by boiling a rooster in ale and spices—but the water at the inn was even worse and the cider nearly as bad.

He finished his dinner and drained his tankard, then went upstairs to his room. He studied the map on the wall for several minutes, planning in his mind a series of movements meant to take him through most of the town in a matter of hours. As he was turning away, his vision blurred; he experienced what felt like a sudden hard blow to his chest. The pain was as sickening as it was intense.

Will reached out blindly for the wall, meaning to steady himself, but he could not find it. As he took an uncertain step forward, he nearly doubled over with another pain. He felt himself toppling, then hitting the floor. His head struck the wall with a loud crack. After that, there was nothing but darkness.

Eighty miles away, at Brakeburn Hall, a very fine coach was just rolling down the long drive between the oaks. The owner of that coach was obviously one who liked to travel in style: nine out-riders kept pace, a pair of footmen went sprinting ahead, and two large mastiffs trotted briskly behind. When the coach stopped at the foot of the stone staircase leading up to the house, there was increased activity on the part of this retinue. The horsemen dismounted and lined up smartly along the avenue. The coach door opened, a panting footman moved forward to let down a pair of steps and assist the occupant as she alighted. Meanwhile, the two dogs bounded up to the top of the stairs, where they stationed themselves on either side of the massive front door.

Inside the house, Miss Allora Brakeburn was sitting in the morning room, knotting a fringe, when a dazed-looking lackey came in to announce Lady Krogan. Wondering at this unexpected visit, Allora put her work hastily aside and rose to her feet, just as a stately figure trailing shawls, scarves, and veils swept into the room, followed by the two golden mastiffs.

"How do you do, Miss Brakeburn," said the dowager. Though she moved with great energy as she crossed the room, it could be seen that she leaned heavily on a silver handled cane. "I hope that I do not intrude."

"Not at all," said Allora, dropping a perfunctory curtsy, at the same time she was taking the other woman's measure. These two formidable old ladies had never met, though each knew the other by reputation. Allora—who seldom felt her lack of inches—was somewhat taken aback. She had not, after all, suspected Will of such a tall and imposing grandmother. "Though I cannot help wondering what could possibly bring you here."

"Your great-niece and my Wilrowan," said Lady Krogan, shedding several layers of sable draperies as she spoke.

Allora frowned. A forthright woman herself, she was not always pleased when others were equally direct with her. She motioned her visitor to take a seat, and the dowager lowered herself carefully into a wing-backed chair, while the two leonine mastiffs settled down on the polished floor at her feet. "I wish to effect a reconciliation between those two children, and I believe you may be of some little assistance."

Allora gave a short, incredulous laugh. "A reconciliation between your Will and my Lilliana?" She resumed her own seat with a small indignant bounce. "No, Lady Krogan, I cannot and will not assist you there. I am sorry to say so, but your grandson's unpardonable conduct on every occasion—"

The dowager stopped her by the simple expedient of talking over her. "It is not of Wilrowan's conduct that I wish to speak; you can tell me nothing that I do not know. Where Lili is concerned, however, I must admit that I was regrettably ignorant—until quite recently, when I made it my business to make certain inquiries. What I learned *then* surprised me very much."

Allora gave a tiny, outraged gasp. "If you believe that you have uncovered any scandal, you are very much mis—"

"No scandal," said Lady Krogan, cutting her off again, this time with an imperious wave of one white hand. "Though much that you obviously wish to keep hidden. To be brief, Miss Brakeburn, I find that you have been training Lilliana as a Specularii magician."

Allora stiffened. There was a long pause, while she struggled to regain her poise. "I don't know what you can possibly mean. Perhaps you will inform me: just what *is* a Specularii magician, and why should I wish to train Lili to become one?"

The dowager shook her head. "Come, come, let us at least be honest with one another. You do yourself no good by pretending ignorance. We are both too old and too experienced to be fooled by such puerile tactics. Could someone like yourself—with such a very wide acquaintance in esoteric circles—really know nothing of the Specularii? Indeed, your evasions only convince me that my sources do not lie."

Allora did not answer. She only sat very upright in her chair, maintaining a stubborn silence. There was nothing that she *could* say. All she could do was try to school her expression to perfect indifference as Lady Krogan went on.

"It is plain enough that Will and Lili left Mountfalcon for the same purpose. Would they not stand a very much greater chance of succeeding, if they worked together instead of apart?"

Allora thrust out her chin. "Where Lili has gone, what she is doing, has nothing to do with Wilrowan. But even if it did, it would not matter. Where Lili is at this precise moment, I do not know, and I have no way of finding it out. That is to say," she added, with a tight little smile, "supposing I wished to influence her on your grandson's behalf—which I certainly do not!"

The dowager regarded her scornfully. "Well, you are a foolish, prejudiced old woman after all. It is too bad. I had expected more of Lili's aunt." As she rose slowly from her chair, the dogs growled deep in their chests and lumbered to their feet. "You might have made my task considerably easier, but as you will not—it hardly matters."

Gathering up her trailing vestments, she moved toward the door, though she stopped on the threshold for a final word. "Lilliana is no longer a child. When she and Wilrowan return, you should treat their marriage with more respect, allow your niece to lead her own life without interference. Otherwise, I warn you: you may very well lose her, and you will have no one but yourself to blame."

Rather than return to Eaudaimanté, Lady Krogan instructed her coachman to take the western road. She allowed one of the footmen to assist her into the coach, made herself as comfortable as possible, then whistled to one of the mastiffs. The big golden dog entered the coach in a single bound, and settled down with his head propped on the dowager's feet.

She groaned inwardly as the coach began to move. Though the vehicle was well sprung and its seats padded, she was growing too old for these long journeys. She had already found this trip a punishing one, and feared she would scarcely be able to move by the time she reached Hawkesbridge. Yet a visit to the Volary suddenly seemed imperative.

Three days later, after a difficult and fatiguing journey, she arrived at the house she maintained in the city, and went directly upstairs to her bedchamber. Dismissing the maid-servant who helped her to remove her shoes and loosen her stays, she lay back against the horsehair bolster with a deep sigh.

The bed was soft, the room was dark, but try as she might to fall asleep, her keen mind continued to work. At last she abandoned all efforts to rest, rose from her bed, and hobbled around the dim bedchamber, leaning heavily on her stick.

She had not really expected much in the way of cooperation from Allora Brakeburn; what she had principally meant to accomplish was to trick Lili's aunt into confirming what had really only been guesses about Lili, the Specularii, and the quest for some mysterious missing object— the true nature of which the dowager's spies had been unable to discover. In this, at least, she felt she had succeeded very well. If Allora *said* nothing to confirm Lady Krogan's suspicions, the expression on her face, even her silence on some points, had been eloquent enough.

"But perhaps I will learn more when I visit King Rodaric," she mused out loud. "I must see how much I can convince him to tell me. Then, of course, there is young Trefallon—who is likely to know considerably more than he actually realizes. In the meantime, if Miss Brakeburn will not send word to Lilliana, I must find a way to communicate with Wilrowan."

Lady Krogan stopped pacing; she stood staring blindly before her, seeing another place, another time, in her mind's eye. Almost three years had passed since she handed the Maglore ring on to her grandson, yet she had possessed the ring for so many years before that, she thought that some lingering traces of her long rapport with the ravens might still remain. "It is at least worth trying."

Crossing to her bedroom window, she drew back the heavy draperies of grey tabby silk and threw open the shutters. A brilliant beam of sunlight came into the room, causing the old woman to throw up a hand to shield her eyes. Gradually, her vision adjusted, and she was able to face the light.

With an immense effort, she pulled a heavy chair over to the window, and lowered herself to the seat. She waited a moment for the ache in her bones to subside. Then she sent out her thoughts across the city—hoping that one or more of the great black birds would hear and respond.

She sat by the window for what seemed like hours, straight-backed, determined, refusing to accept defeat. The ravens *would* come, if her will was strong enough, if she kept her mind focused on her pressing desire.

At last there was a flutter of wings outside; a raven landed on the window-sill. A moment later, another bird joined him. Faint and seemingly far-off, the first raven's greeting was like a broken whisper in her mind.

<I—Crwcrwyl—Captain—trusted spy. What does—wish of me?> A pale blue spark flared and then disappeared.

Lady Krogan concentrated as hard as she could. <*You must tell all the other ravens. Each must pass on the word to as many others as he can. Fly north in search of Captain Blackheart and carry my message.*> She was not certain how much of this was getting through, but she must have succeeded in communicating something, because Crwcrwyl responded by projecting a clear picture of Wilrowan into her mind.

So the old woman gave her message, repeating it three times over, in the hope that in this way it might all be received—if not intact at least in intelligible fragments.

<*We will try. But the way is long—there are—miles to be—perhaps he has spoken—others of our kind in the north. Perhaps we—if so, do you—reply?*>

"No," said Lady Krogan out loud at the same time she spoke the words in her mind. "There is no need for you to bring me any reply. Only make certain that Wilrowan learns this valuable piece of information. It could spare him much worry and grief."

Will had been wandering in darkness for an hour or an eternity when he heard someone speaking inside his head. <*Will—Wilrowan! Breathe, Will, breathe; pull the air into your lungs and push it back out again.*>

He did as he was told. Gradually, the inky blackness turned to grey, and then to a golden glow of candlelight. A pale face was hovering over him, slightly blurred. Then his vision cleared and he recognized Lili.

"Thank goodness, he has come back!" She spoke over her shoulder, to somebody standing in the shadows by the door. "No, Will, you mustn't try to speak or move. Just lie there quietly."

"I must be dreaming," he managed to say. "You can't possibly be here. Lili, I—"

"Hush, Will. Be still and don't tire yourself by trying to speak. Someone poisoned you; if I had arrived even a few minutes later, you would have died. As it was, it was a very near thing."

"Poisoned?" Will tried to sit up, to lever himself up on his elbows, but the room began to spin, all the strength went out of his arms, and he fell back again. He tried to remember where he was, what he had been doing, but the events of the last several days all jumbled together in his mind. In his confusion, he forgot to whom he was speaking, imagined he was speaking to Nick Brakeburn instead. "Was it the woman or was it the Wryneck?"

There was a brief hesitation. "The—woman, Wilrowan? And I don't understand what you mean about the Wryneck."

"The one in Chetterly. Dash it, Nick, I must have told you—you say I was *poisoned*? Eternal Darkness! Don't ever tell my grandmother I was such a fool. If she knew I had allowed myself to drink something I shouldn't, she would never let me hear the end of it."

"Will," said Lili, with a slight tremor in her voice, "it very nearly *was* the end—for you. Now do as I say, close your eyes, and rest for a while. There will be time for explanations later."

Will nodded. For some reason, he suddenly felt enormously sleepy, weary beyond all measure.

The moment he closed his eyes, a wave of sleep seemed to wash over him. He barely heard the sound of retreating footsteps, or the soft click of a closing door.

Out in the berlin again, Lili confronted Sir Bastian. "The Wryneck, sir? I knew there was a Grant killed when Will was in Chetterly. But I never heard there was a Wryneck involved in the plot—or a woman, either!"

"I was as surprised as you were. But what a fortunate stroke of luck for us. Thanks to Captain Blackheart, we now know more than we did about the people we are seeking. This is all most interesting."

Lili looked down at her hands, which were still shaking from the recent excitement. "Interesting?" she said, on a faint, interrogatory note. "I suppose you might say so. But just how many *other* vital details might we be missing, simply because we failed to make an ally of Wilrowan, as I suggested at the very beginning?"

"You did suggest that," said Sir Bastian mildly. "And perhaps I was wrong not to listen to you. Still, there was no harm done. We have this new information in spite of everything—and it is much too late to reconsider now. We could not possibly stay behind and wait for the captain to recover."

The coach swayed as it rounded a corner. The old gentleman gave her a searching look under the brim of his round black hat. "Perhaps, Lilliana, you would like to tell me just how you knew your husband was dying. That was really—quite extraordinary."

Lili looked down at her hands again, weaving her fingers together. She had not really had time to think before, but it *was* extraordinary. As she realized the truth, she blushed to the roots of her hair. "Before I left Hawkesbridge—the night before—Will and I were in sympathy, I matched our heartbeats. I must have forgotten to break our communion when everything happened so quickly in the morning."

A suspicious note came into Sir Bastian's voice. "Captain Blackheart was ill? He must have made a very swift recovery, since he left the city the very next day."

Lili blushed even more furiously than before. "Will was not—sick. I knew it was wrong, but I wanted to see—I wanted to know—" As memories of that night crowded into her thoughts, she continued to blush and to stammer. "I was curious to find out what would—"

"You did it as an erotic experiment," Sir Bastian finished for her. Though he spoke quietly, he sounded disappointed.

Lili nodded, unable to meet his eyes.

"I do not know what to say to you, Lilliana. Others have experimented in much the same way, and almost always with disastrous results. It is a very dangerous practice. I confess that I had thought better of you."

There was a long uncomfortable silence, punctuated by the creaking of the coach. "After all," said Sir Bastian at last, "I should not be surprised. Miss Brakeburn did warn me that Captain Blackheart exerted a regrettable influence."

Lili forced herself to look up at him. "But you mustn't blame Will. Truly, sir, you must not. He could hardly have put me up to anything like that. He had no idea I could even—" Her voice trailed off, as she saw that Sir Bastian was shaking his head.

"Do not distress yourself. One must remember, after all, that you married Captain Blackheart when you were still very young. Your husband having so few morals himself, how could you possibly look to him for guidance?"

Lili sat up a little straighter. It was enough that Will should be held to account for his own sins, without adding hers as well. "Wilrowan was scarcely more than a boy himself," she said indignantly. "Why should I have looked to him for guidance on *anything*?"

"Precisely." The old gentleman reached across the coach and touched her hand reassuringly. "Let us speak no more about it. You acted in ignorance, and I am sure that a word of caution is all that is needed." He settled back in his seat, and smiled at her benignly.

Lili leaned her head back against the lining of the coach, with a sigh of resignation. She was much too tired to argue, and besides, the damage had already been done. Thanks to her own reckless behavior, Sir Bastian was more convinced than ever that Will was a wicked and unprincipled man, whose marriage to Lili could only be deplored, whose influence over her ought to be minimized.

And like her Aunt Allora, Sir Bastian was going to do everything in his power to keep Lili and Wilrowan apart.

39

At Lindenhoff, the winter days were tediously long, made worse by the endless rituals of life at court. Ys was expected to leave her bed at eight precisely, to breakfast for an hour on spice cakes and coffee, then spend the bulk of the morning dressing. Afternoons were reserved for official visits, military reviews (conducted by torchlight in the castle courtyard), and embassy teas. She dressed for the evening at five-thirty. After that, there *should* have been card-parties, elegant suppers, and dancing by candlelight, but these were forbidden with the king so ill. Evenings dragged in the Silver Salon, with dull conversation, bored flirtation, and stifled yawns.

Occasionally, Ys rebelled, spent an entire evening locked in her room, or a morning walking in the snowy gardens. Yet in the end she was always restored to a sense of duty by Lord Wittlesbeck's scolding. His growing influence surprised even Ys, who as a general rule thought little of Humans. But the truth was very simple: for all the servants, guards, and officials she had succeeded in dismissing on one pretext or another, replacing them all with her own choices— people who *ought* to have showered her with gratitude, but who somehow remained curiously aloof—the Master of Ceremonies was her only friend at the palace.

Besides, she needed him to organize the Midwinter Ball. It was the only event all season long that she planned to enjoy, having determined in advance to dance just as often as she liked with Zmaj. Let people make what they would of that! He was her kinsman and it was perfectly proper, though she had an idea that tongues would wag.

But I am entitled to a little *pleasure,* she told herself, midway through a particularly tiresome afternoon spent leaning on the arm of her silver chair, chin in hand, watching two elderly duchesses build card-castles and argue precedence. *Yes, and I deserve a great deal more than that!*

After another hour spent brooding on her various entitlements, she suddenly rose from her seat and proclaimed a desire to visit her aunt. There was a buzz of protest.

"If you wish to send for Madame Debrûle," said the wife of a Parliament minister, "no doubt she will be pleased to visit you here."

"No," said Ys. She wanted privacy and more than anything she wanted *out*: out of Lindenhoff, away from the whispers and the hostile eyes, away from the candles and the open fires.

She rode to the old Maglore mansion in a glass carriage, under a fringed silk canopy. Wherever she was recognized, crowds assembled, waving their fists and cursing her name; without an escort, she would have been terrified. Once she entered the house, however, Ys dismissed her guards and climbed the long staircase up to the second floor alone.

The house looked deserted. Everything was in its place, exactly the way that she remembered it, but as she walked through the echoing halls of the upper floor, as she moved from one empty chamber to the next, she encountered no one, not even a single Goblin servant.

It was only when she reached Madame Solange's private apartments and found Madame sitting with a pen in her hand and a sheet

of closely written paper on the desk before her, that Ys found someone she might talk to.

"Have you dismissed *all* the servants?

Her sometime governess glanced up from her letter-writing. "It
is no longer necessary to keep up the pretense of wealth. There are
a few scullions left down in the kitchen, a groom or two down in the
stables, but that is all."

Ys took a seat, arranging her skirts, smoothing out the fur on her
new ermine muff. She hardly knew what to think—after all, what
had their efforts been *for*, if not to make the illusion of affluence into
reality?

Remembering why she had come, she said briskly: "As you are
interested in simplifying your life, I suppose this is as good a time as
any to broach the subject. I want to know what you have done with
the Jewels from Nordfjall, Tholia, and all the rest."

Madame put down her pen and covered her silver inkwell. "I
thought we had settled this. They are near enough if we should ever
need them. One is in the city of Tronstadt, another in Dahlmark, a
third in Vallerhoven. They do no harm where they are—there is
some advantage, after all, to living in a kingdom which verges on the
Polar Waste. But to bring them any closer together than they are at
this moment would be disastrous. To say nothing of their effect on
the Winterscar Jewel." She turned in her chair, favored her former
pupil with a sardonic glance. "Or would it amuse you to find yourself sitting on top of an erupting volcano?"

"I did not ask you to *give* me the Jewels. I merely want to know
exactly where they are. I know you have taken Aunt Sophie into your
confidence—so why not me?"

Madame smiled that vastly superior smile. "Sophie has played
and will continue to play a very large part in obtaining the Jewels,
so naturally she must be familiar with the plan. When I believe there
is an equally good reason for telling you—then I will do so."

Ys threw down her muff, sprang up from her chair, and began to pace the floor. "I think you need to remember to whom the Jewels really belong. And I am not a schoolgirl anymore, to do your bidding, not some meek little nobody. I am the Queen of Winterscar, after all."

Madame continued to regard her with delicate contempt. "How arrogant you have become. And to think that Sophie used to fear I might break your spirit."

Ys turned on her defiantly. "Break my spirit? No. You have bruised it, battered it, ground it under your heel, but you could never break it. When I think of the years that I endured your abuse——"

Now it was Madame's turn to shoot up from her chair, to speak in a voice of suppressed passion. "I kept you *alive*. Do you think that was easy, with our own kind hunting you? I protected you, nurtured you, taught you——not satisfied with that, I placed you in the exalted position you occupy now." The words hissed between her teeth with her rapid breathing. "I suppose it would be too much to expect a little gratitude."

"Gratitude?" Ys gave an angry laugh. "Why should I feel gratitude for anything you've done? You were the royal governess. It was nothing more than your simple duty."

"My duty, yes." The word seemed to calm Madame, rather than enrage her. She stood with her eyes closed for a moment, apparently gathering some inner strength. When she opened them again, when she spoke to Ys, her voice barely shook. "Some might say I had discharged that duty by rearing Sophie. Some might say I would have been wiser to put her where you are now. She would have made——a conformable empress. But I had to go looking for Chimena's brat and begin the whole process again. It has all been duty for me and never a moment's pleasure. Have I been ruthless in sacrificing others? Yes. But always more ruthless in sacrificing myself. I am a woman with strong feelings, but I have never indulged them. And I never will."

She smiled, completely in control again. "So don't think you can provoke me into saying more than I mean to, or that you can wheedle the information out of me. You will never succeed."

But by now, Ys was growing reckless. "I have not come here to beg or to tease you. I have come to demand what is rightfully mine." Part of her was horrified by what she had already said; part of her was thrilled by her own daring. "I am not helpless. If you have access to poisons, then so have I. If you have followers willing to do whatever you tell them without asking questions, then I have also."

Much to Ys's surprise, Madame only resumed her seat with a laugh and a shake of her head. "One or two, perhaps. Zmaj and possibly Jmel, while they remain under the spell of Chimena's necklace and your sexual favors. But the rest are accustomed to obeying *me*; you will find it difficult to shift their allegiance."

She turned her back on Ys, took up a silver sand-caster and sprinkled her letter to set the ink. "Take that fool Vif for a deplorable example of what the Maglore have become. He agonizes for weeks over anything as trivial as a new waistcoat. To consider switching his allegiance from me to you—that could take him years."

Ys bent down and retrieved her muff. Every nerve in her body cried out for revenge on this woman who had dominated her so completely for so many years. Yet angry as she was, she could see that Madame was quite immovable. "So you refuse to do what I ask?"

Madame dusted off her letter, and folded the paper in half. "To refuse you out of hand would be—impulsive. And I am never impulsive, no matter how sorely I am tempted. I will think the matter over and tell you my answer, but in my own good time."

Preparations for the Midwinter Ball threw the palace into a ferment. The queen, it was said, had determined the event should surpass all others for beauty and splendor. The major-domos and the Master of Ceremonies bustled about looking important, exchanging lists of wines and orders of march. In a vast chamber set aside for the purpose, an army of seamstresses was hard at work on the queen's new ballgown.

In all this activity, one person was largely forgotten. The king remained all day in his bedchamber, growing weaker and weaker as the days and weeks passed.

He was sitting propped up in bed one morning, when Francis Purcell dropped in for a visit. Though the room was but dimly lit, with only the smallest of fires burning on the hearth, the old man was forcibly struck by Jarred's pasty complexion and his lank dark hair.

"If I may say so, sir, I think you should consult yet another physician. One that may finally discover the cause of your condition."

Jarred passed a frail white hand over his eyes. "My dear Francis, I have seen so very many doctors already. I feel as though I have been physicked nearly to death."

"And do none of their remedies provide relief?"

The king heaved a weary sigh. "The better ones do me no harm. The worst—well, I have been purged and bled until I feel like an empty shell." He groaned and slipped further down on the pillows. "I believe my ailment goes deeper than anyone guesses. I believe there is something inherently wrong in the way I am made, some hidden defect, some hereditary taint. Something—something like the disease that killed Zelene."

Purcell bent forward, the better to study his face. "I know of no such defect in your family line. It is true that neither of your parents lived very long, but fevers and hunting accidents are scarcely hereditary."

He hesitated before he went on. "Your Majesty—might it not be possible that it is only your own state of mind that is making you ill?"

Jarred looked up at him with haunted eyes. "My state of mind? Do you mean, Francis, that I am—finally going mad?"

"Nothing of the sort, sir, nothing of the sort." The philosopher

was appalled that he had spoken so carelessly. "I was speaking of—
of a melancholy conviction, which you seem to hold, that you will
never be well again. I am not a physician, of course, but it seems to
me that you may be suffering from nothing more serious than nervous excitation, a wasting anxiety. One I hope you will soon overcome, and rally sufficiently—"

"To do what?" said Jarred, as Purcell's voice died off.

The old man hesitated again. He was reluctant to say anything
that might worry the king. Yet perhaps the truth might have a tonic
effect, might force him to bestir himself.

"I believe, sir, that it is very important for you to be seen in public. The people are distressed by what they hear of your condition.
Then too, they remain unreconciled to your recent marriage. Many
are convinced that the queen exerts a malign influence. They call
her—" Purcell decided against telling Jarred the worst of it. "But if
they saw you again, if they were reminded how much you love them,
how deeply their welfare has always—"

He was interrupted by the opening of a door and the unexpected
entrance of the queen herself. At the sight of her, Purcell closed his
lips, folded his arms, and determined not to say anything more while
she was present.

Yet there was nothing in her appearance to inspire distrust, as
she tripped lightly across the room, made a dutiful curtsy beside
the bed, and dropped a wifely kiss on Jarred's pale forehead. "Are
you bored, sir? Would you like me to sit with you and read for a
while?"

The king made a listless movement. "No, I thank you, though it's
kind of you to ask. The truth is, my head aches, and I want nothing
so much as quiet."

"Of course," she said sweetly. "We will leave you in peace." And
she gave Purcell a significant look across the bedclothes.

Taking the hint, he bowed to the king. With a last uneasy glance

over his shoulder, the philosopher followed the queen out of the
room, through the antechamber, and into the corridor outside.

"It is good that we met," said Ys, as Purcell closed the door softly
behind him. "There is something I particularly wanted to say to you.
We can be private, I take it, up in your laboratory?"

"Indeed," said the old man, leading the way. They climbed a short
flight of stairs, traversed a long gallery, passed through a number of
rooms and doors, and at last arrived in the philosopher's clock-
tower workshop.

Ys came immediately to the point. "When I found you with the
king, you were speaking of the rumors abroad in the town?"

Purcell nodded reluctantly.

"And because the people are restless and disaffected you are inclined to blame me?"

"Not at all," said the old man. "I was telling the king that the *public* blames you. Perhaps with some cause, considering the changes
you have made here. The entire Perys family dismissed, beginning
with Jarred's coachman. Thrown out into the streets, when they
were born right here in the palace! The older ones, too, after a lifetime of service. Do you wonder they retaliate by blackening your
name? Yet what have the people to complain of, really? There is neither famine, disease, nor any other thing abroad in the land to disturb their peace, and they are hardly touched by the changes here."

Ys gave him a calculating look. "You don't think that your own
presence here at the palace contributes something to the public apprehension?"

Purcell was bewildered, this was so unexpected. "*My* presence?
How should my presence 'contribute to the public apprehension'? I
am the most innocuous of men. No one has ever—"

"*That* was before a certain report was recently published, before
it was handed out in the form of broadsheets on every street corner

in the town." With a triumphant smile, Ys reached into the front of her gown and pulled out a roll of papers, which she handed over to the astonished philosopher.

Purcell unrolled them; a quick glance was enough to tell him exactly what he was looking at. He felt all the blood drain out of his face. "May I ask, Your Majesty, how you came by these? I thought I kept them in—a private place, known only to myself."

"I obtained them, after considerable persuasion, from the very same printer who is publishing the broadsheets. How he came by them, I never learned. But these papers, I take it, are truly yours? And the invention they describe, that is yours as well?"

With an unsteady gait, Doctor Purcell crossed the room, put the papers down on the smooth marble top of his workbench. "It is my invention. But the machine does nothing, *nothing* that should cause anyone the least concern. It is—a mere plaything, like all of these others." He indicated with a sweep of his hand the dancing dolls and the other mechanical toys that littered the table.

"So harmless that you kept the plans hidden away? So innocent that for eighteen years you have been afraid to complete your 'Celestial Clock,' which has been standing unfinished in that corner over there, all of this time?"

The philosopher put a suddenly clammy hand to his forehead. "I admit that some of the principles involved might cause apprehension in—certain quarters."

Ys laughed sarcastically. "Apprehension, you say, in certain quarters? A *perpetual motion* machine? Surely, Doctor, you vastly understate the case. And the design of the engine so very sophisticated. In some ways even more sophisticated than the Goblin Jewels. The very existence of these plans argues a reckless curiosity, a meddling in things you had far, far better have left alone—as you must have known when you suppressed them yourself."

"The engine itself is perfectly harmless. If I kept it a secret, it was only because I feared the plans might someday be modified in ways I could never anticipate." Purcell picked up the papers, impulsively tore them in half, a futile gesture, but one that relieved some of his feelings. "Whoever has stolen these, whoever has published them, he is the one who has behaved irresponsibly."

"So you say now," replied Ys, with a toss of her head. "But you should have destroyed them a long time since. In any case, your secret is out. And considering the present state of unrest in the city, surely you must see what irreparable harm you may do, merely by remaining at Jarred's side?"

Purcell stared at her in growing dismay. "You are suggesting that I leave Lindenhoff—desert the king in his weakened condition? But what if he wants me, what if he calls for me?" The old man tottered over to a chair, and without asking leave, he sat down. "Surely, *he* would understand that my motives were harmless. He would never——"

"That may be. But the king needs quiet, he can't endure the least excitement. And there is going to *be* excitement if you remain here, as soon as word of your disgrace spreads through the palace."

The philosopher struggled with the conflicting dictates of his heart and his head. Then he made a helpless gesture. "I am afraid, Your Majesty, that you speak the truth. I will pack up my personal effects at once, and leave Lindenhoff tomorrow morning."

"Thank you," said Ys, not quite able to suppress her satisfied smile. "Your loyalty is commendable. I believe you will spare the king considerable grief by this noble sacrifice."

*S*pring came early to Voirdemare in Château-Rouge. The city was located on the shores of a jewel-like bay, warmed by breezes blowing in from the south. Trees leafed out, flowers bloomed, weeks before the season was anything more than a rumor inland.

Yet the city was dirty, haphazard, and populous. Her high old houses of pink stucco—the palaces and the tenements alike—were often so wretched inside, that with the first hint of spring her population spilled into the streets. There, they cooked their meals and roasted their coffee over communal fires, ate, laughed, danced, duelled, made music—and generally conducted their business, their love affairs, and their family quarrels out in the open air.

To enter Voirdemare from the south during certain months was like attending a weeks-long festival. Great vats of boiling grease were set up in her tiny flagstone squares, for the making of fritters and other delicacies. Butchers gilded their meat with egg-yolks and gold leaf; fishmongers displayed their freshest wares in baskets lined with green leaves. Orange-blossoms, roses, and clove gilly-flowers scented the air. Those who lacked occupation the rest of the year found it now: running errands, arranging assignations, showing visitors the sights of the city. Street musicians, puppet shows, parades—oh yes, life could be very pleasant in Voirdemare, during certain months of the year—if you entered by way of the south.

Entering from the north, it was another matter. In the crowded neighborhoods there, sea breezes never entered. And the poverty was so acute, the misery so intense, the heat and the smoke and the dust and the stench from the brickyards, the tanneries, the potteries, the slaughter-house, and the prison so unremitting—it was like spending a season in an Anti-demonist's Hell.

40

$\mathcal{J}$t was the worst part of the worst part of town: a paradise for thieves, a maze without a clue. It was miles upon miles of battered old houses, with windows boarded up and hundreds of secret entrances and exits. It was the kind of place where people went who wanted to slip out of sight—sometimes, indeed, they accomplished this far more effectively and permanently than they intended—a place where people went when they had something or someone that they wanted to disappear.

By night, these ill-lit lanes and byways swarmed with highwaymen and horse-thieves, with gangs of swashbuckling adventurers in ragged silks and piratical black wigs, with footpads, bravos, and bully swordsmen. By day, they were a hunting ground for cloak-snatchers and pickpockets.

It was early one evening, in the hour between the horse-thieves and the pickpockets, that an oddly grim figure was seen moving through the narrow streets, with long easy strides. Though he was a stranger in the neighborhood, he seemed to know exactly where he was going, for he entered one of the dirty pink houses, climbed two flights of stairs, and walked right in through the door at the top without stopping to knock.

Inside, a man and woman were sitting at a broken-down table by the window, sharing a simple meal of figs, flat-bread and white wine. At the sight of the intruder, they both jumped to their feet, with mingled expressions of surprise and pleasure.

"Raith, my dear fellow. I can hardly believe——" Lucius began, but he was immediately silenced by the sudden and startling appearance of a large silver pistol in the Leveller's hand.

"Excuse me, Mr. Guilian. I must ask you to raise your hands up over your head and allow me to search you, before we can even proceed to the point of explanations."

Luke did not raise his hands as Raith requested; neither did he make any move to escape. He laughed uneasily. "And if I refuse to do as you say, am I supposed to believe that you are going to shoot me? Everyone knows that Levellers——"

"——never make use of firearms," the Rijxlander finished for him. "Neither do we own or carry them. And yet you see this one here in my hand. Are you willing to wager your life that, having so far departed from Anti-demonist doctrine, I will not depart even further by actually firing at you? At this range, I could hardly miss."

Luke considered for several heartbeats, then slowly raised his hands. At his yielding, Tremeur made a tiny sound of protest. "But you can't really be here to arrest him. He has done nothing wrong. He did not—— did not *abduct* me."

"Mademoiselle Brouillard," said Raith. "That Mr. Guilian saw fit to remove you from the care of your guardian, that he even went so far, I am informed, as to take you through a form of marriage, concerns me very little. I may deplore such imprudent behavior, yet I can admire his chivalry. But that he saw fit to remove at the same time an object of great value to the Crown of Rijxland——that I cannot condone."

As he spoke, Raith strode across the room and made a quick but efficient one-handed search of Luke's pockets, extracting, in the process, a small pearl-handled pistol that he found inside the coat.

"An object of value?" Luke was flabbergasted. "I can't begin to guess what you mean. I took nothing when I left Luden, nothing that wasn't mine—except that is, this young lady here and a certain post chaise, for which I paid all the charges."

The Leveller pocketed Luke's pistol, made a movement with the larger one he held in his hand. "If you will sit back down in your chair and put your arms behind you, and if Mademoiselle will do the same—"

Reluctantly, the two resumed their seats. Pulling out two lengths of thin but strong cording from somewhere inside his dark cloak, the Anti-demonist bound first Luke then Tremeur to their chairs.

"Raith," said Lucius, as reasonably as he could, though by now he was seething with indignation. "I can assure you that none of this is necessary. There seems to be some misunderstanding. And I thought we were friends. How you can—"

"Mr. Guilian, we *are* friends. I am binding you to this chair in order to prevent you from making any move that would force me to harm you. Make no mistake about it: whatever violence it might do my feelings to hurt or to kill you, I will not allow you to escape, and I *will* have the object you took with you when you left Luden."

Luke and Tremeur exchanged a bewildered glance.

"I still don't know—but you have already searched me. Pray don't hesitate to search the room as well," Luke said bitterly. "Whatever you are looking for, you won't find it here."

"I know that the Jewel is not here," Raith answered calmly. "Had you kept it in your possession, I would have experienced far less difficulty finding *you*. What I wish to know is where you have hidden it, or who has it now. Then we will discuss what I am to do with you."

Luke threw back his head and glared up at him. "Jewel? What jewel? Fiend seize you, Raith! How am I to clear my name, when you won't even tell me what it is I have supposedly stolen?"

The Leveller continued to regard him impassively. "Very well,

450 ₯· TERESA EDGERTON

since you would have me speak plainly: I am here to recover the Maglore artifact, the Rijxlander Jewel. There is every reason to believe
that it left Luden at the same time you did, and as you had access to
it, the obvious conclusion is that you are responsible."

"Access?" Luke gave an incredulous shake of his head. "But I have
never even *seen* it. Surely the thing was kept at the palace in Luden,
and your spies must have told you: I've never been inside the place!"

"Not at the palace, but at Doctor Van Tulp's, where King Izaiah
kept the Jewel within reach at all times. When Mademoiselle disappeared, he grew uneasy. When he found that the Jewel had also disappeared, he immediately sent for the Princess Marjote, who shortly
thereafter sent for me, and for the Prime Minister."

Raith drew up a chair, turned its back to the table, and sat down
straddling the seat. "When the summons reached him, Lord Flinx
had just learned of his niece's elopement."

"A coincidence," Luke insisted. "What else could it be but a
damned coincidence? Can you really believe that in planning an
elopement I designed to bring anything so large, so immediately recognizable as the Silver Nef? Is this likely? Is this reasonable? And
what would I do with the thing, once I had taken it out of Rijxland?"

Now a flicker of doubt crossed the Leveller's face. "Naturally, we
do not speak of the Silver Nef. What was stolen was far more valuable. It is possible, I suppose, that you did not know what it was
when you took it. Though why you should indulge in ordinary
theft—"

He was interrupted by a sharp cry from Tremeur, who had finally
realized what he was searching for. "My fault—it was my fault. But
I didn't know. Oh Luke, Luke, what have I done? I have embroiled
you in something far worse than I ever dreamed of, but all I meant
to do was buy us time!"

She turned in her chair, wild-eyed and pale, to face the Leveller.
"Can't you see? Luke has no idea, even now, what we are talking about.

It is King Izaiah's emerald pocket watch, isn't it? Lord Flinx ordered me to find it and turn it over to him——months ago——a year ago."

"And you conveniently discovered its whereabouts just before you left Luden?"

Tremeur shook her head emphatically. "I *always* knew where it was. I was the one who helped King Izaiah smuggle the watch out of the palace. I had no idea why he was so attached to it, but neither could I see why he should not have it. So I did what he told me and hid the watch outside the palace. After he arrived at the madhouse, we crept out together one night and buried it in the garden——where I suppose it remained up until the time that Luke and I eloped. Then I left a letter behind for Lord Flinx, telling him where to find it. I thought that if I did that one last thing he wanted me to do, he might——he might be less likely to follow after me."

"It is an interesting story, and entirely plausible," said Raith, who had seemed, while she spoke, to be weighing all the details in his mind. "Unfortunately, mademoiselle, you are so well-known for your storytelling ability, it is difficult for me to accept even so plausible an explanation. Mr. Guilian, too, has a lively imagination. I can hardly suppose this——most convincing account beyond your combined powers of invention."

Luke had been listening attentively all of this time. At first he had been astonished, then outraged, and finally thoughtful. "But where is Lord Flinx right now?" he challenged Raith. "When the princess told you both that the Jewel was missing, did he elect to remain behind in Luden——which would certainly be the act of an innocent man——or has he covered his own escape by pretending to go in search of *us?*"

Again doubt flickered in Raith's eyes. "I believe I will decline to answer such a leading question. This much I will say: Lord Flinx is not in Luden. He left with the intention of searching for you in Mountfalcon."

Luke raised his eyebrows in feigned surprise. "In Mountfalcon? When I told *everyone* that I was going to Herndyke?"

"We knew, of course, that the last place we ought to look for you was in Herndyke, since you had announced so plainly your intention to go there. We concluded between us—the princess, the Prime Minister, and myself—that you were equally unlikely to head further north to Winterscar, where you might involve King Jarred and your other relations in irredeemable disgrace."

Raith crossed his arms over the back of the chair. "It was Lord Flinx who suggested you might be found in Montcieux, where the young lady might wish to seek out some friend of her early years. I was assigned to search for you there, but I chanced to stumble across your trail and followed you here instead."

"And did it never occur to you," said Luke sarcastically, "since Lord Flinx has a house there, that *he* was the one who should go to Montcieux?"

An intent look crossed the Leveller's face. "Now that you mention it, I am somewhat surprised by that. I also admit that my judgement may have been clouded. I was so eager, you see, to send him east. I thought there might be far less grief for everyone involved if I was the one who found you."

Luke made an impatient movement, straining against his bonds. "You say that we are friends, and everyone knows that you despise Lord Flinx—yet you were ready enough to suspect *me* of this terrible thing, and him not at all. How do you explain that?"

The Leveller shook his head. "I should undoubtedly remind you, Mr. Guilian, that under the circumstances I am the one who should be asking questions and demanding explanations." There was a sudden disturbance down in the street, a clash of swords and the sound of running feet, and Raith left his seat and closed the shutters.

"Nevertheless, I will answer you this time," he said, returning to his chair. "I am sorry if what I say pains you. You have always seemed to be the sort of man who thought he knew better than anyone else how things should be done. This being so, I cannot help thinking that you might—with the best possible intentions, meaning only good to come of it—have entered into some conspiracy designed to—" Raith shrugged. "I will not mince words. A conspiracy designed to arrange the world in a more satisfactory manner. Also, if you were given the opportunity to play at cloak and dagger, I do not see how you could possibly resist."

Luke winced, since he had clearly left himself open to these very constructions by his own actions, his own enthusiasms.

"As for Lord Flinx," Raith continued, "his ambitions, though selfish, have always been considerably less—grandiose in their scope. So far as I can see, he would be perfectly content ruling his own little corner of the world."

"But it isn't his corner to rule. He may be the most powerful man in Rijxland now, but when King Izaiah dies, Lord Flinx loses everything."

The Leveller was continuing to listen to Luke with an expression of close attention. "Again you are correct. When the Princess Marjote ascends the throne, in the first surge of popular support which always bears up a new monarch at the time of her coronation, she can have everything her own way. Unless I am much mistaken, that will include choosing her own Prime Minister. By the time her policies come under a closer scrutiny, Lord Flinx should already be established in an embassy post thousands of miles away."

"Then surely you see," said Luke, "that Lord Flinx is a far more likely suspect than I am." Again he strained against his bonds. "For the love of Heaven! Set the two of us free, and then go as quickly as you can to catch the man who is really responsible for the theft of the Jewel."

Raith shook his head regretfully. "I am afraid that I cannot release

454 D· TERESA EDGERTON

you. As much as I am inclined to believe you —as much as I *wish* to believe you—I dare not risk letting you go."

Luke made a loud, exasperated sound of protest. "But neither," said the Leveller, "will I ignore any of the disturbing questions you have raised. I shall certainly do all in my power to find Lord Flinx and discover the truth. But I am afraid that allowing you and Mademoiselle to escape in the meantime is quite impossible."

Tremeur spoke up. "But if you admit we have done nothing wrong by marrying—?"

Raith's large hands gripped the sides of the chair as he hitched it closer to the table. His expression was troubled. "I did not mean to imply that I condone this illegal marriage of yours, only that I understood and sympathized with Mr. Guilian's motives. I do acknowledge that there is a law higher than that of Mankind, and perhaps you both believe you have acted in accordance with that law—perhaps you are even right. Yet you have violated a ban which has been in place for fifteen hundred years. Having done so in full knowledge of the law and the consequences, I see no reason why you should expect to avoid them."

"But the law is so *damned* arbitrary," Luke protested. "So much so, that in our own case it doesn't even make sense. There is some question whether Tremeur is even related to the King of Rijxland. And as for me: I stand within seven degrees of kinship to Jarred, but on the wrong side of the family. I'm not even in the line of succession, and if Jarred dies without issue, I won't even be related to the cousin who succeeds him. The proscription against our marrying is patently absurd!"

"I must confess," said Raith, his dark eyes glinting, "that if this were the only crime of which you stood accused, I would be willing enough to allow you to escape. But you have not been cleared of the other charge against you, and so long as that remains the case, I have no choice but to—" His voice trailed off, and he sat a moment in thought. "Or perhaps I do have a choice in this matter. Rather than send you back to Luden, I could take you with me as my prisoners, to be released when, and only when, I am able to establish your innocence."

Luke stared at him incredulously. "I think you must be joking. Take the two of us with you—bound hand and foot? Or do you mean to accept our parole?"

"It is not possible, or at least not feasible, for me to do either of those things. Yet there are other bindings than rope or iron fetters. You will be bound to me just as surely, but not in any way you might ever have imagined." Raith drew himself up to his full, impressive height, reached into his cloak and pulled out a short length of silver chain. "I am going to place you under a magical compulsion."

And so saying, he poured some of the wine into a dish, set it on fire, and proceeded to pass the silver chain through the heart of the flame. For some reason the whole situation struck Luke as enormously funny. He began to laugh, first softly, then with increasing violence. Tremeur watched him in surprise and concern, no doubt wondering at this sudden hysteria.

"It wanted only that," Luke managed to gasp between peals of laughter. "That you should be a magician along with everything else. My dear Raith, you are the most amazing man I know, but all this time I imagined they had wronged you. A Leveller with a gun in his hand is ludicrous enough—but who could truly believe in an Anti-demonist hexmaster?"

"Not a hexmaster," said Raith calmly, as he took out a piece of chalk and began drawing figures on the dirty floor-boards. "Though the accusation has certainly been made. However, my fellow magicians and I have a different name for what we do.

"We call ourselves Specularii."

41

ill was sitting slumped in a chair with a wet cloth draped over his forehead when Nick Brakeburn pushed open his bedchamber door and came into the room. "Darkness, Will! You look like death. What happened to you?"

"I was poisoned last night," said Wilrowan, cringing at the sound of the lieutenant's voice. "And Lili was here. No, I didn't imagine it. I saw her and spoke with her, and if there is any doubt about that, she left this handkerchief with her initials on it." He removed the cloth from his brow and showed it to Lili's cousin.

Nick examined it, shaking his head. "But surely you don't mean to tell me that *Lili* was part of some scheme to poison you? Be sensible, Will. You probably—"

"Of course she wasn't part of some plot to kill me," Will snapped back at him. "She was the one who saved me. And we have to find her. She left Hawkesbridge under the strangest circumstances and now she turns up here in Chêneboix. I'll tell you the whole of it later. For now, just believe me when I say it's vitally important. She was dressed for travel and seemed to be in a tearing hurry. Inquire at each of the main roads out of the town, ask if anyone has seen a black berlin drawn by four grey horses. The driver is short, stout, and wears a dark wig." He could only hope that Lili and her mysterious companion were still using the same coach and driver his servants had described to him back in Hawkesbridge.

"If you hear anything, *anything,* come back here and tell me at once."

Nick was gone for several hours. By the time he finally reappeared, entering the room with his long stride, Will was already in a fever of impatience.

"The berlin crossed the river into Bridemoor and headed north, just about midnight—and at a brisk pace, too. Still, it might be possible to catch up with them before they reach Fencaster, which is the first city of any size on the north road. The road loops several times, and a mounted traveller cutting cross-country—"

Will jumped to his feet, slipped into his drab riding coat, picked up his hat, his pistols, his powderhorn, and the red silk baldric. "My bags are packed and my horse is saddled and waiting for me down in the stable."

"You promised me an explanation. Or had you forgotten?"

Wilrowan paused on his way to the door. "So I did." He put down his weapons, pushed back his hat, and rubbed the back of one hand across his forehead. "But where to begin, I hardly know. I suspect that Lili has something to do with this search of ours, though I can't think how. Besides some mysterious connection with Sir Frederic Marlowe, besides the fact that she left Hawkesbridge at the same time we did, and the fact she was here last night, she was at the Leviathan when Macquay was murdered. It's not possible that *all* of these things are mere coincidence."

"Excuse me," said Nick, folding his arms, "but I don't quite follow you. What has Rufus Macquay to do with anything?"

"Damnation," Will groaned under his breath. "I forgot that you didn't know everything. Curse Rodaric and his secrecy anyway! He may break me when he hears what I have done, but it's time that I told you the whole. Especially because you are going to have to take charge of the search here, while I go out looking for Lili." And Will gave a quick explanation of the disappearance of the Chaos Machine, and all the important circumstances before and afterward.

Nick listened carefully. "Of course," he said, when Will had finished. "That explains a great many things I have been wondering about. The amazing thing is that I never put all the clues together myself."

"Why should you?" said Will, with a short, harsh laugh. "Why should it even occur to you that you had been assigned to a secret mission and then deceived about the very thing you were supposed to be looking for? If I were you, I would be furious."

"I am furious," said Nick, in a perfectly steady voice. If he *was* angry it was a nice display of the famous Brakeburn unflappability. "But when I consider the matter, I understand Rodaric's reasoning. If people knew of this, I don't even like to consider the consequences." For a moment his composure wavered, and a look of horror flickered across his face, then was gone. "I am glad to be let in on the secret at last, but for all that, I don't think we should be in any great hurry to tell Gilpin and Odgers."

"I will trust your judgement on that. Do whatever you think best while I am gone." Dropping the pistols and the powder horn into his pockets, slinging the baldric over his shoulder, Will was starting once more for the door, when again Nick stopped him.

"Are you certain this is wise, to go on your own? Someone has tried to kill you at least twice and very nearly succeeded both times."

"I'll be on my guard. They won't get me with poison another time, that I can promise you." Will laughed and patted a waistcoat pocket, into which he had already slipped the odd little bottles he had picked up in Hawkesbridge. "I'll test everything that I eat or drink before I so much as taste it."

He opened the door but paused on the threshold. "I have no idea whether Lili has gone in pursuit of the Wryneck and the woman, or has left town following some other scent. I won't know until I finally catch up to her. If she isn't following them, they're likely to still be here in Fermouline, or across the river in Chalkford. If so, you, Gilpin, and Odgers may be in danger. So be cautious, Nick, and stay alive."

Bridemoor was grim and windswept—all pitted granite and smokey purple heath, with occasional patches of yellow broom. The settlements were small, rarely more than a dozen houses and two or three churches, one of them sure to be abandoned. The people raised goats and sheep, and scratched whatever else they could out of the hard, unforgiving soil. It was a lonely country, and Will rode for hours without meeting anyone.

A day and a night of largely cross-country travel brought him and the buckskin gelding to the outskirts of Fencaster, without so much as a glimpse of Lili or the black berlin. Just where the open road gave way to cobblestones and cottages, Wilrowan drew up and considered the alternatives.

He had expected to catch up with the coach just about now. That he had not done so meant one of two things: either he had miscalculated and Lili had arrived sooner than he anticipated, or she had been delayed or had turned aside at one of the minor crossroads further back.

The latter seemed by far the more likely, so Will turned south and back-tracked for about twenty miles, this time keeping to the rutted and winding road the entire way. In the tiny village of Starling, where he stopped to inquire, he learned that a black berlin had suffered a broken axle just south of the village earlier that day. Unfortunately, rather than wait while their coach was repaired, the passengers had taken seats on the public stage and gone on to Fencaster,

while the coachman bought himself a horse and rode off in the opposite direction.

Will could only curse his bad luck. He had passed the stage fifteen miles back. It had reached the city by now, where Lili and her
companion would have effectively disappeared.

And night was falling. Stiff and exhausted after thirty hours spent
mostly in the saddle, Will decided that a good night's rest would best
prepare him for the search ahead. He took a room at the village's
one frowsy inn, ate a wretched meal of boiled roots and what tasted
like underdone shoe-leather, slaked a heavy thirst with some very
small beer, and fell into bed without stopping to undress. The room
was drafty, the bed hard and infested with tiny vermin, but he passed
out the moment his head touched the pillow. He slept until early
morning, when his flea-bites began to itch.

Rising with the dawn, Will swallowed an equally unsatisfactory
breakfast and set off for the city. About ten o'clock, he spotted a
flock of ravens flying overhead, coming from the direction of Fencaster. Thinking these might be the same birds he had sent ahead to
scout the countryside when he left Fermouline, he sent out a greeting. The ring responded by shooting out a ray of dazzling blue light,
and two of the ravens veered away from the others and came wing-
ing back: one landing on the saddle bow, the other on Wilrowan's
shoulder.

The news they brought him was mixed. Nothing had been seen
of Lili or her companion, but of the Wryneck and his female con-
federate they had much to tell.

<There is a fire in Fencaster. Whole streets have been consumed.> This
was the raven on his saddle bow. <The wind is carrying the sparks. One
of them landed on the Wryneck: there was a flash and a sizzle, then nothing
left but a pile of ashes. His death sent all of the other people on the street
into a panic. Several were injured.>

<And the woman who was with him?> asked Will.

<She was carried along by the crowd for a time. When she broke free, we followed her to an inn where she hired a carriage. She drove out of the city, heading west toward the mountains and Catwitsen. But soon it was night and we lost her in the dark.>

Will frowned, trying to make sense of this. <Why should she be in such a hurry to go on? The Jewel has to be moved slowly and in short stages. If she keeps on travelling at such a pace, she'll only carry disaster wherever she goes. Besides that, if she wants to avoid being found, what better way to lose herself than in the confusion caused by the fire? If she kept a safe distance, where better to hide herself than right there in Fencaster?>

<Not if she is a Gobline.> The raven on his shoulder stretched its wings. <For a Goblin or Gobline, there is no safe distance, when the wind blows sparks. And the Wryneck addressed her as "Lady Sophronispa.">

Will shook his head. He did not see how the woman could possibly be a Gobline, even if, for some bizarre reason, she was using a Maglore name. Still, she had left the city. The question now was whether he ought to try and follow her, or go on to Fencaster in search of Lili.

In the end, he decided he had no choice. It had been one thing to go after Lili when she might actually be in hot pursuit of the Chaos Machine, but now that he *knew* which direction the Jewel was heading, he had to follow it. Sending the ravens on ahead, he continued north until he came again to the outskirts of Fencaster. A black cloud of smoke hovered over the ancient half-timber houses, giving the city a sinister appearance. If Lili was there, Will could only hope that she was not in danger.

It was in Hoile, a ramshackle village near a windy cross-roads, that the blow fell. Will had taken a room for the night and gone out for a stroll in the gathering dusk, across a scrubby patch of common ground, when he was violently accosted by three stout villagers. Almost before he had time to react, certainly before he had time to get the pistol out of his pocket, one of the rustics had wrenched the weapon out of his hand, and the other two quickly overpowered him. Under loud protest, they hustled him off toward the village gaol.

"Damn the lot of you! Won't you tell me what it is I am supposed to have done?" Will demanded, as they threw him into a cell and sent him sprawling across a scuffed plank floor. A heavy wooden door slammed shut behind him.

The was a rattle of iron keys, and a face like a huge slab of fat appeared between the bars of a window in the door. "We been asked to hold you on charges of murder and treason back t'Mountfalcon," said a gruff voice.

"Charges of murder and—ridiculous!" said Will, sitting up and dusting himself off. "I've done nothing of the sort. And *who* asked you? You can't arrest me for crimes committed in Mountfalcon without—"Acting on a sudden twinge of doubt, he felt for the carte blanche he kept in an inner pocket of his riding coat and found it missing.

"The lady, she did have a warrant from t'King of Mountfalcon— all signed and sealed 'twas," said the gravelly voice.

Will cursed softly under his breath. It was humiliating enough to be arrested—but with his own warrant? Leaning his back against the rough stone wall, he closed his eyes, struggling to remember. He had a dim impression of a soft pair of hands going lightly over him while he lay poisoned and semi-conscious on the floor of his room at the Cinque d'Or. Had that been *before* or *after* Lili entered the room?

"The 'lady' you said—was it a small plump woman, or a lady of medium height, very composed and attractive?"

" 'Tis not for me to say," the constable replied with a coarse laugh. "You can speak t'magistrate when he do come next month. Mayhap he'll tell you what you wants to know—mayhap he won't.

In t'meantime, you can just sit right where you are and think on your own wickedness."

The next few days went slowly by, as Wilrowan spent most of his time pacing his cell or staring out through the one grated window opening on the outside world, which offered a less than inspiring view of a barren stretch of yard and one twisted thorn tree. Meanwhile, the constable steadfastly refused to answer his questions, and the two bailiffs who took over at intervals proved equally uncooperative. When Will demanded paper and ink, these were grudgingly provided, but after he wrote a letter to Nick, no one would send it.

"And a fine thing 'twould be, you called in t'rest of your gang to bust you out of here!" said the village lawman.

"Very well," answered Will, seething by now, yet rendered cunning by adversity. "Then let me write to King Rodaric at the Volary Palace." This meant a much longer wait before help arrived, but it hardly seemed possible the constable could object. "Or do you imagine *he's* a member of my gang?"

After much urging, and the exchange of several small coins, the constable allowed that he saw no harm in it. "Though whether it happens he'll read your letter, I don't promise, Mr. Blackheart. But I'll find a man t'carry it, right enough, and you'll have to be satisfied wi' that."

"*Captain* Blackheart. If your man gives my name correctly at the palace gate when he delivers my letter, it *will* get in to the king. And if I receive the reply I expect, there will be six gold guineas in it for you."

With the letter sent on its way, there was nothing for Will to do but wait. He was likely to remain where he was for at least a fortnight: a week for his message to reach Rodaric, another for the letter securing his release to arrive in Hoile.

But one cold morning, just after dawn, as Wilrowan lay on his

bed of moldy straw, he was aroused from a half-doze by a loud tapping on the iron grating. He rose quickly and crossed to the window,
before the noise could attract the bailiff's attention.

A raven had perched on the window ledge, a very old bird with
ragged feathers. <*Wilrowan Blackheart. A message from your grandmother.*>

It was not one of his own ravens, and the rapport was tenuous,
the words very faint in his mind. Will was not even certain he had
heard them correctly. <*A message from my* grandmother?!> Lady
Krogan had never used this means to communicate with him before,
and it had never occurred to him that she could.

Even when the raven had repeated his grandmother's message
two times over, Will was not quite certain what to think of it. Could
the words have been garbled along the way? That Lili was for some
reason on the trail of the Chaos Machine, he had already guessed.
But that she and her Aunt Allora could be Specularii magicians—?

Moving in the varied circles that he did, Will had heard vague rumors of the Specularii: a group of crackpots claiming descent from
one of the ancient magical societies, a handful of misguided souls
who actually believed that the Maglore were still in existence. How
could Lili—his sweet, sensible, level-headed Lili—possibly associate
herself with people like that?

When the raven was gone, Will returned to his bed of straw. He
sat with his head bowed in thought, trying to make sense of this unexpected information. For some reason, his thoughts kept turning
back to what the other raven had said to him on the road to Fencaster. *Not if she was a Gobline.* If the woman he was following was not
an Ouph or a Padfoot, could not be a Wryneck or Grant, yet she *was*
a Gobline, that meant—

Wilrowan felt suddenly dizzy and disoriented, as his whole conception of the world turned upside down and inside out. What if the
Specularii were right after all? What if the Maglore *did* still exist and

were behind the plot to steal the Jewels? What if, unknowingly, he had actually been pursuing one of the creatures all of this time?

The answer to that question made him beat his fists in impotent fury against the wall until his knuckles bled. If all this was true, then right at this moment Lili might be in pursuit of the Maglore woman. She and the man she was with might be moving inexorably toward a confrontation with one of the most dangerous and ruthless creatures ever to exist.

And he, Wilrowan, was absolutely helpless to do anything about it, absolutely incapable of coming to her aid, so long as he remained locked up in this cursed cell.

42

*J*t was a respectable house where gentlemen took lodgings, a sedate old house on a quiet street. Ys sat outside in her glass coach, staring at the prim facade and shuttered windows, unable to make up her mind. More and more, she was learning to ignore the conventions, but she was not yet dead to all sense of propriety. Young ladies, even young married ladies, did not visit young men at their rented rooms.

But she had not seen Zmaj in more than ten days; he had not responded to any of her increasingly frantic letters. No one had heard of him leaving the town; no one had spotted him anywhere in Tarnburgh. Ys felt a growing certainty that something dreadful had happened to him.

Coming to a abrupt decision, she left the coach, instructing two of the footmen to follow her inside the house. She had to know the truth, no matter how awful.

Zmaj's rooms were on the second floor (more shabby-genteel than the first) on a short corridor with a worn carpet and a dingy skylight. Ys hesitated outside his door, then clenched one hand into a hard little fist and knocked softly.

The sound echoed dully in the empty corridor, but there was no response. After a minute, she knocked again, this time with more force. Still no answer, no slightest rumor of movement on the other side. Ys was considering that she might tell her lackeys to break down the door, when she suddenly thought to try the handle.

At her touch, the catch slid aside, and the door swung open on a dark interior. Ys felt a sharp twinge of panic. Surely if Zmaj had taken a trip out of town, he would never have left his door unlocked.

"Stay here," she ordered the footmen, and with a dry mouth and a leaping pulse, she entered the flat alone.

The sitting room was cold and stale. Feeling her way in the dim light, Ys moved toward the long window and unlatched the shutters. A shaft of golden sunlight pierced the gloom, turned the threadbare carpet the color of blood. Ys looked around her cautiously, but there was nothing amiss—only a room full of cheap old furniture, and a cloud of dust motes spinning in the air.

She moved on to the bedchamber. Again, the room was in perfect order, his bed made up, his clothes stored neatly inside a pine clothes-press, his other things tidied away in drawers. It was only when she approached the fireplace that she cried out.

There was a mound of silvery-grey ashes upon the hearth, spilling over on the crimson carpet. A pile so small, so fine, you would hardly imagine it was all that remained of so tall a youth. But the Maglore burned exceedingly hot, and much was vaporized when they did, including most of their clothing.

Ys dropped to her knees beside the sooty hearth, heedless of the damage to her silken skirts. Her heart beat painfully hard against her ribs, the blood roared in her ears. Slowly, she put out a hand to touch the ashes, then drew back with a deep, racking shudder. This was no accident, it had been done deliberately. No suicide, either, Zmaj was far too young, and the usual method was the ingestion of poison or ground glass. It was the usual method of assassination, too—death by fire was far too horrifying for even the most vengeful to contemplate. Ys drew in a long, slow breath in order to steady herself. She knew only one Goblin cruel enough, ruthless enough, to burn another Goblin to death.

Her gaze hardened and her back stiffened; all in an instant, she formed an unshakeable resolution. Madame Solange deserved to *suffer* for this, and Ys intended to see that she did.

Madame was preparing to go out when Ys walked in. Handsome in midnight velvet and grey squirrel, but restless and discontented as to her expression, there was a familiar dangerous gleam in her eye which *ought* to have warned her former pupil, had Ys not been so far beyond reading the signs.

"How *dare* you," said Ys, trembling with the intensity of her indignation. "First Izek and now Zmaj. Who are you to shed such quantities of Imperial Maglore blood?"

"I am the one who has guarded and protected you all of your life. The boy had become a danger to you—in some sense, a danger to every one of us. Particularly after your abominable behavior the night of the Midwinter Ball. I urge you to put aside your childish passion, and for once in your life *think*."

Ys stamped one tiny foot. "I *won't* think, it makes me sick to think. My head aches when I'm so angry. How could you do this to me? I loved Zmaj, I—"

"Exactly. Your affair with him had gone on too long, was becoming too obvious." Madame picked up her velvet hat, placed it carefully atop the sleek, dark coils of her hair, and skewered it in place with a long glittering hat-pin. "Besides," she added with a knowing smile, as she examined the result in a small hand mirror, "he had already served his purpose, hadn't he?"

Ys drew in her breath sharply, astonished anew by such uncanny omniscience. "You *knew* that? But I never told anyone; I was hardly sure of it myself. How could you know?"

Her governess shrugged, put aside the mirror. "There are certain signs. Unmistakable to those of us who know them. And when the day finally comes that you announce your condition to the world, there must be no breath of scandal, no slightest suspicion in anyone's mind that the child you carry is not King Jarred's. By your own thoughtless behavior, *you* were the one who forced me to take such drastic measures."

Ys sat down very suddenly on a chair by the door. Her sense of injury was still very strong, but her anger was ebbing. She was beginning to suspect that Madame was right, that she had brought this grief on herself. "But why did he have to die?" she said softly. "Couldn't we just send him away?"

"We?" said Madame, spinning around to face her. "But you told me yourself he was *yours* to command. Had you possessed the good sense to send him away of your own accord, this would not have been necessary. As it was, you left me no choice." On a table by her elbow, there was a pair of scented gloves; she caught up the right one and pulled it on, then repeated the process with the left. "It is time, Ys, that you accepted responsibility for your own actions. You are, as you recently pointed out, no longer a chit in the schoolroom. If you make a threat, no one is going to mistake it for childish bravado— least of all me. You must learn to guard your tongue, to display a little discretion. Otherwise, even *I* won't be able to save you."

Ys put her hands to her head, which was aching intolerably. "You should have explained this to me. Why did you not even try to explain before taking such a drastic step?"

Again came that savage light in Madame's eyes. "I have always found that an object lesson—be it sufficiently sharp—is far more effective than an explanation. That was the only way with your mother, and I knew from the very beginning it would be the only way with you."

"But I'm not Chimena," Ys answered pitifully. "You might have *tried* to teach me more gently. You might have at least tried."

The red lips parted in a scornful smile. "You don't even know what you were when I first took charge of you, do you? You don't remember—or you *won't* remember—what a miserable life you led before I rescued you?"

Ys passed a hand over her eyes. "I have nightmares— sometimes the briefest glimpses of people and places. But no clear memories."

"Then I think," said Madame, "it is long past time that you were reminded."

The houses were old and dilapidated, the streets of Ottarsburg were muddy, dirty, and depressing. The damp was everywhere—as a clammy sweat on all the houses, in filthy puddles down in the streets, in the chests of invalids, in dreary attics and moldy cellars, anywhere and everywhere but where it belonged.

A hackney coach came rattling down a rutted lane and stopped in one of the dismal little squares. Two women, dressed all in black and discreetly veiled, climbed down out of the coach. The taller of the two commanded the driver to wait, as they did not expect to be long about their business.

They walked for two blocks through the mud and filth, holding up their heavy skirts to keep them out of the muck. Then the ground fell away under their feet, and they found they were standing on a high bluff, overlooking a vast network of piers and boardwalks, which stretched as far as the River Scar. A faint breeze from the river bottoms lifted their veils.

They descended a steep flight of stairs to a walkway below, and continued on: past lounging figures of sailors in short woolen jackets and high wooden clogs, past ragged children playing on heaps of garbage, who stopped and stared to see the two strange females go hurrying by. The air was thick with the stench of poverty, fish, and dying river. Finally, Ys and her governess stopped before a ramshackle little building.

When the door of the shop creaked open, when she followed Madame Solange into the sordid interior, Ys was suddenly overwhelmed by a wave of despair. She knew this place: these dusty piles of books and papers; these tottering stacks of battered furniture. She knew this sickly odor, rising off heaps of mildewed clothing. It was the stuff of all her nightmares.

A distant bell rang somewhere at the back of the shop. In response, a door creaked open and a stooped figure appeared on the threshold, silhouetted against the pale light of a horn lantern. As he hobbled forward, all of his attention seemed to center on Madame.

"So—you have returned," said the ancient Wryneck.

"Yes," said Madame, putting aside her veil with a restless gesture. "Though I must say, I am astonished to find you alive after so many years."

"I have been somewhat astonished myself. I quite expected that you would have me silenced. I wonder why you did not?"

Madame shrugged, as though the matter were of supreme indifference to her—as very probably it was. "Perhaps I anticipated that this day might come." She turned toward Ys. "Do you know this place? Do you recognize this Goblin?"

Slowly, reluctantly, Ys raised her veil and gazed wonderingly around her. "I *lived* here amidst all this filth. And this creature reared me—if you can dignify his negligence by such a name!"

"Then you still don't remember it all. You were not a child to be *reared;* you were a wild animal to be broken and tamed. It is often the fate of the orphaned children of Maglore families living in exile. When the parents die, no one is able to teach them, no one knows the way or possesses the necessary strength of will. There have been many such over the years, living on the tolerance of their lesser Goblin neighbors, who are too tender-hearted to have them exterminated. For all that, such children seldom last long. They die as they have lived, like wild beasts."

Ys covered her eyes with her hands. The memories were coming swiftly now, and there was such an avalanche of them, they threatened to bury her. "No," she whispered. "No. I was never anything so vile and degraded as *that*."

"Ah, but you were," said Madame, on a note of triumph. "Ragged, filthy, bestial. As you would be still, had it not been for the infinite pains *I* took over you. Supposing, that is, you had survived at all."

But Ys continued to shake her head. This humiliation went far too deep, was too unbearable. "No," she repeated again and again. "I could never have been like that and be what I am now. If that were true, I could never hold up my head again." With a final despairing gesture, she turned around and fled the building. The door slammed shut behind her.

The crowded little shop was silent for several minutes, until the Wryneck spoke. "So you spared me only for this. She will never allow me to live, knowing that I remember her as she was, knowing I was a witness to her early degradation."

Madame spent a moment longer looking after Ys with a puzzled frown. But when she turned to face the old Goblin, her brilliant dark eyes were as hard as ever.

"No doubt you are right," she responded with a shrug. "But after all—you were always expendable."

43

Omens of spring appeared in the north. As the ice melted and the sun warmed the earth, larches turned a tender green, and purple saxifrage and arctic poppies appeared in the fields. But at Lindenhoff, with the wasting of winter, King Jarred wasted, too. By the time that the larches leafed out, he was unable to rise from his bed. He spent most of his time sleeping; when he was not, he faced a constant parade of doctors.

"His Majesty's blood is in a constant state of ferment," said an elderly surgeon. "He wants further cupping."

"Nonsense," replied a self-important young physician. "The king's condition could only be the result of confluent pustules and a consequent putredinous pestilent disposition of the humors. Bee-glue, cat's-tongue, and laudanum is the only cure."

"Not so," insisted a healer-physician from the University of Vallerhoven—who, like most academics, was strong on theory but had little to offer when it came to prescribing a practical course of treatment. "His Majesty suffers from an acid acrimony and a hectic hydropondriachal heat."

The king suffered them all patiently, allowed them to physick him, sweat him, blister him, bleed him; apply mustard plasters, clysters, leeches, and freshly slaughtered pigeons; give him simples, purgatives, cathartics, and anodynes; dose him with epsom salts, calomel, alkermes and theriac. None of this did him the least bit of good.

But early one morning a new man came in. He was an elderly physician with keen grey eyes and a brisk way about him that made something—some dim sensation of hope perhaps—stir inside Jarred for the first time in weeks. The doctor brought with him a surprising assistant: a roguish old fellow with jet-black hair, a crimson eye-patch, and a jagged white scar that slashed across his cheek under a three days' growth of rough grey stubble. The two men presented such a remarkable contrast between them—the trim physician and his disreputable-looking assistant—that Jarred smiled faintly in spite of himself.

At a word from the doctor, the servants filed out of the room. Approaching the bed, he took the king's wrist between his thumb and two fingers. Inside the frilled linen cuff of his nightshirt, Jarred's flesh was shrunken, the bones seemed as brittle and the skin as fragile as that of a child. "The pulse is very weak, but it is steady. I do not think he will be harmed by a little wholesome excitement—indeed, it may do him a great deal of good."

The physician stepped back from his place by the bed, to be replaced by his colorful assistant. "Your Majesty, do you know me?"

For a moment, Jarred failed to understand him. Then he became aware of several things almost at once: The black hair was a wig; the scar was too spectacularly vivid to be true; he had heard this voice before, a thousand times.

"Francis?" he said weakly. Then, with a marked increase in volume as the full improbability of the situation struck him: "*Francis?*"

"Yes, sir, it is I. Your old tutor, your second father," said the old man, with an emotional quiver in his voice as he lifted the gaudy crimson eye-patch and cast it aside. "I have been forbidden to approach you, but they could not keep me away, not while you remain so very, very ill. My good cousin here came to my aid and smuggled me in to see you."

The faint smile turned into a full-fledged grin. "My dear friend, I can hardly say how glad I am to see you. But in such—such a ridiculous disguise! What were you thinking?"

The philosopher smiled, too, though somewhat shakily. "That no one would suspect staid old Doctor Purcell of such a bizarre deception. That no one would imagine for one moment that the doddering old fellow with his clocks and his tiny machines had enough dash or sense of romance to appear before his king in this flamboyant fashion. And as you can see, I was perfectly correct."

The king closed his eyes; for just a moment, this was all too much for him. "I don't understand. That is, I understand why you left the palace—but how were you forbidden to even visit? I gave no such order."

"It was the queen," said Purcell. "Your Majesty, have you no suspicion of her yourself?" Jarred's eyes flickered open, but he gave no other response. "Shortly after I left Lindenhoff, I discovered that *she* was the one who had arranged to publish my papers. You know, of course, what havoc she has created with the palace staff. One would expect a few such changes—she would naturally wish to advance people of her own—but she appears to be systematically isolating you from everyone that you ought to be able to trust. Under the circumstances, I cannot help thinking she must be responsible for this sickness as well."

"But why?" Now that Jarred saw her so rarely, the fascination exerted by his queen was affecting him less. Though some impression lingered of the pleasure she had bestowed during their wedding trip, the memory of pain was considerably sharper. "I don't say you are wrong, but if you are right, what does she hope to gain? If I die—and it seems to me, Francis, that my life *is* slipping away—then she loses everything when Rupert succeeds me."

Purcell shook his head ruefully. "I have no idea what she hopes to gain. Nor do I know who she really is, with her mysterious past and her Goblin servants. Not who she claims to be. I have spoken with travellers from Montcieux and Château-Rouge—no one knows anything about the Debrûles."

He gave a half-humorous sigh. "If Mr. Guilian were here, no doubt he would spin us some fanciful story, as have some of the wilder imaginations down in the streets, who have named her the Queen of the Goblins—but I am a practical man, and can see no practical purpose behind this plot of the queen's. She cannot hope to rule in your place, for she has neither popular nor political support. And if you were to die—as my cousin, Doctor Wildebaden, and I are determined you shall *not*—she must step aside in favor of Lord Rupert. Unless—" The old man caught his breath sharply. "Unless, Your Majesty, it should happen that she is pregnant with your heir and hopes to be named regent after you are gone?"

Jarred moved his head wearily from side to side. "I don't think so. We have not—we have not shared the same bed for so many months." But as his eyes moved listlessly around the room, he chanced to notice something. Throwing off the bed-clothes, he struggled to rise. "Francis, she may have a way of gaining *both* popular and political support. My music box, the one that sat on that table there for so long—it seems to have disappeared!" He fell back, breathless, against the feather pillows.

The philosopher and his cousin exchanged a puzzled glance, no doubt wondering if the king was delirious. The physician stepped forward again to check his pulse.

Jarred laughed weakly, mirthlessly. "No, gentleman, I am not wandering, though I am undoubtedly agitated. Francis, you remember that jeweled casket of silver and satinwood? The one with a miniature golden city inside, and a hidden movement that played twelve different tunes? Did you never guess what it really was? With your knowledge of clockwork and other machines, I thought you had guessed long ago that our famous Crystal Egg was considerably less than it seemed—and the music box considerably more."

A tense, attentive look came into the philosopher's eyes. "The music box is the Winterscar Jewel? I admit that I knew the Egg was a sham, but as I never had the chance to examine the music box closely—then, too, you kept it here so openly and I had an idea that you must keep the genuine engine somewhere safe under lock and key."

"It seemed perfectly safe where it was. My father and grandfather both kept it right here in this room, and nothing ever happened to it. I thought that to lock it away after so many years would cause people to wonder, people to suspect—people in other countries who had reason to know that the so-called Jewels are all of them fakes."

The two old men exchanged another glance; some unspoken question seemed to pass between them. "But does the *queen* know?" said Purcell to the King. "Did you ever confide in her?"

"I never said anything to anyone. Rupert knows, of course, but it was my father who let him in on the secret, before I was even born. It was only proper, as he was the heir."

Jarred made another effort to rise, and succeeded in raising himself up on his elbows. "It may be that we suspect the queen wrongly. There have been so many strangers inside this room, so many doctors and their assistants—it might have been any one of them. Even without knowing its true nature, they might have been tempted by the precious metals and the gemstones." He fell back again, panting. "Though there are other costly things in this room, smaller and more easily carried away."

Purcell clasped his hands behind his back, began to pace the floor. "I think we must go on the assumption that the queen has it— who else would dare? And if she does, then she certainly has the power to inflict grievous destruction on the city of Tarnburgh. That is, assuming she has the least idea how to manipulate the Philosophic Engine inside."

"Whether she knows or not, even for her to make the attempt could be—catastrophic." Suddenly so tired that he could hardly think, Jarred looked pleadingly across at the two old men. "What are we to do, to get it back again?"

"At the moment, nothing," said Purcell, coming to a halt beside the bed. "But perhaps we will be able to come up with some plan. In the meantime, we must concentrate our efforts on your full recovery."

"How are we to do that? The truth is, I sometimes wonder if I *want* to get well, if the effort to recover is even worth it."

"That is your illness talking, Your Majesty, not the man that I know and respect," Purcell said sternly. He had taken charge now, had slipped back into the long abandoned rôle of schoolmaster and mentor. It was necessary to do so, in this time of crisis. "You will get well and perhaps very soon."

"How?" said Jarred, fretfully. "Have you some miraculous medicine to give me?"

"There is a tonic that should do you some good," Doctor Wildebaden answered in Purcell's place. "But the greatest good, I think, will come when you simply stop ingesting any potion or poison the queen may have been slipping into your food. From this time onward, do not eat or drink anything, unless it should come directly from my hands."

"So," said Madame Solange to Ys, across the mahogany table in the queen's private dining room. "It is to be a reconciliation, is it? After so many weeks of ignoring me, of sending my letters back unopened, you have determined to be gracious and to allow me the privilege of actually breaking bread with you?"

Ys bit her lip and bore the sarcasm as patiently as she could. She had not even been certain that Madame would accept her invitation, had been greatly relieved when her former governess sent a favorable reply. It would not do to put her whole scheme in jeopardy, now, with intemperate language.

"I need your help," Ys said quietly. "I am in desperate need of your help, and I am not too proud to humble myself. I have made a dreadful, dreadful mistake."

"I take it," Madame answered coldly, "that you do not allude to the mistake you made in treating me so shabbily? No, I thought not. But I know my duty, even if others do not. Tell me what it is you have done, and I will do whatever I can to help you undo it."

Ys lifted the crystal goblet beside her plate, took a very small sip. "It is the king. I think I have gone too far and he is actually dying. And he can't die yet—that would ruin everything."

"It would indeed." Madame Solange lifted her own glass and swallowed half the contents. "A pity you didn't think of this before. But am I to understand that you have already ceased to administer the potion that you had from Sophie?"

"I stopped long ago. He hasn't had so much as a taste in almost two months, yet he shows no sign of recovering from the effects."

Madame appeared to consider carefully, twirling the stem of the wine glass in her hand. "There is something that we might try. It may prove effective, it may not. Best, I think, that I should see him first, before we attempt to do anything."

Ys nodded eagerly. "I will take you in to see him directly after supper. That is the hour when I always visit him, after the physicians have all been in. Now that I've been hoping to see him improve, I thought it best not to change my habits, for fear that someone would suspect a connection."

Madame signified her approval with a stately inclination of her head. "A wise precaution. Perhaps you are not so shatter-brained as I had thought."

Ys changed color at this patronizing speech, but she lowered her eyes and tried to look humble. "Perhaps we should begin to eat," she suggested, reaching for the small silver bell that sat on the table.

At the sound of the bell, the door opened and a train of Padfoot and Ouph servants came into the room, bearing a great variety of covered dishes, bringing with them a steamy, savory smell. Though initially Ys had brought only her cook and a single maid-servant with her, by now her entire household staff was made up of Goblins. She had known that this would excite comment, as indeed it had, but she had also discovered that she simply could not bear the repeated touch of Human hands.

If Madame thought anything of this, she uncharacteristically held her tongue, and helped herself lavishly from several dishes. She had always been a large feeder. Ys took less and only picked at her food.

"You do not eat?" said Madame, hesitating between a dish of jellied cockcombs and some damson tartlets.

"Not very much," said Ys, rejecting with a shudder some larks stewed in egg-shells, forcing herself to nibble at a salad made of endives, lettuce, and grapes. "The nausea never seems to entirely pass. Will I feel like this the *whole* time that I carry this child?"

"For some months longer, though it will pass eventually." Madame lifted a golden fork to her lips, then grimaced distastefully. "This tastes very odd. I have never had anything quite like it before."

"Oh dear—" said Ys, on a faltering note. "I had hoped you would like it—it was intended as a peace offering."

"I do not dislike it," said Madame, swallowing, then running her tongue over her teeth. "The spice, whatever it is, does impart a certain—relish to the dish. It is just that the taste is so bizarre. What does your cook call this?"

Ys suddenly put aside her show of diffidence. "*My* cook? This dish was prepared by Jarred's own chef, and I believe that he considers it something of a specialty. I was counting on you not to recognize the taste." Turned reckless with triumph, she was unable to contain her glee. "You've never suffered as I have—never put lip to lip or tongue to skin with a Human male."

Madame put down her fork. "What do you mean?" she asked in a queer, tight voice. "What are you trying to tell me?"

"Only," said Ys, with a wild laugh, "that there was salt enough in that single bite to kill you twice over. You think yourself so damnably clever, and you never suspected at all!"

Madame pushed back her chair and jerked to her feet. As she did so, a spasm passed over her entire frame. She bent double for a moment, then straightened with enormous difficulty, and forced out a reply. "You little fool. Did I say that you had gained common sense? This is the single most foolish thing—" Another convulsion shook her from head to foot and caused her to gasp for breath.

Ys was on her own feet by now, dancing with excitement. "Foolish, am I? But not so foolish that I couldn't fool you. The great Valentine Solange, so vastly superior to all the other short-sighted Goblins—but you never thought of this, did you? You never thought that I would be revenged for all the years of humiliation that you heaped on my head?"

Madame collapsed in her chair. As another pain racked her, she fell forward, facedown on the table. With a tremendous effort she raised herself up on her forearms, lifted her head, fixed Ys in the midst of her exultant dancing with a glance of unutterable scorn and contempt.

"Of course I *knew*. I never thought otherwise. You wouldn't be worth much if you were incapable of *that*." Her eyes rolled back in her head, the breath rattled in her throat, but she was able to push out a few more words. "But—not yet, you little—fool—not until—" Then all of the strength drained out of her, and she fell forward again for the very last time.

44

ilrowan was pacing the worn plank floor of his cell when he heard the sound of a key grating in the lock. The door swung open, and an exceedingly dapper figure in a gentleman's riding dress sauntered into the room. For a moment, Will could do nothing but stare at him; then he found his voice. "Blaise. I have no idea what brings you here, but I've never been so happy to see anyone in my life."

"No doubt," said Trefallon, raising a shapely eyebrow. "As to what brings me here: why it is just the usual thing. Do you think I'm in the habit of visiting gaols except under the necessity of securing your release?"

"Then I am *doubly* glad to see you. When do we leave?"

Blaise stepped aside, gestured toward the door. His coat and breeches were dusty and his boots splashed with mud, but his bow was as cosmopolitan as ever. "Whenever you like. I brought with me an order from Rodaric. The constable heaved a great sigh of relief, and promptly turned over your effects. Apparently, you've not been a model prisoner."

Will's volatile spirits plummeted. He scowled ferociously. "Nonsense. I've been no trouble at all." Picking up his hat and his coat, he strode past Trefallon, through the door, and into the long narrow room where the constable kept watch. Remembering his promise, he scattered a handful of coins on the floor, made a vulgar gesture in the lawman's direction, and proceeded out to the street. There, he found the buckskin gelding waiting for him, already saddled and bridled, along with a leggy chestnut stallion, apparently the property of Blaise.

Will untied the reins, vaulted into the saddle, and was halfway down the village street before Trefallon caught up with him, reining the chestnut in from a canter to walk beside the gelding. "If this is an example of the manners you've shown, I don't wonder your gaolers are pleased to see the last of you."

Will gave a short, explosive laugh. "You couldn't prove that by me. Apparently, I was the first prisoner they've had in fifteen months, and the most dangerous one ever. All the louts and boobies in the district have been in to gawk at me, and I'll swear the constable charged for the privilege." Then he grinned sheepishly. "I *did* say I was glad to see you. Though I still don't know why it was you instead of Nick that Rodaric sent to my rescue."

Blaise was suddenly very much occupied—brushing the dust off of one sleeve, squinting down at the no-longer-perfect polish on his boots—before he could bring himself to meet Will's eyes. "I did stop in Fermouline, with the idea of bringing Nick and the others with me. But they—Wilrowan, the inn where Nick and Gilpin were staying, the Rouge-Croix, it isn't even there anymore. Somebody exploded the place with gunpowder."

"Gods!" said Will. He felt all the blood drain from his heart at the thought of such reckless destruction. "How many people were killed?"

"They dug twenty-one bodies out of the wreckage, many burned beyond recognition. I have no idea if your men were even there, but nothing has been seen of them since. Of course, if they felt there was likely to be another attempt, they would want to lay low. Still, it looks very bad."

Will had a sick feeling that he was responsible, not just for Nick, Gilpin, and Odgers, but for all of the other people who were killed. If he had not shown himself to the Maglore woman on the ferry—

"I'm sorry. I should have broken the news more gently. You have known Nick since he was a boy, and they were all three under your orders. You must feel this—"

"Of course I feel it!" Wilrowan interrupted him savagely. "I was fond of Nick, and it goes to my heart to lose the other two as well. But don't waste your pity on me. He is *Lili's* cousin, and he is—was—only nineteen."

They rode in silence for a time, and the only sound was that of the horses' hooves on the stony road. Eventually, however, Will became impatient for answers. "Just how much about this business have you been told?"

"Everything," said Blaise. "The Chaos Machine, the entire fantastic plot—and the real reason for your bad behavior all winter long."

Will gave him a sidelong glance. "I wanted to confide in you, but Rodaric was adamant. What made him change his mind?"

Again Blaise hesitated, winding the reins around one hand, leaning forward to pat the chestnut on the side of its muscular neck. "There has been no official announcement, but the disappearance of the Mountfalcon Jewel is an open secret since all of the mines had to be boarded up. There have been riots in Hawkesbridge, and I didn't care for the mood or the mutterings that I heard in some of the places I stopped on my way here." Blaise shook his head ruefully. "I know you resented all the gaping rustics back in the Hoile, but as for me, I envy their innocence. The world is changing, Wilrowan, and not for the better."

He remembered something and dipped into his coat pocket. "I recovered this from the constable," he said, handing over Will's pistol. "Along with a number of interesting little bottles and flasks. Which reminds me: when I spoke with the king, Lady Krogan was there. I believe she had something to do with bringing me into the secret; she certainly took an active part in the entire interview."

"My grandmother?" Will was scarcely surprised. "Did she tell you that my wife is up to her ears in this business as well?"

"Yes. Though you said nothing about Lili in your letter to Rodaric. I wonder why?"

Will felt a rush of blood to his face. "Because I couldn't be sure how and why Lili was in it. I am ashamed to say so, but for a time I even wondered if she might not be——on a different side than you and I are. I know it was absurd, but until I learned of her involvement with the Specularii, some part of me doubted Lili. And even now," he added with a gusty sigh, "I still don't know if she was the one who stole my warrant and had me locked up."

"We will ask her when we see her," said Blaise. "And on that note, perhaps you can tell me just where we are going?"

They had come to a brook——clear water running over gravel—— but it was shallow and could be forded. Will and the buckskin led the way. "To Catwitsen, I believe. It's where I was heading before. Unless you have some better idea."

"I know what you know——or even less," said Trefallon, as they came up on the opposite bank.

Will gave him a calculating glance. "You do know something I would like to know. Just why did Rodaric and my grandmother choose you to join me here?"

Blaise winced, as though he had been hoping to avoid the subject. "I'm not altogether certain that I want to tell you."

Wilrowan gritted his teeth; he had a sinking feeling that he knew the answer. "No need to try and spare me. Knowing my grandmother, I can easily imagine. I suppose she said I shouldn't be allowed to wander about without my usual nursemaid."

"Well," said Blaise, "the metaphor in question was more to the effect of lunatics and their keepers, but you have the sense of it." Now it was his turn to look embarrassed. "You knew, then, that I had been writing to your grandmother? I hope you aren't offended by that?"

"My dear Trefallon," Will answered airily, "sooner or later practically *everyone* writes to my grandmother. She has her little ways of convincing them to do so."

The road divided, running north through a stretch of sparse shrubby woodland and west across rocky heath. Will urged his horse down the western road. "But I will tell you something my grandmother *doesn't* know. The creature that Lili and I have been chasing after looks just as Human as you or I, but I've reason to believe she may be a Gobline—and you may draw what conclusions you will from that!"

"Maglore?" said Blaise, with a startled glance. "When and how did you learn *that*? You said nothing of this when you wrote to Rodaric."

Will shrugged. "Suffice it to say that I, too, have my ways of learning things. Though unlike my esteemed grandparent," he added gloomily, "I seem to have a remarkable facility for learning most of those things far too late."

A day's ride took them into the grassy foothills. Goats grazed there among ragged bushes of heather and gorse; golden plovers circled overhead; snipe and grouse started up out of the long grass. Beyond, a range of snow-capped mountains stood tall and forbidding.

Crossing into Catwitsen turned out to be more difficult than Wilrowan had anticipated. A freshly painted white gate had been erected across the road at the border, and a deep rocky trench—still raw and new looking—extended as far as the eye could see. The crossing was guarded by men in blue coats with military-style cockades on their hats. When Will and Blaise drew up at the barrier, two of the guards presented arms and a third man, wearing the insignia of a lieutenant, demanded to see a passport.

"A passport?" Will gave a light laugh, hardly knowing what to make of this. "Are Bridemoor and Catwitsen at war, then?"

"No, sir, Catwitsen and Lichtenwald," replied the Lieutenant. "It is no joking matter. There have been several battles already, and the casualties have been very high."

Will and Trefallon were stunned into silence, this was so far beyond anything they might have expected. "I beg your pardon," said Wilrowan, at last. "I spoke without thinking. I never really supposed—"

"No, sir, most people don't. Half the people we have stopped have said the same thing."

"In any case, we are not from Lichtenwald," said Blaise, restraining with an effort the leggy chestnut, as it danced before the gate. "We are citizens of Mountfalcon. What must we do to obtain a passport?"

The lieutenant gestured in the direction of a large canvas tent pitched beside the road. "You can wait in there until we send for the general. He is the only one who can issue you a pass."

"*General.*" For a moment, Will and Blaise imagined they had misheard him. In a world where "captain" was the highest rank anyone achieved except under the most extraordinary circumstances, the archaic title had an ominous sound to it. There were a handful of ancient majors and colonels in Mountfalcon, dating back to a period of famine and riots sixty years before, but generals belonged to another age of the world entirely: an age of armies, conquest, and invasion. As Blaise and Wilrowan dismounted and led their horses toward the tent, the idea that *large* numbers of men were actually fighting gradually penetrated.

"Ye gods," said Trefallon under his breath. "I said that the world was changing, but I never had any idea of this."

"Nor had I," Will answered him soberly. It was almost unthinkable.

They were still awaiting the arrival of the general at sunset, when the lieutenant came into the canvas tent with a lighted brass lantern. Will looked up from his seat on a low stool, where he had been brooding silently for the last half hour. "Tell me, if you are allowed to, if anyone has passed this way in the last fortnight."

The lieutenant hung his lantern on one of the willow tent poles. "Many have tried, but only Sir Bastian Josslyn-Mather and his granddaughter were allowed to pass. That was ten days ago."

"Sir Bastian Mather!" Wilrowan and Blaise exclaimed in chorus, starting up from their seats. Will because he remembered that name from Marzden's report, and Blaise because he had finally recalled the name of Lili's "civil old gentleman."

"And who is Sir Bastian Mather that he was allowed to pass, when so many others were turned back?" Will muttered under his breath.

"Sir Bastian is a citizen of Catwitsen," replied the lieutenant, evidently taking this for a question he was meant to answer. "He has been living in Mountfalcon for many years, but he was born in Catwitsen, where the Josslyns and the Mathers are very prominent families. The general knew him on sight, and issued Sir Bastian and the young lady a passport immediately."

"How very convenient," said Will, resuming his seat. "How *damned* convenient!" Crossing one leg over the other, he glared up at the lieutenant. "Now that I think of it, I believe that I know—the granddaughter. Chestnut curls, grey eyes, and a fair complexion?"

"Yes, sir, that would describe her exactly. Quite an attractive young lady, if I may say so."

Will ground his teeth. "And they were riding in a coach—or was it an open carriage?"

The lieutenant shook his head. "In a barouche, behind two black horses. A very fine team, if I may——"

"And they were the only ones allowed to pass?" Will persisted. "You are absolutely certain of that?"

"All of the others were turned back. I should think, sir, that the same will happen to you." With a brief touch to his cockaded hat, the lieutenant went out of the tent, leaving the lantern behind him.

Will glanced over at Blaise. "All of the others were turned back—or else slipped across the border in the dark some night. Which is what it may come to for us."

"But we are following the Maglore women—not Lili and this Sir Bastian," said Trefallon, crossing the tent and peering out past the flap to make certain that no one could hear them. "How can we be certain the creature is even in Catwitsen?"

Will jumped up and joined him by the tent flap. In the yellow lantern light, his face was uncommonly grim; there was a dangerous spark in his hazel eyes. "We are following the Chaos Machine, whoever has it. But Lili seems to be better than I am at tracking the Jewel, and where she goes, we should go, too. I can only hope that this 'Lady Sophronispa' has been delayed along the way. She is so dangerous, Blaise, I would far rather catch her before Lili does."

Remembering all of those innocent people blasted into eternity at the Rouge-Croix, he felt his heart grow sick again. "We may already be too late. It may all be over. One or the other of them may be—dead."

45

The ship was luxurious, a great three-master out of Monte Luna in the south, carrying travellers for business and pleasure up and down the coast. But for one of her passengers she might have been a prison, walled and barred. Her comfortable cabins, the ample meals served each day, the gilded splendor of her poop-deck, bowsprit, and taffrails—all of these things were of little account to a man who lacked his freedom, who had already been fretting for many days in invisible fetters.

The cabin Raith shared with his two captives was long and low. The nearness of the carved beams overhead did much to increase Luke's sense of confinement, but the length of the cabin provided room for the incessant pacing that filled so many of his waking hours. Up and down, back and forth, he moved, like a man demented, and his frustration seemed to grow rather than diminish with every transit.

"This is," he growled, "the single most humiliating and degrading thing that has ever happened to me in my life. How long do you think it is going to continue?"

The Leveller answered with a slight shake of his head. "Sometimes a humbling experience can be good for the soul."

Luke rounded on him. "So this is supposed to be for my own ben-efit? The elevation of my mind, the improvement of my character?" Though he spat the words out with considerable heat, he kept his voice very low, so as not to disturb Tremeur, who was sleeping on one of the rosewood bunks.

"What you make of the experience is entirely up to you," said Raith. "Speaking for myself, it is one I would have given much to avoid. If you find the situation distasteful, you may take what com-fort you can from the knowledge that it is almost equally so for me. It was, however, the lesser of several evils and could not be avoided."

Luke glanced over at his slumbering bride. She had fallen asleep fully clothed, rolled up in a plain grey cloak she had acquired in the south. No, not fallen asleep—that was much too gentle a descrip-tion—she had finally collapsed from stress and exhaustion after sev-eral restless nights, and had been sleeping now for about sixteen hours.

When Raith slept was a mystery. Perhaps only when Luke slept himself—which was not very often—and for shorter periods, since he was always awake and alert again by the time Lucius opened his eyes. Whether Tremeur had ever seen the Leveller asleep, Luke did not know. They had had no time to speak privately, not since that first moment back in Château-Rouge when Raith appeared, pistol in hand. Remembering that day, Luke suddenly wanted to know the truth.

"Would you have fired, that day in Voirdemare? If I had attempted to escape before you bound me with this fiendish compulsion of yours, would you have actually pulled the trigger?" Raith was silent—which led Luke to the inevitable conclusion. "Damn and blast!" he said, slapping the palm of his hand to his breast. "You would have shot me down like a dog, for all your former pretensions of friendship."

The Leveller sat down in a mahogany armchair, which had been bolted to the hardwood planks to keep it from sliding. "I am reluctant to say anything that might make you even more uncomfortable than you already are. But since you insist on knowing—I brought the pistol with me solely for your protection. There is something sobering about a firearm; it presents a threat that few can ignore. Had I come into the room unarmed, your pride might have compelled you to offer some form of resistance." His large hands flexed. "In the midst of any physical struggle, I often find it difficult to restrain myself from doing more harm than is absolutely necessary."

"This famous strength of yours," Luke said sarcastically. Though he remembered quite well how easily the Rijxlander had lifted a heavy trunk one day. "But homicidal urges in a Leveller? Who could have ever imagined it? What other secrets are you hiding?"

Raith did not answer, but Luke persisted. "This magical society of yours—how did you ever become a member, in the teeth of your Anti-demonist doctrine?"

"As to that, I felt there was a great work that I was destined to do, one for which I had been singled out by Divine Providence, and that I might best accomplish that work within the ranks of the Specularii. Which, I should perhaps inform you," Raith added, with a grim look, "is a name you will find it impossible either to write or to utter, should you ever attempt to do so."

Luke declined to make the experiment. He had already learned, through repeated attempts, that he was helpless to resist the Leveller's compulsion. He was not about to humiliate himself further by demonstrating that fact all over again.

Though to be perfectly fair—which was the very last thing Luke wanted to be just then—Raith appeared to have too much delicacy to use his power except when it was absolutely necessary. He never, for instance, asked Luke to stop his pacing, though there were signs that he found the habit intensely irritating. Recognizing this, Luke sometimes kept it up even after the restless mood had passed. It was a petty revenge, he knew, but one he seemed to require.

"Why did you ever mention the name to me in the first place, if I am never to speak it?"

"I have been wondering that myself," Raith replied, removing something from his pocket as he spoke. It was a fish-skin box, about four inches square, and it opened up with a flick of the thumb to reveal inside a tiny terrestrial globe made of painted ivory. "Certainly, I should never have done so. But you do have a way of drawing things out of me, perhaps because of the extraordinary sense of friendship I feel for you."

Luke ground his teeth and continued to pace. He would have preferred to maintain a dignified silence, but again his curiosity overcame him. "You spoke of a great work, a divinely ordained purpose. Might one inquire what that purpose is?"

Raith hesitated before replying, taking the exquisitely painted little globe out of its case and pretending to examine it. "You are the historian, Mr. Guilian. Also, you are extremely adept at detecting conspiracies. Perhaps *you* can tell *me*."

Luke considered his own question at considerable length. "You and your magician friends have named yourselves after an ancient society," he said at last, "supposed to have been dedicated to freeing Mankind from the rule of the Maglore. But I hardly think that can be your purpose now, since the Maglore—as every schoolboy knows—are all extinct."

The ghost of a smile stirred at the back of the Leveller's dark eyes. "Are they? But then, that would be perfectly appropriate: members of a society that no longer exists, in pursuit of a race that has long since disappeared from the face of the earth."

Lucius glared at him. "The next thing you will tell me is that you are one of the Maglore yourself!"

Again that flicker of amusement in the Leveller's eyes, as he juggled the tiny globe from hand to hand. "I think, Mr. Guilian, that is the last thing I would *ever* tell you—particularly if it happened to be true."

The ship took a roll, a dip, and a plunge, and Luke clutched at the top bunk in order to keep from falling. Tremeur stirred in her sleep, but did not awaken. As the ship righted herself, Luke shot an angry look across at Raith.

"If we *were* friends, as you claim, you would have taken my word for it that I had nothing to do with the disappearance of the damned pocket-watch. If we were friends—"

"It is not a question of whether or not I am willing to take your word for anything. My own inclinations in this matter are so likely to lead me astray, I dare not consult them. For what it is worth— and practically speaking that is very little—I do in my heart believe in your innocence. Unfortunately for both of us, I do not feel I have the right to act on that belief." He returned the ivory globe to its fish-skin case, and snapped the lid shut.

"And so you hold me helpless and impotent before my wife."

"Naturally," said Raith, with a brief flash of emotion, "since I am willing to do violence to my own feelings, I could hardly be ex- pected to spare yours." Yet his glance softened as it came to rest on the sleeping girl. "If it is any comfort to you, I do not think any of this diminishes you in the eyes of Mrs. Guilian. Indeed, I believe her regard is only strengthened by what you have suffered on her ac- count."

Luke gave him an evil look, and took another restless turn around the cabin. It was no comfort to him at all what Tremeur thought. He was diminished in his own eyes. He had meant to play the hero, to swoop down and carry her off, into a better and nobler life than any she had known before—and only look what a pitiful figure he made instead!

Driven by a sudden surge of love and longing, Luke dropped

down on the edge of the bunk and reached out impulsively to stroke his bride's cheek—but remembering that Raith was a witness to his every action, he arrested the movement in mid-air, and drew back again.

Leaping to his feet, he crossed the floor and flung himself down in another chair. This lack of privacy, this constant constraint on any demonstration of physical affection, made everything worse. In the first blissful days of their union, it had been easy for him to be generous, to forget all the sordid details of her scandalous past, but now it was just one more insult among the many he was forced to endure, that while so many other men had enjoyed her favors, *he* was denied even the slightest intimacy.

On the other side of the cabin, Raith cleared his throat. As was so often the case, he seemed to be able to read his prisoner's mind. "If you must blame someone, I direct your attention to Lord Flinx. He, after all, is ultimately responsible for this distasteful situation, and seems to be guilty of worse things besides."

Luke's eyes kindled, a deep flush rose in his face. "I haven't forgotten Lord Flinx. I know how far he is to blame." Indeed, Luke sometimes thought it was the only thing that kept him sane, thinking what revenge he was going to take on the Prime Minister if and when they finally caught up with him.

Once they had sailed past Rijxland and landed in Herndyke, Raith and his prisoners left the ship and set out on an arduous overland trek. The days that followed passed in a whirl of activity, a blur of fatigue for Luke and Tremeur. Raith was virtually tireless and kept them all to a terrifying pace, though the course he followed was highly erratic and often involved considerable back-tracking. They travelled by coach, carriage, wagon, barge, and cart, on horseback and even on foot, when the mail-coach they entered at Louu was ditched.

As they moved north, they passed into a wild fen country, where the roads were built up to keep them from flooding. A cold wind from the sea ruffled the pools on either side of these causeways; herons waded in the shallows; geese and teal-ducks paddled where the water was deeper. Except in the towns on the coast, where trade was brisk and smuggling was rampant, the people here were herdsmen and small farmers, who supplemented their meager stock by fishing and fowling. They were slow, silent, unemotional folk, who lived in low houses with reed-thatched roofs, and hex-signs made up of stars, hearts, and queer-looking birds painted or carved above their doors. The men wore big boots of water-proofed leather impregnated with fish-oil, and the women had a weakness for rust-colored petticoats and for bright silk scarves, which they tied in their knotted dark hair, two or three colors at a time. On the rare occasions when any of them spoke, they used a dialect so thick that it was nearly impossible for Luke to understand them.

Seldom would Raith consent to stop in any of the houses, or in the lonely inns or hedge-taverns along the way. He and his prisoners carried food and drink with them, and slept on the move—Tremeur most often with her head on Luke's shoulder, or curled up in a corner of the coach or the wagon; Lucius giving way to sudden, overwhelming urges to nap, which he thought must be induced by Raith, so the Leveller himself might snatch a few hours of rest.

There were unforeseen and surprising obstacles.

Once, when travelling on horseback, they were forced off the high-road and obliged to make their way slowly across a quaking bog, because an entire herd of sheep lay dead in the road, struck down by some mysterious disease.

On another day, they stopped to assist a trio of keening, wild-eyed women as they pulled the water-logged bodies of a dozen drowned men out of a ditch. "How did this happen?" asked Raith. But the women refused to answer, and the men could not.

Sometimes, there would be a brief pause in some isolated spot, where the Leveller reined in the job horses, climbed down from the wagon or carriage, and began to cast one of his seeking spells. Of these he seemed to know a great number, and he employed a variety of curious devices: wands, pendulums, needles of magnetized iron. He was frequently seen scratching arcane figures in the soft earth, or sketching them in the air.

"Is that a hex?" Luke asked early one evening, when they had stopped at the edge of a rushy lake. He jumped down from the carriage to get a better look at Raith's activities. "I suppose it must be."

It was the hour before sunset, and a mist was gathering over the water, so that only the tops of the bulrushes were visible. A flight of swans flew overhead. In spite of himself, Luke felt a superstitious thrill pass down his spine.

"It is a pentacle," Raith answered calmly. "A figure much used by magicians and hexmasters alike."

Luke scowled at him. "You speak as though there were some essential difference."

The Leveller went on digging his mystic signs into the damp ground. "Hexes are invariably the work of ignorant rustics, frequently clumsy in their execution, and far more concerned with immediate results than with long-term consequences. As such, no matter how benign his intention, the work of any hexmaster generally leads to unfortunate results, sooner or later. I, on the other hand, am a trained magician. There is a precise calculation in everything I do."

Frogs were croaking in the invisible lake. The mist had crept inside of Luke's clothing, making his linens heavy and dank. "A trained magician," he repeated mockingly. "Yet you are also an Antidemonist—and excommunicate."

"That is true," said Raith, taking out and examining another of his curious devices—this one much like a compass, though with two needles and the signs of the zodiac painted on the dial. "If hexmasters are common in Rijxland, Herndyke, and Catwitsen, so are Antidemonists. Unfortunately, that very proximity has caused the latter to form an unshakeable aversion to *all* forms of magic. It is an aversion which, needless to say, I do not share."

"But does any of this really tell you where Lord Flinx *is*?" Luke was determined to be unpleasant—though it did often seem they were moving at random.

"Not precisely where he is, no. What it tells me is where he has been and where he is not, which can also be useful, though it does take longer to find him that way." Raith's eyes were sunken and shadowed, his skin was dull, yet Luke detected nothing in his voice or his movements to betray fatigue. "But we will catch up with Lord Flinx eventually. When we do, I can only hope that he carries the Jewel with him. If he has passed it on to somebody else, this whole journey may well prove fruitless."

"Pass it on to—why would he do that?" said Luke, with a fleering laugh. "When the whole idea of stealing one of the Goblin Jewels must be to gain power for himself?"

The device in Raith's hand began to give out a low humming noise. The double needles, which had been swinging wildly up until now, suddenly came to rest: one of them pointing to the sign of the crab, the other to the scorpion. "I do not say he would pass it on willingly. But I believe he may be dealing with people more ruthless, even, than he is himself."

"But who could that possibly be?" Tremeur asked, coming up beside them, materializing like the ghost of a drowned child out of the mist. "You don't mean to tell us, sir, that my uncle has been nothing more than a pawn in somebody else's game from the very beginning?"

"I do mean to tell you so. Have I kept you both to such a pace that you have not even noticed the forces at work on every side of us? When we took the mail-coach from Louu, did you hear none of the disturbing news that the other passengers were all discussing?"

Luke thought about that as they all climbed back into their hired carriage, sat down again on the clammy red leather seats. He had been absorbed in his own troubles, yet he had not been deaf or blind—he had simply refused to analyze any of the ugly or frightening things he had seen or heard along the way.

"It does seem as though there is sickness in every village or town we pass through," he answered slowly. "Or that the people are always just recovering from some freak disaster. But that it might actually *mean* something—it never occurred to me."

"Then consider it now," said Raith, taking up the worn leather reins. "Let your imagination run wild. I doubt you will come up with anything more incredible than the truth. If ever there was a time for you to detect evidence of some dread conspiracy, Mr. Guilian, that time is now."

46

eneral Pengennis arrived with the dawn. A lanky gentleman, something past fifty, he had long fair hair streaked
with grey and a fine military swagger. Evidently, he was
perfectly at ease in his brand-new uniform, with its gaudy gold
braid, immense brass buttons, shoulder loops, and archaic insignia.
"If you can prove to my satisfaction that you are in no way connected
with the Crown of Lichtenwald, I will issue a passport. Otherwise,
I am afraid you will have to turn back."

Will was absent-mindedly reaching for his missing warrant,
when Blaise surprised him by stepping forward and producing a
handful of documents. "Blaise Crowsmeare-Trefallon," he said
briskly. "I have here a lieutenant's commission, recently signed by
Rodaric of Mountfalcon, and a letter explaining that Captain Blackheart and I have been sent abroad on exceedingly vital official business."

The general accepted his papers and examined them carefully.
"Blackheart," he said, with a keen glance in Will's direction. "I believe that I had the honor of meeting your wife. She is Sir Bastian's
granddaughter?"

Will bowed stiffly, rather than assent to the lie.

"It seems strange you should both be travelling this way—though separately and on different business."

Will bowed again, even more rigidly than before. The general continued to frown at him for several minutes, then shook his head and turned to Blaise. He asked a number of curt questions and seemed satisfied with the answers, because he scribbled out a pass on the back of the letter and handed all the papers back to Trefallon. He left the tent, but not without another pointed glance in Will's direction.

"Now, why poker up like that and remain silent?" asked the exasperated Blaise. "Or did you *mean* to convince him you are a wife-beater and a brute, in pursuit of your unfortunate bride who has fled with her grandfather?"

Will shrugged. "It scarcely matters *what* he thought; he issued a passport anyway. But as we are asking questions, *lieutenant*, perhaps you'll explain those documents you're carrying?"

Trefallon followed him out of the tent, shaking his head. "Don't sulk, Will, just because Rodaric gave them to me. I admit that I should have mentioned them before, but the truth is—"

"The truth is," said Will, vaulting up into the saddle, and spitting the words out over his shoulder, "it's been decided I might be inclined to lose them."

"Nothing of the sort," Blaise answered patiently, as he untied the reins, and mounted the chestnut. "It's been decided that you are a walking target for the conspirators. Who, we devoutly hope, don't know me—since the Wryneck who *might* have identified me is a handful of ashes blowing through the streets of Fencaster."

They crossed the mountains and descended into the lowlands of Catwitsen, heading west into country made marshy by the confluence of three rivers: the Catkin, the Eel, and the Windle. It was feverish country; many died there during the summer months. This early in the year, it ought to have been pleasant. Yet, though the fennel and the lacy water hemlock were in bloom, though an immense blue sky stretched overhead, it seemed a landscape in mourning. At least once a day, Blaise and Will passed some funeral procession: a dozen black barges poling through the reedy waterways, or a straggling line of veiled women and children toiling up a windy hillside rank with sedge. In every churchyard, there were fresh graves under the silver willows.

For Will, the next weeks were a study in frustration. Twice, when he and Blaise stopped at an inn or a tavern to make inquiries about an elderly gentleman and a young woman travelling in a barouche, they were sent tearing off in some new direction, only to discover in the end that they were following the wrong pair.

Arriving late one evening in the town of Rummeny, they were denied lodgings on the grounds that the inn and all the houses were under quarantine for the Yellow Plague. And when—already impatient for dinner and beds—they rode on to the next village, they were stopped four times in three hours by roving troops of soldiers, who demanded to see their passport.

Even the weather turned against them. For a solid week, it rained heavily. Rivers raged, roads flooded, bridges were swept away, causing numerous detours. When the rain stopped, there was a brief period of calm, followed by a wind-storm so violent, it tore branches off trees and thatch off roofs, and even pulled rushes and cattails out of the ground.

The further they rode into Catwitsen, the worse they found the accommodations. Beds were hard, food ill-prepared, landlords, waiters, and chambermaids surly. One night there was nothing to eat but pilchards. Breakfast the next morning was burnt porridge. Boots went unpolished, linen unwashed, until Blaise and Wilrowan became as dirty and sullen as the inhabitants.

Worst of all, at least for Trefallon, were the volatile moods of his travelling companion. Up one day and down the next, Will's spirits seemed to fluctuate more often than the weather.

The world that he knew was passing away, and he felt responsible. The old ways had not been perfect, certainly, but at least they had been safe, predictable. Wilrowan had always scoffed at those of his friends who preferred a secure and settled life, but now he was finally learning its value—just when it seemed there was no safety left in the world for anybody.

When it looked like his search was about to be crowned with success, he was exalted. When he encountered another disappointment, his mood was savage. On the day it became obvious they had lost the scent entirely, Will and Blaise nearly came to blows.

But late one morning, they arrived in a tiny village on the banks of the Catkin. While Trefallon rode on to make the usual inquiries at a tumbledown tavern across the green, Will stopped off at the more respectable little inn, and walked right in on Lili and Sir Bastian eating breakfast in the coffee-room.

He stopped dead on the threshold, surprised by the violence of his own reaction. Though he had known from the beginning that Lili was not travelling alone, there was something in the sight of her sitting there so placidly, eating herrings and toast with another man, that made his blood burn.

But the savage mood passed. He walked quickly across the room, and bowed to Sir Bastian. "Sir," he said coldly. "I believe that you owe me an explanation."

Lili put out one hand, whether in greeting or in protest it was impossible to say. "No, Will, it is I who—"

But she got no further, as Will hauled her up out of her seat, wrapped his arms around her in a tight embrace, and buried his face in her hair. "You owe me nothing," he answered fiercely. "Whatever *you* have done, no doubt I deserved it. But these other people—this

Sir Bastian of yours, and all your other Specularii magicians—they have no shadow of a right to place themselves between man and wife."

He put her gently aside. "I repeat, sir. You owe me an explanation, and I am still waiting here, impatient to receive it."

Sir Bastian rose from his seat. "It is possible, Captain Blackheart, that I have been misinformed as to your character. Your sentiments, at least, are well expressed, and your demeanor toward your wife impresses me favorably." A slight frown creased his broad high forehead. "But it seems that I need not tell you why Lilliana and I are here. You have been deceived, it is true, but in a good cause. I should tell you, however, that Mrs. Blackheart wished to include you from the very beginning."

Moving out of Will's embrace, Lili turned to Sir Bastian. "Sir, we ought to include him *now*. It's perfectly absurd to continue on as we have, considering how much Wilrowan knows already."

The old gentleman nodded, though a trifle reluctantly. "Things have reached such a desperate pass, these last weeks," he said with a sigh, "I fear that we mustn't be too particular in choosing our allies."

A mocking smile passed over Will's face; he bowed ironically. "Someday, Sir Bastian, I hope to be able to return that compliment."

Yet the tension in the room relaxed just a little. At Lili's insistence they all three sat down around the table, where she poured out some bitter blackberry-leaf tea for Wilrowan and refilled Sir Bastian's cup.

"I trust, Captain Blackheart, that you did not find the accommodations in Hoile—too confining?" the old gentleman asked, as he passed Will a plate of slightly charred toast.

Will gave a start of surprise. "They were not in the least to my taste," he answered, automatically accepting the plate and laying it down on the table in front of him. "Am I to assume, sir, that you are the one I should thank for my imprisonment?"

Lili set down the chipped china teapot so hard and so suddenly the lid rattled. "Imprisonment? What are you——"

But Wilrowan ignored her, intent on Sir Bastian. "I was told that it was a *lady* who presented the warrant."

Lili's mentor took a small sip of tea. Then he took a bite of burnt toast, chewed it, and swallowed it before he answered. "They say that money talks. It may also, on occasion, prevaricate. Are you surprised to learn that the constable in Hoile was induced to lie to you?"

"Not at all." Will raised his cup to his lips, blew on the tea in order to cool it. "Had you paid him enough, I expect he would have strangled me in my sleep. But I certainly wonder why you wanted to deceive me."

"I thought it might serve to discourage you if you thought Lilliana was responsible. I see now that it probably had the opposite effect. My congratulations, Captain Blackheart. I never supposed you would be able to overtake us after such a serious setback."

Things went more pleasantly after that, and they were all eating an amicable breakfast when Blaise came in, expecting to report his failure at the tavern. Taking in the situation at a glance, Trefallon nodded to Sir Bastian, kissed Lili's hand, and slipped into a seat beside Will.

"Had I known you would find them here, I would never have left you alone," he said under his breath. "You surprise me, Will. This is exceedingly civilized. I would have expected a cutting of throats all around."

After breakfast, they hired a private parlor, where they could speak confidentially. It was a small room at the back of the house, with a view of the yard below. Sir Bastian and Blaise took chairs, while Lili and Will sat down together on a window-seat.

Wilrowan took her hand and held it tightly, while Lili spoke. He was surprised to learn that she and Sir Bastian were no longer in

506 ⅅ· TERESA EDGERTON

pursuit of the Maglore woman. "It appears," said Lilliana, "that she passed the Chaos Machine to a fellow conspirator. And though we hear of him in practically every place we visit, he always seems to know that we are coming, and invariably leaves just an hour or two before we arrive."

"But just what does this fellow conspirator look like?" asked Will, staring moodily down at his boots. That Lady Sophronispa had carried the Chaos Machine so far only to hand it on to somebody else struck him as exceedingly odd.

"A gentleman of forty or thereabouts," said Sir Bastian. "He has a smooth tongue and an affable manner, which endears him to innkeepers, hostlers, and waiters, in every place that he goes."

Will glanced up. "A gentleman, you say, and not a Goblin? You are certain he is not one of these resurrected Maglore—or even a Wryneck or Grant?"

"We are moderately certain," Sir Bastian answered. "He is travelling under diplomatic credentials, which seems unlikely for a Goblin. We did rather wonder if he might not be *you* in disguise—except that he had been described as considerably taller."

"And except, of course, for the affable manner," Blaise said under his breath, remembering the weeks just past, with all their tempests and tantrums.

Lili's mentor smiled grimly. "As you say. No doubt this man's affability does much to smooth his way, but there is no reason to suppose he would hesitate to abandon it, if he were cornered.

"If and when we run him to earth, he is likely to prove just as dangerous as the female."

47

ill woke in the middle of the night, and Lili was no longer pressed against his side. Reaching out blindly, he realized that her half of the bed was empty. "Lili!" he said sharply, into the darkness.

There was a soft sound of movement on the other side of the room. "I'm here, Will. Did I startle you?" The words were followed by a rattle, as she unlatched and opened a pair of shutters. A moment later, the room was flooded with moonlight.

A curiously wavering moonlight, soft and shadowy. Dark feathers appeared to be falling past the window. With a shock, Will suddenly understood that it was snowing.

Lili appeared at the foot of the bed, very pale in her white nightdress, with a length of grey woolen shawl wrapped around her. "I couldn't sleep, and now I know why." She opened her hand so that Will could see the lump of cloudy crystal she held in her palm. There was a shrill sound in the room, like a piece of glass vibrating; as Lili moved around to his side of the bed, Will felt the smoke-colored stone in his own intaglio ring begin to resonate.

"The Chaos Machine is moving across country again."

"It has moved in the last few hours, yes," said Lili. "But that doesn't account for such a strong fluxuation in the magnetic currents. Either someone has made a mistake—or they deliberately court disaster, by bringing two of the Goblin Jewels into close proximity."

A sudden blaze of light flashed outside and peal after peal of thunder rocked the entire building. The beams overhead shivered; the walls creaked. The floor under Lili's feet shook so violently, it was almost impossible to keep her balance. Will reached out and pulled her onto the bed with him. Gradually, the shaking and the clatter died down.

"Thunder—in the midst of a snowstorm?" he asked, just before another peal sounded, and the building rattled again with the shock. "Or was it an earthquake?"

"Thunder, I think." There was another flash and another rumble, but more distant this time; the storm seemed to be passing. "Though I've never heard anything like it before. Not—not a natural phenomenon, that much is certain."

Lili climbed out of the bed, clutching at the post in order to steady herself. "You should get dressed and find Blaise and Sir Bastian, while I pack up our things. We ought to leave as soon as possible. This may be our very best opportunity to overtake the Jewel."

Will nodded wordlessly and slipped out of the bed. Throwing on his clothes, he was out of the room in two minutes, and halfway down the corridor—where he all but collided with Blaise, already booted and spurred, coming to meet him. A moment later, they were joined by Sir Bastian.

"I have been restless," said the old gentleman. "I thought that something was about to happen, and my bags are already packed. I will see to the horses and the carriage, and meet the rest of you by the stables."

While Will went off to wake the landlord and pay what was owed him, Blaise went back to his room to pack. In half an hour they were down in the inn yard, impatient to be off.

The horses had already been saddled and bridled, but they were shivering and snorting, dancing with excitement, held under control only by the combined concentration of the two magicians. Blaise tossed the baggage into the barouche, and Will helped Lili to climb in after them. She sat on the seat, muffled up in her cloak, while Sir Bastian took his place on the box. The snow had stopped falling, it was already melting, and light from the stables reflected off the wet cobblestones.

A sleepy hostler lit two lanterns, one for the carriage and one for Wilrowan to carry. Then Will and Blaise mounted in a trice, Sir Bastian took up the reins, and the whole party went careering off into the night.

They travelled through the cold hour before dawn, on past sunrise, and into the afternoon: bowling down the long winding roads that snaked across the mud-flats of northern Catwitsen; fording the broad, shallow Catkin and the chocolate-brown Windle; stopping only when the horses needed to be watered and rested, or when Lili or Sir Bastian desired to take a bearing with her crystal or his pendulum.

At one o'clock, Lili caught her first hint of the sea, carried on a freshening breeze from the west. At two, Sir Bastian pointed out the first flat-bottomed eel boats—half raft, half shanty—which were never seen more than a mile or two from the coast. At two-thirty, they entered the salt-crusted gates of the seaside town of Penmorva.

The streets were crowded with carriages, sedan-chairs, citizens, fishermen, merchants, and sailors, which made the going slow. But as they moved toward the harbor, as the briny scent of the ocean grew stronger and stronger, Lili felt her mouth grow dry and her heart begin to pound with excitement.

"We are closer, I think, than we have ever been before," she said to Sir Bastian, as the barouche rattled down a narrow cobblestone lane between rows of brick warehouses. There was little traffic here, but the way was so narrow, the old gentleman had all he could do to negotiate a passage. "Perhaps we could go more swiftly on foot. I almost feel as though I could reach out and touch—" Then the lane intersected with a dark alley. "To the right," said Lili.

They found their way blocked by a gentleman's carriage, the horses left standing and unattended. Lili and Sir Bastian exchanged a triumphant glance. It was exactly like the carriage they had heard described at a dozen different inns between the border and the sea.

Leaving Sir Bastian behind with the horses, signaling to Will and Blaise who were riding behind, Lili was out of the barouche in an instant and edging past the other carriage. Somewhere inside one of the buildings backing on this alley, she knew she would find the Jewel. But which building? They all looked alike: tall brick warehouses, windowless, featureless, except for a line of heavy double doors, all barred shut. Then she caught a glimmer in the shadows at the far end of the alley, where one of the doors had been left slightly ajar, allowing a faint beam of light to escape.

Will caught up with Lili about ten feet from the open door. He reached into his coat pocket, drew out a pistol.

Lili put a hand on his arm. "No," she whispered, directly in his ear. "Suppose that you were to fire, and you hit the Chaos Machine instead of the man who is carrying it?"

He nodded, put back his pistol, and reached for his rapier instead. He signaled to Blaise to do the same, then turned back to Lili. "Trefallon and I will go in first. We are—expendable, but you are not."

Lili nodded reluctantly and fell back a step. Very cautiously, Will slipped between the double doors and disappeared from sight. Then it was Blaise's turn to vanish. Lili waited for a moment, listening for some signal whether to advance or to retreat, but when there was nothing, she followed Trefallon through the gap.

*   *   *

It was very quiet inside the warehouse. To either side of a wide aisle, there stood casks of brandy, oil, and wine; crates of fruit and rolls of coconut matting; bales of twine, hides, cotton, and to-bacco—piled almost as high as the ceiling. Every twenty feet or so, an iron lantern hung suspended from a crossbeam by a long chain, casting a circle of light on the floor. Will and Blaise moved swiftly and silently, first down the long aisle, then through a half-open door at the end. They found themselves in another large storeroom, look-ing up at a shadowy gallery that encircled the entire room.

The air smelled strongly of sandalwood, cinnamon, tea, and or-anges. Somewhere ahead of them, down some hidden aisle, Will heard a light fall of footsteps on the hickory plank floor. Those foot-steps were coming their way.

Acting quickly, Wilrowan dodged behind a tall wooden crate, and Blaise crouched down behind a trunk, ready to pounce. A mo-ment later, a trim gentlemanly figure came into view, through a gap in the piled boxes.

Clearly unaware of their presence, he moved confidently for-ward, with a satisfied expression on his face, as though his business in this out-of-the-way spot had been entirely successful. Another few steps, and Blaise and Will leaped out at him; one grabbing him from behind and imprisoning his arms; the other placing the tip of a very thin and sharp-looking rapier lightly against his collarbone.

"You will oblige us, sir," said Wilrowan, "by producing the Ma-glore artifact, which you are no doubt carrying with you." As he spoke, his fingers tightened their grip on the hilt of his sword.

The prisoner only smiled gently. "There seems to be some mis-take. I have not the pleasure of your acquaintance, but—"

"—nor will you have, if I allow myself the pleasure of skewering you like a pig," Will interjected, "which I can promise you I certainly will do, if you do not instantly hand over—"

But he, too, was interrupted, by the sudden noise of sliding boxes, which distracted his attention upwards, then caused him to leap back, just in time to avoid being crushed by an avalanche of falling crates and bales tumbling down from the gallery above. Though he was quick enough to escape serious injury, Will was knocked off his feet and sent sprawling across the hard planks. In that same instant, a long lean figure jumped down from the loft and overpowered Blaise.

While Trefallon and the newcomer fell to the floor in a furious struggle, the soft-spoken gentleman slipped quickly past the fallen boxes and raced down the aisle, back in the direction he had originally come. Will was on his feet in an instant. Scrambling up and over the crates that blocked him, he took off in hot pursuit.

He finally cornered his quarry at the end of another aisle, where he was attempting to lift an iron bar and open a heavy oak door. At the sound of Wilrowan's approach he spun around, drew a pistol out of his coat pocket, aimed, and fired. There was an explosion of sound. Will felt a sudden sharp pain in the fleshy part of his upper right arm, as the ball passed through, then a soft thud as it hit one of the boxes behind him.

Meanwhile, Trefallon was engaged in a life-and-death struggle with an unnaturally agile and flexible opponent. As they rolled about on the floor, it came to Blaise that he was wrestling with one of the rare and mysterious Grants. On top for a moment, the Goblin produced, seemingly out of nowhere, a silver-hilted knife with a long blade, which he aimed in a vicious left-hand stroke at Trefallon's throat.

Blaise threw up his arm and managed to deflect the blow, so that it caught in the heavy sleeve of his riding-coat instead. As the Grant drew out the blade and prepared to strike again, Blaise caught at the hilt with his own left hand and tried to wrench the knife out of the creature's grasp. The Grant seemed to be loosening his grip; it seemed that Trefallon was about to gain control of the weapon—when the Goblin doubled up his other hand into a fist and struck Blaise a hard blow to the side of his head.

Momentarily stunned, Blaise lost his grip on the hilt; for a moment he felt the knife graze the skin on his throat. Somehow, he managed to catch hold of the Goblin's arm with both of his and slowly force the blade away. There followed what seemed like an eternity of panting and rolling about on the floor. Then the creature reached out with his free right hand, and snaking his flexible arm through the circle of Trefallon's more rigid limbs—the Grant simply passed himself the knife.

The blade was descending again, this time unimpeded, when a shadowy figure loomed overhead. Something bright flashed in the air, then the Grant cried out, lost his grip on the knife, and went entirely limp.

In another part of the warehouse, Wilrowan required but a moment to recover from the impact of being grazed in the arm. Knocking the pistol out of the older man's grip and picking up the sword he had dropped when the ball winged him, he took the hilt in his left hand, indicating with a movement that his opponent was to draw his own sword. This the stranger did very readily, pulling his rapier out from its scabbard in one smooth, easy movement.

Will was the first to attack, but his opponent was swift to parry. There followed a brief exchange of blows, each man taking the other's measure. Wilrowan was the younger, the quicker, and the more experienced. Ordinarily, the advantage would have been all his, but as matters stood now—when he was forced to fight left-handed, when he was growing steadily weaker with the flow of blood from the shallow wound in his upper arm—he knew he would have to fight for his life.

Thrust and parry, feint, beat, attack, and retreat. As the contest continued, Will wondered what had happened to Blaise and to the others. He was growing light-headed—how much longer could he continue? He attacked high, slashing at his opponent's face, but his blade was deflected; a moment later he was blocking a blow aimed at his right arm.

There was another flurry of blows. Wilrowan gasped for air, but his opponent was breathing hard, too, and did not press the advantage. Then Will saw his chance. Much as he might have liked to disarm the man and question him, he had no such luxury. The stranger took the full length of Will's rapier right through the heart.

"I arrive somewhat tardily," said Sir Bastian to Blaise, "but not, it seems, too late." Something crunched under his feet as he moved around the unconscious Goblin and offered Trefallon a hand up. A barrel of rock-salt lay shattered and scattered across the plank floor. "I trust that you took no harm from this extraordinary creature."

Blaise rose stiffly to his feet. He looked from Sir Bastian to Lili. "I am well enough. But Wilrowan—"

"I, too, am well enough." Will came slowly around the corner, looking pale and shaken. "Although I will ask Lili to take a look at this arm."

Lili made a small sound of distress at the sight of blood soaking through the drab wool, but she set to work at once, very efficiently helping him out of his coat, rolling up the stained shirt sleeve beneath, and probing the wound with gentle fingers. "Not serious at all," she said, with only the slightest tremor in her voice. She produced a handkerchief and a roll of linen out of a pocket in her cloak and contrived a quick bandage.

Meanwhile, Blaise and Sir Bastian were busy with the unconscious Goblin, heaving him up to a semi-sitting position, holding him there, and securely binding his hands behind his back with a piece of dirty hemp rope, which Blaise had picked up from somewhere on the floor.

"Do not allow him near the salt when he wakes," said Sir Bastian. "He may try to suicide, but we want him to answer a great many questions."

As the old gentleman spoke, the Grant showed signs of coming around. He opened his eyes slowly, gazed around him with a confused air. Finding himself bound and surrounded by enemies, he seemed to panic. A wild look came into his eyes, and he attempted to heave himself to his feet.

"None of that!" said Blaise, taking the Goblin firmly by the shoulders and pushing him back down into a sitting position on the floor. Then he cried out in sudden pain, as the prisoner twisted his head and neck at an unnatural angle and sunk his teeth deep into the flesh of one hand.

Sir Bastian caught the Goblin by his lank hair and struck him blow after blow to the head. Yet it was necessary for Will to use the butt of his pistol, knocking the Grant unconscious again, before the jaws slackened and the teeth lost their grip on Trefallon's hand.

"Gods!" Blaise said faintly. He was bleeding copiously, and his face had gone white with shock and pain. "It looks like a Man, but it's little better than an animal." He swayed, and would have fallen, had not the old gentleman reached out to steady him.

"As vicious as his behavior may seem, I believe the creature acted completely without malice. Lilliana, see if it is possible for you to save the Goblin's life, while I attend to Mr. Trefallon's wound. I fear, however, that our prisoner has drunk too deeply of Human blood."

Lili acted immediately, bending down beside the Grant and putting an ear to his chest, listening for a heartbeat. It was several moments before either Wilrowan or Blaise had the presence of mind to realize what had just happened.

"Salt," said Will weakly, as he leaned up against one of the boxes for support. "Your blood is full of it."

"So it has apparently contrived to suicide after all," said Trefallon, with a grimace of distaste. On the floor, the Grant had begun to convulse, his long lean body writhing in a manner horrible to behold. Within seconds, he was dead.

There was a long silence, broken at last by Sir Bastian. "I am afraid to ask," he said, glancing over at Will. "The man we were following——"

"Dead," said Wirowan, with a weary shake of his head. "I am sorry, but I really had very little choice in the matter."

"And the Chaos Machine?" said Lili, rising to her feet, going over to stand beside him. "I beg your pardon, Will. I know that you were hurt, but did you search the body?"

"There was something—not what we are looking for—but I thought you would want to see it, so I brought it with me." Will searched in his coat pocket and drew out something heavy and bright. Lili reached out eagerly to take it.

"A pocket-watch, set inside a single enormous emerald—how beautiful it is." But the moment she touched it she knew: it was no ordinary piece of jewelry.

Her heart sank as she realized the truth. She passed the watch on to Sir Bastian. "I am very much afraid we have been following the wrong man, for—for the last fortnight at least. This *is* one of the Goblin Jewels, but not our own. Where it came from I do not know."

"It came from Rijxland, and it is the property of King Izaiah," said a deep, resonant voice. Everyone turned in surprise. So softly had the intruder entered the warehouse that no one had even noticed he was there.

A tall lean man in a long cloak and a round black hat stepped from the shadows into the light; another man and a dark-haired girl followed after him.

"As King Izaiah's agent," said Raith, extending his hand and removing the watch from Sir Bastian's suddenly slackened grip, "I will be happy to assume the responsibility of returning it to him."

48

The grass over Madame Solange's grave was already long and green—thanks to the long hours of daylight and the swift northern growing season—when a tiny woman swathed all in black from head to toe, with a hair brooch on a ribbon at her throat and a funeral ring on one slender hand, stood looking down at the white marble slab carved with the name "Valentine Debrûle" and the dates "6496–6538."

The first of these dates was—which Ys knew very well—as false as the name. Madame never mentioned her exact age, yet it had to approach a century and a half, since Sophie admitted to ninety-seven and was probably older than that.

"I did you a favor," said Ys. "If I hadn't decided to help you along, you might have felt it your *duty* to linger on, practically forever. As it was, you made a remarkably handsome corpse, everybody said so—and what more than that could you possibly ask for?"

Turning away from the grave, Ys started back toward her waiting carriage. There would be no true night at this time of the year—just a brilliant sunset, followed by several hours of twilight—but the sun was sinking toward the horizon, the shadows were lengthening, and a sudden chill, real or imaginary, caused a shiver to pass over her.

Was it some premonition of evil to come? Ys glanced suspiciously around her and saw a small, plump figure, dressed as she was, all in black with a waist-length veil, coming across the graveyard through the knee-high grass to meet her.

"Oh, Sophie, Sophie!" Ys hurried her steps; she all but flung herself into the waiting arms of her aunt. "Oh Aunt Sophie, I am *so* glad to see you."

Sophie hugged her briefly, then drew back a little to take a long look at her. "How thin you have grown. But I can hardly wonder at that. Such a tragedy, my dear. I came as soon as I heard, as soon as I could, but there were—complications along the way."

Ys shrugged out of her embrace. "*Was* it a tragedy? I don't think so. Madame Solange was getting above herself. I know you were fond of her, but I believe we are much better off without her."

Sophie stared at Ys for a long moment in shocked silence. "Ys," she said very quietly, when she was able to speak again. "You don't mean to tell me that this was *your* doing?"

"She killed Zmaj; she burned him to death—imagine one Maglore doing that to another! She killed Izek, too. She was a wicked, wicked creature, and she *deserved* to die."

"Wicked? Oh, my poor child!" Sophie seemed more distressed than angry. "Valentine Solange was the most idealistic—the noblest of us all. If you don't know that, then you will never understand—" She drew in a long shuddering breath. "Val never did anything for herself; it was all for our glorious cause. She would have laid down her own life. Indeed, she always intended to do just that, but she wanted to see you securely established first. How *could* you do this while we still needed her?"

Ys scowled fiercely, twisting the ring on her right hand. "I *am* securely established. I don't need anybody but you, Aunt Sophie—certainly not Madame or any of the others."

"Do you really believe that? But you can't imagine some of the things that I saw and heard as I travelled north. They say that Catwit-sen is in chaos, and that conditions in Tholia and Lichtenwald are even worse. There is a revolt in progress right now in Nordfjall, ri-oting in Mountfalcon, and strange rumors of floods, plagues, and worse things besides come out of Rijxland. Everywhere I go, Men say that the world is coming to an end, that civilization is crumbling."

"But all this is good news," Ys insisted, throwing back her veil, stamping her foot. "It is what we wanted, after all. It is only a sign of the success of our plan so far."

"Not *our* plan," said Sophie, with a determined shake of her head. "It was Val's plan. Val thought of it, Val executed it, Val knew how it was all to end. Without her to guide us, how can we ever hope to bring order out of chaos? This is no time for uncertainty, no time for indecision. It is no time for us to make even the slightest miscalcu-lation."

Now Ys felt a faint prickle of apprehension. "But she must have *told* you what happens next. She must have explained to you. She trusted you with all of her secrets. Oh, Aunt Sophie, if you are try-ing to frighten me, I wish you would not."

But Sophie only continued to shake her head, more emphatically than before. Stepping away from Ys, she smoothed out the skirts of her black twill gown. "I have no idea. She only told me as much as I needed to know. It was not that she didn't trust me, but the part I played was far too dangerous, the risk of capture was far too great. She said that what I didn't know, no one could force out of me."

For a moment, Ys felt the world sinking away beneath her feet. But then she rallied. "If that is so—then we will just make a new plan. Why should we not? Madame said it herself: we can see months, even years into the future. We don't grow muddled, as the other Goblins do, if we have to think ahead."

"We don't grow muddled if someone like Val is there to explain to us, to map out the whole plan, step by step, and show us exactly

how it will work. But to conceive such a plan for ourselves? We may
be better than any of the others, but neither of us will ever match
Val. She was remarkable—extraordinary. I doubt there is another
Maglore like her in all the world."

"I am," Ys maintained stubbornly. "I am remarkable, too. I can
think for myself. After all, I've been doing it all of these months. You
have no idea how many things I have done without asking Madame.
You weren't here, so you don't know."

Sophie remained unconvinced. "My poor child, I hope you are
not deceiving yourself." She reached out absently, pushed back a
stray lock of her niece's golden hair, which looked very bright
against the black silk and net. "Because if you are—I dare not
think of the consequences. Oh, I wish, I *wish* you had not done this
terrible thing. To think that all of Val's work should go for nothing!"

Ys was beginning to tremble. "Aunt Sophie, you are not going to
turn against me—you are going to stand by me, aren't you?"

"Turn against you?" said her aunt, taking Ys tenderly by the arm,
leading her back toward the carriage. "My poor child, you and I are
the last, the very last in the direct line. I could never turn against
you—no matter what you had done!"

But in the morning, Sophie was gone. When Ys went to visit her
at the house on the outskirts of town, she found the ancient mansion
deserted. A quick search of the premises was enough to convince
her that Lord Vif, Aunt Sophie, and the few remaining servants had
all of them fled during the night.

There was a letter addressed to Ys, on a table in Sophie's bedchamber, propped up by a gilded jewel box. Ys carried the letter
over to one of the windows and drew back the velvet curtains.

"*Ys,*" Sophie had written. "*I dare not stay. Whatever Affection I may feel
for you, there is a greater Principle at stake & I must Obey. Never, never would*

your Aunt Sophie do anything to Harm you, but Stand by Your Side in the days to come—that She Cannot Do.

"As I told you last Evening, we are the Last in the Line of Direct Descent. If anything should Happen to you, then I have a duty to Survive & to bear Children. Val found me Wanting, she thought me too Weak for a Maglore Empress. She believed that Chimena's daughter would better serve the Cause of our People. But whatever I may be Lacking in myself, I may yet produce a Child who will be Strong enough. For this reason, I have taken Jmel with me.

"As a sign of my continued Good Will, I direct your Attention to the contents of a small Box made of ebony & palisander, Which you will find among Val's effects. If you are as Clever as you say you are, you will Recognize the Object for what it is, & you will make Good Use of the Information it provides. Darling Ys, if you cannot be Wise, at least be Cautious.

"Please believe me ever Your Loving Aunt,

"Sophronispa."

Ys read the letter three times through, then crumbled it up in her hand, and turned away from the window, away from the light which seemed suddenly too strong. She brushed a hand across her eyes.

Only gradually could she take it all in: the fact that she was truly alone, that everyone on whom she had ever depended in her life was gone.

But perhaps there was more of Chimena, more of Madame in her than anyone suspected. With a great effort, Ys pulled herself back from the brink of despair. She was determined to survive—yes, and to do more than that! It was not enough to forswear the poison bottle and the ground glass: she must not only live, she must succeed—and splendidly.

In Madame's bedchamber, Ys threw open the curtains, and set to work at once rummaging through the clothes-press and several large trunks; tossing out petticoats, gloves, corsets, gowns, and shawls;

sifting through a collection of ivory busks, tortoise-shell combs, and tiny scent-bottles made of agate and jet. In a small jeweled casket, she discovered an amber pendant in the shape of a tear-drop with a tiny spider caught inside, and a heart-shaped pouncet box made of silver.

Finding nothing in any of those places of any interest, she moved on to the large mahogany desk, where she pulled out drawer after drawer, running a cursory eye over the contents, until she came to a drawer near the bottom, which she yanked out so hard, it fell to the floor with a hard thump.

Picking it up and sliding it halfway back into its former place, Ys drew in her breath sharply at what she saw inside.

Taking up a pretty glass dagger with an elaborate twisted hilt, she turned it over in her hand, examining it curiously, being careful all the while not to touch the blade, for fear it had been treated with some deadly poison. Looking further through the drawer, she brought out bright silk scarves, long jeweled hat-pins, a silver pistol so tiny it might fit entire in the palm of her hand, and even (Ys could not help smiling grimly at the irony) a small clear phial containing a crystalline substance which appeared to be salt. *It is a perfect treasure-trove,* Ys thought, *supposing you happen to be an assassin!*

Underneath it all, she finally unearthed the box made of ebony and palisander woods which Sophie had mentioned in her letter. Ys opened it eagerly and looked inside—and then made a small sound of disappointment. It was only a fan, a frivolous brisé fan of painted ivory. Spreading the sticks, she could not help noticing how very curiously and delicately they had been painted. But why had Sophie written that she might find it useful? For a moment, Ys wondered if her aunt had lost her senses. Or was it—was it merely that Sophie meant to tease and torment her, in revenge for her beloved Valentine's death?

But no, she decided, cruelty for its own sake was quite unlike the gentle Sophie. Ys considered the fan for another moment. She had heard of such trinkets with a deadly secret—a blade concealed somewhere inside, every bit as sharp and dangerous as the glass dagger. But after several minutes examining the fan, she was forced to admit that it seemed perfectly harmless. She dropped it back into its case, was about to toss it carelessly in the drawer—when she changed her mind.

Sophie *must* have meant something. Ys had no time right now to unravel that meaning, but if she took the fan back to Lindenhoff with her, she might eventually be able to puzzle out its secret. Concluding that this would be best, she slipped the slender ebony case inside her bodice between her gown and her corset, and reached out to close the drawer.

Then she changed her mind once more. Picking up the dainty glass dagger and wrapping it carefully in one of the silken scarves, she slid it up inside her sleeve.

49

"Raith," said Sir Bastian, stepping forward to shake the Leveller by the hand. "I had thought you still in Luden."

"As I thought you still in Mountfalcon. It is good to find a friend here, so unexpectedly. But allow me to present my companions: Mr. Lucius Guilian, late of Winterscar, and his bride."

If Sir Bastian saw anything strange in this abbreviated introduction, he did not mention it. A round of further introductions, of eager questions and hurried explanations followed. At last, Raith asked to be shown the man who had been carrying the emerald pocket-watch.

He followed Wilrowan into the next room, and the others all trailed behind. Kneeling down on the hickory planks and turning over the body, Raith studied the face carefully. In death, Lord Flinx's features had taken on a harder, more calculating cast, but there could be no doubt as to his identity. "It appears, Mr. and Mrs. Guilian, that I owe you both an apology, along with your immediate freedom."

Tremeur was silent, but Luke stood glaring down at the corpse with a thousand different emotions at war inside of him. "It appears that somebody else owes me an apology," he said, prodding one limp hand with the toe of his shoe. "I wanted to kill this man myself."

Will bristled up at once. So much had happened, so much blood had been shed—and yet they were no closer, now, to finding the Mountfalcon Jewel. He was ready enough to take this opportunity to vent his frustration. He bared his teeth. "If that is so, then I am the one who has wronged you, sir. I am prepared to offer you immediate satisfaction."

Luke raised a supercilious eyebrow. "Satisfaction from a one-armed man?" He indicated, with a gesture, Wilrowan's bloody bandage.

Will's good hand had strayed to the hilt of his rapier when Raith intervened. "I am under the impression, Captain Blackheart, that we have far more pressing business than any trifling quarrel between you and Mr. Guilian."

Feeling only slightly ashamed of himself, Will bowed coldly to Luke, and Lucius responded in kind. Meanwhile, the Leveller began a swift and efficient search through Lord Flinx's pockets, extracting all of the papers—including the diplomatic passport which had brought the Prime Minister so far.

"This may prove useful," he said, slipping the passport into a pocket inside his dark cloak. "And I think it would be best if no one is able to identify this body—which might only serve to inflame an already tense political situation."

He rose quickly to his feet, and addressed the company. "There is a decent inn on the outskirts of town. Perhaps we should adjourn there, so the ladies may refresh themselves, and we can all meet together to plan our next move."

There was agreement all around, and the entire party left the warehouse and returned to the street. The bodies of Lord Flinx and the unnamed Grant they elected to leave behind, on the Leveller's advice.

"It should give the local authorities something to wonder about," said Raith, climbing into his carriage and taking up the reins. "Though considering all of the problems here and abroad, I hardly think they will concern themselves over much with the death of an unknown man." He nodded at Luke, who was handing Tremeur up to the other seat. "It will be another of those historical mysteries, Mr. Guilian—the kind in which you seem to delight."

Luke laughed bitterly. "One I am happy to leave unsolved. It is a fitting end for such an ambitious man: an unmarked grave in a foreign country. I can only regret that I wasn't the one who had the honor of putting him there."

While Luke engaged a room at the inn and took the exhausted and over-wrought Tremeur upstairs for some much needed rest, the others met together in a private parlor with a view of the harbor, where everyone but the Leveller ate a light meal and they all discussed what ought to be done next.

Where the Chaos Machine was now, it was impossible to tell; it had passed beyond their ability to detect its presence. Yet everything they knew pointed to some ultimate destination in the far north. Whoever had the Jewel now would be travelling overland, as a voyage by sea involved too many risks—the worst one being that the Jewel could be lost forever at the bottom of the sea. "But if we booked a passage ourselves," said Raith, "we might arrive in the north a little behind or even just before this Lady Sophronispa."

After much debate, it was decided that Sir Bastian would take the pocket-watch back to Rijxland, while Raith accompanied Lili, Wilrowan, and Blaise on their voyage.

"You are as fit to advise Lilliana as I am," said Sir Bastian, finally yielding his place to the Leveller. "And far better suited to rapid travel. I must resign myself to assuming what appears to be the easier task."

Raith nodded solemnly. "I will give you a letter for the Crown Princess, explaining just how you came by the Rijxlander Jewel. That should serve to spare you any awkward questions."

Excusing himself from the company, he went in search of pen, ink, paper, and sealing wax. Being provided with these by the innkeeper, he sat down in the coffee-room, pulled out his own pen-knife and a little stone jar filled with pounce that he always carried with him, and proceeded to write out the promised letter. He was just finishing up when Lucius sauntered in and asked to know what had been decided.

Raith described the situation briefly. "But if you mean to ask what is to happen to *you*, that is entirely your own decision. You are free to go wherever you will."

"Does that include accompanying you on your journey north?"

"It does," the Leveller replied, as he folded and sealed the letter, "if you are not heartily sick of my company by now—as I had rather assumed you were."

"That is beside the point," Luke answered coldly. "You say there may be some disaster brewing in Winterscar or Nordfjall, and I agree. It may even be that my home in Tarnburgh is the center of the trouble. If so, I may be needed there. I believe that by travelling with you, I will arrive much sooner than I might otherwise. You have a way of—removing all obstacles in your path."

"As you say," Raith answered calmly. He picked up his letter and rose from his seat. "And perhaps someday you may even forgive me for what has passed between us—forgive Captain Blackheart, too, for killing a man you so ardently wished to see dead."

Luke glared up at him, far from mollified. "I suppose you will say that Lord Flinx is just as dead this way as if I had killed him myself."

Raith paused with one hand on the brass door-knob, and considered a moment before he spoke. "I might say that, if I wished to annoy you." He opened the door and stepped over the threshold. "As I do not wish to do anything of the sort, I think I must be content saying nothing at all."

The next several days saw the departure of Sir Bastian, and the rest of the party roaming the docks in search of a vessel to carry them north. This close to midsummer it ought to have been easy to book a passage, but it proved unexpectedly difficult to find a ship that was even heading in the right direction.

"There be no safe passage by Lichtenwald," said one old salt, whom they met perched on a piling down by the water, carving a walking-stick out of the backbone of a shark. "There were a shipwreck near Zutlingen, all hands lost, and they do say a fleet of fishing boats went out from Ilben two month past and they never come back again."

Wilrowan frowned at this ominous piece of information. The people of Lichtenwald were known to be cautious and discreet, and they never discussed the properties of their Jewel. Yet it was a fact known throughout the world that wood acquired a special buoyancy near the coast of Lichtenwald, and that the jagged off-shore rocks actually appeared to *repel* ships. A ship lost or wrecked in those waters could mean only one thing.

An ancient beldame boiling chowder in an iron pot outside a tavern provided Will's friends with equally unwelcome news. With bloody revolutions going on in Nordfjall and Kjellmark, another one brewing in Winterscar, those who believed there was money to be made, by selling weapons or hiring themselves out as mercenaries, were already on their way. "All other folk means t'stay clear. At least so long as t'Goblin Queen rules in Tarnburgh."

Lili and Raith exchanged a glance.

"The Goblin Queen, is that what they call her?" Lili felt a shiver across her skin, as though there were something fateful in that name, as though it was solely to meet this creature—be she woman or Gobline—and to test her powers, whatever they might be, that Lili herself had been taught by the Specularii all of these years.

The question remained how to reach Tarnburgh and effect that meeting. Three long days of fruitless enquiry passed before the travellers finally met a wood-carver who gave them encouraging news.

"There be t' *Pagan Queen* just in from Finghyll and dropped anchor out t'bay. By all accounts she'm sailing south." As he spoke, he put the finishing touches on the outstretched wing of a harpie fig- urehead, which he was chiseling out of an immense block of white elm. "But that Captain Pyke—they do say he'll do anything for money, you pay him enough."

There was a momentary brightening, followed by flat despair. Will, Raith, and Blaise held a hurried conference down on a windy stretch of shingle beach, where their party had gathered to exchange information. From this vantage point they could see the *Queen* her- self, looking more leaky and disreputable than ever, as she rode the waves just within the mouth of the bay, where she had dropped an- chor. For all that, she might have been a world away for all the good she seemed likely to do them. How could they possibly raise be- tween them a sufficient sum to offer the sea captain? Their separate journeys had already lasted longer, had proved far more expensive than anyone anticipated when they first left home. They were al- ready reduced to pawning some rings and other small valuables, along with selling the horses, in order to pay their passage. A bribe for Captain Pyke was an unforeseen expense. To make matters worse, they had only until the tide turned the following morning to accomplish all this. How were they to do it?

"Allow me," said Luke, breaking in. With the wind ruffling his dark hair and raising the skirts of his velvet coat, he drew out the wallet he carried in an inside pocket. For the last month, he and Tremeur, as the Leveller's prisoners, had been travelling at Raith's expense; the better part of the very large sum he had drawn before leaving Luden was still intact. "I believe that I have enough here to bribe a far greedier man than Captain Pyke."

It was decided that Luke and Raith, being acquainted with the captain, would row out to the *Queen* in order to effect the negotia- tions. This they did successfully, securing a passage as far as Ottars- burg in Nordfjall, though at a considerable cost. The others were pleased to notice that Lucius—having found a way to make himself useful—was in a slightly better temper for the next two hours.

At nightfall, they all went aboard with their baggage, paying two stout boatmen to row them out. The other passengers were just vacating their cabins under vigorous protest, having only just been informed that the ship would be heading north instead of south as planned. When the hubbub died down, the newcomers found that there was ample room to make themselves comfortable, even on a ship so lacking in amenities as the *Pagan Queen*.

Wilrowan went below almost immediately. He had been very quiet, even morose, all evening. Even Luke Guilian and his stinging remarks had failed to provoke a response. Among the rumors they had gathered on the docks there was a story that the Queen of Mountfalcon was dead, that Dionee had died miscarrying what would have been a fine boy, King Rodaric's heir.

"But we have heard so many improbable stories," Lili said soothingly, when she joined him in their cabin. "And so many contradictory accounts. Wilrowan, they can't *all* be true, so why believe this one?"

"Because it *is* true, because I know it to be true," Will said bleakly, throwing himself down on the lower bunk and shading his eyes with one hand. "I saw death in her face when I took my leave of her—though I tried to convince myself it wasn't so. The strain of these last few months—" He passed his palm over his eyes, dashing away the tears. "We may call it, perhaps, a merciful release, if what we have seen elsewhere has come to Mountfalcon, and Dionee holding herself to blame. But to those of us who remain behind—" He choked and could not continue.

Lili did not know what to say, she had no words of comfort to give him, for she had a similar heartache of her own. She had not yet given up hope that Nick might still be alive, that he had somehow been elsewhere when the Rouge-Croix was destroyed, but every day a small part of that hope died, and she came a little closer to believing that he was dead.

50

Alone with Luke in the close confines of the next cabin, Tremeur prepared for bed while he paced. She was all too aware of his increasing coldness, had been growing daily more distressed by the dawning realization that some deep cause of bitterness lay between them. Now, as she put on her night-dress and slipped between the damp sheets of her narrow bunk, the fact that Luke took such care not to look at her filled her with such unbearable pain that she was finally impelled to speak out.

"Luke," she said softly—barely audible over the creaking and the shuddering of the ship, "when we land in Ottarsburg, when the rest of you go on to Winterscar, would it not be better if I stayed behind?"

He stopped his restless pacing, caught off guard by this suggestion—which, to do him justice, had never occurred to him. "If you stayed behind? It may well be that we are going into danger, and if there was anywhere, anywhere safe for you to stay until I could come back for you—but what would become of you in Nordfjall, where you have no friends, where no one knows you?"

"I was thinking of you. You are going home, and who knows what trouble you may find when you get there? If you have the additional worry of explaining *me*, to your cousin the king and all the rest—"

He smiled a twisted smile. "I'm very much afraid that when we finally arrive, affairs in Winterscar will have reached such a crisis that explaining you—your unfortunate past, our questionable marriage—will be the very last thing that anyone cares about." Shrugging out of his velvet coat, he pretended for a moment to be absorbed in a rent he discovered at the back. Then he shook it out, and hung it up on a peg by the door.

"I was thinking of you," Tremeur said again, this time with a catch in her voice. "I will be an additional burden on you."

Finding himself embarrassed for an answer, for once in his life, Luke stood silent, slowly unfastening the six silver buttons on his satin-twill waistcoat. He had been hoping—he did not quite know how—that she had not and would not guess any of the things he was thinking or feeling. He wished that he might explain to her *why* he felt as he did, that he might reassure her it was no fault of hers that he, who prided himself on his originality, should turn out to be such a petty, conventional man. But every time he had thought about speaking, the words caught in his throat, and he realized that the confusion in his own mind was still too great. If he could not justify his feelings to himself, then how could he possibly hope to explain them to her? Sitting down on the edge of her bunk, he pulled off his top-boots, one after the other, placing them very carefully side by side on the floor.

"Why should you think so?" he said at last.

She made a wide gesture with her hands. "These past weeks, the weeks ahead—perhaps it is selfish to even think so, when we see so much misery around us—but you have to admit it has been exciting—truly a marvelous adventure. Far better than anything we imagined when we were back in Luden. You ought to be enjoying it more than you are, and the reason you *can't* must have something to do with me."

Luke turned to face her with a defeated sigh. "It *is* an adventure, but it doesn't seem to be *my* adventure. It belongs to men like Captain Blackheart and Blaise Trefallon. I'm only a spectator. I always thought that if the opportunity arose, I would play a far more dashing role, but the truth is—I'm woefully inadequate. Worse still, while I was gadding about the world searching out imaginary plots, that woman my cousin Jarred has married was hatching her monstrous schemes back home—where I *ought* to have been, where I might have proved useful." He took one of Tremeur's hands in both of his, applied a light, reassuring pressure. "Now how, may I ask, are *you* to blame for any of that?"

Yet he did blame her and they both knew it. He felt that all of his folly, all of his pretensions, were mercilessly exposed. Unfortunately, the woman he loved had been there to see it all. That might be a small sin, compared to certain other sins in her past, but oddly enough it was the one that he found it the hardest to forgive.

At daybreak, the ship set sail; a strong wind sent her scudding north. The days grew longer and longer, the nights were hardly nights at all. They expected to reach Winterscar at the midpoint of the year, at the height of summer.

The *Queen* hugged the coast for much of the journey. Only when they reached Kjellmark would they tack westward across the Mare Frigorium. In the meantime, the wind from the shore too often brought the scent of burning, and great black smokes and other signs of disaster could be seen in most of the settlements as they sailed on past.

One bright morning, Lili met Raith strolling on the upper deck. After an exchange of courtesies, she fell into step beside him. "I wonder," she said, "if I might ask you some questions? If I am too curious, please tell me so at once, but I must say, sir, that I find you something of a puzzle."

Raith smiled down at her. "You mean to ask, no doubt, about the anomaly of an Anti-Demonist magician."

534 ა· TERESA EDGERTON

Lili shook her head. "No. That is unusual, of course, but there is something else. Something I can't help regarding as even more mysterious." Her brown velvet cloak was whipping around in the wind, but the day was fine, and she felt little need of it.

"You see, I thought that I recognized you that first day, when you stepped forward to claim the Rijxlander Jewel. I asked Sir Bastian, and he said that you *were* the one who guided me through the underground maze when I was initiated. But he also told me things that I found—entirely remarkable. I hope you will forgive him, and not feel that he has betrayed your confidence, but he thought it might be necessary for me to know these things, considering the dangers we may very well face together in the near future."

"Of course," said Raith, as calm as ever, as though the matter of which they were speaking were of very little account—and not likely to result in his execution anywhere in the world, if the truth became known. "That was very wise of him. Then as to the question you hesitate to ask me: perhaps you wish to know how a—person like myself ever came to align himself on the side of good?"

"Not precisely that. Sir Bastian tells me there are undoubtedly hundreds, perhaps even thousands of your people alive in the world, most of them living the most blameless lives. Even if he had *not* told me that, it would be impossible for me to believe that any race of beings could be entirely given over to evil. No, what I wish to ask is how anyone—be he Man or Goblin—could dedicate himself to a cause which is so clearly in conflict with the best interests of his own kind."

Raith glanced around him, to make certain they could not be overheard. They were alone on the forecastle, and even if the wind carried their words, anything they said would be blown harmlessly over the water. He turned his particularly penetrating gaze full on her face as he spoke. "But are the best interests of Men and Goblins truly opposed? Surely the Padfoots and the Ouphs—and the majority of the Wrynecks and the Grants—have made it abundantly clear that they wish to live in peace.

"As to the Maglore—my parents died when I was so very young, it is hard for me to remember all that they taught me. As I understand it, for many years there were two factions. One was determined to win back the Empire, and they were ready to do whatever was required in order to do so. The other, essentially pacifist, wanted nothing more than to live their lives in obscurity and safety. They felt that the other party imperiled that safety, and were willing to put their principles temporarily aside and fight a secret war. Unfortunately, the other party proved stronger in the end, and they were destroyed."

"And to which faction did your parents belong?" Lili asked, with a searching glance of her own.

"I have reason to suppose they had been born into families of opposing principles. In any case, they chose to ally themselves to neither party, to live apart from their own kind, and to break all ties. Others had made the same choice before, doubtless others have made it since. As some Men do live in Goblin Town, so it is possible for Maglore families to do so also and to still pass as Human—at least in the eyes of the Human population. But those who do so place their families in jeopardy. If both parents die in this self-imposed exile, there is no one on hand to take charge of the children.

"I was one such orphan, wandering the streets, until one day I chanced to find my way into an Anti-demonist orphanage. The good people there took me in, and raised me as one of their own." His eyes kindled at the memory, but he gave no other sign of emotion.

Lili raised her eyebrows, with a slight incredulous smile. "And they never guessed who and what you were? I find that difficult to believe!"

"They guessed soon enough," said Raith. "How could they not?"

"And yet they kept your secret?"

The Leveller shrugged. "Like most people, the Anti-demonists firmly believed that the last Maglore was exterminated more than a thousand years ago. What were they to suppose upon discovering me? To their way of thinking, it was a miracle: a Maglore child brought forward in time. As vile a thing as he was—a creature who, in his own time and place, had much better not have been born— they felt he had been spared for some special purpose, appointed by a Divine Providence to perform some great service to Mankind, perhaps in expiation for the sins of his forefathers. So they set about making him fit for that task. It was not easy, for them or for me, I can assure you."

For a moment, it was as though some barrier dropped, and his strong, passionate nature was revealed to her. "There is no creature on earth more wild, more willful than a Maglore child. But in time the Anti-demonists tamed me, in time they taught me their faith, in time they schooled me to an absolute conviction that I had been sin-gled out for some great purpose."

"But—you knew all along when and where you had originated."

"I was so very young, so very ignorant." The barrier descended again, but now Lili was aware of the iron control by which he achieved his apparent serenity. "I could not even tell them what year I had been born, nor refute, even in my own mind, the idea that I might have been carried from another time and brought into theirs. And the adults around me all seemed so much wiser than I, that I was ready to accept whatever they told me. Much later on, when I was an adult myself, I found my way back to the neighborhood where I was born, and there I discovered the truth. But by that time, I had already discovered a great many extraordinary things about myself, things which seemed to support the idea that I *was* made and meant for some extraordinary purpose."

The wind had died momentarily, and the ragged sails went slack. Then a series of gusts caused them to fill again. As the wind gained in strength, the ship leaped forward, with the foam flying off of her bow, and a milky white wake boiling behind her. The air was colder now, and Lili took the edges of her cloak in both hands wrapping them around her.

"What had you learned about yourself?"

"My kind protectors at the orphanage first discovered my secret when I became ill again and again after eating their food. But I had eaten enough salt during that time that I ought to have been dead, not ill. You have perhaps guessed that I had an inherent gift for healing. I was able, unconsciously, to neutralize the poison—in much the same way that you did during your initiation. On another occasion, when I was careless with a candle, my arm caught fire. Though someone immediately doused the flame with water, I still bear the mark to this day."

He pushed back the sleeve of his dark woolen coat, rolled up the linen underneath, and showed her a muscular forearm, hideously scarred. "A Human child would have suffered only a minor burn from so brief a contact. *I* should have been reduced to ashes before anyone had time to react."

He rolled down his sleeve again, covering the scar. "Then, too, I am far stronger than anyone I have ever met. Finally, as you may have noticed, I do have an ability to think ahead and to plan much further into the future than most Goblins. When I first discovered these things, I imagined that I was unique."

"But you don't think so now?" said Lili.

"No," said Raith. "I believe I have detected another—superior Maglore—at the heart of the conspiracy to steal the Jewels. To be more precise, I believe I have detected evidence of a mind capable of a plan far more complex and subtle than any ordinary Goblin could possibly devise, but with certain flaws inherent in that plan that a Human might have avoided.

"But at the time of which I speak, I was very far from suspecting anything of the sort. I had heard rumors of the existence of the Specularii. I felt that their purpose and mine exactly matched. I longed to seek them out, to prove myself worthy of membership in their noble order. Eventually, I succeeded, but at a great cost. There is little privacy in Anti-demonist households, and it did not take long for my foster-parents to discover that I was involved in the practice of magic, which is strictly against our Doctrine. So I was cast out, so I was excommunicated. This was painful to me, of course, but as I had been taught that physical and mental anguish were good for the soul, this only confirmed my belief that I had chosen the correct path. I was not being punished, I was merely being tested."

By now, Lili was almost past wondering at the odd motivations of this strange cult. Almost, but not quite. "They cast you out—but still kept your secret from the rest of the world?"

"I do not know, Mrs. Blackheart, the strength of your own religious convictions. But whatever your inclinations, you could not easily over-estimate the overwhelming power of faith among the Anti-demonists. They are not in the habit of questioning miracles. They continue to believe there is some divine plan being expressed through me. Because they do not understand this plan, that is no reason for them to doubt its existence. At the same time, they do not think it wise to allow me a place among them, lest I corrupt their children with evil influences. They cast me out to make my own way in the world, yet their belief that I will ultimately redeem myself remains as strong as ever, and they keep my secret. Now it seems that the time of my testing is near at hand. I hope I will not disappoint them."

Lili turned toward the back of the ship. She stood for a while in thought, with the wind in her face and her hair streaming behind her, before she ventured another question. "Then you don't think that this—all this we have seen, is the beginning of the end of the world, as foretold by your prophets?"

"No, I do not. The Apocalypse, when it comes, will be an Act of God, not the work of Men or Goblins. Once, I believed that day might not be far off, but I can no longer maintain that comforting thought."

"Why comforting? *How* comforting?" asked Lili, shaking her head in wonder at this strange new friend, so calm without, so intense within. He was a creature whose very existence as he stood there before her now was a study in irony——Maglore, Anti-demonist, Specularii magician. How did he live with his own contradictions?

"Because when the Apocalypse comes there will be nothing to do but accept the Will of God, knowing that after the Fire and the Flood there will come Rebirth, knowing that what the Almighty tears down He can easily build up again."

They were sailing past a line of rocks, where there was evidence of some recent wreck. Broken spars floated on the water, and scraps of wet canvas, which had caught on the rocks, flapped in the breeze. "But what Men and Goblins destroy," said Raith, "it will be for Men and Goblins to restore."

he days before Midsummer found Tarnburgh in turmoil, as rumors that the king was dead swept through the city in a matter of hours.

The story seemed to originate with the tradesmen and the common laboring-men, who gathered on every street corner, whispering at first, then shouting the news out loud. In the summer heat, it did not take long for their excitement to reach the boiling point.

In the cafes where the nobility met to eat strawberry ices and drink coffee and cinnamon water, the topic was discussed and debated through three long restless, sleepless twilights. King Jarred had been steadily improving for more than a month— No, he had wasted away and died two weeks ago, and the body was spirited away from the palace and secretly buried— No, no, it was a living Man they had smuggled out of Lindenhoff and carried to a house in the country, that he might convalesce from his long illness, far from the noise and the hurry of his capital city.

But down in the streets, there were very few who doubted that King Jarred was dead. It was the queen who ruled the country now—Ys the upstart, Ys the foreigner. She had replaced all the government ministers with her favorites, just as she had earlier replaced the palace guards and servants.

Where was the king's rightful heir? a hundred voices demanded, as the days passed. Why, he was dead, too, a hundred voices answered—and of the same mysterious malady that carried off Jarred. That Lord Rupert had reportedly been seen hours or days ago, hale and hearty—sailing his yacht around the islands off the tip of Nordfjall, or fishing at his lodge in the mountains—carried little weight with anyone. Even if true, the news could hardly have reached Tarnburgh so soon. These reports must be, no, they were a fabrication invented by the queen, spread by her agents throughout the city to conceal her complicity in the heir's death.

Meanwhile, ill news came from everywhere. It was a time when reassuring words were needed from the palace, but those who inhabited the palace no longer seemed to care for the people. The queen and her favorites lived only for pleasure. They danced for ten, twelve, even twenty hours at a stretch, on the marble dance floor—just as the last Maglore Empress and her court had reveled in mindless pleasure, fifteen hundred years ago, while their world crumbled around them.

Or so the story circulated, and it grew with every repetition. The queen and her favorites were not dancing, they were engaged in orgies of drunken debauchery. Strange rituals were performed daily at Lindenhoff, by masked adepts behind locked doors—cats and wild birds had disappeared from the palace gardens, and their blood was flowing in scarlet streams on the palace floors. Meanwhile, the queen's Goblin servants were busy in the palace kitchens brewing up vats of poison, which would soon be tipped into all of Tarnburgh's wells and fountains, slaying thousands. The queen—

But these rumors came to sudden halt and a new sort of panic passed through the city, when steaming gases began to escape through cracks in the earth just to the north, and ashes were seen blowing on the wind.

51

A t Lindenhoff, Ys was alone in her private apartments. Those down in the city who spoke of dancing and debauchery would have been surprised to learn just how quiet and solitary her life had become. With Madame and Zmaj dead, with Aunt Sophie and the rest so devastatingly estranged from her—without the aid and support of those imaginary sycophants and favorites, better known to the populace who had invented them than they were to Ys—she was growing daily more frightened, more uncertain as to her future.

So Ys paced alone in her rooms, rather than reveal her agitation to the servants. When Lord Wittlesbeck came to call on her, he was turned away by the Padfoot page, who said that the queen would receive no visitors.

As for that gaudy little music box, the Winterscar Jewel: it sat on her dressing table, looking deceptively innocent. Her attempts to establish a rapport with the tiny Maglore engine inside had been responsible for the intermittent explosions of steam and ash which had been plaguing the city for many days now; responsible, too, for the underground rumbling heard in the city since an hour before sunrise.

Ys paused in her restless transit to look at the sparkling, dangerous thing. She shivered at the very sight of it, terrified to think what
might happen if she tampered with the mechanism again—if, in her
ignorance, she upset some delicate, vital balance, and started a
process impossible to halt. She could picture in her mind all too
clearly a city flooded with liquid fire, herself destroyed along with
the rest. But the Jewel was her only chance now, the only way that
she could hope to regain some control in this rapidly deteriorating
situation.

There came a pounding on her door, a voice demanding to be let
in—louder and more vehement than the shrill voices of the Padfoot
servants she could hear in the background. Realizing her Goblins
might not be able to keep whoever it was out, Ys dashed across the
room in a panic, to lock and bolt the door.

But she was too late. The door flew open before she could reach
it, and a stocky young man in the sky-blue uniform of the Palace
Guard entered the room all in a rush.

"Your Majesty!" At the sight of the queen, the lieutenant came to
an immediate halt and saluted smartly. "I bring you an urgent message."

Ys drew a long sigh of relief, realizing he had come to serve her,
not to harm her. Gathering what dignity she could, she smoothed
out the silken skirts of her gown, adjusted the diamond bracelets on
her wrists, and replied imperiously: "Tell me your message at once,
then."

"Your Majesty, there is a mob forming outside the gate. They demand to see you. They insist that you turn over the keys to the palace
and leave the city at once. They—"

Ys stopped him by striking her hands together loudly. "It is not
for the rabble to present me with their demands—or even," she
added sternly, "for you as my representative to carry their messages."

Wheeling about, she moved swiftly to her writing desk, took up a pen and dipped it into the inkpot, and wrote out a quick proclamation. "You may read this to the mob at the gate," she said, signing and underlining her name with a decisive flourish, then handing the paper on to the young officer. "Tell them—tell them this is my answer, which you received directly from me. It is the only answer I will ever give them, so they need not trouble themselves further with more ultimatums."

The lieutenant read through her declaration quickly, shaking his head as he did so. When he looked up again, all of the color had drained out of his face. "Your Majesty, you must realize that if I were to read this out exactly as you have written it, they would tear me to pieces before I was halfway through it."

"If you are afraid to read it, then have it nailed up by the gate. Have other copies written out and distributed to the crowd. What?" she added, with a scornful little laugh. "Do you turn coward even at that? But if they do not receive my warning, if they do not do exactly as I tell them to do, then *you* will be the one to blame when the entire city is de—"

"Madam, I urge you to think," the lieutenant interrupted. "You cannot mean—or if you do mean, it is a grave mistake! You cannot turn them aside with such threats as these. Indeed, you will only enrage them. Be wise, Your Majesty. Be more temperate. If you will not do as they ask, at least send them some soothing message. Buy yourself some time and the frenzy may pass."

Ys fingered the cold white stones at her throat. Conquering her distaste for using the necklace in this way, for initiating that intimate contact with yet another Human creature, she looked the guardsman straight in the eye. "I ask you, lieutenant, to deliver my message. Will you not do as I say?"

A confused expression crossed his face, one of mingled pleasure and distaste, and his face, which had been very pale a moment before, was now suffused with blood. "Yes, madam, I will do as you say." And he turned slowly, and walked dazedly out of the room.

Ys hurried after him to slam the door and bolt it shut. Then she threw herself down in a chair and wept uncontrollably for a quarter of an hour.

It was an exhausting journey from Ottarsburg to Tarnburgh, though Luke provided the money to hire a large and comfortable coach as soon as they landed in Nordfjall, and the hired coachman proved stalwart and invaluable all along the difficult northern roads.

But the countryside was in chaos and strangers were no longer welcome. Half the inns where they stopped refused to serve them, and they missed many meals before their long journey was done. The men grew irritable and contentious—as hungry people will— and Tremeur and Lili turned light-headed.

As they approached the Winterscar border, mountains smoked and rumbled in the distance. The River Scar was in full flood, swollen by snow-melt from the high peaks. In other years, the peaks remained white all through the summer, but volcanoes long dormant were coming back to life, and heat from their vents had melted the snow.

Whenever Lili and Raith stopped to take a bearing with their wands, crystals, and compasses, the results seemed to point in a half-dozen different directions.

Blaise had possessed the forethought to obtain a map before leaving Catwitsen. Now Lilliana and the Leveller covered the face of that map with mysterious markings, and they spent many long hours studying and discussing these notations, while the heavy coach jolted along the rutted forest and mountain roads.

"But what does it all mean?" Luke asked, from the seat facing them, as he craned his neck to get a better look at the unfolded parchment. It was the first civil word he had spoken in many days, but the map with its puzzling notations was exactly the sort of thing which invariably engaged his curious mind.

"It means, Mr. Guilian, that there seem to be Philosophic Engines located in each of the large cities which lie on or near this line we have drawn—which describes an arc more or less similar to that of the Circumpolar Mountains, many miles further north," said Raith.

Under the shadow of his dark hat, the set of his jaw, the uncompromising line of his thin lips was as grim as ever, but his black eyes sparkled with emotion. "Which of the missing Goblin Jewels are in which cities we cannot determine—even less, *where* in each city a Jewel might be hidden. Whether the Chaos Machine is even among them, we cannot tell. It may be that it has not yet travelled so far north as we have, yet it is clear, at least, that many of the missing Jewels are now located within a two-day journey of Tarnburgh.

"This makes us more convinced than ever," the Leveller concluded, "that the person who can answer all of our questions will be found in your cousin's capital city."

Luke was appalled by the changes he saw in Tarnburgh. Riding beside the coachman up on the box, while Raith perched behind him on the roof, he could not resist commenting on everything he saw.

"What has become of her? She was exquisite—the most elegant little city in the world. Now there is mud in the streets, the house-fronts are dirty, and as for her people—" Luke almost fell off the coach in his efforts to see better. "That gentleman there, the one with his wig askew and his lace all in tatters—I'm sure I know him. He was a pompous old merchant, ten years an alderman of the city; now he looks like a man run distracted."

Luke resumed his seat on the box, with an ache in his heart. Nothing he had seen along the way had produced quite the same impact as this ruin of Tarnburgh. "It is hard to believe that so much damage has been caused in this city by one small female."

Before long, the press of moving bodies in the street made it impossible for the coach to go any further. While Lucius paid off and thanked the driver, Raith opened the door and informed the rest of their party that the time had come to go on foot. They piled out of the coach, staring with wide eyes at the tide of dirty, unkempt, and hysterical citizens moving past them.

When they tried to make inquiries, no one was willing to answer their questions, but by listening to messages shouted back and forth by the crowd, Raith and his companions soon learned that Linden-hoff was under siege. An angry populace was attacking the palace, but the guards were putting up a spirited defense. The fighting had already gone on, intermittently, for several days now.

"We *must* get inside the palace before the mob does," said Lili, as she and the other travellers gathered in a doorway. "If the queen has the Winterscar Jewel—if it should be lost or carried off in the confusion—then the entire city could be buried under a sheet of molten lava in a matter of hours. Or if she doesn't have the Jewel with her but has sent it away for safekeeping, then—"

"—then it would scarcely be advisable to allow her to be torn to pieces by revolutionaries, before she reveals its whereabouts," Raith finished for her.

"But how *do* we get inside, past the insurgents, past all of her guards?" asked Will. "For myself, I am ready to make the attempt, to follow any plan no matter how desperate or foolhardy, but we ought to have some *small* chance of succeeding."

The roar of the crowd swelled for a moment, then there was the sound of tramping feet, followed by a vast creaking and shaking, as if some tremendous wagon or immense piece of machinery on iron-clad wheels went rumbling over the cobblestones two or three streets away.

"There is a way that I know of into the palace," said Luke. "One that has seen very little use for fifteen hundred years, and it may well be that no one else has thought of it. If we take that way, our path may be clear."

Moving through the crowd, he had reached out instinctively and taken Tremeur by the hand. Now, he pulled her closer as he spoke. "Lindenhoff was built by the Maglore, though it's been extensively renovated. It was originally a summer palace, but the staff of servants who lived there all year round heated the place during the winter in the usual Goblin fashion: with vents and pipes, and elaborate machinery to bring up heat from the volcanic fires below. The tunnels and underground chambers which house that machinery still exist. While the men who maintained the machines used to enter from the city, some of the tunnels do connect to the palace. Jarred and I often explored down there when we were boys. It is like a great maze, and anyone who ventured recklessly in without knowing the way would soon get hopelessly lost and might wander for days in the dark. But I think I remember enough about those childhood explorations to take us through."

"It may be very warm down there, with the volcano stirring," warned Lili. "It may even be dangerous. But if these tunnels of yours provide our only chance of entering Lindenhoff in advance of the mob—"

The others agreed that it was worth the risk, and that it was necessary to move on to the palace as swiftly as possible.

"However, there is another matter we ought to consider," said Raith. "Once we are in, it may be difficult to get back out again, or to bring the Winterscar Jewel out with us to safety. The mob may mistake us for allies of the queen. We may need friends in the city to speak for us. I know of at least one Specularii magician who has lived in Tarnburgh for many years; if he is still alive he may be able to summon further friends to come to our aid. One of us must go to him, while the rest attempt the palace."

"I will go," offered Tremeur, in a small voice. "If you will tell me where to find him. I *should* be the one to go, since I can be of very little use to anyone at Lindenhoff."

"No!" said Luke, showing an unexpected reluctance to release his hold on her hand. In the midst of ruin, she suddenly seemed very precious to him. His resentment—which now seemed very foolish and petty—had faded, and all of his former affection, his desire to shield and protect her, came surging back. "To make your way through these hysterical crowds alone? A woman and a foreigner—reminding them of the woman they hate? If anything you did or said aroused their suspicions—"

"Then I will contrive some tale on the spot." She managed an unsteady smile. "Luke, you know my powers of invention. I can spin them a story so fantastic, so fabulous, they won't be able to make head or tail of it—while they are trying to puzzle it out, I will slip away."

Still, Lucius was reluctant. "You can't talk your way out of being crushed by the crowd in the midst of a panic. You can't—"

"Pardon me, Mr. Guilian," said Raith. "I find this most affecting, but where the rest of us are going, she would be equally in danger. And while it is certainly romantic, this desire of yours to suffer the worst at Mrs. Guilian's side, I feel bound to point out that it would be of no practical use to either of you."

With a hopeless gesture, Luke released his hold on her hand. "As always, Raith, you are correct. Tell me where this magician friend of yours lives, and I will try to describe the quickest and the safest way to reach that part of the city."

The directions were given and repeated back again, to be certain that Tremeur had heard and remembered them correctly.

"If you cannot find Doctor Wildebaden, then go to an Anti-demonist meeting house," said Raith. "I do not know how they will react if you mention my name. Yet they are good people. At the very least, they will not harm you, nor would I expect them to turn you away."

*　　*　　*

After much searching, Luke located a small shop tucked away under an ancient aqueduct in the iron-mongers' district, one still doing business despite the turmoil outside. There, he and his companions bought lanterns and candles to light their way during their journey underground. Once they had obtained these useful items, they headed for the entrance to the tunnels. It took longer than they had anticipated, pushing their way through the milling crowds in the streets, and Lili and Wilrowan were briefly separated from Blaise, Luke, and Raith. It was only by spotting the Leveller's black hat—rising five or six inches above any of the others as he moved down one of the broad boulevards—that they were able to catch up with their friends.

The first obstacle they faced when they reached the stairs to the tunnels was a wrought-iron grating which completely covered the stairwell and made entrance impossible. The two halves of the grate had been chained and padlocked together, and the hinges on either side bolted into a solid stone facing.

"I don't remember this chain and padlock," said Luke, with a frown. "They appear to be a recent addition, no doubt meant to keep children from wandering inside and getting lost. This grillwork, however, is considerably older; with the hinges and bolts so badly rusted, it may be possible to pull them loose."

He and Blaise set to work at once. Wilrowan—still sporting one arm in a black silk sling—was forced to stand back and watch, as did the Leveller. But when all efforts to wrench the heavy iron grillwork off at the hinges proved futile, Raith stepped forward.

"If you will move aside," he said, bending down and taking hold with his large knotted hands, "I believe I can do this."

As the others backed away, the Leveller took a long audible breath and began to pull. The hinges creaked, the stone to which they were fastened seemed to groan and shudder, but there was no other result. Raith stopped, took another deep breath, seemed to be drawing strength from some inner reserve, and pulled again. Very slowly, the stone began to crumble. A few minutes later, the Leveller stood up, gasping for air, but with half of the grating in his hands.

He stepped back, laying the section flat against the other portion, to which it was still secured by the chain. He said nothing, but indicated with a gesture that the way was now clear and it was up to the others to proceed.

Luke took up one of the lanterns and stepped through the gap, and the others followed him down the steps in a close single file. When he had caught his breath, Raith brought up the rear.

The stairs went down for what seemed a very long time, before finally stopping and opening out into a narrow passageway. The air was hot and heavy. "There may be poisonous gases," said the Leveller, coming up behind Wilrowan.

"Lucius and I will go ahead," said Lili. "He to lead the way, I to draw on my healer's training to test the air. By paying close attention to my own breathing and heartbeat, I should know if the atmosphere becomes insupportable."

Though Will was by no means eager to see Lili play this rôle, there seemed to be no other way to guard the safety of the whole party. He gritted his teeth and kept silent as the group proceeded down the tunnel: first Lili and Luke, then Will and Blaise, with the Leveller still stalking behind.

The tunnel had apparently been carved in solid rock, and the way was long and winding. Every now and again, some cavernous chamber or low-ceilinged tunnel opened on the passage they were following, and several times Luke turned into one of these intersecting corridors. As they passed some of the larger rooms, they caught glimpses of ancient machinery covered with rust and verdigris. Several times, they saw clouds of steam pouring out of broken pipes, and once a rain of burning ashes drifted out of one room. Luke and Blaise caught sparks in their clothes, but were able to brush them off before their coats caught fire.

552 D· TERESA EDGERTON

Realizing, as the others did not, the danger to Raith, Lili looked back to see if the Leveller had passed the opening safely. The hem of his cloak was smoldering. Reacting swiftly, he tore the garment off and cast it aside. Very pale indeed, but showing no sign of panic, he signalled to her that all was well with him and that they ought to move on. Lili lengthened her stride to catch up with Luke.

Twice, their path was blocked by some crack in the earth, opening on the molten depths below. The blast of heated air coming up through these cracks, the glare of incandescent gases, made it impossible to pass, even where the fissures were comparatively narrow. Luke was forced to turn aside and seek some other path through the maze. For a time, he seemed to lose his sense of direction.

"We must be under the palace by now. I found a map of the tunnels in the archives, once, which showed five different staircases leading up into Lindenhoff, though Jarred and I were only able to find one."

But at last he seemed to regain his bearings. His aspect brightened, and he began to move forward with a more purposeful stride. "This is the way; I know this passage. Look here where Jarred and I carved our names in the rock."

Then they were at the foot of a long staircase, and then they were running up it. A moment later, Luke pushed open a door. The others followed him through, and found themselves inside the palace, in what looked like the scullery.

"Now you must show us to the queen's apartments, or to any other place where you think she may have taken refuge," said Raith.

Luke frowned thoughtfully. Since he had only met the woman once, he had no way of knowing how she might react in a crisis. "I will take you first to the Royal Apartments. If we don't find her there, we will try the clock-tower. It is the place *I* would choose if I were in her place."

He started off at a brisk pace and the others continued to follow. Wilrowan hurried to catch up with Lili. "I want you to take this, in case we should be separated." He pressed something smooth and cold into her hand. "Gods, Lilliana! Be careful where you point it. That gun is loaded."

Still moving forward, she glanced down at the pistol. "Will, I haven't the least idea how to—"

"Just aim it, cock it, and pull the trigger. You can do that much, I know. But only at close range and only as your last resort, since there is no time for me to show you how to reload it." As she continued to protest, he shook his head stubbornly. "I will feel much better knowing you have it."

Lucius led the way swiftly through the kitchen regions, across a banquet hall bright with murals, and up a long marble staircase. In the gallery above, they met a party of four guardsmen. No doubt mistaking them for insurgents, the guards promptly attacked.

Drawing their rapiers, Will and Blaise eagerly entered the fray. The Leveller was right behind them. He dispatched one man by kicking the legs out from under him, aiming a sharp blow with his fist to the head. The guard went limp and did not move after that. But a second man dodged his initial attack, and it was Raith who was put on the defensive, skillfully evading the flickering point of his opponent's saber, but unable to move close enough to disarm him.

Luke was in the act of reaching for the sword of the unconscious guardsman, meaning to join the battle and assist his friends, when Lili put a hand on his arm to stop him. "You and I have to go on—I know it is hard," she said with a tremor in her voice, watching her husband wage a left-handed battle. "But I need you to show me the way. The others may follow if they can."

Luke nodded grimly. With a last reluctant glance at the continuing struggle, he took her by the hand and pulled her along, first down the gallery, then swiftly through a maze of luxurious rooms as confusing to Lili as the tunnels had been. "I didn't recognize a single one of those men. And did you chance to get a close look at their faces? I thought there was something—not right with any of them."

"I had heard," said Lili, growing breathless with the pace, "that this 'Goblin Queen' has some power over the minds of those around her, but until now I had dismissed the story."

They were crossing a very large chamber hung in tapestry, when the sound of running footsteps behind them caused Luke to drop her hand and whirl around, and Lili to uncertainly raise Wilrowan's pistol. But it was only Raith racing to catch up with them.

"The—others?" Lili faltered.

"They were both injured and did not wish to slow us down. Captain Blackheart insists that you go on without him."

Lili caught her breath. "He is not—?"

"Dead or dying? No," the Leveller answered firmly. "I would not deceive you about something like that."

She looked to Lucius, as if for confirmation.

"Raith would tell you the truth, no matter how bitter a thing it was. He is not in the habit of telling people comforting falsehoods," Luke assured her, and Lili was forced to be satisfied with that.

52

*L*ong before they reached the Queen's Apartments, Lili smelled smoke.

"I heard rumors of a catapult, when we were down in the streets—one meant to throw flaming brands at the palace and smoke out the queen and her Goblin servants," said Raith, running along beside her. "I did not think they would move so quickly."

Several strides ahead, Luke threw open a pair of french doors and stepped through; the others crowded behind him onto a small wrought-iron balcony. The gardens of Lindenhoff stretched before them, and beyond that expanse of cool green lawns, white gravel paths, and shimmering fish-ponds, there rose another white-and-gold wing of the palace. Lili made a small sound of distress deep in her throat. There was a crimson flicker of firelight behind every window in the opposite wing, and the leads on the roof were melting like wax.

"The fire is still a long way off," said Luke, turning back toward the doors. "We're in no danger yet."

As Lili and Raith followed him through, the Leveller's expression was grimmer than ever. "Unless, of course, they adjust the range of their catapult and something falls on this side of the palace. I suggest we redouble our efforts to find the queen."

Luke assented and the three moved on, as fast as their legs could carry them. "We have nearly reached Zelene's old rooms." Luke threw open a pair of doors and passed swiftly into a large antechamber. A single guardsman stood by the inner door.

"Allow me," said Raith, and the guard was dispatched neatly and efficiently. His body fell down in a heap against the door, blocking their way. Luke took the feet and Raith the shoulders, and they moved him aside. Too impatient to wait for them, Lili was the first one across the threshold by several steps.

Inside the bedchamber, a blonde girl in a grey satin gown turned away from her post at one of the windows, allowing the heavy brocade curtains to fall into place behind her. "How *dare* you—" But at the sight of Lili, followed almost immediately by Raith and Luke, the sentence died unfinished.

A slow look of recognition appeared on the queen's face. "Mr. Lucius Sackville-Guilian, isn't it?" Her expression grew calculating, her manner cool and imperious. "To see a kinsman at a moment like this is a very pleasant surprise. Have you come to rescue me, sir?"

"I think I have come here to wring the life right out of you," he ground out between his teeth. "Where is my Cousin Jarred, and what have you done with the Winterscar Jewel?"

She shook her head, took a step backwards, pressed up against the pale gold curtains. "Jarred is gone, though I don't know where. I suggest you ask the doctors who spirited him away. As for your famous Crystal Egg—you'll have to ask Jarred's doctors about that as well."

But her eyes betrayed her by a momentary glance in the direction of a small table, where a silver and satinwood casket containing a jeweled miniature of the city sat on a blue velvet cushion.

"Thank you, but I think we would prefer the real Jewel instead," said Luke, stepping toward the table. His hand was almost on the music box when his movement was suddenly arrested, and a look of pure astonishment froze on his face.

The queen smiled, fingering the necklace at her throat. "For all that, I don't think you will have it."

As Raith started to move across the room he was struck by the same remarkable paralysis. A curious look of startled recognition passed between the Leveller and the queen. Ys laughed, and stepped lightly toward the table, where she took up the Jewel herself. One hand moved toward the necklace again.

Lili felt a sharp pain in her head, heard a sweet, high voice speaking in her mind. She struggled against the compulsion in that voice, but the more that she fought, the more the voice hurt her. A pulse was beating in her head, a red mist rose up before her eyes, every nerve in her body seemed to be thrilling with agony—yet her years of training as a healer enabled her to put aside much of the pain. Still, the compulsion remained almost unbearably strong, and all the time that the battle of wills continued, the queen was edging one sideways step at a time closer and closer to the open door.

Slowly, and with infinite effort, Lili clasped Will's pistol between both her hands—slowly and painfully she lifted it, until the barrel was pointing somewhere in the vicinity of the curly golden head.

"You may go—if you wish—but you will leave your necklace and the Jewel—behind." Lili forced out the words past the constriction in her throat. She could barely hear herself over the shrilling in her ears, the thrumming of her nerves. "This entire city will—be destroyed—if you continue to tamper with things—that you don't understand. And perhaps I should tell you—Lindenhoff is already on fire."

As if to confirm her words, a tendril of smoke snaked into the room through the open door, and the scent of burning was suddenly very strong. It seemed that Raith's prediction had come true: the men down in the street had adjusted the range of their catapult.

The queen hesitated. Her hand moved from the necklace to the beaded bodice of her gown. Then she gave a brittle little laugh, put

558 ☽· TERESA EDGERTON

down the music box, and unclasped the necklace from around her throat. Dropping it on the richly carpeted floor, she ran from the room.

Gradually, the agony inside Lili's head subsided, and she was able to think clearly again. Released from the compulsion which had rooted her to the one spot, she stepped past the necklace. Still holding the pistol in one hand, she picked up the Winterscar Jewel with the other. The silver and satinwood casket, the tiny golden city inside, it all seemed so fragile, such an inconsequent thing to control the fate of a great city like Tarnburgh.

A voice spoke behind her, and Lili turned. Raith and Luke seemed themselves again, though both were pale and sweating, like men who had just survived some great ordeal. Lucius raised an arm and wiped his forehead with the embroidered cuff of his sleeve.

"She should not be allowed to escape," said Raith, moving toward the door. "I will go after her. But you, Mrs. Blackheart, should go with Mr. Guilian out of the palace at once, taking the Winterscar Jewel with you. If the king is dead as the rumor tells us, you—who already know something of the inner workings of one such engine—have a better chance than anyone in the city of establishing the necessary rapport with this one."

Before Lili could respond, he was through the door; his swift footsteps sounded in the antechamber outside. Luke stepped forward and gently removed the pistol from her hand.

"I think that next time, Lilliana, you may wish to cock your weapon, as though you actually mean to fire. It is likely to prove a far more effective threat if you do."

Raith ran through the palace, trying to keep Ys always in sight. Sometimes, when she whisked around a corner at the bottom of a staircase, when she passed through a room with more than one exit, he lost her for a moment. Then he was obliged to pause, catch his breath, and listen for the sound of her racing footsteps—often over the roar of the fire, which was sometimes just a room or a stairwell or a passage away. Had it not been for his much longer stride, which allowed him to make up some of the time that he lost, she might have eluded him entirely.

Just when he was beginning to truly close the distance, just when he began to believe he must overtake her, she ran through a pair of double doors. Entering the room only seconds behind her, Raith came to a sudden bewildered halt. The room seemed to offer a myriad of exits, of doors both open and closed, of archways leading into endless vistas of chambers and corridors, receding in the distance. How was he ever to choose correctly between such a multitude of possibilities?

Then he realized that he had fallen victim to an optical illusion. The walls had been painted trompe l'oeil: most of these doors and archways did not even exist; they were merely clever examples of the painter's art.

With that knowledge, it took only a moment to detect the true from the false. Redoubling his efforts, he raced across the chamber, through an open doorway, and sprinted down the long stone-flagged corridor he found on the other side.

Even so, he might never have caught up with her, had it not been for the fast-moving fire, which eventually allowed him to corner Ys between a churning wall of smoke and a locked door.

Turning to face him, pressing one hand to the front of her gown as if in an effort to slow her racing heartbeat, Ys was trembling but nevertheless defiant. During that moment of recognition which had passed between them in the room upstairs, she had guessed Raith's secret, just as he had learned hers. But there had been something more, a natural antagonism, as though she had realized something about him that he did not even know about himself.

<*You are just like her! You might be Valentine's twin.*> Her mental ex-

clamation had echoed in his brain, though he had little idea what the words meant. <*Who* are *you?*>

Now she asked that question again, this time hissing it out between her teeth, past her labored breathing. "Who are you—what kind of Goblin are you, to make common cause with these Human creatures?"

"My name—my true name, signifies Fury—and also Retribution." Yet even as Raith moved toward her, he felt a certain reluctance. Had he, in the excitement of the chase, been able to overtake her, he might easily have used his tremendous strength to snap her neck, to crack her spine, to kill her in an instant. There would have been no time then for second thoughts. But to do it now in cold blood—when she was trapped, when she was helpless, when he saw her cringe against the wall, trembling with apprehension despite her best efforts to appear courageous—that went against every instinct.

Nevertheless, a lifetime of discipline, of stern repression of his ardent nature, had schooled the Leveller to put his sense of duty even over his strongest inclinations. And so he continued to advance inexorably. "In your case," he said, with a regretful shake of his head, "I very much fear that my name must also mean—Death."

"Then die!" said Ys, reaching inside the neck of her gown. Something slender and shining appeared in her hand. Before he had time to react, she plunged the glass dagger into his chest, just under the breastbone and between two of his ribs, where it felt like a sliver of fire inside him. As she jerked her hand back, the blade snapped off just below the twisted hilt, and remained there buried in his breast.

As Luke and Lili ran along the gallery toward the stairs, billows of black smoke were already roiling on the floor below, and flames licked at the bottom steps.

"It looks as though the rebels have broken past the gate and set the palace on fire from within." Luke leaned for a moment over the railing, to get a better look. "It seems to be every place at once."

Taking Lili by the arm, he pulled her along the gallery behind him. "We'll have to find another way out. Look, you can see more of the flames through that half-open door. That room is the library and those fine old volumes will go up like tinder, if they haven't al—"

An enveloping cloud of dark smoke put an end to this speech; the rest was lost in a paroxysm of choking and coughing. Yet Lucius continued blindly on. More by instinct than by anything else, he found a door and opened it, pulled Lili through, and slammed it shut behind them. Though the air was better here, it was a minute before Lili could stop coughing and speak again.

"Is there another way down?"

Luke nodded. His face and clothes were smudged and his eyes had turned red from the smoke. Lili supposed she looked much the same, and her own eyes felt dry and burning.

"There is a back stair. We will hope that someone overlooked that particular escape route—or never knew that it existed in the first place."

They hurried through a series of intersecting chambers, until Luke opened a door on a narrow corridor and they both stepped through. The air here was cool and untainted; it seemed they had outrun the fire. At the end of the passage, Lili could see flights of steps leading up and down.

"This way is used only by the servants. I doubt many people even know there are stairs here. There is some advantage to having been raised at Lindenhoff—and to being an extraordinarily curious child!"

Down the steps went Lili and Lucius, through another door, and along another corridor. But now the air grew hot again; it tasted of smoke. "We are on the ground floor. There is an intersecting corridor that you can see just ahead. If we turn left, there is a door to the gardens. It's possible—"

He broke off as they rounded the corner. A wall of flame blocked their path to the door, and flakes of burning ash danced in the air. The fire was too high and too broad to safely jump over. Luke began pulling Lili back in the other direction, but she managed to wrench herself free out of his grasp. "I think—I think I can pass through the flames without being harmed; I've done something like that before." She hesitated. "But that would mean abandoning you."

He shook his head emphatically. "Don't delay on my account. It may be that I'll find another way out, but if I can't—you *must* escape with the Jewel if you can. Too many lives are depending on it." He gave her a gentle push in the direction of the garden door.

Realizing that he spoke the truth, Lili reached out and clasped his hand briefly, then turned back toward the fire. The wall of flame rose up before her, beating her back with its heat. The air shimmered, and bright sparks of burning paint whirled madly on every side of her. For a moment it seemed as though the entire castle was melting around her. Lili held the precious jeweled casket closer, wondering if she really dared to attempt this. It had been one thing to pass her hand through a flame during her initiation, it was another and a far more perilous thing, to step into the heart of fire now.

She remembered what Sir Bastian had said to her. "*You were in a state of extraordinary mental excitement at the time and your powers were very great. But I would not, if I were you, attempt to do any of those things under any other circumstances. The least distraction, even a momentary twinge of self-doubt, would cause you to fail.*"

But I must not fail, Lili told herself. *I dare not.* There was simply too much at stake. She closed her eyes and stepped boldly forward.

She felt only the faintest sensation of heat as she passed through the fire. When she opened her eyes again, she was already several yards on the other side. With a gasp and a laugh of sheer relief, Lili moved on to the door, flung it open, and passed through to the fresher air outside.

*   *   *

She would never know how long she wandered through the gardens, growing more and more exhausted and confused. Walls and gates and boxwood hedges continually rose up to block her way and turn her aside again and again, until—in her fatigue and distress— she finally lost all sense of direction. It seemed that she spent long hours merely walking in circles, while the sun dipped below the horizon, and the midsummer twilight went from grey to deep violet and back to grey again.

At last she came out in an immense stone-paved courtyard, where dark figures moved to and fro against the glaring light of the flames. Whether they were fighting the holocaust or urging it on she did not know, but because she was simply too tired to go on, she sat heavily down on a low brick wall and passively awaited further events.

Minutes or hours later, she heard a soft feminine voice speaking her name. When she looked up, Tremeur was standing just a few feet away. With her were two old men, and a younger man, very pale and emaciated, being supported by the others. The young man was undoubtedly a stranger—Lili had no name in her mind to go with his face—yet there was something teasingly familiar about him, too.

"This is Raith's Doctor Wildebaden," said Tremeur, indicating one of the two old men. "And this is his cousin, who is Luke's Doctor Purcell. And this other man, Lili, is His Majesty, King Jarred of Winterscar, who is not dead after all."

"Then this belongs to you, sir," said Lili, gratefully handing the music box over. "You will know far better than I do what is to be done with it."

"I do—and I thank you for bringing it back to me," he replied, in a voice worn thin by illness. "I fear there will be a heavy price to be paid for my carelessness in losing it. But perhaps it is not too late to avert the very worst consequences."

The second old man, the one Tremeur had identified as Doctor Purcell, helped the king into a waiting carriage, and Doctor Wildebaden offered Lili his hand. "Madam, what the king has to do is best done in some quiet place away from all of these distractions. And this is no place for a gentlewoman. Will you not come away with us?"

Lili gave a weary shake of his head, refusing his assistance. "I can't go without Wilrowan—without my husband. He may still be inside."

"In that case, there is nothing you can do to aid him. And if he and your other friends have found their way safely out of the palace, perhaps they are seeking you even now at my house."

But Lili would not be moved. "He won't go anywhere without trying to find me first. And I won't go until I know what has happened to him. There may, as you say, be nothing I can do to help him—but I can wait for him."

"Then, I will wait with you," said Tremeur, sitting down on the low brick wall beside her, slipping a small cold hand into one of Lili's. "We will wait here together for Captain Blackheart, Luke, and the others."

53

o they sat quietly together, the two dazed and exhausted young women, while the twilight passed away and the sun came up, and the fire continued to burn.

When a tall lean man dressed all in black moved past her, Lili started up, thinking that it must be Raith. But it was not. The man in black was joined by a another, similarly garbed, and they both set to work assisting the fire-fighters.

"They are Levellers," said Tremeur, as Lili dropped down beside her again. "I met an Anti-demonist on the way to Doctor Wilde-baden's. When I mentioned Raith, he said—Lili, he said the Levellers were waiting to hear from him in this time of trial. Though it was very odd the way that he said the name. He pronounced it 'Wrath.' Then he took me to a kind of church, and—they are the most amazing people! They never doubted anything I told them, and they offered to help me at once."

Perhaps, after that, Lili dozed off for a time. There followed a long, long period of grey incoherence, during which she entertained a dim impression that the confusion on every side of her gradually died down.

Then a dearly familiar voice was saying her name, over and over again. Tremeur moved aside, a strong arm encircled Lili's waist, and a lively hazel-eyed face was on a level with her own—very much obscured by smoke and sweat, but not to be mistaken for all that. "Lili, Lili, I thought I had lost you."

She gave a sob of relief and buried her face against Wilrowan's shoulder.

Lindenhoff continued to burn for several days. Though an effective effort was made to keep the fire from spreading to the nearest buildings, no attempt was made to save the palace itself. What could burn did burn, until there was nothing left but blackened brick and stone, and piles of ash.

The city had escaped destruction. She was scarcely recognizable, to be sure, very much battered and smoke-stained, but only a few buildings had fallen during the rumblings caused by the volcano. It was doubtful that Tarnburgh would ever regain her former dignity, or her easy, elegant way of life—even after the smuts and ashes were cleaned away—but she looked like she would survive the end of one civilization just as she had survived the one before it.

From the top floors at Doctor Wildebaden's house, Lili could just make out the smoking ruin that was Lindenhoff. She knew that she had been fortunate to come out of the holocaust alive, fortunate, too, that Will had been spared. Though she could not remember seeing Trefallon in the courtyard—being much too absorbed in Wilrowan—Blaise had apparently been at Will's side all along. According to Will, they had bound up each other's wounds after their fight with the guards, and hobbled to safety together. He had a limp now and Blaise was the one with his arm in a sling, but at least they were both alive. Eventually, old Doctor Purcell had discovered Luke, wandering the streets in a daze. Someone or something had hit him hard on the head; there was a deep gash, and two more days would pass before he knew his own name or remembered much of anything else. But of Raith and Queen Ys there was still no word or sign.

"He would not allow her to escape," Luke insisted, when he recovered enough to be told the news and to return a coherent reply. "They must both have died in the flames. It's not possible that Raith would allow her to escape."

When the fire was finally extinguished, a search was made of the ruins. Several bodies turned up, many of them burnt beyond recognition, apparently those of rioters or guards, as none of them was small enough or large enough to suggest either the queen or the Leveller. Lili, of course, had not expected otherwise. If what people said of Queen Ys was true, there would be very little left—no more than there would be of Raith—not even so much as a rag or a bone. And who would notice two small piles of silvery ash, amidst the ashes of an entire palace?

The Chaos Machine and the other missing Jewels still had to be found and returned to their rightful places as soon as possible, but it was depressingly evident to Lili and her friends that it would be days or weeks before they were fit to travel. Will and Blaise had lost too much blood; Lili had swallowed too much smoke. Both men burned with a fever in their wounds, and Lili had a cough that left her almost too weak to walk. Luke was still disoriented at times, and when he recovered, he was likely to find plenty to occupy him working to rebuild his beloved city. Accordingly, Doctor Wildebaden and some of the other Specularii took up the search, though without Lili and her particular gift they did not expect their efforts to be rewarded with immediate success.

Meanwhile, the volcano had ceased to threaten, thanks to the king's timely intervention. Yet public outrage against the Crown remained strong. Jarred had been as much his queen's victim as any one, but there was still a keen and widespread resentment against him, because of his imprudent marriage. Under the threat of further mob violence, the Parliament met, voted, and deposed the king, putting his cousin, Lord Rupert, in his place. It was as an ordinary man, then, that Jarred was to be tried for the crime of High Treason.

When the day of that trial arrived, Luke had recovered enough to attend. He went to the courtroom along with old Doctor Purcell, found a seat in one of the high galleries, and watched with dismay and a growing sense of outrage as a thin figure all in black was hustled into the dock by some rough-looking constables, and "Mr. Jarred Sackville-Walburg" was accused, berated, and humiliated— by the judge, the prosecutor, and by the immense jeering crowd that had squeezed inside the courtroom to watch the trial.

When Luke's own turn came to speak, he took the long twisting staircase down to the floor and stepped into the witness box with deep misgiving, but the determination to do what he knew to be right.

He came straight back to the house afterward, bitterly disappointed. He had hoped that depriving the king of his crown would prove sufficient to satisfy the mob, but the mob and the court had not been so easily placated.

Luke described the proceedings later to Tremeur. "He said not a word in his own defense, but everyone who knew him spoke in his favor. We tried to remind the rabble what he was really like—how much he loved them always, how diligent he had been in securing their welfare—but people have suffered and they wanted someone that they could punish—someone, that is, besides the hundreds of innocent Padfoots and Ouphs they have already harried out of their homes. It was all that we could do, Jarred's remaining friends, to talk the jury out of imprisoning or executing him. A Bill of Attainder was drawn up. Not only has he been deposed, it is as though his reign had never occured. Every one of his edicts has been repealed, his name will be blotted or struck out from all the histories, and he is banished from Winterscar forever, on pain of death."

Luke ran his hands over his face. "I think—I think in some ways his leaving the country may be for the best. He is a broken man, and it is better for him to lead a private life. He says he will go to Ottarsburg with Francis Purcell, where they will rent a house and set up a business making clocks together. Yes, for Jarred's own sake, this may be best—but the beastly unfairness! That they should heap punishment upon punishment, shame upon shame, when he never did anything but what was required of an honest and honorable man—"

Lucius choked on his own indignation and it was impossible for him to go on. He went upstairs and locked himself up alone in his bedchamber, and was not seen again for many hours.

Luke was calmer a few days later when he explained the situation to Lili. "The truly bizarre thing is that I actually benefit. Officially, there was never such a person as King Jarred of Winterscar, and as for our good King Rupert—who, as it develops, has been invisibly ruling for all of these years—he and I aren't even related. That means that Tremeur and I have been legally married from the moment that parson in Château-Rouge pronounced the words over us.

"Not," he added with a wry glance, "that anyone is likely to give much thought to the ban anymore. Everything has changed too much. Still, I must be glad that my marriage has been regularized—and more so, because my wife shows signs just at the moment of becoming a Leveller."

Lili expressed her surprise with a slight smile. They were in a tiny walled garden behind the house, where Lilliana was gathering roses which she meant to arrange in vases in the dining room and the front hall.

"Oh, yes, I assure you," said Luke. "Her interest is quite sincere. She has always admired Raith, and the congregation here has most favorably impressed her! One of them even told her that this God of theirs can forgive *anything*—supposing that is, one truly repents. I can't begin to tell you how truly taken she was with the notion that all of her sins might be washed away, with a single, heartfelt declaration.

"And really," he added with a shrug, "they are the most extraordinary people. They've taken this whole disaster in stride, and have done more than anyone to relieve the general suffering. So it seems I must make up my mind to being married to—to an exceptionally virtuous woman, and eventually raising a family of exceptionally well-behaved children."

Lili was restless. Her cough had ceased to trouble her, and she was feeling stronger. Will and Blaise, too, though far from recovered, were beginning to complain after nearly a fortnight of inactivity. The only thing that prevented them all from packing up immediately, and setting off in search of the Chaos Machine, was the fact that they had no clear idea where to begin looking. As one day followed the next, Lili continued to hope that some message would arrive from Doctor Wildebaden, but still there was no news, and still she lacked any sense of direction to send her on her way.

She was engaged, one day, in a listless attempt to mend one of her petticoats, in the tiny second-floor parlor which the bachelor physician had turned over to the ladies, when Tremeur came in with a look of intense excitement on her face and a slender parcel wrapped up in brown paper in one small hand.

"Only look how mysterious! A package has arrived with your name on it—but no indication at all where it might come from."

Lili was naturally intrigued. Putting aside her mending, she quickly unwrapped the parcel, uncovering a slender marquetry box made with decorative woods—ebony, she guessed, and palisander. On opening the lid and lifting out the very frivolous object that she found inside, Lili turned to Tremeur with a bewildered smile.

"Now who on earth would want to send me a puzzle fan? It is extremely pretty, of course, but— Oh, I see—there is a message after all." She took out a folded slip of paper from the bottom of the box, and read the note out loud: " '*Mrs. Blackheart. This should aid you in finding what you seek.*' Now how am I to interpret that?"

"Perhaps we should bring in Luke," Tremeur suggested, taking the fan and spreading out the sticks, the better to observe the paintings. "He has a positive genius for deciphering things."

So Luke was sent for and arrived soon after, accompanied by Blaise and Wilrowan. He examined the fan for several minutes, turning it over and over in the process. At last the light of comprehension dawned in his eyes. "It is very simple. On the one side you will find a series of rebuses drawn on the individual sticks, each one translating to the name of a city: as Tronstadt, Vallerhoven, Dahlmark, and so forth. The list itself is highly instructive, if you'll look at that map that you and Raith spent so much time poring over during our journey." He turned the fan over again. "Then, on the reverse side, as you can see—where the pattern has not been completed—most of the sticks have been deeply engraved with a series of ancient characters. They appear—indeed, I am fairly certain— they look to be a series of street names and house numbers." He paused dramatically before going on. "I would say, Lilliana, that someone has very kindly provided you with a key to finding all the missing Jewels."

There were gasps of surprise and delight from the others. "But who has sent this—and can we trust them?" Trefallon asked, with a lift of his well-shaped eyebrows.

Luke passed Blaise the fan and took up the note; he stood looking down at the message it contained, with a smile beginning to form on his face. "It's impossible to be certain, but I think that we may. The writing here, while unfamiliar, should strike a chord with every one of us, so round as it is, so smooth and so legible. It is a pedagogue's hand, a schoolmaster's writing.

"Unless I am very much mistaken, the fan and the accompanying note come from—Raith."

There were nine houses on nine streets in nine cities—houses of brick, and stone, and timber—all of them plain and unprepossessing, yet each of them held a hidden treasure.

Three long weeks after the arrival of the puzzle fan, Lili stood in a tiny entry hall inside the ninth house, with the crystal-tipped wand in her hand. The Jewels from Tholia, Nordfjall, Finghyll, Lichtenwald, and the rest had all been recovered; only the Mountfalcon Jewel was still missing.

It has to be here, Lili told herself. *I am weary of travelling, weary of searching. I want to go home.*

With that thought, the wand turned in her hand. "This way," she said to Wilrowan and Blaise, the only two who had come this far with her. Doctor Wildebaden and his Specularii friends had each claimed responsibility for returning one of the other Jewels to its rightful place, and all had departed before reaching this red brick house in Starkhavn.

Lili threw open a door and stepped through to the very odd room on the other side. It had been furnished as a bedchamber, but there were no less than seven great glasses in ornate frames arranged on the walls. Overcome by a wave of dizziness, she put the tips of her fingers to the side of her head. "It almost seems as though there must be more than one of the Jewels here—they seem to be on every side of us at once."

Trefallon and Will began a swift but thorough search of the room: pulling out drawers, tapping on wall panels, rummaging through the clothes-press. But Lili stood staring down at her hands, which were inexplicably shaking, and wondered what had happened to make her feel so ill and disoriented.

She heard Will catch his breath sharply. "No one move. There is a trap here somewhere, I'm sure of it."

Blaise froze in place. Lili swallowed her rising nausea and glanced around her. What could Will mean? If he had actually seen something, then why not say so? Then, all in an instant, she knew the source of the danger. "The mirrors. Break all of the mirrors!"

There was a crashing and a tinkling of broken glass as Will and Trefallon each took up something heavy and struck at the mirrors again and again. As the last silvery shards fell to the floor, Lili realized that the pain in her head had vanished, her sickness had passed. "In another five minutes, we would have been mad—or dead."

Now the wand pointed unerringly toward a cupboard near the fireplace. Will crossed the room in two long strides, opened the cupboard, and drew out a small rosewood box that he found inside. Then he opened the lid so that Lili and Blaise could see what the casket contained. All three gave a deep sigh of relief at once.

"But how did you know the room was trapped?" Lili asked, fifteen minutes later, when she, Wilrowan, and Blaise had returned to their coach. "There was nothing like that before, when we found the other Jewels."

The driver spoke to the horses and the coach began to move. "Queen Ys is either dead or the Leveller's prisoner," said Will. "But our own nemesis, Lady Sophronispa, is still at large. I think she arranged that trap as a parting gift—though perhaps not her last."

Lili regarded him with a puzzled frown. "Why should you think so? The plot to steal the Jewels has not only been exposed but foiled. I should think she would want nothing so much, right now, as a safe place to hide herself."

"For all that," said Will, raising his voice as the coach began to rattle over a series of bumps, "she remained one step ahead of us every inch of the way. She eluded us again and again—and only consider how many, many deaths she caused in Mountfalcon and elsewhere."

He gave a rueful shake of the head. "I can't help thinking that she was the most dangerous of all the conspirators."

"She might well consider *you* dangerous, and elusive, too," suggested Blaise from the opposite seat. "And therefore to be avoided. How many times did she try to kill? And yet you survived."

Lili reached out with one hand and gave her husband a reassuring touch on the shoulder. "More than that, the Maglore waited for fifteen hundred years to make an attempt to win back their Empire. Who knows how long it may be before they feel ready to try again? And really, why should this Sophronispa be in any hurry? She can expect to live two hundred, three hundred years. She can afford to wait until people like you and I are dead, and nobody else remembers anything about her."

Wilrowan nodded thoughtfully. How could he ever hope to comprehend the motives of this creature who might live for centuries? He had certainly failed to guess what she might do every single time that he had tried it before.

Nevertheless, he had an uneasy suspicion they had not heard the last of Lady Sophronispa.

Epilogue

It was a sad homecoming on a bleak autumn day. The city of Hawkesbridge looked more battered and ugly than ever. Wilrowan wondered if she had slipped further into dissolution during his absence, or whether he was returning with newly sharpened vision after his long absence. The streets were filled with beggars, ragged and weary-looking, and that was one certain difference—but was that all?

"They come, I suppose, from the mining towns," he said to Lili. "Let us hope that as soon as we turn the Chaos Machine over to Rodaric he can begin to set things right again."

As they approached the Volary, Will was struck by the absence of guards at the outer gate, and while there appeared to be the usual number of men on duty at the palace itself, the rambling structure was strangely silent. A lieutenant directed Lili and Will to one of the gardens where the king had developed a habit of walking alone in the afternoons. "I am afraid you will find him changed—almost beyond recognition."

And indeed, it was a sad, weary, and very much diminished Rodaric they discovered wandering amidst the rank, uncontained growth in one of the untended greenhouses. Yet his eyes kindled and his face momentarily brightened when Will placed in his hands the small rosewood box banded in iron, and he opened the lid and saw inside the gold-and-crystal orrery nestled against a green silk lining.

Lili had done what she could, and so had the other magicians, but the tiny spheres and figures were scarcely moving. One of the guards was dispatched to Malachim with a message for Doctor Fox and Sir Frederic Marlowe. Between the three of them, Rodaric and the two professors would make the necessary adjustments.

He closed the box, passed a thin, unsteady hand over his face, where many deep lines had appeared since the last time Will saw him. "Wilrowan—Lilliana—I wish I could find the words to express my gratitude. I did promise you, Will, almost any reward you might care to name—"

"But that was under very different circumstances," Will interrupted, remembering—as no doubt Rodaric remembered also—that the re- ward had been partly contingent on the queen's safety and the birth of a healthy heir. "If you please, sir, I had rather not speak of it now."

They spent a quiet hour with the king, walking through the gar- dens and then up to the giddy wall-walks, during which time he de- scribed to them the events of Dionee's last days. "She felt no physical pain, of that I am certain. It was just that delivering her child took the last of her strength—all that remained to her after all those months of anxiety—and the next morning she drifted off into a deep sleep from which, apparently, she had no desire to waken."

"And the child?" said Will. "I have heard so many conflicting sto- ries. That it was born dead, or died soon after, or that—"

A brief smile crossed Rodaric's gaunt face. "My daughter is alive and well, Wilrowan. She was born so weak and small, for a time we feared she would never survive. But she has rallied in the last few weeks and is actually thriving. Indeed, little Cleone is my one joy, my one reason for continuing on. There will be no remarriage, no son of mine to supplant her—Dionee's last precious gift to me—and I mean to put this kingdom in order again, for her sake alone." He heaved a weary, weary sigh. "When my strength comes back to me. When I recover some sense of purpose—I hope it may not take very long."

Will and Lili took their leave of him soon after that, but not before Will had requested a private audience for the next day. They spent the night in his quarters at the barracks. In the morning, he put on his green uniform for the last time and went to speak with the king.

"Well," said Lili, starting up from her seat when Wilrowan finally returned, several hours later. "Did you resign your commission, as you intended?"

Will removed his tricorn hat with its gay cockade, and stood looking down at it with a puzzled frown, as though he were somehow uncertain what he was expected to do with it. "I did resign it, yes," he said at last. "And naturally Rodaric said it must be as I wished, understanding as he did that there was nothing for me to do here now, with Dionee gone. But he—he offered me something else."

Lili raised an inquiring eyebrow.

"You have seen to what a state our country has come." Will made a broad gesture with both hands. "It has all changed, and Rodaric believes, as I do, that there is no going back to the way things were. But he does feel it is both necessary and possible to reclaim *something*. He wants to send out a company of men to do all that is needful, to settle disputes, to restore order—a sort of army, constabulary, and magistracy combined. This morning, he actually found the energy to make up a list of several good men, but he still needs someone to command them. He has offered me the commission, which carries with it the rank of colonel."

Will tossed the hat into a chair. "I told him I had made other plans for our future, but he insisted that I spend a day or two thinking it over, and discussing the matter with you."

Lili shook her head wonderingly. "But don't you *want* to do this?

578 ⊃· TERESA EDGERTON

I understand that you don't wish to live at the Volary or stay in Hawkesbridge where there are so many painful memories, but what Rodaric is offering you—I think it would suit you *perfectly*."

He made an airy gesture, affecting to make little of it, though Lili could see very well how strongly the idea appealed to him. "Whether I like what he is offering me or not, I had already made other plans. I want to take you home with me to my father's house, as I should have done years ago. I owe you that much at least."

But now Lili laughed. "If you have refused the king on my account, then I am very glad he had the good sense to ask you to reconsider. Oh, Wilrowan, do you really think it would please me to sit back and watch you grow more and more restless at your father's house in the country? Or that I, for that matter, after so much excitement, would welcome a return to such a quiet life?"

He crossed the room in two steps, took one of her hands between both of his. "But what is the alternative? Not another parting between us?"

"I hope not," Lili answered emphatically. "Accept the commission that Rodaric has offered you and go wherever it takes you. I will go, too. No doubt there will be a crying need for physicians everywhere you go, and there will be plenty of work for both of us."

A brighter look came into Will's eyes. "But what of the family we meant to start?"

"A family may come in time. Yes, Wilrowan, I really mean it. No doubt you will make an admirable father, but in the meantime I don't want to see you so bored that you get yourself into all sorts of absurd scrapes—nor do I wish to be bored, either, waiting to become a mother."

Will laughed, took her by the shoulders, and kissed her on the forehead. "Then if you really are very, very certain—I think I will go and speak to Rodaric again, before *he* has the chance to change his mind and withdraw the offer."

"Yes," said Lili, "that strikes me as a very good idea."

He gave her a blinding smile, swept up his hat, and headed for the door. She could hear the light, quick fall of his booted feet as he moved down the corridor to the stairs.